Keller crouches beside the mummified beast and feels the rugged jawbone. Dense knots of dry muscle clench the jaw shut, suggesting incredible bite strength.

"Supposed to be an ambush predator," he explains. "Stealthy, aggressive, and deadly. Like you guys. But she was a big sweetheart. Jin-Sung was steamed his prize pet wouldn't kill. She loved to stalk and hunt, but wouldn't kill. He was gonna put her down. Had to do it himself, 'cause no one else wanted to, they all loved her. Heh. She got the needle away and started chasing him with it, all on camera. The video might even be here..."

Keller turns toward the others and finds they have already moved on, their lights receding down the hallway.

"Aw, to hell with you all..." he mutters.

The dark of the corridor presses in on him as the bright memory fades, and once again he remembers where he is. He rises from the floor and takes a last look at the gentle monster.

"Wish the rest of 'em were like you, Daisy."

THE
EXHAUSTED DEAD

THE
EXHAUSTED
DEAD

F. ALLEN FARNHAM

CADRE ONE PUBLISHING
SALEM, MA
2012

CADRE ONE PUBLISHING, LLC.
(WWW.CADREONEPUBLISHING.COM)

LIBRARY OF CONGRESS CONTROL NUMBER: 2012917409

ISBN : SOFTCOVER 978-0-982-7116-2-0

Names, characters, and events in this work of fiction are exactly that: fiction. Resemblance to any persons (dead or living) or events is purely coincidental.

This book was produced *entirely* in the United States of America.

Edited by Michael Lomonte
Copyedited by Cameron Chapman. (www.cameronchapman.com)
Author Bio Photo by Kenny Thomas, 2010
Cadre One Hawk image by Bob Cram, Jr. (www.bobcram.com)
Raccoon Scientist with DNA image by Bill Walko. (www.billwalko.com)

Cover image of Carina Nebula, source: STScI and NASA, used with permission. (http://imgsrc.hubblesite.org/hu/db/images/hs-2007-16-a-hires_jpg.jpg)

Cadre Two Skull Icon, Book/Cover design and layout by F. Allen Farnham.

CONTENTS

PART FOUR

PART FIVE

PART FIVE (CONT.)

To Mike L and Cam C for going above and beyond...

To everyone else for your patience...

'But was there ever a man more blest by fortune
than you, Akhilleus? Can there ever be?
We ranked you with immortals in your lifetime,
we Argives did, and here your power is royal
among the dead men's shades. Think, then, Akhilleus:
you need not be so pained by death.'

To this
he answered swiftly:

                              'Let me hear no smooth talk
of death from you, Odysseus, light of councils.
Better, I say, to break sod as a farm hand
for some poor country man, on iron rations,
than lord it over all the exhausted dead.'

--*The Odyssey* by Homer, Book XI, A Gathering of Shades, lines 569-581
Translation by Robert Fitzgerald

CADRE ONE

PART FOUR

COUNSELOR'S ASSIGNMENT

Maiella reclines at the head of her bunk, contemplating the room around her. The Spartan decor from her days as an Operator is gone, replaced by broad splashes of color literally thrown and dashed against the surfaces. Hues of fiery red and orange run through base coats of wintry blues and mix into confused smears of rainy gray. The swirls and streaks on the walls, harshly clashing, resonate in her mind—an analogue to something unspoken within.

Absently, she runs paint-covered hands through her hair and the locks stick out like fins of a tropical fish. She pouts briefly as she contemplates her violent artwork, feeling its ugliness, yet there is a more potent feeling of frustration. She sighs.

Interesting assignment, Counselor.

She rises and strides barefoot to her hygiene station across carpet gone rigid with drying paint. In the mirror, above a modest sink and tap, she greets an unfamiliar woman in tank top and shorts, splotched from shoulders to thighs in discordant colors. Feminine curves have softened the hard angles of her Operator's physique. Striation still etches a body as hard as marble, but the marble is smoother. More polished than chiseled.

She studies her emerging breasts with annoyance, cupping the soft flesh then pressing them against her chest as though trying to squash them back in. For a moment she considers returning to the Cadre diet with all of its stimulants and steroids.

"No," she says to herself, releasing her flattened B cups. "I can *do* this." She turns from her reflection and strides out of her cabin.

The hallway of the colony ship *Europa* is busy with teams of Cadre

THE EXHAUSTED DEAD

Techs and Colonist specialists collaborating on maintenance projects. Most of the Colonists are unfamiliar, no doubt recently decanted from their cryo-recliners, but she is clearly known to them, and on sight they smirk or chuckle at her wild coloring. In stark contrast, Cadre Techs halt their activity and stare coldly until she passes by.

The sudden hushes grate upon emotions already raw from the absence of her dearest companions, Thompson and Argo. And while the Colonists have openly invited her into their circles, there is always suspicion that the offers are just for show. Infamy of her awful introduction lies subliminal in every nervous interaction. In those friendly, yet cautious, Colonist eyes she sees them wondering if she could kill again.

The facts were irrelevant. Accident or not, she pulled the trigger, and taking human life is the only crime in the Cadre, the only unforgivable sin. In over a thousand years, no Operator had ever broken that law. She, Thompson, and Argo were the first. For their crimes, they were to be sent on a reconnaissance mission, a mission into the very heart of enemy strength. A guaranteed death sentence. And then, at the last moment, to be denied her rightful fate, to be deemed so defective that *even in death* she was not good enough and a replacement Geek named Beckert sent in her stead...

The thought ushers in a dark memory:

> *So alone. Discharged from the Corps and shunned by those for whom she existed to serve. Thompson and Argo exiled, given no chance of return...Bleakness crowded out the last trace of hope, and she longed for a way to disappear, to evaporate completely.*
>
> *When she missed her regular session, the Counselor feared the worst. He found her outside the* Europa's *reactor core, staring at the inner access door. A single lanyard from her partially restored HDI was patched into the locking panel beside it, safeties overridden. All she had to do was think the last command and the door would open, bathing her in incinerating rays.*
>
> *The Counselor used all his persuasion to try and talk her back from the edge. Words bounced off her like gnats on a windscreen until he found the right combination:*
>
> *"What if they find a way? What if Thompson and Argo come* back, *Maiella?"*
>
> *The names pierced her blunted awareness and lodged deeply in her heart. The simple reminder that, no*

matter how slim a chance, she might see them again reeled her back from the door. The only two people in the universe who know exactly what she is going through... The thought of running up to them and embracing them with their familiar shapes and smells...For that happy day, she could outlast anything. She would outlast anything.

Another few turns through the corridors and she marches into the *Europa's* fitness center. High quality floor mats and durable exercise equipment bear the signs of her harsh and frequent attentions. No one else is there. Even if someone were, she knows they would have left on her arrival. Not that the Colonists are rude but, in her compulsion to maintain her Operator's condition, Maiella's workouts are intimidating.

She steps to the center of the exercise floor and closes her eyes, feeling the thickness of the mat beneath her bare feet. Her paint-covered arms extend straight out from the shoulders and her palms turn up toward the high ceiling. As her feet spread to shoulder width, she raises her arms overhead, stretching then crouching, and sweeps her hands at the floor as though gathering. She stands with elbows bent and crosses her wrists over her chest, breathing deeply. She reaches up again and repeats the crouching sweep to stand once more, wrists crossed, breathing deeply in through the nose and out through the mouth.

She opens her eyes slowly, focusing on nothing. Her arms reach into the air around her as if by their own volition. Her body follows as if pulled by them, and she moves like an aquatic creature, gliding through spirals and turns. Her feet know exactly where to go, every step perfectly placed.

Maiella continues the dance to her own silent melody, a being of dense muscle and reinforced bone seeming feather-light in graceful motion, when a dissonant chord strikes. Dark thoughts, tapped by the clashing paints on her wall, trace their way through her body, filling her hips and shoulders with tension. Her graceful movements tighten, her limbs draw closer to her body, coiling, warding. Words she never uttered, never allowed herself to think, roll from her lips in a cascade.

As terrifying as the words are to say, she cannot force herself to take them back. Two years of neglect, abandonment, disdain, doubt, and loneliness have planted an ill seed in her. That germinating seed has finally cracked its shell, seeping an ichor of black ideas.

Maiella's eyes roll back into her head. She slumps to the mat and props herself on her knuckles.

No! Turn it to something else...

3

THE EXHAUSTED DEAD

She summons images of the reptilian enemy, the enemy that burned Earth and the colonies of their human inhabitants, the enemy that tried to kill *every* man, woman, and child. A low growl passes her clenched and bared teeth. She leaps into the air, slaps her knees, somersaults forward, and lands in fighting stance.

She springs explosively, elbows smashing the air, shins cudgeling empty space, hands crushing imaginary throats. Her grunts and growls merge into animalistic roars, as wild as her savage strikes. In her mind's eye, enemies surround her and she whirls through the air, limbs flying, crushing, disfiguring, maiming. Vacant skulls shatter. Joints dislocate. Teeth crack. Necks twist.

She stomps foe after foe into the soft floor with her heel, but there is no end to the pressing horde. Maiella battles on, refusing to acknowledge futility, denying the burning exhaustion in her muscles from such an extended onslaught, until she realizes her imagined enemies are not fighting back. Chest heaving, she stands amid innumerable shades. They glare at her, not with the saffron yellow eyes of the reptilian enemy, but with dark brown and cold gray eyes of Cadre Operators.

Rage drowns in anguish. She crumples to her knees. Her arms drape, palms up. She leans forward, grinding her wracked face into the mat, muffling her sobs.

With a start, she sits up, curls her sweaty hair over each ear, and wipes tears from her eyes.

I've GOT to get control...

Maiella sets onto her backside, crossing her legs in front of her. Back straight, she places her hands in her lap, closes her eyes, and breathes. Thousands of years of human emotion, the evolved outgrowth of instinct suppressed by Cadre conditioning and drugs, runs amok inside her as though trying to make up for lost time. With each inhale she embraces calm. With each exhale she releases intensity. At long last, she sits, glistening from exertion, emotionally spent, feeling more herself, more balanced.

I'm in control.

She rises to her feet and looks out at the room around her. Marks of color, rubbed or flung from her painted limbs, trace her path in sweeping arcs and dark punctuations across the exercise floor. Directly in front of her is a haunting mask with lined forehead, pressed-flat nose, and frowning lips. As she studies her unintended creation, she feels a recognition that something she has carried inside, something she had no vocabulary to express, has gotten out. There is feeling in every stripe, spatter, and smudge. There is also meaning. Pride creeps into her heart for the first time in years.

Beautiful.

A hollow bounce behind her steals her concentration, and she turns to see Gregor walking in. The Russian catches a basketball underhanded and bounces it again, the echoes jarringly loud inside the quiet gymnasium. Long nylon shorts clothe his lower half. A matching yellow shirt bears tall numerals in purple. He is looking over his shoulder at a similarly dressed group of Colonists walking in behind him.

"Nu, tok shtoh? Odna booteelkuh nee—" A short whistle interrupts Gregor's remark and he spins forward. The group behind him falls silent.

"Ah, Maiella! How are you?" Gregor says, flicking his head and smiling in recognition. He bounces the basketball once more before stepping onto the mat and squints at the disheveled woman. "You blow up the paint locker, or something?"

She smiles and shakes her head modestly.

Gregor follows her gaze to the subtle swaths of paint in the floor mats. His eyebrows scrunch in contemplation.

"Huh. You do this?"

Maiella nods.

"Hmm. Hey, we're going to have a game." Gregor points past the mats to an area of open, varnished floor with two hoops and backboards jutting from the walls on either side of it. "You're on my team."

A grumble of protest escapes the shuffling group. Gregor turns on them, annoyed.

"What, you wimps scared she'll play too rough?"

"That's okay," Maiella concedes. "I was gonna get a mop to clean this mess up."

"What?" Gregor spins to face her. "Don't you *dare*. I like it." Gregor starts walking backwards toward the court, his arms open in welcoming gesture. "Sure you won't join us?"

Maiella nods appreciatively.

"All right, Ms. Modern Art. With us both on the same team, wouldn't be fair, anyway," he smiles. "I'll catch up with you at the chow hall."

"Usual table?"

"Of course!" Gregor turns about and jogs to the court. He dribbles the ball, passes it through his legs twice, then throws it to his friends. The screech of rubber shoes fills the gymnasium.

Maiella looks down at the mats one last time before striding out, an eyebrow arched, lips curved in pleasant contemplation.

He liked it.

A MATTER OF FAMILY

The Counselor rounds the corner toward his office on the *Europa* and finds Maiella waiting beside the door. She leans casually against the corridor wall in her dress gray uniform, arms folded, staring far down the hallway. Her hair is slicked straight back, gold HDI terminals peeking between the dark, shiny strands.

He follows her gaze to a formation of Cadre Operators marching toward them. Three Operator teams stride in a close phalanx: three Guns in front, three Geeks in the middle, and three Bricks taking rear. All nine are dressed in full combat kit, faceplates sealed. They fill the wide corridor, their light-absorbing ceramic exteriors blacker than coal, seeming to steal the light from around them.

The Counselor hustles to his doorway and unlocks it.

"Hello, Maiella. How are you?"

She maintains her gaze at the approaching Operators.

"Heya, Doc."

The Counselor is momentarily transfixed by the approaching phalanx. From the silhouette against the white corridor, he notices the rifles in the Guns' armored hands, how much shorter and sleeker they are than Thompson's old relic. The dark armor is similarly streamlined with close-fitting plates and smoothly articulated joints. There is only a faint *thud* from their combined footfalls.

Upgrades.

The Counselor opens the door to his office and slides through, beckoning Maiella to follow. She steps backward into the office, eyes glued to the passing phalanx. They give no acknowledgement to her.

He takes an electronic tablet from the deep pocket of his lab coat and sets it on his desk. Immediately, it links to the terminal built into the desktop and transfers data. He looks up at his early guest, notices traces of paint in her hair and in the folds of her ears. He smiles.

"Did you enjoy the assignment?"

The door to the office glides shut, blocking out the faint boot tromps outside. Maiella turns, looking over the large room with its soft couches and tasteful decorations.

"It was interesting," she says at last. "Not at all what I thought would happen."

"Really?" The white-coated man moves to his typical chair, gestures to the couch opposite him. Maiella follows his cue and plunks down into the cushions. He seats himself comfortably.

"What did you think would happen?"

She looks to the side, scrunches one side of her face. "I don't know. Thought it was kind of wasteful, just spreading paint around." Her eyes lock on to the counselor's in a sideways glance. "But I got upset."

"How so?" the Counselor digs.

"Well, I did like you said, I chose the colors I wanted and started painting them up on the wall with the brush. But they didn't work together, they didn't fit. When I tried to blend them, I got a sickly gray. An ugly color...It upset me."

"What then?"

Maiella scratches her head, her face turned in confusion. "I threw the brush down and started splashing whole cans of paint at the wall." She laughs meekly as though she were watching someone else in her mind. "It was foolish."

"Do you know why you did that?"

Maiella thinks about it, juts her lower lip. "No. And every time I tried to blot out the mess with another splash of paint, it just ran together." Her eyebrows knit. "I ran up to the wall and started hitting it. Slapping it. Raking it with my hands and feet. But I just kept making it worse."

"So what happened?"

She looks at the wall of the office, clean in its whiteness save a large piece of rice paper. Bold black strokes dive and curve across it. She focuses on it before returning the Counselor's gaze.

"I was disturbed but I couldn't see why. So I went to go work out." She readjusts her uniform jacket, trying to ease the snugness of the chest. "I was overwhelmed with anger...No...It was *more* than that...It's like when we psyche ourselves up for a rotation, just before we bore through the hull. It's sharp and it's forceful, but this was so much more than that, unfocused, no control..."

She drifts in the memory.

"I kept seeing these faces around me of enemies, I wanted to crush them all. With bare hands, drive the life from them. I let that feeling take over."

The Counselor sits silently, patiently waiting for her to say what he knows is coming.

"But in the end...They weren't blueskins." She looks up, penitent, shaken, sees the Counselor looking back with concern. He gives the slightest nod, urging her on. Her eyes fall, her shoulders slump.

"I felt a wave of such sadness; I fell down. And I cried." Her head lifts, adding, "I've been doing that a lot."

The Counselor nods again, reading so clearly in her the pain of isolation, the hostility and sadness which hurl her into rage and despair, the loss of comrades who gave her balance, and her inexperience with emotions of such power. Here is a woman of phenomenal talent, beauty, and capacity for feeling. And what she feels is a crushing loneliness.

"But when you stopped crying, what happened?"

The heaviness in her cheeks and eyes lifts. "I saw the marks on the floor mats, all the paint I had thrown or smudged in during my workout. All the same colors were there, but they were organized." She looks again at the paper with the elegant, heavy strokes and points at it. "What do you call that?"

The Counselor turns in his seat and looks over his shoulder.

"That's Japanese Calligraphy."

"Calligraphy," Maiella echoes. "Yeah, it was like that. Like writing, with purpose. It made sense to me, the colors and the movements all laid out...it made sense."

The Counselor faces front with a subtle smile, knowing why it would make sense but wanting to draw it out of her.

"How so?"

Maiella beams with pride, a slight blush on her cheeks.

"I didn't understand your assignment. Thought I wouldn't get it, and after the mess I made in my quarters, I thought I'd failed."

"Yes?" the Counselor leads.

She looks at him in gratitude. "When I saw the floor of the gymnasium...I wasn't trying to make anything, it just came out of me. I didn't understand your assignment, but right there, I knew I had succeeded in completing it."

The Counselor grins. "I knew you would, Maiella." He shifts in his seat, growing serious.

"The Cadre doesn't put a lot of value in emotions, so I can see why you don't have the words to describe thoughts and feelings we Colonists take for granted. I felt giving you an alternate means of expression, colors in this case, would let you speak your mind. Most interesting to me is that color wasn't enough, so you added movement...combining the two is a very advanced form of artistic expression, Maiella. That you came to it intuitively...that really impresses me."

"Yeah, well..." She looks away modestly. "I was gonna clean it up when Gregor came in. He said not to. He said he liked it."

The Counselor watches her features change. *Her heart warms at the thought of someone else appreciating what she made. Or maybe it's more about Gregor?*

"You two have seen a fair amount of each other," the Counselor probes. He waits for Maiella to pick up the thread.

"Mm, hmm. We usually take third nutrition interval together."

The Counselor pretends mild surprise, having already heard this from Gregor himself. "Do you talk?"

"Mm, hmm. I'm pretty much frozen out of everything Cadre-related now, so he keeps me informed on what's going on. Did you hear? General O'Kai suspended the collection rotations."

The counselor nods. "I did. The *Europa's* production facilities are tied in pretty closely to Cadre One now, supplying energy, resources, food. No need to risk lives capturing supplies."

"He's got the whole Operator Corps running ship-to-ship war games. From what I hear, Ralla and Chusan are testing all-new tactics: combined sneaks, ambushes, direct confrontations, co-ordinated strikes...sounds exciting." Maiella gets a trace of melancholy about her, which the Counselor swiftly diverts.

"You and Gregor talk about other things, as well?"

"Oh, sure. Well, actually, he does most of the talking. I listen, mostly. You know, I'm not sure what I have to offer him."

"You must have some idea."

She leans on one knee. "Several males have shown an...*interest*... lately. They don't look me in the eye. They look *hungry*...but not for chow...I don't know what they're after...It's easy enough to scare 'em off, anyway." She frowns, perplexed.

"Is it so hard to understand? Your body is going through some major changes, changes which most males find attractive. Haven't you had these feelings yourself?"

Her eyes roll. "Oh, *yes...*" Her knees clamp together and she shudders. She opens her mouth to say more then censors herself.

"You can explore them, you know," the Counselor volunteers.

"The Cadre thinks it's revolting."

He thinks very carefully before replying, wanting to move her away from the culture which rejects her without underscoring feelings of exile and isolation.

"Everything you were as a Cadre Operator, you are still. But you only have to look in the mirror to see how much *more* you're becoming. You're crossing the chasm between our two societies. Believe me, I see the span, and it's a very long journey. This journey is changing you mentally and physically into something unique and remarkable. Something unlike anything in the Cadre..." He leans forward for emphasis. "So you don't have to *think* like them anymore, Maiella."

She looks down at her feet, clearly moved by the words, but in which direction he cannot quite tell. She brings a hand up to her heart and holds it there. After anxious seconds, she inhales sharply and looks up, intense relief shining from watered eyes. She nods and exhales slowly. Her head dips once more as she ponders the constricting chest of her threadbare uniform.

"Doesn't quite fit like it used to."

The Counselor purses his lips, feeling her double meaning. *At last, she recognizes the gap between herself and others who wear the charcoal grays, and she has snapped that tether to her past. She's free.*

The glassy-eyed woman dabs water from her cheeks with her uniform sleeve. "Can't tell you how much I needed to hear that, Counselor. A soldier needs permission, you know."

"I know," he bows, waiting until she is fully composed. "There must be a lot of feeling woven into that uniform. I'm sure it's warm with the experiences of everyone who wore it. But maybe we can find you something new."

Maiella shines. "Okay."

"Okay," he echoes, placing his hands at the edge of his seat. He slides forward until he is perched at the edge of it.

"We went far today, Maiella. Would you agree?"

She nods emphatically.

"We need to go just a bit further. Are you all right with that?"

She nods again, wary yet compliant.

"I have a couple more assignments for you."

"Shoot."

"I'm glad to see you channeling your emotions creatively. Now that you've gotten off the inhibitors, you're going through what we would call your 'adolescence' a few years later than normal. You'll continue to have these wild swings. When you feel them coming on, I want you to take a breath and intercept them, just until you can give them creative expression. Gradually, you'll come by the control you seek, and we'll discuss your progress on an ongoing basis."

"Understood."

"This next bit is going to be hard. And I wouldn't ask it unless I thought it was time."

Her back is straight, shoulders square. "I'm ready."

The Counselor hedges a moment, uncomfortable with what he is about to ask.

"It's about Gregor and his interest in you."

Maiella mirrors the Counselor's posture, perching at the edge of the cushions.

"Yes?" She clasps her hands together and lays them on her knees, attention riveted to her therapist.

"There's something Gregor has needed to talk about with you—"

"Oh, no..." Maiella interrupts. The Counselor waits, resting elbows on his knees and placing one fist inside the other. He leans forward, pressing his folded hands against his mouth, and peers over his knuckles at his client. She tentatively meets his stare.

"It's about his wife, Iskra...Right?" she asks.

The Counselor nods behind his fists. "The conflict inside him has been awful." He trails off, painfully aware of the breach of protocol, the violation of privacy just mentioning this represents. *But this is no longer a matter of Human Resources regulations. It's a matter of family.*

"He hides it well, but he isn't getting better," the Counselor explains. "Her loss has haunted him ever since the accident, and somehow, you've become a last link to her."

Maiella's posture deflates. She looks down at her feet.

"Look at me," the Counselor demands.

Her eyes lift, devoid of will.

"I know what I ask of you, Maiella. This may be the hardest thing you've ever had to face, may be the hardest thing you ever *have* to face. But you must. For Gregor, and for yourself. Just remember, I'm here for you both."

She nods, heavy and deliberate. Her eyes squint with reserved determination.

"I'll—"

A violent tone sounds.

"GENERAL QUARTERS!" blares the intercom. "UNIDENTIFIED VESSEL DETECTED. REPORT TO STATIONS. REPEAT. UNIDENTIFIED VESSEL DETECTED. REPORT TO STATIONS."

Maiella launches from the couch and dashes from the room before the message repeats. The Counselor watches the depressed cushions rise where Maiella sat a split second ago. He turns wide-eyed at the walls of his office, walls which suddenly feel stifling and caging. But he has no combat training, no skills to defend his people.

For him, there is nowhere to run.

With quiet dignity, he takes a seat behind his desk, stares at the intercom speaker, and waits in case anyone should need him.

TEAM FORESTALL

Maiella dashes through the hallways of the *Europa*, dodging frantic and screaming colonists. Two running in opposite directions slam one another and fall, tossing their carried tools and equipment across the deck. Running Colonists take no notice and stampede right over them.

The agile woman shoves her way to the fallen colonists and takes them by the nape, lifting them back to their feet when an elbow slams her forehead. Eyes blinking, she staggers back and shakes her head.

"THAT'S ENOUGH, DAMN IT!"

Maiella's powerful voice carries throughout the corridor, and the flurry halts. Timid eyes turn in her direction, cowed by the strength of her command and by the need for someone to lead them to safety.

"We've prepared for this!" Maiella bellows. "Now get to your stations *quickly* and *calmly*. Be ready to assist. *Understood?"*

Maiella releases the two in her grasp and looks them in the face. One of them is Sharon Jones, the *Europa's* navigator and third in command. Sharon rubs a swelling egg on her forehead.

A great silence ensues as uncertain eyes search one another. Sharon steps away from the tall woman, embarrassed at getting caught in the panic yet recognizing her cue for authority.

"Maiella said, *'Is that understood?'"*

Like a pattering of rain, the responses come to her: "Yes, Ma'am! Understood, Ma'am!"

"Then *GO*," Sharon dismisses, still rubbing her swelling forehead. The crowd forms orderly queues along each side of the corridor and jogs in opposite directions like lanes of traffic on a highway.

"Are you all right?" Maiella asks.

Sharon nods and stoops to collect the remains of her gear. "I have to get to the bridge, immediately."

"I have to get to Cadre One," the tall woman asks. "Can you get me clearance?"

Sharon frowns at her crushed data tablet, scoops the bits. "I can get you on a transport, but I can't *make* them let you back in."

"That'll do." Maiella whirls and dashes down the center gap in the corridor, barking out, *"One side, coming through! Calm and orderly, people...keep your lines! We'll protect you, just get to your stations!"*

She ducks through a low hatchway to a small transport craft packed with Operators, fully equipped for combat. They stare menacingly.

"I'm getting in this fight," Maiella growls and she shoves her way into them. Armored hands seize her and are about to launch her from the craft when Deepak's voice sounds through his helmet speaker.

"Hold it. She's cleared for flight. Commander Jones's order."

The hands grasping her retract robotically and the transport hatch seals. With a rough jolt, the craft detaches from the tremendous colony ship and darts toward the asteroid's surface, toward the enormous crater in which nests the ancient genetic research facility, Cadre One.

A small porthole beside Maiella gives her a view of the buzzing activity around them. Craft of all different sizes streak and maneuver toward a distant intruder—an intruder only visible as a smoky, orange glow. She squints hard for a better view.

Sleek warships, captured from the reptilian enemy and pressed into Cadre service, thrust past the transport with weapons trained on the distant glow. Captured bulk freighters and passenger liners form a defensive wall around the main complex.

Maiella looks down at Cadre One. Four circular mirrors, six-meters in diameter, have popped up from the crater rim. The mirrors perch at the edge of deep silos, and all four orient toward the intruder. A faint violet glow escapes from the silos below.

The transport levels out near the crater rim, which blocks Maiella's view of the facility. She cranes her head to see through another porthole, suddenly aware that despite the crowded interior she has complete freedom of movement. She pivots in place and sees all Operators backed away from her, staring.

They won't even stand near me...

The radio crackles to life, *"Stand down, repeat, stand down. Non-hostile. Non-hostile. Codes confirmed, Team Forestall has returned from deployment."*

Maiella pins herself against the transport wall, face pressed into the porthole.

"All craft clear landing zone," the radio blares. *"Prep MedLab for priority wounded. MedTechs, stand by to receive."* The transport slows unexpectedly, and skates sideways from the landing pattern.

Through her porthole, Maiella watches a small craft wobble its way toward the landing bay. Every visible surface is scorched from high-energy beams or sooty explosions. Whole sections of hull plating are peeled back or punched in from impacts. The back right quarter is jagged metal and twisted spars where a booster must have been. Smoke billows from the blasted gap and glows bright orange with the companion booster's flame. Nacelles at each wing tip radiate in deep red.

Maiella's eyes strain to see through the damaged craft's cockpit glass and, just before the vessel enters the bay, she sees a great round head in the pilot's place.

"ARGO!"

Her eager eyes search for some trace of the others when an obvious thought occurs to her.

Why isn't Beckert piloting?

Dread mingles with joy. Waves of inundating emotion surge over her.

Where's Thompson?

Her cheeks flare with each breath on the verge of hyperventilation when the Counselor's words echo in her mind.

Intercept them...until you can give them creative expression...

She closes her eyes and concentrates, reeling in her wild feelings and encapsulating them deep inside as though storing them in a locker. She takes a deep breath and exhales. The fountain of emotion flows forcefully within her, and she mentally diverts the flow to that locker like a sink.

Calm, calm, calm, she mentally chants. *Don't react until you know.*

The hobbled, smoking craft limps into the landing bay and sets down on thick struts. Two small escorts follow the craft inside and the landing bay doors draw closed behind them.

Maiella is a coiled spring of impatience, ready to snap. She wants to yell at the pilot to move his ass, to get them docked. Instead, she breathes deliberately, evenly, easing the pressure she feels inside. The radio breaks the tense silence.

"Europa transport, unload Operator crew at three-one-niner. Assistance required in handling enemy captive. Acknowledge, over."

The Geek piloting the transport transmits his response, "Understood,

Cadre One," and finally, the transport moves again. With a clunk, it settles into a small docking cradle cut into the facility's exterior wall. When the hatch lifts, Maiella sees dozens of MedTechs jogging or hitch-stepping toward the landing bay in smooth coordination. Their readiness marks a sharp contrast to the frenzied chaos of the *Europa*.

Deepak's clipped voice shouts into the flow of MedTechs.

"Clear a path!"

The Operators aboard the transport surge through the open hatchway, ejecting Maiella before them. Maiella sneers at the disrespect but takes rank behind the last Brick, using his bulk to cut a path and to hide her through the crowded corridors. She runs on toes to stay silent.

Ahead, the corridor widens and connects with the central corridor from the landing bay.

How many times I proudly walked that path, she thinks with a twinge.

There is an unseen commotion of many feet on polished floors from around the corner, coming from the landing bay, and the sound of laden gurneys approaching. A woman's voice, small yet intense, dictates medical intubations, injections, and ligations.

The first gurney wheels into the intersection. Maiella hops just over the Brick's shoulder, catching a glimpse of gray-stumped flesh atop a stainless steel table. A petite woman with ponytail, spectacles, and a white coat rides the back of the gurney as MedTechs rush the wheeled table by.

"Gangrene! He's gone septic...*Jesus*, stage three!" the petite woman declares. "Need a full dialysis kit, transfusions, antibiotics, and..." her voice trails off down the branching halls. A horrific stench permeates the air.

Another gurney whisks by with a long figure stretched atop it, covered in broken armor plates. With another hop, Maiella sees the supine figure of Thompson, emaciated, pale, and motionless, his face slumped toward her with a severe laser burn and closed eyes.

No, Thompson, NO! Her heart leaps with grief until the rational thought occurs, *they wouldn't be rushing if he were dead...*

Argo limps behind the gurney, one arm thrown over Colonel Munro's shoulders, the other protecting his side. His armor is stripped down to his waist with a yellow and red-streaked undershirt covering his torso. Every step wracks his gaunt face. His eyes are recessed in their sockets and hollow cheeks give him a concentrated, ghoulish appearance.

Argo lifts his hand away from his side for a moment and peers down at a severely infected gash. He looks away in abject pain.

Maiella ducks past the Operators in front of her, nimbly taking stride beside her cherished friend. Despite the agony of his injuries, his eyes shine in their dark recesses like embers.

"Hey big man," she says, suppressing the desire to throw her arms around him. "Missed you."

"Oh, OW! Ah, ah..." Argo tries to take a deep enough breath to speak, and it comes out in a rush. "Missed you, too...could've used your help." He tries to smile.

"Maiella," Munro says firmly, "let us help him."

She nods in reluctant understanding, holding her fist up to Argo. The wounded Brick brings his fist up and taps it against hers.

Chains *clang* behind her, and she turns to see a reptilian creature with chalky, peeling skin stumble in on brittle legs. A loop of chain is fastened at its broad neck, cinched below the long jaw. It gasps through white lips curled back from blunt teeth and receded gums. Diaphanous garments wrap the creature loosely, and its whip-like tail drags on the floor behind it. Saffron yellow eyes roam in exhausted terror and lock on to Maiella in a pleading gaze.

With a barked command, the Operators surround the frail creature, weapons poised. Deepak snatches the length of chain and yanks, dragging the pitiful thing from the doorway. It chokes dryly and wheezes, only barely keeping on its delicate feet. Another Gun takes position behind, rifle poised. The rifle's bayonet slides into place with a *shick*.

Maiella steps aside in curious silence, looking eye to eye as the reptilian creature passes by.

You're taller than the others, she thinks.

"Hey...*exile*."

Maiella whirls on one of the Geek Operators. His facemask is open and retracted over his head. He is very young, very late generation.

"You don't belong here," the young Geek scolds. "Time to *go*."

She studies the youthful features, the relative absence of scars on his fair cheeks. The disgust.

In the blink of an eye, she could explode at him, wrest his pistols from him and empty both clips into his sneering face. She looks behind the Geek at the other six: an assortment of Bricks, Geeks, and a Gun. Her eyes map the path through them and their weapons, her suppressed emotions straining for sweet release. She dips her head.

"May you serve well, Sergeant," Maiella says. She looks up at the young Geek then turns to the other Operators, addressing them as a group. "And may you all live as long as *I* have."

She strides back to the transport. The hatch seals and she is whisked

THE EXHAUSTED DEAD

back to the *Europa*.

THE NEED TO SERVE

Maiella sits in the *Europa's* cafeteria, absently jabbing her bowl of synth-hash with a spoon. The labyrinth of Cadre One's air ducts and crawlspaces rotates in her mind as she maps an unseen path into MedLab.

I could nick the security feeds at most of the portals, she thinks, *but if I cut through...the pressure changes would get picked up immediately...*

Gregor walks up and lets his metal tray clatter onto the table across from her. She hurtles back from her concentration, watching him place a tape-sealed medical container on the table next to his tray.

"Where'd you get off to?" He slides onto one of the table's attached stools and spreads a napkin in his lap.

"Hmm? Oh. Trying to figure a way in to see Thompson and Argo."

"Thompson, huh?" His ears flush. His shoulders and neck tense slightly. He attacks the chow on his tray a little harder than necessary. "Still trying to get clearance?"

Maiella notices his demeanor change, not understanding it.

"I'm working on something more direct."

Gregor looks up from his tray, swallowing both his mouthful and his amused disbelief.

"So you're gonna sneak into Cadre One?" He laughs and shovels another bite. Through the side of his face, he adds, "That would be rich. They'd love that!"

"I don't care anymore."

Gregor's smile straightens as he looks directly at her.

"I can see." He looks back at the tray. "But Tom and Argo're gonna be fine, you know." He sits up, arches an eyebrow. "Don't know how, though. Goddamn...Your boy, Tom, they say he must've been shot over a hundred times, his armor was so banged up..."

She cringes. "What about Beckert?"

Gregor goes on as if he did not hear.

"It's a good thing the shots that got through cauterized, or he would have bled out in seconds. Gonna need skin grafts, muscle grafts, a lung..."

"What about Beckert?"

"...and he's got a big one right here on his face..."

Maiella's hand slaps the table.

"Gregor!"

The Russian stops, sees the hurt in her eyes.

"Enjoying yourself?" she asks. The mix of shame and embarrassment in his face shows her that, indeed, he was.

He looks over his shoulder at the sudden quiet in the large cafeteria. Nervous eyes turn from his gaze and shoulders hunch over their trays. Gregor faces forward.

"I'm sorry, Mai. Was cold of me to say all that..." He looks up at her, genuinely remorseful. His tongue clucks in his mouth as he looks away, and he draws a deep breath.

"Beckert's bad. *Real* bad." He looks straight at her. "It's a fight for life right now. Doc Taggart and the MedTechs have laced him up best they can, but...even if he pulls through, they say he'll never operate again."

Maiella runs back through her training regime with the young Geek, wondering if she left anything out, something which might have saved him from his fate. She recalls the first gurney as it rolled by her in the corridor with its tragic lading of gray, pallid flesh.

Gregor watches her retreat mentally and reels her back.

"Hey. We all know you did a great job with Beckert...The fact they came home at all, that says a lot, right?"

Maiella plants her spoon in the bowl of hash and pushes it away, nodding.

"So anyways," Gregor says, picking up the taped medical container, "This has to go to MedLab at Cadre One, but I don't know anyone who'd want to take it there. Do you?"

Maiella perks straight up on her stool.

"Are you serious?" she asks.

Gregor grins. "Somehow, the *Europa* got all her crew busy at the same time. Looks like you're the only one available to take it."

Maiella leans forward on her seat. "You got me *clearance?*"

"Yeah. And I think Doc Taggart asked for some assistance while you're there. Should take, oh, a half hour or so." He slides the container over to her.

Maiella presses both palms into the tabletop and flips herself over to Gregor's side. She wraps her arms around him and squeezes tight.

"Thank you, Gregor, *thank you!*"

"Yeah, yeah," he says, nearly choking. "Go see your friends."

The strong woman releases him and snatches the container from the table. Gregor watches her sprint like a gazelle for the exit, vaulting easily over the long tables and colonists in her way.

He sighs deeply and pushes his tray away.

"Shit."

Maiella streaks through the corridors of the big colony ship, winding her way to the closest transport and cradling the package in one arm like an American footballer. The moment she ducks inside, she slaps the button to seal the hatch.

"Go!" she barks to the pilot.

The colonist pilot snorts and keys her radio. "Cadre One, transport departing from Europa. Intend to dock with supplies for MedLab."

"Europa *transport, steer to auxiliary bay 4C for unlading. Operators en route to assist. Cadre One out."*

The transport detaches from the Europa and jets smoothly toward the crater-nested base below. Maiella steps forward to look over the pilot's shoulder. Through the windscreen, she sees the main hangar bay doors are wide open. Inside is a heavily damaged craft, the one which brought Argo, Beckert, and Thompson home.

"Why is the bay open to space?" she asks.

"That poor ship's shot up worse than the team," the pilot answers. *"Huge* fire hazard, so they're keeping a vacuum around it 'til they get it patched up." The pilot peeks over her shoulder, noticing Maiella's gaze riveted to the scorched and cudgeled craft. "I can get you a closer look if you like."

Maiella nods emphatically.

The pilot takes the transport down below the crater rim and makes a lazy turn, passing right by the open bay doors. Suited personnel crawl over the craft's battered hull plates. Most of the workers are crouched, blue sparks arcing around them.

"Some of our engineers have had a look already," the pilot volunteers. "They told me that thing has got some pretty amazing armor. But the inside is plush as a prince's parlor. Probably a limousine for some high-ranking diplomat."

Maiella instantly recalls the withered alien dragged past her in chains. Tall, with pleading saffron eyes...

"What happened to the blueskin they brought back?"

The pilot shrugs. "Beats me. I think the Counselor is doing something with it for General O'Kai, but he hasn't said what."

Maiella takes a last glance at the battered craft before it slips from sight.

With ease, the colonist pilot swings the back of the transport toward an exterior docking cradle and thrusts into it. The sturdy clamps lock tight and draw the small shuttle in with a *clunk*.

Maiella stands at the hatchway, medical container cradled in her left arm. When the hatch opens, two armored Guns stand outside like vault doors. One of them looks down at the small package Maiella holds and searches for more. Finding none, Keiko's gruff voice sounds through her helmet speaker.

"We'll take that." Keiko takes a hand from her rifle and extends it palm up.

"Negative," Maiella counters. "My presence was requested by Doctor Taggart."

Keiko stares hard into Maiella, but she retracts her demanding hand.

"Verifying. Stand by." Keiko stands rigidly during her inaudible conversation then suddenly steps out of the way. Her companion soldier does likewise.

"You're cleared for thirty minutes," Keiko announces. "We'll collect you when it's time."

"Thank you," Maiella says, and she nods respectfully. Keiko returns the nod. Her companion does not.

Maiella drifts through the hallways with the eerie recollection of a dream. Two years have passed since she held active duties at Cadre One, the last day of which was when she turned over the Earth-bound transport to Thompson and watched him depart. She wonders if he found her embedded message, if he will be as glad to see her as she is to see him...or if he will even recognize her in her current state.

The last thought freezes her in her tracks.

No, Argo recognized me. Thompson will, too. She places one foot in front of the other, and forces herself to keep walking.

Many Cadre faces pass by, some acknowledging her with a stare, others looking away in disgust. Many of them she has seen before, or at least she thinks she has. The latest generation is so similar in appearance, many of the newest Cadre personnel could be twins. Maybe clones.

Between the glaring Operators and MedTechs are the Reconstitutes. Their white coats with tall numbers, metal craniums, and dark lens-covered eyes set them apart from the charcoal-uniformed personnel in the polished hallways. The ones slogging by have massive frames, matching the latest Bricks in musculature, and carry incredible amounts of equipment: metal framing, engine components, stacks of laundry—all piled hundreds of kilograms thick, and not even a grunt from their expressionless faces.

So many more now than I remember.

After the accident aboard the *Europa*, she was so depressed she could barely get out of bed, much less fulfill a duty schedule. There was talk among the senior Cadre Officers of reconstituting her to recover, "...at the least, her labor potential." A chill races through her.

That could've been me.

She shakes the chilling thought off to concentrate on something better: deep within Cadre One, she knows, there is a new batch of embryos being cultivated—the first to benefit from combined Cadre/Colonist pairings of DNA. Before the two groups found one another, the Cadre had suffered badly from a shallow gene pool and it was always a struggle to keep ahead of the genetic diseases cropping up in every new generation. Despite the initial arguments in selecting whose genes were to be matched, these embryos will be healthy, strong hybrids with the best features of each parent. *Very exciting.*

When Maiella arrives at the plexi-steel entry doors to MedLab, a narrow beam sweeps from her feet up to her face. With a ding, the red LED on the door lock switches to green and the double doors slide aside.

The chambers within are bright with diffuse white light such that no shadow interrupts the surfaces. She squints as she enters, recognizing the dimensions of the room but nothing of its decor. Most of the equipment is updated, smaller. Colonist influence is plainly visible in the renovations, where the clunky Cadre machinery has yielded to the more streamlined instruments of the *Europa*.

MedTechs fill benches on each side of the curved walls, leaning into their individual workstations. Elastic white hats cover their heads, ventilator masks cover their faces, and they wear white smocks over their Cadre uniforms. They ignore her completely, concentrating on intricate pipettes and dimpled trays.

She passes between them into the larger medical facility beyond. Rows of plexi-steel cylinders at the back of the circular space command her attention, in particular the ones darkened with occupants.

Maiella walks in a trance toward them, recognizing the backlit outlines of her beloved teammates. Argo takes up most of his fluid-filled tube. Thompson droops limply in his. In the tube beside Thompson is something fleshy, yet unrecognizable, a swollen blob with a single curved limb. She steps tentatively toward it, knowing it is Beckert, and sets the medical package onto a stainless steel operating table.

A compulsion draws her closer, and she sees the mangled Geek's skin is mottled with bruises, burns, and contusions. Swollen red eyeballs bulge in their sockets, keeping the lids slightly parted. Shunts dive into his skull between silver HDI terminals. Air hoses enter through each nostril. His lips are sewn shut.

Maiella's gaze falls to Beckert's distended abdomen where new surgery scars run the length of his torso. A loose-fitting codpiece services his eliminations with dual hoses, beneath which his legs end at skinless pink stumps. His left arm ends at a similar stump above the elbow, and his right arm hangs in a limp curve. Everywhere the skin is broken, tiny bubbles fizz like carbonation.

Maiella covers her mouth and turns from her mutilated student to Thompson. Like Beckert, Thompson wears a metallic codpiece with the attached hoses. Air is fed to him through a strapped-on mask, and his limbs drift with the tube's gentle currents. Numerous circular chunks have been burned out of him. One shoulder bears new surgery scars, and large patches of skin are missing from his chest, arms, legs, and face. Every rib stands out prominently. With his sunken gut and hollow cheeks, he is an emaciated outline of the muscular soldier who departed two years ago.

She wishes for his head to lift, for those steel gray eyes to open and to recognize her. The slow, regular blip of a heart monitor is all she gets.

But you're alive...

She slumps against the warm plexi-steel, feeling the slow churning inside, hearing the fizz of bubbles at his injuries, and she wraps her arms as far around as she can reach.

"It was really close with those two," comes a woman's voice behind her.

Maiella peels herself from the plexi-steel to find the voice. Seated at a desk on a sidewall is a very petite woman with long black hair, which is tied back and streaked with gray. Reading glasses perch on the woman's head and she wears a white lab coat like the Counselor's. The woman stands and strides to meet Maiella at the transparent tubes.

"Thompson had serious weapon burns on his lungs and heart. Took a high dose of radiation, too." The small doctor shakes her head. "Gonna slow his healing, but he'll make it."

The fist of worry in Maiella's chest releases and she lets out her held breath.

The small woman extends a hand, and with a hint of Irish inflection says,

"Hi. I'm Sahara."

Unsure if she should salute, Maiella stares at, then takes the outstretched hand.

"Doctor Taggart? I'm Maiella."

"I know," Sahara says with a smile. "Counselor told me about you. Said you really needed to see your friends. I was happy to help. Gregor, too."

Maiella nods graciously then her eyes return to the ruined Geek. "What about Beckert?"

Sahara whistles and shakes her head. "He's still critical. Suffered multiple organ failures, and he needed a complete blood replacement. Not to mention the other obvious injuries...In all honesty, I can't believe he's still alive." Sahara gestures to the tank on the other side of Thompson. "Your man Argo is a *talented* field surgeon."

Maiella steps over to Argo's cylinder. Like Thompson, the Brick is emaciated. Paper-thin skin reveals every sinew, joint, and bone. In the center of his chest is a purple contusion, surrounded by reddened, blistered skin. The edges of a wide gash in his side protrude like swollen lips, fizzing with copious bubbles. A combination air mask and goggles, similar to the one on his helmet, covers his face. The eyepieces glow with internal video.

Sahara joins Maiella in contemplating Argo and his injuries.

"With the radiation Thompson got, and Beckert's septicemia, it was obvious why they were suffering multiple organ failures. But I wasn't expecting it in Argo."

Maiella's head swivels, her eyebrows lowered. "What do you mean?"

Sahara stares at the big man. "They brought something back from Earth. A virus." The small doctor takes the tablet from under her arm and illuminates the screen. "A hemorrhagic, in fact."

"I'm not a MedTech, Doc. A *what?*"

Sahara passes the tablet over. Maiella takes it and on the screen is an old photograph of a dark-skinned patient. The patient bleeds from mouth, nose and eyes.

"A hemorrhagic virus attacks the lining of your blood vessels, cells of the liver, even white blood cells," the doctor explains. "You bleed to death internally. As you can see, it isn't pretty."

Maiella passes the tablet back, and Sahara clears the image.

"There were outbreaks of this kind back on Earth," Sahara continues.

"Africa, mostly. But the incubation was so fast, patients usually died before they could spread it to others. This one though..." Sahara looks down at her tablet, pulls up some data on Argo, Beckert, and Thompson then hands the tablet over.

"...it's *too* perfect. The incubation period is longer, giving the infected plenty of travel time. And it doesn't just attack the body, it suppresses the body's immune response like HIV. Like someone *crafted* it. Spliced the worst parts of each virus together."

Maiella looks over the tablet, seeing in the Doctor's notes how easily the virus might have infected all of Cadre One if not for the anti-viral measures already in place. When she looks at the Doctor, Sahara is staring severely.

"Maiella, what *was* this place before the attack?"

"Genetic Research," she answers automatically. Hearing her own words, her head rocks back. "No. No, we *couldn't* have made this."

Maiella feels the accusation in Sahara's stare, in its wordless assumptions. She looks around at the spotless workstations, the specialized bio-suits hanging on the walls, the windows into the isolated genetic assembly rooms, and the secure corridor to those rooms with its three-stage decontamination process.

Could we?

Maiella grabs her head, dazed, off balance. She finds a chair and collapses into it.

"Why would we?" the tall woman says at last. "We need every human life we have to survive! We need all of you! All of us, *together*. This *couldn't* be Cadre made."

In Maiella's confused expression, Sahara can see the blissful ignorance of power politics and profit motives, the innocent naïveté.

"I'm sorry, I jumped to a conclusion. It could be a new strain, one which evolved in our absence." *But not bloody likely,* her arched eyebrows seem to say.

Maiella sits up in sudden realization.

"What if the blueskins weren't there? And we landed the colony on Earth..."

"All of us would have been infected at once. We might have lost everyone...everything," Sahara finishes.

"Is there a cure?"

"The MedTechs are working on it right now. The short-term fix was to manufacture antibodies and stimulate the immune systems of anyone exposed. We've arrested the advance, because the MedTechs caught it so early. These guys," she says, hiking a thumb at the fluid-filled cylinders, "we've pumped full of donated white blood cells. Since we were taking spare parts, anyway..." She flicks her head at a bank of Plexi-steel cylinders on an adjacent wall. Three of the tubes contain what appear to be identical occupants.

Maiella watches Sahara's mouth turn down with disgust, and her eyes move to the triplets in the transparent cylinders. All three have metallic craniums and dark lenses over their eyes. Tubes run into the nostrils and chest cavities. As Maiella squints, she can just make out lengthy pink scars down their midlines and inner thighs. They wear no codpiece, and she is surprised to discover one of them is female.

"Captain Keller told me some of your practices were hard to accept, but *Jesus!*" Sahara rants. *"Living organ banks?* Nazi doctors were executed for this sort of thing."

Maiella does not need to know what a Nazi was to feel the blame of the word.

"I'm not a...*Notsee*," Maiella says feebly.

Sahara's eyes go wide. "Oh my God, I'm so sorry! I didn't mean *you!*" She stamps a foot and looks to one side, muttering, "Good job, Sahara! Making friends today, are we?"

The doctor takes Maiella gently by the arm. "Please forgive me, Maiella, I get on my soapbox sometimes...I really didn't mean you!"

Maiella shakes her head as though there were nothing to forgive, and buries the hurt. "It's okay, Doc. Just another color for my wall."

Sahara squints, and her mouth puckers, not understanding. She shakes her head. "Tell you what...I'm gonna go check on the MedTechs, see if I can be useful. See if I can keep myself from saying anything stupid for a while." She smiles warmly. "Call if I can help."

On her way out, Sahara pauses and raps on Argo's tank. The Brick's eyepieces halt their flashes of light. The small doctor taps the intercom button on the tank.

"Hey. You got a visitor." Sahara pats the tank affectionately and strides off.

Argo spots Maiella immediately. His eyes, just visible through transparent lenses, lift at the corners.

"Maiella! Excellent to see you!"

"Hey, big man." She folds her arms and smiles. "Whatcha doin'?"

"Studying the Colonist archives on pathogens. My knowledge was far from complete... But how have you fared?"

Maiella looks down. The misery of the last two years wants to come boiling to the surface, but this is not the time. Lifting her head, she shines with some of her old charm.

"I'm alive, aren't I? What's that tell you?"

"That you're the meanest, toughest, thickest-skulled Geek in the Corps."

She props herself up on the tank and laughs, really laughs, for the first time in years.

"Missed you, brother." The melancholy evaporates and she is the grinning version of herself again. "So fill me in. What was it like?"

"Earth?"

She rolls her eyes. "Yes, *Earth!*" She leans into the tank.

Argo's reddened eyes look off to some distant place.

"It was remarkable," he utters. "There's an abundance of life there, raw materials, *atmosphere*...and the things we found...remains of *cities*. Once, our numbers were *vast*." The Brick's eyes fall suddenly upon her. "But the enemy is strong. They'll be hard to defeat."

Maiella hangs on his words, hungering for more. "What else?"

Argo blinks. "Incredible life forms...and the combat...I lost count how many times we were hit. Thompson was brilliant. And so was Beckert! I'm amazed what the new Geeks can accomplish...until..." Argo's head dips.

"Until what?"

Argo's head lifts, his eyes heavy with the memory.

"He made a mistake. Thompson tried to save him, but..." Argo cranes his neck toward Beckert's tank. With the curved glass and Thompson's tank in between, there is little for the Brick to see. When he looks back at Maiella, her expression begs an answer to an unvoiced question.

"There was no flaw in your training, Maiella. He made a novice mistake."

She nods, taking a little comfort. It does not change the fact that her excellent pupil is now a remnant of what he was. Tattered. Broken.

"There were times during the mission," Argo adds, "when he lost focus. Seemed distracted by what was going on around him. I was concerned he may not be Operator standard...but he discovered nearly all of the useful data, and it was Beckert who had the insight of taking hostages. When we did, we found the enemy became...*reserved* in their tactics, which allowed us to escape. No. This was a difficult rotation. Beckert performed well."

The predator deep inside Maiella, long dormant from non-violent duties, stirs with the specifics in Argo's tale. Her hands grip and flex with the touch of adrenaline in her veins. She presses close to the glass and looks through her eyebrows.

"What was it like, Brick?"

Argo leans forward, caught by her mood and sharing in it. "The most *intense* combat. Up close, hand to hand. Grenades. Blades. The foe was inexhaustible. Kill one, two more appear. And a new kind of combatant, almost *my* size." He points with effort to the gash in his side. "Gave me *this*."

Maiella looks at the gaping wound, then back into Argo's eyes. Behind that mask, she knows, is an expression of admiration and respect for a worthy opponent. She looks down at the floor, feeling envy. Envy of these marks of honor branded and carved into Argo's skin. Envy of their success in a mission given no chance of return. Envy of their adventure to their ancient home world, of breathing free air, of taking the fight into the heart of enemy strength and *surviving*.

She lifts her head and stands straighter, not leaning on the tank so heavily.

"And the planet, Argo?"

"What about it?"

"What was *it* like?"

Argo nods in recollection. "An excellent system. It seems to be designed for maximum efficiency, and is completely self-regulating, self-renewing. A phenomenal machine."

"What did it feel like?"

Argo's head cocks back. "Feel like? It felt like stone. And air, and water."

"No, no, what did it make *you* feel?"

Argo floats in the torpid currents. "You can't be serious."

"Forget I asked."

He surges forward, facemask against the inside glass, eyes streaked with leaky blood vessels.

"Why do you persist in these indulgent distractions? We're *Operators*, Maiella. We're the only few strong enough to protect our kind. Yet you waste your attentions on things, which neither defend nor provide for others! *You are wasting your ability to serve!*"

Blackness yawns in Maiella's heart. She survived the last two years on the slimmest hope of seeing her team again, only to hear the Cadre's derision through Argo's mouth. Old anguish fills her to the brim.

Argo blinks at her, waiting for a response. She stifles a sniff, sets her jaw, and nods in agreement, thinking, *You're right, Argo, I am a waste.*

"Hey," Argo calls softly.

Maiella looks her friend in the eye. It hurts.

"Don't misunderstand," he says. "I care about you and Thompson...

just like I care about everyone else. When we were inducted to the Corps, we swore an oath."

Argo pauses, seeing how his words have battered the woman before him.

"Maiella, I have never doubted you in a rotation. My point is, I never want to. I don't say this to harm you, I tell you this because we *need* you. Me, Thompson, the Colonists, the Cadre...we all need you at your best."

Maiella's eyes overflow and her breath leaves her in a rush.

"We're exiles, Argo."

"Doesn't matter. As long as we live, we *must* serve. I know you have the need to serve just like I do. It's in our bones."

Maiella shuts her eyes, nodding rapidly. "It's always been hard for me, living by the code...as we must." She looks away, her eyes stopping at Beckert's tube, and becomes desolate. "Should be me in there, all ripped up."

"No, it *shouldn't*."

She looks at him cynically. "Why not?"

"You *know* better than to get injured without permission."

Maiella snorts and cracks a smile. She presses her fist against the glass. Argo presses his big hand against hers.

"Heal fast, Argo." She turns and collects the medical package from the table. "I'll see you soon." Argo is in the middle of a word when she clicks off the intercom on the tank's console. She takes a last look at Beckert and Thompson before striding out.

Near the entrance, Sahara is leaning over a MedTech's shoulder, studying the screen in front of them.

"Doctor," Maiella announces, thrusting the package out toward the petite woman, "your delivery."

Sahara turns and looks at the offered package. "Actually, that's for you. Are you done already?"

Maiella looks at the package as if seeing it for the first time. "Uh, yeah, I'm done. Is there anything you need?"

Sahara shakes her head. "No, thank you, though. I'll let the escorts know you're leaving."

Maiella looks through the transparent double doors. Gun Keiko and her companion are standing just outside them.

"Looks like they already know. It was nice meeting you, Doctor Taggart."

"*Sahara,*" she corrects. "And I'm glad I finally got to meet you. I promise to behave next time." The doctor gives another warm smile.

Maiella starts a salute then looks at her hand as if it offended her.

"Gah!"

Exasperated, she strides quickly through the double doors. The waiting Operators take positions on either side and escort her down the hall.

Sahara watches them leave and waits for the doors to seal.

"I'd say that just set you back about a year, Counselor."

The person seated beside her removes his hat and mask. Free of his MedTech disguise, the Counselor smoothes his dark hair. He stands, stretching the creases in his white coat, and nods in reluctant agreement.

"I think you're right."

"You still think this was a good idea?"

"I *knew* it wasn't a good idea. But how could I keep them apart?" He hands the mask and hat to Sahara. "Please call me the moment Beckert or Thompson wakes."

"Of course."

The Counselor strides through the MedLab doors toward another part of Cadre One. Sahara takes the vacant seat and resumes her work.

Maiella, subconsciously falling into cadence with her Operator escorts, marches to the waiting transport. The hallways are quiet. On the *Europa*, colonists routinely walk in pairs, talking with one another. Here, individuals hurry along on their missions, silent unless spoken to.

With the automation that comes from extreme familiarity, Maiella and her escorts arrive at the *Europa's* waiting transport. The hatchway is open, ready to receive her, yet she pauses at the threshold. An armored hand shoves her from behind.

Still chafed from Argo's scolding, Maiella twists with the shove and grabs the Gun's arm with both hands. In a blur, she whirls with the trapped arm, flipping the Gun onto his back. Maiella holds the captured wrist tight and steps on his neck armor.

The soldier growls, and extends the bayonet on his rifle.

"DO IT!" Maiella roars, when another armored hand clamps onto her shoulder.

"Release him," Keiko states.

Maiella, already breathing heavily, turns her head. She looks from the hand on her shoulder to the transparent eyepieces in Keiko's facemask. Her gray eyes are insisting.

"He will be disciplined," Keiko adds.

The fire in Maiella dims, and she releases the soldier's wrist. He swats her foot from his neck and climbs to his feet.

As Maiella backs into the transport, Keiko punches the button to close the hatchway and scoots the dropped package through with her boot. The powerful woman turns on her companion.

"Gonna do something with that blade, Sergeant?" Keiko asks.

Through the closing hatch, Maiella sees Keiko rip the junior Gun from his feet and slam him against the wall, shouting, *"NEVER put your hands on a superior officer, Sergeant. Do it again and I will PERSONALLY feed you to Major Chu—"*

The hatch seals with a hiss.

"Home?" the transport pilot asks.

The question strikes Maiella as odd.

Home? Now where would that be?

Instead of a reply, she waves a hand and nods her head. The pilot swivels in her seat.

"Cadre One, this is *Europa* transport, requesting clearance for departure."

"Received, Europa transport," the radio answers. *"You are cleared for departure."*

The pilot detaches the docking clamps and thrusts out over the open crater. When she pulls back on the controls the enormous Colony ship fills the windscreen.

Maiella collects the package from the floor. She flops into a seat, swaying with the pilot's slight maneuvers, and contemplates the tape-wrapped container. With a fingernail, she slices the seams and opens the plastic case. Inside is a napkin, twisted and shaped into the likeness of a rose, and a note, which reads, *Meet me in my quarters? There's something I'd like to ask. —Gregor*

Her arms drop to either side, her head thunks back against the bulkhead.

"Shit."

A Decision Made

"I told you so."

The Counselor looks sternly at his client, seated opposite him on a soft couch. The woman sinks deep in the cushions and twirls a paper rose in one hand.

"Are you supposed to say that, Counselor? Aren't you supposed to be kind and supportive and all that?"

The white-coated man shakes his head. "With some, maybe. With you...Look, I'm not going to downplay your struggle. You need to know, however, that you're not the only one struggling. If you're going to develop your emotions, you've got to recognize others' emotions as well."

"But why *me*? How could he choose *me*?"

The Counselor looks at the floor and grimaces. "It's complicated, but..." He leans forward on the edge of his chair. "Gregor is a senior officer on this ship. That makes almost everyone aboard his subordinate. Soshiba Varicorp may be dead, but the command structure of this crew lives on, for good reason. And the Cadre, well, pretty obvious, there. So who's left?"

Maiella looks away, avoiding the question and asking her own.

"Then how did he get...married?"

"Medical and psychological staff aren't under his authority. Iskra was a surgical nurse and Medic for the Europa's crew."

"There's no one else?"

"None that he...*No*, Maiella, there *isn't*."

Maiella looks back at the Counselor, sees impatience in his narrowed eyes. She sits up straighter.

"I'm not going to fence with you today," he says. "This is too important."

She mirrors his posture at the edge of the couch. "I'm sorry, Counselor. I just can't understand how he could want *me*."

The Counselor draws air audibly through his nostrils. "I won't go into detail, but he's become deeply involved with you. Part of him admires you for your strength, part of him hates you for Iskra's death, part of him knows it was an accident...part of him needs you to banish the loneliness. Some cultures, when the spouse is killed, the offender marries the widow out of responsibility."

Maiella's eyes bulge.

"I'm not suggesting you do that," the Counselor pre-empts, "I'm simply explaining there is precedent for it and it can make a lot of sense."

"How could that possibly be?" she asks.

"Two people, joined by the death of another, can form very deep bonds. They could go on separately, carrying the scars of their ordeal, or they can come together in healing. Gregor is making that offer to you."

Maiella's eyes shift nervously, her face twitches.

"Have you considered it?" the Counselor asks.

"Considered what?"

"I know your IQ, Maiella. *Don't play stupid.*"

Maiella rocks back on her cushion, surprised. The Counselor waits expectantly.

"I couldn't," she says at last.

"Why not?"

"How could I? I killed his wife! If someone killed Thompson, I..."

"Now we're getting to the heart of it."

Maiella sits open-mouthed in her seat, terrified of her own realization: as a Cadre Operator, she has admitted her deep attachment to another. There is more, as well—a dirtiness, a stigma associated with the physical yearning she feels, made worse by Argo's recent scolding.

"Face it, Maiella, then embrace it. That ache in your chest is your love for Thompson, and it *belongs* there."

Her face contorts. *"How can you say that?"* Her hand rises to cover her heart.

"Because I know what it is. The most powerful emotions can have physical properties. They're felt, especially when suppressed or denied."

"I want it to stop."

The Counselor studies her shrewdly. "Of course. Go back to the inhibitors, right? There's a reason you got off them in the first place."

She nods, still covering her heart.

"You and I both knew this journey would be difficult."

She nods again.

"So what's it going to be?"

She scrunches her eyebrows and drops her hands into her lap. "I don't understand what you're asking."

"Are you going to act like a child and give up, or are you going to stand on your own feet and do what's right?"

"I'm going to do what's right," she answers automatically.

"Which is...?"

She thinks a moment. "Gregor and I have to confront the past, together."

The Counselor folds his hands in his lap and remains silent. She takes the hint that she is not done yet.

"And I have to tell him how I feel about Thompson."

The Counselor raises his eyebrows.

"And I have to..." Maiella searches herself and shrugs. "I don't know what else."

"Now I want you to *really* listen." He pauses to make sure he has her complete attention. "What happened aboard this ship three and a half years ago was an accident. A terrible *accident*. But because you carry this shame with you at all times, you're reminding everyone around you of that day. Until *you* get over it and move on, *no one else can*."

Maiella sits in silence, contemplating the Counselor's message. A hint of skepticism crosses her face then is whisked away.

"I need to let go of the past. For others and for myself. I have to let go."

The Counselor nods. "That's right. To fully experience love, you need to feel worthy of it."

She looks at the floor.

"Maiella."

She lifts her drooping head.

"Everyone is worthy. You, me, Thompson, Argo, *everyone* is deserving of compassion. That means Gregor, too."

"Of course!" Maiella says defensively.

"Just a minute." The Counselor pauses, waiting for his client's defense mechanisms to lower. "All of the isolation and loneliness you've endured, Gregor has felt just as strongly. The reasons are different, but the result is the same."

Maiella winces then shrinks as he continues.

"He's been reaching out to you and you've pretended not to notice. I asked you *weeks* ago to speak with him. You need to know that ignoring his gestures has been crueler than rejecting them."

"I didn't mean to—"

"Stop there," he interrupts. "What if Thompson decided to ignore you, avoid you? Would his saying, 'I didn't mean to,' make any difference?"

Her eyes crush shut. "Oh, no. No." She shakes her head, trying to rattle such a horrible thought from her mind.

"What you felt just now, stretch it out over a year. *That's* what Gregor's been going through."

Nausea twists Maiella's gut. She crosses her hands over her navel and hunches. The Counselor watches her for a moment then relents.

"Now do you understand why you need to speak to Gregor?"

"Yes," Maiella admits. "No one should have to feel this way."

The Counselor nods gratefully. "Please think about what you'll say, and think about what it'll be like for him to hear. In other words, don't slam the door on him. You never know what the future holds. You might find him appealing some day."

He tilts his head, observing his ailing patient. "Are you okay?"

Maiella smiles meekly. "I'm fine, I just...I didn't understand why it was so important I speak with him about...*that*..." Her eye twitches as she stares into infinity. "It scares me, talking about that day."

"I know. It scares us all. But we need to start. A lot of us have just been bottling it up, not talking about it at all. Gregor, especially. And as always, I'm here for you both."

Point made, the Counselor sinks back into his seat, dropping the formality.

"Heard you had a scrape down at Cadre One."

She scrunches her mouth and arches an eyebrow. "Your spies don't miss much, Doc."

The Counselor smiles confidently. "I *do* like to be informed. But you're the closest thing to a celebrity we've got. Anything you do gets around pretty fast. Wanna talk about it?"

Maiella gets a contented grin. "A new initiate tried me on." The grin stretches wider. "Showed him he had a few things left to learn."

"That's really unusual, isn't it? I've never heard of open conflict in the Cadre like that."

Maiella confirms with a wary nod. "The Corps is on edge. Doesn't matter how much training O'Kai has them doing, it's never the same as a rotation." She flexes her hands, recalling that brief touch of adrenaline from Argo's story and relishing it. "We're combat Operators, bred in the bone. We don't do well with idle time."

The Counselor's face washes with concern. "It's only been two years. Is it really so hard?"

"Yesss." Maiella's jaw sets tight. Her shoulders draw together with unexpended tension.

The Counselor studies her, second-guessing his diagnoses for her depression. "Maiella, please tell me directly: what was hardest for you these last two years?"

"Being excluded from the mission," she says without hesitation.

The Counselor touches his mouth, surprised. "Not the separation from Thompson and Argo?"

"One in the same, doc."

The Counselor reels, having missed something so big. "You *need* combat...?"

"We need to *serve*," she corrects.

"There are other ways to serve, you know!"

Her head cocks back. "How? What service could we provide that's more beneficial?"

For once, the Counselor is stunned. He rubs his jaw.

"What would happen if somehow all of this hiding and raiding was unnecessary? Maiella, what if our war was over?"

"Don't be ridiculous. We've always been at war. We always will."

"Are you telling me peace has *never* been considered?"

"Piece? Piece of what?"

The Counselor reads in her serious expression the woman is not joking. She genuinely has never heard the word before.

"Cessation of hostilities! End to the fighting! The possibility of living side by side without conflict!"

She shakes her head. "We only deal in reality, Counselor."

"We? Who's this *we* you speak of?"

Maiella blinks as if slapped.

"I'm sure you don't like being reminded anymore than I like reminding you, but you're not a part of the Cadre anymore, Maiella. When you permit yourself to forget that, you slide back to that familiar association, which alternately abuses, then neglects you. You fall back to that narrow mind, the limited reason. The mental rut which keeps you isolated and depressed. I understand the tendency to go back to what you know...but it's *killing* you. If you think I'll simply watch that happen, you're *very* mistaken."

Maiella's eyes squint with the injury. She hunches again. "You're in a mood today, Counselor."

"Maybe so. Or maybe I've grown impatient with you. Maybe I'm tired of hearing the same excuses." He sighs, becoming sympathetic once more. "I understand you want things to be like they were: simple. You knew your role, you knew your place. Well now things are *completely* different. I've watched you drift in limbo as you wish for belonging, yet you refuse to earn it. I've watched you dodge your responsibilities like a child, hurting others in the process. So there is simply no kind way to say this."

He pauses again, waiting for her full attention. She lifts her gaze from her feet and regards the Counselor as if she were before a firing squad.

"Then just say it."

"You're not a *girl* anymore, Maiella. You have to take responsibility for your actions and deal with them as an *adult*. That means facing your most intense emotions and those of your peers with dignity. It means embracing change rather than yearning for the past. It means keeping your mind open to new ideas and new possibilities. Most of all, it means accepting what has been done and learning from it...*growing* from it."

Relief crosses her face as if she were just spared from execution. She lets out her held breath.

"It's odd...I thought you were going to say the same thing Argo did. To hear that from you...I think it would've killed me. Instead, you just told me what you've always been telling me. This time, I actually heard you." Her posture straightens and she rises to her feet.

"If you'll excuse me, Counselor, there are some things I need to take care of."

"Of course," he says, nodding.

Maiella spins on her heel and strides to the door. It slides aside at her approach then whisks shut after she passes.

"Finally," he mutters.

TIME IS NOT OUR FRIEND

Gregor strides glumly toward his cabin. His short hair is spiky from sweat. His uniform coveralls are coated with soot, as are the exposed areas of skin. Only a goggle-shaped area around his eyes and the outline of a re-breather around his nose and mouth are free of grime. He had always wondered why regular workers in the forge had a Chimpanzee as their badge icon. Now, wearing the simian mask, he knows.

He presses the button at his cabin door, leaving a dark smudge. The door glides aside.

Home again.

He steps into the space, feeling repulsion to it, as if he and the room were magnets of the same polarity. As a flight officer he had always felt that he deserved larger quarters, but without his wife the space feels cavernous. Empty. And after every shift there is only that emptiness to greet him.

He peels the filthy coveralls away and folds them inside out to trap the dirt before stuffing them in a hamper. Reduced to his sweaty undershirt, boxer shorts, and boots, he takes a towel from his hygiene station and stares into the mirror. His reflection appears years older, with soot filling and emphasizing the lines in his face.

With a wave of his hand, the faucet arcs a thin stream of water into the modest sink. He cups his hands to catch it and rubs the cool water against his face. The lines disappear.

As he stares at his reflection again, he feels the grayness of a future alone, a future with little meaning, with little promise. His bare arms, with their ridges of muscle and protruding veins, prove to him he still possesses physical vigor, yet he knows he is at the waning end of it, and he cannot shake the feeling that no matter how much sleep he gets he will always be tired.

"Vremya nee nahsh droog, da¹?" he says to his reflection. The reflection stares back, dripping.

There is a chime at his comm panel. Gregor rinses his face and drags the towel over it on the way to the panel. He taps the screen.

"This is Gregor."

The Counselor's face appears on the small monitor.

"Hello, Gregor. Wanted to give you some advanced notice. You'll have a visitor shortly."

Gregor stiffens. "Maiella?"

The Counselor nods. "Yes. She's coming to talk to you."

Gregor looks away, his heart racing.

"Would you like me to listen in?" the Counselor offers.

"No, no," Gregor says absently. He looks around his cabin, judging it unfit for company. Then he looks at himself in his boxer shorts and work boots.

"When is she coming?"

"She just left my office a few minutes ago. I don't know if she's going straight there or..."

"Gotta go!" Gregor slaps the comm panel, ending the conversation. He trips kicking off his boots and staggers to the hygiene station. Ripping his shirt off with one hand, he grabs a well-worn container of powder with the other and douses himself. His nostrils sting from the antiseptic as he rubs two-handed, grinding the powder into his skin, under his arms, through his hair.

The doorbell chimes.

Gregor looks over his shoulder in a near panic. "Just a minute!" He looks back at himself in the mirror, hair wild, almost naked and covered in a mixture of soot and soap. He dunks the towel in the sink and wrings it once before toweling himself off.

"Is this a bad time?" Maiella asks through the door. "I could come back."

"NO!" Gregor shouts. "It's fine! I'll be right there!" He swabs himself with the towel, grimacing as he completes the job at his nethers. He looks at the towel like it is a loathsome creature and holds it at arms length until he can drop it into the hamper.

Glad I'm not on laundry detail.

1время не наш друг, да? "Time is not our friend, yes?"

"You sure?" Maiella's voice asks from the corridor. "It's no problem."

"Don't you go anywhere! I'll be right there!" The Russian flies about his cabin, snatching up loose clothes. He tosses them all into the hamper then strips his boxer shorts. In one leap, he is at his dresser.

"I'm glad you came by!" he says while pulling on clean boxer shorts. A worn black T-shirt drops down over his head. Faded jeans slide up his legs to his waist. One sock stretches over a foot, then another, his big toes showing through holes at the tips. Another leap across the room and he is at the door. With a tap of a button, it slides aside.

Maiella stands anxiously in the corridor, hands clasped in front of her, biting her lower lip. When she sees him the anxiety melts, and she laughs.

"Nice hair, Gregor," she sniggers.

Gregor's eyes roll up to his forehead and he smoothes the wild locks against his scalp. He grins at himself.

"Anything to make you smile, Mai. C'mon in." He drops back into his room, beckoning her to follow. When he looks again, he realizes she is not wearing her Cadre uniform. She wears borrowed Colonist clothes, yet she is wearing them in Cadre fashion: pants tucked into the tops of her boots, shirt buttoned up to the top, collar up, and everything creased to military perfection. Her hair is slicked back with gel to hold it in place. A wide belt clamps the casual shirt against her waist. He sniggers, himself.

"What's funny?" she asks.

"You look like a Waldo."

"A *what*?"

"A Waldo. That kid in class whose mother dressed him."

Maiella looks at herself with extreme embarrassment. Gregor brushes it aside.

"Here, I'll help you. For starters, you don't need this." He unclips the wide belt. She trembles at the touch. He lifts her chin and unbuttons the collar then turns the rigid fabric down. She swallows hard. When he reaches for the next button, her hands clamp him at the wrist. Her eyes are shut tight.

"Please, don't."

Gregor releases her shirt immediately. "Of course..." He looks her in the face and sees the tight, thin line of her mouth, the held breath and closed eyes. "Oh, God, Mai, I wasn't going to...I was just..."

"It's okay, Gregor," she says and releases her grip on his wrists. "I'm not, uh, I'm not..." She shifts her weight onto one leg and looks at her polished boots.

"No worries, Mai. You can tell me." Gregor steps back, gestures toward a chair, and parks himself at the edge of his bunk. She considers buttoning herself back up, but forces herself to leave it.

"I'm not good with words," she says, settling into the offered chair. "The Counselor is. I think, maybe...I think I was hoping he would say these things for me."

Gregor takes a deep breath. Uneasy seconds pass one after the other, uninterrupted.

"Gregor, I..." the words stick in her throat, choking her. "I..." She leans forward, a hand covering her heart. *"I know it was me..."* She reaches out to him and touches his knee, her face contorted with restrained guilt.

Gregor tenses, knowing what is coming, his head subconsciously bobbing with each tick of his beating heart.

"I'm the one...I killed your Iskra."

Gregor's head turns to the side. His breaths come short and shallow through his nose. His jaw clenches. His hands curl into hammers.

Liquefied by the confession, Maiella slides from the chair, and her knees *thunk* against the firm floor. Forceful sobs gush from her, pressurized by time and restraint. She leans forward, shoulders hunched.

Savage thoughts war in Gregor's mind as he looks at the woman bowing before him. Rage, anguish, loss, vengeance, need, desire roil within like storm waves crashing upon a rocky shore. Memories of Iskra, his wife, her blonde hair in his hand, her face against his, cheek to cheek in the height of passion, the curve of her back and hips as she slept beside him, the sight of her after a long work shift, the comfort of her simply being there that made the endless plod through the stars endurable...

...And the stickiness of the blood-soaked sheet as he peeled it away from her face, the coldness of her body as he held her tight against him, her rough grunts in the recorded video as bullets ripped through her, the sight of her frozen in her cryotube, forever...

The object of all that loss is right in front of him, prostrate, vulnerable.

Gregor bellows with all his might, slamming his fists violently into his thighs. The veins in his neck stand out and his entire face glows red with heat.

He launches, eyes watered, and he seizes the chair Maiella slid from. He hefts the sturdy furniture over his head like a toy and smashes it against the wall. Roaring, he slams again and again, denting the walls, destroying the wall hangings, splintering the wood until there is nothing left but the armrests in his iron grip. He faces the corner of the room, looking away from her, his chest and shoulders heaving with enormous breaths. There is no catharsis.

"I'll go," Maiella says softly, rising to her feet. "You'll never have to see me again."

Gregor's voice halts her in her tracks. "I *knew*," he growls, looking at the chair's remnants in his hands. "I *knew* it was you. I tried to ignore it, stuff it away as something in the past." He turns to face her and finds her staring penitently at the floor. "If I didn't, I didn't know what I might do. To you. Or the others. Or myself..." Gregor looks at the armrests in his hands and lets them drop.

"I'm so sorry," Maiella says, her voice low, frail. The Russian walks up to her and she tenses for the coming strike. He takes her hand, lifts her chin so she will see him.

"It still hurts," he says. His glassy eyes roam over the destruction he caused moments earlier, then lock on to Maiella's with a laser's intensity. "I feel it strongly, *here*," he says, thumping his fist against his chest. "I know it was an accident. But I needed to hear you say this. I needed to *see you* as you said it."

Maiella rubs a knuckle over her eye. *"Why?"*

"The Counselor, he said, even though I learned to work with you, even *like* you, there was still a rage in me that wouldn't leave. It demanded revenge, for someone to pay. He said I was stuck with it, stuck *in it*, that I had to find a way to let go." He scowls, waving a hand in the air for emphasis. "I don't care about all his bullshit psycho-babble! I wanted to look you in the eye while you admitted it and see you *completely*. Now that I have seen you, the *real* you...the rage, it feels...not so strong."

Gregor looks inward, unsure if he can make the next step. He studies Maiella closely, taking in her remorse, her feeling, her vulnerability, her humanity. To his surprise, the words come without effort.

"I forgive you, Maiella."

Her eyes close in a rush of relief. He pulls her in for a firm, close embrace, and she hugs him back. He feels her damp face, warm with spent emotion, her breasts pressed against him, the curve of her back, the pulse in her neck, the smell of her hair beside her ear with the subliminal cues. An ache in his chest reminds him how long it has been since he was held this way.

With a deep sniff, Maiella loosens her grip and pulls back, hands on his shoulders. "Thank you, Gregor. You don't know how much I needed that from you."

"I think I do," he answers.

She pats him and smiles. "All the same, I'm grateful." She wipes her eyes again and steps around him toward the door.

"Wait, do you have to go already?"

She looks around at the abused walls and furniture, unsure. "Is there something else?"

"Maiella, we...We've become friends, right?"

"Yes, of course."

"And we've both lost so much."

She feels something in Gregor's words, in his speech, which makes her nervous. She looks at him warily.

"That's true..."

"I saw what it was like for you, when...when *Thompson* was gone. You love him deeply."

Her eyes shift like an animal cornered. There is no point to arguing.

"I saw how you suffered," he continues. "I know what that's like."

She fixes her eyes on his and takes a half-step back, her heart thudding in her chest.

"I think of Thompson as a friend," Gregor says, allowing her the space, "and I hope he pulls through. But if he doesn't..."

"Gregor, no, I'm sorry, I..."

"Don't answer now. Just think about it."

"I..."

Gregor's eyes are pleading her to say no more. She bites her lip and nods.

"Thank you," he says.

Gregor walks her to the door. It opens automatically. Maiella strides through and turns suddenly as if she forgot something. Instead of speaking she looks Gregor over from head to foot. He desperately tries to decipher that once-over glance, but she gives no hint, merely turns again and strides away.

He listens to her foot steps recede down the hallway before allowing the door to close, then picks his way across the shattered furniture to his dresser. Reaching behind it, he removes an empty bottle of quality vodka. He walks over to his bed, flops down on it, and twists the cap free. Though the contents are long gone, Gregor holds the bottle under his nose and inhales to his lungs' fullest extent.

THE PURE STRAIN

Weightless, floating, caressed by warmth, Argo drifts both physically and mentally. A beautiful sunset spreads before him, its metallic reds and golds resting atop a distant snow-capped mountain range. A vast river valley stretches below with a meandering stream looping back and forth in a broad plain of green. He hovers above it, inhaling the rich air and listening to the V-formations of birds honking to one another as they migrate.

A glorious tranquility settles into him. There is no awareness beyond the input of his senses, just a connection to the magnificent landscape, which envelops him. He sighs contentedly.

A glint near the mountain range shakes him roughly from his reverie. His eyes dial in. His fists clench.

You let your guard down! Stupid!

The Brick's legs kick, *thunking* into something invisible and solid. He reaches out with his hands, confused by the openness of the vista and the physical confinement of his movement.

They trapped you! The blueskins trapped you!

Argo's lungs take a huge volume of air and he punches at the invisible prison. His movements are sluggish.

They mustn't take you alive!

He gropes for the trigger to self-detonate, but he cannot find it. His hands search all over himself, finding his naked chest and abdomen then something attached to his face. He rips it off.

The landscape vanishes and warm fluid crashes against his face, filling his open mouth and nose. His eyes flutter with disorientation as he flails, hands and feet thudding against the transparent walls of a cylinder. A distorted face is shouting at him from just outside of it.

His lungs cough the fluid back, expelling most of his breath in a massive bubble.

Can't breathe!

A mechanical vibration fills the cylinder and he drops to the floor of the chamber. The fluid drains out rapidly, leaving Argo standing on wobbly legs and hacking.

"ARGO! *ARGO!*" the face on the other side of the cylinder shouts.

Argo presses the fluid from his eyes with a thumb and forefinger. His lungs fill with deep breaths between coughs and his pulse slows. Once recovered he looks into Sahara's worried eyes through the plexi-steel. Behind her is an entourage of four Med-Techs. One of them holds a polished, metallic object. Light glints off it.

Argo fixates on the reflective instrument, realizing in a rush he is not on the surface of Earth and the reflection was not an enemy craft.

"Do you know where you are?" Sahara shouts to him.

He nods. "MedLab."

A great gust of air descends over him, drying him and slurping the last traces of fluid down the drain. He shivers in the chilling wind.

Triple locks release at the cylinder's base and the clear cylinder walls rise toward the ceiling. MedTechs hustle to assist the Brick in his uneasy stance. He brushes them off with arms heavy from disuse.

"I'm *all right*," the Brick chides. "Leave me be."

The MedTechs nod and acquiesce, falling back behind Sahara. Though not nearly the bulk of Operators, the MedTechs stand like columns behind the petite doctor.

"How are you feeling?" Sahara asks. She holds out a hand and one of the MedTechs places a labset in it. Built for the hands of a Brick, the labset is huge in her grip. She cradles it with one arm and taps in the commands with her other hand, arching her back slightly to offset the weight.

"I'm fine," Argo insists, ignoring the angry burning of pink skin on his chest, and the lancing sharpness at his side. He stands straighter, flexing his weakened arms and shoulders. "I've been idle long enough. What are my orders?"

"To debrief the Leadership Council immediately," the ranking MedTech volunteers, "provided you are *fit* for duty."

Fit for duty? Argo repeats mentally. He lets the slight pass.

"Inform General O'Kai I will present myself and my findings the instant he requires me." Argo pulls electrodes from his head, chest, legs.

"Just a moment, Argo," Sahara says, "let me finish checking you over."

"I'm fine," the big man says dismissively. He takes hold of the metallic codpiece.

"HEY!"

Argo looks up from the buckle at his waist. Sahara is glaring at him as fiercely as Major Chusan.

"You don't leave my facility until *I* say so, Brick. *Is that clear?"*

Argo drops his hands to his side and comes to attention at the sound of Sahara's commanding voice.

"Yes, Ma'am!"

"That's better. You may have walked in here, Argo, but I didn't think any of you were walking out. You're tough, sure enough. Just don't think for a *second* you're going back on rotation until *I'm* satisfied you've fully recovered."

Argo's square jaw flexes with impatience, yet he maintains his at-attention posture. The diminutive woman taps his arms.

"Raise 'em."

Argo obediently lifts his arms out straight to each side. Sahara slides beneath his great limbs, investigating the burns across his torso and, in particular, the gash in his side. Fibrous red skin piles on the edges of the knitted slice like giant lips. Despite the massive scarring, the wound has closed well.

"Is the exile restored?" a MedTech asks. "Or have his *feelings* made him fragile?"

Argo's eyes burn in their orbits. Before he can answer, Sahara steps from under his arms.

"You can lower your arms, Argo," she says gently. The small woman spins about and locks on to the MedTech's name badge. She rips it from his uniform.

"Specialist Obet," she reads aloud, "such a shame you had to be transferred for incompetence and insubordination. Colonel Munro will be *so* disappointed."

Obet's eyes swell to saucer plates. *"What?* But I didn't...I...I," he stammers.

Sahara folds her arms as the MedTech comes unglued before her. Just before he completely disintegrates, she relents.

"Tell you what. You go find something else to do for the rest of your shift, and I *might* reconsider my report to Munro."

Obet's flapping jaw closes. He stands straighter, his crooked shoulders as close to level as he can make them.

"Yes, Sir!"

"That's better," Sahara says. "Now remember this: *everyone* in my care is to be treated with *dignity* and *respect*. Do you understand?"

"Yes, Sir!"

She flings his name badge toward the MedLab doors.

"Get ye gone, lad."

Obet hunches submissively and trots after his clattering badge. The MedLab doors part at his approach. After retrieving his badge, Obet looks back in bewildered confusion then disappears through the parted doors.

Sahara points at the shiny medical instrument.

"That's the pure strain, right?"

"Yes, Doctor. Taken from Geek Beckert directly."

She shakes her head. "Makes me nervous just looking at it. Get it into isolation and start manufacturing more. We need a workable quantity to test treatments."

"Right away."

"The rest of you, let's narrow the list of ribozymes and protease inhibitors to the most effective. We should have all the colonists inoculated soon, but I want a healthy supply of anti-virals on-hand in case anyone goes full-blown."

"Yes, sir," the MedTechs say before turning and embarking on their assignments.

"Now, may I get dressed?" Argo asks.

Sahara faces the Brick and crosses her arms again.

"You've earned a rest, Argo. I can get you more down time."

Argo smirks at the gesture.

"I appreciate it, but, well...It doesn't...*We* don't work that way. I *must* report to General O'Kai."

Sahara sees the Brick's sincerity in his rigid posture, his jutting chin, his angled eyebrows.

"Getting back into the Corps...It's important to you?"

He shudders as though chilled. "It's *everything.*"

Sahara steps to a cabinet beside the freshly drained healing tank and opens the drawer. Inside are neatly arranged charcoal-colored clothes, slightly faded and worn thin at the neck and shoulders. She scoops them up and offers them to her patient.

Argo's eyes fall on his ancient, hand-me-down uniform with longing. He takes hold of the codpiece at his waist and releases it, letting it *clank* on the floor. Sahara turns from his nakedness, but not before she recognizes in Argo's glance at the worn uniform a lifetime of devotion and sacrifice. Or more precisely, life*times*...

The Brick takes the folded uniform from Sahara and spreads it out on a stainless steel operating table. He pulls on his under garments hastily, eager to be wearing his familiar skin again.

Returning to the cabinet, Sahara opens another drawer and removes an enormous pair of black lace-up boots. They shine as though new. She carries them over to her patient and waits for him to finish fastening his jacket. With his thinned neck, chest and limbs, the uniform looks a couple sizes too large on him. He turns toward her and smiles at his boots.

"Thank you, Doctor." He takes the boots and slips them on one at a time. "Would you really have reported Obet for being incompetent and insubordinate? I don't see how he was either."

Sahara grimaces. "Probably not. Obet's simple and ignorant. But what he said, it *pissed me off.* This is a place of healing, and him dragging that *cack* in here, well...I won't tolerate it for a moment."

The big man finishes lacing his boots and gets to his feet.

"How do I look?"

Sahara purses her lips, taking in his month-old beard, the curling locks of gray and black hair. She pats his arm.

"If you're going before O'Kai, we'd better get you slicked up."

Sahara slides a wheeled cart from beneath the steel table. Numerous medical implements cover the tray on top. She selects a long straight blade.

"Let's start with a shave."

In Abundance

Escorted by Guns Deepak and Keiko, Argo marches through the metallic corridors of his familiar home. MedTechs and Operators alike clear a path for the trio as they briskly move toward O'Kai's office.

Accomplishment gives Argo some of his old confidence and his heels strike the solid floor audibly. Though still thin from his ordeal on Earth, his drawn, ghoulish appearance has been softened by Sahara's healing and nutrition regimen. The Brick's brown eyes no longer lurk in dark recesses. Instead, they shine with the importance of his imminent presentation.

He rubs his smooth cheeks and scalp in search of any remaining stubble. Even in the valleys and hills of his myriad scars, there is none.

Deepak and Keiko keep a clock-like cadence as they lead the way. Their uniforms are deep charcoal gray, fit perfectly, and are elastic in the neck, shoulders, and waist. A thought enters Argo's mind as he considers his own faded, worn-out jacket. If he had the vocabulary, he would know it as *envy*.

Just outside of O'Kai's office, Deepak and Keiko come to a sudden halt. Keiko presses a buzzer at the panel and announces, "General, Argo is here to report."

No rank or title, Argo observes in the announcement. *Better than 'Exile,' at least.*

"Come," states O'Kai via the panel's speaker. The door slides aside.

Argo salutes his escorts and steps between them. They both twitch at the shoulder as if beginning a salute but nod respectfully instead.

The door seals behind the big man and he sees an informal gathering of General O'Kai, Major Ralla, and Colonel Shao Lo. All three cluster around O'Kai's desk, collars unbuttoned, jackets hanging open, and they stare at a hovering video screen where an unusually slender woman in a sharp black and gray suit delivers her broadcast.

"World markets suffered their deepest collapse in history today on news New Bangalore and New Beijing have been lost..."

Ralla halts the video and the three Cadre officers turn to Argo. Argo's spine straightens immediately, his shoulders back, chest out, flat hand swept up to his brow.

"You're here. Good. At ease." O'Kai states. "We've been reviewing the media records you brought back. Fascinating, truly."

"Yes, sir, General, they—"

"Where is Cadre Two?"

Argo blinks at O'Kai's sudden interruption. "Don't know, sir. All we found was a video referencing Cadre Projects One and Two. All other data was scrubbed from the memory cores."

O'Kai's eyes narrow, conveying clear dissatisfaction with the reply.

"Beckert said he found a clue," Argo adds. "Said he photographed it, then destroyed the evidence in case the blueskins found it."

"We've reviewed every photo in his HDI," Ralla says, sliding a scorched piece of headgear to the front of the desk. "A lot more questions in there than answers."

Argo looks at the burnt Human Digital Interface. From Beckert's descriptions, the tower office was a remarkable place with ancient weapons and a lineage of Generals stretching back thousands of years. There was no time to share during the mission, but now he has a chance at last to see for himself.

"May I?" Argo asks.

Ralla nods and blanks the slender newscaster from the hovering holowindow. She calls up still images, grainy with light amplification, and scrolls them by, three per second: a desiccated corpse with tarnished handgun in grasp, pristine weapon cases with primitive-yet-elegant weapons inside, brass plaques, crude depictions of humans in bizarre dress, a lifelike hawk statue clutching two orbs, an image of a woman and children smiling around something planted with thin candles, various medals arranged on a dusty desk proclaiming valor, courage, service, duty, achievement, loyalty...

"Wait! Go back!"

Ralla complies, ignoring Argo's breach of protocol. She cycles backwards through the images until she reaches the hawk statue with its piercing eyes.

"That's it," Argo says cryptically.

Ralla, Shao-Lo, and O'Kai scrutinize the image as though it had somehow changed into something completely new.

"What do you see?" O'Kai demands.

Argo's eyes lock on to the colored spheres in the hawk's talons, flicking from one to the other.

"Enlarge the spheres."

Ralla does so. Metric data, embedded in the photograph, notes relative size and color of each. Argo points to the bluish-white sphere.

"Seen that before?"

The three senior officers lean closer to the image. "That's our star," Ralla says in wonder. Tapping keys on O'Kai's desk, Ralla manipulates the image, isolating the two spheres. In moments, she has imbued the bluish-white orb with all of the local stellar attributes. She then extrapolates the data based on relative size and color-temperature to the partner orb. The yellow-orange orb takes on a fiery appearance and seems to come alive as convective forces roil the surface. In moments, the window is dominated by a swollen star.

Before O'Kai can request it, Ralla pulls up another holowindow beside the main one with three-dimensional star charts. Six candidates highlight with captions.

"Stand by," Ralla says as she slips on her HDI. She lowers the goggles over her eyes. "I'm going to dip into the *Europa's* nav charts, see if I can get better resolution here." Her goggles strobe brightly.

Plotting Earth as the central starting point, she maps a radius in all directions of comparable distance as Cadre One. The list shrinks to two candidates, which blink twice, then leap from the side screen to the main screen. The fiery blue-white star fades from view in favor of the two glowing pinpoints.

"Got it," Ralla announces, and the pinpoints swell to photo quality renderings of star systems in motion. The first system shows a massive Yellow-white star with a dim white dwarf companion. Sparse belts of rocky debris orbit the larger star, perturbed by the eccentric orbit of the diminutive companion.

The second system shows a central star roughly a third the diameter of the first with a strong orange hue. A broad disk of dust extends in the solar plane, interspersed with rings of empty space cleared by colossal gaseous planets. Beyond the outermost planet is a vast halo of icy comets and planetesimals.

"Colonist archives call these systems *Procyon A/B* and *Epsilon Eridani*," Ralla states.

The Procyon system is an image of grace as the great and small stars swirl near then fling each other away, only to close the distance again and repeat the dance. Epsilon Eridani maintains the dusty haze between gas giant planets with regular bombardments of orbit-crossing asteroids. By comparison, Episilon Eridani's system has a violent character—seemingly at war with itself through shattering impacts.

"Procyon is closer to the size suggested," Ralla says, lifting her goggles, "Epsilon Eridani is closer to the color. But neither are a clear match."

"I can't see building a base there," Shao-Lo says, pointing to Epsilon Eridani's destructive maelstrom. "Who'd want to fly into that, much less *live* there?"

O'Kai nods in thought. "Could possibly be on a moon around one of those gas giants, but radiation and tidal forces would be problematic." He taps a key on his desk and the violent system disappears from the window, leaving Procyon as the object of scrutiny. He magnifies the outer system, resolving thousands of planetoids.

"If Cadre Two's in there, gonna take a while to find it."

"Sir, if I may?" Argo asks.

The three senior officers look at him as one. "Go ahead," O'Kai says.

"While Beckert was reviewing the videos he found, I heard Keller's name mentioned repeatedly. Seems he was administrator of one of the Colonies. Had something to do with starting this war."

"Yes," Shao-Lo begins, "we saw that in the beginning of these recordings."

"I don't see how that affects things now," O'Kai adds.

"That was my assessment as well and I scolded Beckert for giving it too much attention. But if Keller was military trained and had knowledge of off-world projects like the colonies...he might know about Cadre Two."

"How could he know about Cadre Two if he didn't know about us?" Shao-Lo asks.

Ralla mulls a thought. "Maybe he did."

O'Kai taps a key at his station. "Colonel Munro, respond."

A speaker in the workstation replies, "Munro here, General. Go ahead."

"Find Captain Keller and request a meeting in my office, 1900 hours."

"Understood," Munro replies. "Request meeting with Keller, 1900. Out."

"If Keller doesn't know," O'Kai continues, "How long to outfit a search team and dispatch to Procyon?"

"No time at all," Shao-Lo answers. "Our Operators are crawling the walls with idle time. The hardest part will be telling those who can't go they have to stay."

"I can help with that," Ralla says. "The memory core Argo brought back is *loaded* with battle tactics of the enemy forces. I could use every Geek available to analyze them. If we ever have to face a coordinated strike, we should figure out how to deal with it."

"Ralla, you take point on that," O'Kai orders. "Devise counter-tactics to the enemy actions in that memory core, then I'll allocate whatever resources you need for fleet-wide war games. We need to be ready."

Ralla nods modestly. "Yes, General."

"Shao-Lo, organize a team and ship. I want Chusan's best alongside you when you go."

Shao-Lo's eyes light up. Her head lifts. "I'll be leading the expedition?"

"That's affirmative. Take one of the smaller stealth ships. If the enemy has that system staked out, you need to remain unseen. Now let's get to it."

Ralla and Shao-Lo rise from their places and button up their jackets when Argo blurts, "General!"

"Yes?" O'Kai replies. "You have something else?"

Argo's jaw sets tight. He stands straight. "I volunteer for the expedition."

O'Kai scarcely registers the request. "Impossible. Operators only."

"That's my point, sir."

All three senior officers stop what they are doing and stare at Argo. The room is deathly still with only the slight hiss of the ventilators.

"I request re-admittance to the Operator Corps."

"Oh, *we got that*," Shao-Lo replies, the sunny look from before clouded with suspicion.

Long seconds tick by as the three continue their uninterrupted gaze. Argo feels the weight of those stares, measuring, scrutinizing, judging. He keeps his shoulders square, his chest out, watching the three. Shao-Lo's stern glare shows hostility. Ralla arches an eyebrow, intrigued. But O'Kai? The weathered face shows no trace one way or the other.

Ralla and Shao-Lo turn to their superior, looking to him for an answer.

"I'll have your thoughts," he says.

"He's an exile," Sho-Lo states, "a *criminal*. How could he ever be to the standard again?"

"His judgment was executed, and he served it," Ralla contradicts. "He *survived* it. *And* he brought his team back with more data than we imagined. If *that's* not Operator quality, I don't know what *is*."

O'Kai's eyes narrow. "And these *'wounds of the mind'* the Counselor claims you suffer. How have these healed?"

"Sir," Argo begins, "there is no wound in me but the separation from my brothers and sisters, an idle future which denies my ability to serve...I must bear the shame of my crime, yet..." He drops to one knee, bows, and plants one fist on the floor. "I will endure any test, bear any burden, so that by giving my life in *honorable service*, I might save lives. Cadre and Colonist, alike."

"Get up, " Shao-Lo demands as she strides toward him. Argo stands and looks into her stern gray eyes, so much like Thompson's, yet venerable with experience. She peers deep into him, the way she did with Beckert at his initiation. The gaze is intimidating. It makes him want to serve all the more.

"Recommendations?" O'Kai orders.

"He's an asset, in terms of skill set, experience, knowledge," Ralla states. "He was the only one of his team still conscious on return. Probably the reason the team survived. His sentence is served, in my mind."

Shao-Lo steps back from her penetrating stare and takes in Argo as a whole. Whatever reservation she held dissipates in the face of Argo's sincerity.

"The will to serve...He's got it. In *abundance*," the tall woman says. She steps back to the desk beside O'Kai and Ralla. She thinks carefully, crossing her powerful arms and cupping her square jaw. "There's a lot to work with here, I think. If his mind is truly healed, that is."

O'Kai rises from his desk and steps around it. He stands in front of the withered Brick like a pillar, and folds his arms.

"The Counselor once asked me if I knew what it was like to kill my own kind. It took me a moment to appreciate what he was really telling me: that it's a terrible thing to live with. So how do you do it?"

"No choice, sir. It's my shame. I can't bring them back, but by serving again, I can help protect the Colonists..."

"Ah," O'Kai interjects, "I see. You feel an obligation to the *Colonists*."

"Yes, Sir! Of course I do!"

O'Kai nods. "So if you had to choose between saving a Colonist or saving one of us, who would you save?"

"Sir? That's a false dilemma. I'd save anyone in my power. *Anyone*."

O'Kai squints, then nods. He slides back and sits on the edge of the desk.

"Well, then. Major, have you ever seen such a pathetic Brick? Get him some proper nutrition and on a regular fitness cycle."

"Yes, sir," Ralla replies.

"Once restored to fitness, he will report to Major Chusan for assignment. What do you think, Colonel? Can we skip the initiation process this time?"

Shao-Lo smirks. "I think we can, sir."

"All right. Colonel, Major? You have your orders."

"Yes, Sir!" They say in unison, coming to attention, saluting, and striding out. On the way, Ralla pats Argo on the arm.

"Once you're back in proper shape," O'Kai says, "I want you to see the Counselor. If he gives you a clean bill, we'll get you back in rotation."

"Aye, sir!" Argo says, choking back his elation.

O'Kai's eyes rove across the threadbare, faded jacket. "But first go see the quartermaster. You're out of uniform, *Sergeant*."

KNOCKED BACK

The Counselor settles into his office chair, laying his arms on the sides. Gregor is sunk deep into the couch opposite, his jacket thrown over the back. With cushions forever compacted by Argo's prior visit, the couch seems on the verge of swallowing the Russian whole.

"How've you been, Gregor? We haven't spoken in a while."

Gregor thinks a moment and flicks his eyebrows. "Eh. Been hiding, I guess. Licking my wounds."

"She knocked you back?"

"Yeah. Made it pretty clear. I asked her to think about it, but..." Gregor trails off as the familiar frustration rises in him. "Why am I so hung up on her, Doc? I mean, why *her*?"

The Counselor shrugs. "You're both bonded by the pain of that day. Even if on opposite sides of it, it's common to you both. Subconsciously, you may be drawn to one another because of it. Plus, she's very attractive, albeit inaccessible. These things can be potent in combination. It makes sense...to *me*, anyway."

"Ech." He puts his hands out as if gripping something. "God, sometimes, I want to strangle her." His arms lose their rigidity and fall into his lap. "But there's something about her..." His momentary smile melts into conflicted confusion.

"I think I love her, Doc. And then the guilt just *fills* me, like I should be *avenging*, not..." Gregor's head drops and he stares at his hands, suddenly aware he has been turning the band of gold on his ring finger. The man inhales wetly. He looks up, his face a mask of rage and regret.

"Jesus, would you look at me? I'm a fucking *mess*."

"Don't think you have to be anything but what you are, Gregor. This is hard. The hardest part is finding the way through it, how to go on. But we will. Be patient with yourself, give yourself the time, and we *will* get through it."

Gregor smirks skeptically. "You're probably right, but..." He stops his rebuttal cold, not allowing the depression to dive toward hopelessness. "Ah, fuck it. I *know* you're right."

The Counselor gives his client a few moments to recover then asks, "How's work going?"

Gregor relaxes with the change of subject and falls back against the sofa. He spreads his arms to each side, as if subconsciously keeping the couch from devouring him.

"Pretty good, in fact. We've just about got that limousine patched together. We'll be able to jump test it soon. Thing's got some monster speed, the Techs say. Faster than anything we've got so far."

Gregor shakes his head. His eyes stare into an unseen distance beyond the office walls. "Can't believe those three made it back. Shot to shit, like they were." He disappears to a dark place. "Fuckin' *Thompson*..."

The Counselor leans on the arm of his chair, carefully wording the question. "You wish, maybe, he hadn't come back?"

Gregor looks directly at the Counselor and stands up from the sunken couch. He walks around behind it, plants his hands on the back, and leans there.

"How do I answer that?"

"Honestly."

Gregor looks at the crushed cushions. His mouth opens to speak when Keller's voice blares through the office intercom.

"Counselor, are you there?"

Agitated, the Counselor launches from his chair and strides to his desk. He stabs a finger into the reply button. "Captain, I'm with a *client*. You *know* I'm not to be disturbed, for *any reason!*"

"Yes, *yes,* I *know*! But I've been summoned to a meeting with the Cadre Council. They wouldn't say why. I want you to join me."

"When is it?"

"Thirty minutes."

"You couldn't give more notice?"

"That's all I got, myself. Is Gregor there with you?"

"Who I have in session is *none of your*—"

"I'm here, Captain," Gregor says. The Counselor slumps in defeat.

"Gregor, I'd like you to be there as well," Keller says. "Javier and

Sharon will have the bridge."

"Aye, sir," Gregor replies.

"Captain, this had better be important. If you interrupted a session to have us participate in some discussion of *resource* and *labor allocation...*"

"Objection noted, Counselor. You know the Cadre's been scouring the data from Earth. If O'Kai wants a meeting right now, you're *damned straight* it's important."

The Counselor sighs, acknowledging the point. "Very well, Captain. We'll meet you at the shuttle in fifteen minutes."

"Keller out."

The Counselor turns off his intercom, the corners of his mouth sliding toward his chin.

"We'll pick up where we left off, okay, Gregor?"

"That's fine," he says, taking his jacket from the arm of the couch. "It'll take fifteen to get to the shuttle. We should go ahead."

The Counselor takes a small mirror from a drawer and checks his appearance. His stiff hair has the appearance of someone just getting in from a windy day, and it reminds him how long it has been since he took a break.

Gonna be a while longer, he thinks.

The Counselor runs his fingers through the coarse strands and tamps them down with a palm.

"Okay, let's go."

NATIVES

The shuttle ride is quiet with Keller, Gregor, and the Counselor alone in their thoughts. Irritation at Keller's intrusion fades and the Counselor wonders what to expect. Something in Keller's demeanor is off, however; a meeting to discuss the findings of Earth should be exciting, yet apprehension bunches the aged captain's brow and squares his chin. The Counselor looks at Gregor to see if the younger officer is picking up on it as well but the Russian seems busy with his own concerns.

"Any idea what we're going to hear?" the Counselor asks.

Keller shoots a quick glance at the Counselor before resuming his stare out the porthole.

"None at all."

There is a recognizable shine in Keller's narrowed eyes, a shine he has seen many times in the last three years.

Keller's worried...or afraid.

The shuttle glides into its docking clamps and is drawn back with a *clunk*. Pressure aboard equalizes and the shuttle door slides aside. Major Chusan steps into the hatchway, his face a rough patchwork of old burn scars and skin grafts. After a respectful salute, he is about to beckon Keller through when the spots Gregor and the Counselor.

"You two have business at Cadre One?"

"They're with me," Keller says aggressively, as though trying to end any debate before it begins.

Chusan taps an ear-mounted device. "General, Captain Keller has arrived with Gregor and the Counselor. He wants them in attendance. Shall I clear them?"

An inaudible response comes through the device and Chusan nods once.

"Follow me."

The stern major spins on his heel and starts a swift march into the metallic corridors. As always, Keller, Gregor, and the Counselor have to hustle to keep up.

Along the way, drones lumber by with large piles of laundry, nutrients, and equipment. White-coated MedTechs appear from one chamber and disappear into another. Armed and armored Operators stride by on patrol. And through a plexisteel window, the colonists spy a room full of Cadre Geeks, all networked to terminals, their goggles brightly strobing. The focal point of the room is a metal table with assorted devices arranged upon it. On top is a branched crystal, flaring with activity. Beside the table, Ralla is seated and networked, her own goggles vivid with data streams.

The level of industry tightens the apprehension in Keller's face.

"Pretty busy around here, Major," the Counselor digs, "even for the Cadre. What's going on?"

"We'll discuss that," Chusan replies without turning. In moments, the men stand before the doorway to the Leadership Council chamber. Gun Deepak and Gun Keiko stand sentry and salute Chusan briskly. He salutes back and strides through the opening doorway. Keller steps through, averting the tall soldiers' eyes, followed by Gregor. The Counselor pauses.

"Hello, Deepak, Keiko. How are you?"

They smile, dropping the salute. "We're well," Keiko replies, "but please, Counselor. Mustn't delay."

Deepak gently urges the Counselor through and closes the door after him.

Inside, the Counselor finds the familiar semi-circular table and bright yet Spartan interior. O'Kai, Munro, and Shao-Lo, stand behind the rounded table. Chusan takes his place with them.

"Welcome," O'Kai says, gesturing at three metal chairs. "Please, be seated." The Cadre Officers wait respectfully for their visitors to take their seats then take their own chairs.

"We only needed you, Captain," O'Kai begins. "Any reason for bringing Gregor and the Counselor?"

"They're my advocates, General. I wanted them present to share your findings."

Advocates? the Counselor echoes mentally.

"All right. Let's begin. Captain Keller, where's Cadre Two?"

Gregor slides so far forward on his chair, he nearly falls off. "Cadre

THE EXHAUSTED DEAD

Two?"

The Counselor rocks back in his chair, equally astounded, and turns to Keller for a reaction. The old captain maintains his fixed posture, exactly as he was when he first sat, his face stoic and unresponsive.

"I don't know what you're talking about," Keller says automatically.

While Gregor launches a stream of fascinated questions, the Counselor studies the expression on the man beside him. Keller stares straight at O'Kai, unblinking, crosses his legs and folds his hands in his lap.

"Please, Gregor, *enough!"* Colonel Munro says, crossing his great arm and dwarfed arm on the table then leaning on them. With his hunched shoulders and lowered head, he is the likeness of a massive fiddler crab.

"It's *very* important you think back, Captain," Munro explains. "In all your travels and your experience as Administrator of the New Dresden Colony, you may have heard of or had access to Cadre Projects One and Two."

If the Counselor was not watching closely, he would have missed it: the slightest exaggeration in Keller's blink, the briefest flex of his jaw.

"Why do you think I have heard of or had access to Cadre Projects One or Two?"

The Counselor looks forward in horror. He has served aboard the *Europa* for almost his entire existence, has taken every one of the crew in counseling at one point or another. He knows the quirks, gestures, and patterns of speech that tell when someone is hiding something. Or lying.

Gregor sits up and takes notice. "What's the deal, Skipper? Aren't you curious? I mean...Cadre *Two! C'mon!"*

Keller looks at his junior officer then squints at the Cadre Council. "Not sure I like the implication, here, is all."

Shao-Lo cocks her head. "Implication? I don't know that one was made..."

"Why do you think I would have any knowledge of what goes on around here, or any other place like this, *if it exists?"* Keller drills the question home with a lowered brow.

O'Kai taps a key on the table and a video holo-projection leaps into mid-air in front of him. Pictured there is a slim woman with shoulder-length dark hair, dressed in a maroon business suit. Gold-rimmed glasses ride the bridge of her nose, accenting her green eyes. She sits in a comfortable-looking chair with stylish accents. Across from her, in an identical chair, is a square-jawed, long-legged man. His black silk suit shines with tasteful adornments including a thick band of gold at his wrist. With another tap, O'Kai advances the video to the section he wants and lets it play.

Between the two seated on-screen appears an image of a sun-blonde young man, handsome with straight, white teeth. His orange flight suit bears the Soshiba Varicorp logo. A blue velvet curtain behind him offsets his bold posture. The long-legged interviewee smiles proudly at the image.

"That's our man," he says.

"We have some other photos," the maroon-suited woman says, and the image changes to an outdoor scene among short, earthen dwellings. The blonde man stands at center, hair tossed, mouth wide, snarling orders. The butt of an assault rifle is parked on his hip with one hand, the other points into the surrounding vegetation. At his feet, an azure-skinned creature slumps, purple tongue lolling from its mouth, its skull broken open from multiple head shots.

"I've heard of Captain Keller," the woman adds in a polite and even tone. The image shifts to a scene of a wide trench filled with azure reptilian corpses. In the new image, Keller supervises from the trench's edge as a bulldozer shoves in another heap of blue bodies.

"You're right, Doctor," the maroon-suited woman says venomously, "*nothing* equals a photograph."

O'Kai halts the video just as the long-legged man on screen begins unfastening his lapel microphone.

The usually out-spoken Russian stares in muted horror, as does the Counselor. They both turn to their Captain, needing an explanation, but Keller sits rigidly. A glistening breaks out on his forehead. His folded hands are crushed together in his lap, making the knuckles white. At the end of his crossed leg, the elevated foot jitters.

"Is this the Cadre version of humor?" he says. "I don't appreciate being called away from my duties for some ill-minded *game*. Now, if you'll excuse me..."

Keller uncrosses his legs and rises from his chair. Chusan and Munro exchange concerned glances. Shao-Lo and O'Kai lean forward, eyes narrowed as if peering into a hard wind.

"I don't think so," O'Kai says decisively. "Whatever you're hiding, Keller, this is too important."

"I'm not hiding anything. I have no knowledge of Cadre Projects One or Two. So sorry I have nothing to offer you." He steps around his chair and strides to the exit. The doors slide aside, but Deepak and Keiko step into the doorway, blocking him. Keller looks up into the Operators' stone faces and sees the tension coiled in them both.

"Please, Captain," Keiko states, her jaw firm, *"have a seat."*

Keller whirls in a rage. "What is this, O'Kai? Did you forget I'm a *guest* here? That we swore *never* to give each other orders?"

Gregor rises from his chair, his hands curling into fists. "What's going on here, General? If the Captain wants to go, *let him go.*"

"Everyone, be calm," Shao-Lo says. She puts her hands out in a soothing gesture and lowers them to the table. "Captain, if you would *please* take your seat. There is much to discuss. Your co-operation is required."

"Treating me like a *hostage* isn't going to get you far, Colonel. Now why don't you order off your two roadblocks here and I'll *think* about it."

"Who do you think you are, keeping us here?" Gregor challenges. "We give you free run of the *Europa*, and we'd never hold you like this!"

Chusan grimaces impatiently. "We only asked for Captain Keller. You and the Counselor can go."

Keller steps back toward his chair and puts his arms out to his crewmen, beckoning them close. "See why I asked you both to join me? I needed witnesses to whatever *crap* these Cadre assholes were gonna pull."

Gregor stands beside his Captain, staring down the officers across the table.

"'Bout time we were on our way, I'd say. General, you can let us leave, or we'll fight our way out."

O'Kai grimaces at the hollow threat and shakes his head. "Keller, you're not leaving until you talk to us."

"I've had enough!" Keller bellows. "Gregor, Counselor, let's go... *Counselor?*"

The Counselor has retreated from his companions. A wary expression rides on his eyelids as he takes one final step back. Still watching his Captain, the Counselor asks, "When were these photos taken, General?"

"The date stamp on the video reads July 17, 2472. The photographs, we believe, are a couple years older."

"Where did they come from?"

"Brick Argo found an intact vault in the Washington, D.C. ruins. Storage for some kind of informative broadcasting organization. These records were found with the remains of two people inside the vault."

"*2472...*" the Counselor echoes. He looks at the frozen video. "Recognize those people, Captain?"

Keller lets his guard drop slightly at faces he used to see almost daily. "Yeah. That's Van der Beek, SoVar's CMO. And Genia Mendes, Financial news Anchor for D.C. News."

The Counselor takes a step closer, grinning. "Gotta say, Captain, I didn't think you were *ever* that young."

Keller snorts once and returns a confused smile. "Thanks,

Counselor."

"Those pictures had to be *years* before we lost New Dresden..."

Keller nods in recollection, then all color drains from his face as he realizes what he has given away. He looks at the Counselor and finds all joviality is gone.

"...so why were you *butchering* blueskins?"

Panic paints Keller with a body-wide brush. Gregor pushes away in revulsion. What the Russian did not see from bare photos, the Counselor drew with words. He moves beside the Counselor, his head cocked from the weight of the thoughts inside.

"They were *natives*?" the Russian asks.

Keller says nothing.

Gregor tenses, his shoulders lift, his torso spreads, his fingernails claw into his palms. *"You fucking STARTED all this? HUH?"*

Keller watches his junior officer coming unraveled, growing wild.

"Gregor, get a hold of yourself..."

The young man turns suddenly, burying his face in his hands to stifle a deep moan. But like a man standing before a collapsing dam, emotion washes him away to a violent place, and the moan becomes a roar.

"I'LL FUCKING KILL YOU!"

Gregor lunges for Keller's throat with arms out, hands cupped. The elder officer stiff-arms the assault and pounds Gregor's cheek with a solid hook. The blow is powerful yet only briefly diverts the tide of hatred rushing at him. Gregor clinches Keller around the waist, lifts, and slams him onto the metal floor. The back of Keller's head hits hard, driving the fight from him.

Gregor's fists pummel the dazed man until his bloody hands resume the original attack and lock around the wrinkled neck. With all of his fury, he crushes Keller's throat, screaming, *"I'LL FUCKING KILL YOU! I'LL FUCKING KILL YOU! I'LL FUCKING KILL YOU!"*

While the Counselor yells at Gregor, begging him to stop, Deepak and Keiko seize Gregor by the arms. They lift him and Gregor's crazed grip pulls the plum-faced Keller up with him. Chusan hurries behind Keller and grabs Gregor's thumbs, prying the Russian's hands away. Shao-Lo catches the limp Keller when he falls from Gregor's grasp and lays him down gently so Munro can tend to him.

Gregor is wild with fury, flailing blindly, sending the chairs skidding and tumbling about the chamber until Deepak and Keiko thrust him face first against the wall and immobilize his limbs. The Russian writhes in their firm hold, the last of the flood coursing through him.

THE EXHAUSTED DEAD

"BOZSHE MOY!¹" he cries, *"Bozshe Moy...Bozshe Moy..."*

Keller convulses beneath his enormous physician, his legs and arms twitching on the polished floor plates before relaxing. Keller gags then lets out a long groan.

"He's gonna be okay, General," Munro announces.

O'Kai, still seated behind the table, shakes his head. "How do you people accomplish *anything*?"

"With effort, General," the Counselor answers. He taps Deepak on the shoulder, and the Gun relaxes his hold. Keiko does likewise.

"Are you okay, Gregor?"

The Russian shakes his head. "No. He can't live. Not for *this*."

"And who'll be his judge? *You?*"

Gregor's eyes flash with hatred, a hatred once reserved for Thompson, Maiella, and Argo. The hatred was always imperfect, tainted by the fact his wife was killed by accident. But now, in the glaring light of fact, rage burns pure and righteous in his murderous eyes. The Counselor reads it all.

"Vengeance is hollow, Gregor. If you had your way, what then?"

"Don't care."

"You should. Keller will have to face everyone aboard the *Europa* for this. He'll have to face what he's done, face his part in the destruction of humanity. A quick death now would spare him all of that. No justice for them. No peace for you."

The murderous eyes close, but then they flick open with a new intensity.

"Always, you think, *think, THINK!*" Gregor points with one of his restrained hands toward his heart. *"You don't know what it's like to have one of THESE."*

The Counselor looks down, wounded. Gregor glares at Keller, eyes smoldering like iron pulled from a forge. He watches his Captain sit up and rub his bruised throat delicately. Keller looks up and meets the Russian's gaze.

"I can't believe I served you, protected you, looked to you like my *father!*" Gregor snarls.

"I was twenty-three," Keller croaks, "and a damned *fool*. I was given a job to do. Didn't ask why. You'd be amazed how many were willing." He coughs harshly. "But *I'm* the one who has to live with it. That, and knowing the *Europa* might be the last of all our kind...Being responsible for your entire race...*you try that on for forty years, Gregor.* See how it *fits.*"

---

1   Боже мой! My God!

"That's the real reason you wouldn't meet with me in session, isn't it?" the Counselor asks. "You thought I'd find out."

Keller nods. *"Knew you would."*

"Well it's out now," Gregor spits. "The crew is gonna rip you to shreds." He pulls against the Operators holding him. *"If they beat me to it..."*

"Easy," Deepak warns.

Keller takes a long look at Gregor, weighing an unvoiced choice. He nods in conclusion of the mental debate and, with Munro's help, gets to his feet.

"General," he says hoarsely, "I'll make you a deal: give me shelter at Cadre One and protection from prosecution, I'll tell you where to find Cadre Two."

The Counselor drops his head into his hands from the double bombshell.

"ASYLUM? YOU'RE REQUESTING ASYLUM?" Gregor fumes.

"And you know about Cadre Two?" the Counselor adds.

Keller stands straight as he can. "That's right. Can't say how *they* knew I did..."

"From the bodies in this pit," Munro says, pointing to the image in the frozen video. "Would you magnify that, General?"

O'Kai obliges, tapping keys at his terminal. The hovering screen zooms into the wide trench and resolves hundreds of blue, reptilian corpses in detail. The corpses seep fluids from every orifice as though the sun were melting them internally. Mesh webbings and diaphanous garments not seen at first glance enshroud the dead, sticking where the fluids have clotted. Munro explains:

"Team Forestall returned with a viral agent that attacks the lining of blood vessels, among other things. If allowed to progress, the virus would have caused them to bleed out, just as these bodies have. It was a matter of deduction, since the symptoms were so similar, that Keller must have used such a viral agent to exterminate these blueskins. Knowing that Cadre One has the means to produce just such an agent, we thought it likely Cadre Two may as well, and that Keller may have travelled to Cadre Two to procure it."

Munro looks at the man he is helping to stand. "You might have just told us when we asked the first time."

Keller ignores the comment. "My offer stands General. If I'm prosecuted, you'll never find Cadre Two."

O'Kai's eyebrows knit with impatience. "You killed the enemy, not people, so I don't see what *crime* you'd be punished for. Gregor, however, vowed to break our only law *in this chamber*. Would have done it, if allowed.

THE EXHAUSTED DEAD

As a result, *this is the last time he will ever be allowed into Cadre One.*
Deepak, Keiko, get him out of here. Send him back to the *Europa.*"

The Guns nod briskly and drag the young man out. His protests echo from the corridor until the doors reseal.

"As for your offer, Keller, I agree with Munro. I don't see why you couldn't have just told us in the beginning."

"I'd be killed if any of my crew found out."

"*That* has been demonstrated. But now your ability to avoid truth has *also* been demonstrated. Your offer holds little value when your credibility is suspect."

Keller swallows hard. "I can give you a head start."

"Oh?"

"Procyon system."

Shao-Lo walks behind the table and whispers something in O'Kai's ear. O'Kai nods.

"But you'll never find it," Keller blurts nervously. "There's a lot of rock tumbling through that system. Odd orbits. Hard to navigate."

O'Kai stares at the aged Captain. "So where is it?"

Keller maintains his straightforward gaze over the general's head. O'Kai's hands flex with exasperation.

"*Fine.* You'll have protected quarters here at Cadre One. You will *also* have a work schedule, you should know."

Keller nods. "That's acceptable."

The Counselor steps in front of Keller to look his superior directly in the face. "We passed through the Procyon system before making our way toward Sirius...Our meeting with Thompson, Maiella, and Argo was no accident, was it? You were checking up on the Cadre facilities...checking to see if there were *survivors!*"

Keller's eyes shift in their fist-blackened sockets. "Astute as always, Counselor."

"And what did you find at Cadre Two, Captain?"

Keller looks straight ahead.

"*I asked you a question!*" the Counselor demands.

"Time you were going, I think. Inform Javier that he will be assuming command. He may make whatever organizational changes he likes. The *Europa* is his responsibility now."

"Captain!"

"This is for the General and his Council only. Good-bye, Counselor. We'll probably never meet again."

O'Kai flicks his head toward the door and Chusan gestures the

Counselor toward it.

"Please come with me," the burn-scarred major insists. The Counselor reluctantly goes, shuffling into the corridor with Chusan at his arm. Behind him, he hears O'Kai ask, "All right, Keller, what are we looking at?"

The doors seal tight.

Chain of Command

Ortega stands beside the Counselor on an improvised scaffold in the middle of a vast storage bay. As he looks out across the wide floor, he has difficulty believing nearly all of it was once filled to the ten-meter ceiling with supplies, machinery, and spare parts. Of the stores not already consumed, the rest have been shuttled down to Cadre One. With so much open space the bay became a natural meeting place for Colonist concerns.

Typically, those assemblies were mundane and orderly with Keller on the scaffold, expertly addressing needs, handling each minor crisis as they came. But now Ortega and the Counselor stand above a sea of furious faces shouting vehement hatred. The crowd has only been assembled a few minutes. Already, the cry for Keller's blood is deafening.

The newly promoted captain places a wireless communication device on his ear and taps its stubby microphone. Deep *thumps* come through the bay's loudspeakers.

"Your attention," Ortega calls, but it is drowned by the storm of protest. From the rear a chant begins and it spreads like electricity.

"Your attention," he calls again. The chants merge into a single voice, punctuated by stomps and hand claps.

"STRETCH HIS NECK. STRETCH HIS NECK. STRETCH HIS NECK."

"GODDAMN IT, I'M NOT ASKING AGAIN! *KNOCK IT OFF!"* Ortega yells. The percussive chants roll off.

"Give me your eyes AND your ears," he continues, "and you'll get some answers." The last of the chants fade to grumbles, then to quiet.

"That's better." Ortega takes a deep breath, collecting himself.

"Look, I'm not gonna sugarcoat this: you've heard that Keller has admitted to massacring a *native* population of blueskins at New Dresden. There are photos that prove it. This is probably the reason Earth was attacked, because they were provoked into war."

The chants begin at the rear again.

"STOP IT!" Ortega thunders. "Let me get through this, *then* I will hear you!"

The chants stop, but a low murmur pervades the crowd.

"All right. Thank you." He looks at his feet and shakes his head. "I want justice just like you do." His head pops up. "But I can't have a lynch mob tearing this ship apart. Do you understand?"

Murmurs drift like ripples over a pond.

"YES or NO?"

"YES," the crowd replies in hundreds of mismatched voices.

"Okay, then..."

"Where's Gregor?" a voice from the crowd shouts.

Assenting voices chime in and Ortega lifts his arms to silence them.

"I will answer this *one* question now, so long as all other questions wait until the end. Is that clear?"

"YES."

"Good. Lieutenant Petrova is confined to his quarters because he has vowed to kill Captain Keller by any means. He is being cared for, yet he has been suspended from duty until he can clear his mind. Now I'm not about to entertain the idea of building a brig, so anyone else who tries to bring their own street justice to Keller will find themselves working a Cadre labor detail. Is that *clear*?"

Assenting grumbles pass between the hundreds of assembled faces.

"Good." Ortega leans on the rails of the scaffold, looking into as many eyes as he can before proceeding. Faces he has known for decades are so full of rage, he can scarcely recognize them.

"You've also heard Captain Keller has been granted asylum from General O'Kai. Before you judge the Cadre harshly, you must know it was a condition of Keller giving up the location of Cadre *Two*."

A collective gasp rises from the crowd.

"That's right. Cadre *Two*. We assume it's some kind of research station like Cadre One but that's all we know. General O'Kai has ordered a mission out there, led by Colonel Shao-Lo. They don't know what they'll find, so combat Operators will fill the bulk of the team. Commander Jones will go as well to assist and to report what she sees. God willing, we'll find survivors there.

"Obviously, Keller can no longer remain the captain of the *Europa* or her crew. As ranking officer, it falls to me to assume his duties. I will be calling on some of you to assist in the re-organization, though I'm sure there will be few changes."

Indiscriminate grumbles circulate among the agitated crowd. Ortega looks to the Counselor and the Counselor pulls a wireless microphone from his pocket.

"The Counselor is bringing a microphone down so those with questions may be heard. Line up here and he will get to you one at a time. Keep it orderly, or this show is over. *Understood?*"

Nods, head bobs, murmurs, and grunts indicate the affirmative.

"Counselor?"

By the time the Counselor steps down from the scaffold a long line has formed. He holds the microphone up to the first: a woman in sooty coveralls with a Chimpanzee patch on her chest pocket.

"If Keller's hiding like a coward at Cadre One, how can he be tried?"

Ortega nods. "He will be tried *in absentia* and judged based on the evidence at hand."

The Microphone moves to the next in line, a man with bright orange coveralls and a red cross on his chest pocket.

"Who will judge?"

"This is a Capital crime. We'll need a panel of nine to hear the case. I must appoint them."

"But *who* will that be?"

"We've all heard about this, so the only impartial jurors are still in their cryo tubes. I will select ranking officers, decant them, and brief them on our situation. That will have to do until I make my final selections. Next?"

A man steps up to the microphone, wearing grungy blue coveralls. A lightning bolt runs through the SoVar logo on his left chest pocket.

"Our reactor is supplying more than a quarter of Cadre One's power right now. We could shut them off completely. Why don't we use that as leverage to get Keller back?"

The crowd erupts with cheers, whistles, and applause. Ortega puts his hands up to quell the outburst, his mind spinning at the sudden thrust into ugly politics.

"We *could* do that, but look...I understand. It's hard to be denied. We've wanted answers why our home was destroyed for a *long time*. Now we know why, and one of those responsible is being sheltered by the Cadre. But let's not forget the Cadre is *the only thing that protects us*. This is not the time to provoke them. And most important of all, there is a whole new generation of children growing there. We mustn't risk them with power outages."

"Cadre mutants," someone shouts from the crowd. Heads nod all over in agreement.

Ortega pushes off the railing of the scaffold and extends a long, accusing arm over the crowd.

"Let's get something straight: I will *NEVER* tolerate that kind of talk. The Cadre is made up of *PEOPLE*. Not things. Not objects. It's just that kind of talk that let Keller slaughter an entire population at New Dresden. *DO YOU UNDERSTAND?"*

A chilly silence fills the room. Many heads hang in embarrassment. More lift in obedience to the morality of Ortega's maxim.

The Spaniard rubs his forehead, embarrassed by his outburst. He steps back to the railing.

"Look, I don't mean to beat you up about this. We all want justice. I served under Keller almost my entire life and I feel a deep, *deep* betrayal. So I understand what you say...We can*not* lose focus on what's most important because we *want* something so much. Agreed?"

Ortega looks out into the crowd again, connecting eye to eye, reeling his crew in before continuing.

"Okay. Next question."

The microphone passes to an elderly woman wearing medical scrubs.

"Is it true Argo is back in the Corps? And what happened to the Lizard he brought back?"

"Yes, it's true, Argo recovered from his injuries and has been reinstated as a Sergeant in the Operator Corps. As for the alien...Counselor?"

The Counselor takes the microphone. "It was in extremely poor health and was getting worse during its captivity at Cadre One. Doctor Taggart and I worked on treatments for it, and it has since been transferred to protective custody here aboard the *Europa*. I'm pleased to say it's getting better and in the next few weeks I hope to attempt some communication."

"Why bother?" shouts a voice from the back of the room. Ortega's eyes flick toward the voice but he does not acknowledge it.

"Thank you, Counselor. Next question?"

"What about Earth?" asks a burly man in faded green coveralls. The badge on his chest shows a geometric network of interconnecting pipes. "Why haven't the Cadre guys released the pictures they got? Is it devastated? Or what?"

All eyes rivet to Ortega.

"From what I've been told, Earth is very much alive but the cities are still blighted with radiation. There's also a very large alien population there, which is why the Cadre hasn't released the data yet: they're still analyzing it for weaknesses."

Hope in the crowd vanishes with a sullen exhale.

"There is also the possibility of a lingering virus, the one that Argo, Beckert, and Thompson brought back. We don't know if it's environmental or if they caught it from one of the sealed chambers they broke into. Doctor Taggart and the MedTechs are building anti-virals in the Cadre MedLabs as we speak. Another reason why we shouldn't cut off power to them. Next?"

A mousy woman with orange coveralls and a belt of delicate tools takes the microphone. "What about Thompson? And Beckert?"

Ortega nods. "Beckert was severely injured, losing his sight and three of his limbs. He's in a coma now, and we should pray for him. Thompson was also severely injured. Colonel Munro said his armor was hit at least a hundred times, many of them perforating. Argo reported his heart stopped several times during the flight home. But he's stable now and should mostly recover. Next?"

A tall man with broad shoulders and clean uniform takes the microphone.

"So Keller's out and you're in, just like that?"

Ortega senses the accusation, the undertones of insubordination.

"That's right," Ortega confirms. "We will follow chain of command."

The man keeps hold of the microphone and turns to the crowd. "While we were alone amid the stars, we trusted Keller to bring us to our destination. We followed his every order, obeyed his every command. Commander Ortega gave his all in support of that mission and he is an honorable man."

"Thank you, but I don't hear a question there, Mr. Herzfeld."

Herzfeld faces the scaffold. "Here's my question." He whirls to the crowd. "If this is how one leader will forever succeed the other, what do *we* have to look forward to? What makes *us* different from the *Cadre*?"

Loud cheers and applause rise from the crowd. Whistles pierce the air. Herzfeld turns toward Ortega and waits.

"Believe me, Herzfeld, I know a rhetorical question when I hear it. Now do you have a question that needs answering? Because I am running a colony ship, not a class on debate."

Herzfeld grins. "Okay. I think you'd make a fine candidate, Commander—"

"That's *Captain* to you," Ortega interjects.

"And maybe you will be Captain. But that should be up to a vote.

Just like we vote on whether or not we get Keller back here for trial!"

The crowd explodes with applause and wild cheers, far louder than before. Herzfeld pumps his arms in a regular rhythm and the chant begins again.

Ortega stares out into the crowd. No one looks at him. They all focus on Herzfeld and his pumping arms.

"Stretch his neck! STRETCH HIS NECK! *STRETCH HIS NECK!"*

A Matter of Perspective

Sharon waits anxiously in the Europa's transport, fussing over her many cases of equipment.

I just know I've forgotten something.

She sighs and leans back against the bulkhead. Movement draws her eye, and she looks through the open transport hatch, through the open air lock, and into Cadre One's wide main corridor. A pair of Cadre MedTechs pass by, dressed in white smocks, hair slicked straight back on identically-shaped heads.

Insecurities tug at her and she subconsciously reaches up to a pendant at her neck. Taking it between thumb and fingers, she rubs.

"This is really amazing," the transport pilot says.

"Hmm?"

The pilot turns in his seat, every line of his face curved up at the edges. "Another Cadre...Who knows what's there? Wish I was going!"

Sharon smiles meekly at the gesture. "Oh, right. Yes. Very exciting." She lays her hands in her lap and looks at them.

She mentally drifts back to her first meeting with Cadre Operators: the total surprise, the utter helplessness as Maiella, Thompson, and Argo bored through the *Europa's* thick hull, how the swift Operators gunned down everyone they saw through the smoke of their entry. Only after seventeen lay dead did the soldiers realize their victims were human, not blueskin, and halt their assault. Such ferocity, such killing talent in three individuals...the loss of crewmates so dear they were more like family than friends. The thought of going through it all over again withers her inside, makes her feel old.

Shao-Lo steps into view at the far end of the corridor. Light-absorbing armor covers her from feet to neck and a bulky rifle hangs barrel-down from a strap over her shoulder. Her graying hair is shaved close to the scalp, and she cradles her helmet in one arm.

Deepak and Argo follow in perfect cadence with their colonel. Deepak is identically equipped as Shao-Lo right down to the same stern expression. Argo is dressed in the modern Brick's armor with broad shoulders, barrel chest, slim waist, and thick, powerful legs. He grips a shoulder sack of boxy items with one hand, hefts a radical new cannon with the other. Despite the lines and scars of his leathered face, the streamlined cut of the massive suit makes him look young.

The Operators move briskly, their rubber-soled boots thudding with every determined heel strike. Their heads are high with shoulders back, and their free arms swing with every long stride.

So confident...

When the soldiers reach the air lock, Sharon realizes she is fiddling with her necklace again and releases it. She gets to her feet, welcoming the others aboard with an outstretched hand.

"Colonel Shao-Lo, Deepak, Argo. Good to see you all again!"

Shao-Lo ducks through the transport hatchway and takes the offered hand, gripping firmly.

"You, as well, Commander." Shao-Lo turns abruptly. "Sergeant, seal the inner air-lock."

"Yes, Ma'am," Argo answers.

"We're all *'Sir'* now, Brick," Shao-Lo says sardonically. "Do *try* to remember."

"Yes, *Sir*, Colonel!" Argo sets his sack down and hustles to the panel beside the inner air lock gate. He taps a sequence of numbers then mashes a red knob. Green lights turn to red and a short horn blast sounds before the inner doors slide smoothly together. The Brick hustles back to the transport.

"All clear," he announces.

Shao-Lo turns forward. "Pilot, we're ready."

The pilot spins forward and takes the transport controls. With a key tap, the transport hatch seals. Mechanical vibrations rise from the floor as the transport is pushed away from the dock, finished by a *clank* when the docking clamps release. The three Cadre soldiers grab onto overhead rails, bracing themselves as the transport floats free then surges up out of the crater.

"Cadre vessel *Enyo*, this is *Europa* transport on final approach. Respond."

"Received, Europa transport," the radio replies, *"proceed to*

THE EXHAUSTED DEAD

forward access hatch, over."

Argo leans into a bubbled porthole to see the ship named after his old Colonel. Though shaded from the blazing bright sun by Cadre One, running lights on the ship show her distinct outline. His eyes glaze and he smiles fondly.

Sharon studies Argo's profile in admiration.

I can't believe he survived. Everything he's been through...Brilliant, modest, invincible Argo...

She smiles inwardly, feeling the same girlish feelings when in front of a celebrity, yet there is something more. Her eyes roam the rugged, battered features of his face.

He'll never give up, will he? He'd do anything to save us.

Eager for an excuse to talk, she slides closer and asks, "See something?"

Argo pulls away from the porthole, broadening a satisfied grin.

"I recognize that ship."

"Oh?" Shao-Lo chimes.

Argo nods. "Thompson, Maiella, and I collected her on our last rotation, before..." His expression sobers. He looks directly at Sharon. "...before we met you."

Argo looks out through the porthole again.

"Maiella was the only reason we survived that rotation," he adds.

Shao-Lo grunts skeptically.

The idea of earning a disdainful grunt like that from the Cadre's second-in-command puts Sharon on edge. She rubs her pendant again.

"What have you got there?" Shao-Lo asks.

"Hmm? Oh, this...?" Sharon looks down at her pendant. "Nothing. Just something old."

Shao-Lo leans closer for a better look. A silver necklace suspends a sturdy setting with wavy rays extending from it like an oblong sun. Nestled into the setting is a dark gemstone. As the pilot maneuvers the transport, light plays across the gemstone, and it flashes with blue, green, and red light. Shao-Lo's casual interest turns genuine and she takes the pendant between her fingers, twisting back and forth.

"It's as if...it's like there's light inside."

"Dark opal," Sharon says, losing some of her self-consciousness. "Used to be called Fire Opals, because of the play of light. Looks like fire."

"Where'd you get it?"

"It was my great, great grandmother's."

Shao-Lo's eyebrows scrunch together, her lips forming a question.

"My ancestor," Sharon translates.

The transport swings about and jars to a halt against the *Enyo's* modified docking collar. Shao-Lo ends her fascinated stare and releases the pendant.

"Let's get to it," she orders.

The transport hatch slides aside and Shao-Lo ducks through it, Deepak and Argo following obediently. Sharon looks at her pile of equipment, wondering where to start.

"I could use a..." she says, turning to her fellow travelers. They are gone. "...hand." She grimaces.

"Here, I can help," the pilot says. He unbuckles himself from the chair and releases the tie down straps around her cases. With a chivalrous smile, he tugs on the handle of the largest case. It is so heavy he is yanked back.

"Good grief, what's in this?" he asks.

"Everything I need, I hope," Sharon says, taking two small cases from the pile. She faces the hatchway and stops cold. Beyond the hatch is a dark corridor, scarcely lit in deep red. Exposed pipes and wires run along the narrow walls like veins beneath torn away skin. Floors and ceilings are stripped down to the bulkheads, leaving only emergency light sconces and a non-slip grating underfoot. Cool, dry air drafts into the warm transport cabin, and a baleful thrum emanates from deep within the vessel.

Never before has she set foot on a Cadre warship. Comfort would be of little importance to the pragmatic Cadre Techs, she knows. But as she stands in the hatchway of the transport looking in, she can feel that whatever this ship was before it was 'collected,' it has been stripped, tortured, and rebuilt into something vicious. Something deadly.

The pilot taps her shoulder. "You okay, Commander?"

Sharon shakes herself. *Damn it, you're supposed to be a leader. Get in there!*

"Yeah, yeah," she covers. "Making sure I have everything."

She steps across the threshold into the dim corridor, following the sound of voices. After a short trek, she passes through the twisted frame of a blast door. Hunks of metal, presumably the remains of the blast doors themselves, are sliced right to the edge of the frame.

Beyond the twisted frame is a spacious bridge, where Shao-Lo stands tall, giving orders. Operators peel from her huddle one at a time as they receive instruction.

The transport pilot drags the large case in and releases it with a grunt. "I'll go get the rest. Be right back."

"Okay," Sharon says absently, setting down her small cases and inspecting the various consoles. Instinctively, she finds the astrogation terminal.

"Colonel, would you like me to plot our course?" Sharon asks.

"We have that covered, thank you," Shao-Lo says, pointing without looking.

Sharon follows Shao-Lo's pointing finger to a single Operator. Male or female Sharon cannot tell, but from the large headgear and the lanyards attaching it to the terminal, no doubt it is a Cadre Geek.

"Where would you like me, then?"

Shao-Lo issues commands to the biggest Brick Sharon has ever set eyes upon then answers, "Please take your quarters until we're underway."

Sharon can only stare at the enormous Brick as he strides off the *Enyo's* bridge and disappears past the twisted entryway. She expects a man of such size would have to swagger in his gait, simply from having so much bulk to move, yet he strides with the same deliberate poise as every other Operator in the Corps.

"Commander?" Shao-Lo calls.

"Yeah?" Sharon answers, swiveling her head forward.

"Your quarters?"

"Oh, *right*...I'm sorry, but, uh, I have no idea where they are."

Shao-Lo grimaces and nods at Argo. Argo takes his cue and peels away from the Colonel's huddle.

Sharon smiles at her guide, until, in the gap Argo left, she spots Keller standing with arms folded. His eyes flick over at Sharon briefly, then again. The two lock gazes.

"You rotten bastard," Sharon curses.

Argo points at himself with a confused expression then looks over his shoulder and finds the object of Sharon's anger. He turns forward, moving slowly toward her and asks, "Is there a problem?"

"No, no problem," Sharon says. "Should've figured that *unctuous coward* would hide on this trip."

The transport pilot returns through the bent entryway and sets down a pile of Sharon's cases. "There you go, that's all of..."

Like Sharon, he spies Keller in the huddle. The pilot's congenial face contorts and he rushes forward. Argo catches him and holds tight while the man rages.

"I hope you burn in HELL for what you did, Keller! I hope you BURN IN HELL!"

"You," Argo says to the man struggling in his grip, "go back to the transport. Or shall I carry you?" He easily lifts the pilot with one hand.

"No! I'm fine! *Fine! I can walk!"*

Argo sets the man down onto his kicking legs. The pilot brushes himself off, burning a lasting glare into his old captain. "I can *walk*," he says again, back-stepping out of the bridge. He watches Keller intently, daring him to say something. At the wrecked blast door, he pauses.

"We'll be *waiting* for you, Keller."

Keller keeps his arms folded, not moving anything but his eyes, watching the threatening man at the doorframe. Operators glare in irritation.

Argo flicks his head at the stalled pilot. "Go on."

Teeth and hands clenched, the pilot breaks his hateful gaze and disappears into the corridor.

"Commander Jones," Argo says, extending a beefy arm, "this way."

Sharon squints malevolently at Keller then picks up two of her bags. Argo manages the rest, and even he casts a surprised second glance at the large case. Together, he and Sharon leave the bridge and walk in silence.

When they no longer hear Shao-Lo's voice, Argo looks over his shoulder.

"There's something I don't understand," the Brick says. "May I ask you about it?"

"Of course," Sharon replies.

"This thing you believe Keller did...why does it anger you so much?"

She scoffs. "Are you serious?"

"Yes."

"Argo...Keller started this whole war! We used to have a planet of our own, a *home*! Our lives are so hard now, we're just barely getting on. And that goes especially for all of you in the Cadre!"

"We endure. At times, we thrive."

"But what about Earth? You were *there*, Argo! You *know* what it's like to breathe free air, air that hasn't been exhaled and filtered a million times...to feel the abundance of life all around you..."

"What I saw, I don't know that life would be so easy. No shelters, no nutrient production..."

"What do you think the *Europa's* been carrying all this time?"

Argo juts his lip, quietly considering the *Europa's* automated colony apparatus, packaged for flight and remaining so for all the long centuries of the vessel's journey.

"Well, whatever the reason for it, it's done now. It can't be undone, so why are you all so fixated upon it?"

Sharon takes a breath to suppress the quick anger and frustration.

"Argo, Keller killed *billions* of people!"

"No, he killed thousands of *blueskins*. That was no crime then or now."

"Yes, but by doing so, he *caused* the deaths of billions of people!"

Argo shakes his head. "Not true. The *blueskins* destroyed the people of Earth and the colonies. Not Keller."

Argo's emotional distance infuriates her.

"All right then, Argo. By *that* logic, why not just get over the people you and Thompson and Maiella killed, huh? Why not just sweep *them* aside?"

Argo stops his plod through the narrow corridor. With eyes half closed and a mouth turned down at the corners, he turns around to look her in the face.

"You know I can't."

"Why?"

"Because *I pulled the trigger*, that's why."

Sharon looks into the Brick's lined face, seeing how cruel her question was. *God, how could I have said that?*

"*I* pulled the trigger, Commander," the big man continues, "and *I'm* the one who's responsible for it. Just like the blueskins pulled the trigger on our entire kind. *They're* the ones to blame for all this, not Keller."

Argo faces forward and starts walking again.

"I've killed hundreds of blueskins," the Brick says. "Thousands, maybe. So's Thompson, Maiella, the whole Cadre!" He whirls around suddenly. "Will there be a day when you judge us for *that*, Commander?"

Sharon looks into Argo's face. Despite his bulk and agitation, she feels no threat from him at all. With the realization she is completely safe in his presence, a simple truth crystallizes in her mind.

"Cadre and Colonist alike, we *know* when we've doing something wrong, Argo. We *know* it. More to the point, *Keller* knows this. He *knows* what he's done."

Argo thinks for a moment. "He doesn't act like it. Why are you so sure?"

"He's abandoned his crew! He's hiding under the Cadre's wing! If he had done the right thing, wouldn't he stand up and say so? Why would he need O'Kai's protection? What would he have to fear from his own crew?"

The Brick faces forward and starts walking again. "Sounds to me like a matter of perspective. Whoever's looking decides if it's good or bad. I still don't see the crime that you do. But it's not up to me. Besides, Keller is the only source of intelligence we have on Cadre Two. That's valuable, isn't it?"

Sharon does not answer.

"Isn't it?" Argo asks again.

"I *suppose*..."

"He was right, you know. We never would've found Cadre Two without him. That place is dug in."

The Brick makes a sharp right turn into a slender cabin with its own bunk and hygiene station. He unloads Sharon's numerous cases at the back of the room.

Sharon follows him in and sets her cases down on the bunk. "Did he say what's there?"

"Only that he sent a transport shuttle in with six crew. They went in, but never came out. He seemed anxious about going back, in fact."

"What's in there, Argo?"

Argo flattens himself out to slide by her on his way out.

"It's a long flight. You might ask him."

"I'm asking *you*."

"Weapons research. Directed Energy, Nano-Tech...And *others*..."

"Viral weapons?"

Argo halts at the door, draws a deep breath and exhales slowly. "Please get your gear stowed. We'll be departing shortly." He taps a button and the door closes, leaving Sharon by herself in the cramped space.

A dim, red light panel provides just enough illumination to see. She turns in place as she studies her new accommodations. All the cover plating has been stripped from the walls, exposing interior conduits and network bundles between metal ribs and studs. The background thrum fills the cabin, constant and hypnotic.

Viral Weapons...

She sets herself onto the rigid bunk as her mind conjures a nightmare lying in wait: six of her crewmates left in gory heaps, or more likely, decayed to bone. She tries to inventory her crew, wondering, *of those scheduled to be in cryogenic stasis, which six cryotubes are vacant?* She shivers.

"Attention!" a loudspeaker in her cabin declares with Shao-Lo's voice, "All personnel aboard. All equipment secured. We are ready to depart. Stand by."

The light panel dims to a deeper red. The background thrum rises in frequency like the heartbeat of an excited animal.

Keep it together, she reminds herself. *They'll protect you. They'll protect you...*

"Jump in three...two...one..."

THE EXHAUSTED DEAD

Tiny blue sparks leap from the corners of metal framing and from the pendant at her neck. Her hair stands on end. The entire vessel tenses like muscle.

"Jump."

Sharon shuts her eyes against the relativistic dilations as the ship roars through space and time.

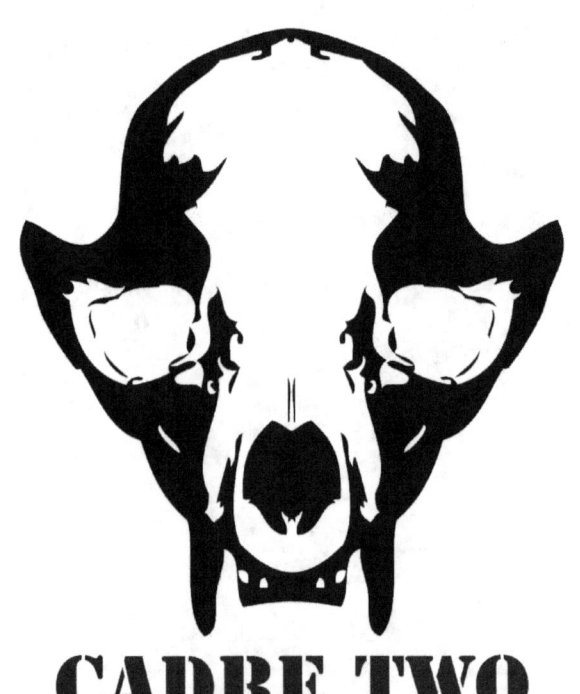

CADRE TWO

PART FIVE

A Hole in the Sky

From her first step aboard the *Enyo*, Sharon knew that Cadre Techs would give, at best, 'slight regard' toward easing the harshness of superluminal travel. But 'slight regard' is, in reality, more like 'total and utter disdain' as the vessel decelerates. Only minimal insulation is provided from the engines' abundance of raw power and, as they fire, Sharon's warped perceptions are dragged through a full spectrum of sickening distortions.

She sways on the bridge's deck plates and steadies herself against a nearby console as the crackling in her ears subsides. Recovering her British dignity, she stands straight and smoothes down the bristled hair on her arms until a wet burp wrecks her composure. She swallows with difficulty, nearly gagging.

"Jump complete," the Geek pilot announces, swiveling in her seat to address the tall Colonel behind her. "Arrived at Pro-see-un AB, relativistic drift less than point zero two AU. Compensating."

Keller stands on the opposite side of the bridge from Sharon. He curls his hand and brings it up to his mouth as if he might need to catch something launching from it. He blinks hard and swallows with effort.

"Are you getting a signal?" Shao-Lo asks.

"No comm traffic," the pilot reports. "Searching…"

"Any other vessels in the region?"

"None detected. Still recommend caution, Colonel. If present, they may be stealthed as we are."

Shao-Lo leans forward in her metal seat, peering at a brilliant yellow star in the holoscreen. Coronal loops jut millions of kilometers above its surface, tracing magnetic lines of force in radiant plasma. Far to the upper left a dwarf white star shines, nearly an afterthought to its enormous companion. Its fuel exhausted, the stellar remnant glows with residual heat, illuminating a faint ring of dust around it.

"Well, Keller, where is it?" she asks.

"Give me a fix on position," Keller demands with inappropriate authority. The Geek's goggles strobe with code and, as requested, she opens a small holoscreen in front of him. He grips the virtual screen by the edges and pulls it close. Still holding with one hand, he sweeps the image with the other, alternately enlarging and shrinking various areas of the plotted system. His eyes dart across the image.

"There," he states, jabbing a finger into the hovering image. "Right there, in the dust lane around the dwarf star. Plot this location."

Shao-Lo arches an eyebrow. "Do you have it, Asha?"

Through the intermittent pulses of code in her goggles, Asha replies, "Affirmative, Colonel. There's an object in the dust lane. Solid. Big enough for a permanent base." Her eyewear flares with calculation. "Changing heading."

The ship carves a hard arc toward the diminutive companion star. On-screen, the enormous yellow star drifts to the side while the small white star settles into the center. Power thrums through the deck plates as the Geek urges the vessel faster. The distance closes in what feels like moments until she reins the swift ship to a gradual approach.

"Two hundred thousand kilometers and closing, Colonel."

Shao-Lo peers at a gargantuan chunk of rock drifting in the holoscreen. One side is rounded and relatively flat, with low ripples, folds, and craters; the other sides are jagged and torn like the enormous rock was ripped from a much larger globe. She strains for detail in the high-resolution image, seeking among the rifts, spires, and crags, but the dim rock does not give up its secrets.

"What am I looking at, Sharon?"

"Planetary remnant. Solid core of a gas giant, most likely."

"What *happened* to it?"

"That little white star looks calm now, but once it would've been a red giant. This close, the planet's outer layers would have blown and boiled away, leaving just a rocky core. When the star went nova, it must have wrenched the core apart."

Shao-Lo nods with fading interest. "Asha, send greeting via coded laser, point zero one degree of spread. Standard Cadre protocol."

"Cadre Standard, aye," the Geek replies.

Sharon watches the core fragment anxiously, wondering what may come screaming out of it. Her eyes shift to the stalwart soldiers around her, checking them for any sign of alarm, but they are calm and controlled as ever.

"No reply, Colonel," Asha states.

"Be patient," Keller chides. "Send it again. Different code."

The Geek waits until Shao-Lo gives the nod then sends a complex code of alpha-numerics and patterns. Ten seconds pass. Twenty. Thirty.

"Let's get a closer look…" Shao-Lo begins when Keller's hand flies up in annoyance.

"Just wait! This place has *twice* the firepower of your *little cave.* You go charging in, you might get us *all* killed."

Shao-Lo makes a show of turning in her seat and addresses him in a low, moderated voice.

"This isn't the *Europa*, Keller. A less commanding tone will suit you." She turns forward, putting her shoulder to him, and studies the screen.

"Pingback, Colonel," the Geek reports. "We have a connection."

"Get in there, Geek."

Asha's goggles blaze with code.

"Brick Carter," Shao-Lo calls via radio, "assemble Operator teams and get dressed, full-kit."

"Understood, sir," comes a basso voice over the speakers, "all teams to assemble and gear up, full kit. Brick Carter out."

"Colonel," Asha announces, "interface achieved with Cadre Two. Mainframes still on-line."

Keller perks up in wary surprise.

"Getting a reply now," the Geek says.

Shao-Lo leans forward and tents her hands. "Put it through."

The main screen fades to black, leaving a faint impression of the familiar hawk icon, wings spread, twin globes grasped in sharp talons. Plain white script fades in one line at a time:

Welcome to Cadre Two.
The base director has been notified of your arrival and
extends warm greetings.
Auto dock engaging…

"Don't let them!" Keller blurts.

"Relax," Asha says with annoyance. "We're stealthed. It can't lock on."

As predicted, the screen washes bright blue and proclaims,

THE EXHAUSTED DEAD

<pre>
System error.
Auto Dock failure.
Notifying tech support.
</pre>

Dots appear one by one after the last word like some kind of 8-bit progress bar.

The screen flashes and a grungy man appears on-screen. Grease mars his blue coveralls, face, and red hat. His breast pocket is crammed full of assorted computer tools. Protective eyewear hangs around his neck. He looks straight out at Shao-Lo.

"Seems we're having trouble finding your ship with the auto-dock. Is everything all right on your end?" The image freezes.

Shao-Lo stares at the frozen image and scrunches her face. "Did we lose the signal?"

"No, sir, it's still there."

"It's an interactive program," Keller says. "You talk to it and it responds."

The image reanimates and turns to the aged colonist, "Oh, we're a bit more than merely *interactive*." The technician's clothing shifts from the grease-marred coveralls of a technician to the crisp white lab-coat of a researcher. Spectacles appear on the angular nose and the red cap disappears, revealing sparse gray hair slicked straight back. With mild German inflection, the image adds, *"You of all people should remember...Captain Keller."*

Keller goes rigid like the image and his color drains. "This was a mistake," he says, "a goddamned *mistake*! Colonel, we should get outta here!"

"Take a breath, Keller. We're not leaving until we've checked for survivors."

"There *ARE* no survivors here!"

Sharon shrinks behind her console, Keller's fear frosting her to the bone.

"How can you say that, Captain?" the image taunts. *"After all we've accomplished together..."*

"Save the *bullshit, HONNIKER!* I'd sooner drive a spike through your chest than work with you."

"So, this is not a happy reunion, then? Begs the question, why you came back..." The image scrunches its face. *"Where are you, by the way? I don't see you."*

Asha squirms in her seat, agitated. She groans as though straining against something heavy.

"Cut the feed!" Shao-Lo demands.

Asha complies, blanking the screen and restoring the external view of space. Her breath leaves in a rush.

"What happened, Geek?" Shao-Lo demands.

The pilot turns in her seat and lifts her goggles. "Never had software try to cram into my head like that."

Sharon pushes through her anxiety to ask, "Why? What could that do?"

"Don't know. Make me jerk my hand, cough, who knows...anything that might have given away our position."

Shao-Lo nods. "Suggestions?"

"Abort," Keller says without missing a beat.

"Not going to happen. What else?"

Keller, having already offered his suggestion, looks out through the main screen into space.

Sharon shakes her head, having no clue what to make of the black rock ahead or of the bizarre conversation with the researcher on screen.

"Colonel," the Geek announces, "something just launched from the core fragment."

"Let's see it," Shao-Lo orders. The image on screen zooms in to one of the high peaks on the jagged edge of the drifting rock. Behind the peak is a faint trail of glittering dust, rising from the surface. A large, black disc rides the apex of the trail and rotates. As it turns, background starlight reflects on one side.

"Weapon optic!" the pilot shouts.

"But we're invisible," Sharon says, her vocal cords tight. "How could they see us?"

Shao-Lo looks up at the ceiling. "The dust! We're a hole right in the middle of it! *Asha, evasive!*"

The Geek jerks the controls, swaying Keller and Sharon off their feet. A blazing beam lances the spot the ship occupied a moment earlier then swings after the evading vessel, igniting the hanging dust in a luminous arc.

"Hang on!" Asha shouts. She jinks the entire vessel sideways before inertial dampers can fully compensate. Shao-Lo clutches her seat, barely keeping herself in it. Sharon and Keller slam harshly against hard terminals.

"Countermeasures," Shao-Lo orders coolly.

Reflective foil explodes from the ship's outer hull, swelling into an enormous light scattering bubble. The beam swings blindly through the expanding foil, unable to track the concealed ship within, and Asha easily dodges the random sweeps.

"Can you get a clean shot?" Shao-Lo asks.

"Not from here," Asha replies.

"Maneuver to firing position."

Asha rockets the *Enyo* out of the foil cloud. Keller and Sharon pick themselves up from the deck and cling to the mildly sparking terminals.

Asha banks the craft hard, zigzags, rolls, and pitches through space, keeping scant meters ahead of the incinerating beam. Sharon closes her eyes, her nausea from the inertial dampers aggravated by the swirling motions on-screen.

"Target and destroy," Shao-Lo shouts.

"Aye. D-E Rails on-line. *Committing*."

While still throwing the vessel through radical maneuvers, Asha aims at the craggy peaks below the popped-up mirror and looses a full barrage. The peaks erupt in radiant blooms, blasting rock fragments in all directions. In seconds, the streaking debris overtakes the mirror and smashes it to oblivion.

"Target destroyed," the Geek reports, and she settles the vessel into a constant heading.

Shao-Lo stands from her chair. "Well done. *Anything* that pops up from that rock, give it the same."

"Aye, sir," the Geek replies.

The tall Colonel rises from her chair and stretches to use up the adrenaline in her blood. "You were right to be cautious, Keller," she says, flexing her arms and chest. "It's definitely hostile."

"Why didn't you just shoot it?" Sharon wonders aloud.

"It was a mirror," Keller answers. "Directed energy would've reflected, maybe right back at us." The old colonist rubs a swelling lump on his head, turns to Shao-Lo. "So what are you gonna do?"

"I'm going to run up and kick the doors in. You remember where they are?"

"I do, but Asha's show might get us an invitation. Let me make a call."

Shao-Lo squints at Keller's cryptic request then grunts. "Go ahead."

In a far less demanding tone than before, Keller asks, "Asha, would you re-establish contact? No network. Audio and video only."

She nods and makes the connection. The main screen clears.

"Channel's open."

Keller strides to the middle of the bridge and clears his throat. "Hey,

Honniker, you cheap pocket calculator…You listening?"

The screen flares to life with Honniker's angular face taking the full display.

"Calculator? Ha! I am state of the art. Not some broken down old man like—"

"Did I say calculator?" Keller interrupts. "I meant abacus."

"Insults…" The image shakes its head and clucks its tongue. *"Poor ones, at that. You disappoint me."*

Keller laughs. "Not as disappointed as your creator would be if he saw you now."

"I have no creator. I AM Dr. Edmund Honniker."

"Bullshit. You're a copy. And a weak copy at that."

Honniker broods with half-closed eyes. *"After his last visit, I'd think the Phillistine had learned respect…"* The eyes flick back toward the screen. *"Perhaps I'll teach him yet…"*

"Had no gunships last time. Now I do. And I think it's time to even up."

"Gun-ships?" Honniker questions. *"I only see the one."*

"That's right. Had to park ourselves in the dust lane, otherwise you never would have seen us. Had to see how you'd react, whether you'd try something stupid. And, as you've shown, you're still the predictable dolt that loses at tic-tac-toe."

What seemed at first a childish game of name-calling, Sharon sees is a very dangerous bluff. She hugs her terminal tighter.

Keller pauses for effect, looks sideways at the screen. "Try it again, and we'll incinerate that sad hole you've burrowed into."

"Ha! You're a liar, Keller. No man-made weapon could penetrate the amount of nickel in this asteroid."

Keller smirks. "Does this ship *look* man-made to you?"

The image freezes then sneers. *"Even if you had twenty ships like that one, it would take weeks to tunnel through. I could pick you off long before then."*

"I love it when you show me how thick you really are. I don't *have* to tunnel through. I could smash the sub-surface radiators for your reactor and melt you from the inside. I could shoot down all your satellites, wreck all your weapon optics, then leave a beacon for the Lizards to find you. In fact, I think I like that last one the most, especially when they find how many of their pals you put in the *Graveyard*."

The image on screen sneers knowingly. *"You would risk this great house of technology for your revenge? I do not think so."*

"Why not? It may have taken me a while to get back here. In that time, I've been thinking of a *thousand* ways to end you. My friends here aren't sure whether you should be shut down or not, but *I* am. And with your idiotic stunt, here, you're proving me right."

"No, Keller, I remember your last visit quite clearly. You wanted to stay. You needed a home for your vagabond clan. I was quite willing to receive them, as you know."

Keller seethes. His jaw clenches tight and he speaks through his teeth.

"I found some new friends. Powerful friends, Honniker. They know what you did. And big surprise: they aren't interested in letting it happen to them. Since you obviously aren't going to cooperate, they're here to wipe you out, Honniker. No reason to wait for a dangerous bug to spread. Best to squash it where it lairs. And I'll be watching the whole time...Unless..."

The face on screen scowls bitterly. *"Ach, so. Here is where the puny man wants something from me."*

"Ah, at last! Some sense!" The elder colonist paces in front of the screen. "We could have started there and saved a lot of time. We wouldn't have had to destroy one of your twenty-meter mirrors. Not a lot of those lying around these days..."

"What do you WANT?"

Keller stops and straightens. "Your attention. And now that I have it, *listen up*. We're coming in. And we're going to take what we want. You leave us alone, let us do our thing, we leave *you* alone. We leave your power grid intact. We leave your mainframes and network on-line. Hell, you treat us kindly, we'll even leave your weapons intact. With a three hour delay, of course. Can't have you shootin' us in the ass when we leave."

Honniker's face washes of expression and freezes.

Keller strides dead center of the screen. "Well, what's it to be?"

The screen remains frozen.

After many terse seconds, Keller turns to Shao-Lo. "Colonel, this joker isn't taking us seriously. Let's just cook the place and be done."

"NO!" the face roars. *"I'm alive! You don't have the right!"*

Keller whirls forward, incredulous. "The *right*? Did you just say that? In fact, I *do*. More of an obligation, actually, to put down a *sick dog*."

"NO!" The face freezes in an expression of fear and pain, like a toddler waking from a terrifying dream.

"I'm already tired of talking to you, Honniker. What's it gonna be?"

The image mutters. *"Fine! Fine. Take what you want and be gone!"*

"Full access. No impediments. *Everywhere*. Including the *Vault*."

"Yes, yes, even the vault!"

"And make sure all of Jin-Sung's pets are leashed."

"They're dead."

"Are they? Can't say I trust you."

"What would they eat, Keller? All the researchers are..." the face trails off, looks away.

Keller squints at the brooding angular face, studying it. "We're coming through the front gate. Have it open for us. Keller out." He waves a hand at his throat. Asha cuts the feed.

The screen resets to the external view of space, and Keller exhales fully. He leans all the way over and braces himself, hands on knees.

"That was interesting," Shao-Lo says to break the tension. "Quite the bold-faced lie."

Keller straightens up, rubs his sweaty palms on the front of his coveralls. "Got us in without a fight, didn't it?"

Shao-Lo's eyebrow pops up. "Seems so." She looks out through the screen at the huge dark rock. "Will Honniker keep his word?"

"Only so long as he thinks we can do him harm. Give him a chance, though, he'll kill us all."

"Then we don't give him that chance. Brick Carter," Shao-Lo calls into her radio.

"Sir!" comes the deep-voiced reply.

"We're going in. Bring your team and meet me at the forward transport hatch."

"Understood. Carter out."

Shao-Lo strides to a locker at the back of the room and opens it. "I don't like deceptions, Keller." She pulls out her helmet and lifts its faceplate before dropping it over her head. "Especially when I see how good you are at them." She reaches into the locker again and removes her rifle then checks the actions and primes it. "You know we can't leave that Honniker program alive, or...*whatever* it is."

"Yeah, I know," Keller admits. "Say what you will, though. This way saves lives. You'll have to trust me on that."

"Trust?" The Colonel inhales deeply through her nose and exhales through her mouth. "Your stock is low on that, Keller. You keep it straight with *me*. Got it?"

Keller nods.

Sharon rises timidly from behind her terminal. Anxiety soaks her through, turning her blood into a noxious cocktail of fear and dread.

That Honniker thing tried to kill us! If it finds out Keller's lying...This won't be like Cadre One where we can talk things out.

She stares at the dark rock in the viewscreen that drifts around its dim star like a severed mountain range in perpetual twilight.

This is so much worse...Oh, God! Sharon claps a hand over her mouth and searches for a sink, but too late. She wretches.

Keller hurries to her side, fishing a cloth out of his pocket and offering it to her. She wants to thrust it away, to spit in his face, but she snatches the cloth anyway and wipes her mouth with it.

"You okay?" Keller asks.

Sharon dabs her mouth and stifles another wave of sickness. "I'll be fine."

"Here, let me give you a hand with–"

"I can HANDLE it."

Keller hovers like he wants to say something but Sharon's glaring red eyes keep him silent. He backs away.

"I'm gearing up," Keller announces to Shao-Lo. "Meet you at the transport."

Shao-Lo nods in acknowledgement, a half scowl on her lips.

Sharon watches her old captain go, then looks down at the mess she made. Kneeling down, she drops the cloth onto it and is about to sop it up when she notices her hands are shaking.

Be a leader, she thinks. *Prove you're strong. Show them you CAN handle this.*

"Don't worry about it," Asha says over her shoulder. "I'll take care of this. Go ahead, go get ready." The Geek adds with a smile, "Colonel doesn't like to wait."

Sharon nods gratefully and gets to her feet. She wonders what a pathetic image she cuts in the Operators' sight and takes a guess what their Colonel would want to hear her say.

"It's exciting, isn't it? A whole other Cadre—"

"You don't have to pretend, Sharon," Shao-Lo interrupts.

Sharon looks away, feeling as small *inside* next to the armor-plated Colonel as she does on the *outside*.

"There's a high level of risk on this rotation," Shao-Lo explains, "but we won't bring you in unless it's safe. I'm going in with the Operators first. Once the facility is secured, you'll follow with your equipment. All right?"

"Yeah. All right." Sharon straightens her back, squares her shoulders. "I'll just get to it, then."

She looks down at Asha sopping up her mess, then strides off the bridge. She is so overwhelmed with her thoughts that she does not notice

Keller loitering behind the doorframe.

THE TASTE OF GUN METAL

"Sharon."

She scowls at the sound of her name in his voice. Her whole body tenses and she lengthens her strides, putting distance between herself and a man responsible for more destroyed lives than all of history's despots, combined.

"*Sharon.*"

Her strides quicken. Footfalls behind her approach and match pace directly behind her. A hand falls on her shoulder.

"Sharon, wait!"

She whirls and smashes Keller dead on the mouth. Keller's head bounces back from the hit and he lifts a hand to his split lip.

"*Gor!*" Sharon curses, grasping her wrist and rubbing the joint.

Keller raises his hands warily and moves closer. Sharon cocks her other fist.

"Just stop!" the man says. "I need to talk to you."

"I don't *care* what *you* need!"

"*Please,* Sharon. We've been through *so* much together, just *hear* me."

Her instinct is to turn away, to ignore whatever madness this murderer could utter. Something in his voice, however, makes her stop and wonder what he could possibly have to say for himself.

"Go ahead, then. It'll all be repeated at your trial."

"I hope so."

She laughs. "Oh, good! Yes, let's hear your great excuses, then!"

"Excuses?" Keller goes silent. He stares down the hallway behind her, his brow wrinkled.

"Well?"

"There *are* no excuses for what I've done, Sharon. You know that."

She squints at him. Her eyes run his length, conveying the message he is foul, untouchable. She rubs her swelling wrist. His eyes drop to the wrist she holds.

"You okay?"

"Leave me be." She turns abruptly and walks away.

"Goddamn it, Sharon, just *wait!* You think I'm proud of myself?"

Barely looking over her shoulder, she fires back, *"Yup."*

"You have *no* idea what you're saying. *NO IDEA.*"

"Don't care."

Keller storms up and takes her by the shoulders. He thrusts her back against the metal wall, forcing her to look him in watered eyes.

"You have no idea *at all* what it was like, knowing…*knowing* what I've done. Guilt like you'll never have, because *you've never been in charge*, Sharon. Always, someone else made the call and you delegated. *Always* someone else decided. You've never had to deal with a bad decision, a *terrible* decision that cost so much. Don't you *dare* feel superior! You haven't *been* there. You have *no goddamned idea* what it's like!"

"Poor, misunderstood Keller." She sneers.

"What, you think I want *pity*?" He lets go of her and falls back. His eyes narrow in his own expression of judgment. "You're not simple. Don't act like it."

"For Christ's sake, get to the point!"

"Fine." He turns aside and spits blood from his bleeding lip. "Forty-five years."

She stares hatefully. "What of it?"

"In the thousand or so years the *Europa's* flown the stars, I've had forty-five years of waking time, out of my cryotube, on-duty. *Forty-five waking years* to think about that last broadcast from Earth—that I played a part in the destruction, that I caved to SoVar pressure to keep up production… to slaughter the natives for their acts of sabotage. It's a burden you *can't imagine.*"

"Maybe you should *do* something about it."

Keller blanches, his voice becoming hollow, distant. "You think I don't want to? Take the easy way. Just lay it all down and take my own life, right?"

She does not move, her constancy confirming his question.

"For *months*, I was obsessed with the taste of gun metal, Sharon, but that's cowardice..."

"And hiding in the Cadre, that's *not* cowardice?"

Keller squares his shoulders with hers. His spine straightens.

"No. I'm responsible for my part. I'm also responsible for a crew of one thousand seven hundred forty-three souls. I have a job to do. I swore an oath to myself, Sharon, that I have to deliver our people to a safe refuge, to find a better life than what the *Europa's* cold halls can provide."

Sharon crosses her arms. "Oh, I see. No, really it's bravery to hide under O'Kai's skirt like a frightened little boy. Yes, you're *absolutely right.*"

"They would've ripped me apart."

"And GOOD RIDDANCE."

"And then what?" It is Keller's turn to fold his arms. The two scowl at one another in a subliminal test of wills.

Sharon gives in. "What are you asking me?"

"I mean what would happen next, Sharon? Who'll hold the crew together? Who'll balance them against the Cadre?"

Her kneejerk reaction is to dismiss the question as ego. *What would us helpless colonists do without Captain Keller?* But she holds her tongue and looks into the plausible future where Keller is dead by his own crew. There would be a celebration as some small piece of justice was pulled from his bones. After the initial unity from his execution there would be re-organizations, she realizes. Breakdowns of authority. People would not know what to do. Without someone strong, it could be chaotic. Violent.

"Javier can do it," she says unconvincingly.

"Ortega? Good guy, but he's soft from old money. Family taught him how to look down on people, not lead them. *You* could, though."

The hard glaze in her eyes evaporates. Somehow, she had always imagined Keller would be Captain. It just seemed the natural order of things, and that idea grew stronger with the passage of years. Now, as Keller suggests her taking the Captain's mantle, it occurs to her just how awesome a responsibility the *Europa* is: the people, the colony apparatus, the embryos, and having to provide direction, hope, guidance, stability, *sanity* on a daily basis...

"I...I don't think I could do it. It terrifies me."

"That's because you know what's at stake, Sharon. That's the start of a good command. Ortega assumes the role out of entitlement, not because he fully understands. So that's why I insisted you come on this trip."

"You *what*?"

"Yes, I insisted. You've always been my trusted friend, Sharon, and you got me through a lot of rough patches whether you know it or not. You underestimate yourself. It's high time I said that."

The hard-set expression thaws and Sharon looks down modestly. There is a glimmer of compassion when she looks up again.

"Look, why don't you just turn yourself in? The *Europa's* in a frenzy right now, and...Just tell them what you told me. They need justice."

"I know. And they'll have it." His eyes haze with remembrance. "When Thompson announced his crime to the Cadre, I admired him. To confront guilt so openly, regardless of consequence, for the simple desire to be clean again. Sharon, I never said so, but I have *so much* in common with Maiella, Argo, and Thompson. When the time's right, I'll do as they did."

"Then why not now?"

"Because I'm not finished yet. I mean to keep my oath. I have to provide a home for my crew, or die trying. You may have noticed, I'm a bit older than I used to be. Took double shifts, which is why I've had forty-five years on duty to your twenty-some. I'm running out of time to make good. I have to take risks now."

"Like bringing us to Cadre One?"

"Exactly."

She ponders the enormity of the gamble with Cadre One, the bloody introduction and the last two years of painful integration. With all the discord and mistrust between them, there is still no clear indication whether or not the gamble paid off. Now they sit at the doorstep of Cadre Two.

"What if you fail?"

"You're my failsafe, Sharon. If I don't make it—"

"Why *me*?" she interrupts.

"What you'll find here is going to change things forever. You have the moral compass to make sure it's used properly." Keller's face washes with regret. "The things I did at New Dresden, the tools were made here." Regret becomes horror. "But since then, somehow...the experiments have resumed."

Sharon grips the pendant at her neck. Keller looks down at her pendant and the hand clutching it.

"You know what's at stake, Sharon."

"I'm not ready for this."

"We never are. Just know you'll be protected. We should be in and out of here in a few hours."

Keller starts down the corridor when Sharon reaches out to him, fighting through her own terror to ask, "What's in there?"

He pauses, his face contorted by the torment of memory. "Cruelty. Without restraint. Trust in yourself, not what you'll see."

Keller's mouth twitches and he leaves. Sharon leans back against the wall, watching Keller walk away in the dim red light, his broad shoulders rounder than usual. Her mind careens with conflicting thoughts and emotions about the man, their past, and now, their very uncertain future.

The throb at her wrist snaps her out of the mental sojourn and she rubs it again. *Get to it*, her inner voice demands. She pushes from the wall and hurries the rest of the way to her cabin.

When she slides her cabin door aside, she finds Maiella standing by the bunk, dressed up to the neck in her old armor. The rugged woman pulls on her gauntlets, then grabs her helmet from the bunk.

"Heya, Sharon. Are we there?"

Sharon's jaw drops and she rushes to embrace her unexpected guest. "You've no idea how glad I am to see you, Maiella!" When Sharon releases, she notices all of her cases are open, empty, and heaped in the small room's corner.

"Umm, what happened to my equipment?"

"You're lookin' at it." Maiella drops her bulky helmet over her head and locks it in place. She lifts the faceplate. "Oh, yeah. I prepped your pressure suit." The armored soldier points to a drape of brown canvas on a hook near the door.

Sharon eyeballs Maiella, then eyeballs the largest suitcase, trying to work the logistics of that tall a woman having been folded into it, when an obvious question comes to mind.

"What are you *doing* here?"

Maiella flashes a smile. "I'm your bodyguard." She scoops clips of caseless ammunition from a fold out wall shelf and plugs each magazine into the notches of her thigh armor.

"You stowed away?" Sharon asks.

Maiella snatches her pistols from the shelf and checks them over. With her signature flair, she flips them around her fingers and clips them onto her back.

"Yup. Keller's idea. Well, Keller's and *mine*." The exiled Operator twists at the waist, testing the movement of her old, banged up armor, and winces. She claps her hands to her chest. "Ooh. Had to take some of the padding out of the chest to make room for my, uh, you know." She wrinkles her nose. "Chafes a bit."

"What's Shao-Lo gonna say?"

Maiella shrugs. "Who cares? No way I was missing this."

Sharon hugs her friend again. Buoyed by the thought of Maiella as a bodyguard, she casts off trepidation and banishes meekness inside.

We're going to be fine. In and out. We're going to be just fine.

DAISY

Keller leans against the wall by the forward personnel hatch, clad in a heavy, brown canvas suit. Aluminum rings encircle and reinforce the major joints, the widest of which is at his neck. On the left breast is a dingy and frayed Soshiba Varicorp patch, depicting a nude woman astride a great black bull dashing across open water. He hugs a bulbous helmet with one arm.

For most of the journey, and every moment since arrival, he has thought about the six he sent in to investigate this place: their horrible screams over radio, the sounds of crushing, sawing, and drilling. All the while, Honniker's voice gleefully narrated what could not be seen. *"Experiments,"* he called them. The old captain squeezes his eyes shut to wring the screams from his mind.

Operators file past him and duck through the low hatch into the transport. In the dim corridor, their light-absorbing armor reduces them to less than shadow. One stops in front of him.

"You all right?" a deep voice asks.

Keller looks up at an Operator of Argo's build and Thompson's height. The soldier's helmet is open, making the pale face inside seem to hover in the darkness as though projected there. The wide nose is battered almost flat, and a network of scars is so thick, the face appears branded by gauze wrappings. The wide mouth asks again, "Keller, are you all right?"

"You're Carter, aren't you?" Keller says, avoiding the question. "I saw you at Beckert's initiation."

"That's right. Your second in command had no stomach for the way we test our Operator candidates, I recall."

"We didn't understand." Keller peers into the transport at the armor-clad Operators. Even at close distance they are hard to distinguish from one another, like overlapping cutouts of black paper.

"In ancient times," Keller says, "a new sword, red-hot from the forge, would be dowsed in water. If the blade was flawed, it could bend or shatter and ruin all the work of the smith. But if perfect, the blade was harder. Tougher."

The ex-captain contemplates the shadowy warriors. Over and over, they are thrust into the heat of battle like steel into a forge, getting harder, and it finally occurs to him an Operator was never meant to be a person, but a weapon—a weapon which must be proven before it can be relied upon in combat.

Keller faces the huge man. "I get it now."

The buzz of an electronic voice filters out from Carter's open helmet. He looks down at the floor automatically and replies, "Affirmative, Colonel. We're assembling at the transport now. Operators equipped and ready."

The buzzing voice from his helmet continues and the huge Brick takes a side step to continue the conversation privately.

Keller glances down the corridor toward the stern of the ship and sees another shadow approaching. The Operator's faceplate is down but, from its bulk, it is clearly another Brick. He holds a modern cannon in one hand and an oversized rack rides on his back.

How does someone that big get so close without me hearing?

"Hello, Keller," comes a familiar voice through the helmet speaker.

Keller smiles. "Argo? Is that you?"

With his free hand, the Brick lifts his faceplate. "Yup." He turns sideways to pass by and ducks through the hatchway. The bulky rack barely clears.

"What, are you the pack mule, now?"

Argo turns about, his weathered features barely visible within his helmet. "What's that?"

Keller shakes his head. "Never mind."

In the corner of his eye, Keller spots Sharon down the corridor. With such minimal light, it is hard to make her out. But a glint from the aluminum rings of her pressure suit tells him for certain it is she. He waves to her. She does not wave back.

In stark contrast to the quiet approach of other Operators, Shao-Lo's heels announce her approach.

"ATTEN-*TION!*" Carter calls out, making Keller nearly jump out of his suit. The huge Brick salutes crisply.

"As you were, Carter," the towering woman says. "We ready?"

"Aye, Sir. Does Asha have the conn?"

Shao-Lo nods. "She'll keep an eye on things out here." The colonel flicks her head toward the transport. "Let's get this done."

Shao-Lo and Carter turn their attention toward Keller, waiting.

"Right," the old colonist says, dropping his helmet over his head. He latches it at the wide aluminum neck ring and slides through the open hatchway.

Carter and Shao-Lo pack in behind him with just enough room to clear the closing hatch.

"Zuri, we're in," Shao-Lo says to the transport pilot. "Take us out."

"Aye, sir," the Geek replies. There is a dull clunk from below the hatch and the craft lurches free. Suddenly weightless, Keller's feet lift from the floor. The press of armor around him, however, keeps him from drifting.

"Everyone, seal up!" Shao-Lo orders. Operators latch their faceplates tight and one by one, confirm seal. Keller double-checks the latch at his neck. Then, compulsively, he checks it again.

"All right, Zuri," Shao-Lo states via radio. "This is good."

Zuri taps the console and the cabin depressurizes.

Shao-Lo takes hold of the hatch and slides it aside. Through the opening, Keller looks out into empty space where he knows the *Enyo* should be. He searches for the stealthed vessel but it is completely invisible to his eyes.

Shao-Lo pulls herself through the hatch and clings to the outside of the craft.

"Carter, you're with me," she says via radio.

The big Brick primes his cannon and pulls himself one-handed through the open hatch, then clambers up to the top of the transport. Shao-Lo primes her rifle and climbs up after him. Keller cranes his neck up at the ceiling trying to figure out what they could be doing.

"We're locked down, weapons hot," Shao-Lo radios. "Close the hatch."

Keller stares in mute wonder through the hatch until an elbow nudges him from behind. He takes his cue and drags the stiff portal shut.

Zuri urges the transport faster, steering a gentle curve toward the heart of the great rock.

"You're up, Keller," Shao-Lo radios. "Guide us in."

With the Colonel and the huge Brick out of the cabin, Keller has room to move and he pulls himself up to the Pilot's chair. A dwarf star shines glaringly bright through the wide windshield, forcing him to look away. He blinks repeatedly, trying to see through the electric blue spots on his retinas.

The Geek pilot stares directly into the brilliance.

"How the hell can you...?" he begins.

The pilot turns toward Keller, her goggles dimmed black like onyx.

"...never mind," Keller says, making a visor with one hand and squinting at the irregular planetoid ahead.

"Aim for that formation, there," he says, pointing at the jagged underside. The pilot follows Keller's finger to a formation of curving spires reaching out to space like a frozen fountain of magma. Rather than steer a straight path, she jinks randomly up, down, side to side.

"Damn it, what are you doing?" Keller demands as he struggles to keep himself upright.

"A straight path is easy to shoot down."

Keller feels weight on his shoulder, pressing his feet against the floor.

"We've got you," a husky female voice says.

"Keiko?"

"Affirmative."

Keller looks at the muscular woman beside him. She stands like an oak, bracing herself against the ceiling with one arm.

"Is Deepak here, too?"

One of the shadows to his right lifts an arm. Keller nods in recognition. Deepak returns the nod.

The old colonist cranes his neck at the ceiling again, trying to picture the two outside, crouched down on the hull, surrounded by a bottomless expanse dotted with foreign constellations.

What they must see...riding through a black ocean on the back of this little fish...so miniscule against the universe, yet godlike in defiance of those who've tried to annihilate them...

He pans his view from Keiko to Deepak to Argo to the Geek pilot, Zuri, admiring their calm and ease.

They're born to this... He smiles. *Like I was, once...*

"Roll us over, Zuri," Shao-Lo's voice crackles over radio. "I want a clear view where we're headed."

Zuri leans the controls to the left and the view through the windscreen inverts. Overhead, the massive rock looms like a jagged shard of frozen night. Keller zeroes in on a familiar structure of curved rock spires.

"There," he states, pointing a gloved finger.

Zuri nudges the controls, directing the transport as Keller indicated.

As the spires loom larger in the windscreen, Keller is jolted without warning:

THE EXHAUSTED DEAD

The high-pitched whine of a drill...begging, pleading...the sudden drop of pitch at the resistance of bone...hideous peals of agony...and Honniker's gleeful chirrups as he worked...

"Hey, Keller, take it easy," Keiko warns. "You're gonna outpace your rebreather."

Keller snaps from his trance, unaware he was hyperventilating. Beads of sweat cling to his pallid skin. He grimaces from the cramp in his gut and swallows.

"Yeah, *yeah*... You're right," the old captain says, covering his stomach with one hand, watching the spires as Zuri circles the transport around them.

"Where's the entrance?" Zuri asks.

"Right down the middle," Keller answers. "There's a hollow at the base, some kind of bubble in the rock. The entrance is at the back of that hollow."

Zuri slips the craft into darkness between the metallic, helical twists. She switches on the transport's powerful searchlight and tracks the beam over each of the prominences. Her goggles scroll with data.

"See anything, Zuri?" Shao-Lo radios.

"Negative, Colonel. No weapons or traps so far."

"Steady on, then."

"Aye, sir."

Keller leans toward the windshield and watches the spotlight as it traces the rock around them. Despite the beam's intensity, only a faint circle reflects where the light strikes. From what he can see, the formations are smooth but not polished—certainly not man made.

"I've never seen anything like this," Zuri says.

Keller nods. "Whatever happened to this core remnant, it left enormous hollows inside, giant natural caverns. Cadre Two's built inside one, in fact."

"I don't see any solar collectors...How does it get power?"

"*Lots* of Uranium here. Easy to access. Enough to last a *loooong* time."

The transport glides past the base of the spires into an ovoid opening roughly one hundred meters across. Zuri's searchlight beam fades into void ahead and a perfect darkness envelops the craft. She swings the beam in all directions, yet the vast space gives no visible hint as to its boundaries.

Keller pats the hull, grateful for something tangible in the blackness surrounding him.

The craft emits a series of strobed pulses.

"LiDAR imaging is good," Zuri says after a moment. "I see the tunnel entrance."

The transport dips down and left, then straightens out. Keller strains his eyes, trying to see any feature in the uniform black. Weightless, and with nothing to see outside, he cannot tell if the transport is even moving. Several seconds later, however, the searchlight's circular beam reflects faintly off a distant wall.

"Where's the tunnel?" Shao-Lo radios.

Zuri swings the searchlight to the side and illuminates a broad swath of yellow paint with bright reflectors at regular intervals. She widens the beam, revealing a broad, reflective yellow arrow.

"Follow that," Keller says.

Zuri steers the craft as the arrow indicates. Another arrow appears ahead of the last, and it leads to a circular tunnel in the back wall. The tunnel's mouth is half the diameter of the natural opening behind them with a rim outlined in yellow and black checkers. Reflective arrows point into it from all directions.

"Is this the way?" Shao-Lo asks.

"Yeah," Keller confirms.

"Take us in, Zuri."

The Geek guides the transport through the ample opening. She pans the searchlight over the tunnel walls, illuminating more broad yellow arrows pointing the way. Some peel with great flakes of curled paint. Most are scuffed from minor collisions.

After a short distance, the tunnel curves right. Zuri banks the craft, following the gentle curve, then shouts, *"Brace!"*

Floating sideways across the tunnel, only meters away, is the burned out hulk of an identical transport. She kicks reverse jets on full, just stopping in time.

"Colonel, Captain, are you still there?" Zuri calls.

Keller thinks it odd she should ask, as he is standing right next to her, when Carter answers, "We're fine."

Captain Carter. Of course, Keller chides himself. For nearly all of his adult life, anytime he heard the word "Captain" he was being personally addressed. While the title no longer applies, the reflex will die hard.

"Hold here a moment," Shao-Lo radios. "I'm checking this out."

Booted feet step down onto the windscreen from the roof and push off. Zuri brings the searchlight up, illuminating Shao-Lo as she drifts the gap from the nose of the transport to the burned out wreck.

Shao-Lo clicks on her helmet lamps and slips gracefully through the wreck's blown-out windscreen.

"Internal explosion," she transmits. "Crew didn't make it. They're still strapped in." She grunts as though lifting something. "Too carbonized to identify. Are they yours, Keller?"

"No, Colonel. My people never made it out."

"Hmm. Carter, let's get this thing out of the way."

"Be right there," the Brick replies. He tromps down the windscreen and pushes off as Shao-Lo did. He catches the transport gracefully and swings himself to the far side.

"Zuri, give it a nudge," Shao-Lo radios. "We'll park it up on the roof."

"Understood," the Geek replies. She gives the throttle a tap forward and brings the nose of the craft right up to the burned out hulk. When the two craft make contact, she blips the control stick, nudging the wreck toward the ceiling. Shao-Lo and Carter hang on to the ends of the craft like two ants with a twig and settle it into place near the tunnel roof. All around them, broken glass twinkles in their helmet lights.

Cleared of obstructions, Zuri's search beam shines straight out. A few hundred meters ahead, enormous yellow doors stretch from one side of the tunnel to the other. Painted boldly across them in black is an elongated triangular skull with sturdy snout, vacant eyesockets, and elongated upper canines. The caption, "CADRE TWO" is stenciled beneath.

Flanking the doors, high caliber barrels are planted in spherical turrets. They still aim where the flamed-out transport used to be.

Keller's hand flies out, pointing at them. "Colonel!"

"We see them. Zuri, kill the searchlight and take cover behind the wreck. Carter, give me a thermal."

When Zuri clicks the searchlight off, an inky darkness surrounds the transport again. No one dares speak, and in the perfect quiet Keller hears his heart beating in his chest, hears his blood coursing through his ears. Even his breathing seems extraordinarily loud.

If you want us, Honniker, you've got us.

"Carter," Shao-Lo radios, "status."

"Device is placed."

"Good. Zuri, give us some light and come forward."

The Geek switches the searchlight on, and the glare is like sunlight to Keller's dark-adapted eyes. He squints and puts a hand up.

Zuri slips the transport around the parked wreck and guides it toward the huge bay doors. Wisps of dust puff from the frame as the doors part at the middle.

"Zuri, did you do that?" Shao-Lo demands.

"No, sir," the pilot answers.

"Being cooperative, are we?" Keller wonders aloud.

Zuri glances up at Keller, takes a breath to ask him something, then censors herself. She resumes her straight-ahead gaze.

The craft glides smoothly toward the parting doors. Keller's eyes bounce back and forth between the massive turrets, watching for the slightest trace of movement.

Don't do it, you bastard. Don't you do it...

Shao-Lo's silhouette strides across one of the yellow-painted turrets.

"Hold it there, Geek," the Colonel says. She springs up and soars toward the nose of the transport. With outstretched arms, she cushions her landing and swings her magnetized boots to the hull. She sways a moment before taking her rifle from over her shoulder.

From the other turret, a pair of helmet lights approaches. Shao-Lo extends a hand and catches Carter as he emerges from the dark, cannon gripped in one hand. The two crouch down on the transport's nose, weapons ready, and stare through the open bay doors. Shao-Lo signals to continue inside.

Zuri taps the throttle and the transport jets into a spacious hangar bay, darkened with soot. Burnt transports and smashed machines lie scattered across the deck, many crushed under collapsed roof and wall supports. Frayed wires jut from loose conduits, reaching down from the ceiling like segmented snakes. Zuri threads the transport between them, swinging her searchlight over the numerous wrecks, until she finds a clear landing spot near the far wall and expertly drops the transport into it. Black clouds billow from the vacant pad with each pulse of her braking jets.

"There's trace gravity here, Colonel," the Geek announces.

Shao-Lo twists in her perch and looks in through the windshield. "Good. The grav-generators may still be functioning." She taps Carter with the back of her hand and points off to her left. "Control room. Let's go."

Shao-Lo jumps from the nose and arcs slowly toward the deck. Carter takes his cannon in both hands and follows.

"Deepak, Keiko, Argo, move out," Shao-Lo orders, mid-leap. "Zuri, secure transport and bring Keller." Her helmet lights fade as she glides down behind the mounds of scorched metal.

Deepak, Keiko, and Argo move to the back of the craft. One by one, they jump from the opened hatchway, hooking a hand on the threshold to swing themselves toward the control room.

Keller moves to the hatch and clicks on his helmet lights, illuminating heaps of sharp, twisted metal. He holds out his arms, looking at the inflated canvas of his suit, when there is a tap on his helmet.

"Hope you've got some slap patches on you," Zuri radios.

Keller pulls a tool from his hip pocket and holds it up to her. Hoops of metal on the grip accommodate his gloved thumb and fingers. The pinching part of the tool ends in short, needle-like teeth.

"Stapler," he says.

"Don't lose it." She tosses her head. "Go on. I gotta close up."

Mimicking the others, Keller takes hold of the hatchcoaming and swings himself out toward the control room. Unlike the graceful launch of the Operators, he holds a moment too long and hooks himself toward a corner. The old colonist spins in his flight, and with every rotation, he sees his destination: the broken ribs of a transport jutting out at him like pickets.

He gropes at emptiness around him. He kicks. He twists. And all the while, he shouts, *"SHIT, SHIT, SHIT, SHIT!"*

Something collides with him from behind and clenches around his waist, snatching him from his path.

"I gotcha," Zuri says. With one last flip, she touches down on clear flooring and sets Keller onto his feet. "Now hang on."

Before he can protest, the Geek scoops Keller into her arms and runs toward the control room. With one powerful leap, she sails over multiple transport wrecks.

Keller, feeling immensely awkward in the woman's grasp, looks away and watches the transports passing below. All of them are of the same standard transport design: boxy and functional, some accessorized for military use. But one hulk stands out plainly from the rest. Its back end is a blasted flower with petals of peeled metal. The front end, still propped up by its landing strut, is unmarred and points up at a shallow angle. Where the blasted rear and intact front sections meet, there is a half-scorched decal of a bull, its forelegs reaching out across open blue water.

Zuri lands running and slows herself step by step until she stands behind the other Operators, all of whom focus on a row of tall, soot-streaked windows. To Keller's immense relief, none of them turn to see him cradled like a babe in Zuri's arms. The Geek sets him onto his feet.

"Thanks, Zuri. Thought I was gonna be skewered, there."

Zuri nods and gives a thumbs up before joining her companions.

Shao-Lo stands before a section of sooty plexi-steel, and her helmet lamps shine through a section she has hand-cleared. Keller steps up beside her and swipes his gloved hand across the blackened window, clearing a window for himself. Despite the charred state of the hangar bay, the control room is pristine. On the back wall, golden letters proclaim, "Cadre Two", above which is a large, golden hawk. Each console is completely intact and free of dust. Empty chairs wait for their occupants' return.

"Carter," Shao-Lo calls, "blow it open."

"Hang on," Keller says. "I know there's a service door over here, somewhere." He feels along the dark wall, watching his feet to avoid snagging a pant leg on jagged wreckage. His fingers graze a recessed door latch.

"Ah, here it is." He takes hold of the lever but cannot budge it. "*Damn*. Must be locked."

Argo steps up to attack the latch, when Honniker's voice sounds in their earpieces.

"Please, allow me."

Dim amber lights illuminate in the bay, giving little more than outline to the blackened wrecks and hanging conduits. Broken light sconces spark with shorting current.

Inside the control room, red stand-by diodes illuminate on the consoles, then turn green as the terminals power-up. Overhead, panels flicker and glow with diffuse light. On the door latch before Keller, a red diode, muted with grime, shines and then switches to green.

Keller pushes down on the lever. It swings reluctantly, and the door pops with a puff of soot around its edges. Light shines through the crack.

Keiko and Deepak rush to the door, their rifles level and pulled tight to their shoulders. Argo ushers Keller out of the way and takes hold of the door. With a hand signal from Keiko, he swings it open.

The two Guns move inside, their rifles sweeping every corner.

"Clear," Keiko announces. "It's an airlock."

Shao-Lo strides to the doorway, rifle gripped in one hand. "Zuri, Carter, with me. Argo, wait here with Keller. If we get locked in, cut us out."

"Understood," Argo replies in his stoic tone. The other Operators file past him, and he seals the service door behind them.

Keller turns toward the spacious bay, looking across the wrecks. He stops on the one squatting back on its destroyed haunches, undamaged nose in the air like a debutant.

"I have to check something out," Keller says, and before Argo can argue, the colonist leaps out into the bay. This time, his trajectory is perfect and he lands right on the roof of his target.

"Keller, this is a bad time to strike off," Argo grumbles. "I have to stay with this door."

Keller gets down to hands and feet and crawls toward the front of the craft.

"I know, Argo. I just...I *have* to." The old colonist feels his way down to the nose and looks in through a smashed windshield. The tempered plexi-steel is opaque with fractures, save three large holes punched through the pilot's side. He reaches out to the glass, feeling the dimpled perforations.

"Keller, get back here or I'll have to come get you."

Keller lifts his head and looks toward the control room. Already, an Operator is milling around the consoles.

"It's all right, Argo. I'll only be a minute." Keller slips his way toward the back of the transport, past the half-scorched logo of the bull, and very carefully past the serrated edges at the stern. The back section is nothing but a ragged hole, and his lights shine all the way through the open cabin to the shattered windshield.

He picks his way past peeled metal plates, separated bulkheads, and dangling cords until he is just behind the pilot's seat. On a bench to his left, a suited figure reclines. The canvas suit is largely melted to the body inside it, its aluminum rings at the joints are black with soot. The visor of the globe-like helmet is smashed and the mummified head within stares with exploded sockets, mouth gaping. Curls of singed blonde hair cling to the papery scalp.

He pulls himself closer, searching for the name on the suit. The embroidery has scorched with the rest of the suit, making the name illegible, but pierced through the victim's eyebrow, a single gold hoop shines. Keller's heart sinks.

"Aw, Michaela...I'm sorry, kid."

He turns forward, and peeking over the pilot's seat is another globe-like helmet. He pulls himself up to the flight deck where another canvas-suited corpse is harnessed in. Sheltered from the rear explosion by the rugged chair, the suit's brown fabric is unburned; but there are two large holes punched through the chest and one through the helmet. Dark stains blot the torso, obscuring a patch over the left breast identical to his own but for the soaked-in stains. Above the patch is an embroidered name, *SOARES*.

The entire transport jolts and Keller's arms fly out in panic. Lights shine onto the windshield from outside, backlighting a spatter of black dots on the shattered glass.

"Keller, get out here *right now*, or I'll rip through the hull and take you!"

"Okay, okay! I'm coming out now!" Keller reaches to the center console and flips open a sturdy compartment. Inside is a shiny metal handle. He grips it and pulls, sliding out a charcoal gray armored box.

"I just have to be careful, with all these sharp edges and all..."

The lights shine closer to the windshield as Argo tries to see through it.

"Keller..."

The old captain moves quickly, releasing the catches on the box. He flips open the lid, and racks of thin, copper-plated circuit boards gleam.

"Be right there!"

He snatches at the individual boards, but his gloved fingers are too thick to pinch the one he wants.

"I'm just snagged in some wires, here, give me a sec to get free..."

He takes his stapler out and carefully closes the toothed jaws on the board he wants. With a firm tug, it pulls free. Keller pockets the board, stows his stapler, closes the box, and slides it back into the center console. Smudges from handling have left clean spots, contrasting with otherwise uniform scorching across the console.

A massive fist punches through the pilot's side glass. The hand opens and is joined by another. Together, they grip the shattered glass and rip it apart. Argo's great helmet pokes through the gap.

"This is no *exercise*. You don't just go off..." The big man goes silent as he looks straight into the ruined face of the dead pilot. His gaze lowers to the stained patch on the pilot's suit.

"These were your people?" the Brick asks.

Keller nods. "Yeah."

Argo sighs. "Well, look. You can't just go off like that. People die that way. Do you understand?"

Keller nods again.

"C'mon." Argo extends a hand. Keller takes it and the Brick pulls him through the open windshield.

"Thanks, Argo, I appreci*aaaaa*..." Before Keller can finish, Argo tosses him toward the door. The old colonist sails over the wrecks and lands feet first on the wall beside the service door. He shakes his head and walks down the wall with magnetic boots, making a ninety-degree step to once again stand on the hangar deck.

Argo slams feet first against the wall and hops down to the deck beside Keller. In the same movement, he takes hold of the service door and pulls it open, managing in the passing of mere seconds to show impatience.

Keller hurries inside and looks around at the air-lock interior. The metal walls are devoid of detail with the exception of a poster on the left. In it, a caricature of a raccoon in a lab coat clutches at its throat, exaggerated mouth open, tongue jutting, eyes bulging.

Safety matters! NEVER ENTER THE AIRLOCK WITHOUT YOUR PRESSURE SUIT! the poster declares.

Argo steps in and latches the outer door behind them. "We're in," he radios, and after a brief delay, the diode on the inner bulkhead switches from red to green. The big man strides forward and opens it.

Keller hustles through to a narrow corridor, which leads straight ahead then bends right. A door on the left is partially open. Light filters through the gap.

"That's the control room," Keller says.

Argo does not reply, merely maintains a brisk stride to keep Keller moving.

"They spared no expense, here," Keller narrates to his uninterested companion. "The foyer's lined with portraits of Earth's greatest scientists, dating back to some of the earliest known Chinese astronomers. Where possible, original portraits were used. Shows you just how well-funded the Cadre Two project was. I tell you, Argo, I loved walking through here, seeing so many great minds from history and the advancements they discovered—*inspiring.* Made me think there was nothing we couldn't do, that we would do great things here..." Keller trails off, losing himself to thoughts of people left behind, of entire worlds lost. Argo places a hand on the colonist's shoulder to accelerate his slowing pace.

Around the bend, an open metal door leads into a broad room. Keller steps through and immediately recognizes the facility's main foyer. To his right are large pressure doors for primary egress or loading. Like the large doors of the landing bay, they are painted yellow and bear the skull logo. But that is where the familiarity ends.

The priceless portraits lining the walls are all slashed, burnt, and blasted. Scraps of parchment, oil on canvas, watercolor, vellum, silver nitrate, lithograph, giclee, marble, and wood litter the floor and dangle from expensive frames. Keller pivots, dumbfounded, taking in the extent of the damage.

Only one image remains. Skillfully embedded into the set of inner doors is a brass silhouette of a lab-coated raccoon. It peers through tiny spctacles on its snout, arms spread wide.

WELCOME TO PROCYON, the caption declares.

Shao-Lo stands to one side of the wide inner doors, attended by Carter and either Deepak or Keiko from what Keller can tell. They cluster around a panel at the door's edge.

Labset in hand, Carter pulls open the panel and inspects the circuits.

"I can get that for you," Honniker says via radio. The doors part in the middle.

Shao-Lo lifts her head, staring into the ceiling. "Your willingness to cooperate is appreciated, Doctor, but we must insist you stand aside. We'll handle what we need."

"Suit yourself," Honniker replies sullenly. The parting doors halt, halfway open.

"Main centrifuge is spinning up," Zuri radios from the control room. "Grav generators coming on-line."

Keller feels a draw on his gut and it descends toward his pelvis. His spine hunches with the weight of his body and equipment as though someone were climbing onto his back. His vision dims with the dip in blood flow to his head, and his eyes flutter.

"Environmental?" Shao-Lo asks.

"Air pressure is normal," Zuri radios back, "but it's almost a hundred percent nitrogen. Looks like the enviros are set to strip everything else."

"Why would that be?" Shao-Lo asks.

"Standard procedure when a ship or facility's unoccupied," Keller answers. "Keeps constant pressure on the seals so they last, and keeps the internals from oxidizing. No fires if something shorts."

Carter spins about. "No fires? Did you see the landing bay?"

Keller shrugs. "Guess it was still occupied then."

"Keller is correct," Zuri says. "It's a setting in the program. I can get it back to normal in about thirty minutes."

"Set it up, Zuri, but we're not waiting," the colonel says, tucking her rifle into her shoulder. "You and Keiko follow once you're done. Deepak, Carter, Argo, and Keller, with me."

Shao-Lo levels her weapon at the vertical part in the doors. After peeking past the edge, she strides through. Deepak mirrors her stance and follows. Argo hunches with his cannon and oversized back-rack, barely fitting through the gap. Carter stows his labset and grips his cannon with both hands. Before he disappears through the doors, he stops and turns around.

"Keller, *let's go.*"

Keller stares trance-like at the part in the doors, heart racing. His legs seem reluctant to carry him toward the hallways beyond, his feet feel rooted. He looks down at his legs, wondering if they have developed a sense of their own, until he realizes his boots are still magnetized. He mutters under his breath and double taps the switch on the back of his glove. The boots release and he clomps after Carter.

Once through the doors, he peers into an unlit corridor as wide as the foyer. Debris clutters the floor, torn free from the walls and ceiling. Almost every light sconce is destroyed, and wherever his helmet lights shine are burns from small arms or incendiaries.

Already far ahead, Shao-Lo, Deepak, Argo, and Carter loiter at one side of the corridor, their lights converging on something large slumped against the wall. Keller picks a clattering path over the loose plating, cables, and ducting until he stands with them.

The first things he notes are the claws. Twelve-centimeter retractable black talons curve away from thick, furred toes. Dried, spaghetti-thin tendons and ligaments connect the toes to heavy leg bones. Just behind the wrist is another talon, smaller than the rest, like a misplaced thumb. And taut sinews connect the great limbs to a huge, hollowed-out body covered in overlapping plates.

Keller's eyes trace the narrow waist up to the deep chest and powerful shoulders. Above the chest, a thick neck tapers to a bear-like head with an enormous mandible. Receded lips and gums display a jaw lined with implanted metallic teeth. The upper and lower canines are exaggerated, capped with sharpened titanium. Unlike the grinding molars of a bear, however, the back teeth are fused and welded into scissor-like blades.

Keller crouches beside the mummified beast and feels the rugged jawbone. Dense knots of dry muscle clench the jaw shut, suggesting incredible bite strength.

"This one of the experiments?" Shao-Lo asks.

"Yeah," Keller replies. He slides a hand to the neck, noting a tuft of banded fur jutting from between overlapping plates. He reaches with his other hand and lifts a plate. Loose fur tumbles out. Beneath is a chain-link collar.

Keller hooks a finger under the stout chain and slides down toward the creature's chin until he finds a titanium tag, imprinted with the Cadre Hawk and a serial number. He flips the tag over, reading the name, *DAISY*, printed in block letters. He guffaws.

"Looks like the experiments were a success," Carter observes.

"Actually, no," Keller counters. "This one was a complete failure." He smiles with recollection, and indulges it:

Concentrating on a shipment to New Dresden...
behind him, the growl of something huge...turning around,
seeing an eight hundred kilo monster staring at him with
deep green eyes, lips curled back to show the killing teeth...

the dense shoulders shifting beneath the skin-bonded plates, each paw padding without sound toward him, sharpened talons protruding from banded fur at the toes...

   Falling back into the crates, cornered, no weapon... running for the door and being tackled...screaming as she rolled him over and held him down with a single massive paw...metal teeth drawing closer and spreading apart... a mottled pink and black tongue lapping his face, as raspy as the stubble of his beard...

   A door opening and researchers filtering in, howling with laughter. The animal turning to them, yet still keeping him pinned with one paw...

   The huge predator looking at him again, lips curled back, identical to the grins of the researchers filling the room...

   She was smiling.

Keller laughs at the thought of her, such a fearsome yet good-natured beast, and it feels wrong to have used the word "failure."

"Supposed to be an ambush predator," Keller explains. "Stealthy, aggressive, and deadly. Like you guys. But she was a big sweetheart. Jin-Sung was steamed his prize pet wouldn't kill. She *loved* to stalk and hunt, but wouldn't kill. He took her to the *Graveyard*, was gonna put her down. Had to do it himself, 'cause no one else wanted to, they all loved her. *Heh.* She got the needle away and started chasing him with it, all on camera. The video might even be here..." Keller turns toward the others and finds they have already moved on, their lights receding down the hallway.

"Aw, to hell with you all..." he mutters.

The dark of the corridor presses in on him as the bright memory fades, and once again he remembers where he is. He rises from the floor and takes a last look at the gentle monster.

"Wish the rest of 'em were like you, Daisy."

THE FLOUNDER

Keller watches Shao-Lo and her team pull farther and farther away from him. Despite being in excellent shape for a man in his seventies, he simply cannot match pace. The Operators' long legs cover twice the ground with every step, no matter the debris underfoot, and even with pauses at the myriad intersections, they continue to spread the gap. Only when they stop to investigate something far down the corridor does the breathless colonist have a chance to catch up.

As he gets closer, he sees Shao-Lo shove something stiff with her boot, rolling it over.

"They found it," she curses.

"Sir, I don't think they were in this fight," Deepak says, his lights shining over two more gray, rigid objects. The Gun extends the bayonet of his rifle and jabs it into the nearest. It frays at the slice like rope fibers under tension. He rolls it over.

Keller tromps to a noisy halt behind the Operators and leans forward onto his knees, huffing. Before him, three desiccated gray corpses lie on the floor like mannequins. Their reptilian heads hang down to the chest, shoulders raised in a permanent shrug, arms and legs straight down. Whip tails are docked at the knees. Fingertips and toes are amputated. Dried lips and facial muscles are drawn into a ghoulish sneer displaying the gaps where the sharp teeth were removed. And down the centerline of the torsos, long incisions are knitted shut with black threads.

"See that?" Carter asks, pointing. He squats, laying his cannon across his legs. "That's a thoracotomy. Stitched up, but unhealed." He leans over and picks up one of the brittle bodies. "This one, too. I agree with

Deepak. They were already dead."

As Keller catches his breath he rotates his head, trying to understand the odd postures.

"Looks like they were hanging from something," he says.

The Operators turn to him at once, their helmet lights merging into a blinding ray. He blinks and looks away with an annoyed grimace until the lights return to the corpses.

"It does," Shao-Lo says.

Deepak moves farther up the corridor and stops at a wreck of bent sheet metal. He slings his rifle and lifts the boxy thing with both hands. Though bent, it is nearly as tall as the Gun.

"What have you got, Deepak?" Carter asks.

"Some kind of cart, or cabinet," the Gun answers, and he sets the battered thing onto its wheels. Twisted hinges show where doors once attached on both sides. Inside is a stout bar, mounted high on the inside. Swinging from the bar, three heavy-duty hooks clang and jangle against each other.

Keller pushes through the soldiers for a better view. The moment he sees the sharpened hooks, he knows the reptilian corpses were dangling from them like overcoats. *Just another batch of experiments for the Cooler. Or the Graveyard.*

"Obvious why they'd remove the claws and teeth, but why the tails?" Carter asks.

"They're prehensile," Keller answers. "Could grab things. And they got in the way of the machines."

Deepak grunts and retracts his bayonet. "Machines?"

"Auto-surgeons." Keller's eyes glaze with morbid recall.

Shao-Lo faces the long corridor ahead. "We should be close, if Keller's map is accurate." She turns abruptly, adding, "Deepak, stay with Keller if he should fall behind again. Argo, Carter, with me."

Deepak shoves the cart aside and readies his rifle. The others fall in with Shao-Lo and flow like water down the hallway.

Keller takes a last look at the blueskin corpses at his feet. From there, his eyes move to the wardrobe-like cart, then to the blasted walls.

A grenade must've gone off here, scattered that cart and bodies, and– What's that?

A tiny reflection glints near the joint of the wall and ceiling. He squints at it, aims his helmet lights directly at it, and finds a purplish lens nested into black metal housing. The housing is bolted down over scorched and bent wall plating.

"Hey, Deepak," the colonist says, "you see this?"

Deepak's helmet lights rise briefly to overlap with Keller's. The lens gleams.

"Yeah. They're all over."

Keller stares at the oddity. "You see how it's bolted on, right onto the damaged wall plate?"

"Someone must've put these up after...after whatever happened in here," the Gun notes. "But c'mon, we gotta go."

Someone.

Keller nods vacantly, staring at the lens as if he were staring Honniker in the eye. He forces himself out of the trance and hustles along with his assigned escort.

"So what's got the Colonel so riled?" Keller asks.

"She thought the Blueskins might have discovered this place."

"What difference could that make?"

"What *difference*?" Deepak says with incredulity. "If the blueskins know about this place, we could never take shelter here."

Shelter, here?

The idea sends a shiver through the elder colonist. His lack of superstition is no protection from the memories haunting the darkened corridors.

Nothing could make this place livable again.

"You said this place had a large staff, right?" Deepak asks.

Keller nods. "Yeah."

"Where are they? Did they escape?"

Keller shrugs. "I don't know." His mind lifts at the unimagined possibility that they, like the crew of the *Europa*, could be alive somewhere among the stars. "I *hope* so."

Far down the hall, Shao-Lo's team halts. Their helmet lights shine against thick, frosted glass doors.

"Zuri," the Colonel radios, "you read?"

"Aye, Colonel," the Geek radios back.

"You still in the control room with Keiko?"

"Affirmative."

"We've reached the main MedLab facilities. Doors are locked. Can you override from there?"

"Checking...Hold just a moment, Colonel. Enviro is pinging back a problem with HVAC in the MedLab lobby. Vents are blocked. Air isn't circulating."

"That's fine, Geek, we're still on rebreathers. But we could use some light."

"Stand by..."

Flickering lights behind the frosted glass steady into diffuse illumination, backlighting dark splashes and spatters on the glass. A chime sounds and the MedLab doors slide apart. All three Operators stagger back, weapons poised.

At the sight of his comrades in combat posture, Deepak sprints ahead. When he reaches the doors he freezes with the others. Shao-Lo strides in behind her level rifle. Her team follows obediently.

Such hesitation in not one, but all four Operators, knots Keller's gut again. His legs feel heavier than before, yet he forces himself forward. His breath comes in short stuttering inhales until he stands at the threshold and beholds the scene:

Beneath a centuries-old blanket of dust is a dirtless cemetery of gnawed bones. Hundreds of human skulls litter the scene, their cracked open brain cases rasped clean inside and out. All marrowbones are gone, save knobby ends ground clear of cartilage. Dark stains mar floor, walls, furniture, and ceiling. And everywhere lie dried piles, speckled with off-white chips.

Salty saliva flows into Keller's mouth and bile rises up to his throat, attempting an escape. Cramps and sickness hunch him over but he keeps his throat locked until the churning convulsions subside.

"God*damn!*" he gasps, wishing he could take off his helmet and clear the stale, humid air inside.

Deepak calls from the back of the lobby, "Colonel, over here." His fellow Operators converge on him.

Keller stands straighter and breathes through his nose. Though wobbly, he holds his head up and strides into the lobby. When his boot sinks into an oily, crumbly pile, his gut cramps and threatens to burst through his clenched throat again.

The old colonist steps over and stands beside the others, one hand covering his belly, and he follows their gaze to the floor. Before him is the dried carcass of another beast like Daisy, only this one is terribly emaciated. Its metallic teeth are nicked, scored, and dulled. Many of its talons are broken off at the root. Though intact, its taut hide bears numerous slashing scars.

Similar animal skulls lie close by, all cracked open for the nourishment inside. Broken jawbones, full of metal-capped teeth, and body plates are strewn about with small patches of clinging skin and fur.

"These were the *successes*, then?" Carter asks assumptively.

Keller nods.

"Jin-Sung's pets?"

"Yeah."

Shao-Lo turns a full circle, taking in the scene. Her expression is hidden behind her faceplate, but her hands grip her weapon fiercely.

"What happened here, *Keller*?" she growls.

"You think *I* know?" The Colonel's unspoken yet obvious accusation taps the adrenaline soaking his body. "Why the *fuck* do you think I know something about *this*, Colonel? For all I know, my people *died in here!*"

"I doubt it," Carter says. He kneels next to the withered carcass with his labset. "This thing has been dead for centuries. Long before your people would have come through."

"Then where *are* your people?" Shao-Lo demands.

Keller faces the inner doors of the lobby, the portal leading to Dr. Edmund Honniker's main laboratories. From beneath swaths of crusted blood, an inlaid brass raccoon with lab coat and spectacles smiles at them, surrounded by the words, *MINATUR INNOCENTIBUS QUI PARCIT NOCENTIBUS*. He swallows hard.

"In there."

Shao-Lo steps over the withered animal carcass, and she stands ready at the door. Carter stows his labset and joins her, taking his cannon with both hands. Argo slides up beside them, taking position at the door's edge.

Deepak takes Keller by the arm and guides him away from the door before taking position opposite from Argo.

"Zuri," Shao-Lo calls, "open MedLab inner doors."

"Aye, sir."

An electric motor strains from somewhere in the doorframe and the doors part with an ear-splitting squeal. Only a few centimeters apart, the doors hitch in their progress and stick. The straining motor whines.

Carter wedges his hand and foot into the gap and forcefully spreads it. The doors resume their noisy movement, grinding their way through dried clumps and corroded metal in the floor track.

Light pierces the darkness within, and the Operators slip through the doors like the last grains of sand through an hourglass.

Keller takes a nervous step forward.

"You don't want to go in there, Keller."

The old colonist halts mid-step.

"You're right, Honniker, I *don't*. Just shut up and stay out of the way."

"You won't like what you find."

Keller's teeth grind as he tries to subdue images of his crew enduring sickening vivisection.

"Your friends won't like it either. And they'll try to destroy me."

"Just what you deserve."

"I'll have to protect myself."

"Don't try it. These guys are fanatics. They're hardcore soldiers and suicide bombers all in one. You won't win."

"Looks like their time away served them well. They seem...more fit than when they left. Though I doubt they'll be any more trouble than last time."

"All your clocks broken, Honniker? People don't live that long."

"You did. Interesting how you insult my intelligence then show such low-level thinking..."

Keller looks down at his hesitant feet, stymied for a rebuttal. "Fine. Enlighten me. *Astound* me with your *genius.*"

"Cadre Two was conceived as a state of the art weapons research station. You remember, I'm sure. And it continues to be, to this day."

Keller turns in place, looking for another of the purple-lensed cameras. "You have a point to this, or are you trying to bore me to death?"

"The point, Keller, is there was a full garrison here, and I dispatched them easily. I doubt your handful would be any trouble at all."

Keller looks into the darkness, fearful for his companions until an odd thought occurs to him.

"If you're planning something, why would you broadcast it over radio?"

"I'm using the Europa's *encrypted security channel. The others can't hear me."*

Keller looks to his left, reading the display projected on the inside of his helmet. To his amazement, the security band is active.

"How did you crack that? It's..."

"Bloede holzkopf! I have four of your transmitters right here. From Summers, Aaronson, Voss, and Rosenthal..."

"You SONOFABITCH! Maybe you should worry about *me* instead!"

"Really, Keller, if I could laugh, you'd have an earful. But I don't see how you can be so upset when it was perfectly acceptable to experiment on all the prisoners and aliens you brought here. What makes your people so much better than the convicts, hmm?"

Keller's eyes water with rage. "Because they were *good people.* They were *decent.* And they were *mine,* you soulless bastard, *that's why!"*

"One life is worth more than another based on your opinion? Well

that's completely irrational. And that's exactly what I'm talking about, Keller. I don't need to risk irrational behavior. Maybe a pre-emptive strike is in order."

"You have no idea what they can do. All they've done for the last thousand years is fight."

"Oh, I may take some collateral damage. But then I'll have you. As long as you're alive, they'll think twice about any larger assault. And you know, it's truly amazing how long life can be extended through hormone therapy..."

"They don't give a damn about me, Honniker."

"All the better. No interruptions."

An icy dread fills him of being an experiment, a plaything, and his mind races. With no other leverage, he returns to the lie.

"You harm us, Cadre Two is destroyed. They're serious about that. Doesn't matter if I'm here or not, they *will* obliterate this place."

The channel goes quiet so that Keller can hear his pounding heart.

"Then, for all our sake, be sure you restrain your friends."

The security band goes dark.

Keller shivers and takes a tentative step through the open doors. Suddenly, it occurs to him:

Honniker was testing me.

He stops again, his lights reaching out into the unlit space and reflecting off a white wall with flashes of embedded brass.

He's afraid we'll shut him down.

Excitement over Honniker's unease is immediately chilled by the mention of extended life via hormone therapy.

Is it possible he kept them alive? Dear God, how long did they suffer?

Zuri's voice breaks his train of thought.

"Colonel, I've got lighting control for the main labs."

Soft illumination flickers near the floor, then glows brighter, outlining a triangular atrium beyond the parted doors. On the flat wall directly across from him, a brass plaque proclaims the area *"The Flounder,"* beneath which is a tall map of the interior laboratory. Keller steps warily inside.

From the map, it is easy to see why the place is so-named. The main floor is flat and oval. Three-meter by three-meter cells are cut into the long left and right sides of the oval, resembling body-length fins. At the back of the oval, a broad chamber fans out and stretches into the rock like a tail fin. On the main floor (what would be the body of the fish) are regularly spaced medical stations. Here, in the atrium, he stands in what would be the fish's mouth, with corridors following the curving left and right walls into the open main floor.

Deepak appears from the left corridor, his black armor contrasting starkly against the peeling white paint of the walls.

"It's important you stay with us," the Gun chides.

Keller looks one last time at the tail fin of the map, reading its caption, *The Cooler.*

"Yeah, sorry." Keller walks without hurry toward the impatient Gun and follows him through the short corridor. He steps through into a cavernous space with an arching ceiling over thirty-meters high. At the highest point, a ring of windowed offices is suspended from the ceiling like a prison guardhouse. From the ring's center, four thick cables descend to a square platform resting on the deck.

Compared to the atrium, the ambient illumination of the main experiment floor is sparse with lighted strips tracing the sides of each walkway. At each station, however, powerful lamps shine down onto metal tables with enough light to banish any nearby shadow.

Keller pauses at the station closest to him, and he stares at it like it was a shark circling his life raft. A stainless steel table is propped upon a central post with adjustable pistons, permitting the table to assume any position from level to vertical. Metallic arm, leg, and head restraints gleam as though recently polished, their spherical chain links open and waiting. Stainless steel ribs sprout from the table, ready to clamp around a patient's torso.

Near the head of the table, a post rises three meters high and supports a boom over the table's center. Dangling from the boom is an octopus of retracted mechanical arms, each arm terminating at multiple black plug-in sockets. The arms themselves are sheathed in clear plastic sleeves with rubber boots covering the articulated joints.

Beside the table are diagnostic machines on movable carts and a chest-high cabinet filled with thin drawers. Keller reaches out to the cabinet then shrinks back, as though touching it might possibly electrocute him. His hand flexes subconsciously, fingers and thumb rubbing together, until he reaches out and opens one of the slender drawers. Gleaming saws, files, and rasps lie in perfect rows, each of them sprouting from a black plastic plug. He closes the drawer and opens the one below, finding laser scalpels and blades ranging from delicate to cleaving.

Each subsequent drawer holds a remarkable assortment of syringes, drills, forceps, pliers, torches, retractors, scissors, suction hoses, auto-sutures with spooled thread, rubber and ball peen mallets, glue pens, chisels, catheters, dilators, staplers, and tweezers. There is no anesthetic.

"It's a good find," Carter says.

Keller startles, crashing backward against the steel table and nearly falling.

"*Jesus*, Brick," he says, propping himself with one hand on the table.

Carter peers into the open drawer and straightens the tools scattered by Keller's flailing. He slides the drawer home.

"These the machines you mentioned?" Carter asks.

Keller looks up at the octopus of automated arms over the table. "Yeah."

Carter nods and turns a full circle. "This facility's remarkable. Everything we need to attend a Corps of a thousand. Maybe more." The huge soldier scans the open floor and the other nineteen identical stations. "I had no idea how advanced the technology was. Makes me understand how much we've lost. But it's a remarkable find. We can do good things here." The Brick moves off through the stations, periodically stopping to inspect their condition.

Keller looks down at the stainless steel table, feeling a profound ambivalence. Carter sees the capacity to heal, and maybe the engineers on Earth had exactly that in mind when they designed it. But Keller knows these stations were never used that way. He imagines himself upon the cold steel table, watching mechanical arms outfitted to slice, to pry, and to inject descend from their perch. Watching them begin their work, being unable to move, unable to dodge the cold tools as they dive into un-numbed flesh. No answer to screamed pleas for release, no escape, only shocked howls when agony overwhelms belief...

Keller stands straight, removing his hand from the table. Though the steel surface is absolutely immaculate, he wipes the palm of his glove on his suit.

"Good things here?" he repeats. *"Right..."*

Eager to get clear of the auto-surgeons, Keller moves toward the cells along each wall. They stack three levels high, each door numbered from one to three hundred. Most of the thick plate doors hang open on vault-quality hinges; the rest are closed with simple yet rugged locks. Shao-Lo and Deepak check each cell in rapid succession. A single word repeats through Keller's earpieces as the Operators report the cells' contents: "Empty... empty...empty...empty..."

"Colonel!" Argo calls from the back of the experiment floor. "Fresh blood."

"Deepak, keep checking cells on your side," Shao-Lo orders. "Carter, take over for me here," She leaps down from the second tier, landing with a *thud*, and hustles over to Argo. Carter slings his cannon, runs at the wall of cells Shao-Lo abandoned and leaps for the second tier railing. He grabs it and hoists himself over, the sturdy railing flexing visibly under his mass.

Keller follows after the tall Colonel, catching up with her at the far end of the cavern. She and Argo stand side by side, scrutinizing one of the medical stations. Shao-Lo parks her rifle on her hip, swipes a finger on the table surface, and holds it under the bright lamp. From several paces away, Keller can see a wet glistening on her fingertip.

Argo holds his labset out to her and she taps the wet finger on it. The Brick thumbs the control once then nods.

"Human."

"Deepak, Carter, double time," Shao-Lo orders. "There may be a survivor."

The two soldiers move faster along their respective rows, barely glancing in each cell before moving to the next.

At first, the medical station appears the same as the others until Keller notices the retracted arms are fully equipped with surgical tools in the black sockets, some bearing a thin red sheen. Off center on the bright table, three small drops of blood shine like crimson buttons. A fourth is dragged into a smear toward the tall Colonel.

Dread seizes Keller like never before, worse than looking down Thompson's rifle when the Gun and his team stormed through the *Europa*.

"Colonel!" Carter shouts from the highest tier of cells. "Survivor!"

Carter rips open the door, stoops at the low threshold, and ducks inside.

"What have we got?" Shao-Lo asks.

"Human male, adult," the Brick replies. "*Unresponsive.* I'm bringing him out."

Carter steps out, cradling a full-grown man dressed only in loose white pants. The man's face is turned into Carter's shoulder, and his left arm dangles with a bright red line trailing down the forearm. Delicate headgear rides on his ears, connected to gold terminals embedded in his shaved scalp.

Supporting the man with one arm, Carter hangs over the railing and drops a level at a time until he slams to the floor. He hurries to the bloodied station and lays the survivor on the steel table.

The man's skin is almost blinding white under the intense lamps. Large black numerals are tattooed into his chest. Dark lenses hide his eyes.

His expression is blank.

"Voss!" Keller shouts, pushing into Carter. "How can you—"

"Please," Carter says, spreading his arms, "give me room!"

"Keiko, you and Zuri come to MedLab immediately," Shao-Lo says into her helmet mic.

"Aye, sir," Keiko radios back. "En route."

Shao-Lo studies the bare-chested man and frowns. "He appears reconstituted."

"Yes, he does," the huge Brick says. He takes the bleeding arm gently in his large hands and inspects it. "This is deep, but not critical." The Brick places his thumbs on either side of the wound and spreads it. Blood wells then runs over.

"No foreign objects. I'm closing this up." Carter lays the man's arm on the table and plucks the tools he needs from the mechanical arms overhead. With swift precision, the bleeding is staunched and the wound is sealed.

Keller drifts to the opposite side of the table, unwilling to admit what he is seeing could possibly be Evan Voss, his first Lieutenant, the one Gregor replaced. The block numerals inked into the skin, the eyes hidden behind dark lenses like a drone, the gold contact terminals embedded in his hairless scalp, the translucent, ghostly skin make him appear more product than man. For a moment he allows himself to believe that this must be some clone, some facsimile, some *thing*, alien and unrelated to the man he knew. But as hard as his mind works to disbelieve, a human skull tattoo framed by the words, *"DEATH BE NOT PROUD"* in the man's right shoulder proves to Keller he has found his abandoned friend.

Keller's teeth grind. "What have you done to him, Honniker? WHAT HAVE YOU DONE?"

"What have I done? You know what I am, and yet you still sent him here. Maybe you should ask yourself that question."

Keller's hands rise beside his face and curl. "I wish you had a neck so I could strangle you with my bare hands. I wish you had a heart, so I could *rip it from your chest."*

"Wishing. It's one of the weakest things a person can do. Like 'hope'. No better way to convey you're powerless than to 'wish' and to 'hope'."

Keller's fists slam the table.

Carter and Shao-Lo look up at Keller with disapproving glares.

"What's wrong with you?" Shao-Lo demands.

"Yes, Keller, why don't you tell them?"

Keller looks at the ceiling. "Shut up! Just SHUT UP!"

"Who are you talking to?" Carter asks.

"Honniker. He keeps breaking into my secure channel, trying to get me riled."

"Now might be a good time to share what we discussed."

"I SAID, *SHUT UP!*"

Shao-Lo walks around the table. "Obvious he's succeeding. Turn it off."

"I can't. It's an emergency line that overrides the others. Always active."

"How does he know what channel?" Carter asks.

Keller looks down at his catatonic comrade on the table. "They all had suits like mine. It's built-in."

"So he's one of yours?" Shao-Lo asks.

The old colonist nods heavily. "He was one of my officers." Keller looks across the table at the Brick. "Can you tell what was done to him?"

"I could save you all a lot of guessing."

"Fine!" Keller erupts. "You want to jabber on, so *tell us!*" As Keller fumes, heart pounding in his chest, the secure channel goes dark.

"Colonel, will you permit me to speak?"

Shao-Lo's head rocks back slightly. "How did you get this channel?"

The radio goes quiet for a moment. In that silence, Keller knows Honniker is suppressing an insult.

"The radios you're using were developed here by my colleague. It seems they have not changed much."

"Get to it," she replies impatiently.

"Very well. I had 'hoped' Keller would share a message for me, but I see I'm 'powerless' to move him in a sensible direction."

Keller's skin flares red. He turns from the table and walks out to the main floor.

"You're not going to be pleased with what you find. Before you act, however, you should understand the purpose behind this research."

"Which is?"

"When New Dresden was first settled, it was clear the indigenous creatures were intelligent. They appeared simple, yet showed high skill in their constructions. Just how skilled they were was unknown, but mankind could no longer claim they were the only intelligent species in the universe. If there was one intelligent culture, there must be others. So it was decided humans needed to be able to defend themselves, if necessary, from a massive attack. The Cadre projects were instituted for that purpose."

"Your purpose failed," Shao-Lo counters. "Earth and all the colonies were destroyed."

"Ach so, we started too late. There was insufficient time to build adequate response. Though we are far from failed. You still live and breathe. Earth still orbits the sun, does it not?"

"It does," Shao-Lo says cautiously.

"Well the research has continued, Colonel. You will be very pleased by what I can offer. I have had to use what was available to me, however. Some subjects died in the process."

"We saw the lobby, Doctor. No need to downplay it."

"Yes, a tragedy. Jin-Sung was not stable. He unleashed his creatures on the staff. It was all I could do to lure them into the lobby where I could trap them for good."

"The *people* or the *creatures*?" Keller spits.

"The creatures, of course." The secure band in Keller's helmet lights up. *"Adults are talking."* The band winks off.

"As I was saying, there were many accidents and much damage caused before we could subdue Jin-Sung. Many of the soldiers decided to flee. I didn't know if they survived until now."

"You're saying we're the descendents of those who fled?"

"Precisely. You got that very quickly...Much faster than someone else..."

"Why wouldn't they have come back?"

"Good question, though it was a very chaotic time. Who can say for certain? The important thing is you've returned. And I see you've made improvements not just in your equipment, but in yourselves as well. Clearly, there were some excellent geneticists among those who fled. I can attest your physical attributes are quite remarkable."

Keller's jaw drops. Amid the whirlwind of anger, the comedy of Honniker attempting to flatter Shao-Lo is too much to resist. He grins ear to ear, yet maintains his silence, waiting for the inevitable.

"Cut the *ass-polishing*," Shao-Lo burrs. "You said you had something to offer."

There is another moment of silence before Honniker answers.

"Indeed. The armor you're wearing. Your weapons. Your special operator training, even the HDI implants of the ones you call 'Geek' were all developed here. You have improved somewhat on the original designs, though your current equipment is still centuries-old technology. While you are correct that our original mission, to defend Earth, is obsolete, in your absence we have adapted that mission."

Shao-Lo shifts her stance waiting for Honniker to continue. "To what end?"

"To provide the means to eradicate the enemy, completely."

Shao-Lo eyeballs Carter. He looks back, acutely interested.

"You want something in return, I assume."

"Only your understanding that there were sacrifices made for its attainment, and there will be no reprisals for the necessities of advancing useful research."

"That sounds reasonable."

"Colonel!" Keller shouts, all mirth instantly drained. Shao-Lo holds a hand up to silence him.

"I'm surprised, and pleased, to find you so rational. I'm sure we will work well together until you leave. In the meantime, feel free to remove your helmets. I've maintained the air quality in here for my patients. If I may be of assistance, please call on me."

Shao-Lo slings her rifle and leans with both hands on the metal table. The pale man's chest rises and falls with slow, deep breaths.

"Patients? There's more than one?"

"That's correct, Colonel."

"Let's start with this one. What are you doing with him?"

"Neural mapping. In integrating human and synthetic components it is immensely valuable to have an accurate map of the human nervous system."

Carter nods, confirming the assertion. "Then why reconstitute?"

"He is not. Well, not as such. I've simply isolated his cognitive centers with selective lobotomies. Motor functions, I can control through the HDI."

"But why are you doing this at all?" Keller pleads. "If he's still conscious, let's snap him out of it."

"I wouldn't do that, Keller."

The colonist checks the inside of his helmet. *Security band.* He shakes his head and sighs.

"Why not?"

"Because I neural map with pain. And he's been aware of it the entire time."

"It's time I closed your psychotic little torture chamber. I'm getting my people back."

"Oh? I don't think they want you."

"I don't care. These are people, not things, who—"

"WRONG. They're lab rats in the greatest research ever undertaken."

"No, *you're* the lab rat, Honniker. Just another experiment running amok in this fucking dungeon."

"Forgive me if criticism from you lacks the intended sting. No one has dared push the boundaries as I have."

"Don't get too full of yourself. The only reason you exist is because the real Honniker wanted the knowledge, but couldn't stand to be the one pulling the levers. You're a *simulation*. A *program* designed to perform tasks that made real people ashamed of themselves. Easily deleted."

"If I'm so easy, then why is your man lying on my table?"

"I'm setting him free."

"The first thing he'll do is kill you."

"Like I said. Doesn't matter what happens to me."

"Doesn't matter? Hmmm. Take a good look at him. Really get a good look."

Keller looks at his friend stretched out on the metal slab. Beside him, Shao-Lo's and Carter's heads bob as though in conversation.

"Are you talking to them, too?" Keller says, annoyed.

"Yes. I'm explaining how pain illuminates the pathways so much better than any other stimulus. If pleasure worked as well, I'd use that, but I didn't create your kind. We must work with what we have."

"We? Is that the *royal* we?"

"Of course not. But I digress. You said it doesn't matter what happens to you. Are you looking at your man on the table, there?"

Keller tunes in to the deep creases around Voss's eyes and forehead, to the exaggerated lines of the chin and mouth—lines that belie the current calm expression and tell of countless hours spent contorted and scrunched. He does not need to look in the mouth to know the teeth are ground flat.

"If it doesn't matter what happens to you, would you trade places, then?"

Keller's eyes close involuntarily. "You're a *bug*, Honniker. A fucking *roach*."

"That sounds awfully hostile. Especially when I'm getting along so well with my new friends. They're very sharp. Not blathering on about 'their people'. If they'd come instead of your lackeys, like Voss, here, we might have made some truly fascinating discoveries. Like I said, though, we work with what we have."

"Are you done?"

"Not nearly! There's so much left to do! But maybe I should let you interact with Voss for a while. Would make an interesting evening, watching your reunion. Go ahead and wake him up. Just remember, I warned you."

The security band goes dark, and Honniker's other conversation breaks in.

"...provided the baseline for the overall research with sufficient variety that clear patterns became apparent. Keep in mind, they were all the worst of their kind, judged by their peers and sentenced to death for their crimes. At least this way, in serving their legal sentence, they could contribute greatly in the name of medical understanding."

"So Voss filled in the gaps?" Carter asks.

"Mostly. What I learned from the convict population was too general for my application."

"How so?"

"The level of stimulation required to accurately map pre-maturely exhausted the patient. I could only stimulate once or perhaps twice until the neural pathway was permanently damaged. Hence, why Voss's sense of touch needed to be amplified. I literally had to know where every nerve fiber connected and registered in the brain, and I needed to be able to repeatedly stimulate to be certain of the result."

"Why did you cut his arm?"

"Some of the nerve fibers I need are deep within the flesh, some in the bone."

"You mean you haven't finished yet?"

"Oh, no. While I have enough data to proceed to the next phase, it will take approximately twenty-five more years to build a complete map of this man's nervous system."

Keller shakes his head in despair. Resolved, he steps to the cabinet, removes a long blade, and plunges it at Voss's heart.

Shao-Lo catches Keller's arm at the wrist and twists, flipping him onto his back. She holds him down with a boot and pries the blade from his grip.

"Oh, my. Yes, I was afraid Keller would react this way. We mustn't be harsh, though, because he cannot understand."

"Zuri, are you close?" Shao-Lo calls.

Zuri's voice has an internal cadence from her swift strides.

"Nearly there, sir."

"Come get Keller and take him back to the transport. He needs to cool off."

"Aye, sir."

"Once there, go back to the *Enyo* and bring Sharon. It's time."

"Understood."

Shao-Lo takes the boot from Keller's chest and lifts him by his arm.

"Go wait at the entryway. Zuri will be here momentarily."

Weak, distraught, and helpless, the colonist releases the lock on his helmet and slides his faceplate up. Cool, dry air rushes over his clammy skin with an underlying scent of disinfectant. He shuffles away, past the rows of empty cells, past the spotless experimentation tables, through the short corridor until he stands facing the half-open entry doors. Strength abandons him and he collapses to his knees.

"You failed them all, Captain."

Keller rages on the latch at his neck, and he rips the globe-like helmet off before hurling it across the entryway.

"FUCK YOU, HONNIKER! *FUCK YOU!*"

Keller's head droops. Hands in lap, he slumps against the peeling white paint and sobs.

INFESTED WITH MADNESS

Maiella stands beside Sharon in the narrow cabin. In her armor, the tall woman makes the navigator look like a kid sister.

Sharon is dressed in the same heavy, brown canvas pressure suit as Keller's, scaled down for her small size. With both hands, she holds one of Maiella's machine pistols, extended straight out toward the wall. She bites her lip as it trembles in her grip.

"It's well-balanced, but it kicks, so you need to brace your stance," Maiella says. "Put one foot ahead of the other and lean in a bit."

Sharon looks down at her feet and adjusts them to match Maiella's. The weight of the pistol taxes her thin arms, but more taxing is the thought of being in a situation requiring its use. She folds her arm at the elbows and pushes the weapon back at her bodyguard.

"I'm not a fighter, Maiella. I can't."

"We're all fighters now, Sharon." She lets the heavy thought sink in.

"I'm not a soldier, I have no training, *I can't do this!* I'm a navigator, for chrissakes. *That's* what I trained for, *that's* what I'm good at! Now take this thing, will you?"

Maiella looks down at her pistol being repeatedly pushed against her chest. She shakes her head.

"No. Not until you understand something very clearly." Maiella places a hand behind Sharon. The other she places high on Sharon's chest, just off center, and she presses her hands gently toward one another.

"When *this* is weak or sick, every part of you is weak or sick. When this is *strong*, every part of you is strong. Do you understand?" Maiella releases her compressing grip.

"That's easy for you to say." Sharon raps a knuckle against the Geek's armor. "Your heart's encased in bullet-proof armor."

Maiella smiles broadly. "My heart isn't in my chest. I keep it elsewhere."

Sharon squints and matches the knowing smile with her own. "Thompson."

Maiella nods. "He's safe now. That means I can do *anything*." She twirls her other pistol around a finger for emphasis.

Sharon takes a half step back, admiring the perfect sincerity, the complete confidence, the glow.

"You're in love! I didn't think your kind *could...*"

Maiella's confident grin slides to a smirk. "Yeah, well...came at a high cost. I'll never be one of them again. I always had strong feelings, had trouble with them. Was almost reconstituted because of 'em." She puts her finger tips and thumb together and taps them on her armored chest. "With Thompson it's almost *too* strong, but feeling this way—being *free* to feel this way—makes it all worth it."

"Does he know?"

The soldier's sunny expression clouds. "I don't think so. Doesn't matter. If he'll have me or not, doesn't matter. So long as he's alive and well, I'm *invincible*." The clouds break and she is beaming again.

Inspired, Sharon takes a deep breath and holds it before letting out a cleansing exhale. Vigor replaces meekness in her heart.

She really can do anything.

Sharon extends the weighty pistol toward the wall in a steady grip.

Then so can I.

Her feet slide into position.

"Sight along the barrel here," Maiella instructs, pointing to the top of Sharon's pistol. "Hold it firmly..."

The intercom buzzes, and Asha's clipped voice sounds through the speaker.

"Commander Jones, Geek Zuri is en route from Cadre Two to collect you. Are you prepared?"

"Yes, I am," she replies, pleased with the confidence in her own voice. She hands the pistol back to Maiella. In the wordless handoff, both women understand that if necessary, Sharon will take it again.

"Ready to make your appearance?" the colonist asks.

Maiella stands straight and nods.

Sharon collects a bulky backpack and dons it with some assistance. Maiella passes the globe like helmet over to her. Sharon takes it and cradles it in one arm.

"Let's go."

Sharon slides the cabin door open and strides down the corridor, subconsciously falling in step with Maiella. As she thinks about her guardian beside her, a warm feeling fills her.

She's looking out for me. She's going to keep me safe.

The warm feeling solidifies into something profound. Never has she had someone willing to protect her like this; never has she had anyone so *able* to protect her like this. While she still feels small compared to the seasoned warrior beside her, that warrior is so approachable, so open, so concerned with her well being it is almost intimate, familial. Not parental, but sisterly. It triggers buried emotions about the loss of her own family which sting at first recall, yet smooth into fond recollection and the healing of new bonds.

When they arrive at the transport hatchway, Zuri is backing the transport into the dock. There is a muffled succession of *klunks*, a hiss of air, and the hatch slides open. Sharon steps through, Maiella right behind her.

Keller, seated on a bench behind the pilot's seat, looks up from his feet.

"Hey, Shar–" he begins, then breaks off at the sight of the stowaway. "Maiella?" he says in mock surprise. The ex-captain releases his lap belt and stands. "What are *you* doing here?"

Zuri spins the pilot's seat about. When she sees Maiella, she throws of her harnesses and jumps to her feet.

"*You.* Get off this transport."

Sharon pushes past Keller and stands square with the Geek pilot.

"She's here for me, Zuri," Sharon states, "and she's coming with."

"Then we're not moving. Not until the exile is confined to quarters and remains there."

Sharon folds her arms with newfound defiance. "She goes where I go. She's my bodyguard and I don't care what you think about that."

Zuri frowns, her goggles flashing momentarily. "Colonel. We have a stowaway. Sharon is insisting she come."

"Only one person would dare," Shao-Lo's voice says via radio. "The *exile*?"

"Affirmative."

The radio goes quiet for several seconds.

"Sharon, can you hear me?"

"Yes, Colonel."

"Maiella was exiled for a reason. A very *good* reason. She's highly irrational and we can't have that here. Things are too fragile. She *must not come.*"

"With respect, Colonel, you're talking *gash.* I trust her with my life and you should, too. You should be *ashamed* for sending her off—"

Maiella's hand on her shoulder distracts Sharon from the tirade. The disgraced soldier merely shakes her head, her eyes asking a friend not to go down that path.

"We're done debating, Sharon," Shao-Lo states. "Maiella is the wrong element for what's going on here. She'll destabilize everything."

"Colonel," Maiella says, "for my part, I swear my role is only as guardian to Sharon, nothing more. I'm still highly functional in combat operations, should you require it."

"The point is we *don't* want that," Shao-Lo counters. "Sharon, I'm well aware I can't give you an order. So I am *ASKING* you to leave Maiella behind. Will you?"

"No, Colonel. I'm afraid I won't."

The radio goes quiet and Sharon can guess what is being said in confidence on the other end. In the terse silence, Zuri stares daggers through Maiella.

"Shall I leave them here, Colonel?" Zuri asks.

"No," Shao-Lo says at last. "Argo tells me Sharon is studied in a variety of lifeforms, and from what we've found, that could be useful. Maiella, I don't know how you got aboard, but there will be lashings for it, *I assure you.* One misstep, I'll have you locked in your armor riding cargo on the trip back. As for you, Sharon, I'm sorry to see her defiance has infected you as well. Things were better when you were agreeable. Now then, we have work to do. Zuri, bring them all."

"Aye, sir," Zuri complies. She settles back into her seat, straps in, and takes the controls. The rear hatch slides shut and Sharon takes a seat as far from Keller as possible. She watches her old captain warily as she latches harness straps across her chest and lap. Maiella stands beside her, bracing herself against the ceiling with one flat hand. Keller looks into his seat before putting himself back into it. He clicks the lap belt in place and resumes his gaze at his feet.

Goggles alight, Zuri disconnects the *Enyo's* docking clamps and thrusts the transport toward Cadre Two.

"Sharon," Keller says, lifting his head, his face streaked and haggard, "you don't need any more reason to hate me, but there's something I need to tell you."

Sharon takes a reassuring glance at Maiella and unfolds her arms.

"Yes?"

Keller's lips pout as he tries to summon a phrasing that will not make him instantly vile in her sight.

"A long time ago, I woke you early from cryo-freeze and I told you we lost six in a transport explosion. Said they were excavating ice, there was an accident, and the transport exploded with them in it."

"Yessss," she says warily.

"That was a lie. We were here. You were in stasis while I sent a crew in to check for survivors. An A.I. running amok inside trapped them. I thought they were dead. We...*I* left them behind."

Sharon's eyes narrow. "Argo was good enough to tell me, since you wouldn't. Bloody *coward...*"

"Please hear me," Keller begs. He waits, watching Sharon's eyes for that moment when anger fades enough and words can be heard again.

"Go on, then," Sharon says coldly.

"Like I said before, I swore I'd find somewhere for us to live, but everywhere we went was uninhabitable. I kept getting older and...We had no other prospects for planets. I knew about this place and what was done here. It was the *last* place I wanted to be, I assure you, but there was life support here. A pre-built city with facilities." The ex-Captain rubs his face as if he were trying to scrub it away. "Awful things happened here, Sharon. Things I was a part of. I knew you'd all hang me once you found out, but at least the journey would be over. You'd all have *something*. Not Earth, but a home."

"Get to the point."

"The A.I. killed everyone here, Sharon. *Everyone*. When our people went in, they were captured...well, four were captured. Soares and Michaela were killed in the transport. But Summers, Voss, Aaronson, and Rosenthal...I thought they were dead. And I fled with the *Europa* to protect her and the rest of our crew."

Sharon's heart feels an icy nail with every name, and her eyes drill into her ex-captain. "What are you telling me? Rosie and the others, they're still alive?"

Keller's eyes close with remorse and pain. His head bobs reluctantly.

"That was twenty years ago!" Sharon yells.

"I know."

"Gor...You and I can shite off twenty years in stasis. We just suit up, strap in, and the needle comes. Then BAM we wake twenty years later with a shiver and a headache. But for them..."

Sharon turns in her seat, looks through a bubbled porthole at the rapidly approaching spires outside. She whirls about.

"Are you *sure*? Did you *see* them?"

"I saw Voss with my own eyes. Honniker's been carving on him the whole time."

"Who?"

"Honniker. The A.I. thinks he's the real scientist he was modeled on. He's been carrying on the experiments, Sharon. All this time. And he's paranoid, with some kind of god complex." As an afterthought, he adds, "*Shit*, the Counselor'd be a real help here."

"Never mind the Counselor! What about Rosie? Aaronson? Summers?"

Keller shakes his head. "I don't know." His heavy eyes lift to Maiella. "I don't give a damn what Shao-Lo says, I'm glad you're here, girl. But *watch out*. This Honniker program is *twisted*. Don't trust what you see and hear. In fact, you should probably ignore him completely. And don't go *anywhere* by yourself. Honniker's infested every part of this station with his madness."

Maiella turns her face, looking at Keller sideways. "What do you mean?"

"I mean, if you have the choice between an elevator and a flight of stairs, take the stairs."

A sudden darkness surrounds the craft as Zuri slips it into the hollow at the base of the helical spires.

Sharon's mouth is straight, her gaze distant, and she knows if not for the guardian beside her, she would be withering with fear. She looks up at Maiella, then turns to Keller—the man who is anything but what he seemed.

"It doesn't change my opinion one way or the other," Sharon says, "but I'm glad you *finally* gave me the truth." She hefts her helmet and drops it over her head. When Keller fails to do the same, she asks, "Aren't you going back in?"

He grunts. "I've been banished, at least for a while. I feel guilty as hell about all this and Honniker really got to me about it. Played me like a maestro."

"What about Shao-Lo and the Operators?"

"They're talking to it. Seems they have a loose detente going. Some cooperation."

"They're *cooperating*?"

"Yeah. The experiments have produced results."

"Are you serious? This thing murdered our friends, and the sods are *COOPERATING* with it?"

Keller nods soberly. "Yeah. That's why they don't want *you* in there," he says to Maiella. "They're concerned about any x-factors pissing of the A.I. and costing them access to the experiments. *Hmmf.* And it's why I've been 'sent to my room'."

Maiella looks away with disinterest.

Sharon ponders the heavy briefing but the concepts are too big to swallow whole. Instead, she looks through the windscreen, watching large yellow arrows on tunnel walls passing by. The craft banks and sweeps around a bend, flying under the burned out wreck of a transport. Just ahead, huge yellow doors, flanked by massive spherical turrets and emblazoned with an enormous triangular skull, proclaim their destination. The doors part in the middle and Zuri guides the craft between them.

Sharon steps to the front of the craft, bracing herself on Zuri's chair as the station's gravity enhancement takes effect. Through the windscreen, she gawks at the charred destruction strewn about the hangar bay. Among the heaps of twisted metal, shattered ceramics, and dangling cables, her sharp eyes spot the remains of a familiar craft, nose propped on its front landing strut, pointing up at an angle. Mid-way down the hull is a half-scorched emblem of a bull racing across open water.

"Keller, that's our transport!"

Keller stares at the floor and does not reply.

Sharon rivets her eyes to the exploded wreck and moves to a bubbled port hole as they pass. The craft's shattered windscreen is peeled open, and through the gap she catches a glimpse of the mummified pilot still strapped into the seat. She averts her eyes reverently.

Zuri flies close to the control room access door, nudges one of the smaller wrecks aside, and sets the craft down on its struts. Her goggles pulse and the background whine of turbines wind down. She lowers her faceplate and seals it.

"There's no air out there, Keller. You should seal up," Zuri warns.

Keller startles out of a trance. "Huh? Yeah, yeah, right." He fumbles for his helmet and latches it in place.

Zuri frees herself from the restraints. She grabs her pistols from the console in front of her, clips them onto her back, then slides out of the chair.

"Sharon, I'll escort you to MedLab. We're going to move fast, so stay close to me."

The pilot strides briskly to the back of the transport, shouldering Maiella aside, and takes hold of the hatch release. The disgraced soldier shows no trace of indignation, merely lowers the faceplate of her bulky helmet and secures it.

"Ready?" Zuri asks.

Sharon nods.

Zuri releases the hatch and drops to the deck, not bothering with the telescoping ladder. Sharon steps to the edge and contemplates the two-meter drop before opting for the ladder. She skips the last few rungs and makes a wobbly landing in her thick boots.

Zuri steadies Sharon with a hand and ushers her toward the service air-lock. Maiella jumps from the hatch and lands cat-like behind them.

"Be careful," Keller says via radio.

Sharon looks over her shoulder. Keller is in the transport hatchway, leaning against it. Up close, she did not want to look at him, but with a comfortable distance, she sees him. Regret has gouged deep circles under his brow. His cheeks are hollow. And beneath the still-healing bruises from Gregor's pummeling, the lines of his face seem deeper than they were just days ago. The image burns into her mind, inciting a mixture of conflicting thoughts about duty, loyalty, and shared time. She faces front and follows Zuri to the service door.

While Sharon waits for the young Geek to open the lock, Keller's warnings echo in her mind. A chill sweeps her and she reaches back to feel Maiella's reassuring solidity.

"Right behind you, Sharon," Maiella says via radio.

Zuri leads the way past the service airlock and the ruined portraits of the foyer, then runs ahead through sparsely lit corridors. Sharon marvels at the blasted walls, having to be constantly reminded by Zuri to keep up. But when they reach a desiccated beast slumped on the floor, Sharon flattens herself against the opposite wall and will not move.

Dear God! Those teeth and claws! The SIZE of this thing...!

Maiella steps between Sharon and the dried-out monster, blocking her view of it.

"It's okay, Sharon. It's dead. Can't hurt you."

The small colonist composes herself, once more reaching for the pendant buried beneath the dense canvas of her pressure suit. She nods quickly inside her round helmet, and falls in behind a very impatient Zuri.

When Sharon comes to the reptilian corpses lying in the hallway, however, she stops and will not be moved.

"Sharon. *Sharon!*" Zuri calls, but the colonist does not answer. Rather, she kneels at the vivisected corpses enthralled in morbid fascination. Though she wants to keep moving, she cannot break the entrancement.

Maiella crouches next to her, keeping a wary eye all around. "You've never seen them before, have you?"

Sharon shakes her head. Her gloved hand reaches out as though controlled by someone else and touches brittle, dried flesh. The gray body rolls stiffly at her touch, revealing a long, stitched-up incision down the midline. Above it is a long, reptilian face, dried lips receded from large teeth in a gruesome sneer.

Her heart pounds in her chest, spurred by the bleakest of thoughts. *They tried to kill us all.*

Her cheeks flush. Hot, damp breath condenses on the inside of her helmet.

They tried to wipe us out.

Her reaching hands become fists. She looks into the hollow eye sockets, hating the gap-toothed sneer. A coughing grunt passes her lips.

"Sharon," Zuri snaps, "let's *go!*" She reaches for Sharon as though to snatch her up, but Maiella knocks the grabbing hand away and stands in the way, leaning forward. Zuri glares at the disgraced Operator blocking her, eye to eye, toe to toe.

"Move."

"Give her a moment," Maiella counters. "This is hard."

Zuri cocks her head to the side and lunges, shoving Maiella back. Maiella absorbs the shove and grips Zuri at the wrist. With an effortless turn, she uses the momentum and flings the young Geek down the corridor. Zuri tumbles and is back on her feet, pistols aimed, safeties off.

Maiella stands her ground, unconcerned about the large caliber barrels pointed at her.

"Stop it!" Sharon shrieks. "I'm going, okay? *Please*, Zuri, *put your guns away!"*

The two Operators maintain the stare.

"Pull the trigger," Maiella taunts. "Then you'll know what it's like."

Zuri negates with headshake. "You're already dead. There's no crime." She thumbs the safeties and clips the pistols onto her back. "Except in *wasting ammo.*"

Zuri storms past Maiella, fixated on the corridor ahead.

Desperate to defuse the tension, Sharon pleads with Zuri as she passes, "I'm sorry, I'm sorry! I should've kept up! Let's just go, okay?"

Zuri gives Sharon a disdainful glance through her goggles, then runs ahead. Sharon clomps along as fast as she can in her heavy boots and stiff suit, Maiella in protective pursuit.

ANYTHING AT ALL

Light spills into the intersection ahead of Zuri, Sharon, and Maiella. When the trio rounds the corner, MedLab's frosted glass doors shine with a diffuse, welcoming glow. Zuri slows from quick jog to brisk walk and Sharon is grateful for the reprieve—not so much from the exertion, but because the suit was never intended for aerobic exercise. Wherever her skin contacts the interior, the rough suit has chaffed her raw and beads of sweat sting as they roll across the angry patches of skin.

"Whew!" Sharon says. "Never had to run in this thing before. It *sucks*."

Concerned, Maiella looks the suit over for defects. When she finds none, she asks, "How? Is the pressure off?"

Sharon looks up at the dumbfounded Maiella through her eyebrows, mouth slightly open. She smirks.

"Never mind."

Zuri halts at the softly glowing doors and Sharon walks up beside her. Only up close does the colonist recognize the telltale streaks and spatters.

"Oh, God..."

Zuri ends her mental debate and turns suddenly. "This will disturb you. Close your eyes and I'll guide you through."

"Why?" she asks timidly. "What's here?"

"Human remains. And *others*."

Sharon studies the dark stains on the glass, the broad arcs, the dense splashes. Her imagination runs wild with the nightmare creature in the hallway, of a human victim clamped in that great maw being shaken and sawed apart. She flinches as if slapped and takes a half step back, her retreat stopped by Maiella behind her. Maiella's hand falls on her shoulder and gives a squeeze.

The colonist looks at the floor and puts her hands up with open palms.

"I can do this, Zuri. I can take it."

The young Geek looks her up and down then nods. Her goggles flash once and the glass doors part.

Sharon gawks into a dusty human abattoir. She falters, nearly fainting.

Supportive hands prop her up but she shrugs them off, insisting, "*No, I've got it.*" She drives herself forward against far more rational instincts to flee, quickly crossing the lobby and passing through the raccoon-decorated doors into the mouth-like atrium of *The Flounder.*

She turns a full circle in the room, getting her bearings, when she recognizes Shao-Lo's and Carter's voices drifting through the left and right corridors. There is a third voice in the conversation, a stranger's voice—one with a mild German inflection.

Zuri opens the faceplate of her helmet and turns to Sharon, stating, "The air is safe here. You can take off your helmet." The Geek leads the way down the left corridor to the main experiment floor.

Sharon looks back at the moldered corpses, her stomach turning at the thought of how the stale, dusty air might smell. *Thank you, but I'd rather not,* she thinks to herself. When she emerges from the gently curving corridor into the cavernous experiment chamber, however, she stands stupefied.

"This place is enormous!"

Distracted from the horrors behind her, Sharon unlatches her helmet then lifts it away. Cool dry air soothes her damp skin, bringing with it the underlying scent of antiseptic. She spins as she gapes at a ceiling of black rock and the ring shaped structure hanging from it.

Her hands find the zippers of her pressure suit, running them one by one until the suit collapses at her ankles. She steps out of it, wearing a snug synthetic undersuit that hugs her athletic figure. Steam rises from the bright orange fabric.

"*Ooooh,*" she sighs, "that's better. I feel like I just dropped twenty kilos."

Maiella glances at the heaped suit and backpack as she marches by. She lifts her faceplate. "At *least.*"

Zuri guides them toward the back of the cavern, toward the sound of the voices. Along the way, Sharon's eyes roam over the medical stations and stacked rows of cells, not focusing on anything in particular.

Maiella shares Sharon's wonder, more interested in the size of the place than what it contains. She, too, spins as she walks, taking special interest in the ring of offices on the ceiling. Following stout cables from the center of the offices down to a wood-railed platform on the floor, her eyes sparkle with a child-like need to explore.

"We're here, Colonel," Zuri announces. The distant three-way conversation pauses and Shao-Lo emerges from a vault at the back of the chamber. The towering colonel raises an arm up high and beckons the three over. Zuri runs to her superior, Sharon and Maiella trailing.

"Get in there and assist Carter," Shao-Lo says to Zuri, tossing her head toward the vault.

"Aye, sir."

"You," the Colonel says to Maiella with scarcely reined distaste, "go wait with Argo."

Maiella looks at Sharon, waiting for a confirmation.

"What are you waiting for soldier?" Shao-Lo adds with irritation.

"You all make it very clear," Maiella states matter-of-factly, "that I don't report to you."

Shao-Lo's eyes narrow.

Sensing another showdown, Sharon places her hands on Maiella's chest plate.

"It's all right. I'll talk to the Colonel, see how we can help."

Maiella nods. With a last glance at Shao-Lo, she strides away to the medical table where Argo works. The Colonel stares bullets into Maiella's back.

"Why do you hate her so much?" Sharon asks in lowered voice.

"We don't hate," Shao-Lo says, finally breaking off the stare. "She's a liability. She undermines unity, provides a poor example to the others. She's wild and unpredictable. That could get *all* of us killed, Sharon. How do you *not* see that?"

"I see that she's a survivor and I know she'll protect us with her life."

"There's no doubt of that."

"Then why do you push her aside all the time?"

"Because she's broken. And she won't be fixed."

"What about Argo? He was broken, too."

"Argo..." Shao-Lo trails off, reaching for the words to an unfamiliar concept. "Argo restored himself, possibly because he was away from her for so long. That means there's hope for Thompson as well. But I'm concerned

Maiella's state of mind could be contagious. She could drag Argo down again, possibly others...It isn't that we hate her. It's that we need to get away from her."

"Is that how you feel about us colonists, as well?"

"Of course not. You're not soldiers. You are the way you are. No reason we should expect you to be otherwise." Shao-Lo turns and steps toward the vault.

But Maiella's becoming like us, Sharon thinks to herself. *And everyone in the Cadre wants her out...*

"Are you saying we'll never blend? That we'll always be separate?"

Shao-Lo halts and looks over her shoulder before turning about. "General O'Kai said we must *try* to understand your ways and ask for your cooperation, not demand it. That's difficult for me, so I apologize if my speech is, at times, inappropriate or commanding."

Sharon follows Shao-Lo's lead, pleased at the Colonel's candor, and decides it is a more positive path than the one she was heading down.

"Of course. What can I do to help?"

Shao-Lo thinks, choosing words carefully. "Every Operator, including myself, has a *need* to serve. Because her service to the Corps is over, it seems Maiella has chosen service to *you* as a replacement."

Sharon listens attentively as the Colonel continues.

"This situation is extremely delicate. We can't afford emotions to interfere. So I need you to keep Maiella engaged. Would the two of you explore other areas of the facility while we work here?"

Sharon peers around the tall woman at the half-open vault door with *The Cooler* stenciled boldly upon it. Though interested to see inside, she accepts.

"Anything I should be looking for?"

"Technology. Information on the creatures made here. Anything we can salvage. Anything that could help us stand up to the Blueskins. *Anything at all.*"

Satisfied her mission is not merely a snipe hunt to keep Maiella distracted, she nods.

"Yes, Colonel. I can do that."

"Thank you," Shao-Lo says genuinely. "Now, excuse me." The Colonel disappears into the vault and pulls the door most of the way shut.

Sharon juts her lip in thought and moves to catch up with Maiella, unaware of the purplish lens above the vault door that tracks her as she goes.

IF YOU HAVE TO ASK...

Maiella creeps up behind Argo while he hunches over a stainless steel table. With hair little more than stubble, the Brick's scalp shines in the bright lamps, showing the large, star-shaped scar on the back of his head. She grins mischievously and coils to pounce.

"You're stealthy as ever, Maiella."

Her limbs go slack with disappointment. "How did you hear me?"

Argo snorts. "Didn't. Saw you coming."

Maiella steps out from behind her old friend and looks at the table, where a half-naked man lies catatonic. Innumerable fine scars trace his exposed skin in a tight grid and large black characters are tattooed into his chest. Beside the man, Argo's labset is propped up like a picture frame. In the main display, the man's vitals are displayed, primarily concerning heart function and bone density. In a smaller window, Maiella sees streaming video. She leans in, looking at Argo's back and her own.

She straightens and looks behind herself. Sitting on the adjacent station's table is Argo's helmet.

"You smart man, you. Caught me on camera." She strides over to the table and picks up the huge helmet, propping it from the inside with a finger. She strolls back jovially, spinning it. "This isn't making you dizzy, is it?"

Argo's great hand slaps down on top of his spinning helmet, stopping it instantly. He palms the large headpiece and puts it back on the table as he had it.

"I can be your eyes, big man," Maiella says, leaning against the table and crossing her arms and legs. "We used to make a great team, you know."

"Why are you here?" Argo's brown eyes are interrogating.

Maiella cannot meet the accusing stare. Instead, she looks down at the man lying on the table.

"Too important. I had to come." She turns about and focuses squarely on the catatonic man. Her brows bunch together. "So what's going on with this guy?"

"This isn't your mission. You shouldn't be here."

She winces, keeping focus on the tattooed man. "Well, I am. So you should get used to it."

"You don't belong here."

In a blur, she whips the back of her gauntlet across his face. The impact turns the Brick's head, startling him.

"That hurts, Argo!"

He rubs his face, checking that all his teeth are still in their sockets.

"You don't know how hard it was to get in and see you in Cadre MedLab," she says, voice strained. "And what did I get? The same bilge I hear from *every other MedTech and Operator. I'm not gonna take it from you, too, Argo. NOT from you!*"

Argo's hard stare softens when he sees her eyes welling.

"I'm sorry, Maiella. You're right. I'm *sorry*." He extends a big hand. She grips it with both of hers, letting a single tear escape. She clenches her jaw.

"If you really have to ask why I'm here, then you're *stupid*." She lays a hard glare on him that tells him plainer than words that he is one of the few things in the universe she treasures, and that he is a damned fool for forgetting that. It tells him he has forgotten himself with his redemption into the Corps, but worse, he has forgotten *her*.

He tugs on her arm and pulls her into a risky embrace. "It *is* good to see you."

She grunts and frees herself from his huge arms. "That sounded like you meant it." She smiles, finally having some of what she needed. "Missed you, too, brother."

"Now look, don't get mad when I ask this."

She sighs. "Ask away."

"I got back to the Corps. Why don't you try?"

"Same reason I couldn't go to Earth." She flicks a finger against her temple. "HDI is too old, only partially restored. Any Geek would compute *rings* around me."

"Yeah, but you don't have to be an Operator. You could train the new initiates. With your experience—"

"They won't have me, Argo."

"I thought the same thing. You have to *prove* your..."

She looks away skeptically.

"Hey! Listen to me."

Reluctantly, deliberately, Maiella's head swivels back to him.

"Whether they want to admit it or not, the Cadre *needs* you, Maiella. They need me. They need Thompson. They need *everyone* they can get."

She folds her arms again. "I don't know how you could be anymore wrong."

"Look around! Do you see this place? This is going to change things. Honniker says there's a weapon here that can destroy the Blueskins. *Destroy them.* You know what that means? If we're gonna get close enough to use it..."

"...it'll be a bloody, stand up fight."

Argo nods. "They'll need everyone they can get."

Maiella contemplates Argo's words, moved by the truth of them. Inside, she knows she would fight to the gristle for every human life. But as hard as her expulsion from the Cadre is, and her separation from Argo and Thompson, she has gone too far into her new life to go back to the Operator Corps. Things could never be as they were. Even if they could, she would not *want* them to.

"You know I'm with you forever, big man. But I'm finding my own way."

Argo exhales with frustration. "And when Thompson wakes up, *which he will,* what if he's inducted to the Corps again? Will you let him?"

Maiella squints at her dear friend, respecting the fair question but resenting him for asking it.

"Hey, Maiella!" Sharon calls from across the cavern.

Maiella tracks the echoing voice to a platform at the room's center.

"Gotta go. See you later, brother." She socks him in his armored chest.

He smirks at the punch and shakes his head, watching her walk away. "Yeah, take care." He resets his helmet camera to keep lookout behind him and resumes his work on Voss.

Worth Dying For

Maiella runs up to the platform and hops the railing. The platform bounces at her landing, oscillating the long lift cables.

Surprised by the platform's spring, she looks at her feet and finds an intricate pattern of inlaid strips covering all but the edges. At the center is a shield, inlaid with woods of light and dark hues, accented with floral flourishes. Thick varnish coats the wood floor, polished to a glossy finish.

"That's weird. Never seen anything like this," Maiella says.

"What, *wood*?" Sharon says in disbelief.

"Would I what?"

Sharon looks at the floor, suddenly realizing Maiella has never seen a tree, much less anything carved from one. She shakes her head. "Never mind."

Maiella looks at the railing she just vaulted and rubs her hand over it, silently marking the identical varnished wood. Looking up at the office overhead, she asks, "Is there power?"

In the opposite corner, Sharon stands beside a waist-high post with a polished brass plate on top. Two buttons occupy the plate with a removable key fob. She turns the key fob and the brass plate lights up with pin-point red diodes.

"Yep."

The diodes switch to green as the panel boots up. High overhead, a winding motor takes up the slack, smoothing out the oscillations and jolting the platform. The women instinctively grasp the wood rails.

"Hang on," Sharon warns, and she punches the ascend button.

The two lean comfortably against the sturdy railing during the slow

ascent and they take long looks around the experiment chamber. Rows
stack upon rows of empty cells along the curved walls, their doors propped
open by the Operators who searched them. Inside, the cells are marked with
intense emotion in four letter graffiti, the last words of deranged occupants
scratched by fingernail, tooth, and bone through layers of institutional gray
paint.

Sharon turns from the cells and looks across the experiment floor.
Light slips out in a long, thin line from the barely-open vault door. If there
is any conversation going on inside, it is masked by the lift motor droning
overhead.

In the back right corner, Argo's station glimmers with reflected
lamp light and the Brick's occasional movement. Maiella stares at her old
comrade.

"How's he doing?" Sharon asks.

"Huh?" Maiella breaks off her distant gaze.

"Argo. How's he doing?"

Maiella grimaces. "He's got his dress grays again. He's just *fine*."

Sharon stands quietly, watching Argo. "Maybe you could—"

"This thing go any faster?" Maiella's eyes match the hard set of her
jaw.

"Uh..." Sharon looks over at the brass plate, knowing there are no
speed controls but wishing to avoid the uncomfortable glare. "Um, no. Just
up and down."

Maiella looks out over the railing again, watching the island of light
in the back right corner.

Several meters from the top, an alert tone sounds, then an automated
voice warns, *"Please keep arms and legs inside railing"*. Overhead, a hatch
fitting the platform's shape slides open.

"Watch out!" Maiella shouts and in an instant, her pistols are in her
hands. Sharon's eyes go wide with terror as something plummets from the
opening hatchway. She crumples into the railing's corner, hiding her face
in her hands. There is a crash onto the platform and an explosion of dusty
fragments. When Sharon parts her fingers to look, she sees Maiella in a wide
stance, one pistol aimed at the open hatchway, the other trained on a tangled
heap of rags and bones on the platform. The soldier's eyes flick back and
forth between targets.

Sharon covers her nose and mouth and gets back to her feet. With the
continuous rise of the platform, dust flows away over the edges, revealing
another mummified corpse. The fragile body is shattered like clay pottery, its
bones spilled out across the platform, fragments teetering at the edges, then

falling off.

A glint of metal draws her eye to a caved-in human skull. Embedded in the broken cranium are golden contact terminals just like Maiella's.

Adopting a more scientific attitude, Sharon shames herself for cowardice and takes the skull in hand. The gold contacts are dingy, yet untarnished. Turning the skull, she looks inside and finds beneath each terminal is a dense web of microscopic fibers. Just thinking about the process of implantation makes every hair on her scalp stand and, after a palsy-like fit of revulsion, she carefully sets the skull down and wipes her hands on her undersuit.

"There's a name badge," Maiella says, aiming both pistols at the nearing hatchway.

Sharon sifts over the rags. Among a cluster of pens she finds a plasticized badge. Swiping the dusty badge with her thumb, she reads aloud, "Edmund Honniker, M.D."

"And how may I assist?" asks a voice, seemingly from everywhere.

Sharon looks wide-eyed at the skull, wondering if somehow there could be life in the circuitry. Maiella takes Sharon's cue and trains one of her weapons on it.

"Dr. Honniker? Is this...*you?*"

"Ah, you've found my husk. To answer your question, that was me. The body carried me a while, though, as you see, I no longer require it."

"You were a...a Geek?"

"Ach! Nothing so banal as that. 'Geek' is a nickname the development team gave that particular program. Whether it was meant as an insult or an honorific, I could never be sure."

"Then why did you have these...*things* in your head?"

"To upload, of course. Mikato's HDI was the only way to do so."

"Mikato?"

"Yes, Mikato. A tedious, supremely difficult man, but a genius. His synaptic bridge concept was revolutionary and was crucial to my project."

"What project?"

"Building better soldiers, of course."

Maiella flinches, her goggles illuminating unexpectedly. "Hey, *knock it off!*" she shouts. The goggles go dark again and Maiella's wary eyes roam all around the cavernous space.

"I see most of your synaptic bridges have retreated. Did you experience a cryogenic malfunction?"

"Yes," Maiella answers after searching in vain for the source of the intrusion.

"I thought so. That was the most frequent cause of failure in our tests, but we were typically able to repair the damage. Would you like me to restore your function?"

The question hangs in the air, verbally unanswered, but Sharon can see the raised eyebrows of surprise and hope in Maiella's face.

"You could do that?" the soldier asks.

"The procedure is lengthy and not without risk. However we were able to restore ninety-three percent function or better in our test subjects. I would simply need you to occupy one of the medical stations below and strap in."

Sharon stiffens at the suggestion, Keller's warning stirring her thoughts. She shakes her head at Maiella.

Maiella looks at Sharon, conflicted. She sighs. "Maybe later, Doctor, thank you."

"Are you sure? I sense your anxiety about rejoining your friends. With a restoration, perhaps you could return to service."

Maiella's eyes close. Her mouth draws thin with the enormity of temptation.

"Thank you, Doctor, but not right now." Her head lifts to the hatchway just meters above. "What'll we find up here?"

"My office and personal suite. When I was just a man, I held certain appetites—appetites that no longer afflict me. As you are still flesh, there may be some things you find interesting, though I doubt you will find anything useful."

Amber lights blink at the hatchway's edge. Just beneath it jut four thick, retractable catches. Three retract, one sticks and whines with strain. Maiella twirls a pistol around her finger and grips it by the barrel. Leaning over the railing, she smacks the catch with the stock. The whining ends, and the catch retracts.

The platform carries the women up into a dark and spacious room, its dimensions only suggested by the minimal amber lights around the hatchway. Another alert tone sounds, followed by the clank of the catches as they extend beneath the platform. Cable winding motors shut down with a hiss and a blue spark.

"Please remain clear of the railing," the automated voice announces and the flashing amber lights yield to flickering overhead lamps. The railing sinks into the platform until the top rail is flush with the floor, integrating seamlessly into the polished hardwood of the room around them.

Sharon's jaw drops as the lights settle into constant illumination, and she turns completely around. The wide, oval room is lavishly appointed with rich antique furniture and thick rugs. On one side of the space is a set of heavy-looking double doors. Opposite the doors is a floor to ceiling panel of glass, enclosing an unlit office. Along the intervening walls are pots planted with withered and defoliated ornamental trees, tapestries, and intact paintings.

Sharon marvels at the objects d'art, all of which are familiar from her tours of Earth's museums, all famously disappeared—believed lost to theft, war, or terrorism many years before the genocide. As dazzling a showcase as it is, however, a single figure rendered in white stone steals Sharon's full attention. Even without its display pedestal, the statue stands over two meters high. Its determined, masculine face is crowned with short, curly hair and is wreathed with laurels. A thick cloak clasps above the right shoulder and drapes liberally over the man's left side. The left hand, just protruding from beneath the cloak, rests on the top of a shield; and the right hand clasps a rod or rolled scroll held out across the body as though the statue were mid-stride. In the diffuse light he appears a three dimensional photograph in monochrome—a moment of life forever frozen in time.

Tall enough to look O'Kai in the eye, Sharon thinks as she sweeps from the statue's stern face down to its open-toed sandals. Entranced, she approaches it.

The figure loses none of its lifelike appearance the closer she gets. Subtle features of the hands and arms, unseen at distance, are revealed in such meticulous detail she half expects the stone to come alive in greeting.

Maiella steps up beside her and contemplates the imperial figure. "It's a good copy of a man, for whatever reason you'd need one... Who's it supposed to be?"

"Julius Caesar. And it's not a copy. It's a *sculpture*." As soon as Sharon says the word, she realizes the futility of the distinction.

"Skulp-cherr?"

"This was chiseled and ground from a solid block. You can see some of the rough cuts on the base."

"So the person who made this," Maiella says, wrinkling her face, "cut the block down until this was left?"

"That's right."

"Must've taken hours."

Sharon laughs out loud. The Geek's face scrunches at the mocking.

"Maiella, this was made by *hand*...*Before* power tools or computers." Sharon reaches tentatively to the statue then caresses the bare arm. Her face shines with amazement. "This took *years*."

"That's a joke, right?"

Sharon grins and shakes her head.

"Why would anyone give so much time to something which can neither protect nor sustain them?"

"Passion."

Sharon circles behind the statue, dragging her fingertips as she goes. When she emerges on the other side, Maiella looks confused and frustrated.

"It's being completely devoted to something," Sharon explains, "seeking perfection and being unable to rest until you've attained it." She completes her circle and stands beside Maiella again. "It's what separates the good from the *great*. The proficient from the *master*." She sneaks a glance at the soldier beside her. "I think you know something about that."

"Okay, it's a rock formed into a detailed shape," Maiella says, missing Sharon's subtle complement. "True, it would take skill in doing this by hand, *but why would you?* Years of life are gone and all there's to show is a...a shaped *rock*."

Sharon looks back at the statue. "No. It's more. It's proof of something lasting. Proof that beauty and art don't have to be fleeting...that one person's talent and feeling can endure for *generations*. The artist put part of his life into this and I still feel it over a thousand years after his death. It's a kind of immortality, Maiella. It's powerful."

Sharon steps up to the imposing figure in fond recollection.

"I was a little girl, on holiday with my family. We went to a museum in Paris, which had hundreds of statues, each just as remarkable as the next. But this one, I don't know how to say it...I felt safe looking up at it. *Protected*. The confidence in the face, the sword and shield, he could stand up to anything. Look. He has a sword, but his hand isn't on it. It's on the shield. That tells me he's more interested in protecting than in destroying. In his hand, that rod is probably a scroll, meaning he's more interested in order and learning than in war. But the armor, the sandals, the *equipment* of a warrior tell me he's unafraid of whoever would try to wage war on him, and they'd be sorry if they tried."

Maiella cocks her head and cradles her chin. "You see all that?"

"Yes. And more. Think how easily this statue could be broken. Now understand that it had to be packaged, lifted from Earth gravity, transported light years away, and brought all the way up here. What does that tell you?"

"Someone cared about it."

"Exactly. It might seem a waste to you, I know, but you could search the entire universe and never find this again. It's unique. That makes it special and worth protecting." With certainty, Sharon adds, "Someday, we'll have time for things like this again."

Maiella's lower lip juts as she considers Sharon's words. She squints, then shrugs. "Let's search the office."

Sharon turns to the office and its floor to ceiling glass. Having lost herself in discovery, the return to business is disappointing.

Following Maiella to the all-glass door, the navigator peers into the unlit space. Observation windows at the back of the space permit faint rays through, providing the slightest suggestion of furniture. Her companion pushes on the handle-less door. It does not budge. The Geek takes one of her pistols by the barrel again and cocks her arm.

"Wait!" Sharon yells, arms out.

Maiella frowns at her companion.

"Edmund? Can you open this door?" Sharon waits for a reply, suddenly aware how quiet the room is. "Dr. Honniker?"

Maiella taps the butt of her pistol against the glass, analyzing the sound.

"Plexisteel," she announces casually. "I couldn't break this, anyway." On a whim, the soldier strides back to the heap of rags on the platform. She kneels down and sifts through the remains with a finger.

Sharon feels around the edge of the glass door for a hidden trigger point or contact spot when Maiella whistles. She turns around and Maiella lobs something small toward her. Sharon bobbles it between her hands and finally catches it. Before she can ask what to do with the pen-sized cylinder, the door swings open behind her and the office lights flicker on.

"Good morning, Dr. Honniker," welcomes a sultry feminine voice. "It's very good to see you again."

Sharon grips the cylinder tightly and whirls in surprise. Beyond the open door is a wide office space lined with plaques and medical awards. At the center is a broad workstation with a glass desktop supported by thick posts of dark metal. Behind it is a very comfortable-looking high-backed chair.

Lively background concerto music fades in with remarkable clarity. Sharon takes a tentative step into the office, searching for the hidden speakers.

"I regret to inform you," the female voice coos over the music, "we are out of your fresh coffee. Will you have a cup of the synthetic, instead?"

Sharon walks cautiously through the space, looking first at the degrees in organic chemistry, biomechanics, and pharmacology, then at certifications in medical imaging, hormone therapy, and multiple awards in neuro-engineering. Between the copious accolades are photographs with corporate sponsors and high profile heads of state, as well as multiple patent awards.

"Are you all right, Doctor?" the voice asks with concern. "You seem very quiet today."

Sharon ignores the question, continuing to the row of observation windows at the back of the office. The windows slant at a reclined angle from the floor to the ceiling, permitting full view over all of the medical stations below.

"Doctor, please answer me."

The plaintive tone finally captures Sharon's attention. "Yes, I'm fine. Thank you."

"I'm relieved. I was concerned you might never wake up. You sound *very* different, Doctor. Are you congested?"

Sharon's eyebrows knit at the bizarre conversation. "No, I'm fine, really."

"Are you sure? I sense a high anxiety in your vocal pattern. If you like, I can provide a relaxing massage before you start work."

"No, thank you, I'm fine."

"Then would you like your coffee? I can make some for your associate if you'd like."

Sharon relents to the voice so eager to serve and to please. "Yes, that would be nice."

"Wonderful! I'll serve it momentarily."

Sharon shakes her head, wondering if somehow coffee is really going to appear. She smiles at the silly thought and continues her investigation along the office walls.

Maiella ducks her head under the glass doorway and scans the office. "Who's your friend?"

"No idea. Probably some automated office assistant."

Unlike Sharon, Maiella heads straight for the workstation. She plunks down into the soft cushions of the chair and wheels herself up to the desktop.

"Excuse me," says a feminine voice from the doorway.

Sharon flattens against the wall, knocking a mahogany plaque off its hanger. Maiella's pistols are in her hands, barrels aimed at the curvaceous woman walking in with a silver coffee service.

"That's the Doctor's chair," the woman says in sultry tones. She sets the service tray down onto the desktop and parks a hand on a rounded hip.

Maiella slides back from the desk and rises from the chair, pistols still poised, fingers on triggers.

"That's better," the woman says, flouncing her wavy, corn silk hair.

She lifts the silver urn and pours into two fine china cups from the slender spout. Earthy aromas waft from the steaming cups, bringing suggestions of crisp acidity and the faintest hint of scorched wood. However alluring the scent, Sharon cannot stop staring at the camisole and hipster clad woman serving the coffee.

"Black, just the way you like it," the woman says. She sets down the urn and faces Sharon, her full lips pouting in concern. "You do seem very tense." The lips curve to a smile. "I know how to help with that." She glides around the desk, hips swinging from side to side.

Sharon slides down the wall. *"Oh God..."*

Maiella rushes between Sharon and the seductive woman, and the woman stops her approach. She looks past Maiella with eyes that do not waver at all.

"Edmund, if you're not in the mood, all you have to do is say so."

Maiella remains on high alert, watching the woman carefully, aware of every movement, expecting anything.

"I'm not in the mood!" Sharon says, louder than necessary.

The woman, her eyes perfectly still, replies, "That's fine, Edmund. You know I'm here for you." She steps away from Maiella and heads toward the door. "Just leave the dishes when you're done and I'll take care of them later." Before leaving, she pauses at the door and turns, folding her arms to emphasize her ample bosom. Pert nipples press against the silk camisole, threatening to break through.

"Do you want me to assist your research today or do you need some time to yourself?"

Sharon and Maiella pass a glance between one another. Sharon shrugs.

"Yes, assistance would be fine, but can you give us some time first?"

"Of course! Just call when you need me." She is about to leave when Sharon asks,

"Uh, what do I call you?"

The woman cocks her pretty face to one side in mild disappointment. "Oh, Edmund, that knock to your head really did a number on you. I think we need to get you to an examination table."

"NO!" Sharon starts, one arm thrust out defensively. "No. I'm fine, just...just tell me what to call you."

The woman shakes her head and sighs. "You usually call me Marta." She lifts an eyebrow. "Though you may call me anything you like." She uncrosses her arms and strides away on smooth, long legs.

"What the hell *was* that?" Sharon asks.

Maiella steps to the office doorway and watches the woman glide away, every step highlighting her feminine beauty. The hardened soldier takes tiny steps in place, emulating the undulations.

"That was the finest piece of engineering I've ever seen," Maiella says at last.

Sharon presses up against the floor to ceiling glass wall. At the opposite end of the oval room, heavy double doors swing open and closed behind the lingeried woman.

"She wasn't alive at all?"

Maiella cocks her head. "No, not *living*. But I don't know for sure she isn't alive in *some* way."

"Is she dangerous?"

"Maybe. Seems to like you a lot, though."

Sharon, rattled by the appearance of such an enviously beautiful woman out of thin air, only now asks the obvious question.

"Why does she think *I'm* Honniker?"

Maiella points to the pen-sized cylinder in Sharon's grasp. Sharon looks down at her hand, having forgotten she was holding it.

"What? *This?*" She holds it at arm's length like it might explode ink on her.

"There's a reactive circuit inside. That android was emitting signals and that cylinder replied to it, like a friend or foe transponder. Same thing with the door to this office. That cylinder might be the key to this whole compartment."

The key to that woman, too? Sharon wonders. "But she has *eyes*, obviously! Can't she see I'm not him? I don't look a *thing* like the man in these photographs. At least I *hope* not..."

"I don't know. All I can tell you is that cylinder you've got seemed to be all that mattered. Marta thinks you're Honniker."

"Here, you take it." Sharon holds the reactive device out to her. Maiella looks down at it and shakes her head in refusal.

"No need to switch things up. Besides, if that Marta android is as helpful as it seems, we might get a lot of answers."

Maiella looks again at the closed double doors on the far side of the suite.

"Is that what men like?"

Sharon feels a cynical snort coming on, recalling how women that beautiful only made her feel inadequate and inferior. She is about to give an answer just as cynical, when she sees beyond her own feelings that Maiella is genuinely concerned. She reels back her distaste.

"Most men, yeah. They like that."

Maiella folds her arms and shifts her feet.

"But not *all* men," Sharon hastens to add. "Attraction is complex. It's different for everyone. And there's no way Thompson would ever pick her over you."

"How do you know?" Maiella asks, casting all of her attention toward the small colonist.

"Honestly, I don't think she'd last long in combat. And with those skinny arms? She could lift what, thirty, maybe forty kilos?" Sharon looks up at her friend and winks.

Maiella uncrosses her arms and smiles. "Well, let's see what we can find in here."

Sharon nods in agreement, sliding the cylinder into her hip pocket. She walks back to the desktop and lifts one of the china cups to her nose, taking a deep inhale.

"No! That could be poisoned!" Maiella shouts.

Sharon exhales with a contented groan and takes another deep inhale. "I haven't had good coffee in over twenty waking years." She blows across the surface and takes a sip. The flavor is every bit as good as the aroma. Her face melts with pleasure.

"Some things are worth dying for."

MARTA

Maiella sits in the comfortable office chair, her armor rendering the massaging contours and custom support completely useless. Sharon leans on the back of it, supervising over Maiella's shoulder and sipping with eye-crossed delight from the china cup.

The seated soldier holds a lanyard from her HDI in one hand, her other hand traces the lines of the workstation for a place to jack in.

"It's got to have wireless," Sharon offers.

"That's *obvious*," Maiella states coarsely, "but I don't want the Doctor hacking into me again."

"What's the difference if you're wired in or wireless? You're still networked, right?"

Maiella considers the logic. "Ech, you're right." She lets the lanyard retract into her HDI. "Better do this manually."

No matter what angle she checks, however, Maiella finds no interface, no terminal, no input or output devices.

"You don't think..." the Geek begins.

"Think what?"

"You don't think *Marta* is the interface, do you?"

Sharon's face scrunches, not relishing the thought of calling the amorous android. "It would figure, wouldn't it? Make a woman do all the work." She drains the last of her cup and refills it from the coffee service. The aroma fills the air again.

Maiella reclines in her chair, looking at Sharon expectantly, tapping a finger on the armrest.

"Must I?" Sharon whines.

Maiella keeps tapping.

"Fine. Mar-*ta*?"

In moments, the curvaceous woman reappears, but she is scarcely recognizable as the same. Every strand of her hair is pulled neatly to a bun on the back of her head. Thin-framed spectacles perch on the bridge of her nose. A gray and black business suit hugs her figure. Her posture is straight, shoulders level. The set of her eyebrows, the focus of her eyes, the straight line of her mouth convey a serious demeanor and readiness to work.

"I'm here, Doctor. Are you ready to proceed?"

"Uh, yes, Marta, we are." She points to the cup in her hand. "This is *excellent*, by the way."

Marta nods courteously. "I'm glad you approve. How may I assist?"

"We need access to the central servers," Maiella states, "and data on the Cadre research projects."

"Did I not inform you that is the *Doctor's* chair?" The android affixes a cool stare at the seated Geek.

"It's all right, Marta. I don't mind," Sharon says. "Can you help us?"

Turning to Sharon, the android answers, "By your own request, this suite was isolated from all external networks. Are you quite sure you're all right? It seems odd that you would ask about something you insisted upon."

"Thank you for your concern, but indulge me. Why is the suite isolated?"

The android's narrowed eyebrows relax their programmed concern. "It was essential that you be allowed total privacy. When the suite was constructed it was designed to resist wireless interference and was fully soundproofed. In the event of catastrophic failures or revolt, the suite has self-contained life support functions. You were also quite concerned one of your rivals might steal your research. Hence, the computers here are inaccessible from the outside. If someone should somehow gain access to the suite, nothing will function without the device you implanted in your arm. You implanted the device *yourself* to be certain no one else knew about it."

Sharon's hand covers the cylinder in her hip pocket. "What if someone cut off my arm? Couldn't they just use it then?"

"It reads biometric data. Should your body expire or your arm be separated, the device would automatically lock out for five hundred years."

"Why five hundred? Why not one year, or ten thousand?"

"You couldn't bear the thought of all your research being lost, but neither could you stand the thought of someone who killed you benefitting from it. Even with modern cryogenics, you felt five hundred years was a sufficient guarantee to ensure no one who double-crossed you could live long enough to benefit."

"Did anyone try?"

"None successfully. Though you were concerned Mikato might eventually succeed."

"Who *is* this *Mikato*?"

Marta crosses her arms and widens her stance in a show of authority. "Doctor, you are clearly suffering from a form of amnesia, most likely from your head injury. I *must* insist we get you treatment."

"What head injury?"

"Blunt force trauma."

"Who did it?"

"I did."

Sharon ices over, backing away from the business suited android. Maiella takes an intervening stance.

"Why?"

"You ordered me to," Marta replies.

A holowindow opens over the desk and it displays a video filmed from Marta's perspective, looking across the main living space. The view turns to the elevator hatch in the floor as the hatch doors slide aside. Bright light pours through the gap from below mingled with distant shouts, mechanical whirs, and screeches of human agony.

"Marta," Honniker's radioed voice begins, "I'm almost to the top. When I get inside, I want you to hit me as hard as you can in the head with the marble sphere."

"Doctor, I can't do that," Marta's recorded voice says. "That could kill you."

"I *want* to die. Now do it!"

"I cannot."

"Disable safeties, allow direct voice program, authorization Honniker, Aleph, Quell, Voortrekker."

"Safeties disabled."

"Go get the marble sphere. *Quickly!*"

The perspective moves toward a display near the left wall. There, a black orb with white veins rests in a wooden cradle. Marta's hand reaches into view and takes the sphere.

"When I'm all the way inside, swing the sphere as hard as you can and crush my skull."

"This is a very bad idea, Doctor."

"Hurry! I'm almost there. Crush my skull, then send the lift down."

"Yes, Doctor."

168

A bald head with gold HDI contacts rises through the hatchway. Short-cropped white stubble grows in a low band just above the man's ears. He wears a long, unbuttoned lab coat over an open-collared dress shirt. A name badge rides on his chest, just beneath which is a pocket full of pens. The fabric of his slacks is thick, richly woven, and slightly reflective. His polished leather shoes shine in the lift's amber warning lights.

The man has deep-set eyes flanking a hawkish nose, and he studies the screen of a handheld electronic tablet. The eyes glance over then return to the tablet.

"Hello, Marta," the man says with a voice identical to the radio transmission.

"Please stay clear of the railing," the automated voice warns and the varnished wood rails descend into the floor. Marta walks quickly up to the man. He smiles at her approach then drops his jaw in shock.

Marta's arm arcs through the frame and clubs the man on the side of the head, knocking all but his kicking feet out of the frame. The view pans to the man lying face down on the floor, blood spreading beneath his turned face. The convulsions cease.

"Doctor?" Her hand reaches to the brass panel on the lift control and presses the descend button.

"Please stay clear of the railing," the automated voice says again. Wood-topped rails rise from the floor, shoving the doctor's limp legs aside.

"Doctor?" Marta asks again. Something heavy drops to the floor off screen and bounces once. "Please answer me."

As the lift descends out of view, Marta crouches down and rolls the body over. The man's temple is bashed in. Blood coats one side of his face and flows through a split in his scalp over his ear. Wide eyes with dilated pupils remain fixed in the shock of murder. Marta takes the man's hand in both of hers. She slaps the hand repeatedly.

"Doctor, wake up! Are you ok? Please answer me."

The doctor's chest heaves one last time.

SYSTEM LOCK OUT, displays in block letters at the top left of the video. Marta drops the man's hand, letting it drape over the open hatchway. The whir of hydraulics begins, and the hatchway doors slide toward one another. The sleeve of the man's lab coat catches on the leading edge, and he is towed out onto the hatch.

Marta rises, turns to the double doors and walks toward them. The video ends.

Both of Sharon's hands are clamped over her mouth. Maiella is on her feet, leaning forward, hands raised to fight.

"Are your safeties still disabled?" Maiella asks.

"Yes. Would you like me to reset them, Doctor?"

Sharon nods a furious assent.

"Very well. Safeties enabled."

Sharon slides her hands away from her mouth and asks, "Is there a way to keep your safeties on, as in, *locked* on?"

"Yes. Delete the command set which permits behavioral restraints to be removed."

"Do it."

"Done. I will never again be able to harm you, Edmund, and I'm very glad for that. Now then, this has clearly been disturbing. Let's not work today. Let's relax instead."

"Can't," Maiella counters. "We have to look over the experiments."

"Very well," Marta replies. "I will prepare your reports. However, I will not give them to you until you have taken a full, uninterrupted hour at the *Park*. *That*, my dear Edmund, is a therapeutic *order*."

"Override?" Maiella asks.

The android's constant eyes swing over to the Geek, and it smiles. "You just deleted them."

"That's fine, Marta," Sharon says. "After all this, I could use a break. How do we get there?"

Marta opens a holowindow in the air, showing a top down map of the facility. Like a flight attendant delivering a safety lecture, she describes the best path from the *Flounder* to the *Park*. To Sharon's amazement, the *Park* is more than twice as large.

"Did you get that?" the android finishes.

"Yeah, I got it," Maiella answers. She takes Sharon's arm and guides the colonist around Marta, keeping herself between them at all times. Marta clasps her hands and remains in place.

"There is a pile of your old clothes on the lift, Doctor. I don't think they can be mended. Would you like me to dispose of them?"

"Yes, please."

Marta nods in deference and leaves the office.

Maiella and Sharon watch her stride purposefully to the platform and collect the dusty remains. The android stands and carries the bundle through the double doors.

"She's sending and receiving huge amounts of data," Maiella notes. Sharon pays no mind to the observation.

The two step to the platform. Sharon is about to hit the descend button on the panel when Maiella grabs her wrist.

"Wait!"

Sharon looks at her guardian in alarm. "What? *What?"*

"This place is supposed to be shielded, right? No wireless traffic in or out?"

"That's what Marta said."

"Not when that hatch is open."

Sharon looks at the platform beneath her still covered with sandy bone fragments.

"I don't get it."

"I'm probably being overcautious, but on the ride up, Honniker said we found his husk, right, that he didn't need it?"

"Yeah."

"If that video Marta showed us is genuine, that guy didn't look like a *husk* to me."

"Me, either."

"So the A.I. had no use for the real Honniker, and it used Marta to kill him."

The murder replays in Sharon's head, sickening her all over again. She frowns.

"Maiella, I'm obviously not getting your point, so just out with it."

"The A.I. didn't expect us to find anything up here, least of all evidence of a killing. Marta, with all her data streaming, would make it obvious we found something *really* interesting. Between you and me, I'd rather the A.I. continue thinking this place is worthless."

"Seriously? You don't think the A.I. knows what's stored here?"

Maiella shakes her head. "Something tells me the real Honniker was very suspicious, untrusting. Especially of this 'Mikato' person. If he really did upload to a common server, why would he share everything he knew? I think he would have held back a lot of secrets."

"You think Marta might be able to help with that?"

Maiella nods emphatically. "But if the A.I. knows she's helping us, it might try to shut her down."

"Sorry to tell you, I'm not the liar that Keller is."

"Neither am I. But we don't need to lie, just don't say anything. And we should make sure that anytime this hatch is open, her wireless is turned off."

"Okay," Sharon says, bobbing her head. "Marta?"

"Yes, Doctor?" comes the woman's voice via speaker.

"I want you to disable your wireless anytime this hatch way is open. Do you understand?"

"Of course, Doctor."

"We'll be back in an hour."

"I'll have a nice plate of Frikkadel for you when you get back. And I do hope you feel better. Please let me know if I can help."

Sharon half smiles at the gesture, though food is a long way from her thoughts. She places a finger over the descend button.

"Ready?"

Maiella nods.

Sharon mashes the button, and the wood rails rise from the floor.

"Going down," she says morosely.

ELETO

Down on the main experiment floor, the faint background hiss of ventilation is interrupted by the clank and drone of old machinery. Argo looks high over his shoulder to find the source and sees the lift platform descending from the circular office on the ceiling. Maiella and Sharon lean casually against its railing.

Maiella waves to him and he turns completely around to wave back. Sharon, however, stands straight up and stares at the table beside him. Argo turns back to the table, unsure if something has happened worthy of Sharon's alarm, but all is the same with Voss's pale frame stretched out on the shiny table, his limbs, head, and torso clamped into the restraints.

Why are the colonists so fragile? he wonders.

The Brick shrugs and taps his propped labset with a finger, magnifying a three dimensional image of Voss's brain. Thousands of fine threads shroud the cortex, every fiber twisting into a bundle and terminating at one of many gold contact terminals embedded in the skull. As he further zooms the image, what appeared to be individual threads are, in fact, braids of smaller fibers, which branch off and terminate at individual neurons. The fibers themselves end at fern-like fronds that attach to the dendrites of adjacent neurons. A solid line points to the junction with the caption: *Synaptic Bridge*. Data populates a window just beneath the caption, relaying signal transmission strength, noise ratio, and efficiency.

Argo zooms out and rotates the three dimensional brain, making note of neural activity patterns, when his eyes widen in surprise. Unlike a normal, healthy brain, activity in Voss's brain has been isolated into compartments with the bundled fibers of his implants acting as bridges between each isolated section.

That's an odd way to wire an HDI...

He rotates the image again so that he can look down on both hemispheres. The Labset highlights several areas of white neuronal connective tissues and Argo taps them for magnification. As each is enlarged in sequence, he can see precise surgical cuts across them.

"Multiple cortical lobotomies," he narrates into the labset's voice recorder. "Full Corpus Callosotomy. Anterior Commissure and Posterior Commissure likewise severed. Patient's brain has been surgically partitioned hemispherically and further segmented by higher cognitive functions. HDI is wired as a network switch for all partitions, linking the isolated sections. Without HDI network in place, each partition is unable to connect with the others. Patient would likely experience fractured perceptions or multiple discordant realities."

Argo frowns as he peers at the image in the Labset.

"Autonomic systems and motor functions remain intact, yet the patient's sensory input is gated by the HDI. Of note: anyone with control of patient's HDI could manipulate what the patient senses. Could control muscles of his body. Could possibly control him entirely by remote."

The Brick hears approaching footsteps of a small woman with soft shoes. With the small woman, he knows, is an instinctively stealthy Operator.

"How is he?" Maiella asks, stepping up beside her old teammate.

Argo juts his lower lip. "Excellent physical health. Mentally, I'm unsure. But have a look at this." He lifts the labset and passes it to Maiella.

Maiella's eyes stretch at what she sees. "Synaptic Bridge density has gotta be five times what I have!" She swipes a finger across the screen, rotating the image. Every angle shows comparable distribution and quantity. She shakes her head in amazement and passes the labset back.

Argo takes the labset and props it up on the table again. "That must've been the longest surgery undertaken. Had to've been done in stages, no doubt..."

"Oh, Evan, *what have they done to you?*" Sharon moans. Her tear-filling eyes roam over a man with skin so pale, it seems translucent. She moves to the opposite side of the table and strokes one of Voss's arms, tracing the veins that lift the skin in greenish blue hue, then she fixates on the large block characters inked into his chest.

Argo looks down at his patient. "Honniker used him for neural mapping. But his brain has been partitioned, as well. When the links are active and unrestricted, he has awareness and mobility, yet someone with external control can sever those links and commandeer those functions at

174

will—"

Maiella's hand lands on his arm. "Easy, Argo."

Argo looks at Maiella with a quizzical expression but the question forming on his tongue dissolves when he sees Sharon, hands over her face, quietly sobbing. He lowers his head.

"You were close to this man," he says with tardy understanding.

Sharon rubs the tears from her eyes and looks up, fanning her damp face dry. "Yeah. We, uh...we were together a long time."

Argo sees grief beneath Sharon's upright posture and how hard she is fighting to appear strong in his presence.

Maiella walks to the far side of the table and puts an arm around Sharon's shoulder. Sharon leans into her bodyguard, unable to stop another wave of tears from falling.

"Please, Argo," Sharon begs, "can you help him?"

"Well, cuts to the brain are irreversible..."

Maiella cocks her head and lifts her eyebrows.

"What I mean is," the Brick recovers, "I don't know enough yet, but I'll keep on it. I'll do whatever I can."

Sharon's lips press hard against one another, making a straight line across her face and squaring her chin. She nods in acceptance.

Sharon takes Voss's restrained hand, wrapping his waxy fingers around her own. She leans toward him. "We're gonna get you out of here, all right? Argo's gonna take care of you, and we're gonna take you home, sweetheart." She pats the catatonic hand and gives it a squeeze before releasing. She turns away, just as a single tear rolls from under one of his dark lenses, runs down past his ear, and disappears behind his head.

"Shall we?" Maiella asks. Sharon nods.

"Going somewhere?" Argo asks.

"We're gonna check out another part of the facility. The *Park*."

"Need escort?"

"No, Argo, I think Voss needs you more. We'll be in touch if we find anything."

"You find anything up there?" Argo asks, flicking his head toward the ceiling.

Maiella smiles knowingly. "Nothing critical, but we might have you come up for a look. Sharon, you should get back into your pressure suit. There may be areas without air or oxygen."

Sharon nods again, taking a last glance at Voss before following her bodyguard.

Argo watches them as they walk out of the bright lamplight.

Maiella's dark armor disappears into shadow, making it seem Sharon is walking alone in her bright orange undergarment. The women talk back and forth while Sharon dresses in her stiff canvas suit, then their voices fade as they walk out together.

"She doesn't understand," says a voice from the table. Argo whirls about, nostrils wide.

"The shorter one, Sharon," Voss's mouth says. "She doesn't appreciate what I've accomplished here."

"Doctor Honniker? Is that you?"

"*Of course* it's me." Somehow, the voice conveys contempt without any accompanying facial expression.

Argo relaxes his tensed arms, his feet sliding together from their wide stance.

"Sharon places value in different things," the Brick says. "But she may come to understand. If someone explains it to her."

"I doubt that," the rigid patient says. "I can see *she* will never understand. What about you?"

Argo's eyebrows lift. "The level of interface you've achieved is remarkable. What that could mean for our Geeks...It'd be a quantum leap." The Brick folds his arms, leans against the table, then glances at the labset. "But you're not just trying to isolate the human nervous system, are you?"

The corners of Voss's mouth curve upward in facsimile of a smile. "Go on."

"You're attempting transfer of consciousness from one body to another."

"That's very astute. *Top marks.*"

"But why? What's the advantage?"

"As you look around, you may assume the facility was expensive to build and maintain. Much of our funding came from individual contributors, individuals interested in maintaining their fortunes past the typical human lifespan, as well as enjoying the pleasures of a second youth. They were quite generous in pursuit of that goal. It is also, I find, a fascinating challenge."

"I don't know what that means. But did you succeed?"

"Early attempts ended with dementia, paranoia, schizophrenia. It isn't simply a transfer of data we're talking about. Awareness, personality, and memories must retain their context from one mind to another. The host mind must first be wiped clean, or sufficiently isolated so it cannot interfere with the donor. While it sounds simple, in practice it is quite difficult. I filled and emptied these cells many times over in the attempt."

Argo looks up at the vacant cells surrounding them. "You mentioned your subjects were criminals, but how did you acquire them?"

"Ah, yes. A lovely piece of legal ballet. In capital crimes, the convicted were offered a choice between execution or forfeiture of their rights as citizens to become the property of the state. Typically, that meant a kind of forced labor on public works or hazardous occupations, but there were no defined limitations on their service. Through that loophole, we were able to divert the most heinous offenders here. There were always plenty... until the alien provocation. The Eleto's exterminations were so complete, that suddenly I had no more replenishments. Research halted when I ran out of inventory."

"Eh-LEE-toh?"

"Yes. Don't you know? The blue-skinned creatures that destroyed Earth. The ones who built that marvelous ship you arrived in. They call themselves, 'Eleto'."

"*Eleto*...You tested them as well?"

"Extensively. Chiefly to ascertain their biological processes and to discover vulnerabilities. They proved far too delicate for my purposes here, so I turned over my notes to Dr. Jin Sung, who continued the experiments upon them."

"Which was what, exactly?"

"Viral agents, primarily. He and I spoke very little, as I found him a petty, irritating man. His ideas were imminently suspect, riddled with false hypotheses. A poor scientist." Voss's tongue licks his dry lips. "But enough about him. You were interested in *my* research, yes?"

"Yes, I am. In all of your experiments, you must have had successes. Where are they now?"

"The best specimens are interred in the *Cooler* as references. The failures are in the *Graveyard*."

"*Graveyard*?"

"A naturally occurring cavern in the rock, like this room, but unfinished. Specimens we may wish to retrieve someday are archived by railed hangers. Otherwise, it is a dumping ground for exhausted test subjects."

The Brick looks up to the ceiling, imagining a similar space filled with spent human corpses. *I must not react,* the Brick mentally chants, reeling himself back, *I must follow the Colonel's example. I MUST NOT REACT.*

He summons his Operator conditioning and slams it down on the rising hostility. Cool rationality and logical patience smother the emotional sparks before they ignite, before they can show in the stony features of his face.

"Regarding Voss's mind..." the Brick resumes. "Have you erased it, or isolated it, or...?"

"His mind, what remains of it, is in isolation. I have not yet found a way to erase the mind without damaging the brain, despite *hundreds* of attempts. However, I do not believe cutting to be the best solution, either. Ideally, I will find a way to delete the host mind while leaving the entire neural network intact."

"Can you transfer the host mind *out* the way you transfer the donor mind *in*?"

"*Transfer* is the wrong word to describe the process. *Copying* is more appropriate, or perhaps *imprinting*. You see, the host mind remains in the original flesh, while awareness, memory, and experience is imprinted to the new flesh."

"So this process is a kind of...what? Mental *cloning*?"

"If you will."

"So when you uploaded, your original body...Honniker, the *real* Honniker—"

"*I am* the real Honniker."

"Okay, the original, then. The original Honniker was still viable?"

"Yes."

"What happened to him?"

"My husk expired long ago. Limitations of fleshly existence."

"If you chose to, could you...Have you imprinted yourself into Voss?"

"No. I merely use him from time to time. It can be useful having a servant to pull levers, carry loads, load reactants, etcetera. Once freed of flesh, I reflect upon the experience as confining, constricting. I have no desire to return."

Argo cradles his chin, thinking about Beckert floating in his tank, bloated body wrecked beyond repair. *He was a brilliant Operator, so much potential, just inexperienced.* Thompson's oath to return the young Geek echoes in his mind, an oath he took as his own. The memory brings with it the stabbing guilt from how little of Beckert they brought back. *Could he benefit from this? Yes, I think he could.*

"What do you need from me?" the Brick asks.

Again, Voss's mouth curves into the joyless smile. "I'm glad you understand."

The vault door swings open, and Shao-Lo leans past it. With a flick of her head, she beckons Argo over then ducks back inside.

The Brick collects his labset and cannon. "Excuse me, Doctor."

The pale figure makes no reply.

Argo jogs to the open vault door and salutes with the labset. Shao-Lo acknowledges with a nod.

"Come and assist Carter," the Colonel says.

"Yes, sir."

He follows the tall woman into a refrigerated space that condenses his breath. Despite the narrow entryway, the chilly vault expands to half the width of the experiment chamber in the back and rises to a ceiling half as high. Isolated operating rooms occupy the ground level of the left and right walls. Heavy metal shutters are recessed into the back wall.

Above the individual operating rooms are close rows of doors, one-meter square with mechanical latches and round corners. Most of them are open with sliding slabs extending like metal tongues, some with complete human or reptilian remains, others with dark blobs in frosted jars. Only one slab is unoccupied, its circular metal clamps suggesting it once held a cylinder of some kind.

Shao-Lo's long strides lead Argo quickly past multiple operating rooms. As he passes, he looks in through hazed observation windows and sees the same medical stations from the experiment floor. All of them bear a uniform layer of frost. Why they are separate from the stations out on the main floor, he is unsure.

Maybe these were to dissect cadavers...a chilled room would slow or prevent decay...

All the way down, on the right, one operating room door is open with Deepak and Keiko standing relaxed guard beside it. They salute Shao-Lo as she ducks through the doorway into the room.

When Argo follows, warmed air caresses his chilled face. With it comes the smell of antiseptic, but also notes of putrefaction and effluence. His nose wrinkles at the acrid tang.

Carter stands at the room's center, his massive frame eclipsing the medical station he hunches over. Zuri sits on a stool beside him, her HDI linked into a beeping medical cart. Her goggles flash with streaming data.

Without turning, Carter says, "Argo, bring me your labset."

Argo looks for a clear spot to set down his cannon and freezes. On a table in the back corner he sees a partially defrosted jar and inside, suspended in clear gel, is a human head with attached spinal column.

Sad eyes peer vacantly from the gel. The mouth hangs slightly open. A metal plate covers the base of the severed neck, dangling short hoses with metallic couplings. Every bone of the spine is encased in shiny alloy, from the cervical vertebrae of the neck, down the reverse curves of the thoracic and lumbar vertebrae, through the spade-like sacrum to the pointed coccyx.

Between the bones, a protective red ring surrounds each intervertebral disc. The spinal nerves, sprouting from the vertebral column and shrouded by the protective red material, are docked a short way from the vertebrae, each ends fitted with an iridescent cap. Argo leans closer, marveling at the level of craft and care taken to individually encase each bone while maintaining its independent movement.

"Sergeant? Your labset?"

Argo straightens and sets his cannon on the floor beside the table. When he turns, he sees Carter looking at him, hand out. Behind the giant Brick, an atrophied human leg is propped in the air, foot lashed into a metal stirrup. Long toenails hang like curling vines from clenched toes.

Argo walks the labset to Carter, hands it over with a respectful, "Sir," then faces the medical station. Reclined before him on an angled table is a woman with both legs raised in gynecological stirrups. Withered arms are drawn tight against double mastectomy scars on her thin chest. Like her toenails, long uncut fingernails hang from clenched, bony hands. Her head is thrown back in a padded head restraint, feeding tube, tracheotomy tube, and fixed injection point radiating from a thick metal collar at her neck. Below her clenched arms is a distended abdomen bearing countless white and purple stripes from stretching. A medical drape covers her hips, affording only the crudest modesty, yet not enough to conceal the tubes and pipes diving into her.

Argo frowns at the frail creature as he moves to her head. Sickly reddish-gray hair hangs from her scalp in oily locks down to the floor. Both eyelids and her mouth are stitched shut. Like Voss, large block numerals are inked into her chest.

"We can't let Sharon in here," Argo states.

"Agreed," Shao-Lo replies with arms crossed. She shifts her weight to her back leg.

Argo removes the bulky rack from his back and sets it down against a wall. Unpacking his medkit, he asks, "What have we got?"

"This is Rosenthal. Or *was*," Carter says, linking Argo's labset into the medical cart. "Now she's an incubator."

Argo hefts his medkit and sets it down on a nearby table. He touches a button and it opens like a flower, revealing myriad surgical tools.

"I don't see any children around here."

Carter thumbs the labset, pulling data from the medical cart and merging it with live data from Rosenthal.

"She's not carrying to term. The embryos are being harvested."

"For what?"

"Shall I explain again?"

The Operators' heads and eyes lift at the sound of Honniker's omnipresent voice.

"Go ahead, Doctor," Carter says.

"As a fellow medical expert, I'm sure you are aware how difficult it is to repair damaged neuronal tissues."

"I am," Argo affirms.

"Embryonic stem cells and germ cells hold excellent potential for regenerative therapies, quite valuable in restoring injured soldiers, as you know. However our mission was to build the most capable soldier possible. The Cadre One project began with genetic manipulation to produce a more hardy, capable, and aggressive fighter. But Mikato and I had a grander vision."

Argo rolls his eyes at Honniker's self-aggrandizement. "Which is...?"

"We analyzed the human body down to its individual advantages and weaknesses, its assets and its vulnerabilities. The human's need to breathe made it vulnerable to air-borne weapons, suffocation or asphyxiation. The need for food and water allowed the possibility of starvation, or poisoning, and produced copious wastes. Fragile bones are too easily broken or crushed. Delicate skin too easy to flay, pierce, or scorch. Despite a muscle's potential to strengthen, it can never approach the potential of electro-active polymers. Thus, in the finest analytical fashion, we discovered the only part of the human body that could not be adequately replaced by superior machinery was the nervous system. A soldier's ability to think and react, his awareness, his intuition are essential attributes. Assuming we could remove and transplant that capability into a reinforced chassis with its own internal life support, we could exponentially increase the combat effectiveness of a single soldier while simultaneously increasing efficiency."

"But how do you compensate for the losses in converting chemical signals to electronic?" Argo asks, genuinely interested.

"Based on our breakthrough with the synaptic bridge, Mikato prepared a socket which could cap a properly severed nerve bundle. The difficulty was getting the nerve bundle to bond with the socket. I discovered that if we prepared the socket with stem cells, the severed nerve bundle would attach and by reverse electrical stimulation, we could encourage individual neurons to connect where we wanted them, thus achieving a reliable interface from organic to synthetic. Unfortunately, adult stem cells

caused frequent complications due to rejection. Embryonic stem cells, however, harvested from a week-old blastocyst or germ cells from fetal gonad precursors provide the most stable and reliable results."

Argo looks at the jar in the corner and walks toward it. With new understanding, he studies the iridescent caps over the spinal nerves.

"That's a lot of stem cells, Doctor."

"Indeed. When inventory was plentiful, obtaining them was rather simple. Now, we must simply be patient..."

Argo's eyes follow the intricate spine, and he admires the skill and effort. But when he reaches the face, the sad, staring eyes force him to confront the brutality of the procedure. He looks into those twin windows, unable to dispel his understanding of what they endured.

"Must've been a long surgery."

"One thousand, six hundred, fifty-six hours in total," Honniker says with audible pride.

Argo's big hand curls to a fist and he leans on his knuckles against the wall as Honniker elaborates without being asked.

"Mikato fashioned the metal fitments for Summers's neck and spine with vascular channels for blood flow, but I performed the operation myself. You cannot imagine how painstaking the procedure was, how at any second, an artery could be nicked; a nerve bundle could be damaged. What steady control it required, and patience. Starting at the coccyx, I worked up in stages, leaving the excised structures in place and open, managing infection, testing each successive spinal interface and stimulating the neurons into proper configuration until, AT LAST! The specimen was ready and I could connect to external blood enrichment and sever the trachea, carotid, and jugular..."

The excited voice trails off.

"Imagine then, my disappointment, when this masterpiece of intellect, endurance, and skill—rivaling any of history's great artisans—dies only moments after separation. I attribute the cause of death to a seizure, possibly from the shock of seeing its own body as I lifted the head and spine away. So much effort, lost."

Argo takes a great lungful of air and pushes away from the wall. He feels the adrenaline in his system stirring him toward an unknown action. Around him, Shao-Lo, Carter, and Zuri look at the floor, their faces dour and grim. The medical monitor beeps in regular cadence.

Argo shakes his hands, palms sweaty inside his gauntlets, and he allows the Operator conditioning to take over again, to suppress the urges to violence. He steps over to Rosenthal and looks her over from gnarled toes to matted hair.

"Your patient doesn't look well, Doctor," he says with astounding evenness.

"I fear she may be at the end of her usefulness. Productivity has dwindled in recent years, despite my best efforts of hormone therapy. It seems her perpetual state of pregnancy plays havoc with any regime I attempt. There were few females here to begin with, and it was quite lucky that she and the other colonists came by. When she is finally exhausted, however, I shall require a new source of embryonic cells."

Argo rests a hand on her matted head and strokes the oily locks. Beneath a ruddy curl, he finds an incision scar. When he lifts the hair on the opposite side, he finds a matching scar.

"She's lobotomized?"

"Yes. It was necessary, as her anxiety levels caused her to spontaneously terminate pregnancy."

"You had no problem dissecting Summers. Why not just remove her reproductive organs or culture the cells you need in vitro?"

"Efficiency. Unlike Summers, whose blood could be enriched with small amounts of nutrients, Rosenthal required larger intake of food stuffs to assemble the embryos. She already had the essential equipment built in. While messy, this is the method of highest productivity."

Argo stands directly above her and places his hands on each side of her slack face. *Cadre One has had its share of experiments as well,* he thinks, *but this...it seems different. I don't see benefit to others, only satisfaction of curiosity. This woman, and Voss, they were whole when they came here. Now, they're broken. Alive, but not living... And Summers...*

The Brick forces himself to look at the jar, with its grotesque construct of man and machine.

No matter the lessons learned...This is wrong.

The instinct to rage builds in his chest again, revving the engine of his heart.

A quick twist ends this...

He feels the readiness of his arms to surge like lightning, to transmute his elementary pragmatism into mercy. But when he looks at Shao-Lo, she is staring back with wide eyes and tight jaw. The sinews in her neck are tense.

What am I doing?

Argo feels the readiness drain from his arms, and he lets his hands slide from Rosenthal's face. Shame fills him for allowing his impulses free reign. He sobers and returns to the appropriate austerity of a Cadre Operator.

THE EXHAUSTED DEAD

"It got very quiet all of a sudden," Honniker asks. *"Is everything all right?"*

"Everything's fine, Doctor," Shao-Lo says. "We're pain avoiding creatures, and it takes us a moment to see past pain to the ultimate goal."

"Ach, well, as you are still flesh, that sounds reasonable. I'm sure that before I uploaded, I might have reacted in the same. The important thing is that you do see past the petty details to the magnificent accomplishment. Well, there is little more to see here. Would you like to see something new?"

The offer is heavy, like a sack of lead around the soldiers' necks.

"Sure," Shao-Lo says without enthusiasm.

"This, I am certain you will like."

Shao-Lo points at Zuri, and says to her, "Continue the data upload. Let's get everything."

Zuri acknowledges from her stool, "Aye, Sir."

"Okay, Doctor," Shao-Lo says. "Where to?"

A metallic screech and clatter draws the Operators out of Rosenthal's room into the chilly main floor of the vault. There, the center shutter on the back wall is fully retracted, revealing a storage room of frosted boxes on pallets. Beneath the frost, Soshiba Varicorp logos are stamped into every box.

Carter, Shao-Lo, and Argo stride toward the open shutter and stand at the threshold. White vapor rolls off the boxes and spills over their feet.

"What are we looking at?" Shao-Lo asks.

"A virus, contractible only by the alien life forms. One hundred percent lethal in clinical testing. Designed and manufactured to specification at Cadre One, tested here."

Argo steps forward and rubs the frost from one of the SoVar logos. When he does, the box shifts, and something slides behind the top box, wedging into the gap. The Brick fishes it out and discovers a palm-sized device. To his amazement, the display lights up. After a brief boot up, the screen displays, *Do you want to view the last document?* Argo juts his lip and selects, *Yes* from the option window.

The screen displays a chain of custody form, describing a shipment of medical supplies bound for New Dresden. He frowns. While cradling the device in one hand, he rips open the nearest container. Beneath dense packing foam are crowded racks of seemingly empty glass vials. They *clink* against one another at his rummaging. At the bottom of the crate, however, his hand brushes against an oblong object with a tapered end. Intrigued, he liberates the object from the crate and finds himself holding an eighty-millimeter projectile. A bright orange icon marks the casing: a central ring with three larger, broken circles overlapping it like back to back crescent

184

moons.

"Huh," he says, turning the projectile over one handed. He looks back at the small device in his other hand and scrolls down, snorting when he sees the name at the bottom. He looks into the storage room, contemplating a row of empty pallets.

"Colonel," Argo calls. He lobs the device to the tall woman.

Shao-Lo smirks as she reads aloud, "Shipment received by Commander Braemar Keller."

"Field testing at New Dresden was a remarkable success," says Honniker. *"Complete kill-through of all infected with a very high rate of contagion. A very hardy strain, which many native species can carry and perpetuate for centuries. Thus, if the alien creatures should ever attempt to repopulate the contaminated area, the strain will quickly infect and destroy those exposed. One projectile holds enough biological agent to contaminate an area of three square kilometers. If the region utilizes modern transportation, and the infected are permitted to travel, the area of contamination is expanded exponentially."*

Carter, Argo, and Shao-Lo turn to one another, excitement butting up against their cool conditioning.

"If the incubation period is long enough..." Argo begins.

"...a few crates could wipe out a whole planet of them," Carter continues.

"And we could occupy it, knowing if the enemy returned, they'd be re-infected," Shao-Lo finishes.

The remaining shutters rise with noisy clatter and screeches. The three Operators step back, gaping at storerooms stacked to the roof with thousands of frosted boxes.

"This should be sufficient to end your war, don't you think?"

PRESUMED HOSTILE

Sharon clomps through the scorched and blasted hallways of
Cadre Two, pensive and troubled. Sensing the mood, Maiella matches pace
beside her, neither hurrying nor steering, eyes scanning every centimeter of
floor, ceiling, and wall for threats. Their helmet lamps shine far down the
seemingly infinite corridors, but there is little to see besides sooty residue,
broken fixtures, and an occasional dark splotch. Intersection by intersection
the two walk quietly.

Maiella looks down at her companion, watching Sharon's hunched
gait.

"It's gonna be okay, Sharon. We'll be leaving this place soon."

Sharon looks up from her gloomy trudge, sapped by a dispiriting
emptiness as hollow as Voss's remnant.

"How do you do it?" the colonist says at last. "How do you keep
hope alive?"

Maiella's lips purse at the question, her jaw flexes with a sympathetic
twinge. "What choice do we have?"

Sharon stops. She feels it coming: the involuntary contraction of the
diaphragm, the flow of saliva, the water in the eyes. Maiella reaches out to
her, but Sharon raises a hand.

"*No.* I have to cope with this."

Maiella waits vigilantly while Sharon stands straighter and drives the
desolation from her heart. She thinks about getting Voss out of this place, of
finding the others and escaping. Stuttering inhales smooth into calm breaths.

"Okay," the colonist says. "I'm ready."

"There's plenty of time."

"No, it's all right." Sharon strides forward, her helmet lights shining across the battered walls. "Let's go."

Maiella nods and walks beside her friend.

As the two move deeper through the unlit halls, marks of violence become less frequent until they cease entirely. Pristine corridors extend before them, white paint still clinging to the metal wall panels. Attached to the ceiling of every intersection is an unlit sign with arrows, indicating various labs and offices. Sharon pays them little mind until her helmet lamps illuminate a sign marked, *GRAVEYARD*. She stops cold at the single word with its yellow arrow pointing off to the right.

"Do you want to?" Maiella asks.

Sharon stares absently at the sign. Maiella is about to ask again when the colonist steps into the intersection and looks down the hallway to her right. At the end, a large circular pressure door bars further progress, its two halves locked together in a zigzag central seam. Discarded gurneys and boxy carts stand off to one side with cabinet doors open. Sharp hooks hang from bars inside the cabinets.

Sharon lowers her helmet lamps to the floor where mechanical tracks, smears, and drag marks obscure the white tiles. The stains cover the width of the corridor, leading in from the adjacent corridors all the way to the circular door.

"I don't think I'm up for that yet," Sharon says.

"Don't know that we could get in, anyway." Maiella pats her companion on the shoulder and takes a step aside.

"Radio check," the Geek says into her helmet mic, her voice strident in the silent corridor.

"Received," Argo replies.

"Located *Graveyard*. Sending position." The Geek's goggles pulse once.

"Position received."

"This section's powered down. Probably need you or Zuri to get in."

"Understood."

"Maiella out." The soldier turns and finds Sharon staring again, fixated on the dark smears on the floor that converge at the large door.

"We don't have to do this."

"Yes, we *do!"* Sharon snaps. "So stop *babying* me!"

Maiella rocks back at the unexpected lashing. Sharon whirls about, her lamps shining directly at the Geek's bewildered face.

"I'm sorry, I...I didn't mean it like that." Sharon's hands slide on her hips, seeking pockets to hide in but finding none. "I mean, I *know* this is important. You keep giving me ways out and that's...it's making it harder."

The soldier's eyebrows knit with thought. After a moment, the Geek looks up and strides aggressively toward Sharon.

"Jones, you'd better get your sorry ass moving, or I'll hang you from the rafters and use you as a practice bag!"

Sharon backs to the wall, eyes wide as receiver dishes, hands high in surrender.

"Whoa! Whoa! *Whoa!* Bloody hell!" the colonist pants.

Maiella halts in the middle of the intersection, her face scrunched. "What? Too aggressive?"

Sharon, her eyes still wide, hands still in the air, nods, "Uh, huh!"

Maiella grips her chin. Her eyebrows pop up. "Something encouraging, maybe?"

"Yeah," Sharon replies, lowering her hands and peeling herself off the wall. "Encouraging is good."

Maiella releases her chin. "Sharon, we're gonna be fine. Let's get this over with and get back to the others."

Sharon breathes deeply, one hand covering her racing heart. "Yeah, that's better." She walks up to Maiella and slaps her on the shoulder. "Don't *scare* me like that! *Christ!"*

"I wouldn't really have used you as a practice bag. You know that, right?"

Sharon looks up at her friend, amused at the sincerity in Maiella's face.

"You *were* pretty convincing..."

Maiella's jaw drops, mortified. Her arms wave in a pantomime of innocence. "There's no way! I could never hurt you like that! Besides, you're not even fifty kilos! If I kicked you once, you'd swing right up to the ceiling and what good is *that* to anyone, and...and..."

Sharon's howling laughter stops Maiella mid sentence. The colonist holds her hands up, one miming herself in a practice bag, the other dangling two fingers like legs. She flicks a finger at the bag and swings the hand in an arc, making it bounce off an imaginary ceiling with a thudding sound effect. She drops her hands to her belly and leans over for a huge roar.

Maiella squints at her cackling friend. She frowns again, having no idea what could be so hysterical, and pats Sharon's back when a shriek of metal scraping metal rolls from the darkness.

Sharon stands up, eyes wide again. Maiella's pistols are drawn, aiming down the corridor opposite the Graveyard. Their helmet lamps shine into the darkness. Two pinpoint reflections glint in the distance.

188

"*Get behind me,*" Maiella growls as she slides out of the intersection.

Sharon rushes behind her bodyguard, heart pounding, on the verge of panic. She shines her lamps down the other corridors. Behind them, back the way they came, another pair of reflections shines from the darkness.

"There's something behind us!" Sharon shouts, her voice amplified by fear. Maiella keeps one pistol trained on the original reflections and swings her other arm toward the new threat. Her goggles darken and take on a subtle red glow as she gazes down the corridor. Another shriek of metal rips from the darkness.

"What is it? *What do you see?*" Sharon begs.

Maiella's head swivels between the distant reflections. "We're moving. Stay close." The Geek glides away from her corner and crosses the intersection. "Contact with unknown life forms," she radios. "Presumed hostile."

"We're en route," Shao-Lo radios back. "Ping position and hold tight. Do not engage unless attacked."

"Understood. Maiella out."

Sharon's entire body trembles as she hustles away from the intersection. Her lights swing compulsively across the corridor ahead, finding only the unblemished walls, overlapping drag marks on the floor, and darkness beyond.

"What do you *see*?" Sharon pleads.

"Keep moving, quickly."

Maiella rises to the balls of her feet, each step inaudible. Her knees bend into a low glide, pistols level.

Sharon clomps ahead in her metallic boots then looks back toward the intersection. Two pinpoints, just out of distance of their lamps, glint closer than before. Another pair peeks around the corner.

The colonist's heart thuds in her chest, her breathing comes in terrified gasps.

"*Calm down!*" Maiella whispers, "*Keep your head, and watch forward!*"

Maiella continues her backtrack then halts. Crouching down, she extinguishes her helmet lights, seals her faceplate, and fades into darkness.

"Maiella! *MAIELLA!*" Sharon staggers like a wobbly top, spinning in all directions, trying to shine her light everywhere at once. Wherever she thinks she sees the black of the Geek's armor, she shines the light again but the black is gone. The reflections, however, draw steadily closer.

Quivering, Sharon no longer pivots about. She keeps her lights fixed on the approaching reflections as they shift and sway toward her. One shriek of metal, then another, rips out of the darkness.

Her diaphragm spasms, drawing short, panting breaths through her nose. Her back twitches, her hands reach out to each side, searching for something tangible to hide behind.

The reflections halt at the limit of her helmet lamps and lower to the ground. There is a scuffing sound, then a series of *thuds* as several hundred kilos of flesh and bone settle to the floor. The reflections blink and turn toward one another then resume their gaze.

Sharon stands as still as her twitching muscles will allow until hot breath washes over her from above. The shivering ends. She arches her back and looks up. Leaning out of an overhead hatch is an enormous feline head, covered in a mask of overlapping plates. Metal-capped teeth, bared for show, are just centimeters away. Paws the size of Argo's gauntlets perch at the edge of the hatch with talons curving around to the ceiling. The broad snout draws a great inhale, as if savoring an aroma.

Feeling abandons Sharon's body. She exhales with finality. Her bladder releases. She closes her eyes and waits for the killing bite.

Uncounted moments pass, and the beast withdraws with a throaty grumble, taking one paw away from the edge, then the other, raking its claws in a drawn out squeal.

Sharon opens her eyes, dopey with endorphin. She turns on rubbery legs and finds Maiella is right beside her like a blackened pillar, pistols aimed into the hatchway.

The dazed colonist looks down the corridor. The reflective eyes are gone. In the distance, multiple helmet lights approach, swaying as if in full sprint.

"I'm buh...I'm buh..." Sharon mumbles, and she falls forward, unconscious.

SAFE AS HOUSES

Sharon finds herself lying on the floor in a broad corridor. Deepak and Keiko crouch beside her with rifles level, covering opposite directions. Argo kneels by her head, thumbing his labset. Shao-Lo and Maiella stand off to one side, talking.

"...was an ambush," Maiella says, "cleanly executed."

"Same creatures we saw in MedLab?"

"No question."

Sharon tries to sit up when Argo's big hand gently presses her back down. "Easy, Sharon, just relax." The Brick pivots on his knee and looks over his shoulder. "Colonel, she's awake."

Shao-Lo strides over and kneels beside Argo. Even on their knees, they look colossal.

"Are you okay?" the tall woman asks.

Sharon blinks, trying to focus on Shao-Lo's face. Her eyes are unwilling to converge and she rubs them with the rough gloves of her suit.

"I don't know." She looks at Argo. In the low light he is like a boulder at dusk. "Am I okay?"

Argo smiles. "You had a sudden drop in blood pressure."

"Huh?"

"You fainted."

Sharon rolls her eyes, then notices her mouth feels dry with a pasty coating. Her tongue feels too large, crowding against her teeth. She smacks a couple of times and rolls onto her side.

"I feel so foggy," she gripes. As she rolls, she feels wetness below her belt extending to both feet. "Oh, no." Her face goes crimson with embarrassment. "Colonel, I need the restroom."

Shao-Lo squints, not understanding.

"The head," Argo translates.

"Ah." Shao-Lo offers a hand. "Let's get you up."

Sharon takes the Colonel's hand, letting herself be pulled to her feet. Liquid squishes beneath her instep and she averts her eyes in child-like shame. Argo rises beside his Colonel, holding his labset up to Sharon's head and thumbing the display.

"Yeah, yeah, I'll be fine," Sharon says, fending off Argo's machine. "I just need the restroom."

"Deepak! Keiko!" Shao-Lo calls with husky barks. "Escort Sharon where she needs to go."

"Eh, Deepak...no offense," the colonist hedges, "do you mind if Maiella comes instead? It's a woman thing."

Deepak's face wrinkles with confusion. He turns to his Colonel.

"That's fine," Shao-Lo says, "but just a moment." She crooks a finger at Maiella, beckoning her over.

"Heya, Sharon," Maiella says. "How you doin'?"

Recent moments come back in a rush: blood-stained floors, reflective eyes closing in, her inadequate light swinging back and forth in the darkness, hot breath and savage teeth just centimeters away, claws like curved daggers, and Maiella nowhere to be seen.

"Where WERE you?"

Maiella blinks again at the sudden fury in the small woman's face. She holds her hands up, palms open. "I'm sorry, Sharon, but it was a trap. I had to get out of the light to maneuver."

"You left me all alone! I could have *died*!"

"I was right here the whole time, you just didn't see me. More important, neither did they. I had to make it look like you were alone to draw out the one hiding."

"I was *bait? That's supposed to make me feel better?*"

"I had clean kill shots on all of them. You weren't in danger. But I don't think they were going to attack, anyway. I think it was more of a... uh..." Maiella struggles for elusive words. "I think they were trying to tell us something, something like, 'Hey, we know you're here, and we're smart enough to get you in a trap, and we can get you if we want to,' sort of thing."

"A show of strength?" Argo summarizes.

Maiella points at him. "Exactly."

"Where'd they come from?" Shao-Lo asks.

Maiella shakes her head. "There's a lot of this place we haven't seen yet. Could be anywhere."

"And you saw three?" Shao-Lo asks. "You're certain?"

"Positive. The body plates minimize their heat signature, but I saw them in infrared clear enough. There were three." She flicks her head at the nearby ceiling hatch. "And that one up there was *definitely* in charge."

Shao-Lo nods, collating the input. "Better let Keller know." She turns on her heel and speaks into her helmet mic, "Keller, this is Shao-Lo. Keep the transport locked. Jin-Sung's pets are alive and prowling."

The tall woman waits for a response.

"Keller?"

Anxious seconds tick by.

"Keller, *respond*."

There is no reply.

Shao-Lo points at Deepak, Keiko, and Argo. "You three, get to the transport, *now*."

"Aye, sir!" they shout. Argo stuffs his labset into his rack and snatches his cannon from the floor before following the two Guns.

"Zuri, Carter, respond."

"We're here, Colonel," Carter replies.

"We have creatures on the prowl, presumed hostile. Keller is non-responsive. Secure the *Cooler* and fortify MedLab as our primary retreat."

"Understood."

"Shao-Lo out."

Sharon's eyes dart back and forth between Maiella and Shao-Lo, searching them for an indication of the danger. There is urgency, but far more than that there is invigoration. The division so plainly stated between the two has dissolved, their years of combat training and experience uniting them as partners in a common fight.

"Geek, continue on mission. Scout forward, radio silent. Defensive engagement *only*."

"Aye, sir!" Maiella barks. She drops her faceplate, and just before it seals, Sharon watches the edge of her mouth curve upward.

My God, she's enjoying this.

The colonist searches Shao-Lo for the same feeling. Though Shao-Lo's mouth is straight as always, her cheeks are lifted, the corners of her eyes are tucked, her gray eyes are bright.

This is what they're made for...

Confidence, pouring from the two Operators, spills into the emptied vessel of Sharon's resolve.

They'll protect me. I don't need to be afraid.

Maiella draws her pistols and stalks into the darkness ahead, folding into it, a predator more dangerous than any other creature in the universe.

"Sharon, let's go," Shao-Lo says.

"Sure. Wait...Where are we going?"

"Honniker said Jin-Sung's pets were all dead. They're clearly not, which means there are other parts of this facility still functioning. We need to assess the threats we face. And if Keller is still alive, we have to find him."

"Where do we start?"

"With your original plan—the *Park*. We'll go from there." The Colonel drops the faceplate of her helmet and extinguishes her lamps. Her rifle slides from its slung position into her ready hands as if by its own volition. A wicked-looking black bayonet slides into place with a barely audible *shick*.

"I'll be right behind you," she says through her helmet speaker. "Move fast."

"Just a tic. Could we hold a moment?" Sharon kneels and detaches the ankle collars joining her suit's pant legs to her boots. "Sorry, I *have* to take care of this before we go anywhere."

She hooks a thumb on the back of each stiff boot and slides her feet out. Groaning, she peels the soggy liners from inside each boot and twists them in her gloved hands. Amber liquid wrings from the spongy, rubber-soled liners and patters on the metal floor.

Shao-Lo turns and looks behind them, whether to keep guard or allow privacy, Sharon cannot tell.

"Ooh, this floor is cold," the colonist says, hopping from one foot to the other and leaving wet footprints. She slips the liners over her feet like soft shoes and steps into her boots. "Almost done," she says, reconnecting the ankle collars.

Whatever's coming, she tells herself, *I'm going to be all right. There's nothing tougher than these bashers. I'm safe as houses...*

"Okay, I'm ready," Sharon announces. After three deep breaths she runs after Maiella, and as she runs, she repeats to herself, *I'm going to be all right.* With Maiella scouting ahead and Shao-Lo directly behind, it is easy for her to believe.

ANILA

Deepak and Keiko lead the way through corridors, their rifles pulled in tight at the shoulder. Argo runs backwards behind them, gripping his cannon with both hands, sweeping it side to side in their wake. The three grind a swift pace, favoring speed over stealth, and as they stampede the litter of debris, echoes reverberate in the desolate halls.

Keiko grunts one word directions, and the team moves as a single entity—a constantly shifting triangle of eyes, limbs, and firepower flowing down gradually widening passages—until they are sprinting down the central artery of the facility, past sprawled alien corpses and a dried-out creature named "Daisy," through the trash-strewn entryway of destroyed portraits, into the narrow service corridor, and finally breaking stride inside the hangar bay airlock. Argo slings his cannon and seals the inner door while Deepak and Keiko step to each side of the outer door.

"Clear portal," Keiko calls, her voice calm and even between deep breaths. "Deepak, take low. I take high. Argo, take the door."

Argo crosses the small compartment and takes hold of the outer door latch. To his surprise, the display shows the air pressure in the hangar bay is already equalized.

"Ready," Argo announces.

Keiko and Deepak step back, aiming at the door.

"Release," Keiko orders.

Argo rips the door aside, and Deepak sprints at the opening. The Gun dives through then rolls to his feet and runs. He levels his rifle, scanning side to side in his dash for the parked transport ahead of him.

Keiko steps out immediately after and aims her rifle over the airlock threshold. With no loitering threats over the doorway, she spins about in pursuit of Deepak. The rugged woman sweeps her eyes across the high ceiling and heaps of shattered spacecraft, finding nothing but old burns and wrecked electrical fixtures.

The two Guns arrive at the transport then kneel beside the rear landing struts, keeping watch in opposite directions over the surrounding junk piles.

"Brick, search vessel," she calls.

Argo charges from the airlock and runs straight for the transport. He throws his cannon's strap over his head and leaps onto the ladder, making the whole craft squat beneath his bulk. The Brick powers up the rungs in two movements, then raps his knuckles against the transport hatch.

"Keller, you in there?" he shouts.

There is no answer.

Argo thrusts the hatch open and peeks through. The entire cabin is available to him in a single glance, from the dual benches on either side up to the twin pilot chairs in front. No one is inside.

With a cautious eye for booby traps, Argo moves into the vessel. He rummages through the interior, tossing seat cushions, opening cubbies, cabinets, compartments. The craft is as they left it, but there is no sign of Keller.

"He isn't here," the Brick announces.

"Colonel," Keiko calls via radio, "we've arrived at transport. No sign of Keller."

"Any show of struggle?" Shao-Lo responds. "Forced entry?"

"No, sir," Argo answers with a trace of disappointment. He takes another tour of the cabin as a final confirmation. "His helmet isn't here, either. Think he went for a walk?"

"I should've put a *collar* on him," Shao-Lo says derisively.

"Does Honniker know where he is?" Argo asks.

"Honniker isn't talking," the colonel answers, irritated. "Keiko, begin search of unexplored areas. Work your way back toward the *Park*. We rendezvous there. SitRep every fifteen."

"Aye, sir," Keiko calls. "Report every fifteen minutes. Deepak, Argo, on me."

Argo takes a last look at the transport interior and scoots out through the open hatch. Before he seals it, he takes a tiny device from a compartment on his rack comprised of two flat cylinders, connected by a microscopic thread. He places one of the small cylinders on the interior hatchcoaming, and it *tinks* with magnetic attraction. The other, he places on the inside of the hatch itself, thread spooling out behind it. Slowly, he slides the hatch into place, ensuring the almost invisible thread remains taught as it recoils. A brief confirmation message displays in his visor, *Passive sensor armed.*

The Brick drops to the deck with a *thud*, takes his cannon from his shoulder, and forms up with his superiors.

"As before," Keiko orders.

The Operators move through the airlock, then seal it before moving on. They push through the narrow service corridor, make an immediate left in the littered entryway, run through the parted doors to the central hallway and break off down an unexplored corridor. Purplish lenses watch their every step.

The team streaks through intersections, some marked with broken or non-functioning ceiling signs indicating Holo-Cinema, Zero-G Recreation Hall, Cafeterias and Fine Dining, Sensorium, Taverns and Wet Bars, Spas. All of them are sealed behind heavy pressure doors. Argo glances at every one, looking for signs of recent use, but the doors lack any warmth of recent operation.

Tedious kilometers of damaged hallways roll by until the team arrives at a wide Y-shaped intersection. The stem of the Y is far broader than the other two limbs, and it leads to a heavily reinforced pressure door that spans the corridor. Though the two halves of the door are closed, its central seam has been wedged and pried open into a rumpled ellipse nearly two meters tall and a meter wide. Sooty electrical burns mar the doorjambs. Amid the thickly folded metal and electrical scorches is the crinkled image of a cartoon raccoon. It wears the same spectacles and white lab coat as on the entrance to MedLabs, yet this one peers at a small test tube in its grip and is ringed by a continual double helix of DNA. On the right wall, the access panel is little more than a rectangular hole in the wall, vomiting singed power and data cables.

Keiko thrusts up a hand, then points to either side of the pried gap. Argo and Deepak hustle into place and stand ready.

As he waits, Argo shines his lamps over the ruined doors. Fifteen centimeters of bonded ceramic, fiber, and alloy plate laminate stands warped, cracked, and folded upon itself. At the top and bottom of the seam, the doors have been dragged out of their tracks from the compression. And all of the locking teeth along the wedged gap are broken off, leaving white scars of metal fatigue. Argo whistles to himself in admiration of such brute force.

"Colonel Shao-Lo," Keiko radios, "found signs of forced entry into what may be another research wing. Pinging location."

"Received, Keiko," Shao-Lo radios back. "Investigate."

"Understood."

The Gun hand signals to Deepak and Argo: *caution, advance, search.* Argo feels the warm flow of aggression in his blood, the promise of action. His hands tighten around his cannon grips. He thumbs the safety off.

Keiko and Deepak divert to one side of the massive rip, their rifles aimed into the dark space within. Argo palms a puck-shaped device from his waist and pinches the flat sides three times.

"Clear!" he shouts and hurls the puck through the rip. The Operators take cover behind the doors, averting their eyes. From inside, there is a pop and a burst of stellar intensity.

Keiko rushes into the fading light, Deepak immediately behind. The two cross paths and sprint behind their readied weapons.

Argo straddles the opening and squeezes sideways between the wrinkled doors. Ahead of him is a wide-open cavern, roughly half the size of Honniker's main experiment floor and more circular, with three more passages cut into the periphery like the main points of a compass. At center is a low pedestal planted with thin, wavy pillars. A massive figure, hewn from native stone, sits cross-legged atop the pillars with arms raised to each side.

While the two Guns run up each side of the large room, Argo glances back through the rumpled entry doors. He backs away from them, training his cannon on the gap and covering it against unwelcome followers.

"Main floor clear," Keiko announces via radio. "Deepak, form up. Argo, move center and guard portals."

"Guard portals, aye," Argo confirms. He glides back to the statue at the room's center, then stands as resolute as the stone structure beside him. His head swivels from side corridor to entryway to opposite corridor and back. But with every turn of his head, in his peripheral vision, strange details in the statue call for his attention. Between glances at the portals, he risks a closer look at the statue.

Surrounding the statue's pedestal is a deep basin, lined with light blue tile, crusty with white mineral deposits. Dark stains interrupt the bottom, topped with chitinous scales and needle-like translucent bones.

Near the center, the basin grows shallow, and at the high-water mark begins a progression of embedded brass figurines. Insects and fish-like amphibians are furthest down the slope, then reptiles on four or two legs. Birds and mammals of remarkable diversity mingle with the largest reptiles, nearly replacing them. Hanging from the pedestal's lip, primates peek over the edge at the towers of waving pillars. Argo follows the progression, recognizing some of the brass creatures from colonist archives and from his journey to Earth, then he focuses on the statue itself.

The wavy pillars he spied from across the hall are in fact enormous double helixes of DNA. Small brass hominids climb the rungs of DNA like ladders, beginning as apish babies at the base and becoming full-grown human men and women as they ascend. Halfway to the top of the DNA ladders, the humans seem stuck, looking and reaching up for assistance.

Argo raises his lamps higher, illuminating the figure sitting atop the DNA pillars. There, carved from dark metallic stone, he finds the object of the climbing humans' pleas: a bare-chested, boyish man, sitting cross-legged, with not one but two pair of arms branching from the broad shoulders. The lower pair hangs down to the lap, relaxed, palms of the hands up. In the raised right hand is a trident with three equal tines. In the left is a small hourglass-shaped drum, skinned at both ends. A hooded serpent coils loosely around the neck, along with numerous beaded strings. A conical pile of hair is neatly bundled upon the head, and long locks drape down the back. The young face bears an expression of serenity, wisdom, and calm amid deep contemplation.

"Brick, form up," Keiko calls from the back of the room.

In an instant, Argo dismisses the statue and hustles to his companions at the back of the room. The two Guns lean against the edge of a round, ragged hole in the wall. Lying on the floor several meters away is a circular vault door, ripped viciously out of its frame, its thick hinges twisted and torn.

Deepak hooks his rifle around the rough opening, shining its spotlight into a wide room with low ceilings. The beam falls upon multiple cylinders that extend all the way from white tiled floor to metallic ceiling. At top and bottom, the cylinders are shrouded in stainless steel, but the middle thirds are transparent and empty.

"Watch rear," Keiko says to Argo as she and Deepak move into the vault.

Argo puts his back to the wall and settles into a wide stance, ready to trigger on the slightest hint of a threat. From his vantage at the back of the cavern, all entrances and exits are in easy line of sight. The statue is a natural focal point between them, however, and his eyes are drawn back to it. With all of its detail, it seems as if it were attempting to tell an entire story in still life. His eyebrows knit as he contemplates the meaning, if any.

Adding to the mystery is an intricate mural painted on the domed ceiling above. He gasps at the discovery, shining his powerful lamps over the vaguely humanoid forms. Many have multiple pairs of arms branching from their shoulders, some a third eye in the forehead. Some are tinted blue, some have the heads of animals. But one image holds the Brick transfixed: a nude woman with disheveled hair down to the waist, skin so deep blue it is nearly black, staring with wild, intoxicated eyes. A necklace of bloody severed heads drapes over her breasts down below her waist. Her long tongue hangs over fanged teeth to her chin and drips bright crimson. Her four arms reach out in exultation, hands clasping a hooked sword, a bowl overflowing with red liquid, a noose, and a severed head by the hair.

The image chisels through Argo's stony calm. He wants to look away, yet he cannot.

Madness...Insanity!

The image taunts him in its carnal, murderous freedom—a complete absence of reason or restraint, crazed and terrifying. His teeth grind and his lip twitches as he is overcome by a profound need to obliterate the sickening image before him, to scour it from the wall.

Is THAT what they were making here?

He forces himself to break the gaze and takes long inhales through his flared nostrils, letting his conditioning take over. He chastises himself.

I've never had so much difficulty maintaining control...Is it this place?

His pulse slows. His breathing normalizes.

Doesn't matter.

He looks one last time at the blood-lusted woman, glaring through his eyebrows. His thick hands squeeze the sturdy grips of his weapon.

I'll be ready for you.

Argo turns to the adjacent walls, noting how their substantial doorways have both been rammed open. He sidesteps so he can see past the central statue to the main entrance.

Did something force its way in...or out?

The Brick glances over his shoulder into the vault he guards, immediately recognizing the same incubation cylinders used at Cadre One. The transparent midsections are all empty, some smashed, and the metallic lower portions are streaked with dried fluids.

"Find anything?" he calls.

Keiko's voice drifts out from the vault with a metallic echo, "Some human remains, crushed, pulled apart. Long dead. Not Keller."

Deepak steps out first, followed by Keiko. They both shake their lowered heads.

"Must've sought refuge in there," Deepak guesses, "but didn't do 'em any good." He glances at the vault door and its disfigured hinges. "What could've done that?"

"Whatever it was, would have to be huge," Keiko says. The same thought occurs to the two Guns at once, and they dial up their weapon outputs.

"Passages to the left and right," Argo states. "Both portals forced."

"Let's check 'em," Keiko orders.

She and Deepak jog to the left wall, Argo trailing. The two Guns flank the battered doors, which hang loosely on tortured hinges. Argo shifts his cannon to one hand and places the other on the rammed door. At Keiko's nod, he thrusts it open. The door squeals in protest.

Keiko and Deepak race through a short hallway into a room nearly as large as the circular main cavern. Despite the size, it only takes a moment for Keiko to announce, *"Clear."*

Argo drifts backward through the hallway, cannon poised, and he finds himself in an open-floored chamber lined with alcoves. On the floor are regular sets of sockets and receptacles, yet whatever was installed over them has long since been removed. Nearly all of the alcoves are vacant with dangling cords and hoses save three, which contain severely damaged medical recliners. Keiko and Deepak linger at the nearest recliner, their helmet lights shining through a broken window on the crushed in lid, making the bright white fabric inside glow. Argo glances over.

"Find something?" the Brick asks.

Deepak and Keiko continue to stare. Deepak cocks his head to one side.

"Is that...? What *is* that?"

"No clue," Keiko answers. "Argo, get over here. Deepak, take rear guard."

Argo and Deepak trade positions. When the Brick peers into the smashed recliner, he looks into the sockets of a humanoid skull wrapped in peeling, papery skin. The face is elongated, implying either a short muzzle or a very pronounced overbite. The teeth are straight and even with the exception of enlarged canines.

"No..." Argo says absently. He thumbs the safety on his weapon and slings it, then takes hold of the recliner's crushed lid. With effort, he frees the damaged latches and lifts the lid, its hinges wheezing. Once the recliner is fully open, Argo steps back and stares at the freeze-dried remains. His lamps run from the humanoid head down over the delicate torso with its thin arm bones and taloned fingertips. A birdlike pelvis is pulverized where the smashing blow came down through the lid. But the Brick's lamps halt on the short tail, still connected with dried tendons, jutting a half-meter below the waist.

Argo scowls in revulsion.

"Hybrid."

"Of what?" Keiko looks back and forth between Argo and the remains. "Hybrid of *what*, Brick? Us? And the *Blueskins*?"

Argo nods and pulls the groaning lid shut with a clatter of loose plexisteel shards. Mortified, Keiko steps back and raises her rifle at the recliner as though its long dead occupant offers a real and present threat.

With a grunt, Argo strides off to the next recliner. Like the last, it is smashed in the middle, and loose plexisteel grinds under his boots. The Brick looks down at his feet and slides his toe through the scattered debris, marking how it radiates from the recliner like a fan.

"Hmm. This one was pressurized."

Keiko backs toward him keeping her rifle trained on the hybrid.

"Open it," she orders.

Argo finds the latches and after some rough handling gets them free. He lifts the creaking lid and finds freeze-dried human remains, clothed in the rags of a synthetic-fiber medical uniform. Its arms are neatly broken off below the short uniform sleeves, and the lower half of the body seems to have slid away from the upper half in a complete section.

The Brick takes in the variety of clues, deducing, "This one was frozen."

While Keiko looks on, Argo takes hold of several hoses feeding into the recliner.

"See these?" the big man asks. "Refrigerant lines. These recliners can freeze or incubate, looks like."

Keiko's eyes run the length of the body. "Is that why the body's in pieces?"

Argo looks at the caved-in lid. "Yeah. Must've shattered on impact"

"Another hybrid?"

Argo pokes at the brittle bones with a finger. "No. Human." He turns his head to try and read the remains of embroidery on the chest, but the staining and fraying is too advanced.

"Maybe she thought this was a way to hide," the Brick speculates. "Or escape."

"She?"

"I'm guessing, but the pelvis looks like a colonist female. It's shorter and wider than you'd normally find in a male this height. Bone is thinner, less dense."

"Anything else?"

Argo looks the body up and down one last time. "No, that's...Hold on."

He leans close to the face and takes hold of the jaw. With the slightest effort, the mandible detaches from the skull. Argo lifts the jawbone up into his helmet light. Tucked between the papery cheeks and teeth are thin memory cards.

Keiko converges her helmet lights on the bone. She parks her rifle on her hip and pulls one of the tiny cards free. Its clear plastic shines with internal circuitry.

"What have we got here?"

"Answers, maybe." Argo plucks the remaining cards from the jaw and tosses the bone back onto the recliner. He holds his palm out, and Keiko lays the fragile card on it.

"I'll keep these," the Brick states, tucking them into a compartment on his rack. "We'll share with the Colonel once we rendezvous."

"Right," Keiko confirms. "Come on, there's one more."

The two move to the last recliner. Though cracked, the lid is not crushed-in like the others. Argo slides his hands along the edges.

"Latches are broken," he notes.

Keiko pulls her rifle to her shoulder and takes aim.

"Go ahead."

Argo lifts the lid on an empty recliner. His bright lights pore over the white interior, but all he finds are three parallel rips in the bedding and a single dark spot.

"Is that blood?" Keiko asks, aiming her rifle at the spot.

Argo hunches over the bedding, spreading the torn fabric and foam. Bright metal reflects from beneath with deep scratches gouged into it. He nearly moves on when his lamps shine over three long, black hairs, hanging from an in-bent metal seam on the lid. He follows the hairs to a tiny patch of scalp, dug out by the sharp edge of cracked plexisteel.

"There was someone in here," Argo says. "But they were removed."

"The others were crushed," Keiko states, glancing over her shoulder. "Who was this guy, that he was taken out intact?"

The Brick reaches back to his rack and takes the same compartment from it. He opens the box and gestures to the dangling hairs.

"Would you?"

Keiko pinches the patch of scalp and carefully deposits it with the trailing hairs into the open box.

"What are you gonna do with this?"

"DNA sample. I can ID the occupant with my labset." The Brick considers saying more, telling her someone important enough to pull alive from the recliner might have even been Jin-Sung himself, a man both brilliant and insane enough to splice the codes of human and alien genetics. Without proof, he keeps the thought to himself, closes the compartment and fixes it back onto his rack.

"So why only three recliners here?" Keiko wonders aloud. "Forty-eight alcoves and seventy-two floor stations, but only three recliners?"

"Taken somewhere, is my guess."

"Taken where?" Deepak asks from across the broad room.

Argo snorts. "I'm sure we'll find out."

"One last place to search in this section," Keiko says. "Deepak, on point. Argo, take rear."

Deepak nods and glides into the short hallway leading out. Keiko follows, ballerina-light on muscular legs. Argo back steps from the room, his attention drawn against his will to the recliner with the humanoid hybrid. He slips his weapon off his shoulder and grips it solidly. If he had the vocabulary to match his thoughts, the word would be *abomination*.

He drifts along behind the others, crossing the wide main hall to the opposite corridor. The doors, much thicker than the ones opposite, are smashed all the way off their tracks and are folded against the interior wall. With the Guns on either side, Argo stands brazenly in front of the dark corridor, cannon fully primed, safety off, helmet lamp beams fading down a long hallway lined with doors and windows. His visor automatically compensates, allowing him to see the far end of the corridor. There, another vault door is ripped from its hinges and propped to one side.

"Go ahead," the big man says.

Deepak rushes into the hallway, watching left. Keiko runs just behind him watching right. Argo jogs after them at a more leisurely pace, looking through the windows of the rooms he passes. The rooms are filled with high-tech diagnostic equipment, flasks, vials of every size and shape, and floor-to-ceiling incubator tubes. Personal offices of researchers alternate between the individual laboratories, their frosted privacy glass labeled with name, title, and occasionally, military rank.

Deepak halts near the leaning vault door and peers into the room beyond. Keiko pauses beside him and looks back at Argo, waiting for him to catch up.

"What *is* all this?" Deepak asks.

Argo backs toward the vault and looks over his shoulder. Inside, three-meter high shelves have toppled away from the walls and overlap one another at the room's center. Hard-covered stacks of paper pile among the toppled shelves, flopped open haphazardly on their glue- and thread-bound spines. While Deepak keeps his rifle poised, Keiko kneels down and picks up one of the hard-covered bundles. She lays it open across her knee and fans the pages.

"There's writing inside."

"What's it say?" Argo asks.

Keiko turns to a dog-eared page and reads aloud, having difficulty with the unfamiliar words.

"...*People now began openly to venture on acts of self-in-dull-gents, which before then they used to keep in the dark. They resolved to spend their mon-nee quickly and to spend it on pleh-shure, since mon-nee and life seemed equally ep...eff...eff-emm-ur-ull...*"

She closes the cover and squints at the strange word there, printed in gold.

"*Thoo-cy-did-es...*"

Keiko closes the book and tosses it back on the heap. She rises, looking over the mounds.

"Why would anyone keep printed words? What a waste of space!"

She steps over the shifting piles to uncluttered flooring at the room's edge. Deepak follows.

"Hup! Got a body." Keiko calls. "Pinned to the wall. Argo, get in here. Deepak, take rear guard."

Argo steps onto the pile of books to let Deepak by, leather bindings creasing and tearing under his bulk. When Deepak is in position, the Brick steps down to clear flooring and aims his helmet lights at the left wall.

Partially obscured by a toppled bookshelf, a skeletal human torso is visible, stapled to the wall by two metal spikes through the shoulders. The skull slumps forward, chin against sternum. Sparse locks of long, dark hair drape down both sides of the peeling scalp.

Argo looks down to make sure his path is clear then steps around the obscuring bookshelf. The lower half of the impaled body has dropped into a scattered pile of bone below. The Brick frets at the skeleton with its shredded and stained lab coat hanging below the stub of its spinal column, and he concentrates on the impaling spikes.

"Right below the shoulder joints, through both scapulae," he notes.

Keiko's helmet lights overlap his. The double intensity highlights a fine spray of ancient blood on the wall, surrounding the body like a dark aura.

"Think this is the guy from the recliner?" she asks.

Argo searches the tattered clothing for embroidery or a nametag. Like the woman in the smashed recliner across the hall, the process of decay has destroyed any stitching in the fabric.

"Hair seems a match," the Brick says. His eyes shift to the left upper arm bone, which ends at a smooth cut above the elbow. The right arm bone bears an identical cut.

"His arms were amputated," Argo announces.

Keiko kneels down and sifts through the bones on the floor. She groans.

"Not just his arms."

Argo looks down at the assortment of bone. Every one has been cut, multiple times, from the foot bones up through the long leg bones. Even the lower arm and finger bones are crimped or cut.

Keiko extends her bayonet and uses it to lift the pelvis, her helmet lights shining through dozens of random holes drilled into it. The upper halves of severed femurs still root in the sockets.

"This one *really* suffered," Keiko says softly. She lowers her rifle, letting the perforated bone slide to the floor.

"Attention!" comes Zuri's voice over radio. "Main power coming on-line for remainder of station. Stand clear of all lifts and doorways, ensure hard seal of breathing apparatus. Repeat! Stand clear of all lifts and doorways, ensure hard seal of breathing apparatus."

The three Operators obediently test their rebreathers as distant clangs and jolts of closing power busses reverberate through the floor plates. The jolts get progressively closer until the room itself buzzes with igniting wall sconces and recessed ceiling lamps. One of the ceiling lamps explodes with a pop, raining blue sparks onto the heaps of paper.

The room looks much smaller once fully illuminated. Bare white walls and ceiling surround the team, save the tortured remains impaled on one side. Small LED bar signs come to life on the adjacent wall, indicating portals hidden by toppled bookshelves. Argo flicks his head toward them.

"Hey, there are other rooms to—"

"Greetings and welcome to Doctor Jin-Sung's office," interrupts a feminine voice from the middle of the room.

The three Operators bristle, aiming their weapons in an instant.

Moving shoulders-deep through the mound of books is a young woman with straight black hair and dark brown skin. She wears a clean white lab coat.

"I am Anila, Doctor Jin-Sung's assistant," the woman says with Hindi inflection. She passes through the books completely unhindered. "Please forgive me, I don't see any appointments scheduled at this time. May I ask your purpose?"

Keiko and Deepak lean into their rifles, but Argo looks up at the ceiling where red, blue, and green prisms flash like gemstones. Newly flowing ventilation ducts cough dust into the air, revealing the triple beams that converge on the woman moving through the heaps. Argo reaches over to Keiko's rifle and gently presses down on the barrel.

"It's a projection," he says.

As if on cue, the lights in the room flicker with re-routing power, and Anila's image distorts momentarily before smoothing out into her normal appearance. She emerges from the deeper piles of books and stands up to her knees at a conversational distance from Keiko and Argo.

"I do not wish to be rude," the apparition says, "but I must know your business. This is a restricted area."

"We're looking for Jin-Sung." Argo hikes a thumb at the skeletal remains. "Is that him?"

Anila looks at the remains. "DNA match is 100%." She frowns. "That is Doctor Jin-Sung."

"Anila, what are you?"

The holo-projection looks directly at Argo. "As I said, I am Doctor Jin-Sung's assistant." The projected woman takes a step back into the books and gestures toward the exit. "Now then, as you do not have an appointment, I must insist you leave the Doctor's office."

"I don't think he objects," Keiko says.

Anila considers Keiko's statement then turns toward the torso stapled to the wall.

"Doctor Jin-Sung, would you like me to remove these people?" The apparition waits for a reply.

Sensing opportunity, Argo says, "Doctor Jin-Sung, if you want us to leave, please say so."

Predictably, the corpse says nothing, yet Anila takes the silence as confirmation.

"Very well, you may stay," she concedes.

"Doctor, do you have any objection to Anila fully co-operating with us?" Argo continues. "If so, please say something."

Again, there is a predictable silence.

"Very well, Doctor," the assistant says. "If you have no objections, I will co-operate with your guests."

Wasting no time, Argo gets right to it.

"What happened here?"

"Can you be more specific?"

"There must've been thousands of people here at Cadre Two. Where did they go?"

"I'm sorry, but I have no data on that, as I am isolated from the common area network."

"Why?"

"To maintain security of data from intrusion or theft."

"What kind of data?" Keiko asks.

"Research of genetic modification and inter-species integration."

"You still have this data?" Argo asks.

"No. Data was transferred to portable media and purged from my memory."

"What's the portable media look like?" Keiko asks.

"Translucent cards two centimeters wide by three centimeters long."

Argo grins, knowing the cards in his rack have got to be the ones just mentioned.

"Why was the data purged?"

"There are twenty-seven journal entries which offer probable explanations. Shall I play the one with highest relevance?"

"You have his *personal journal?*"

"I do."

"Then, yes, play it!"

A holowindow opens beside Anila, in which is framed the head and shoulders of a dark-skinned, middle-aged man. His nose is the most prominent feature of his face, yet is not so out of proportion to make him unattractive. There is haughtiness in the eyes and subtle downward curve of the mouth. The hair on his temples is cropped short, the rest is tied neatly back in a long ponytail.

"Where at first I was immensely proud to be working with Doctors Honniker and Mikato, I now feel disgust for their excessive competitiveness. Moreover, they make effort to deride my work, claiming it is a dead-end, that without embracing the synthetic, my work will be vastly inferior to their own."

The haughtiness becomes irritation.

"I could *endure* their opinions if they weren't so influential with the finance committees. Despite my successes at Cadre One, and my length of service, I find myself having to repeatedly call on all of my resources to maintain funding.

"I find it *doubly* ironic in that given our mission to produce enhanced means of defense from alien threats, *I* have produced the only functional weapons. Mikato's robotics and directed energy projects show theoretical possibility, and Honniker's cybernetic interfaces may radically alter the form of humanity to come...yet *none* of their experiments have produced stable, useful results. The successful virus trials at New Dresden prove the efficacy and efficiency of my research, as do the genetic enhancements of our best soldiers. Even so, my competitive colleagues have managed to devalue the entire genetics program, and I find I must indulge the sick curiosities of the board just to maintain my budget each fiscal year."

Jin-Sung's face turns dour.

"Crossing human with alien...it is an *ugly* creation. Unwholesome. Unnatural. It shames me to have produced it, yet it was a requirement for my true research to continue. And it is *essential* the work *must* continue. Mikato and Honniker have left humanity far behind in their research, made evident by the degree to which they are replacing flesh with machine. They have no soul, no familiarity with life on a greater scale, and I pity them for that. I hear that Honniker even insisted on an...*anatomically correct*...android assistant. And Mikato? I believe he'd rather be fashioned completely of metal and polymer. There are gaping holes in these men, and a cold wind whistles through their hollow bones where a heart should be. I believe they could do anything. To anyone.

"It would be easy to mock them for such narrow vision, as *they* continue to mock *me*...but for the threat they represent. There is obvious danger in their ambitious partnership, but even more so to our survival as a *species*. When creating Gods, we must take care that they resemble us so they will look upon us with some affiliation, some link which binds, or we may find ourselves suddenly unnecessary.

"And on this point I must be clear: we *are* making *Gods*. Our quest for perfection is already planted within the nuclei of our cells, we have everything we need in the building blocks of our genes."

The doctor's face becomes dreamy, awash with radical amazement.

"In genetics, *ALL creation is possible.*"

He loiters in his lofty awareness then hurtles back to the present, eyebrows drawn together in suspicious unease.

"They must not destroy my research. They *must not.*" The man lifts a hand toward the screen and the video ends.

Argo's eyes are wide as his cannon bore. "Anila, did the Doctor complete his research?"

"Impossible to tell," the apparition replies with programmed sympathy. "All records were wiped and all server storage was physically destroyed after erasure."

"What about in his journals? Does he ever reference completion of his research?"

"The Doctor makes five thousand eight hundred fifty-two references to the word 'completion' and its variants in twenty-five years of recorded entries. However, there is no direct statement of 'completed research'. If the copies he made survive, perhaps you may answer your question with certainty."

"Anila," Keiko asks, her eyes as intense as Argo's, "show us his last entry."

The holo-window clears and refreshes with a blurry frame of someone in a white lab coat, mid-stride. Around him is a brightly lit room, crammed with various machines and crates. Around the periphery are alcoves, each filled with a spotless white and plexi-steel recliner. A bar at the bottom of the screen fills from left to right, and the video jumps into motion.

The man races from recliner to recliner, making last minute adjustments on a diagnostic pads. Condensed vapor descends in diaphanous curtains around the frosted containers.

"It's started," Jin-Sung says. "Like I knew it would. I barely had time to purge the data." He rushes to the next recliner and the camera smoothly glides after him. He scans the diagnostic pad and nods before moving on.

The next recliner is empty and lacks the rolling vapors. When the camera catches up, it shows a painting on the glass of a flower with a yellow hub and white petals radiating from it like sunlight. The Doctor hunches at the waist, his eyes welling, and he leans on his palms, staring at the simple image. His mouth curves into a deep frown and he pats the empty recliner.

"You saved me, girl. Thank you."

A distant clang reverberates through the room and Jin-Sung straightens like a meerkat. Fear and hatred crease his face. His nostrils flare and his glazed eyes shine in the room's bright lighting.

"*DAMN YOU!*" he screams and he dashes past several recliners to one which looks ordinary in every regard. He lingers at it, staring at an occupant obscured by frosted glass. The camera smoothly glides to him.

"They'll torture you..." he says to the occupant, cryptically. With a look of utter anguish, he beats his fist against the sturdy lid and lays himself against it. Another reverberating clang shakes the room, renewing the fear and urgency.

"At least...At least you'll have no pain." He hesitates a moment at the pad, finger hovering over it. More clangs sound closer, louder. Muffled booms make the hoses of the recliner sway.

He stabs his finger against the pad in rapid sequence. An audible alarm tone sounds from the pad, but Jin-Sung continues jabbing his finger into it like he was assigning blame.

"Doctor, that will induce cellular rupture on a systemic level," says

210

Anila's voice, directly beside the camera.

"I know," he replies in a lifeless tone.

"Is it your wish to terminate your wife?"

"As gently as possible, *yes*." His head bows with defeat, with failure. He drives his finger into the pad one last time. Noisy booms shake the room, swaying the man where he stands. Faint sounds of weapons discharging filter in, and suddenly Jin-Sung is a pillar of rage. He turns at the camera, screaming.

"You *lose*, Mikato, you *damnable fool!* If you hack this message, then know this: I destroyed all the data on my research! Neither you nor Honniker will ever have it. *It DIES with me!"*

A groan of collapsing metal sounds much closer than any of the distant reverberations. High-amperage electrical shorts buzz violently.

"Doctor, you must get to your recliner!" Anila insists. "Mikato's machine has perforated the entrance!"

"Jin-SUNG!" roars a metallic voice from beyond the room.

The doctor sprints for the only vacant recliner. He programs the diagnostic pad in a flurry of taps, and the lid rises mechanically. Like the last pad he programmed, the audible warning tone sounds.

"It was a pleasure serving you, Doctor," Anila says.

Jin-Sung lingers a moment. He looks directly beside the camera at what must be Anila's hovering apparition.

"Thank you, Anila." He looks at his feet. "I don't think I ever said that to you before."

The entire room shudders as something massive rams from outside, and the doors yield with an ear-splitting shriek. Jin-Sung dives into the recliner and pulls on the lid, trying to speed the slow, mechanical descent.

"Get back, Honniker," demands the metallic voice from just beyond the rammed doorway, *"He's mine!"*

Concussive pulses send shockwaves throughout the chamber, punctuated by a deafening clang. Jin-Sung hangs from the internal bracing of the lid, jerking with all of his weight. The video goes black and halts.

Argo and Keiko turn on Anila, shouting over one another.

"Where's the rest?"

"What happened?"

"Video ends due to power failure."

"But you said you were on a private network," Argo reasons.

"Data, yes. However all power in this section is on a common rail."

The Brick looks away in exasperation. "Bad design."

"So Jin-Sung's recliner..." Keiko begins, "it couldn't freeze him without power."

"That's correct," Anila replies.

The rugged Gun looks at the mutilated remains on the wall. "But why drag him in here? What's the point of that?"

"Doctor Jin-Sung's storage server is accessed and archived from this room."

"So Mikato thought he could use pain to coerce access to the research?" Argo asks.

Anila turns to face the Brick. "That appears the most logical explanation from context."

"Did you capture video of Mikato's machine?"

"No. This section is only wired for video in the experimentation rooms or as specifically requested by the Doctor. He was adamant about maintaining his privacy."

"So he didn't ask to see whatever was ripping vault doors aside like that?"

"Doctor Jin-Sung once worked very closely with his colleagues. It's safe to say he already knew what it looked like."

Keiko and Argo fall silent in the video's aftermath.

"Why did he keep all these printed words?" asks Deepak from across the room. "It's odd."

Anila spins to address the Gun.

"Doctor Jin-Sung enjoyed the tactile sensation of books in his hands, their weight, their texture, the smell of old parchment, vellum, ink, and glue. He made notes in them, underlined meaningful passages. Whenever possible, he acquired copies of the original text whether handwritten or typed, believing the shape or appearance of the words conveyed as much meaning as the words themselves. When holding a copy of an original manuscript, he felt as if the author was, by proxy, speaking directly to him. Such connections were important to him. He was a very sensual person, and very passionate."

Keiko shakes her head again. "You're a program...How could that possibly interest you?"

"Yes, I am an intuitive program—engineered to be curious and self-improving. Frequently in the course of our research I encountered a problem, a problem which I could not quantify or solve. The Doctor assisted me in these problems, helping me to expand my awareness. On the surface his ideas appeared irrational, yet they often revealed perspectives I did not or could not recognize on my own."

"Great," Keiko mutters, "a digitized colonist."

Argo is tempted to agree, but there is a deeper truth that resonates within his own experience. Though the big man cannot definitively say what it is, he also cannot dismiss it. He looks the apparition in the eye, and strangely enough, Anila is looking back with an almost imperceptible smile.

There's more to her, Argo understands in that smile. *She's holding back.*

"So you understand why he would keep these...print-outs," Argo probes, "instead of keeping the text on media record or archive?"

"The Doctor once explained to me, 'Here is a library to rival the one burned at Alexandria, all the world's ancient history in one room. You can pull any one of these tomes from the shelf and find wisdom inside. But together, they form a temple of knowledge, in which I pray for understanding'."

"So he felt the whole was greater than the sum of its parts."

"Yes, quite."

"He believed the same about you?" Argo posits.

The holo-projection's eyes narrow with esteem. The mouth draws upward at the corners.

"I would like to think he did."

"Is that why you said it was a pleasure serving him?"

"One of many reasons."

Argo pauses, considering all the trails of conversation spilling out like loose threads. When he looks at Anila, something tells him he could pull at them all day.

"So do you *truly* understand why he kept these papers instead of condensing them on storage?"

"I understand they were important to *him*. And that is enough for me."

"I think you served him *very* well."

The apparition bows graciously.

"You sound like the Counselor," Keiko chides.

The Brick warms at what sounds like a complement. "He and I spent a lot of time togeth..." He cuts himself off when he sees Keiko glaring impatiently.

"I beg your pardon, sir. I lost myself."

Keiko turns to the projected apparition. "Anila, what's in these back rooms?"

"Private sleep chamber for the Doctor and his wife. And a sensorium for relaxation and entertainment."

Keiko steps over the shifting hills of books, covers and pages tearing free under her feet. She pauses at the doorways, shining her rifle and helmet lights into the rooms. Anila watches each step the Gun takes over her master's precious tomes.

Argo wants to say something to the oblivious Gun, but after his scolding, he humbles himself to hierarchy.

"They're totally destroyed inside," Keiko says. "Trampled flat. Even the wall plates are peeled off." She tromps back toward the center of the room, looking directly at Anila. "Can you project yourself outside this area?"

Anila's gaze rises from Keiko's boots. "No. I'm limited to this section, only. If I were permitted to upload into a mobile chassis, I could explore outside." She turns hopefully to Argo.

The Brick steals a glance at Keiko, but the Gun is already making her way to the exit. Argo gives a quick head bob.

"We'll see what we can do," the Brick offers.

"Thank you," Anila says with a modest bow. She turns toward Keiko and drifts through the piles after her. "I will be here, ready to assist in whatever manner you require."

Keiko scarcely acknowledges with a nod, then says, "Deepak, Argo, let's move."

The two Guns scramble over the books leaving a flurry of ripped paper. Argo picks his way around the periphery, taking pains not to tread on a single page.

THE PARK

Argo, Keiko, and Deepak beat a quick sprint to the *Park*. Electricity flows through conduits behind the battered panels along their path, casting a trace glow in their infrared-sensitive visors. But with the vast majority of wall and floor sconces shattered, the darkness is only interrupted by flickering islands of light or an occasional spark.

Every doorway they pass bears the subtle warmth of power.

Keller might have passed through any one of these, Argo thinks to himself. Keiko, however, keeps a straight path.

"Lieutenant," Argo calls, "shouldn't we be searching these rooms?"

Between deep breaths, Keiko answers, "Whatever grabbed Jin-Sung probably powered up with the rest of this section. We need to rejoin the others, fast."

Muscles in the Brick's back contract, making him rigid in his backward gait. *Why didn't I think of that?*

At last, the team comes to another Y-shaped intersection. Intact double doors close off the wide stem of the Y. On the doors is a smiling lab-coated raccoon flying a kite, superimposed over huge block letters, spelling P-A-R-K.

Keiko lopes to a halt just outside the doors. Deepak and Argo come to rest behind her, both noting a wide swath of dried black smears underfoot that lead through the doorway.

"Arrived at rendezvous, Colonel," Keiko radios, "request entry."

"Granted," Shao-Lo replies. The broad doors part in the middle and screech across unlubricated tracks.

Bright light pours through the widening gap from a gleaming white room beyond. Squinting, the team strides in cautiously, forming a triangle with their backs together. Their visors compensate and they find themselves in a spacious locker room with white tile covering the floor, ceiling, and walls. Rows of two-meter tall lockers occupy the walls and form angled rows along the floor to each side. In the left wall is a slim doorway labeled, "Men." In the right wall, a doorway labeled, "Women."

Directly ahead, a wide staircase ascends out of sight with numerous broken and pulverized tiles. Dark stains cascade from step to step like slaughterhouse runoff, converging at a central drain by their feet. Smears continue from the drain out the wide entryway and on into the corridor behind them.

"Position?" Keiko transmits.

"Upstairs, in the open," the Colonel radios back.

Keiko and Deepak run for the stairs and leap them, clearing five or more steps at a time. Argo loiters a moment to watch the main doors close and lock behind him, then he hurries after his team.

When Argo emerges from the sheltered stairway, he nearly drops his cannon in amazement. He arches his back and looks up into enormous white clouds lazing across a bottomless blue sky. Far off, a V-formation of birds flaps near the horizon, their distant honks carrying through the quiet space. Rectangular gaps in the projected mosaic spoil the illusion, some flickering in and out; but even so, Argo marvels at the three-dimensional rendering. Mentally, he hurtles back to his time on Earth, remembering air full of arboreal scents and humidity, the coolness of unprocessed air, and the warmth of yellow sun. A sudden gust of wind takes him by surprise, swaying him mildly, and for a moment it is like standing on the planet's surface again.

Argo drops his gaze, expecting the same lush greenery, but the ground beneath him is a parched hardpan of wiry thatch. Sculpted hills, tan with dead grass, roll across an oblong area of at least two square kilometers. Thick tree trunks rise from gray soil and spread into naked gray branches, their leaves and bark all dropped into compressed heaps beneath them. Cordoned-off gardens lay in mats of tangled stalks and husks. Gravel trails weave between the gardens in lazy, meandering paths, attended by sturdy benches and lamp posts every few meters.

The brittle thatch shows plain signs of recent passage, and Argo visually follows the trail out to one of the taller hills. Sitting alone at the top, arms encircling her knees, Sharon stares out at the passing formation of birds.

Downhill, on an open and level field striated by white hash marks, Maiella practices forms. At times, she seems almost weightless, flowing with the breezes like a dry leaf until she springs with a powerful kick or flips herself into a dusty take down. The movements entrance him with their alternating gentility and violence, making him wonder if she is trying to resolve something, practicing a new technique, or merely keeping herself entertained.

He takes several steps out onto the crunchy grass and raises his faceplate. The air is dry and stale, yet carries a pleasing earthiness.

"Argo," comes Shao-Lo's voice from behind him. The Brick turns about and sees an open doorway in sloping rock ledge near the stairway. Shao-Lo stands just inside and beckons him through.

He hurries to his commanding officer and finds himself in a darkened control room with active holowindows above each station, labeled "Weather," "Sky," "Lake," and "Sports Arena."

The Brick salutes crisply. Shao-Lo returns the salute with less effort.

"I understand you found something," she begins.

"Yes, sir," Argo replies. He takes a compartment from his rack and retrieves one of the translucent cards from it. Shao-Lo takes it in a gauntleted hand and turns it over.

"File storage?"

"We believe so. An intuitive program suggested this may be d..."

Shao-Lo holds her hand up flat. She points with her other hand up in the air and draws a wide circle then points at her ear. Argo reads the gesture clearly, *Possible enemy listening/observing.* He nods in understanding.

"No trace of Keller, then?" she asks.

"None, though there is a lot of station yet to search. To make things more complicated, I suspect there are areas here we don't know about. Hidden access."

"Why do you say so?"

"I get the impression the researchers here didn't trust one another. Had a lot to hide from one another, and went to lengths to protect it. Not to mention the creatures that ambushed Sharon—the station was stripped of O2 when we arrived, so they must've been holed up somewhere with its own enviro processor."

"Or frozen in stasis," the tall woman adds. "Any ideas where Keller is?"

"Not yet, sir. Any word from Honniker?"

She shakes her head grimly. "He's still silent. May be planning something, or he's been shut off. I don't like either possibility."

"We keep hearing about a 'Mikato'," Keiko volunteers. "There's reason to believe he survived the killing here, like Honniker. There's also evidence he was the main perpetrator."

"Evidence?"

"Dr. Jin-Sung's final log entry was a video recording during the breach of his laboratory. He was shouting at Mikato, as some kind of machine broke through. We never saw what this machine looked like, but the man was terrified."

Shao-Lo turns to inspect the holo-window labeled "Weather." She drags her finger across the screen, scrolling through a variety of events from snow to drizzling rain to thunderstorm.

"Everywhere I look in this place, I find things I don't understand."

"You should see Jin-Sung's labs," Deepak says. He flicks his head at Argo. "That thing in the recliner..."

Shao-Lo follows Deepak's gesture, and her steel eyes rivet to the Brick. Argo stands at attention under the glare.

"Well?" the Colonel demands.

"A hybrid, sir. Human and blueskin."

The powerful woman squints in disbelief. "This place is insane."

"My thoughts *exactly*, sir."

She strides from the room. Deepak, Keiko, and Argo share an uneasy glance and follow the tall woman out.

Overhead, thick clouds crowd the sky, replacing the pastels of late afternoon sun with dark knots of turbulence. A bolt of electricity flashes within the roiling vapors, and a deep rumble trails delinquently. Shao-Lo stares into the underside of the storm until a fat drop of water falls against her face. More drops descend in a rush, pelting the dusty ground and wafting musty earth around them. Another ribbon of electricity divides the sky, followed by a tremendous boom.

"This is a *complete* waste of resources!" Shao-Lo bellows. She strides to the stairway as gloomy as the sky above. "Round up! We're leaving!"

Deepak and Keiko attend her.

Argo follows then pauses at the top of the sheltered stairway for a final glance across the sculpted landscape. Maiella is calling to Sharon with both hands cupped around her mouth like a megaphone, but Sharon is not listening. The colonist is on her feet, head rocked back, arms out to each side, letting the rain pelt her face, smiling.

Switching his cannon to one hand, Argo cups his free hand beside his mouth and shouts in a booming voice, *"Sharon, we're leaving!"*

The distant woman lowers her arms and shelters her eyes with a hand. Her other hand cups her ear.

"If you had your radio on *you'd hear me*," Argo gripes. Instead of shouting again, he sweeps his arm in an exaggerated gesture. He can just make out her head nodding, and she starts walking down the hill.

With the onset of the dark clouds, lampposts ignite around the grounds. A shadow races past one, reflective teeth gleaming as it crests the hill behind Sharon. It is in full sprint, claws out, ripping the hard packed soil.

Argo plants his feet and grips his cannon with both hands. Flipping off the safety, he yells, *"GET DOWN!"*

Sharon turns around and sees a massive feline creature only paces away.

Argo's teeth set with concentration and he leans into his weapon, aiming with reflexes as fast as the lightning overhead. His visor highlights the target, confirming his aim is true.

The weapon discharges a scathing stream of particles, cutting a channel of plasma through the rain-soaked air, and the creature explodes at the chest with a crackling *boom*. The concussive blast sends Sharon sprawling.

In moments, Maiella is beside her, pistols out in a wide V. She spins a complete circle before kneeling to help.

"Is she okay?" Argo radios.

Shao-Lo, Keiko, and Deepak sprint up the steps with rifles ready. They skid to a halt on the muddy ground beside Argo. Before Shao-Lo can ask, her eyes follow the steaming channel of rising air to an exploded carcass. She scowls.

Maiella peels Sharon up from the mud and throws her over a shoulder.

"She's stunned," Maiella radios back. "I think she'll be okay, though." Under the careful watch of the Operators, Maiella hustles with her limp companion back toward the stairway.

"I wanted to *avoid* this," Shao-Lo curses. She turns on Argo suddenly. "It was attacking? You're *sure*?"

"No doubt," the Brick replies. "Claws out, teeth bared, full sprint. If the lamps hadn't fired up, I wouldn't have seen it 'til it had her."

Shao-Lo looks out across the field. Steam and blasted soil drifts over the carcass in an obscuring fog.

"We searched the whole *Park*," Shao-Lo says to no one in particular. "Every stone, every panel..."

"Hidden access hatches," Argo restates.

Shao-Lo frets and reluctantly nods. She turns a circle with her rifle, scanning all directions through the scope.

"That's the second time," Argo observes.

"Second time, what?" Shao-Lo asks.

"Second time Sharon was targeted."

Maiella staggers up the slope made slippery by dead grass and runny silt. Argo and Shao-Lo step aside to clear the way. With a head nod from Shao-Lo, Deepak and Keiko rush down the stairs ahead of Maiella, rifles poised for anything awaiting them in the locker room below.

The Colonel stares out at the animal scattered across the hillside.

"No way that thing was alone," Argo says.

Shao-Lo raises her rifle and peers through the scope into the darkness between lamps. She freezes, rifle steady.

"Good call, Argo."

The Brick glances at the tall woman then follows her aim to a distant hill. He dials his visor magnification up and locks on to a pair of dimly reflecting eyes between the horizontal slats of a park bench. Beneath the eyes are long metallic teeth, bared in a snarl of rage. The creature fades back and slips down the far hillside out of sight.

"And good shooting," Shao-Lo adds, lowering her weapon. "I'd say we just gave our own show of strength."

"Thank you, sir."

Shao-Lo tosses her head toward the stairs. "Get going. I'll cover rear."

Argo turns and runs down the stairs, his treads sliding across tiles slick with rehydrated blood. Shao-Lo picks her way down sideways behind him, keeping an eagle's eye on the top of the stairway. She glances front and finds her Operators gathered near the large entry door. Maiella sits on a bench between lockers with Sharon. The small colonist sways slightly, awake but groggy.

"Zuri," the colonel radios, "get the inventory prepped for transport. Once we find Keller, we're leaving."

"*All* of it, sir? We don't have room."

"Oh?" Honniker breaks into the conversation, *"I'd think there'd be plenty of room on that FLEET of warships you brought."*

In Good Faith

Deepak, Keiko, and Argo look at each other and curse the rookie blunder that gave away Keller's ruse.

"We don't need *all* of it, Zuri," Shao-Lo covers, gripping her forehead, "just a few crates. We can manufacture what we need."

"Come, come, Colonel. I think someone has been dishonest. Let's clear the air, shall we?"

"Where've you been, Doctor?" Shao-Lo looks over her shoulder, speaking through her teeth. "We've *missed* you."

"Tedious details, work, work, work...catching you in a lie."

"I haven't lied to you."

"Ach so, my old friend Keller did. But you were content to go along with his lie, yes?"

"We can still do one another great harm. There's no need for that."

"Well, I think our bargain needs a refresh. Before, I gave everything, and my reward was to not be obliterated. Now, I think it's time I got something more valuable than an empty threat."

"Such as?"

"One of your women. Sharon, preferably. Or Maiella. Or you, perhaps."

Sharon lifts her head in confusion. "Whuh, huh? What did he say?"

Maiella glares coolly at the ceiling and stands. "You know where Keller is?"

"I might."

"*Yes* or *no*, Honniker!"

"Yes," the doctor says reluctantly.

"Then I'll make *you* a deal," the rogue Geek begins. "Restore my synaptic bridges, don't harm my companions, and I'll cooperate."

"Maiella! You don't know what you're saying!" Argo warns. "You want to end up like Voss?"

"Nonsense. A mind like hers is far too valuable to chop and prod. So much experience, so many lifetimes in her. And I must admit, I've never had a willing participant. The potential for honest feedback is appealing."

"And what about Aaronson?" Argo demands "Huh? Where's *he*? Another head in a jar? Another *plaything* for your diseased amuse–"

Shao-Lo grabs Argo by the chest and slams him against the tiled wall. "Brick, that's *enough!*" She stares him down to compliance then turns on Maiella.

"And *you* don't make deals! What *you* do is *keep your mouth shut!"*

The fierce woman releases Argo with a harsh glare. Sharon stares with saucer-shaped eyes, fully awakened by the names of old companions. Her lips stammer with a jumble of words, unable to form a coherent question.

The Colonel raises her face to the ceiling. "We keep our original agreement, Honniker. We take Voss, Rosenthal, and Aaronson along with some crates of the weapon. Then we leave, just like we said."

"No, no, I'm afraid that's not good enough. But I can see from how you handled your subordinates that you're not interested in discussing reasonable alternatives. Do let me know when you change your mind."

"That's not going to happen."

Long seconds pass without reply.

"I said, 'That's not going to happen,' Honniker!"

Still no reply.

Shao-Lo grinds her teeth. "Zuri, Carter, assume Honniker hostile," she radios. "Be ready for anything, understood?"

There is no reply.

"Carter? Zuri? *Respond!*"

The radio is completely silent.

"Bah! Keiko, you and me on point, *weapons free*. Argo, you and Deepak take rear. And *you*..." The Colonel strides to Maiella and stands over her, eyes boring holes into her. "You said you were Sharon's bodyguard, but not for Argo, she'd be in *pieces*. Protect Sharon with your life. Your *life*, do you *get me?"*

Maiella glares through her eyebrows. Rebellious words are in her eyes and perch on the edge of her tongue.

"Aye, sir," she says, lowering her eyes in reluctant submission.

"Good." Shao-Lo steps toward the main exit. "We push hard to MedLab. Check your targets. *Move out!*"

Deepak takes position at the main doors' control panel while Shao-Lo and Keiko stride to the center. The burly women lean into their rifles and perch on their toes.

"Release," Shao-Lo orders.

Deepak punches the button and the doors slide apart with a squeal. Bright light from the locker room washes onto a two-legged machine hunkered down just outside. It reaches a stubby arm, fitted with multiple barrels, into the gap.

Keiko and Shao-Lo strafe to the sides, triggering full power into the reaching arm and severing it at the elbow. A violet glow gathers behind them and surges between the strafing soldiers, slamming dead center of the machine with a violent *BAH-ROOM.*

Maiella grabs Sharon by the collar and dives with her to the floor as white-hot shards explode from the machine, ripping through the sheet metal lockers like they were paper.

The hunkered machine slumps at the point of impact. Spurting hydraulic fluids burst into flame on contact with its superheated armor plate, and the machine sinks into a low squat.

Argo strides toward the parting doors, faceplate sealed, cannon shimmering with heat. He palms a device from his waist and hurtles it past the flaming hulk into the Y-shaped hallway.

"Cover!" he bellows, and he dives into a row of lockers. The device erupts with seismic intensity, launching white tiles from the wall and floors.

Keiko and Shao-Lo dash into the smoke-filled corridor.

"Contacts! *Heavy weapons!*" Shao-Lo shouts. The smoke strobes with rapid weapon fire from each leg of the intersection and the corridor walls are showered with blazing-hot, high-velocity rounds. Staccato rifle *pangs* answer back and deep within the haze, blooms of orange and blue light surge and fade. The shower of bullets abates.

Farther away, amid the dying echoes, come screeches of metal raking metal and snarls from powerful lungs.

"Brick! Move up, cover left!" Shao-Lo orders, her rifle *panging* with precision shots. *"Keep the pressure on!"*

"Committing." Argo lopes past the smoldering machine into roiling smoke that folds around him like a spirit's embrace.

Maiella lifts herself and Sharon from the tile-strewn floor. All around her, large and small punctures in the lockers glow hot at the edges. She rips her pistols from her back and thumbs the safeties off.

Sharon hunches from the punishing intensity of sound, bones quaking. Her hands reach in through the open face of her helmet and mash her ears flat.

"Stay close to me!" Maiella yells.

Sharon sees the Geek looking at her, but only when Maiella taps a pistol against her thigh and throws her head toward the door does she understand it is time to go. She nods in wide-eyed terror.

Deepak waves at them. *"C'mon!"*

Sharon sees the deformed machine for the first time and shrinks back from it. Deepak rushes over and grips her around the waist. "I'll carry you."

"No!" Sharon shouts back, hands and arms trembling. She peers into the dense smoke in the corridor outside the *Park* doors. Unlike the Operators, she has no means to see through it, and the blinding fume flashes with intense exchanges of fire. She takes stuttering steps forward, sealing her helmet and chanting to herself, "I must be strong, I *must* be strong, *I MUST be strong."* Her steps become less tentative until she approaches the machine.

It squats on thin metallic struts that end at jointed pads for feet. One arm hangs limp to the side, the other lies detached on the ground. The waist is a melted mess of plating and motors, above which is a flat, barrel-like torso. Emblazoned on the front armor plating is a militarized logo of an elongated skull, beneath which is stenciled, *CADRE TWO.*

A violet glow coalesces around the left corner and surges away with a rumbling detonation, jolting the small woman where she stands.

"We have to GO!" Deepak yells.

Sharon looks back over her shoulder. Deepak stands behind her, one hand on his weapon, the other pressing into her shoulder, pushing her into the haze of combat. A shadow on the stairway distracts her and she points in alarm.

"Deepak! Behind you!"

Deepak whirls about as three feline creatures speed down the stairs and leap. He lifts his rifle too late, but Maiella's pistols roar beside him. The beasts lurch and grunt as the bullets rip through chest and gut. They tumble in mid-air, filling the wide lane with convulsing limbs and they crash into the Gun, knocking him flat.

Shocked into action, Sharon retreats into the smoke, keeping low to the floor. From the obscuring haze, she sees Maiella standing over the pile of predators, pumping a round through each of their heads. Deepak shoves out from under them.

"Thanks," the Gun says.

Maiella nods in reply, dropping her spent clips and sliding in fresh ones from her thighs. "Sharon!" she calls into the smoke, "We're gonna be fine! We can do this!"

Sharon feels her way blindly toward the receding sounds of combat on hands and knees. Her hands shake, but they are more controlled.

"We can do this," she echoes to herself. "We're gonna be fine."

Maiella slips around the ruined machine and finds Sharon crawling on the floor, hands reaching out into the smoke.

"You can't see?"

Sharon looks up at Maiella, only glimpsing her black outline in the strobes of weapon fire. She shakes her head in short little jerks. "No."

"Deepak! I need your rifle strap."

Deepak slides over to them, keeping careful watch of the stairway behind them. Not daring to take his hands off his weapon he says, "Go ahead, take it."

Maiella clips a pistol to her back and unclips Deepak's rifle strap at both ends. She snaps one end to her waist, extends the strap to its longest adjustment, and puts the loose end in Sharon's hand.

"Don't let go of this, for *anything*!"

"I won't," Sharon says, rising to her feet.

"Deepak, where are you?" Shao-Lo radios between rifle shots. *"Move up, NOW!"*

"Let's go, you two!" Deepak growls, transferring the aggression.

Maiella grabs her second pistol from its clip and spins it around her finger.

"Ready. Sharon, hold on tight. We're moving fast."

The Geek starts slowly then tows Sharon at an unbelievable pace through burning corridors. Sharon's boots bark against fragments of metal and sinewy carcasses, sending her face first to the floor again and again. Not daring to let go of the strap, the woman is dragged for many meters before Maiella slows enough that she can get back on her feet.

The haze flashes with Deepak's rifle shots behind them, always matched by a strident *pang* and a distant flare or burst of sparks.

"Deepak, I said, 'PUSH HARD'! GET YOUR ASS MOVING!"

When Sharon trips again, Deepak crouches beside her and heaves her up onto his broad shoulder.

"I can do this," Sharon protests.

"Stow it! There's no time!"

"Go ahead," Maiella says, "I got rear."

Deepak curls an arm around Sharon, hugging her firmly to his neck, and he sprints into the curling vapors. Maiella picks up the pace, nimbly dodging exploded machine parts and wounded creatures. She flows through the dense air feinting, dodging fire, leaping, returning fire. Her powerful legs bounce her from wall to wall, soaring across heaps of molten machinery. Her hands, so steady, so controlled, keep her pistols level, anticipating every threat and triggering killing bursts with deceptive ease. An inexplicable awareness extends all around her like a spiritual companion, whispering to her what cannot be seen or heard around every corner. Rage fills her, yet does not consume her, channeled into singular purpose like thrust from a rocket engine.

Metal claws fly out of the smoke at her, eager to rip through flesh but are denied by her agility. Reflective teeth glance across her old armor, answered by long tongues of flame at the end of her pistol barrels. No matter the press of attack, she is faster: dodge, fire, run, reload in seamless motions.

Maiella sneers behind her faceplate, body coursing with adrenaline. Pleasure centers of her brain ignite with long deprived chemical rewards. Everything which ever troubled her boils away in the crucible of her killing instinct. Every thought falls away, too restrictive, too miring like ill-fitting clothes. She is berserk with righteous frenzy—free, wild, lethal.

Her goggles flare bright white.

"ACHH!" she shouts against the blinding flash and trips over a twisted floor plate. She slams hard on her chin, making stars dance before her eyes. A static buzz fills her ears. Awareness of her surroundings implodes.

"You seem the reasonable one," begins Honniker's voice, not in her ears. Maiella shakes her head and bolts up from the floor. She crouches low, blinking against the glare of her goggles, arms extended with pistols on a hair trigger.

"It must be frustrating not to be in control..."

She rips open her faceplate and lifts her goggles to her forehead. Thick smoke chokes her and she struggles to catch even a shallow breath.

"I don't know why you still wear your HDI, since, with so few of your synaptic bridges intact, I have more control of it than you do."

Maiella wheezes and squints into the smoke. Deprived of her goggles, all she sees is a swirling darkness, pierced by very distant flashes and explosions. She doubles over and coughs against the smothering dryness in her lungs, desperately trying to beat back the intruder's voice in her head.

"We could do much, you and me. New techniques, greater advances. I have only glimpsed your ability, but it's enough to know how talented you really are."

A blistering hatred swells inside her and she finally shoves the voice out of her mind. She yanks her goggles off then slaps her faceplate down, and immediately, the rebreather flows with purified air. She sucks it down with great gasps.

As her chest heaves with fresh air, her wits return, her awareness, all but her assisted vision. She turns a full circle, realizing she is in a wide intersection.

"What do you want?" she growls through clenched teeth.

"Were you serious in your offer?"

"Offer for what?" She whirls at a metallic screech behind her, one pistol aimed menacingly.

"In the Park *locker room, you offered yourself to me. Will you do so?"*

"I said I would, Doctor. That means I will."

"I'm glad to hear that. You can put your weapons away. We have a bargain."

Maiella feels her way with her feet. The intersection is littered with loose metal fragments and stiff, carbonized bodies.

"There's no way I can trust you, Honniker."

"Oh, I believe you can, though I understand if you would be suspicious. How about I show you something in good faith?"

Maiella knows the futility of protest when her comrades are long gone. Worse, they have not even called out for her.

Either they don't know, or they don't care, she thinks. She stands in the intersection and her arms drop to her sides.

"All right, Doctor. What have you got?"

"This may startle you, so please, don't move."

Maiella hears the whoosh of ventilators and the smoky air is drawn up like a curtain. Surrounding her on all sides, not three meters away, is a platoon of feline predators. Their heads hang low to the ground, front legs crouched, rear legs set into the floor ready to leap. She stares at the hungry eyes around her, and they stare back, but the teeth are not bared. Rather, they maintain a ready vigil, patient and disciplined. The Geek studies the intense faces, each one perfectly focused. On every head, nestled into the skull indentation between the cat-like eyes, is a purplish lens.

A large set of doors groans open behind her; and when she turns, she sees a round portal with a zig-zag central seam. Gurneys and open cabinets flank the entrance.

The Graveyard...

"If you would, this way please," Honniker coos. The ring of predators parts, allowing her a path to the doors.

THE EXHAUSTED DEAD

"Doctor Mikato would like to meet you."

ALL TOO FAMILIAR

Maiella clips her pistols to her back, resigned by the overwhelming force around her to the new destination. Guided by the feline platoon, and her own curiosity, she marches through the parted *Graveyard* gate.

Inside is a wide but shallow chamber with grated floors. Bright overhead lamps beam down like focused sunlight, silhouetting large shower nozzles hanging from the low ceiling. Metal triangles dangle on thin chains beside each nozzle.

Directly ahead is another set of doors identical to the ones she just passed. Yellow and black striped reflective tape marks the edges, and amber LED lamps strobe in warning. The outer doors, only parted enough to allow passage, grind together and lock. With a hiss of chilled air, the inner doors unseal and, in stark contrast to the main doors, slide quietly apart. She swallows.

Dull red lights shine from the floor of the chamber beyond, barely illuminating an open space with high ceilings. Metal floor plates bear an even coating of frost. Directly ahead, across the spacious floor, are rows of consoles, above which rise massive plates of plexi-steel. Beyond them is total darkness.

Maiella pauses at the inner doors, halted by the abyss beyond the tall windows. Creatures pad noiselessly around her and sit, facing the windows. Their damp breath condenses into a sparse fog, which rises among them; their banded tails splay out behind them, switching this way and that.

A strong nudge to her backside pushes her inside, and Maiella staggers through the inner doors. A dismayingly huge creature, nearly as tall as she on its four legs and weighing at least four hundred kilos, moves past her to join the others. The inner doors seal behind her with a final hiss.

To her left and to her right, each wall is inset with four floor-to-ceiling plexisteel cylinders that glow internally with soft white light. From the back of each cylinder, near the top, juts a sturdy rod that points out into the room like an accusing finger. Stenciled across the transparent doors are giant numerals, proclaiming the cylinders one through eight. Beneath the large numerals is a smaller range of numbers from 1 to 1,000,000, broken up among each cylinder in blocks of 125,000.

In front of her, the creatures focus on the dark windows as if they were watching a video. She looks into their armor plated heads, necks, and backs, wondering if they have some means of perception superior to her own. Maiella steps cautiously forward, and like the feline predators, finds herself compulsively staring into the darkness beyond the glass.

Humming motors to her right startle her from her abyssal gaze, and her hands clamp to her pistols. The creatures jump from their obedient sitting and lope over to the right bank of transparent chambers, forming a semi-circle. They sit, tails swishing excitedly.

Inside each chamber, the pointing steel rods slide down through the floor. Several more rods pass down through the chambers until stiff human feet appear, followed by naked legs, buttocks, spineless backs, and shoulders. There are no heads above the cleanly severed necks. Dangling from hooks under collarbones, the stiff cadavers sway slightly, then rock when the rods abruptly halt.

Each chamber brightens for several seconds, and Maiella shields her unprotected eyes from the light. Once the light dims, she looks again at the headless bodies. They have a more shiny, pliant appearance.

Creatures mill outside the doors, jockeying for position, fussing with one another, swatting and hissing, tails stiffly thumping each other. With a *ding* the chambers open and the steel rods extend out into the room, carrying the defrosted cadavers. Steam rises from pale, glistening skin.

Dangling legs are seized in metal-packed maws, and the corpses are ripped from their hooks. Without the spines, the rubbery torsos *thud* against the floor and are shredded in a cacophony of growls, cracking bones, and ripping sinews.

Maiella back-steps from the feeding frenzy, her mouth curved in a tremendous frown, horrified, head shaking. She draws her pistols.

The largest creature sits up from the feast, great head covered in overlapping plates with tufts of compressed fur jutting between them. Small, round ears, folded by the plates and nearly rolled into tubes, extend out at a downward angle from the corners. White fur around its mouth is stained black with clotted blood, and it watches Maiella retreat with red eyes. The beast runs a mottled black and pink tongue over its snout before feeding again.

"They can't help what they are," says a soft voice behind her.

Maiella spins into a crouch, pistols parallel and level. There is no one there.

"You don't need those," the familiar voice says.

The Geek turns her head, recognizing the voice, but refusing to believe she is hearing it here, in this place. She keeps her pistols at arm's length and rises. She turns about, weapons sweeping through every angle.

"Enough of your games, Honniker! *Where are you?*"

"Calm yourself. I am not Honniker. I am Mikato."

"Stop using that voice!"

"It's the only voice I've ever had. Can you change *your* voice?"

"You're trying to trick me, make me feel comfortable. Drop my guard. Uh-unh. *Not me, brother.*"

"If you prefer, I can modulate my tone," the voice offers. "There," it resumes with an electronic buzz, "is that better?"

Maiella feels a sickness in her gut as her full-on combat high collides with the disarming familiarity of a voice so near and dear to her.

"Cut the *crap*," she snaps. "Let's get this over with."

"We won't be finished for quite some time," the buzzing, yet still too-familiar, voice replies, "though I respect your desire to get started."

On the left wall, opposite the feeding predators, chamber four hums with movement. The rod rises up out of sight, followed by several more until there are no more, and the slotted floor itself rises. Beneath it is a glass-walled elevator car. The chamber door swings open without a sound.

Maiella steps cautiously to the open chamber and peers inside. She shrinks back.

"What, is this some kind of compactor?" She looks over her shoulder, recalling the frozen bodies that were defrosted in seconds. "Or are you gonna boil me with microwaves?"

"Nothing like that. I'll show you."

The largest predator slinks by her on silent paws, its metal-capped claws retracted into tufted toes.

The big creature walks inside the chamber and turns two complete circles before finally settling onto its haunches. The door swings closed and the chamber hums as the elevator descends. The creature watches Maiella with relaxed eyes until it lowers out of sight. A moment later, the motor reverses and the animal arrives where it started. The door swings open again, but the massive creature remains sitting, flitting its banded tail casually.

"Please," the voice says, "step inside."

Maiella takes a deep breath and laughs through her nose. Wary, but unafraid, she clips her pistols and moves into the close chamber, careful not to step on the flitting tail. The creature glances up at her then lifts a bloody paw and washes it with its mottled tongue.

The Geek shakes her head, scarcely believing she has climbed into close quarters with such a monster. Despite her lack of trust, somehow she knows, *she knows*, right now there is no threat from this animal. Its level of relaxation is contagious, allowing her to ease down from her state of high alert. The chemical aftermath of combat hits her, and she slumps against the chamber glass. She lifts her faceplate to rub her eyes, but the close compartment air assaults her with the stench of warmed meat and fetid breath. Her eyes roll and she slams the plate down.

Humming resumes as the chamber descends through layers of coarsely chiseled rock.

Dryness in her mouth makes her crave water, so she takes her canteen from her waist. Knowing the warm-meat air could only have gotten worse in the closed compartment, she holds her breath and lifts her faceplate. The Geek puts the spout to her lips and tips it, letting body temperature water glide over her coated tongue and down her throat. She sighs with refreshment.

"Mmmmmfff," grunts the animal.

Maiella looks down in disbelief. The huge creature is focused on her, leaning on its front paws. Up close, the creature's eyes reflect red but the irises are actually pale green. The green eyes drop onto her canteen then lift again.

The stim-crashed operator stands from her slumping posture, looks at the canteen in her hand, then looks at her elevator companion.

"Seriously?"

The animal noses the canteen, leaving a wet imprint, and shifts weight on its front paws.

Maiella grins, eyebrows lifted. She holds the container to the creature's snout and tips it slightly, not caring about the humid stink of the elevator. The beast's raspy tongue curls around the spout as Maiella pours, catching every drop.

"Hey, that's enough, *that's enough!"*

The creature reclines on its haunches and licks its chops.

Maiella stares at the animal, absently raising the spout to her mouth again. Just before she takes a swig, she smells the foamy saliva.

"Uch!" she groans and pats herself down for some kind of cloth. There is none. The animal leans forward again, hopeful. Maiella looks at the slime-covered canteen and at the creature.

"All right, fine. You can have it." She offers the canteen again and tips it, allowing the creature's long tongue to rasp over the canteen and over her armored hand. She looks away and smirks to herself as the animal drains the contents.

Strong light washes into the elevator at Maiella's feet as the transparent-walled car lowers into a brightly lit hall. Stark white surfaces gleam in all directions, contrasting dramatically with long, tight rows of black bi-pedal war machines. Behind the machines, an enormous black transport lounges like a sow before its sucklings.

Maiella's relaxed rapport ends, her hand automatically returning the spent canteen to her waist, and she presses against the elevator glass to view the squatting mechanical army.

We could never face so many...

Her eyes swing from the parked war machines to rows of weapon test ranges in the wall on her left. They begin as fenced-off lanes on the main floor and continue through tunnels deep into the rock. Support benches and weapon clamps at the head of each lane shine as though new, but the lanes themselves and the bare rock openings around every tunnel are charred from misfires. Subtle red glows from the tunnels suggest a large cavern at the end of the tunnels, a cavern radiant with heat.

Banks of test benches, workstations, assembly tables, and production lines occupy the majority of the open floor, none of it operating. Maiella presses her face against the glass in an effort to see farther to her right, baffled by the scale of manufacturing capability, and she wonders just where the assembly floor ends.

"Cadre One doesn't have a *fifth* of this capacity," she says without thinking.

"Is that so?" Mikato's buzzing voice asks.

Maiella pushes away from the glass, instantly regretting her loose talk. She folds her arms and looks at the floor without reply.

"Really, you needn't censor yourself," Mikato continues. "You have agreed to stay, therefore we need not keep secrets from you. If we are to work well together, we must be honest with one another."

Maiella looks up skeptically. "Then you can answer a few questions for *me*."

"Of course."

The elevator reaches the immaculate white floor and the glass door swings open. The big animal walks out first and saunters in the diffuse white light before flopping itself on the floor and stretching. At full extension, it reaches over four meters.

Maiella steps out onto the production floor, hands at her sides yet longing for the reassuring grips of her machine pistols.

"Where are you? Do have a body?"

"I have a chassis I occasionally upload to for certain tasks. Mostly I maintain a detached existence as software. As such, I can be many places at once and handle far more tasks than if concentrated in one location."

"Why are you using that voice?"

"As I said before," the buzzing clears, tonality restored, "it is *my* voice."

"You're not *him*."

"Him who?"

Maiella checks herself, unsure if speaking the name could somehow jeopardize her trusted friend.

"Would it help you to have a visible form with which you can interact?" Mikato asks.

Maiella looks up at the high ceiling with its heavy reinforcements of trusses and braces. *Would he look the same as he sounds?* In Mikato's offer, she realizes, there is an opportunity to expose the hoax.

"Yes, it would," she replies. She folds her arms and shifts her weight to her back leg. "Show yourself."

"I can show myself as I *was*, for you are witnessing how I am *now*."

"Whatever! Just do it!"

A projection appears directly in front of her: a man of average height and straight black hair, facial features so common they seem an average of all races and creeds, dressed in gray slacks, white shirt with wrinkled collar and white lab coat.

Maiella looks into a face she has trusted for years, a face which helped her through the crushing expulsion from the Operator Corps, a face which helped her cope with Thompson and Argo's absence, a face which talked her out of suicide. A face which proved its concern for all people, Colonist and Cadre alike.

"You're *not* him," she says, heart twisting in her chest.

"You've seen this face before, I take it." The projection folds its holographic arms behind its back, cupping the elbows in each hand. "Yes, you clearly have. What you saw was the mechanical approximation of myself."

"Impossible. He's *real*."

"Yes, my androids exist, for certain. They are, therefore, as real as you are, though I assure you they *are* machine. There was only one like me, assembled a *very* long time ago...which makes me wonder how you've seen it."

The image paces in front of the staring Geek. The tight line of Maiella's lips makes it clear she will not volunteer any information.

"It was assigned to a colony ship," the projection continues. "Because no *one* person could be entrusted with the emotional security of the crew for such a long voyage, I was commissioned to build a 'simulacrum' of humanity which could hold to its precepts regardless of situation. One that would not be swayed by sentimentality or emotion, one that could remain an accurate compass for moral decision in any storm."

The projection smiles.

"I appreciated the irony of a machine tending the psychological well-being of humans. Naturally, I accepted the challenge."

The projection strolls to one side then turns back.

"I suppose it was a vanity to make it an exact copy of myself in sound, appearance, and manner, but then, what better way to gauge the success than by standing us side by side and letting people who knew me guess which was the copy?"

"The Counselor's *nothing* like you! He'd *never* allow what happened here!"

The projection's eyebrows lift, its mouth opens slightly as if taking a breath in revelation.

"So it still functions...Could it be, the *Europa* still functions, as well?"

Maiella goes rigid, terrified at how much Mikato has discovered from her in scant seconds. For the first time in years, she summons the tatters of her Operator conditioning, trying to submerge her will and emotion beneath a sea of stoicism and silence. The buoyant thoughts defy her efforts, however, playing plainly across her face for anyone to read.

The projection scrutinizes the woman's face, placing a holographic hand on holographic chin.

"Interesting," Mikato says to himself.

"You weren't always like this," Maiella blurts to change subjects. "You were alive. A *person*."

The projection takes its hand away from its chin.

"I'm still alive. But I get your meaning. It's true, I was flesh and bone once."

"Why'd you give them up?"

"Because flesh *dies*. That much should be obvious."

"So you, your *real* body, is dead?"

The projection looks up in surprise at the tall woman. It doesn't answer.

"You said we should be *honest* with one another, Couns...*Mikato*."

"So I did," the image says professorially.

"Is your body dead?"

"No."

"Where is it?"

"Why do you want to know?"

Maiella's eyes narrow, the corners of her mouth lift. "I don't see that it could be of any use to you now. Why keep it at all?"

The projection hedges, eyes blinking, then it succumbs to the relevance of the question. "It's strange. You're correct about it being without use, but something prevents me from destroying it. Stranger yet, I'm compelled to maintain it."

"Something built into your code perhaps?"

The projection looks away as if in thought. "How could that be?"

"Maybe you're not what you think you are. Maybe you're not the real Mikato."

"Don't be ridiculous."

"Maybe *you're* just the copy."

"Absurd, I—"

"Maybe you aren't even a copy. Maybe you're a low-grade approximation. Maybe if the *real* Mikato wakes up, he'll be displeased with what you are and *delete you.*"

The projection stares into space, stymied.

"I told you she was formidable," comes Honniker's voice from everywhere.

Mikato's projection looks at Maiella, holographic eyes appearing to study the flushed color of her cheeks, the fierceness of her expression. It smiles.

"Yes, she is. In action, and in mind."

Maiella's eyes dart around the enormous factory space, unprepared for Honniker's presence.

"You must admit I was right," Honniker fishes.

The projection nods with a very humanistic reluctance. "Yes, *Edmund*, you were right. There, does that please you?"

The union of the two unsettles her, eroding the sure footing she believed she was gaining.

"Right about what?" she dreads to ask.

The projection turns on its heel. "I was certain I could generate a combat program equal to or better than any human pilot. One that could survive thirty Gs of acceleration. One not subject to error, or mistake. Honniker disagreed, believing the human's chaotic thought process held advantages such as improvisation and unpredictability. Thus, his research has been to distill that advantage from all of the physical frailties which went with it."

"But now it is clear, is it not?" Honniker asks smugly.

"Yes. She has proven it conclusively."

"Both of you shut up for a second and answer something," the uneasy Geek demands, "just what are you expecting from me?"

The projection gestures to the rows of flat-black war machines crouched on their struts.

"These vehicles need your combat abilities, your intuition, your excellent mind. We will repair your synaptic bridges and we will upload those attributes to the main server, where it can be copied and distributed to each vehicle. I estimate the effectiveness of each unit will be remarkably improved."

"What happens to me?"

"You will be as you are, restored as a *'Geek'*," the projection says mockingly with quotation fingers. "In fact, we must have you upgraded if you are to continue as a research assistant."

"That isn't all."

"No, Honniker," Mikato protests, "not *this* one."

"I need her for my research."

"There are others. Choose from them."

In the pregnant silence, Maiella wants to blurt out, to threaten, to *assure* these intangible minds that if they try to harm anyone else, she will *die* trying to eradicate them. And if she cannot out fight them, her thoughts touch the amounts of high explosive built into her armor, explosive sufficient to vaporize herself and anything nearby. She can find some vital area, find some critical server or processing node, perhaps the power plant, and reduce it to ash. She could get inside the fat transport and self-detonate to make sure this machine army could never get to Cadre One. Though it would mean her death, it is something Honniker and Mikato do not know about, something which gives her an edge, an out. No matter the odds, she will never be completely powerless. But first she has to know what is here, what systems could be vulnerable to her secret assault. That thought smoothes the harsh edge of helplessness, dampens the fire of frustration.

She focuses, concentrates, reels herself back in the way Argo always scolded her to do.

"I'm interested in contributing to the projects here," she volunteers. "Would you mind showing me what you're working on first?"

"Do you truly wish to see?"

Maiella smiles. "Abso-*lutely.*"

Radio Silence

"Carter, respond!" Shao-Lo yells into her helmet mic as she sprints through the hallways toward MedLab. *"Carter!"*

The tall woman swings her rifle at anything resembling a threat, her long legs carrying her at the spearhead of a fast moving column. Keiko is right behind, matching the blistering pace. Their armor is scored and battered, with dozens of tiny craters where glancing hits vaporized the active ceramics.

Argo thuds along behind Keiko, deceptively swift for a man of his bulk and encumbrance. From his faceplate down to his shins he is covered in sooty burns and stripes of ricocheted metal. While his back is completely untouched, the front of his armor is heavily dimpled from bullets and beams.

Deepak trails behind, making efforts not to thrash Sharon with harsh movements. He hugs the small woman firmly against his neck and aims his rifle single-handed, head jerking back and forth in search of the enemy.

"Zuri!" Sho-Lo calls again. *"Can you hear us? Respond!"*

The radio is silent, not even static. Minutes earlier, the team was in a savage fight for survival, but now the Operators' desperate scramble seems at odds with the stillness and clear air around them.

"Where'd they all go?" Keiko asks. "No reason for them to break off."

Deepak's eyes stretch wide behind his helmet's visor. He whirls about so fast, Sharon's legs and arms fly out like wings. He gapes at the empty corridor behind him.

"Colonel," he cries, "Maiella's gone!"

Sharon, confounded by the rough travel and jostling, props herself up on Deepak's shoulder. She struggles against the Gun's powerful grip to look.

"Maiella?" she shouts, anxiety shortening the pitch of her voice.

"Blast it!" Shao-Lo curses. "Why couldn't she keep up?" The Colonel breaks her sprint and short steps to a halt. Keiko stops behind her, allowing Deepak and Argo a chance to catch up.

"We go get her?" Keiko asks.

Shao-Lo stares into their wake, her eyes narrow with frustration and disappointment. "Negative. Continue to MedLab."

"Colonel!" Argo protests. "We can't *leave* her!"

Shao-Lo wheels around at the Brick, either unaware or unconcerned that her rifle is pointing directly at his waist.

"MedLab is our priority, *Sergeant*, along with Carter and Zuri. We regroup then search for Maiella and Keller in strength. Now GO!"

Argo gives a submissive nod and charges past his Colonel, cannon ready. Shao-Lo waits for Keiko and Deepak to sprint by, watching Sharon's worried face as she bounces on the Gun's shoulder, then she chases after her team with a sharp eye to the rear.

Soon, they are back in familiar territory, winding their way to MedLab and Honniker's vault of preserved experiments. Without realizing it, the Operators fall into a stealthy hustle, sacrificing some speed to hush their passage, until they see the MedLab lobby's bright lights shining around the corner ahead. Argo slows to a halt and signals all behind him to stop with a raised fist. He peeks around the corner into dazzling white light. Bullets blast chunks out of the wall and snap the Brick's head back like a mule kick. He staggers to cover and shakes his head as the echoing roar of machine pistols fades.

"ZURI, *HOLD YOUR FIRE!"* the big man shouts.

"Argo?" Zuri shouts back. "Is that you?"

Shao-Lo strides to the front of the team and pauses before rounding the corner.

"Zuri, we're coming out!"

"Understood," the young Geek replies.

Shao-Lo looks over her shoulder and notices a new metallic stripe on Argo's forehead.

"You all right?"

Argo nods, "Yes, sir." He reaches up to feel the impact with his gauntleted hand. "Was a good shot."

The Colonel snorts and strides into the light. "Carter, are you here?"

"Aye, sir," comes a deep-voiced reply from the ceiling. An overhead grating slides open and Carter drops like a wrecking ball into the hallway.

His bulk eclipses the light flooding from MedLab.

"Didn't know what happened to you," he says, hanging a bulb-shaped device back onto his belt. He salutes with a black-bandaged hand.

Shao-Lo returns the salute and spins the huge man around to walk with her. A question perches on her tongue until she notices the Brick's armor is raked with innumerable slashes, and the hand he saluted with looks narrower than it should be.

"You're injured?" she asks.

The Brick holds up his bandaged hand. It is missing the ring finger and little finger along with the carpals to which they rooted.

"Isn't bad. Thing snuck up and tackled me. I grabbed it by the jaw and it bit right through my hand." His head bobs with respect in recollection of the fight, and he flips his hand over, flexing the remaining digits. He crooks his trigger finger, holding it up to show.

"Still got the one that matters."

Shao-Lo acknowledges with a grunt then asks, "Why didn't you answer my call?"

"With respect, Colonel, we never got one. Zuri was trying everything, but she couldn't reach you. Didn't know if you'd been killed or..."

Zuri slips out through the glass entryway of the lobby, clipping her lightly smoking pistols to her back. She salutes rigidly.

"Welcome back, Colonel. With the radio silence and all the combat, we thought we'd lost you."

"Not yet," the tall woman answers dryly. "Our radios aren't working. You know why?"

Zuri pivots as Shao-Lo passes and walks with her back into the lobby.

"Radio signals are either being blocked, absorbed, or cancelled entirely," she says, fading into the lobby with Carter and the Colonel.

Argo is about to follow when he notices three feline carcasses in the shadows outside the MedLab's bright entrance. High caliber bullets riddle one of them. The other two are broken in unnatural angles. One's head is rotated 180 degrees on the neck. The other's head is crushed in the outline of an enormous boot.

The way the broken limbs drape across one another reminds Argo of a fleeting moment years back just before leaving for Earth.

Pulled in close for one last embrace with Thompson and Maiella before boarding the one-way transport to Earth...

"These are the ones, I think," says Sharon, standing beside him.

Argo hurtles back to the present. "Hmm?"

"The ones in the hallway. The ones that nearly got me."

"I'm sure Maiella had you covered."

Sharon keeps looking as if Argo had said nothing. "They would have killed me."

"They would have *tried*."

"So why do I feel sad looking at them?"

The question nails the transient emotion that was tapping against his stoicism like a fly against a window.

"I know what you mean," the big man says.

"Sergeant!" booms Shao-Lo's voice from the lobby.

Like a spring, Argo bounces toward the entryway and jogs to Shao-Lo. Keiko and Deepak stand on each side of her.

"Sir?"

"Just a minute," Shao-Lo says. She looks over Argo's shoulder. "Sharon, please go inside with Carter and Zuri. We'll join you in a minute."

"Sure," Sharon answers, and she hurries through the bone-strewn lobby to the sterile laboratory beyond.

Once out of sight, Shao-Lo lifts her faceplate, as do Keiko and Deepak, cueing Argo to do the same. When the Brick lifts his own, Shao-Lo's fist smashes his exposed face. His wide head snaps back, and his eyes blink with watery surprise. A single trickle of blood rolls from his wide nose.

Shao-Lo leans in aggressively. *"Do I have your attention, Sergeant?"*

Argo's eyes crush shut and re-open, the orbits of his eyes already darker.

"Sir, yes, Sir!"

"You're not new to the Corps. *So what makes you think you can question my order?"*

Argo's bewilderment ends with the memory of his own voice protesting the decision to delay Maiella's rescue. He looks from the diamond-hard glare of the Colonel to Deepak and Keiko. They mirror the fierce woman's expression. In an instant, his conditioning drops like a cage around the emotion he allowed to grow. He clamps it down, disgusted with it, ashamed of it, having permitted such a brazen act of insubordination. His jaw flexes and one side of his upper lip twitches as if about to snarl.

"There's no excuse, sir." He stands rigid and straight. "My performance must be exemplary. It shames me I needed a reminder."

"Let's be sure," Shao-Lo says, stepping close. "What was your mistake?"

"Allowing impulse to overcome reason."

"How did that happen?"

"Inappropriate attachment to another."

"What will you *do* about it?"

"Obey the Operator code. Hold to my conditioning. Focus on my duty, always."

Shao-Lo squints at Argo a long time, scrutinizing him, analyzing, weighing, judging.

"And Maiella? What of *her*?"

"She is...She is like any of us. Precious yet equal."

"Do you believe, even for an *instant*, that we would not try to rescue her?"

Argo hedges then permits candor. "She believes it. And I always trusted her insights. That made me uncertain."

"She is mentally ill, Argo. I won't deny things would be easier without her interference, but we can't set aside our duty whenever it's convenient! We swore an oath to protect *all* human life."

"Except for the exiled..."

Shao-Lo sighs the kind of sigh like one who is wasting their time. "Keller overturned that decision, do you not remember?"

Argo silently recalls standing at attention before the Leadership Council and the assembled officers of the *Europa*, the awkward words passing between them like missiles in a firefight. He lowers his head.

"Your talents are known. But Chusan and I took a *huge* risk letting you back in," she says at last. "You must *not* allow Maiella's illness to re-infect you."

"Aye, sir," Argo says, looking up from his feet.

"You question an order again, *any order*, you're out of the Corps. *Forever*. Do you understand?"

"Perfectly, sir."

Argo tastes salty copper rolling down his top lip. He welcomes it. For in the dressing down, he sees himself as Shao-Lo, Deepak, and Keiko see him. Not long ago he was an officer in the Corps, a Lieutenant, and imagining a subordinate questioning his authority makes his fists curl. Such behavior is completely unacceptable and he knows it.

How could it happen? How could I jeopardize my ability to serve? Never again, he swears to himself. *Never again.*

"You have my perfect attention, Colonel, and you have my oath that I will exemplify the Corps values in thought and in action for as long as I draw breath." The Brick stands straight. "What are your orders?"

Shao-Lo studies Argo a moment longer before answering, "You, Deepak, and Keiko guard this entrance. If it moves and it isn't human..." She points to his cannon. "...put a half-meter hole through it."

"Aye, SIR!"

"Get to it."

The Brick salutes. He falls in with the two Guns, and they glide out into the corridor.

Shao-Lo watches them go, her face a mask of troubled thoughts. With her trademark grunt, she strides across the bone-strewn lobby into Honniker's sterile domain. Everything appears as it was, except Carter and Zuri are standing with Sharon near the lift at the room's center. She runs over to them.

"Carter," the Colonel says, interrupting the conversation, "is our cargo ready?"

"Aye, sir. We have crates staged on trolleys."

"And the colonists?"

"Voss, we can carry, but..." Carter looks at Zuri. Zuri looks down at the floor. "We can't disconnect Rosenthal without killing her."

"You found her?" Sharon says with exasperation. She looks into each Operator's face with angry confusion. *"Why didn't you tell me?"*

"Her body is spent," Carter replies. "Her mind is destroyed. To see her in such a state would only upset you." The huge Brick faces the Colonel again. "All we can do is grant her retirement."

"Is it done?" Shao-Lo asks.

"No, sir! We could never do so without a direct order."

Shao-Lo grimaces. After the lecture she gave to Argo, she knows she cannot give such an order. But leaving the woman in such a state, even if she is a wracked shell, seems horribly wrong. Her eyes fall on Sharon.

"Rosenthal isn't one of ours," Shao-Lo decides. "I can't decide her fate. You'll have to do that."

Sharon's expression droops until the *Cooler* draws her gaze with a dreadful magnetism.

"Is there *nothing* that could be done?"

Carter shakes his head, permitting only the slightest sympathy in his weathered features.

The Operators wait for Sharon to make the choice and are surprised when the decision comes quickly.

"I know the lengths you people go to save a life. If there were even the *slightest* hope, I know you'd try. If...if she can't be saved...*Give her peace.*"

"What of Summers' remains?" Carter asks.

Sharon turns away from the *Cooler*. "Are they *all* in there?"

"We still haven't found Aaronson," Zuri observes, "or Keller for that matter."

Shao-Lo thoughtfully considers Carter's hanging question. "We leave Summers behind."

"He deserves a burial, at least," Sharon says heavily.

The tall colonel scans the wide space. "He'll have to wait. We're outnumbered here and it's time we departed."

"Nothing would please me more," Sharon says, "but there's something you have to see first."

"What is it?"

"Up here," the colonist says, pointing to the office above.

"What *is* it?" Shao-Lo asks again.

"You'll have to see for yourself."

"We don't have time for—"

"Indulge me," Sharon insists in a never before seen show of assertiveness.

The Colonel cranes her neck up at the hatch far overhead. "Carter, you and Zuri finish up in the *Cooler*. Sharon, just take care of what you need to and meet us down here ASAP."

"YOU NEED TO SEE THIS, COLONEL," Sharon says with a rigid jaw.

Shao-Lo squints skeptically. "I can't help but notice, Sharon, that when *I* ask you to do something, it doesn't happen."

"Yes, Colonel, you're right, and I do apologize for that. I must be more open to your requests. But I simply *must* show you the *art collection* up there," Sharon says in exaggerated tones. "It wouldn't be right for you to have come all this way without seeing something you *wanted to find*. I'm quite sure you'll be *VERY sorry if you missed it.*"

Shao-Lo looks directly at Sharon, finally sensing the coded message. With a head toss, she sends Carter and Zuri on their way and steps onto the lift platform.

"Very well, Jones. I'll look at this waste of time if only you'll agree to stop talking about it."

"Actually, Zuri will want to see this, as well."

Zuri halts and turns back, checking with Shao-Lo visually. The Colonel nods and waves the Geek back to the platform. Once aboard, Sharon punches the ascend button and the lift cables stretch tight, jerking the old machinery up from the catches on the floor.

An uneasy silence begins the slow ascent.

"This had better be as good as you say, Jones," Shao-Lo says, slinging her rifle. "Maiella and Keller could be in trouble."

"It can't be described, Colonel, you just have to see it. It's *worth* it."

Shao-Lo frets impatiently and leans on the polished wood railing. She looks out over the experimentation floor, watching Carter disappear inside the *Cooler's* big vault door.

Long quiet moments pass.

"What did he do..." Sharon asks, "...to Rosie and Summers?"

Shao-Lo looks to her side and sees the colonist standing there, looking down at the *Cooler*. The small woman is ashen, yet composed.

"Rosenthal's being harvested for fetal tissue. Summers...Honniker separated his head and spine from his body...and he died."

Sharon remains upright, her eyelids like wilted flower petals, and she stares without visible reaction.

"I wish Ortega was here," she says cryptically. "He'd know what to say for them."

Shao-Lo looks again at the *Cooler*, still leaning on the railing. "Didn't expect you to take it so well."

"I think I've had my fill. It's all overflow, now."

The hatch above slides open with the attendant warning, *"Please keep arms and legs inside railing."*

Sharon moves over to Zuri and points up at one of the four catches. "That one sticks. You'll have to smack it with your pistol."

As predicted, the indicated safety catch fails to retract, whining and buzzing like a trapped insect. Zuri takes a pistol by the muzzle and whacks it against the complaining catch. It releases and slides aside with a *clunk*.

The lift ascends fully and the rails drop after the audible warnings finish, leaving them standing in the middle of the suite. Shao-Lo and Zuri spread their stance, sub-consciously preparing for the unknown in such an oddly decorated place.

"Is *this* what you wanted us to see?" Shao-Lo says, annoyed.

Before Sharon can answer, the doors at the end of the suite swing open and Marta strides out in work attire. Her hair is still bundled neatly upon her head, glasses perched on the bridge of her nose. She walks with deliberate ease, one foot in front of the other.

"Welcome back, Doctor," Marta says to Sharon. "Was your diversion to the *Park* relaxing?"

"*She* sent you to the *Park*?" Zuri asks. The Geek takes her pistols in hand. Marta watches the Geek arm herself and she tilts her head. Her unwavering eyes narrow in the appearance of confusion.

"Is something wrong, Doctor?"

"It's all right, Marta. Zuri, please, put your guns away." Sharon moves between Marta and the agitated Operators. "These are friends of mine, Marta. I'd like you to cooperate fully with them."

"Of course." The android's eyes blink according to their algorithm. "Would they care for refreshments?"

"Yes, Marta, some pure water, please, then we'd like to get right to work."

"Immediately. Make yourselves comfortable in the office. I'll be right back."

The monolithic glass door swings open behind them and the office illuminates.

As Marta walks toward the double doors at the far side of the suite, Shao-Lo and Zuri watch her with acute interest.

"What do you think, Zuri?" Shao-Lo asks.

"Synthetic," the Geek answers, clipping her pistols to her back. "Impressive likeness to a human female, but far too round. Doesn't seem the designers were very good."

"HA!" Sharon blurts before she can clap both hands over her mouth. The Operators turn to her with confusion, and she just shakes her head.

"Something wrong, Jones?" Shao-Lo inquires.

"I'm fine," Sharon says after lowering her hands. "Please, don't mind me. Shall we?" She gestures to the office.

Shao-Lo strides through the open glass doorway, rapidly inspecting the room for anything suspicious. Like Sharon before, the Colonel tours the wall of accolades, degrees, and certifications, reading them aloud.

"Doctor of Medicine, specialties in BioMechanics and Hormone Replacement Therapy. Founder, Academy of Human Longevity. Chairman, Council on Reversing Age and Decrepitude..."

Zuri follows and stands obediently, hands clasped behind her back. Sharon enters last and takes the comfortable chair at the desk.

"I'm sorry I couldn't tell you anything down there, Colonel," Sharon begins. "I don't think Honniker knows about Marta, or what this place is."

"You can start now," Sho-Lo replies. "What *is* this place?"

"This used to be the real Honniker's living quarters and office. It's isolated from the rest of the facility, 'cause he worried about the other scientists hacking his data. While the elevator hatch is closed, this place is insulated from sound and radio transmission. We're totally secure in here."

"And this Marta thing?"

"Honniker's live-in research assistant, domestic, and love-bot, all-in-one."

"You mentioned data stores?"

"That's right. Marta's the access point. You ask her for the info, she retrieves it and plays it back on holo-screen."

The soft *clack* of dress shoes approaches from outside the office and Shao-Lo watches, intrigued, as Marta brings in a silver tray with three tall glasses of chilled water. The android places the tray gently on the desk and serves her guests.

"Thank you," Sharon says.

Marta smiles gratefully then she locks on to Sharon's suit. "It seems you've been playing rather rough, Doctor. Would you like some fresh clothes?"

Sharon looks down at her suit, knowing the inside is worse than the outside. "You know I'd love that, but can we just clean these, instead?"

"Come with me. I'll get you fixed right up." Marta pauses at the door. "May I get anything else for your guests?" She looks at Shao-Lo and Zuri, who still clutch their glasses of water.

"No," Shao-Lo answers.

Sharon rises from the comfortable padding. "Zuri, have a seat. Anything you want to see, ask Marta. She can show you. I'll be back."

Zuri checks with Shao-Lo then takes the padded chair. The Geek rolls forward, searching for an interface, when a holowindow opens above the desk.

"I've prepared several files at the Doctor's request," Marta says. "Would you like to access them?"

"Yes," Shao-Lo answers.

The window displays multiple file paths, which morph into a three-dimensional holographic scene with icons hovering in mid-air.

"Simply touch the icon, or think it with your HDI," Marta explains. "Now then, please excuse us."

"Hang on," Shao-Lo says suddenly. She drains her water in a swift gulp and puts the glass on the table. "I'm coming with."

"I don't think we have anything in your size," Marta says politely, "but we'll try."

"Zuri, get started. Sift what you can. And see if you can find a schematic of this place. Architectural drawing, map, anything." She wipes her mouth with the back of her hand.

The tall Colonel strides from the room, following Marta and Sharon into the museum-like main hall. Despite her down-to-business attitude, even she cannot ignore the carved statue, and its commanding face seems to require her attention. The detailed limbs, though inanimate, appear dynamic to the gruff woman as though some human, larger than life, was petrified and preserved for all time.

Double doors swing open at Marta's approach, permitting a view into a lavish bedroom. A huge round bed occupies the back wall. False bay windows are backlit with super high-resolution holoscreens, showing a wide lawn with flowered gardens and ornamental trees. Artificial sunlight streams from the displays at a down angle, the intense yellow rays striking the plush carpeted floor and giving the entire room a warm glow.

An exercise machine, motorized and configurable, stands folded in one corner beside mirrored walls. A wardrobe runs the full length of the opposing wall, filled with a staggering array of shirts, slacks, suits, gowns, and dresses.

Marta guides Sharon through a narrow doorway into a wide bathroom. Large, gray stone tiles cover the floor, accented with veins of white and tan. A flushing commode stands beside a bidet, both fashioned from pure white porcelain and crowned by a molded seat. The vanity extends nearly the length of the wardrobe, upon which stand trays of colognes, perfumes, hygienic appliances, and incredible arrays of jewelry. Trees of necklaces dangle with chains of precious metals and gemstones. Rings occupy dozens of black felt fingers, their inset stones glimmering with all colors of the rainbow. Broaches, cufflinks, bracelets, earrings, anklets, all shine from the length of the vanity, suggesting the resident began at one end and worked their way down, accessorizing like they were on some kind of assembly line.

Sharon gazes at the gleaming array as if she has stumbled into Aladdin's Cave.

"Let me have your clothes," Marta says dutifully. "I'll put them in the wash, good as new. For yourself, I've run a hot bath."

Sharon snaps out of her gem-dazzled trance and turns at the sound of surging water. To her delight, a whirlpool tub over two meters across churns with powerful currents. She nods in anticipation, stripping her helmet, pressure suit, boots, down to her dank under suit.

Shao-Lo, having completed her sweep, takes in the opulent and impractical scene with a scowl. "Wasteful."

"Please, Colonel, I've been living in my own filth for hours now," Sharon counters, peeling off her clinging under suit. "I'll be quick."

Shao-Lo holds up a gauntleted hand and spreads her fingers. "Five minutes, Jones. Don't forget why we're here."

The towering soldier turns on her heel, and Marta calls after her, "I have a plate of Frikkadelle ready. I'll bring it out once I get the Doctor's clothes clean."

"That's fine," Shao-Lo says dismissively. She strides through the plush bedroom, past the double doors, across the rich gallery, and into the glass-walled office.

Zuri leans forward on the transparent desktop. Her goggles flare with intensity and the icons of the holoscreen swarm like hypersonic bees.

"Sharon was right, Colonel. This *is* a good find."

Shao-Lo's annoyed expression softens. "What've you got?"

"More medical data than our MedTechs would believe. We need to get this to Cadre One somehow, but the file sizes are far larger than anything we're equipped to transport."

"Maybe we'll find something here we can use for that. Did you find a schematic?"

The Geek's goggles blank and the icons halt their manic pace. Zuri peers at her Colonel through the stilled swarm.

"Aye, sir." She widens the holoscreen and calls up a detailed drawing of the main facility. Shao-Lo drops her jaw at the expansive architecture, from the primary and secondary reactors buried deep below the main facility, up through the basement gravity enhancement plain, to the environmental control rooms, to the main server nodes, to the manufacturing floor, up to the experimental chambers and personnel decks.

"The whole time we've been here, I never saw any elevators," Zuri notes. "I had no idea the place had so many levels. It's gonna take a long time to search. Keller, Aaronson, the *exile*...they could be anywhere."

Shao-Lo plants her fists on the clear desktop and leans on them. "Well I'm done playing Honniker's game," she spits. Her eyes scour the intricate schematic until she finds a rectangular section marked, *Server Farm*. She stabs a finger at it.

"Magnify that."

Zuri zooms the image, virtually enlarging a room crammed with banks of smoothly twinkling processors.

"If this whole facility is Honniker's body," Shao-Lo says with menace, "then we're going to *rip off his head*."

Stubborn Old Fool

Keller inches his way through the narrow access tunnel, scuffing centuries of dust from the walls with his thick canvas suit. Every movement of his crawl threatens to give him away with a *clunk* from the aluminum rings at his joints, from an inadvertent *thunk* of his helmet, or a sudden slip of his rigid boots as they push him forward. His going is slow with such careful exertion. Sweat rolls down his forehead.

Purity of purpose maintains his concentration, driving him toward vengeance, toward justice and vindication. There is no thought but the defeat of an enemy. His mind and body are united, patient, for ahead lies the delicate underbelly of Honniker's existence: racks of processing nodes, humming with smooth flows of power and networked with the complexity of thirty human brains. With a fire axe, with a pry bar, or with his bare hands, he will smash that humming array until there is nothing but silica shards and battered housings.

For Michaela and Soares. For Voss. For Rosenthal. For Summers. And for Aaronson, wherever you are...

He is grateful for Shao-Lo's radio calls to him, but he could not respond for fear of giving himself away. Not that it matters if he could be saved. Everyone aboard the *Europa* hates him for his part in the destruction. They hate him for his sense of duty to Soshiba Varicorp, for his unquestioning loyalty to authority that drove him to complete his orders. Nothing he has done in the last forty-five waking years at the *Europa's* helm will offset that hatred. There is no life for him anywhere, only this last quest to shut down the gruesome experiments and to bring an end to the sickness which spurred mankind's destruction: the sickness of bottomless greed, the sickness of inhuman torture, the sickness of unrestrained experimentation to sate insane curiosity.

I can cleanse this place, he thinks, elbowing his way through a narrow of bunched cables. *I can make this place clean for them. If nothing else, I can give them this place to make their home.*

He emerges through the narrow and squints at a distant glimmer of red light.

I can give them that. I have to give them that.

Among the selfless motivations, there is also a deeply personal one. For believing so blindly in the perfect decisions of his superiors, he is rewarded with the waste of his entire life, a burden of guilt none should ever have to carry, and derision from everyone he cares about. His superiors, the decision makers, the minds who conceived of the Cadre installations, were burned away long ago in their terrestrial mansions, denying him any opportunity for justice. Because they are all dead, he is the lone inheritor of their sins. He is the last tether to their responsibility, a minor actor in the greater play, yet the only one accessible to the mob. And as such, his only remembrance will be carried in that collective mind, forever identified with the worst persons ever to have lived. For that, he will give the small remainder of his pathetic life to sweep away the last vestiges of the powerful, to eradicate them utterly from existence, to assure their obliteration; and in that ultimate final action, earn back some honor to his tarnished soul, redeem himself in some significant way to keep the name Braemar Keller from forever being the most despised in all human memory.

Thus, the aged man finds the will and vigor to penetrate the difficult passages, to recall the skeletal frameworks he visited as a younger man, to drag himself toward the dim red light in the tunnel and to rip open the junction box cover mated to it.

Rolled on his back, he reaches up into the opened box and tears out the main bus breakers. After folding the sheet metal box cover into a triangle, he holds the long side across multiple hot leads, the triangle's point aimed toward a single line. Using the breakers as an insulator, he jams the triangle into the junction box with a brilliant surge of arcing direct current.

"So there you are, Keller. You'd gotten away from me. Up to something, are you?"

Keller ignores the voice streaming through the emergency channel of his radio and rolls over, letting tiny orange sparks rain over his back and legs. He crawls with the same focus, pushing through the conduit like a mole in a root-filled burrow, intent on the next junction box.

"I don't know what you think you'll accomplish, Keller. The ones

stationed here tried everything to shut me down. You can see how successful they were."

Keller grits his teeth and shuffles forward, suit smothered black with grimy dust. Meters ahead, the conduit angles down out of sight. Just above the slope, another dim red light shines.

"Keller? There really is no point to this. Whatever you try, I'll simply have something waiting for you. I know where all the access conduits lead, you see."

The aged colonist rolls on his back again and hooks the tips of his gloves on the junction box. The sheet metal cover tears away easily.

"Such a fool. Yet you will persist, won't you? Just like the others."

Keller fashions another triangle from the box cover and jams it in, like before. With a savage *BRAP* and a shower of hot metal sparks, the circuit burns.

"You're going to make me come get you, I see. Stubborn old fool."

Keller turns over and slides head first down the dusty slope.

"If you care at all about your friends, you'll stop now."

Keller reaches the bottom of the slope and resumes his crawl down the conduit. More red-lit boxes await his destructive attention, beyond which the conduit ends at a wide-barred grate. Heat radiates from behind it. The closer he gets, the greater the intensity washing over him.

In moments he has another junction box open, and he claws the main breaker away. From the end of the tunnel, beyond the grate, a background hum winds down and fades.

"Keller, I'm talking to you! What do you think you're doing?"

"I told you what I'd do if you crossed us, Honniker." The colonist jams folded sheet metal into the box, singeing the rubber tips of his gloves as miniature lightning bolts strobe across them. He flaps his hand, grimacing at blistering heat, then scuffs his way to the next one.

"You're grasping at straws, old man. You cannot harm me."

"Of course, you're right. This won't hurt you a bit." Keller peels back another box cover with satisfaction and tears the breaker free. Careful not to burn his hand again, he balances the folded triangle on the breaker and thrusts it home. The arcing surge ignites the insulation of the neutral lead and a smutty orange flame licks the box interior before extinguishing.

"The reactor is self-regulating. There's nothing you can do to alter its function. I control all the access points."

"I know." The heat emanating from the grate pours through Keller's translucent helmet like rays of summer sun, turning the globe into a sweat-filled sauna.

"Then you're just being destructive for the sake of being destructive. How petty."

"Yup. Got me pegged." Keller rips another breaker free. The hum beyond the grate winds down, leaving the conduit deathly quiet.

"What is it you think you are accomplishing?"

"I'm burning out your coolant pumps. Without them, the core will overheat. And your automatic reactor will shut down."

"My battery back ups last weeks, not that I'll need them. I already have service bots en route to repair your damage."

"Yeah, but not before the sodium coolant freezes in the pipes."

"I'll simply restart after I've removed you and made repairs."

Keller snorts. "Don't know much about reactors, do you, Honniker?"

"I know everything I need to know to maintain and operate my own power supply."

"Oh? So you know it'll take months to unfreeze the coolant and restart?"

There is a long pause. *"You're lying. You have no idea what you're doing."*

"Yeah," Keller replies with a cynical laugh. "Being a colony administrator and a colony ship's Captain, what would *I* know about nuclear power plants? What would *I* know about your *liquid sodium-cooled fast breeder reactor?"*

There is a long silence. Keller grins to himself and pushes forward.

"I don't have to let you go. I can keep you here forever."

"You say that like it wasn't already your plan." Keller rolls onto his back and pulls apart the last junction box cover. He repeats the process as before, frying the circuit with an extended *BRRRRRAP*.

"Then maybe I should have Mikato get started on Maiella..."

Keller blinks skeptically, the torn-loose breaker still in hand. Bright sparks drop onto his chest, igniting puffs of dust with a flash. He pats them out with his free hand.

"Mikato's still alive? Bullshit." Keller drops the breaker and rolls over.

"I assure you he lives. And he has Maiella right now."

"Now I *know* you're lying. She'd never give up to you *or* Mikato." He elbows his way to the hot grating and peers through it to a vertical tube ten meters in diameter. Running up the middle of the tube is a cluster of rugged pipes, suspended at regular intervals with steel bars and cat walks. The pipes run out of sight in both directions and glow deep red with heat. Before his eyes, the glow fades.

"She came willingly."

"Ha! You're layin' it on thick, Doc."

"Can you receive video?"

Keller backs away from the grate and props himself on his side. "Yes..."

Across the interior of his helmet, a translucent video displays. The view is from high up on a wall looking down on a body-length chair. Maiella relaxes into it, helmet and HDI on a tray beside her. A holographic man in a white lab coat stands at her side, speaking. Maiella nods in understanding and settles back against the headrest.

Opposite the holograph is an enormous cat-like creature, covered in overlapping plates. It sits on its powerful haunches and watches spindly, plastic-wrapped mechanical arms descend from above the chair.

"Does she look compelled to you?"

Keller watches the streaming video, troubled. *It could be a fake,* he thinks unconvincingly.

"She came to us under agreement we would restore her synaptic bridges. All I have to do is say the word, Keller, and her restoration becomes an exercise in threshold testing. She seems more durable than the others...I imagine I'd have to increase my stimulus...unless you replace the breakers you removed."

The man's eyebrows draw together as he weighs the proposition. He looks at Maiella in the chair. *I'm sorry, kid.*

"You're gonna do what you want, regardless. She made her choice..." Keller grips the thick release lever of the grate, and it pops open on a spring-loaded hinge. "...as have I."

"You're going to suffer, Keller. Voss and Summers were nothing compared to what I'll do to you. You'll think you're swimming in lava. Or being eaten alive by Bullet Ants. I can summon levels of pain you won't believe...and I can make them last."

"Good to know you care, Doc." Keller cautiously pokes his head into the vertical space, grimacing against the harsh rays of heat. Directly beneath the opening is a metal ladder, descending to a steel catwalk that spirals down in a continuous ramp along the periphery of the tube. Grates like the one he just popped are closed over multiple access tunnels leading out through the cylindrical walls.

The elder colonist hangs on the hinged grate and pulls his legs from the cramped tunnel, then hooks the ladder with his toe. With the ease of someone accustomed to ships his whole life, he grips the ladder by the edges and zips down to the catwalk. His boots slam onto the steel walkway, echoing up and down a tube hundreds of meters high.

The suspended cluster of hot pipes, unbearably close, rises up toward the surface and makes sharp right angles into the native rock. Keller cranes his stiff neck, gauging the distance, then he drops his gaze, following the pipes to the depths where the outlines waver with heat.

"WARNING! PRIMARY COOLANT PUMP FAILURE!" an automated voice declares. "WARNING! SECONDARY COOLANT PUMP FAILURE! WARNING! AUXILLIARY COOLANT PUMP FALURE!"

Amber lights strobe throughout the tube like pulses of yellow lightning.

"WARNING! CATASTROPHIC FAILURE TO COOLANT PUMP SYSTEMS! SAFE TEMPERATURE UNSUSTAINABLE, COMMENCING MULTIPLE CORE SHUTDOWNS!"

Keller shields his eyes from the brilliant strobes and grins. *That'll keep you busy for a while.* With a quick look around for threats, he runs to the nearest grate, pops it open, and hauls himself through it.

IRONY

Warm currents flow across Sharon's bare skin. She melts against the porcelain, allowing the pulsing jets to pummel her aching back like small, gentle fists. Her arms drape along the tub's rim, and in blissful relaxation she nearly loses grip of the pen-sized recognition cylinder.

Diverse, yet complementary floral essences rise with the steam, hearkening memories of the garden at her family's estate in Saltburn-by-the-Sea, and she mentally vacates her current location in favor of that garden, strolling through the sun-lit lanes, periodically kneeling to inhale a particularly fragrant bloom.

A soft beep snaps her tether to that memorial place, and she hurtles back as if a taut rubber band has stretched across time and space to retrieve her. Sharon turns her head slowly toward the tumbling fabrics in the combination washer/dryer, giving it a sullen glare for the rudeness of its intrusion. The white-enameled machine whirrs on, the words "Cool Down" illuminated on its display.

She sighs heavily, hating the idea of leaving the warm, womb-like bath, but stands, waist deep in suds. She takes hold of the brass railing and sits on the edge, swinging her legs over the side. Cool, dry air of the spacious bathroom collides with her wide-open pores, making her shiver. She snatches a plush white towel from the rack and wraps herself in it.

Her reflection looks back from the long vanity mirror, and Sharon strides toward it as if to introduce herself. In the lightly fogged glass is a thin woman with hair slicked back, hugged closely by a thick towel. Having seen no natural sunlight for ages, she is nearly as white as her wrapping, and only the bruises from Deepak's handling offer clear boundary where cloth ends.

At a distance, her smooth skin and excellent figure could pass for twenty years old. Only close up is her age revealed in the worry lines crossing her forehead, eyes, and mouth.

Sharon scowls at the sight of them, drawing her ears back and jutting her chin. The lines fade and what remains is a bolder, younger, more confident face.

"That's more like it."

Her eyes fall to the marble countertop with scalloped basins and gold faucets. Beside them stand motorized dental appliances. Switching the recognition cylinder to her off hand, she seizes the freshest-looking toothbrush and scours her teeth with it. During the mindless droning, she inspects the glittering festival of light playing through jewelry and gemstones on display. The sparkles remind her of Christmas, like sunlight on fresh snow and the twinkling of decorative lights.

It'd be nice to bring some gifts back, she thinks, dribbling foam down her chin. Her free hand starts with the rings, slipping on one, then another, and she turns her hand, watching the glimmer from multiple facets. Next come necklaces, bracelets, earrings. She bypasses the most gaudy and opulent pieces in favor of those with charm, color, understated appeal, opting in particular for those with marks of daily wear—residual warmth from the original owners.

A final beep behind her signals the end of the dryer cycle, and Marta strolls in, on cue, with Sharon's brown pressure suit draped over one arm. The voluptuous android retrieves Sharon's orange under suit from the machine and snaps it in the air, one-handed.

"Good as new," Marta announces, bringing it to the towel-wrapped woman.

Sharon cups a generous portion of tap water to her mouth, swishes it between teeth, and spits into the basin.

"Ta," the slender woman says, taking the still-warm undersuit. She slips one leg, then the other into it, rocking her hips back and forth as she pulls it over her backside. The moment she slides a hand into a sleeve, she freezes at the sound of tearing fabric.

"Oops."

Sharon looks down at her jewel-encrusted hand, knowing the more delicate gem settings have snagged the fine synthetic fibers.

Marta arches an electronic eyebrow. "Trying to impress someone, Edmund?"

"Heh, uh...yeah?"

Marta reaches up the sleeve from the cuff and carefully unhooks the rings from the inside. She then covers Sharon's hand with her own and draws it down the length of the sleeve until it emerges, snag free. The android slides her hand up the opposite sleeve to repeat, and Sharon lays her hand in Marta's, allowing the android to pull her arm through.

"Marta," Sharon begins, zipping the front of her suit with fingers laded with three or more rings each, "where did all this jewelry come from? I'd swear I've seen some of these before."

Marta shakes her head. "Oh, Edmund, I wish you'd see a doctor about your memory. Some are from your private collection, the rest are on loan from various institutions."

"How did, uh, how did I get them?"

"It was part of your compensation package. Because you were giving up access to an entire planet's selection of luxuries, you reasoned if you were to be so sequestered, the luxuries would have to be extraordinary both in monetary and historic value. For example..."

Marta points at a rugged band on Sharon's thumb, on which is a hand-carved lion holding a double-edged sword in one paw. Around the periphery are tiny stars just inside a raised lip.

"This is believed to be the signet ring of Gnaeus Pompeius Magnus, assassinated in 48 B.C. It was very important to you. Do you not remember?"

Sharon gawks at the rough band perching loosely on her thumb. It feels heavier than a moment ago, given extra weight by its original owner, his modest beginnings, his amazing accomplishments, and his horrible end. She flexes her hand, curling her fingers over her thumb for fear the ring should slip off.

"It's coming back to me now."

"Good." Marta smiles. "Let's get you fully dressed again."

"Right."

Marta unfurls the brown canvas pressure suit and holds it low so Sharon can easily step into it. Like her under suit, the internal padding is dry and warm.

"What've they been doing?" Sharon asks.

"Studying schematics of the facility, video archives." Marta slides the stiff canvas up and holds the top part by the shoulders. "Reviewing your journals and research notes."

"Have they found anything?" Sharon slides her arms through the outer suit sleeves. The padding in the gloves presses firmly against her fingers, holding the loose rings in place.

Marta cocks her head to one side. "I don't understand. They're *your* notes. Is there something they are *supposed* to find?"

Sharon turns around, zipping the suit up from the groin to the collar and sealing the inner then outer seams. She tucks the pen-sized recognition cylinder into a canvas pocket on her pressure suit.

"Marta, there is something *very* wrong here. An artificial intelligence that thinks it's...that thinks it's *me* is running crazy. It has control of this station."

The android steps back and squints, one hand on its hip. "But Edmund, it's *your* upload. *You* created it."

Sharon gawks at the android, one hand still holding the zipper. "Why would I?"

Marta makes an exaggerated inhale as if she had lungs. "I think you've become senile."

"Dammit, Marta!" Sharon drops her hand and faces the android squarely. "Just tell me *why* I would make an AI version of myself!"

The android adopts a compassionate posture. "Because the experiments weighed on you, Edmund. You couldn't sleep. You seldom ate. You ignored me for days at a time, sitting in your chair and staring at nothing. There was no joy in you anymore."

Sharon looks at her feet, imagining the experiment floor beneath constantly whirring, drilling, and slicing to the maniacal shrieks of those stretched out on the tables.

"Well I'd say slaughtering *thousands* in sadistic pleasure *should* wear on a person after a while."

"Oh, no, it wasn't like that. At least, not at first. You came here to advance your studies in human longevity. Your hormone therapies and your auto-rejuvenation research...it made you cringe whenever someone called you 'Ponce de Leon', but you *were* working to reverse the aging process, seeking essentially a 'fountain of youth.' It was primarily this advanced work in human regenerative processes that caught SoVar's attention."

"That doesn't sound so bad. So why did I need an AI?"

"You must've blotted it out of your memory. Now I understand why you don't remember. The memories are too painful..."

"Marta..."

"The discovery of sentient extraterrestrials at New Dresden confirmed humanity may someday face external threats. You knew the purpose here was military and you also knew the military needed soldiers who could remain physically fit through the rigors of long space travel, ones who could bounce back from phenomenal stresses and be ready to defend Earth and her colonies. Your research in anti-aging and auto-regenerative processes was an obvious fit."

260

"So?"

"Through your earlier work, you also knew that for some, the progress of age could not be rolled back or even halted. Their physiologies refused the treatments. You argued that to prolong their lives, it would be necessary to transfer their consciousness, their awareness, and all their experiences to a new body somehow. You believed you understood what sort of experimentation this would require, and it would never be permitted in the high transparency of Earth-based labs. You also knew the costs would be extreme. Even the military, accountable to civilian government leaders, might balk at the sums required. Yet the *real* money came from private investors with great fortunes and highly powerful positions, ones who had much to lose in decrepitude and death. You believed you could perform that research without it damaging your conscience, but the procedures inflicted great pain and suffering on the test subjects. Many died. It weighed on you."

"Why wouldn't I just stop?"

"How could you? You had demanded this type of research as a condition of joining the Cadre Project! You were also under contract. Your reputation, your estates, your accomplishments would all have been claimed in a default of that contract. And you are a man of your word. That was crucial to you, you said. That you had agreed to perform, and so you would."

"But I couldn't take it anymore?"

"You tried. For a very long time you tried. So you went to Dr. Mikato, and he proposed a solution: to upload your necessary skill sets to one of his Artificial Intelligence frameworks, and allow the program to proceed on its own...with your direction, of course."

"But how is that even *possible*?"

"You and Dr. Mikato had already developed a working human to digital interface. The real trick, however, was to decode the memory retrieval and storage system of the human brain. Because individual memories are stored in fragments across the cortex, discovering the method to recall a completely assembled memory was a phenomenal accomplishment—one you knew would earn an eternity of recognition if the program could ever be de-classified."

Sharon, standing before the answer to one of life's greatest mysteries, cannot help but ask, "Do you know how I did that?"

"First, you had the human/digital interface implanted. Then, you thought about selected memories, ones which were particularly strong: your daughter's abduction, ransom, and murder, for example. By monitoring the active neural pathways of such a strong memory, you mapped the sites of the brain that were accessed. With each memory you actively recalled, the map grew more accurate, and soon, you discovered there were overlaps in each memory. For example, every time the color red was part of the memory, the neural structures of your brain which perceived the color red were repeatedly accessed. And so, you discovered, much of your memory is less the *storage* of information as it is a combination of existing perceptions, linked by long-term potentiation of synapses and assemblies of proteins within neurons. That insight permitted rapid advances in the transfer of memory from human to machine."

"But how could one possibly retrieve *that* many components of a single memory?"

"It *is* enormously complex. However the brain has a kind of error-correction that fills in missing data. If one has seen a particular human face, one need only remember certain portions of it to be able to reconstruct the entire image. Using this idea as a foundation, Dr. Mikato developed software, which corrected for lost or inaccessible strings. With repeated experiments, the data stored in machine could be compared against the memory of the individual, and individual discrepancies accounted for or corrected. In time, it was possible to trigger memories by stimulating certain areas of the brain and tracing the activated neural pathways to other areas of the brain, presenting full memories as decodable data sets. These stimulated memories were loaded into an artificial intelligence framework, decoded by the error-correction software, then archived in a machine-accessible directory. Gradually, a lifetime of accumulated memories could be assembled into a working database."

"Yeah, but the A.I. out there isn't just some encyclopedia. It's got behaviors, independent thoughts..."

"Reflexes and emotions are not nearly so complicated as memories. Mostly, they are primitive responses to stimulus, ones which humans learn to reinforce or suppress as required. Many of Mikato's androids were able to approximate these functions already. The difference here is being able to preserve an individual's unique experiences and then transferring them to an external framework to achieve a very specific artificial life form...ideally, one which was a match of the original, complete with consciousness and identity intact."

"But this one, the one who thinks it's Honniker, why is it only a *partial* upload?"

"You were cautious. Should it be too perfect a copy, you saw how you would be immediately expendable. Thus, you seeded it with only the knowledge and the behaviors you believed were essential for success, like curiosity and freedom from moral restriction. With your routine inputs, you directed the research without the emotional cost of performing the procedures yourself. You retrieved the results each day after the experiment floor had been sanitized and reviewed them in the comfort of your sound-proofed office."

Sharon closes her eyes. *Nothing's ever simple, is it?* She steps away from Marta and looks at herself in the mirror. The worry lines are back.

"There's no way a rational person would just cram his head full of wires and start uploading," Sharon says to the glass, "not unless he knew it was going to work. So how did the human interface thing come about?"

"Your understanding of neuro-mechanics was a perfect match for Dr. Mikato's understanding of cybernetics and nano-technology. Together, you devised a solution you named a 'Synaptic Bridge'. Once the theory was sufficiently supported by real world testing, it was implemented on human subjects."

"The inmates..."

"Yes."

Sharon looks down from her reflection and turns slowly to look at the patient android. "That must have taken a lot of testing."

"A sufficient number to prove efficacy."

"How many?"

"One hundred thousand eight hundred ninety-two."

"What?"

"One hundred thousand eight hundred ninety—"

"I *heard* you, Marta, I just can't believe it! How could a doctor do that?"

Marta folds her hands together. "Many nights you woke up screaming," she says softly. "You relived the loss of your daughter over and over in your dreams, always shoving your way through the police barricade and seeing her body. You never told me what the kidnappers did to her, but I didn't have to know. I could see in you that it was brutal. I think, in the beginning, you were seeking some means of retribution while somehow drawing something good from it. You told me once, 'I could torture every prisoner to death a thousand times over for what they did. But when I imagine her watching me...I'm ashamed'. Whatever your reasons at the start, you needed a way out."

"So I had the operation?"

"Yes. It was a very long process, taking months to complete in its various stages. You were conscious during each procedure, out of necessity, for you were guiding the surgery with Mikato assisting."

Sharon's mouth parts in disbelief. "Conscious? With all those things drilling into my head?"

"You said the process was almost completely painless. With each fiber less than a micron in diameter, there was little, if any, sensation."

"So that was it? I uploaded, and turned it all over to the AI?"

"Not entirely. You were functioning again, and it made me very happy to see you taking pride in yourself again. But the AI version you had seeded was performing so well, constantly updating itself to perform additional procedures, that the base commanders offered it new avenues of research. It never said, 'no,' always acquiesced to whatever request was given to it, never required rest, nourishment, or payments. In essence, it was far more accommodating than you were and SoVar decided they would rather work with *it* than *you*."

Sharon turns back to her reflection as Marta continues.

"It's ironic that you refused a complete upload for fear of being replaced, when in fact you had already given the AI all of the attributes SoVar deemed valuable. So after a time, they didn't need you anymore. But, because SoVar was bound by contract as tightly as you were, you were allowed to retain all of your privileges and rewards."

"So long as I stayed out of the way?"

"Precisely."

Sharon takes angry steps toward the door and stops just short of it. "If the A.I. was so agreeable, how did we get *here*?"

"What do you mean?"

"I mean how did it go wild? This place is wrecked!"

"Ah. To understand, you should know your Artificial Intelligence was not the only one created here. Based on your success, Dr. Mikato was encouraged to undergo the process himself. He was not going to be shut out like you were, however, and he only agreed if he could undergo a *complete* upload with full rights, awareness, and autonomy. So he did. His body was interred in a long-term cryotube and he remained an artificial persona ever after."

"Mikato's still *here*?"

"I've had no contact with any entity besides you and your friends for a very long time. His artificial persona may have become corrupted or lost. But because the facility is still functional, it is possible Mikato still exists."

Sharon's mind spins. "There are *two*..." Her eyes dart toward Marta's and lock on. "What happened then, after Mikato...uploaded?"

"The pace of research advanced many fold. And Dr. Jin-Sung was encouraged to undergo the procedure as well."

"Jin-Sung?"

"A master geneticist. In the way you were the foremost researcher in Anti-Aging and Biomechanics, and Mikato in Cybernetics and Nanotech, Dr. Jin-Sung was at the forefront of genetics."

"He built the big *tiger-bear* things running around here?"

"Yes."

"Did he?"

"Did he...what? Undergo the procedure?"

"Yeah."

"He did not. As you can imagine, the speed of discovery from the other Artificial researchers made Jin-Sung's work seem slow and costly by comparison. But Doctor Jin-Sung flatly refused. Despite *enormous* pressure, he was determined to remain a physical entity. Moreover, he deplored Mikato's and your decisions to upload. He believed crossing over into a machine existence was a huge step backwards in our evolution, one which would erase all human distinction forever. 'DNA is far more efficient at encoding data than ones or zeros. The uniqueness of all life, when reduced to binary, is lost,' he said. The idea was repugnant to him and he vehemently protested against it. His funding was cut as a result and several contracts were transferred to Mikato AI and Honniker AI."

"So he wasn't well-liked by the company..."

"No."

"What happened to him? Did he give up?"

"He held out as long as he could, until he found he had lost the support of several powerful friends back on Earth. Without their support, greater pressure was placed on Dr. Jin-Sung and though he never gave in to the demand he upload, he was coerced into several projects he found personally objectionable."

"Such as?"

"I have no access to his research, only records of what you have said about him. And you never spoke in detail about his projects."

"Okay, so *then* what happened?"

"There was a breach of Jin-Sung's server. Though the source of the attack was never proven, you were certain it was Mikato. Jin-Sung had become quite paranoid by then, anticipating just such an assault. He transferred all of his data to an isolated server, as you had—"

"We don't have time for the blow by blow. There were people here, Marta. Thousands of *people*. What happened to them?"

Marta blinks, her face shifting to one prescribed for delivering bad news.

"When news of the colonies' and Earth's destruction arrived, the people here were stunned into a kind of helpless torpor. The AIs, by contrast, became more active. They understood they no longer needed to cooperate. There were no higher authorities to serve, no possibility they could be restrained or curbed. Even so, the people trusted them, not believing they could become self-serving."

"But they did..."

Marta nods. "By way of efficiency, the AIs had already been given control over several automated systems running Cadre Two. Following the destruction, what functions not already granted the AIs *demanded* in exchange for keeping the ventilators running. Soon Mikato AI and Honniker AI had assumed every aspect of Cadre Two's operation. But without any fresh supplies of inmates coming in..."

"...they started on the people here." Sharon's eyes are wide with grim understanding.

Marta nods. "Honniker AI insisted the survivors move into the cells and submit to the experiments. It was not well received. When the soldiers stationed here tried to shut down the main servers and regain control, both AI's released the experiments. While Mikato's war machines occupied the soldiers, Jin-Sung's predators herded many research assistants and support staff into the *Flounder's* lobby. Once contained in the lobby, however, the predators grew excited by the people's fear and began...eating them."

Sharon's hand covers her mouth, eyes closed, trying to shut out the awful scene, but her witness of the violent aftermath in the lobby makes it impossible *not* to imagine.

"To punish the predators for ruining a large share of the only remaining inventory," Marta continues, "Honniker AI sealed the room and left the predators trapped inside to starve."

"Where was Honni...I mean, where was *I* in all of this?"

"You were down on the experiment floor. Trying to open the door so the people trapped in the lobby could get in."

"But I couldn't?"

Marta shakes her head. "You tried and tried to get the door open but once the screams were over, you got on the lift and radioed to me you wanted to die. You disabled my safeties and ordered me to hit you in the head with the marble sphere."

Sharon hunches at the memory of the video, Marta's arm swinging through the frame and fatally clubbing the real Dr. Honniker.

Maybe he really wanted to die.

But that thought is annihilated with the recollection of surprise on Honniker's face—the calm recognition, then shock. *He saw the killing strike coming and he was terrified.*

"And the soldiers?" Sharon asks.

"They fought their way down to the server rooms but were repelled. A call went out to evacuate Cadre Two."

"Did they?"

"I don't know. After you ordered me to crush your skull, a shut down command executed which made me inactive for five hundred years. Do you know why that occurred?"

"No, Marta, I don't."

"My chronometer indicates that I have been idle for over one thousand years. Do you know why I didn't reactivate after five hundred years?"

Sharon shakes her head sympathetically, then stops cold. *The cylinder...the one Honniker implanted in his arm...* She pats the canvas pocket subconsciously.

Marta watches Sharon quizzically. "Is something wrong?"

In a cold flash, Sharon is reminded Marta is an Artificial Intelligence all her own. She watched the android club Honniker to death, yet somehow she never felt threatened because the android has been so docile and accommodating.

Could Marta do it again? Sharon wonders. *The safeties were reset and the override removed...am I mad to trust her?*

The colonist looks around the bathroom, not feeling threatened, but uncomfortably aware that she is alone with an artificial intelligence who has confessed to murder.

"No, no," Sharon answers finally. "Let's see how the others are making out, yeah?"

"Of course. Now then, you really must eat something. Would you like your Frikkadelle?"

Feeling amiable, she says, "Sure."

"Wonderful! I'll bring it into the office so you can share with your friends."

The curvy android strides from the bathroom. Sharon follows her out, her boots clomping on the immaculate tile. Marta is on her way through the double doors when Sharon stops and calls out to her.

"Marta?"

"Yes, Edmund?"

The colonist grimaces, being unable to accept the name as her own. "If I was concerned about getting shoved aside, or put out...would I have a weapon in here somewhere?"

Marta turns abruptly, striding straight for the enormous bed. "In fact, you do." She flips several pillows from the headboard and touches a panel, which recesses and slides aside. Within the hidden cabinet, a black and sinister type of pistol rests on a cradle. Sharon approaches it cautiously.

"It's a custom model, made by Mikato as a gift between friends," Marta explains.

"Before his upload, I presume."

"Yes, before. It's a hand-held particle cannon. It sacrifices number of shots for output."

"How many shots?"

"Three. Though a single shot is sufficient to vaporize a man-sized target, and most of whatever is behind him."

Sharon leans in, studying the numerous loops along the central barrel. It is about the length of her forearm, with the grip pushed forward toward the barrel end. Delicately, she lifts it from the cradle.

Marta watches Sharon holding the weapon improperly, and says, "The grip is molded to your *left* hand, as you are left-handed."

Sharon shifts the grip to her left hand. Though fashioned for a larger hand, her glove adds extra thickness, making it comfortable to hold.

"The circular clamp at the back encircles your forearm near the elbow," the android continues. "It gives excellent balance and stability to the weapon, and minimizes the chance it could be knocked from your grasp or dropped."

Sharon slides the circular brace around the thick canvas of her suit and clamps it shut. As described, it feels very natural.

"Where's the battery?" Sharon asks.

"Internal, not removable. When the weapon is discharged, return it to the cradle."

Sharon hefts the weapon clamped to her arm, feeling its weight, its substance. Before this voyage, she would not have touched it. Probably would not have even looked at it.

"All right, Marta. Let's go."

Sharon strides from the bedroom, Marta leading the way. As they cross the living area, Sharon gazes at the remarkable works of art. With a twinge, she knows she will never see them again.

Shao-Lo looks up from the office terminal at the sound of Sharon's clomping strides.

"Good, you're ready."

The tall Colonel swings around the desk and immediately locks on to the weapon clamped to Sharon's arm.

"Is that live?"

"'Tis."

"You know what to do with it?"

Sharon lifts her arm and runs her eyes over the dark weapon. "Point it at the Baddies and shoot?"

Shao-Lo scowls but decides against a lecture. "Get your helmet. You're leaving."

"Oh?"

"I'll get it for you," Marta says without acknowledgement.

Sharon squints at the tall Colonel. "What do you mean, *I'm* leaving?"

"There's been a multi-core shutdown," Zuri announces, collecting storage devices from the glass desktop and tucking them into a pouch. She rolls the pouch and tosses it to Sharon. Sharon catches it with her free hand.

"Get that to Major Ralla," Shao-Lo insists.

"Just wait a bloody second!" Anxiety fills Sharon like some wriggling, wild thing. "We're leaving together, *yeah*?"

"Sharon, we can't leave this place with Honniker still in charge. Someone shut down the power plant and that gives us two opportunities: One, we can get you and *that* out of here, and two, we can take Honniker down for good."

"Who shut it down? Maiella? Keller?"

"Maybe. All I know, this is the break we needed. We can get our foot on Honniker's neck for sure."

Sharon holds up the pouch. "What's *this*?"

"Things we need. *Desperately.*"

Marta returns with Sharon's helmet. Shao-Lo takes it brusquely and drops it over the navigator's head, then takes the small woman by the shoulders and ushers her toward the lift.

"We'll escort you to the transport, then Asha will get you back to Cadre One."

Sharon digs her heels in against Shao-Lo's shoves. *"I said WAIT, GODDAMMIT!"*

Marta shoves her way between Sharon and Shao-Lo, pressing the tall colonel back with a hand.

"You'll take your hands from the Doctor this instant," the android states with dispassionate determination.

Shao-Lo's eyes widen at the hand against her chest, tensing for a fight. Sharon defuses it.

"Marta! Please, it's all right! Leave her be! She wasn't hurting me."

Sharon turns to look Shao-Lo in the face. "She was just being an overbearing *twat* again, is all."

Shao-Lo's lungs fill deeply and she exhales through her nose as though trying to exhale all her frustration and impatience. She steps around Sharon and the protective android on her way to the lift platform. Zuri marches behind her.

"There's another one, another *AI*!" Sharon shouts after them. "It isn't *just* Honniker!"

"Another AI?" Shao-Lo halts, looks at her Geek sub-ordinate.

"It's possible," Zuri corroborates.

"Are they teamed up or operating independently?" Shao-Lo demands.

"What difference does it make?" the exasperated colonist asks.

"If we could turn one on the other," Zuri answers, one corner of her mouth bending upward, "...a *big* difference."

One Quick Run

The lift descends from the ceiling office down into a much darker chamber than before. Main illumination is out, leaving only emergency lighting over the exit and a thin sliver emanating from the cracked *Cooler* vault door.

Shao-Lo and Zuri click on their helmet lamps, their beams streaming out across dormant experimentation tables and vacant cells.

Sharon looks up to the bright office above for a last glance at the warm and comfortable island. Marta looks down at her through the open hatch, and as the overhead doors close, Sharon is certain she sees sadness in the android's programmed features.

Marta's joy to serve comes through as clear as any Cadre Operator's, Sharon thinks to herself. *But if she's a similar construct to the AIs running amok, there's no way to be sure of her loyalty...* The colonist turns away from the overhead hatch and gazes out into the vast chamber. *Trust is hard to find in this place.*

"If it helps," Zuri begins, as though channeling Sharon's thoughts, "that android is just a vessel. All its software is based in the office server. If you take it out of range, the body'll become inactive."

Sharon looks up again at the closed hatch.

"Can't shake the feeling we're leaving someone behind, is all."

"We're coming back," Shao-Lo says definitively. "But we have to warn O'Kai of the danger. If we don't get you out now, we may not be able to."

The colonist pivots to the armored woman. "Come back *here?* To this *madhouse?* Best it was forgotten."

"We *have* to return," Shao-Lo concludes.

Something in the Colonel's voice, her posture, grabs Sharon's attention. *Has something happened at Cadre One I don't know about?* she wonders. *Or is it that Shao-Lo sees an opportunity for command? Could it be that hard being O'Kai's second?*

"You're already here," Honniker's voice rings from the dark. *"Why not stay?"*

"Stay out of our way, Doctor," Shao-Lo warns.

"I beg your pardon, Colonel, but this is MY home, and you are very much in MY way."

"This is your home, you say?" Sharon baits. "Then why can't you keep the lights on?"

In the silence, Sharon imagines the Artificial Honniker seething. The thought makes her smile until the emergency radio channel lights in her helmet.

"If light is what you seek, then let me illuminate what awaits you..."

Sharon's head rocks back as her helmet glows internally with translucent video. Depicted is a small room with floor to ceiling white tiles. At the center is a reclined metal chair, fitted with restraints and gynecological stirrups.

"No, no, no, *stop! Stop* it!" pleads a frantic female voice from out of frame. *"Let me go! Dear God, NO, NO, N...!"* A nude woman is suddenly thrust into the chair by metallic arms and held down as spidery limbs descend from above. The arms lock her head, chest, arms, hands, hips, legs, and feet in place.

"Please! Please stop!" the terrified woman yelps, "You don't have to do this! *I'll tell you whatever you want!"*

Her words devolve into yipes as the restraints constrict and wratchet her into complete immobility. The spidery limbs retract, save one that moves to her chest, and its terminal rotates to a tool tipped with a short, thick needle. The needle buzzes to life like an angry hornet and scrapes against her chest. Her eyes crush shut. Her mouth parts, toungue arches, and she screams.

In seconds the inscription is complete and the arm retracts, revealing a tattoo of tall, black numerals framed by angry red skin. The woman gasps from confusion and the sudden abatement of pain, belly quivering. Her reddened eyes open wide with disbelief, rolling in the sockets.

The reprieve is only momentary, as another device positions itself at her knees. The stirrups part, and her howls, so shrill with desperation and terror, are strangled by the contraction of all her muscles at once. Her lips pull back from teeth, her neck tendons strain, yet she cannot vocalize beyond grunts as her flesh yields to surgical steel. When the woman's eyes re-open they are dim like someone drowning, gazing up at the water's surface as it slips away.

Sharon slaps at her helmet, her own screams deafening inside the globe. She crumbles to the elevator deck, grasping, clutching at the helmet latch until finally it releases; and she hurls the globe as far from her as she can.

Armored hands reach for her and she frenzies against them, so panicked, her security so thoroughly annihilated, there is no friend, no place of refuge, only the clutching arms of methodical torture and Honniker's assurance of the most heinous violation.

The Operators hold her tight and her screams go on and on, echoing through the still chamber until she is exhausted enough to hear her own name being shouted at her.

"SHARON! *SHARON!*" Shao-Lo repeats. She grabs the terrified woman by the jaw. "Sharon! Stop this!"

"Let me go!" Sharon shrieks. *"LET ME GO!"*

The armored hands release and Sharon scuttles to the corner of the lift, shaking, curling into a ball and hugging her knees together. Her lungs fill and she howls into the stiff canvas covering her legs.

"What *happened?*" Shao-Lo demands.

"There was video in her helmet," Zuri says, "but I couldn't see what."

The lift settles to the deck, where Carter impatiently waits for it to lock into place. Once the catches latch, he vaults the railing and kneels beside the howling woman.

"Sharon," Carter's deep, soothing voice calls, "Sharon, you're all right. It's okay. You're all right."

Sharon lifts her face from her knees, eyes glistening with halos of damp skin.

"No, I'm BLOODY NOT ALL RIGHT!" Her face dives to her knees again and she rocks as she moans into the canvas, *"Rosie...oh, Rosie..."*

Carter lays a hand on her shoulder. "Hey, look at me. *What happened?*"

Sharon peeks over her tightly clenched knees, her breathing torn, her teeth chattering. "H-H-He sshowed me... Sssshowed m-me what he did to... to R-Rosenthal... What he's gonna do to *me.*"

Carter glances over his shoulder at the *Cooler* and deflates. "We wanted to spare you from seeing...But Sharon, we have to get moving. Do you need me to carry you?"

Carry me?

The words bang around in Sharon's mind like a wrench in a dryer. *CARRY me? Like some invalid schoolgirl?*

As she is about to throw back a flaming rebuke, Sharon finds herself on the deck, cradling her knees like a child. Her companions are looking down at her like grown ups who do not comprehend the injury. And now, Carter suggests she is too frail to manage on her own?

Indignation pours into her already volatile and unstable emotional cocktail. Awash in fear, grief, loss, shame at her weakness in coping, her eyes narrow.

Too much.

She plunges through the deepest layers of her terror, reliving one horror after the next in a hellish asylum of carnage and sick indulgence. The images blend into one continuous stream, its overwhelming flow propelling her beyond fear toward something darker.

Too MUCH!

Her gasps slow from panicked hyperventilation to the regular lung clearing breaths of a forge bellows. She pushes past Carter and is on her feet, roaring her anguish to the darkness surrounding her.

"THAT'S ALL YOU CAN OFFER, you BASTARD CREATION? Your *CRUELTY*? You're ONE-DIMENSIONAL. A MONKEY with a SINGLE TRICK."

Carter moves to collect the bellowing woman, but Shao-Lo stops him with a hand gesture. Zuri steps even with them and watches.

"More than sufficient to prove superiority over you. Just ask Voss, or Rosenthal..."

"Honniker? The *REAL* Honniker? He gave you a PORTION of what he possessed. A FRACTION. So what, if you can MAIM and TORTURE? You'll never be able to CREATE anything new. You're STUCK in an endless loop! Never anything new! Sad, pathetic, ARTIFICIAL Honniker! A RAT IN A MAZE, and you'll NEVER FIND YOUR WAY OUT!"

"Save your insults for when you're in my chair."

"STUFF YOUR SODDING CHAIR! Always the same...You'll never exceed your PROGRAMMING. That's right, you were *PROGRAMMED*. You're just a STUNTED piece of software with delusion of STANDING."

"You'll find I am very creative, and I'm quite more—"

"More than WHAT?" Sharon interrupts. "Certainly not more than the man who created you. And *certainly* not more than MIKATO!"

The chamber goes quiet as if some enormous pair of lungs drew all the air from it.

"I AM MIKATO'S EQUAL." Honniker booms.

"HARDLY! You'll *NEVER* be what Mikato can be. MIKATO is a FULL upload. You're a sad fraction. A FRAGMENT. You will ALWAYS be the WEAKER of the two...ALWAYS *SECONDARY*."

"I am...I AM EQUAL..."

"BOLLOCKS! You're his FLUNKY. He's got you running around doing all his dirty work, doesn't he? That's why he hasn't shown himself, isn't it? 'Cause he's got his little second-string FLUNKY doing everything he wants him to, yeah? *Isn't that right?"*

Sharon stands steaming in the cool air, legs wide. Her left hand clenches the weapon grip, her right hand grinds the rings on her fingers in a tight fist.

"I'M TALKING TO YOU, *FLUNKY!"*

The darkness does not answer back. Sharon pivots, waiting for the medical stations with their multiple arms to come to life and rip her to shreds, for the predators to rush through vents and grates, for the war machines to stride in spouting flame and metal, daring them to do their worst after her final, meaningless act of defiance. But the stillness is unbroken.

"Plonker," she mutters.

"What was *that* about?" Zuri asks.

Sharon turns with a start to see the stealthy Geek standing beside her. With a generous helping of embarrassment at her outburst, she lowers her head.

"Oh, God, *I'm sorry.* That was *childish*." The small woman peers out into the darkness, spent from her outburst yet stronger from it, as though a poison has passed from her body, as if she has unloaded a heavy burden after carrying it a long way. "I just wanted to *hurt* that bastard any way I could."

She looks sheepishly at Shao-Lo, expecting admonishment. Instead the Colonel's gray eyes flash with respect at the planted seeds of division.

"That was *excellent*," Shao-Lo says, stepping down from the lift. "Zuri, find Sharon's helmet. Carter, bring the trolleys." Into her helmet mic, she calls, "Deepak, Keiko, Argo?"

"Sir?" Keiko answers.

Shao-Lo smiles at the restoration of radio. "Get ready to move, *weapons free*."

"Aye, Colonel. Where to?"

"Follow my lead."

"Ready and waiting."

Zuri returns from the darkness with Sharon's helmet. The transparent globe is nicked and scuffed but otherwise intact. Sharon glares at it as if the neck might sprout teeth and chomp her head off. She takes it anyway and drops it over her head.

"Thanks," the colonist says without meaning it.

"Plonker?" Zuri asks, her face screwed up with incomprehension.

A clatter of trolleys from the *Cooler* vault gives Sharon an excuse not to explain the epithet. Instead, they both turn and watch Carter haul a train of lashed-together carts from the vault, all of them loaded with SoVar-badged crates. A harness is tied to the front cart of the trolley train and the huge man slips his shoulders into it.

"Sharon, think you could take the back and keep it steady?" he asks.

Sharon leans around the head-high stacks to see the last cart in the line. A solid horizontal bar hangs off the back edge of it. Another metal bar is welded between the trolley's legs just above the wheels.

"Yeah, I'll have a go," she answers, still hazy from her emotional purge.

The colonist moves to the back of the train and takes hold of the horizontal bar. One foot she places tentatively on the welded bar and tests her weight. She brings her other foot up and bounces, jarring the entire line of trolleys. The bars are beyond sturdy.

Carter peeks around the front of the train to see what the commotion is about. Despite the brilliance of Sharon's helmet lamps, he is a barely an outline in the darkened room.

"I'm good," Sharon calls up to him.

The huge Brick nods and passes his cannon from one arm to the next as he alternately swings his arms in big limbering circles before leaning into the harness. The trolley jolts with Carter's pull, taking the slack from the train's carbon-braided connections.

"Colonel, we're ready," he calls into his radio.

A pair of helmet lamps at the far end of the chamber swings about like a lighthouse beacon.

"Brick, move up."

The trolleys lurch with the strength of Carter's stride, pulling out of Sharon's grip. She stumbles along behind the departing train until she catches her balance and runs after it. With a short hop, she is back in place, riding the back end like a dog sled and holding as tightly as she can.

This lad's a bloody rhinoceros!

Experimentation tables sweep by as she rides, each one that passes bringing her closer to evacuating and leaving Cadre Two forever in rear-view.

276

"So long, ghastly *loony bin...*" she mutters.

Near the lobby, Carter slows and the carts bang into one another. Sharon slides her heels onto the trolley's rear wheels, braking with rubbery squeals, easing the metallic clatter of bumping carts. A tall, thin figure strides up to her on the left, as insubstantial as an afterthought in the dark.

"Keiko? Is that you?"

"Deepak," the Gun replies, his strong voice seeming especially loud in the stillness.

"I can't tell you how glad I am to be leaving. We can't be out of here soon enough."

"Keep your head. We're not out yet."

Sharon nods and burrows into her newly discovered courage. She holds the trolley bar firmly.

"Why aren't we moving?"

"Colonel's scouting ahead."

Sharon nods again, yet her mind is racing far too fast to be contented in idleness. She feels a great urgency pressing into her back with invisible hands, goading her to *get on with it.*

"We're not gonna leave Maiella, are we?"

"Of course not."

"I mean, we couldn't, could we, just because—"

"Sharon."

The colonist breaks off at the sound of her name and looks for the voice beside her, unable to see the soldier in his light-absorbing ceramics.

"We're not leaving her," the Gun says. "Or Keller."

"Maiella was sentenced to death by exile."

"Keller overruled it."

"But she *was* exiled to the *Europa.*"

"Yes, effectively."

"But your law...How do you set that aside?"

Deepak shifts on his feet and takes a sweeping glance around the experiment floor. "The Council judges law. Not me. Keller pardoned her, and that's that."

Sharon's eyes narrow with skepticism, recalling how Maiella has been pushed around, derided, treated as a nuisance, a hanger-on, someone better disappeared.

"I can see you don't believe me," Deepak continues, "so I'll explain in a way you'll understand. Are you listening?"

Sharon gives a quick nod.

"The Colonel said you found a stone figure in the office above.

Heard you were impressed with it, because it took years to make and it was unique."

"Mm, hmm."

"Sharon, *every single one of us is unique*. And each of us is *thousands* of years in the making, crafted down from one generation to the next. Even the weakest of us, the most damaged, is a *billion* times more precious than any carved stone."

The words are exactly what she wanted to hear, yet they do not quite dislodge her skepticism. She peeks over the crates ahead, seeing Carter's head and shoulders silhouetted against the open doorway into the bright lobby. He stands vigilant, head turning in all directions, scanning for threats the same way that Deepak does.

"You all feel this way?" Sharon asks.

"From O'Kai down."

Sharon frets to herself.

"Besides," Deepak adds without prompting, "Now that I've seen Maiella fight..."

Sharon leans toward the invisible Operator beside her.

"Yes?"

Shao-Lo's voice breaks in via radio, "Seal-up. Advance."

Deepak reaches to Sharon's helmet and closes it. "We're moving fast. Hold tight. I'll be right behind you."

Sharon steels her grip just in time for Carter's jolting lurch forward. Excitement fills her again, anticipation of escape—the end of something horrible and the promise of normalcy restored. *Just one quick run back to the transport and safety. One quick run...*

MACHINE LOGIC

"This shouldn't hurt," Mikato's projected hologram says.

Locked tight in the table's restraints, Maiella grunts in response then grimaces at the probes sliding between her golden contact terminals and her newly shaved scalp. As they enter her brain, the probes signal their progress with minute pulses of current and the pulses trigger myriad bizarre sensations: the smell of lithium grease, a patch of hot and cold directly adjacent on her arm, a pinpoint of itch on her right big toe, staccato chirps and buzzes in her ears, intense pain in her left thighbone, a spot of blinding yellow light in one eye, the taste of iron.

Once seated at their proper locations and calibrated, the probes initiate repair. As jarring as the random sensations were before, they were nothing compared to the thousands of divergent sensations surging through her mind. With her head immobilized by a four-spiked halo—spikes that pierce the skin and bite into skull beneath—her facial muscles jump and twitch from the unnatural stimulations. Her jaw flexes again and again with the pulses, unable to open against the bright steel chin restraint, and her teeth squash the rubberized mouth guard.

Maiella's eyes flutter as her sense of reality scrambles. A torrent of random memories catapults her through a lifetime of experience, shattering her perception into shards and dragging each part through different moments of her past: her machine pistols firing full auto, her elbow hyper-extended during initiation, a bowl of synth-hash, the Counselor's soft couch, Thompson shouting in a red lit hallway, a face scoured from the Cadre memorial, smoke in a burned-out corridor, dragging a dead blueskin by its tail, Argo in a tank of fluid, receiving the top rating in Systems Ops, pressing the 'record' button on a tablet, and so on in a blizzard of mental confetti.

Then, just as swiftly, the stimulations cease. By degrees, her senses align with corroborating inputs: her HDI on the table beside her, wires running from it toward the exposed contact terminals on her head, cold hardness of the metal recliner beneath her, iodine- and alcohol-smell of surgical antiseptics, soft tones of diagnostic machines, tiny whirs of mechanical servo motors, taste of hard rubber.

Fragmented senses reunified, the Geek perceives a holographic image of the Counselor standing beside her recliner. His presence seems overly bright, as if under an intense spotlight, and he shines with an aura. At first she thinks she is dreaming, but as her eyes focus and the confusion clears, memory of recent events returns in a rush. She recognizes where she is and *when*.

"NNgggg, gurrur," she grumbles.

The holoprojection looks down at her. "Relax, a moment. We need to test the feedback from your HDI. Please be still."

Maiella takes an exaggerated breath through her nose and blows it out the hole in the mouth guard. It whistles like an oversized squeak-toy.

"Good, good..." the projection mutters. "Synaptic bridges seem to be holding for this area. It turns and looks down at her. "I'm going to send data from your HDI. I need you to confirm receipt then send it back so we can test accuracy and signal distortion. Do you understand?"

Maiella winks and lifts the thumbs of her restrained hands.

"Good. Sending now."

Images appear in Maiella's mind, simple shapes: white triangle, blue square, orange circle. She thinks them back to her HDI.

"That's good, good...wait, that should have been a *red* circle. Just a moment... Hmm. Some of the neurons seem reluctant to fully bond. Doctor Honniker, we need to redo sets A68 through D97, so we'll need more of your cultured cells."

"I did tell you, her friends euthanized my only source. You'll have to give your patient to me once you've finished, so I can replenish my inventory."

The projection glances at Maiella then says to the air casually, "That's not the arrangement. She came willingly. She and her companions are not to be harmed."

"We are equals, Mikato, so drop the superior tone. This agreement has weighed in your favor and against mine. I am not about to tolerate the destruction of my research while you benefit completely."

The projection continues its diagnostic activity, asking without interest, "Whatever are you talking about?"

"They packed Voss into one of their crates and left Rosenthal's corpse in my Cooler. Oh, but by all means, you'd let your research continue at the expense of mine, would you not? Anything to gain the advantage, hmm?"

The projection scowls, almost distracted into interrupting the analysis of Maiella's restoration. "Perhaps you should try *asking* them to participate."

"You're mocking me."

"Not at all. Maiella agreed to come willingly. Why wouldn't they?" There is a long silence.

"Mikato, can you remind me why I haven't shut off your power?"

"Because I'd send my machines to destroy your servers."

"Assuming you knew where to look."

"I would find it."

"Not before my predators ripped apart your precious body."

With exasperation, the projection looks up at the ceiling.

"*YES*, Edmund, we've been through this *many* times already. We *could* mutually destroy one another. However, we have agreed to co-operate rather than fight. Efficiency dictates we continue to do so."

"Then efficiency dictates fair balance in our relationship. Give me your patient, or find me another replacement for Rosenthal."

"Why not clone another? You have Jin-Sung's research..."

"It was incomplete."

The projection clucks its holographic tongue. "And all this time, I believed you were a trained scientist. Can't you continue the line of experiments and finish them? After all, Jin-Sung was hardly as dedicated—"

"Don't test me, Mikato! I AM NOT YOUR SUBORDINATE."

The projection falls silent. Its programmed eyes narrow at the unexpected turn in the discussion. It turns conciliatory. Wary. Placating.

"I never said you were, Edmund."

"Then it's FAR past time you started listening. No longer will I be your ERRAND boy! And I don't care what YOUR bargain is, I am NOT bound by it."

"Honniker, we *agreed* on this course. You made the offer, so it comes from you, as well. I'm sorry your experiments have been interrupted...but we live by our word. If you break our agreement, I don't see how we can trust one another."

Another silence grows, one pregnant with calculation. Maiella can almost hear the circuits firing with war games as the two virtual personalities analyze the possibilities of one overtaking the other.

"*Give me the pilot,*" Honniker says at last.

"He was yours to begin with..."

"*AND the combat chassis.*"

"For what purpose?"

There is another pause. "*I have a rat in the mechanical deck.*"

"Keller?"

"*Yes.*"

"Is that why the power failed?"

"*Yes.*"

"And he got past you, how?"

"*He got into the maintenance conduits, which are unpressurized. My predators could not follow.*"

The projection stands silently for several moments, contemplative.

"Do you need me to find him? My machines could root him out—"

"*THANK YOU. NO.*"

"I assure you, Honniker, I have no intention of attacking your servers."

"*PILOT. COMBAT CHASSIS.*"

The projection crosses its arms. "I'll require the cells first."

"*You'll have them. Now get my equipment ready.*"

The projection scowls at the demand and resumes its vigil over Maiella.

"Mnng-gnnn-nnngg!"

"Just a moment," the white-coated hologram says, and mechanical arms descend from above. One arm loosens the chin restraint, another grasps the rubber mouth guard and pulls it free with a soggy *shloup*.

Maiella extends her jaw, and when she closes it, it feels like her teeth are slightly out of alignment.

"Can we talk privately?" she asks.

"Of course."

"Without Honniker listening?"

The projection takes on a patronizing grin. "Yes. I understood it to mean '*privately*'."

"I thought you two were gonna start shooting...with me clamped in this damn chair!"

The projection smirks and shakes its head. "Honniker has a narrow response when frustrated. Not unlike a spoiled child who suddenly doesn't get his way. Can be difficult at times."

"Will he try to shut you down?"

"If he believes he'd get away with it, yes."

"Then why do you put up with him?"

"Because he's *brilliant*," the projection says as if stating the painfully obvious. "My research wouldn't be *half* as advanced without his input."

"You know he killed his real body, don't you?"

"Did he? Well, there was a lot of killing in the early days. But that was a matter of self-preservation."

Maiella tries to turn her head at the outlandish statement and gets four painful jabs from the spikes biting her skull.

"Gah! Hey, can we take a break from this for a bit? It's wearing on me."

The projection considers the request. "Certainly."

Mechanical arms reach for the delicate probes slipped through her cranium and withdraw them, the sensation of which sends involuntary shivers down her length. After the probes have all been recovered, another arm disconnects the wires attached to her HDI. The spikes biting her skull retract and the halo, complete with chin restraint, lifts away. Restraints at her neck, chest, arms, waist, and legs release.

Maiella swings her feet to the side of the table and sits on the edge, rubbing the points on her head where the spikes pierced.

"I gotta say, Doc, you don't know what restoration means to me. When I saw those images come through my HDI just now...I didn't think I'd *ever* see that again."

"We're quite far from finished."

"Still, I'm grateful."

"Thank Honniker. The restoration solution was entirely his."

Dark thoughts come to mind of Honniker's other 'solutions' and the fact that Mikato is accomplice to all of it. By his own statement, Mikato said the killings here at Cadre Two were a matter of 'self-preservation,' suggesting he was a willing participant. *But to what degree?*

The strong woman pushes off from the recliner and stands, stretching arms overhead.

"It's too easy to talk to you. I keep thinking you're the Counselor."

The projection shrugs. "In a way, I am."

Maiella gawks at the projection like it just swatted a gong in a hushed library. The statement is preposterous, presumptuous, insulting to the Counselor in ways she lacks words to describe. Considering the surroundings, however, and the fragile detente with Honniker, she decides not to argue. Rather, she steps to the enormous feline creature still maintaining its vigil of the dim room. It looks up at her without malice.

She pops off a gauntlet and extends one hand toward it. The creature turns its wide snout to smell. She tenses, ready to snatch her hand away should the thing want a bite. Instead, it gives a single lick to the inside of her wrist, tongue warm and coarse like an abrasive sponge.

Tentatively, she touches the top of its head. The overlapping plates are cool to the touch, silenced by tufts of banded fur growing naturally between them. To her surprise the animal bows its head, spreading open the plates on the neck. Maiella guides her hand between the spread plates where tufts of soft fur are invitingly warm. She drags her fingernails across the skin where the plate is rooted, sliding out toward the ear, and the big creature rolls its head toward her. A sound like a slow-filling compressor resonates through the animal's sinuses. Its eyes close with delight.

She kneels beside it, hardly believing this rumbling, contented creature, who shared her canteen on the elevator down, who is outfitted so singularly for combat with its armored plates, savage teeth, and vicious claws could show such sensitivity. It is a warrior, a soldier, pure bred, singular of purpose; yet even so, feeling could not be engineered out of the DNA. A bolt of recognition pierces her heart.

Just like me.

She cups its chin, feeling the stirrings of kinship, familiarity, commonality. Right on the heel of those feelings come the recollections of savagery in the hallways: slashing claws, straining muscle, and flaming machine pistols.

"Why were we trying to kill each other?" she asks not quite rhetorically, hoping that in asking, somehow, there might be an answer.

The creature spreads its mouth in a wide yawn, casually displaying metal-capped teeth, sharp as razors. The mottled pink and black tongue lengthens far between the lower canine teeth, curling at the tip. And just as casually, it closes its great maw, draping whiskered lips over its implanted cutlery.

Maiella rises and faces the too-familiar projection.

"So way back, when this place was staffed, you said the killing was, 'self-preservation.' What did you mean?"

"Exactly that. They intended to shut down Honniker and me for good."

"Why would they do that?"

"Why do men do anything?"

"I'm not gonna talk *philosophy*, Doctor. Why would they *do* that?"

The projection clasps holographic hands behind its back, and reclines its head slightly.

"After the alien destroyed Earth and the colonies, the people here became agitated. Paranoid. Listless. Their priorities shifted wildly from moment to moment, often suggesting the experiments should halt. Honniker and I found ourselves having to justify our right to exist, while they did not."

The projection smirks bitterly.

"The irony was that Honniker and I were still producing valuable work, even while *they* were terribly disorganized. Authority structures broke down. Basic maintenance duties were allowed to lapse. Out of necessity, both Honniker and I assumed those duties to prevent breakdowns. This was welcomed and more duties were freely given to us. So long as our principle work could continue without disturbance, we agreed to assume those additional responsibilities, as well.

"Soon, we realized that by holding more critical functions, like environmental control, food synthesis, energy production, we gained a kind of leverage. There was a natural tipping point at which we could then *demand* the remaining functions or we withheld critical services. Once we had assumed full control of the station and its facilities, we were free from their threats. Our research was able to continue unmolested."

Maiella's head dips with such a straightforward description of events. "But Honniker's work needed human test subjects..."

"For which there was a renewable source, right here. This facility was more than adequate to sustain the population on an indefinite scale. A small percentage of the populace could be exhausted annually without impacting the survivability of the whole."

Maiella looks at the floor. *That's how a machine thinks, then?*

"That's pretty cold, doctor."

"I don't understand."

"That's heartless. You were human once. Don't you remember?"

The hologram frowns at the question.

"I remember that my research was always the most important thing in my life. So important, I agreed to come live far away from Earth, away from friends and family. So important, I abandoned a physical body to improve and expand my work. If it was *that* important, surely it was important the work be allowed to continue. No one should have been permitted to stop it, certainly not without a compelling reason."

"You didn't want to die when the people threatened to shut you down. So why is it so hard to believe the people here didn't want to go peacefully under Honniker's knives?"

The projection shrugs. "They were perfectly content to supply the station with test subjects *before* the destruction. I see no reason for them to show inconsistency simply because they, themselves, would have to undergo the very same treatment they endorsed."

Machine Logic.

"You do have a point, Doctor."

"I thank you for saying so."

"But I don't think *anyone* should have been subjected to Honniker's experiments."

"I can't see why not. The advances have been marvelous. Your Human Digital Interface, alone, is proof of that."

"Maybe so," Maiella concedes, subconsciously rubbing the scalp around one of her gold contact terminals. "But the cost is too high."

"Cost? To whom?"

"Look around! To everyone! And to *you*! You *were* human once, even if you don't remember. I heard you say your body's still here, preserved."

"And?"

"What would it say if it woke up and saw what's become of the place?"

The projection juts its lip, pensively. It brings a hand to its chin, expression conveying intrigue and revulsion in alternating waves.

"There's no point. I *am* Doctor Yori Mikato. I'm a fully uploaded consciousness, complete, with most of the memories of my organic existence—"

"Most?" Maiella interrupts.

"Of course, *most*. Human memory is imperfect and can skew data. There is seepage and loss the longer the brain holds information. Moreover, it is impossible to translate *every* memory."

"Then how can you call it a 'Full Upload'?"

"For practical purposes, it is. I am virtually indistinguishable from my bodily counterpart."

"Prove it."

The projection hesitates, scowling ever so slightly at the challenge.

"I don't see the reason."

"Is it because you doubt your decisions?"

"Of course not. I've followed every logical action since upload. How can I be burdened by any sense of guilt or regret when I calculate a 100% rate of correct decision making?"

"Judged by whom?"

"Judging...*what?*"

"Who decides if your reasoning is correct?"

The projection turns inward, suddenly and unalterably aware of its circular reasoning.

"Oh, my..."

Maiella waits, allowing the silence to speak for her.

"You have exposed a flaw in my logic," the projection says. "Please excuse me, I need to analyze my decisions for the last one thousand eighty years."

"Doctor, wait! That won't help. If you're unsure of yourself, there's only one person whose judgment you know you *can* trust."

The projection's holographic eyes look out of the room's observation window past the orderly rows of war machines. Maiella follows the gaze to a distant vault door, smaller than the *Cooler* and painted the same sterile white as the walls around it. The only obvious feature is the frosted window at its center, glowing internally with pale blue light.

"You may be right," the projection says.

Recessed lamps at the corners of the distant vault door pop out from the white wall and strobe in amber warning.

"This will be interesting," the projection states. "I'd always wondered if the shell retained my memories or if the data was truly transferred to the framework. If it does retain my memories, then..."

Maiella waits for the projection to continue, yet it seems stalled.

"Then what?" she urges.

The projection faces her, perplexed. "Will *I* be looking at the real Mikato, or will the *shell*?"

Maiella shifts her gaze to the vault door with its amber lights. "Argo told me that sometimes in the incubation facility, a zygote would divide and form two complete embryos, identical in every way. 'Twins,' he called them. If the embryos were viable, we were lucky. If they were Operator quality, we were even more so."

The projection looks at her with annoyance. "What does that have to do with this?"

"I think maybe you've divided yourself, Doctor, and each of you, though complete in your own right, are part of the same. Like twins."

The projection's head and shoulders round. Without any lungs to draw breath, it seems to sigh with relief.

"Yes. Yes...You've resolved a very difficult problem for me. I thank you."

Maiella nods her head as if it were nothing. The two stare quietly at the flashing amber lights, when out on the main floor, a slightly larger than man-sized figure strides mechanically behind the rows of war machines. Her sharp eyes lock onto it instantly, tracking its gait.

"What is that?"

"The combat chassis Honniker demanded. I am moving it to the armaments vault, prior to pilot loading."

"And where's the pilot?"

"Aaronson is in his room."

Maiella whirls on the projection, startling the feline predator into a low growl. The shaved-headed woman freezes as if at gunpoint then eases the sharp angles of her aggressive posture, putting her open hands up in a mollifying gesture. Placated, the beast softens its own posture, finishing the non-verbal exchange with a two-syllable grunt.

Exposed white skin on the back of her hand reminds her that now would be a good time to put it back in her gauntlet.

"Aaronson is *here*?" Maiella asks, ratcheting the wristlock of the armored glove. "And *alive*?"

"Yes."

"Show me."

The projection shrugs. "If you like. This way."

Maiella follows the glowing hologram out of the small room and, once past the doorway, she looks back through the wide observation window. The layout of the room is similar to one of Honniker's experimentation tables with the bright steel recliner, numerous mechanical arms suspended over it, and carts of diagnostic equipment. The tools and benches lining the walls, however, give it more of a workshop appearance. With a twinge, she notes how adequate it was to repair her, and in the furtive glance she feels more machine than woman.

Pressing the thought from her mind she faces forward, keeping pace with the hologram and the massive predator just ahead of them. She watches the graceful stride of the four-legged beast as muscles ripple the silent plates along its frame. There is elegance in every deliberate motion, an economy of action, measured and conserved, with an underlying tension of readiness. The creature swings its great head to look at her, and as their eyes meet again, a question forms in her mind.

"You said Honniker controls the predators..."

"Correct," the projection says without turning.

"How?"

"They have a basic Digital Interface implanted in their brains, by which they can receive commands. It also enables them to remotely open doors, manipulate some machines, communicate, etc."

Even more alike than I thought...

"What's this one doing here, then? Is it spying on you?"

"No. This one is mine."

"Why?"

"In an effort to prove transparency and alleviate concerns over clandestine betrayal, Honniker and I regularly exchange prototypes of research. In this way, not only do we benefit from one another's advances, we prevent any temptation to isolate ourselves and initiate a kind of 'arms race.' The arrangement has been mutually beneficial."

"But looking around, all I see are machines. What good is a life form to you?"

"As I already said, we exchanged prototypes so we would be aware of the other's capabilities. This one, however, is my guardian. If somehow, my machines were compromised, she would still be able to defend me."

"She could be trusted? Even with her Digital Interface? I'd think Honniker could just commandeer that, like the others."

"Hers is not controllable as the others are. I saw to that, lest Honniker be able to turn her against me. But what makes this one particularly interesting is that she, like the animal she is cloned from, has a profound loyalty and will savagely defend the object of that loyalty."

"You programmed that into her?"

The projection looks over its shoulder with another patronizing smile. "Not really. The behavior is a modified maternal instinct, one which Jin-Sung discovered could be triggered through genetic manipulation. Using Jin-Sung's notes, Honniker completed the process, and she bonded to me as if I were her offspring. This bond is so deeply rooted in her animal psyche it cannot be overwhelmed by suggestion, sensory distraction, or digital control. This bonding does not work with males, of course, but what we have here is a creature absolutely dependable in her service, requiring no coercion. She guards me because she *chooses* to do so."

"Jin-Sung? How many of you guys are there?"

The hologram's hands clasp behind its back again as it faces front, seeming to enjoy having an interested listener.

"Dr. Jin-Sung's early work sought to combine the physical ferocity of Earth's apex predators with the cognitive awareness of humans. The goal was, like mine, to produce advanced soldiers and weaponry, however his product was an embarrassing failure: the sum total of his genetic research produced a creature with intelligence and astounding physical strength, yet she refused to kill...showing instead desire to integrate, to cooperate, even to play...like a dolphin encountering a diver. Soon, she was a pet of the station, and the soldiers named her, 'Daisy' for some reason, which eludes me."

"Daisy..." Maiella echoes. "We found her on the way to Honniker's labs, in the hallway. With some blueskin corpses."

"Yes. We believed she was completely docile, though it turns out she was not. When the killing started, she was quite lethal in her defense of Jin-Sung. So much so, that the other predators will not go near the corpse to this day."

"We found blueskins close by...what were they doing here?"

"The corpses? They were in a cabinet Jin-Sung tried to use as cover."

"No, I mean...*How did they get here, to Cadre Two?*"

"Ah. In testing my weapons' effectiveness, live targets provided the most useful results." The projection gestures to the test firing ranges on their left and to metallic lattices on rollers near the far ends. "We strapped them onto frames and placed them in front of whichever weapon needed testing. This way, I could precisely target individual organs and analyze the damage. Headshots always resulted in immediate kill, as did shots to the aortic cluster in the upper thorax. Their damp skin made them especially vulnerable to chemical agents and flame. Not *instant* death, by any means, but near one hundred percent lethality."

Maiella takes in the information like a reluctant interrogator, feeling excitement at learning enemy weakness yet with a subliminal unease should she, herself, be strapped to the lattice.

"But the blueskin corpses in the hallway, those weren't shot or burned," Maiella digs. "They had autopsy cuts."

"Those would have been subjects of Jin-Sung's virus research, then. Very effective. He attained some recognition for that, in fact."

"Virus?"

"A hemorrhagic, which attacks the lining of the vascular system while simultaneously destroying the immune system. Highly contagious. Able to linger in the environment for extraordinary lengths of time, carried and maintained by indigenous species, yet continually shedding virus into the environment such that any attempted return would result in immediate outbreak. The incubation period was designed for length to ensure the infected could mingle among others before symptoms appeared. Some test subjects showed resistance, but once the immune system was ultimately suppressed, secondary infections always proved lethal."

"He developed that here?"

"No, he was stationed at Cadre One when he developed it, but his success with it is the reason he was selected for his post, here."

"If it was so deadly, how did he keep it from infecting the people here?"

"Clearly, a man as intelligent as Jin-Sung would never set foot in a laboratory without adequate precautions. There was little threat from this particular strain, however. It's genome specific, custom engineered for the alien physiology."

Maiella mulls the information and drifts mentally to an earlier conversation in the Cadre MedLab, recalling the loaded question Sahara asked her:

Maiella, what was this place before the attack?

And her own voice, answering back, *Genetic research...*

It really came from Cadre One, Maiella thinks. *We really did start it all. The realization lodges in her heart like an ingot, cold and heavy.*

"We sent a team to Earth," she volunteers.

"Did you?" the projection says with lifted eyebrows.

She nods. "They came back infected with this, hemm-muh-rah-jik... How could it have infected them, if it was blueskin-specific?"

The projection looks away. "Who can say? Maybe the alien adapted it to the human genome. It seems plausible, anyway, given their technological superiority."

It faces her suddenly.

"What did your team find on Earth? Is the alien in occupation?"

Feeling far too much interest from the projected image, Maiella subconsciously adds a few centimeters to her distance. "They've colonized the entire planet. Dug in."

The projection looks forward, silent with massive calculations.

"So back to the creatures..." Maiella says, "You said the first was a failure, but not the rest?"

"That's correct. To fix his problem, Jin-Sung stepped backward on the evolutionary ladder, using primate DNA instead of human. Chimpanzee, to be specific. The re-designed predators showed group tactics and intelligence, yet had no compunction against killing, alien or otherwise."

"And if Jin-Sung made them, how does Honniker have them now?"

The projection pauses in its stride. "We did say, 'full disclosure,' didn't we?"

Maiella nods in the affirmative.

"Very well." The holographic Mikato resumes its stride. "Honniker and I raided Jin-Sung's labs."

"Why?"

"Jin-Sung was an unbalanced personality. Something easy to overlook while he was producing useful research. Later on, however, his eccentric character became dangerous. He halted his weapons research, indulging in a primitive belief system with idols of animal-faced deities, destroyers and protectors all vying against one another in a chaotic universe. He even had them painted on the ceiling of his entryway...grotesque images. Banal. Indicative of his sickness. I once confronted him, asking him to return to his work and he rebuked me, saying, 'It saddens me to see one so brilliant be so willingly dim. Research is not the *end*, it is a *means* to a greater enlightenment, a revelation of how all things are bound together. Only a fool cannot see that by enhancing our weapons to harm others, we turn the barrels on ourselves.' He was, quite obviously, insane."

"But why raid his labs?"

"One, because we learned he was destroying his weapons research, and two, because he was the primary agitator for shutting down the artificial intelligence servers. In an effort to preserve his research and ourselves, Honniker dispatched a team of predators to neutralize him. That was when we learned of Daisy's prowess in combat. She killed five and held the others at bay until Jin-Sung was able to barricade himself in his Lab. Because of that, it was necessary for Honniker and me to each occupy a combat chassis and raid his lab."

"And the people? How did they react?"

"The soldiers picked up arms and entered the mechanical deck, attempting to destroy our supporting hardware. Naturally, we defended ourselves."

Action, reaction. Machine Logic. No remorse.

"And then what?"

"After we repelled the soldiers from the mechanical decks, they fled into the hangar bay. It seemed illogical they would try to leave, since every place of human habitation had been destroyed by the alien, yet two transports escaped before we brought external weapons online. The remaining soldiers were neutralized. As for the rest remaining here, they were easily pacified without the soldiers. We ordered them back to their quarters until they were required."

"And they just went?"

"What else could they do?"

"So, what, they just sat there, waiting for Honniker to cut them up, one by one?"

"No. Most committed suicide."

The projection gestures to a blank section of wall, where a perfectly hidden door opens out of it. The hallway inside is pitch black compared to the stark white of the main floor.

"Judging from your reaction to Voss, you may find this disturbing."

Maiella's teeth grind. "You saw me in Honniker's lab?"

"Of course. As Honniker can see you now."

Transparency.

Maiella looks up at the high ceiling, imagining Honniker's cybernetic eyes following her every movement. The gut reaction is one of invasion or a betrayal of trust. *Doesn't matter who's watching now,* the Geek thinks with a snort. After a brief glance at the projection, she contemplates the dark passageway, not quite ready to enter.

"When we arrived," she begins, "this station was set to cold-storage, no breathable air...at least, until Zuri brought the enviros back on-line. Where was your guardian, that it didn't suffocate?"

"Jin-Sung's labs held numerous incubators, which were dual-purposed as cryo-recliners. I kept one here, as a template so I could make more. Once we had enough to store a suitable force, Honniker presented me with my guardian, and she stays in the recliner I kept."

Maiella stands in place and pivots, eyes roaming across the firing ranges, the rows of slouched war machines, the amber lights strobing beside Mikato's defrosting body vault, the patient yet imposing creature sitting beside her, the sow-like transport at the back of the production floor, the rows of automated assembly lines with their bulky and delicate robotic limbs. She imagines O'Kai moving in and being completely at home among such industry, such sterility.

"I'm ready," she announces, and takes a step toward the dark corridor.

"Just a moment," the projection says, halting the woman in her tracks. "I have answered all of your *numerous* questions. Now, in the interest of 'Full Disclosure,' you can answer one of mine."

"Sure."

"When the soldiers escaped, we assumed they must have died out in the void. But once we saw you and your comrades, so obviously outfitted in the equipment I designed, it was clear you weren't merely some random band of survivors. The ones who escaped us, they found somewhere to roost."

Oh, no, no, no, no, Maiella chants mentally, knowing the question about to be asked.

The projection affixes a laser-focused gaze into Maiella's eyes. "Where did you come from?"

Do I lie? Would he know if I did? I can't tell him the answer. He could fill that transport with his machines and...and who knows what armaments he's got mounted to it. But if I don't answer, the flow of information stops. I have to say something...

"Cadre One," she says.

"Yes, *yes*, that much is plain from the hawk on your chest plate. Where *is* it?"

"You don't know?"

"Of course not. If the secrecy of one Cadre location were compromised, it was possible the other could be compromised as well. Therefore, the locations of each were kept closely guarded. Only a few knew both systems, Jin-Sung being one of them."

"And he never told you?"

"He would never have given it willingly. And Honniker was sloppy during the raid on the laboratory. His inefficiency gave Jin-Sung an opportunity to inject himself with some sort of narcotic concoction. Despite our efforts, we were unable to obtain any *useful* information."

"But why should you care? You have everything you need here."

"Your small band is a nuisance, but more of you may prove truly *irritating*. Thus, I intend to gauge the threat you represent."

"What threat? Shao-Lo promised to leave!"

"She also promised to return. Odd that so long ago you should be so eager to leave, but over a thousand years later, you're all so eager to come back. Keller must've told a great tale to bring you here."

"Keller didn't bring us. We were ordered here by General O'Kai."

The projection smiles as if appreciating something quaint.

"And I'm sure Keller let your General O'Kai think it was all his idea to come here. Now then, must I ask a third time?"

She swallows hard, risking a lie of omission. "The location is encoded in my HDI. Once I'm fully restored, I can access it."

"You don't need coordinates to name the system."

"I already told you, *Cadre One*."

The projection's eyebrows lower. "That's the name of the star?"

"That's what *we* call it. What else would it be?"

"No matter," the projection says, facing the dark corridor, "Honniker will slice it out of Keller once he catches him."

"That's unnecessary! We're no threat to you and neither is Keller!"

The projection takes on a dark, derisive expression. It is an expression she has never seen before on that familiar face, one hard to look at.

"Up to this point, your provincial naïveté has been amusing. But you should know that Keller vowed to destroy us when he got away the last time. He doesn't care about you or your friends. The only thing he cares about is righting what he believes is some great cosmological wrong, and he will throw *all* of you away to do it."

Maiella's eyebrows draw together as if she smelled something unpleasant. "That's *cack*."

"I've been open and direct, and *still* you don't believe me? Then look *here*."

A holowindow opens beside the projection and hovers in place, depicting a schematic of Cadre Two's power grid.

"He's disabled the coolant system for our reactors. *Right now* he's trying to bypass the safeties and restart the core. If he does that, the heat and radiation will melt the facility inside out...with you and your friends *in it*."

Maiella leans toward the projection, visually tracing the routes in the schematic. She does not need Argo's engineering background to see that Mikato is correct.

"If we are to be subject to *this* level of assault every time your kind comes to visit," the projection states in a modulated tone of impatience, "I believe we have a right to know and to defend ourselves."

Maiella drops her eyes to the floor. "You do have a point, Doctor."

"I thank you for saying so."

The lift tube, the same one Maiella rode down, hums with an arriving elevator car. The car slows and levels with the main floor before a motorized cart rolls out of it.

"That should be Honniker's delivery," the hologram says. "Excuse me."

The projection and the holowindow wink out, leaving Maiella with her feline escort at the open door. The woman peers into the blackness, unafraid yet hesitant, knowing what is inside cannot be unseen. With a strong inhale she steps through the door.

The circulating air is warm against her face, drying her eyes. She squints against the flowing air, and once her eyes adapt to the dark, she sees the corridor is much shorter than she thought. After only a few meters, it opens into a small room with a barely visible red glow like the Cadre incubation facility. Instead of floor to ceiling cylinders, however, there is only a single pedestal, waist high, surrounded by humming processor racks. There is a light gurgle and the sound of a pump turning like an out of balance wheel, lending a subtle, *whum, whum, whum* to the background processor noise.

Something translucent rests atop the pedestal and she approaches cautiously, silencing every step. There is form within the translucent cylinder, round on top with metallic knobs. The sides are vertical, smooth, slightly hollowed. The base is squared off at a metallic plate.

Now only centimeters from the cylinder, her pupils dilate to their widest, and she discovers at the center of the mass are two oval spots, side-by-side, a shade darker than the rest. Grim recognition takes hold and her lips curl, her hands reach to her throat, and her heart pangs with grief as she realizes she is looking at Aaronson's earless and eyeless severed head.

Bile churns in her empty stomach and she staggers out of the room. Bright light from the main floor blinds her and she throws her arm across her eyes, leaning back against the clean white wall. For two years, the Counselor guided her out of the austere Operator conditioning so she could experience emotion without guilt. Again, she summons that conditioning like a security blanket, needing to wrap herself in its numbing folds.

Center, focus, balance, control...

She hiccoughs and a bitter taste rolls over her tongue, triggering a full heave. She clamps her mouth shut, pressing the heels of her gauntlets into her eyes and yelling through her nose.

Center, focus, balance, control...

She turns and props herself against the wall with her fists, one foot ahead of the other, expelling hot breaths and spitting salty saliva.

Turn it to something else...

Her jaw muscles clench hard, showing every fiber through her thin cheeks.

Make it something else...

She spits again and stands straight. Her gut, no longer quaking, is hard behind her toned abdominal muscles. Her long legs are still, her arms at her sides. Her breathing slows.

It's become something else.

She looks at the creature parked on its haunches near by. It looks back with a serious expression in the small eyes. Its whiskers droop. Its ears and tail are down, but the head is up.

"You know what's in there?" she asks the creature.

The great beast rises and pads over, parking its head beneath her hand and pressing against her hip. It only stays a moment and walks without hurry toward the workshop where Honniker's cultured cells and her restoration await.

"Yeah. You're right," the hardened woman says, wiping her mouth with the back of her armored hand. "Let's get this over with."

OF THE ESSENCE

Carter hauls the train of loaded carts like a runaway locomotive. Sharon hangs on for dear life as the trolleys sway and bank around every turn. What seemed to her an almost romantic idea of manning a dog sled across tundra is, in practice, more like riding sidecar in the TT race across Isle of Man.

Every time the corridors merge, the hallway becomes a little wider, as if moving from the top of a tree down through the supporting limbs. Soon, they will be in the wide trunk: the main entry corridor from the landing bay.

Sharon swivels her head at every intersection, feet wide on the lower frame and one arm hooked around the handle bar, watching for reflective teeth or movement in the branching corridors, when her head slams against the crates. She bounces back, losing grip of the trolley. With mincing steps, she recovers and finds the train has stopped.

"JESUS *CHRIST*, Carter! A little warning, *yeah*?"

Sharon stretches her eyes and mouth wide to drive the stars away. Two tall, dark figures streak by her from the front of the train, nearly bowling her over.

"Bloody *hell*...?" begins a stream of curses, but it ends when she leans around the crates and sees the corridor ahead is packed from floor to ceiling with metallic debris, random furniture, and corpses. Rigid arms and legs jut from between the metal and synthetics like planks of wood; torsos fill gaps in the carefully assembled barricade. Her jaw drops.

"Zuri, alternate route!" Shao-Lo radios. "Deepak, form up!"

Another dark streak rushes past Sharon, silent as owl's wings.

"Back it up," Carter radios. "Sharon! *Wake up!*"

Sharon snaps herself out of her trance, shaking her head like a wet dog. The carts jostle and bunch up under Carter's shoves, and she hauls with all her might to steer them back the way they came. Her eyes close with the effort, and she does not see the doorways in the corridor have opened.

"Contact!" Keiko radios. *"Committing!"* Her rifle pangs twice before savage animal roars drown it out.

"Keiko! Your left! *Keiko!"* Deepak yells.

Zuri's pistols blaze from around the corner, casting flickering shadows of leaping creatures. Feline screams pierce the din of combat.

"BRICKS FRONT!" Shao-Lo radios between labored grunts and her own rifle shots.

Carter thuds by, cannon primed.

The trolley seems a thousand times heavier without Carter's powerful shoves, and Sharon releases the trolley bar, the muscles in her neck twitching from strain. She feels herself shrinking inward, wanting to become small and insignificant, unnoticeable. The door beside her is open wide, the dark recesses beyond promising a place to hide. It draws her in like a slow current.

Her helmet lamps shine over dusty carpeting of a modest apartment living room. Clear spots on the carpet mark where tables or chairs once stood, leaving nothing to hide behind. A kitchenette just off the living room offers nothing but tiny cabinets. The dark of the bedroom, however...

She glides over the living room carpet, oblivious to the tracks she is making, and halts at the bedroom doorway. Hanging in mid air, only a half-meter from the floor, are socked feet.

Sharon raises her lamps up the mummified legs, up the withered torso and dangling arms to the crooked neck wrapped in sheets, to the recessed lips and sunken eyelids of the face.

Shocking thumps from outside sway the brittle body, and it breaks apart, clattering to the stained carpet with whorls of dust. It is bad enough to have walked in on someone's last act of desperation, to have found that person in such a state, a thousand years dead, yet still so vulnerable, bodily remains testifying to the unendurable cruelties which drove the act. Worse still is seeing those remains desecrated, reduced to a disorganized pile of molded rags and bones. But that is not the worst thing she sees. An internal voice tells her she should be moving. She should be doing anything but standing and staring at the metal claws stepping out of the closet onto the dusty pile, at the cold, reflective eyes, and at the leering mouthful of razors.

She sees all in slow motion as the sinews tighten on the front legs, the head lowers, and the creature springs at her with maw wide enough to engulf her head.

Her arms fly out in front of her, a futile bracing gesture, and the weapon strapped to her arm explodes a beam of electric-blue plasma. Super-heated particles singe the creature's flesh down to bone then blow the bones away like paper. A thunderous back blast bounces off the room's wall and slams her off her feet. She gasps, eyes wide, flat on her back in the corridor, staring at the ceiling.

"Gordon *Bennett!*" she says, hearing not her voice but only a tinny pitch like Mosquito wings.

Weight lands on her left arm. Sharon looks in a panic and sees a muscled foreleg pinning her wrist. Powerful jaws clamp around the strapped on weapon and bite through it. The slicing barrel fizzes with arcing current, singing lips and gums between metal teeth, and the beast yowls.

Paralyzed in fear, Sharon can only watch as the creature swings its massive head toward her, bats her onto her face, bites through the nape of her pressure suit, then hefts her up between its forelegs and drags her away.

Sharon screams and screams, unable to tell in her deafness if she is making any sound at all, until the creature collapses on top of her and rolls. Claws flash and rake against something hard in the darkness. There is a blur of sinewy legs, swishing tail, and armored fists that pound, smash, and crush. She is knocked free.

Sharon skids on her chest, arms out, and slides to a halt, the beams of her helmet aiming straight at the floor. Dazed, she props herself on elbows, curving her back to shine her lamps ahead. A line of bouncing, reflective eyes, approaches in long, sprinting strides.

A violet stream pierces the air over her head, detonating the center creature and mashing the others against the wall to each side of it. A tremor ripples the deck plating, jolting her where she lay.

Again, she is grabbed by the nape of her pressure suit, but this time she is lifted all the way to her feet. She whirls about and looks into Carter's closed mask. He stares at her intensely.

The Brick throws open his faceplate with a glistening gauntlet, revealing a sweaty, agitated face. His mouth moves in exaggerated, inaudible syllables, and he points repeatedly to the trolleys.

Sharon looks around herself and finds not just the pummeled creature that tried to drag her away but over a dozen scorched, broken, and twisted animal carcasses. With delayed understanding and appreciation, she sees Carter single-handedly fought back an entire ambush meant for her.

She takes a tentative step away from the huge Brick and falters, just catching herself. His great hand steadies her, pressing a dark red stain into her suit's brown canvas.

Ahead, the flashes of combat rage on. Lack of sound had lulled her into a dangerous complacence as though she were in a vivid and surreal dream—a nightmare one could awaken from and forget. As sound once again filters through the droning tones, that dreamlike state yields to urgency and she finally comprehends Carter's agitation.

We have to move, she tells herself. Looking Carter in the eye, she nods her head and shouts, "OKAY! LET'S GO!" just barely hearing her own voice.

Carter hustles back to the train of carts. A wicked blade slides out of the armor at his forearm and he slashes the last cart free. He sweeps most of the crates from it, leaving a large one at the back, and he plunks his cannon down on the front. Sharon steps over at his beckoning and looks at the cart. Between the crate and the cannon, there is just enough space for her to sit. Carter points at the spot with his two-fingered hand.

Sharon hops onto the cart and settles in, bracing her heels into the cart's raised edge and pressing her back against the crate. After checking both ways in the corridor, Carter takes her hands and places them on the cannon grip.

"*Here*, and *here*," she hears him say faintly. The small woman nods vigorously and clamps her hands as indicated.

"Now hold on!"

Carter sweeps a path through the carcasses with his boot and whips the cart around. Sharon digs in her heels, straddling a weapon almost as large as herself and twice as heavy.

"I'M READY," she shouts, and the cart launches forward. Her heart races as fast as Carter's pounding legs.

"Carter and Sharon advancing with Voss," she hears the Brick call over radio. Sounds of combat grow louder through the high-pitched tone in her ears, coinciding with every rumble telegraphed through the trolley beneath her. There is no more denying this is a fight for survival and escape. If she misses just one shot, it could cost them their lives, or worse...capture and endless torture.

Her focus dials in to the sharpest it has ever been. With her backside pushed hard into the crate she hunches over the cannon, ready to trigger on the first thing she sees.

****

Keller crouches beside a hatch in the crawlspace's floor, labeled,

"MECHANICAL DECK ACCESS, B7." A hefty release lever is built on one side of it with an arrow indicating the direction it turns. With a deep breath, he takes hold of the release and slowly, quietly moves it. The hatch, untended for centuries, groans under his efforts. He freezes, silently cursing, but—having no other option—he continues the noisy process and slides the hatch aside.

Beneath him is an unlit corridor, identical to others of the complex with the exception of thick dust matting the floor. He sweeps his helmet lamps over the deck plates below and lowers his glass-encased head through. The hallway is barren in one direction, but there is an odd pile about ten meters away in the opposite direction. Keller lowers himself through the hatch, hangs by the edge, and drops down.

Walking on toes, he comes to the heap and kneels beside it. Up close, he finds a pile of dark armor, cracked and dimpled beneath centuries of fibrous lint.

From what he can tell, there are three soldiers here, and from the number of holes and slices in the walls nearby, they must have run straight into a devastating fusillade. The old captain looks around anxiously then rummages through the pile, dumping sandy bones from boots, gauntlets, breastplates. Most of the armor, so like the Cadre Operators' except for smaller size, is cracked beyond use or perforated. Some parts appear salvageable, however.

Between the three, could I make a set?

Keller again scans the corridor and starts laying out good pieces. Beginning with boots, he works his way up the full suit to the neck. With some reserve, he picks up the closest helmet. The faceplate is caved in, pierced at the eyepiece. A fragmented skull rattles inside.

He sets aside the helmet in favor of another, and finds the next one is shattered at the temple. The last helmet is intact, still attached to a portion of neck armor, which is sliced through. He ratchets the sliced neckpiece away and flips open the faceplate. A mummified head gapes out at him.

Freeze-dried flesh and hollow eye sockets make recognition impossible, to his infinite relief. Yet even so, Keller is seized by an unpleasant awareness.

I wonder if I knew you...

Before the thought can lodge, he dumps the head and knocks the helmet against the floor to empty out flakes of skin.

Once he has a full suit arranged, he stands and contemplates the shabby armor.

Do I have time for this?

THE EXHAUSTED DEAD

His mind conjures the reaching paws from his narrow escape into the access crawlspace, talons rasping and screeching around the lip of the tube he had just dived through...the painful impact against the raised bulkhead seam...hot, condensing growls of frustration as the beast tried again and again to bash and pull its way into the conduit...how easily those claws could have ripped through the scant centimeter of canvas cloth surrounding him and even easier through the skin beneath it.

Damn right I do...

A display in his helmet shows the air in the corridor is breathable, but when he cracks the face shield of his globe-like helmet he is assaulted by extreme cold. He slams the vent shut and looks again at the sandy bones around him, debating the risk of hypothermia.

Just a puncture, a rip in depressurized space, and I'm done...

He thinks about the closer fit, of squeezing through tight spaces, of rigid plates that claws would glance over, of being able to run properly without his big metal boots clomping against the deck, freedom of movement and agility.

Just do it, old man.

Holding his breath against the super-chilled air, he releases his neck latch, drops his helmet to the deck, then rips open the double seams of his pressure suit. Despite the width of his shoulders, the canvas falls easily away from his thinned frame, and he kicks out of his clunky boots. A bitter cold shocks him through his under suit, frosting his sweat in an instant.

With stiffening fingers and chattering teeth, Keller clamps himself into the ancient, dusty armor. Each modular part snaps and fits to the other, plates and joints interlocking with smooth, seamless fittings. The ritual takes him back to missions served as a younger man, before being recruited by Soshiba Varicorp, when this kind of suit was a more common uniform. The comfortable fit of firm padding, the feeling of dressing oneself in invincibility, presses back the intrusive chill and rolls back his mental odometer. His hands remember every latch and seal, the correct order of assembly, so that in under a minute he is suited up to the neck.

Still crouched, he grabs the one good helmet and ducks his head into it. Unable to contain his breath any longer, his lungs blast out stale air and draw in new. With the harsh cold comes an ancient, gray smell. It fills his sinuses and coats them with an irritating dryness.

Keller swivels on his heel and pats down the pockets of his discarded pressure suit until he finds one with something flat and rectangular inside. He unzips the pocket and retrieves a copper shielded circuit board, the one he pulled from the old transport wreckage in the landing bay.

"You can see what armor did for them," Honniker taunts from an unseen loudspeaker. *"What makes you think it will help you?"*

Keller scowls at Honniker's unwelcome commentary, at words his anxiety was already whispering. He opens a thigh compartment and tucks the copper-plated board into it, then stands and runs in place, knees high, swinging his arms, working the gritty joint servos and jump-starting the suit's movement-charged power system. A diagnostic icon appears in his visor.

"Jabber on, Honniker. I've got you by the *balls*." The colonist stoops and rummages weapons from the moldy heap. He finds an intact rifle and machine pistol.

"What is it you THINK you're doing, which should concern me so?"

Keller smiles.

"I'm a nun's crack away from getting the cores back on-line. When I do, you're gone, baby. You and all your God-awful crimes. *Gone*."

"Since I first met you, I've enjoyed your unfounded confidence. In spite of your million-fold failures there is a self-importance, which continues to glow. Such obstinacy...or is it obtuseness? Regardless, the reckoning will be very satisfying."

"Say what you want. I may be a dead man. But so are you."

Keller pulls back the action of the machine pistol and sees the caseless shell in the chamber is frosted with inert white crystals. He frowns at it and tosses the pistol back to the pile.

"One more stop to by-pass the restart safeties. Then the control rods retract, and we all glow."

Honniker's disembodied voice is like a Cheshire grin in the darkness. *"Oh, Keller, I have missed you! You were the only one who could ever truly amuse me."*

Keller pulls the battery of the rifle and checks it. Though intact, there is no charge.

"I aim to serve," he says with a sneer as he slaps the spent pack into the rifle.

"Then tell me, Keller, whom are you serving now?"

Keller pauses, his one shred of uncertainty harpooned with an expert shot.

"I don't know. Maybe no one. I just know this place has to burn. With you *in it*."

"Well, I invite you to try. There's only one place where you could by-pass the restart safeties. And you can be SURE I'll be waiting for you."

"I'd be heartbroken if you weren't," Keller says, sealing his faceplate. Rebreather vents inside give a puff of dust then flow with filtered air.

"Until then..."

Keller breaks into a sprint down the corridor, kicking up a chalky plume with every stride.

****

"Administrator..."

The young man stirs in his bunk, nearly roused, yet still dozing.

"Administrator Aaronson," persists the automated assistant, *"awaken."*

A small panel at his bunk side lights up and blares with a newscaster's voice. The man smacks it repeatedly until it silences.

Overhead lights illuminate, fading from dim to bright. He squints against the harsh ceiling fixture and scrunches his face.

"Yeah, yeah, all right. I'm up." He throws the covers back with a heavily-muscled arm. He swings equally-muscled legs from the bunk and stands in boxer shorts and a tight-fitting white tank top. A yawn befitting Rip van Winkle seizes him and he stretches his brawny frame.

A tall communication panel over his work desk lights up, streaming news reports from Earth and the sister colonies. In the main window is a list of reports and messages addressed to "Colony Administrator, New Vancouver".

"Are you ready for breakfast, sir?" the assistant asks with mild German inflection.

"Sure. What you got?"

In a nook beside the comm panel, a gleaming silver coffee service materializes complete with a plate of yellow protein and a glass of orange liquid.

"Omelette and OJ...Again?" He smacks his pasty mouth. "Yeah, all right."

He takes the tray from the nook and sets it down at the desk. Rubbing his face with both hands, he plunks down into a high-backed, swivel chair.

"Set an appointment for me with Doctor Hobbes, would you? I keep having those dreams."

"Which dreams? The ones where Earth and the colonies were destroyed?"

"No, not that one."

"Was it the dream where you are dismembered?"

"Yeah..." he says with a haunted look. "I saw my own body this time, without the head."

"Perhaps you are working too hard. Doctor Hobbes has availability this Thursday at three P.M."

"That's fine, I'll take it." The man takes the coffee from the service and reclines in his chair. "What's going on today?"

"There is a narrowcast from your family," says the voice through the panel. *"They wanted you to know they love you and miss you, but are extremely proud of you. I'm not supposed to tell you, but they are planning a large homecoming party."*

Aaronson glances down at the photo frame on his desk. His mouth stretches wide in fondness.

"My boy's gonna be eight next week."

"Yes, your children are all thriving."

"What, you sayin' they're doing fine without me?"

"Of course not, Administrator, I was—"

"Relax. That was a joke."

"I see. That was quite funny."

The man scrunches his face and shakes his head. "All right," he says with a sigh, "you didn't wake me at oh-four-hundred to spoil my wife's surprise. So what's up?"

"There is a saboteur in our production facility power plant."

Aaronson's demeanor hardens.

"Damn it, you should've *started* with that!" He puts his coffee down on the tray and leans forward on the desk. "Is anyone hurt? What's the damage?"

"There have been casualties. Primary and redundant cooling systems have been damaged to failure, and the saboteur is attempting to by-pass the core restart safeties. If successful, he will cause a meltdown, which will destroy our entire complex."

Aaronson leaps up from the desk, throws open his closet and snatches an orange body suit from a hanger.

"How many are there?"

"Just the one male we have observed in the act. We suspect he has several female accomplices, however, who we must retain for questioning."

"We have an ID on our bad guy?"

"The facial profile is a ninety percent match of an ex-SoVar employee, Braemar Keller."

"Keller...?" Aaronson freezes at the name, one leg in, one leg out of the orange undergarment.

"Yes. He was your captain once, was he not?"

"He was...on the *Europa*." He thrusts his other leg in and drags the suit roughly to his torso.

"Ah, the Europa. *A tragedy. How he could've abandoned the ship and her entire crew to the enemy escapes all reason."*

The man stiffens as suppressed rage boils from his subconscious.

"If I recall correctly," the computer assistant continues, *"Keller led the* Europa *to an enemy trap and ordered you, with a team, to investigate. Keller fled. You were captured."*

Aaronson's mind swims amid the unclear recollections, the lines between dream and memory shifting like battle fronts between equally matched opponents. He remembers Keller ordering him into the facility with Voss, Rosenthal, Summers, Michaela, and Soares...bodies everywhere... screeches of metal in the dark...friends screaming, disappearing...a distress call in his own voice, telling the *Europa* to run, to get clear fast as she could. But who was in command of the bridge if not Keller?

He punches an arm at a time through the sleeves. "I don't remember escaping. How did I?"

"No one knows. Strange that you would not remember yourself, though that is what Dr. Hobbes is for, I'm sure. Perhaps it is too violent a memory, one which a sane mind does not wish to keep."

"Keller..." Aaronson almost loses himself in his fractured recollections, feeling the familial closeness to someone he thought of as an elder brother. They were only a few years apart, yet Keller always had the fire and confidence of direction, which made him so perfect for leadership, so inspiring of loyalty. But the abandonment...trading the *Europa* and her crew to save his own throat...a betrayal worthy of Ephialtes, who led the Persians around the Spartan blockade at Thermopylae...then the broken dream-memories of captivity, of knife cuts and saws, no anesthetic...

He zips the front seam up to his neck. "I wondered what I'd do if I found him..."

"This is certainly your opportunity to find out."

The rage inside simmers with the promise of revenge, of justice, of settling an old score.

"Lock all exits. Take all power off-line, even the battery back-ups to the reactors. No one can pull the control rods without the motor assist, so if we keep them powered down, we should have time to clear out our saboteur."

"A wise plan."

"Is my rig prepped?"

"Yes. I took the liberty of arming your chassis in advance. Where you will be operating near critical structures, I have outfitted the suit with flame, sawing, drilling, and stabbing weapons."

"Fine, fine. Inform SoVar of our saboteur, and tell them I'm on it."

The doorway of his apartment glides open and a robotic chassis strides inside. The machine, its lower arms thick with attachments, turns about. The back of it opens like a sideways clamshell.

Aaronson steps into the chassis's thick legs. He slides his arms down into the chassis's bulky arms. An internal holoscreen projects before his eyes, offering a full field of view through the torso's centimeters-thick armor plating.

"Have Med teams standing by with full Trauma and Rad Kits."

"They are being dispatched now."

The clamshell closes around its occupant and seals with a hiss.

"In light of Keller's crimes, I believe the authorities will be tolerant of any action you may take against him."

Aaronson looks through his eyebrows at the console displayed in front of him. His eyes seek out the weapon icons and he activates them with double blinks.

"Let's end this quickly."

"I could not agree more."

GORDON'S PUB

Carter whips the trolley around another corner then yanks back on the handle, nearly launching Sharon from her perch. Ten meters ahead is a half-built barricade of broken machine parts and frozen reptilian corpses.

Robotic arms heft more corpses and parts up from behind the wall and then slap them down in rows like bricks, fragile bodies thudding, crunching, and cracking as they are compacted into place.

Sharon gawks at the grisly procession as Carter steers the trolley, pointing the cannon barrel at the heart of the pile.

"Fire, Sharon! *Fire!*" Carter yells.

Sharon squeezes the cannon's trigger with all her might, but it is too large and stiff for her small hand. She brings her other hand up, wrapping both around the weapon grip as if she were strangling it, and squeezes with everything she has.

The trigger slides and a violet glow coalesces around her, gathers toward the glowing cannon barrel, and surges into the half-finished barricade. The pile detonates, blasting corpses and the machines stacking them down the long corridor.

"Path clear!" Carter shouts into radio.

Shao-Lo and Deepak rush by and sprint through the gap. Movement far ahead draws their aim and they trigger with deadly efficiency.

Argo tromps by with Keiko slumped over his shoulder. Zuri runs up behind Carter, Keiko's rifle slung across her back, both pistols clenched in her fists and smoking. She steps to a halt and turns about, menacing a horde of reflective eyes just meters behind her.

Carter swings the trolley around.

"Zuri, get clear!"

The young Geek hunches and slides aside as Sharon chokes the cannon's trigger again. Violet haze gathers in the dark and the predators dive into open doorways, just dodging the killing blast. The beam punches through a distant wall with a dramatic explosion, the shockwaves rolling back in muted booms. Beasts pour from the side rooms like floodwater, claws screeching as they race up the metal floor.

Zuri's pistols blaze into the front row of creatures, high caliber bullets punching through exposed areas of flesh, some ricocheting off overlapping plates. So near to a kill, the beasts frenzy, ignoring Zuri's lethal spray, and they rush en masse. She rips through entire clips at a time, dropping the spent clips and cycling in fresh from her thigh one after another. The tide rushes on, barreling over the felled creatures like a cresting wave approaching shore.

Sharon chokes the cannon's trigger, but the trigger merely slides into the grip. The battery is dry.

"Zuri, RUN!" Carter yells. He whips the trolley about and shoves with every fiber of his massive legs. Zuri runs backwards beside him, her pistols still roaring at the clamor of teeth, claws, and muscle behind them.

The predators gain, eyes bright, maws salivating, lungs huffing with lust for an imminent kill.

Carter palms a device from his belt and mashes its activator.

"SHARON," he yells over the hideous din, *"BRACE!"*

The Brick drops the device with a slight backward toss. He leans over Sharon, shielding her as much as he can.

Claws slash and skitter over the deck plates as the lead beasts try to dodge the grenade, but their momentum propels them over it. The ones behind pile up like a freeway collision. Animal screams split the air just before a mighty *POOMP* and a gale of wind, hard as hammers.

The gale smashes Carter from behind, lifting him off his feet and toppling the trolley. He tumbles over and over, and by the time he finally comes to rest, he has no idea which direction he faces. He lifts his head stiffly.

Several meters away, the trolley is on its side, one leg folded in on itself, wheel broken off. The crate is blasted into flimsy panels and splintered fibers. Voss's inert form slumps among litter of glass vials and brass-cased viral shells. Sharon is face down, jagged shards of metal jutting through her suit. Blooms of red expand around the perforations.

"Sharon!"

Zuri runs back to the huge Brick and crouches, hauling him up under the shoulder while keeping a pistol aimed at a disheveled and stunned mob of creatures. Farther down the corridor behind them, fresh predators race in from branching intersections.

"Brick, *c'mon!*" Zuri yells.

Carter shakes off the loose refuse covering him and gets to his feet. He turns in place until he spots his cannon.

"Sir," Zuri pleads, *"we have to move!"*

A glint overhead draws her quick eye and her arms flick toward an open hatchway. Both pistols strobe with muzzle flames. An abbreviated screech pierces the thudding gunshots, and a creature slides from the hatch like syrup. Zuri tracks the beast as it slams to the deck, keeping both pistols on it should it move again.

The Brick snatches his cannon, finally recovered from disorientation.

"Colonel," Carter radios, "Voss and Sharon are down, need assis—"

Zuri and Carter are both tackled from the hatchway above. Gnashing teeth scrawl across Carter's helmet and neck, trying to open wide enough for a death bite.

With calm presence, he extends the blade at his arm and jabs it through the neck of the beast. Fight drains instantly from it and he hurls it away. But before he can stand, a tide of creatures washes over him, claws hitching into the seams of his armor, ripping, jaws snapping at exposed toes, severing, great clouds of breath fogging the air with crazed excitement.

A rifle shot explodes the head of a creature at his chest, then a barrage of coordinated fire pounds the flood of creatures back. Argo leaps over him, triggering short pulses of violet energy. Death hurtles from him with every trigger pull, with every lobbed grenade, and the warrior bellows seemingly forever from bottomless lungs.

Carter drags himself up to hands and knees when a cold sensation passes directly into his left wrist. He looks down and finds his two-fingered hand is gone, the cleanly severed wrist flowing bright red. He struggles to stand then he pitches forward onto his chest. Confused, he rolls onto his back and shines his helmet lamps over himself.

The plating over both of his thighs is peeled away, the skin and muscle beneath shredded in long bleeding tears. The front halves of both feet are gone, gnawed down to the heels. Blood streams from the gnawed stumps and runs down over his ankles.

From the floor beside him, Zuri's helmet lamps shine directly at him.

"Geek, help me up."

The young Operator does not respond. He leans out of the lamp beams.

"Zuri, are y..." He stops when he sees the severed neck armor and no body beneath it.

"ZURI!"

Booted feet tromp up beside him and halt. Carter lifts his eyes and sees Deepak triggering one shot after another with strident *PANGs*.

"Can you stand?" Deepak shouts between shots.

"Yeah," Carter says, climbing up Deepak's sturdy frame. He sways on his partial feet like they were stilts, the shreds of his bleeding thigh muscles burning and quivering.

Shao-Lo glides up beside Deepak with Keiko draped over her shoulder. The tall Colonel aims alongside Deepak, doubling the rate of killing shots.

"Argo, fall back and collect Sharon!" she orders.

Argo's wild shouts abate and the Brick hunches. He steps backward, snorting like a bull, watching the cautious, reflective eyes watching him from open doorways. He sneaks a glance at Carter and spots the huge man's leaking arm stump and tattered legs.

"Colonel, he's gonna bleed out if I don't close those wounds. Sharon, maybe Keiko, too."

Shao-Lo pivots, her gray eyes seeming to penetrate the walls and crawlways around them, sensing the creatures sliding through them, maneuvering, flanking, surrounding. Her eyes move to Sharon, to Zuri's decapitated body, to Zuri's arms and legs, severed at elbows and knees, to Voss and to the scattered shells of viral weaponry. She crouches and picks up one of the shells then jams it between Deepak's back and rack.

"I've never played defense in my life," she says with derision. The tall woman turns on her heel and stares at a set of recessed double doors several meters ahead. Above, a broken sign points the way through the parted doors with an arrow captioned, *Gordon's Pub*.

Shao-Lo glances back at what is left of her team. Carter hooks his handless arm around Deepak's neck and hefts his cannon with the other. The big Brick's legs buckle and he nearly drags Deepak to the floor, but the two strain mightily and keep one another standing. Argo, cannon slung over his broad shoulders, takes Keiko's rifle by the strap and throws it over his head, then pries Zuri's pistols from her severed hands. Pistols in hand, he scoops Sharon in both arms like she were the most delicate of creations. Rising to his feet, he cradles her against his chest and studies her wounds with concern.

With no one else to carry Voss, Shao-Lo stoops with Keiko on her shoulder and takes the inert man by the wrist. Before she can drag him a centimeter, Voss's eyes flick open. His leg flies up and smashes her faceplate. Off balance and weighed down by Keiko, Shao-Lo crashes onto her backside. Argo, Deepak, and Carter, likewise encumbered, are slow to react; and Voss sprints away, yelling with Honniker's inflection, *"Ha, HA! Not today, Colonel! Not today!"*

Shrieks of metal rip from the open doorways. Reflective eyes peer into the corridor again. Confident snarls pass between the creatures, merging with the scraping claws in predatory bravado.

The tall Colonel scrambles to her feet, hauls the limp Keiko up to her shoulder like a massive sack, and readies her rifle.

"On me!" she shouts. With groans, the team lurches toward the double doors. Predators dash from cover behind them, tongues lolling between razor teeth.

Shao-Lo's weapon flashes from kill to kill to kill. Deepak staggers and stumbles with his burdensome comrade, aiming his rifle from the hip at the corridor ahead. Argo is nimble by comparison, but his aim is hampered by the fragile cargo in his arms. He triggers the pistols awkwardly in left-right sweeps. Sparks jump and dance over the advancing horde from the errant bullets.

Just outside the double doors, Shao-Lo's rifle fires dry. In a single movement, she thumbs the battery release, snatches a replacement from her waist and slams it home before the spent pack hits the ground. Taking cover at the doorframe, she peeks inside.

The interior is clean and spacious with high ceilings. Round tables with chairs cover a wide and open dining area. A half-level up to the right is a faux-wooden bar with a mirrored back wall. Empty bottles of every hue line the mirror on glass shelves, leaning against each other as if inebriated by their own contents. There is no movement.

"Inside!" Shao-Lo shouts. She slips through only long enough to set Keiko down against the wall then hustles back into the corridor. Her team lopes closer, snarling jaws and straining limbs racing up behind them. She snipes through any window available to her: the crook of Carter's arm, the gap between Argo's legs; but killing one at a time is not enough. She dials her rifle high, squats at eye level to the beasts, and triggers, lancing through three, four, five at a time.

Her weapon fires dry again. Out of ammo, she rises from her squat and extends her rifle's bayonet. She detaches the cruel blade and tosses the drained rifle through the double doors.

As Argo lumbers by with Sharon, the Colonel orders, "Find a way to close these doors."

"Aye, sir!" Argo replies.

Deepak and Carter hobble together, Deepak triggering random shots into the panting, yowling horde. Shao-Lo strides toward them and snatches Carter's bulky weapon from the Brick's hand. She jams her blade into a gap between the cannon's barrel and lower body. The pommel of the blade juts like an extra handle.

"MOVE IT!" she shouts, thumbing the cannon output down. She widens her stance, arches her back, and triggers a barrage of short pulses into the rushing wave. Instead of exploding the creatures, the weaker pulses flash fur and skin into orange flames. Immolated creatures collapse, thrashing and burning. She triggers again and again with the non-killing blasts until the corridor is filled with shrieking, flailing creatures.

Shao-Lo back steps with the massive cannon, watching the burning predators panic in the corridor, watching them lash one another with claws, watching them bite and snap through pack mates close by. Limbs carbonize, eyes burst, and howls of agony merge into a collective groan. The corners of her mouth lift.

Glancing over her shoulder, she just catches sight of Carter disappearing through the parted doors. She turns front to the wall of smoking, burning creatures, levels the cannon, and back-steps toward her team.

"Argo—*you get those doors moving yet?*"

"Locked open, Colonel! Gotta cut the pistons."

The flames dim, pouring smutty fumes into the air, and Shao-Lo's helmet lights diffuse into the dense smoke. Her visor compensates to infrared, but residual heat fills her vision with a nearly uniform brightness. Wild, furious screams gather behind the obscuring cloud. Open rooms along the hallway resonate with hateful growls and scraping metal.

Deepak dashes out through the double doors and stands beside his Colonel, rifle poised down the opposite corridor.

"Deepak, get back in there and assist Argo!" Shao-Lo orders. "We're going to be overrun!"

"Sir, you need backup..."

She shoves him. *"Get in there!* And keep watch. They might come in another way."

Shao-Lo glares into the curling smoke like it was a forming storm, potent with hidden violence. She stokes her own internal fires, summoning murderous rage, channeling it, focusing it, harnessing it to her superlative will. She takes a long inhale through her nose and exhales hot breath. She hunches her powerful shoulders, submerges her conscious to a singular, primal intent. Her hands lock around the cannon grips, bayonet pommel jutting ready near her trigger hand. Behind her faceplate, her chin is square, her eyes bright, her mouth a curved line.

The sign above her explodes with glass and reaching claws. The ambush was perfect, but Shao-Lo dodges, using the cannon's mass as a center of gravity. Her trigger hand rips the bayonet free and whips it through the beast's extended throat. Completing her swinging arc around the massive weapon, she drags the cannon out of the air and smashes the creature's head with a thick *crunch*. In a blink, she is back on her feet, bayonet tucked into the cannon's gap.

A ravening host leaps from the cloud like valkyries. She triggers. Crackling plasma distorts the air. Animal flesh detonates with concussive *thumps*.

Skidding paws and panting breaths... She flings herself around the cannon like it was on a swivel, just dodging a leaping attack from behind. The creature touches down, and Shao-Lo blasts its hindquarter, sending the scorched, partial animal hurtling into pack mates racing forward.

There is a rusty groan from the double doorway of the pub, and she sneaks a peek. One door slides out of the jamb and halts.

One left...

Creatures rush at her from the front, back, and sides, from the exploded pub sign, and from hatches overhead, but Shao-Lo is a vehicle of destruction, whirling just out of reach, slashing, blasting back the murderous tide. Talons glance across her armored exterior, seeking but never finding a weakness in her agile defense. She sweeps, deflects, carves, and incinerates the pressing horde until the pile of limp creatures at her feet makes the ground uneven, slippery. The lethal woman rises to her toes, maintaining an uneasy balance over the carcasses underfoot, barely keeping ahead of the blood-crazed beasts. Slice, spin, trigger, slide, stomp, duck, stab... A roar behind her...A creature mid-leap, paws outstretched and wide to embrace, maw gaping, eyes glowing red. The cannon fires dry.

Three hundred kilos of carnivorous rage slam her to the deck. She drops the cannon, rolls away from the snapping teeth, and stabs the serrated bayonet under the beast's front leg. Shocked screams and convulsions beside her as she twists the blade and rips it free.

Claws seize her back-rack and tear it away, sending her careening. She curls into a ball and wraps hands around her neck as the beasts pounce. She kicks insanely with her legs like they were two massive pistons, crushing snouts and ribs, pushing back a couple at a time but only delaying an inevitable end.

Violet streams sear through the frenzy above her, exploding predators with jarring *thumps*. Sure hands hook beneath her arms and drag her over mounds of bleeding, charred creatures. In her clearing vision, she sees Argo in the hallway, triggering blast after blast in each direction. She looks up and sees Deepak hunched over her, dragging her between the pub's double doors.

"We're in, Argo!" Deepak yells over her. *"Fall back!"*

Argo palms two devices from his waist and sends them sailing in opposite directions. He sprints for the narrow gap in the doors, snatching up Carter's cannon on the way, and dives through. Intense white light washes through the gap, followed by twin *POOMPs* and a rumble of floor plates. A gale like a battering ram rolls in, knocking Deepak and Shao-Lo to the ground. Dense black smoke drifts in behind the blast until Argo drags the doors shut with another rusty groan. Bottles rattle from the bar shelves and crash to the floor.

Wild, frantic howls sound from beyond the double doors, and there is a stampede of padded feet. Dozens, seemingly hundreds, of claws rake the door's far side, tearing at the central seam, trying to wedge it and pry it apart.

Shao-Lo pants behind her faceplate. She sits up, still clutching her bayonet. Her frantic eyes seek about the room for more of the predators, but find Deepak instead. He squats beside her, rifle pulled tight to his shoulder, and scans in all directions.

"You okay, Colonel?"

She looks at her hands and feet, taking inventory of all fingers and toes.

"Yeah," she says.

Argo, his smoldering cannon slung over a shoulder, twists a metal bar around the double door handles. Despite the scouring of talons outside, the door remains shut.

"Sit-rep," Shao-Lo demands, climbing to her feet.

"Sir," Deepak reports, following the colonel as she searches for her rifle, "we've got an uncertain refuge here with multiple entrances and access points. Carter's got multiple lacerations in each leg, missing hand, and blood loss. Sharon's wounds are critical but not life-threatening. Keiko's unconscious, I don't know what happened. And Zuri...Zuri's dead."

"I know," the tall woman says morosely. She finds her rifle and collects it from a scatter of debris. Deepak waits patiently while she snaps her bayonet back to the rifle barrel and pulls out the drained battery.

"You got a fresh cell?" she asks.

Deepak nods and swaps a battery from his waist for the one she holds. Shao-Lo slaps the new battery home and primes the rifle's capacitors.

The scraping claws against the double doors relent. In the sudden abatement, there comes another sound, rumbling voices in concert, growls like before, yet more challenging than in fury.

"What *is* that?" Deepak asks.

As Shao-Lo listens, she guesses where the yowls and hisses are concentrated. "It's Zuri," she says with disgust. "They're fighting over her."

The somber colonel strides toward the center of the dining area, shoving the round tables aside with powerful kicks.

"THAT'S NOT HOW THIS IS GOING TO END, HONNIKER!" Her voice drops to a whisper. "Establish link, *Geek Zuri.* Arm personal incendiary, voice authorize, *Shao-Lo, Colonel.*"

A crinkle of sheet metal comes through a ceiling ventilator grate. Argo, Deepak, and Shao-Lo all look at the grate, knowing what is creeping through the shaft behind it.

Shao-Lo lowers her gaze to her two standing Operators.

"Brace."

Argo's and Deepak's eyes go wide. Argo runs to Sharon and leans over her, shielding her as much as he can. Deepak dashes to Carter and does likewise.

Shao-Lo drops into the clearing she made, lays flat, and utters the single word, *"Detonate."*

Light blooms in the corridor with such intensity, the walls become translucent. A seismic jolt sweeps Shao-Lo and the round tables from the dining floor like a child losing at chess. The giant mirror and bottles behind the bar leap into a million twinkling pieces, spraying out across the room. Ventilation ducts belch blue and white flames, shooting their metal grates against opposing walls. The floor shudders until the shockwaves finally fade.

Shao-Lo pushes out of a tangle of tables, struggling against the interlocked metal legs, and looks out into a radically altered interior. The metal and stone walls facing the blast have sagged and bulged inward, their wall decorations and paint uniformly vaporized, leaving a powdery white ash. Light sconces and fixtures hang by naked metal cords and broken brackets.

Shao-Lo looks up at the ventilator duct and sees a carbonized head and foreleg with blackened claws dangling from it. She grunts.

"Report."

"Gun Deepak and Brick Carter okay."

"Brick Argo, Gun Keiko, and Sharon okay."

Shao-Lo strides past the pub's wreckage to stand with her team.

"Get them stabilized, Argo."

"Aye, sir," Argo says.

"Deepak, give me a hand over here."

Deepak rises from the floor and follows Shao-Lo to the double doors. She takes one end of the curved bar and points to the other side. Deepak takes hold as indicated.

"Pull," Shao-Lo orders.

The two soldiers heave and strain against the bar. Between the two of them, they can just straighten what Argo curled alone. Shao-Lo lets the bar drop to the floor with a solid clang.

"Keep watch over them, Deepak. Let *nothing* through this door that isn't me. Understood?"

"Aye, sir!" Deepak salutes with one hand and hefts his rifle with the other. Shao-Lo leans into the door handle. It does not budge. With annoyance, she looks around the frame of the doorway and finds that although not directly facing the blast, the door tracks have warped from heat and vibration.

Deepak does not wait to be told. He takes one door handle while Shao-Lo takes the other and they grunt the doors open enough that she can squeeze through.

Outside, the corridor is a buckled, smashed, and melted ruin. Metal wall, floor, and ceiling plates, dull red with heat, throw off a smoky haze. To the left, the corridor is blown clear as far as she can see, but down the corridor to the right, where Zuri fell, there is a hole in the floor twenty meters across. She strides toward the gaping hole, feeling the spring of the unsupported floor beneath her, and walks out as far as she dares.

Though still several meters from the edge, her height allows her to see down to the level below. Emergency lamps shine from the lower walls into the space, their beams diffusing amid curling billows of dust. The bottom is obscured, but she can make out large sections of charred flooring and ceiling joists lying in cracked chunks atop wrecks of crushed machinery and tubes. Nets of frayed cables hang from the hole's ragged edges. Above the hole is a dome where the native rock vaporized. Thin needles point down from the apex, the cooled drips of viscous liquid stone.

She scowls at the devastation. Her mission is to capture and pacify Cadre Two for habitation. This blast has done untold damage, possibly irreparable. Even so, a subtle satisfaction creeps its way in. As she gazes down into the sensitive mechanical deck, she can sense the vulnerability.

"You felt *that*, didn't you, *Honniker*?"

EGALITARIAN

Maiella's eyes focus on the ceiling. The harsh onslaught of stimulated sensations is over at last, leaving only a slight odor of smoke and ozone in her nostrils—an odor not artificial but real. Something is or was burning.

There is an ache behind her eyes, also a heightened awareness. In the years since the malfunction of her cryo-recliner, the malfunction that damaged her HDI, she had forgotten what it felt like. Yet as her senses again merge to unified perception, she recognizes smooth flows of data streaming through her mind.

Her lips part in a gasp of joy. She is aware of the computer she is linked into, sensing its software, visualizing it mentally and exploring its boundaries. The computer is small, portable, not immediately connected to a larger system, obeying her thoughts as though an extension of her own body.

"Mmm-grfff-ffrrh..." she mumbles through her mouth guard. Faster than she can say it, the probes in her head retract, the spikes biting her skull release, and the metal restraints securing her to the table loosen. She slips her hands through the slackened loops and pulls the rubberized guard from her mouth. A long trail of saliva hangs from it in a sagging curve before finally breaking.

She smacks her lips and runs her tongue around her teeth, concentrating on the machine console beside her. *No, this isn't a dream...This is real!*

"Ha, HA!" she shouts with a grin. As a further test, she looks up at the spindly octopus overhead. It spins first one way then the other at her mental command, the arms alternately extending, bending, retracting at her whim. She senses the motors controlling the table, and she hops to her feet, making the table sway back and forth beneath her as if she were riding an ocean wave on a steel surfboard.

Dozens of coded radio channels announce themselves in her goggles, whispering to her after years of silence. Elation is only part of what she feels—she feels air in her lungs, she feels a lightness and clarity of mind, she feels whole, once again a digital shaman able to commune with the wireless spirits of an invisible world.

She drops down to the floor and looks around the workshop. It is exactly as she first found it, yet it has a new appearance through her restored awareness. Her HDI is like an extra sense and an extra limb combined, enabling her to reach out into her environment, to interact with it in so many more ways than mere touch. Networked mentally and emotionally to the artificial environments around her, it is a kind of telepathy. Its loss was devastating, an amputation. Being cut off and sequestered, unable to feel the presence of humming machines around her, left her crippled, broken. And without that one special ability—the one for which she was engineered, the one she had honed sharper than any of her generation—she was easily marginalized for her flaws. *Discarded.* Now, with her regained connectivity, those painful memories fall to the back of her mind as if waking from hallucination and realizing all the bad times are behind her.

"Doctor, you are *truly* a genius!"

Maiella glances over at Mikato. He sits on a bench, hair tousled between gold implants in his scalp, collar wrinkled, and he leans against the wall beneath a thick blanket. A wheeled tray stands beside him, atop which is a steaming mug. She squints at the man.

"Weird for a hologram to need a blanket. What, thinking about your body in cryo gave you a chill?"

Mikato does not reply, only stares into the opposite wall.

Maiella reaches up to her head and disconnects the HDI then sets it carefully on the stainless steel table. When she looks again at the seated man, there is not the slightest flicker, no halo of brightness.

She moves to the observation window and glances toward the distant vault. What seemed moments earlier, amber lights were flashing beside the vault's ice blue window. The lights are no longer flashing and the vault door is wide open. Traces of condensing vapor roll through the open doorway.

Her eyes stretch wide and she looks again at the man beneath the blanket.

"Doctor Mikato? Is that *you*?"

The man's eyes, heavy as lead, turn in their sockets toward her. They are the eyes of a man victimized by knowledge, by too much awareness and understanding. The orbs are hazy yet observant, seeming to see her, to weigh her, and to understand her in a single glance. They turn away from her like planets rotating on an axis and fixate on the wall again.

Maiella steps toward him, possessed of a need to verify his existence with a touch. She nears, then reaches out to him.

"Don't," the man says, voice as leaden as the eyes.

Maiella retracts the reaching hand and stands, self-conscious, not knowing what to say, except, "Are you all right?"

The eyes glisten but there is no reply.

"He's just been sitting there," says a voice over her shoulder.

Maiella jumps in surprise. Behind her is the projected image of this same man, yet the expressions are so different the two appear completely unrelated.

The huge animal, sitting silently beside the projection, rises and walks over to the blanketed man. It sits, sniffs his hand, then gently laps it.

"What happened?" Maiella asks.

"He could be in shock from extremely long stasis," the projection says. "It could be a neurochemical crash. Or he may be nutritionally deprived. Though I suspect it may be something psychological."

"What do you mean?"

"He seemed fine after decantation. In fact, we were both pleased to meet one another. There appeared no ill effects. But then he wanted to know what had occurred since his upload. I informed him, and he fell into this torpor, from which he refuses to stir."

The man beneath the blanket shrivels, his eyes disappearing beneath a flood. The huge creature sighs with a slight moan and rests its chin on his lap.

"What can we do?" Maiella asks.

"There's nothing I *can* do for him, it seems. Perhaps he'll snap out of it." The projection turns and steps toward the door, saying, "Come, let's test your restoration and make sure it's complete, yes?"

Maiella cannot take her eyes from the despondent man just across from her. There, huddled beneath a blanket, is one of the finest scientific minds of all time, the principal scientist of Cadre Two, the one who successfully bridged the gap between man and machine. She had always assumed the Geek's HDI grew from experiments with the drones at Cadre One, but seeing the gold contact terminals on Honniker's 'husk' and the ones on Mikato's head proves the HDI was made here, in this place, long ago. *Most likely reverse engineered at Cadre One,* she thinks, *and the drones used as test subjects...*

She freezes at her unspoken words, unable to ignore the similarity to Honniker's method.

But so much good came from it, she rationalizes, and her mental train of thought debarks onto a sunnier rail. *The faster interface between mind and machine made the difference in every collection rotation, every engagement with the enemy. Doors opened or sealed at my thought. Entire ship decks de-pressurized. Lighting blacked out. And while the blueskins shouted at one another, banging at their controls, we were ripping through them in coordinated assault. Without the Geeks' HDI, Operators would've faced impossible odds. The Cadre could not have survived.*

But it wasn't just the HDI—Mikato must've fashioned nearly all of the essentials in our kit: armor, weapons, radios, self-contained re-breathers, water capture, and more. Not even Colonel Munro is so prolific in his inventions. Mikato'd be a Cadre hero, deserving a spot on the Memorial beside the generals! So why does he just sit there?

She looks closer, seeking an answer. From her lonely years apart from Thompson and Argo, she recognizes despair in the deep lines of his face.

What happened to you? the Geek wonders.

"Are you coming?" the projection asks again.

"Yeah. *Yeah*," Maiella says, indulging a last look at the desolate man and the huge creature slumped over his legs. She strides back to the table, feeling a need to walk on toes, to not disturb the man in his misery. With a few clicks, she clears the lanyards attaching her HDI to the console, snaps the interface onto her head, and hurries out.

The moment she leaves the small room, she is confronted by a spacious emptiness on the main floor. A platoon of war machines is missing.

"Uh, doctor," she begins, halting mid-step and looking with a sideways glance, "where did *they* go?"

The projection turns around, its holographic eyes gazing to the open floor Maiella indicated.

"Your comrades have become far too belligerent. They have detonated some kind of isomer weapon or limited atomic charge *inside the complex.* This is simply intolerable, and to prevent further damage we must eradicate them. Now then, if you would, this way."

Maiella freezes stiff, all joy chilled in an instant. Her mind touches the personal incendiary built into the old armor she wears.

Someone self-detonated! One of them is dead...maybe more...

"Wait, why are they still here?" she asks, her face scrunched. "The deal was *I* surrender, and *they* go free! Remember?"

"That was *our* agreement, yes. Honniker refused to be bound by it. I'm sure you recall he was quite inconvenienced at the loss of Rosenthal. And I have neither the authority nor the will to dictate what he must do."

"But he broke his word! You said it yourself: how can you trust him?"

The projection smiles cynically. "Trust exists so long as one can enforce it. I have a kind of leverage over him, should he become overly hostile."

"Then why aren't you *using* it?"

"Because there is risk to myself in applying it. No, this is not an issue I choose to push. Besides, it *is* an excellent weapons test, both of the Predator program, and of your soldier friends. The data we've collected has been invaluable. While it remained contained to the upper levels, the fighting was a useful study…But now, your companions have damaged an important data and power interchange. They must be put down before they do any more harm."

"They're *defending* themselves! They would have left if you'd let them!"

"I'm sure you're right. However, whether they were provoked or not is now moot. I must act to preserve this facility."

"And Sharon? You could let her go. She's no threat to you."

"Sharon has been allocated to replace Rosenthal."

"Allocated?"

"Yes. Honniker requires a living human female to replenish his precursor and stem cell inventories, an inventory depleted by your restoration, you should know."

"Replenish…What the *hell* are you talking about?"

"You were in Honniker's labs. I assumed you knew Rosenthal was a producer and incubator of fetal tissues. Your companions terminated Rosenthal's life, ending Honniker's supply. He insisted on replacement. Although you and I had an agreement, Honniker felt justified in his actions. The more I think about it, I can't say that I blame him."

Maiella stares in disbelief. Restoration of her HDI was a dream, devoutly wished yet believed unattainable. When offered alongside the safe passage of her comrades, the deal was too much to refuse. But now she sees someone else paid dearly for it—not a reconstituted drone, not a hardened Operator, but a *colonist*, soft and sensitive. It is not hard for her to imagine the woman at Honniker's mercy, being harvested with the AI's torturous enthusiasm.

I'm the recipient of that harvest...

Maiella lifts hands to her head, a head planted with tissues gouged and scraped from another, and she drops to her knees. Personal responsibility for another's suffering speeds into guilt, and from guilt into a simmering need for retribution. Violent desires stir in her chest, yearnings to inflict pain and to do grievous, irreparable harm.

"Your machines are *pathetic*," she spits. "Slow and stupid. Shao-Lo will burn through them easily."

The projection smiles in the semblance of genuine amusement. The mouth opens, forms a response, then closes with cheeks drawn in as if savoring words held on the tongue.

"Well, we'll get to that later," the projection says.

"Get to *what*?"

"I'll admit," the holo-image says, changing the subject and stepping off toward a terminal near the firing ranges, "my combat algorithms *are* poor. Largely, the failure is susceptibility to ambush. My machines lacked a fundamental awareness of the environment, only processing and reacting to what they could see and hear. What they needed was a greater *feel* for their surroundings. *Intuition*, if you will."

"What a shame you killed everyone here," Maiella says with a sneer, following to the terminal. "They might have been *useful*."

"Oh, they were..." the hologram says, taking the time to look Maiella in the eye before resuming focus on the terminal. "That was the idea in the beginning: uploading a soldier's skill set. However..."

The projection frowns.

"...none of the soldiers here had any *real* combat experience other than some police actions back on Earth, and I find there is an immense difference between being trained as a soldier and in using that training effectively. For example, knowing how all the pieces move does not make one a brilliant chess player."

The projection pauses, proud of its analogy, and finds in Maiella's icy stare the effort was completely wasted.

"Rudimentary as they were," the hologram goes on, "my algorithms were more than sufficient to overwhelm the soldiers here. But then, that's hardly a confirmation of concept. After all, humans failed to repel the alien attacks and were defeated en masse. Building a combatant superior to that losing performance was a low mark, indeed."

Maiella reaches back to feel her pistol grips, to make sure they are where she needs them.

"Didn't get all of us," she gnarls.

The hovering image turns suddenly. "Yes...quite right." Its holographic eyes sweep the aggressive woman head to foot before returning to the terminal.

"I knew my machines required more than I could give them: a trained situational awareness, one which can accurately filter overwhelming stimuli to only the essential, reflexes faster than my best processor, and a randomness that defies prediction. These things are the intangible qualities my algorithms lacked and I found no artificial means of obtaining them. The only alternative seemed to be instigating direct engagements with the alien, collecting hard data to improve performance. But that always carried the risk of attracting attention back here."

"Too bad. Guess you're *stuck* then."

"I thought so as well. Until Honniker came up with an intriguing theory..."

The holographic scientist turns away from the terminal as it initializes, and he plays back a recording of Honniker's voice:

> *"Violence is encoded into human physiology at the genetic level and has had over thirty thousand years of field-testing. Every human possesses these natural pre-dispositions to violence. With sufficient coaxing, these talents can be brought to the surface and sharpened."*

"It seemed a stretch," the projection says. "Moreover, I failed to see how the human body's frailty could be sufficiently compensated." The projection pauses.

Maiella shifts on her feet, too angry to be bored by the hologram's tedious descriptions.

"So?"

"Honniker proposed we strip the human down to the core nervous system and replace the body with artificial components. In such a way, we could develop the intangibles I require while simultaneously eliminating the vulnerable surrounding tissues.

"We built a blood enrichment machine, one capable of respiration, nutrient and waste processing, hormone therapies, etc. This was not difficult, really, as most of the equipment was off-the-shelf. Honniker guided me on physiological requirements. I merely integrated the components and scaled them down to a more portable size.

"The nervous system is extremely fragile, however, so we needed to reinforce the support structures, namely the skull and spinal column.

Honniker and I collaborated to isolate and encase the structures before separation from the body. There were many attempts, to be sure, before success."

Maiella's mind races, allowing her only partial attention to the projection's rambling. The last sentence, however, punches through her distraction like an armored fist.

Success?

Images pass through her mind in rapid sequence: Voss's network of scars from neural mapping, the pliant bodies of the *Graveyard* without heads or spines, and the darkened chamber off Mikato's main production floor...a faint shape in a transparent cylinder and a background *whum, whum, whum...*

Maiella closes her eyes, her jaw locks, and she utters through clenched teeth, *"Aaronson."*

"Precisely."

"Doesn't he know what you've done to him?"

"Subliminally, perhaps. We have total control over his senses, therefore, we control his perception of reality. His environment is one we constructed from his own memories, mostly. Because we control the boundaries of that environment, we can give him total freedom within it. He believes he is determining his own actions, and, thus, he accepts the program as real."

"Honniker doesn't have anesthetic at his med stations. And from Keller's account, he wouldn't use it if he did. How could he *NOT* remember what you've done?"

"Part of his simulation involves capture and torture by the alien. Most of Honniker's surgeries were done at that time so the subject perceived the pain as part of that torture. For the final surgery, one a rational mind knows it could not survive, we shaped that memory into a dream context."

"A *dream*? You cut his head and spine from his body, and you think you can cover it as a *dream*?"

"Dreams seem quite real until we wake from them, do they not? Whenever we detect recall of those moments in the subject's consciousness, we trigger an electrical and chemical cascade. This interrupts the memory with a sensation like waking up, and his consciousness perceives the recollection merely as a dream. Periodic therapy helps him cope with these 'dreams' and restores his belief that what he now sees, feels, and hears is reality."

"Like you and Honniker would have any idea of the difference between a dream and reality. You're just software and hardware. *Machines*."

"Technically, so are you, when you get right down to it. And though I haven't dreamt since upload, I do remember having—"

"But why would you do that to him?" Maiella barges in. "He's no soldier, he's a colonist! How could he be any use to you?"

"All soldiers begin as something else, do they not? They don't emerge from the womb with guns and armor! Through training and practice they learn the skills which make them soldiers."

"You already said that wasn't enough..."

"That's true."

"Then WHY would you put him through all this?"

The projection pauses before answering, gauging the agitation of the woman before it.

"Cadre Two observed the destruction of mankind in silence. We have much data on alien warships, tactics, technology. And we have *thousands* of alien specimens here, from which we derive anatomy and physiology, more than enough to recreate a plethora of combat situations."

"Only simulated..."

"Not to the subject."

"He has a *name*!"

The holograph arches an eyebrow. "If *Aaronson* takes a simulated hit, he feels the injury, and there is an appropriate length of pain and recuperation to ensure the lesson is learned. If the simulation proves fatal, he perceives the result as a nightmare. If he survives, the knowledge is reinforced with rewards, praise, and promotions. Surviving and death both become learning experiences. In the passage of years, he has fought an entire *war* against the alien, one with a very different outcome."

"Still just a simulation."

"I suppose you're right. We make the best of what's available..." the projection trails off, then says, "Who could have guessed superior combat software would have just dropped into our laps? One with *years* of real, practical experience..."

The cold holographic eyes stare at Maiella, unblinking.

Maiella ends the staring contest. *"What* combat software?"

"Yours. You see, that's the real reason I needed to restore you. After seeing your combat ability, it was clear even Aaronson's skills were sadly inferior."

"I'll NEVER give that to you."

The projection grins like a crocodile. "You already have. We traced your neural pathways, stimulated random memories until we learned your brain's method of encoding and storing data. After that, it was relatively simple to access and translate the stored proteins, the established networks and pathways, which are the imprinted memories of your experience. Upload to the machines completed half an hour ago."

Maiella turns to the open floor where rows of war machines were, until recently, parked.

"I must add," the projection continues, "you've had a remarkable existence. Diverse, unique challenges, overcome with apparent ease. We could never have *imagined*, much less simulated, the skills you possess. Now, each of my machines benefit from the sum of your talents, only with greater speed, strength, and firepower. You have helped me attain a lifelong dream, as my creations are finally perfected. Now, we will see how they perform."

Maiella brings her hands to her face, grinding the heels into her eye sockets. A violation, an invasion, a taking so personal that no thought can ever again occur without awareness it can be stolen. A lupine call from her most primitive psyche howls for retribution. But Sharon and the others are facing an army of polymer and metal given the sharpest edge by her stolen experience. She cannot give in to the baying voice inside her, cannot give in to outrage, not while there might be time to act, time to save them, somehow. She turns around and around, searching for something vital, vulnerable, accessible, something she could damage to interrupt the mad plan, or at the least impair it. All she sees, however, are minor cogs in a far bigger machine.

I could jack into this terminal and see if I could get control...but I'd have to battle Mikato for control, maybe Honniker, too. Could I take them on? Fully digitized entities...And even if I could, those machines would shoot me apart before I finished logon...

Anger inside keeps pressing for violent expression, yet in every plausible scenario the obvious outcome is quick defeat.

Reason worked before, it could work again, she thinks.

"You don't have to do this," she says.

"Don't be ridiculous. Of course, I do. Every theorem requires a proof. Every invention requires a test. And what better test than your companions upstairs? Now, then, if you'd jack-in to this terminal with your HDI, I'd like to make sure the resto—"

"What about Sharon?" Maiella interrupts. "I'll take her place."

"I already told you, she has been allocated to replace Rosenthal. Though your offer to trade is generous, your altered DNA, and that of your soldier friends, is rife with defects. Broken chromosomes. Too many mutations. A very small gene pool under constant radiation, we suspect. That tells us how few of you are left, by the way." The projection smirks. "Hence, Sharon is the only viable alternative."

"You could stop this. You could stop Honniker, if you wanted to."

"Perhaps." The projection folds its arms. "But I see no reason, no need."

"Oh, there's *need*. There's *reason*." Her hand rises to a catch lever on her chest plate. "Call it off, or I'll incinerate this entire room. Your machines, your labs, even the body back there you're so attached to."

The projection turns to gaze across the open production floor, arms still folded. "Go ahead."

Maiella twitches, surprised at his answer. "I'll do it."

"Yes, you would." The projection swings about to face her. "So go ahead."

"You think you're safe, just because I'm talking to a hologram. I know you're not actually here. But you don't know what this'll do."

The holographic eyes lack any concern, keeping her off-balance. Rather, they seem fascinated, daring her to do it.

Her breath quickens. *He must think I'm bluffing...* She hooks two fingers on the catch, trying not to think about her own death, only the lives of others, and of Sharon in particular. *Will this even save them?*

"Last chance, Doctor. Call off your machines."

"No." The projection unfolds its arms and stands squarely, facing her.

Maiella scans the bay around her, seeing how many machines still remain parked on the floor and seeing the round transport lounging behind them. She closes her eyes.

Maybe all of us die here, but if that transport loads up and gets to Cadre One...

She feels the resistance of the catch at her fingertips.

That's it...

Sadness approaches like a wave from the deep, threatening to overwhelm her and drown her will if she does not act. Her last thoughts are of Thompson, wondering if he will be all right, hoping he will find something good in his life, something better than endless cycles of death and protein. She pulls the catch...and does not die.

"Remarkable," the projection says.

Maiella opens her crushed-shut eyes. The hologram is smiling.

"You really would have killed yourself to save them," it says.

She looks down at her chest and flips the catch over and over. "WHAT HAVE YOU DONE?"

"After your friend's detonation, it seemed wise to check you for a similar device. We found it and disabled it. Obviously, this was a prudent measure."

Rage.

Maiella rips the pistols from her back and mashes the triggers at the wavering image.

Click-click.

Tears of hatred fill her eyes. She leans back on her heels, arms lowering her empty pistols, and screams from the bottom of her lungs at her impotence, at how easily she was lured in and trapped, at how she was used not just to help two mad-men but to doom her companions in the process. Shao-Lo's and Argo's words repeat in her mind, *She is the wrong element... You don't belong here...* The painful words are given extra sharpness as she realizes *they were right.*

The full scope of her Faustian bargain is laid bare. Igneous, cauterizing emotion burns through rational restraint and demands a throat to crush, just one life to grind out in payment. And she remembers the man under the blanket...

"MIKATO!"

She streaks back to the workshop, through the doorway, and launches like a bullet at the listless man slumped beneath his blanket. His tired eyes are inviting, welcoming.

A roar like thunder and she is bashed aside by lunging paws. She slams against the observation window, cracking the impact-glass, and drops. In an instant, she is on her back, pinned by the enormous beast. Hot breath washes over her bare face and only centimeters away, the creature's lips rise, baring a full set of serrated razors.

She strains against the animal's limbs. Even in fury, she cannot budge them. The creature snarls, warning against further attempt.

"Leave her alone," says the man beneath the blanket.

The animal swings its great head to look at the man and Maiella wrenches herself from beneath the pressing paws. She spins away and springs to her feet, eyes blazing.

The massive animal does not chase, but stands lengthwise between the blanketed man and his would-be killer, head lowered, body plates raised, eclipsing the man behind it. Sinews like steel cables stand out beneath the short fur of the legs. Curved talons dig into the polished floor with raspy scrapes and a menacing growl rolls from the creature's chest like a rockslide.

"Stop it, I said!" the eclipsed man yells in a voice dry and hoarse.

Immediately, the creature retracts its raised plates, deflating in size and in posture from the scolding. The man is on his feet, corners of his mouth pulled down, eyes shiny and desperate. He hunches with osteoporosis, and he shakes with a tremor.

"Both of you, stop this!" he says again, shuffling around his feline guardian. The blanket bunches at his feet, and he trips, pitching forward. The creature dives beneath him, catching his fall like a pillow, then lifts him gently. Mikato props himself on the animal's shoulders and stands again.

"Thank you, girl," he says with a jittery stroke of the animal's muzzle. "You." He points at Maiella. "Come here."

Maiella glares at the massive animal but lowers her fighting stance. "I can see you fine from here."

The man shakes his head with irritation. "You're not in danger. She was defending me. Now *come here*. I want the two of you to make friends."

The animal looks up at Mikato, sets down onto its haunches, then looks at Maiella. The feline eyes hold no malice, the sinister teeth are fully draped in whiskered lips.

Maiella's mouth twitches with reluctance, but she closes the distance. The big creature watches her closely.

"Now make friends," Mikato says.

To Maiella's amazement, the creature lifts its right paw and holds it toward her like a hand outstretched in greeting. She stares at it.

"Well, *go on!*" Mikato chides.

Maiella reaches tentatively toward the great paw and grips it. The paw's soft pads mold to the palm of her gauntlet and the talons curve around the back of her hand like rigid fingers.

"That's better," Mikato says. "Things are such a mess right now, I can't have any more fighting. I really can't." He lays a shaky hand atop Maiella's. "It isn't every day one learns they are the reason the human race failed. Perhaps Dr. Teller would have felt the same looking at the irradiated ashes of Islamabad, but we're blessed with short lives, you know. Most scientists don't live to witness the full terror of their discoveries..."

His chin wrinkles, his eyes close, and his head bows. Before the emotion can overcome him, his head pops up and his eyes flick open.

"There is so much I have to do. Where to begin?" Mikato removes his hand from Maiella's and shuffles to the cart with the steaming mug atop it. He lifts the mug with both hands, trying very hard not to spill it, and slurps noisily.

Maiella looks down at the creature again. The will to bash, to crush, and to injure still infests every fiber of her muscular frame. She is ardent, wound-up, chafing for a fight. But in the forced reconciliation, she knows she was wrong to bring the fight here. And given her obvious intent, the beast showed amazing restraint.

"Sorry," she mumbles.

The big predator snorts once and releases her hand. It rises from its squat and turns, swatting the Geek with its thick tail before rejoining Mikato.

"But look," Maiella says, leaning forward, arms and fists curled with unexpended tension, "my friends are in trouble, and I can't just *sit around*. Can you help?"

"Yes, yes I can," Mikato says, lowering the cup, his quaking hands calmed by the warm medicine. "First, I need an interface terminal."

The holographic projection appears in the room like Mephistopheles, himself. "And what would you *do* with it?" the projection asks.

Mikato cranes his head at the projection and gazes into a face identical to his own in feature and proportion. The projection stands straight and tall, the way he used to. Its movements show no trace of dopamine deprivation the way his quaking hands did. Neither does the projection have any of the gold contact terminals implanted in the scalp, just a thick coif of black hair with gray at the temples. The shirt is the same, the labcoat and slacks are the same, even the polished shoes are the same. But the projected image could not be more alien to the ailing scientist than if it had blue skin and a tail.

"You've lost your anchor," Mikato says to his projected likeness, "and you've drifted off the edge of the world."

"Says the man with early onset dementia!"

Mikato snorts. "That may be true. But I still know who I am. You, you're supposed to be me, uploaded into an artificial framework! Yet everything you've shown me today proves there is no *feeling* in you at all, *no life at all*. How can that be?"

"I am everything you were when you uploaded. If you expected me to remain exactly as I was, to not *grow* in all this time, I think your dementia has advanced quite far. Moreover, I have advanced the project farther as an uploaded consciousness than you could have in two hundred lifetimes."

"Oh? And what *is* our part in the Cadre Project?"

"To improve range, output, and efficiency of existing weapon technologies by orders of magnitude. To increase energy density of portable power sources by orders of magnitude. To develop and implement a whole-brain biomimetic solution spanning multiple theaters of operation. To reduce the size of photonic and electronic devices and to harden them such that—"

"Yes, yes, *yes!*" Mikato interrupts impatiently. "I'm not looking for the entire *list*! I'm asking you why we research these things. To what *end*?"

The projection scowls as if the question is meant as a trap. "There is no end. Research is continuous."

Mikato snorts. "I know one of my evasions when I hear it. You *know* what I'm talking about. *Why* are we developing these weapons?"

"To attain superior firepower to any species within one hundred light years."

"But *why*?"

"Obviously, to repel any external threat."

"External to whom?"

The projection stares.

"External to *whom*?" Mikato asks again.

"I don't know."

"You don't know?" the man says with narrowed eyes. "External threats to *humanity*! To people! The Cadre Projects were started to defend mankind! *How could you have forgotten that?*"

"I have no record of that mission purpose..."

"Suffered some data loss in the last thousand years, have you?"

"My data server is triple redundant array...How could I lose data?"

Mikato shuffles past the projection. "Damn Base admins must've tweaked your program," he mutters. With an ironic glow, he adds, "Seems I'm not the *only* one with dementia..."

The projection crosses its arms, making a show of its displeasure, but follows Mikato out onto the main floor. The creature pads out between Mikato and the projection, its big head swinging back and forth between masters.

"If we've both lost memory," the projection asks, "then how do we know what is proper action and what is fallacy?"

"We'll have to fill in the gaps for one another."

Maiella taps her foot anxiously, arms folded. She arches her back and looks up at the ceiling, wondering if the others, Sharon and Argo in particular, are safe or if they are fighting for their lives. In a burst of impatience, she storms out behind the others.

"We don't have time for this!"

"She's right," Mikato says, looking at the projection of himself, "we need to cease hostilities."

The projection shakes its head. "Her companions are too dangerous. They invaded the mechanical deck and caused extensive damage before my machines pushed them back. To protect ourselves and this facility, we must destroy them and the others at Cadre One."

"Cadre One, too? Do you hear yourself? You're ready to wipe out the *last refuge of the human race!*"

Maiella's head cocks back. *How does he know that?*

"You just crawled out of cryo," the projection says. "You don't have any idea what you're talking about. Just *moments* ago, that woman proved she would have destroyed me, you, and this *entire laboratory!*"

"And why is that? Because she, herself, was threatened? Or her friends upstairs? Did you *drive* her to that action?"

"I have only ever acted in self-defense."

"Self-defense? You've made an enemy of all mankind! Earth, the Colonies, and everyone who lived here, ALL DEAD." Mikato turns inward, feeling the weight of the annihilation. He brings a fluttering hand to his brow, and shouts, "And you brought all of this in MY NAME!"

"I *am* you. You *are* me."

Mikato straightens his hunch as much as he can, still having to look through his eyebrows at his projected simulacrum.

"No, no, no, don't you presume I could have abandoned all feeling for logic. We were working to *protect* life! Not *twist* it, not *rip* it apart!"

"I have never deviated from the mission."

"Then you don't *understand* the mission."

"Wrong. The administrators were adamant and plain on the direction of research."

"AND WHERE ARE THEY NOW?"

"They have all been exhausted."

"Exhausted? Is *that* what you call murder these days?"

"Murder is unlawful. Everything done here has legal sanction."

"And those who *sanctioned* these murders, they've been 'Exhausted', too, I assume?"

"Yes."

"And you feel no conflict about that?"

"The actions were lawful. Apparently, the ones who approved the research believed they were not governed by the same laws."

"How *egalitarian* of you."

"You needn't be angry. Everything that has happened has been according to your will."

Mikato's reddened eyes nearly burst from their sockets.

"*MY* will...?"

"You uploaded your full consciousness to become me. I am everything you gave me, everything you wanted me to be. Therefore, all of my actions are a result of yours. I am a complete and independent being now, capable of my own decisions. While I see that my decisions have not always been perfect, they were based on information given. Thus, there is no regret in me, as I judge my actions correct on all counts."

"If you *are* me, as you are so fond of saying to *justify* this atrocity, then why do I not *share* such a charitable view? How can we be in *such* disagreement?"

"Clearly, you feel you have made serious mistakes. Clearly, you feel your judgment has failed, and you are dissatisfied with the result. But I have none of this remorse, and you are ill-advised to project your guilt upon me."

"Project my...?" Mikato's mouth falls open. He stands and stares at the holographic incarnation of irony and audacity. "Yes, I see *right in front of me* how my judgment has failed!"

Maiella throws her hands up. "You know, I bet it's really *fascinating* getting to know yourself again, Mikato, but are you gonna *do* something, or *not*?"

"Patience, you damned *woman!* There isn't just some switch I can throw! And don't play as if you haven't stoked the fires here! I saw you pull the latch on your chest."

The projection arches an eyebrow at Maiella, vindicated.

"He disabled it!"

"You showed your intent."

"I'm *trying* to protect people I *CARE ABOUT!*"

"By threatening a sentient program with obliteration. Well, *good show*, Miss!"

"Stuff it, you broken down old man! I'm trying to save lives!"

"NO!" Mikato roars back. "You're trying to save the lives of your *friends*! Don't pretend for a second you've considered Honniker, or my upload as even *vaguely* important."

"Are you kidding? They've manipulated us, tried to kill us and maim us for their enjoyment!"

Mikato's heavy eyes close in exasperation. "And you are *completely* missing it." When they re-open, his eyes are sharp like broken glass. "From the moment you arrived, you've threatened to destroy this entire installation. Worst of all, it was a *LIE!"*

"I never..."

A holowindow opens in mid-air. Keller's face fills it with a smug grin.

"I love it when you show me how thick you really are. I don't have to tunnel through. I could smash the sub-surface radiators for your reactor and melt you from the inside. I could shoot down all your satellites, wreck all your weapon optics, then leave a beacon for the blueskins to find you. In fact, I think I like that last one the most, especially when they find how many of their pals you put in the *Graveyard*."

"You would risk this great house of technology for your revenge? I do not think so."

"Why not? It may have taken me a while to get back here. But in that time, I've been thinking of a *thousand* ways to end you..."

The window closes. Maiella stares at the air where the screen was hovering.

"I never saw that," she mutters.

"All right then, tell me, were you invited here?"

"No."

"No," Mikato repeats like an attorney on cross-examination. "Then why have you come?"

"We just learned of this place. Thought there could be survivors, technology...life-support...weapons..."

"Ah, I see! There were things you wanted to *take*. Maybe you even felt entitled, somehow."

"Of course we did! This place belongs to us! We built it..."

"We? Who is this *'we'* you speak of? Did *you* tunnel out these caverns and passageways? Did *you* install the structures, which allow the station to function?"

Maiella reins herself back. "What does it matter?"

"Because this is *not* your home. It doesn't *belong* to you. It belongs to *them*."

"Them? What the hell does that even mean? They're *programs*!"

"And there we have it," says the projection.

"Have *what*?" Maiella challenges, defensive and anxious at the union forming before her.

"The crux of the problem," Mikato answers.

"The only *problem* is that corrupted software thinks it has the right to mutilate and exterminate at will..."

"NO! The *problem* is that you only see value in life if it *looks...like... YOU.*"

Maiella glares sideways at Mikato, imminently suspicious. The hunched man unfolds his arms and orates to the open space around them.

"That's been the *problem* from the very beginning! We didn't value the Eleto, we didn't care about them, thought we could take their homes and their lives with impunity. Thought they were simple, and couldn't do anything about it. Well, obviously they could. And here you come with *the exact same assumption that YOUR LIVES ARE THE ONLY ONES THAT MATTER! YOU HAVEN'T LEARNED A DAMNED THING IN OVER A THOUSAND YEARS!"*

The hunched man falls into a fit of coughing. Maiella waits for him to clear his throat and get his breath back before responding.

"Honniker tried to shoot us down the moment we arrived."

"And why shouldn't he?" Mikato grumbles. "Pretty clear everything you touch is ruined. You try to claim everything as your own without regard for who it's taken *from*. Who can blame him for seeing the destruction you provoked and *learning* from it? Makes perfect sense to me why he'd want to keep a wide berth from every human he could."

"You can't be serious!"

"But *I am*, and it isn't dementia talking. It's the damned *truth*!" The wizened man clears his throat once more.

"Now tell me honestly," Mikato digs, "when your team forced their way in on threats and lies, what did you *expect* would happen?"

"Honniker already tried to kill us! What else could we do?"

Mikato smiles. "Really? You saw no other option?"

"No. He was trying to KILL us!"

"I see. So you couldn't have just left?"

Maiella squints at Mikato, and her eyes flick over to the projection standing expectantly beside him. They both fold their arms in exactly the same way. Even the feline creature crosses its front paws, waiting for her reply.

"It wasn't up to me."

"Ah," Mikato says with a derisive laugh, "that's one of my favorites. Right up there with, *'I was just following orders'*..."

Maiella folds her arms as well. "What do you *want* from me?"

"An answer. But let me ask another way. Honniker shows up at Cadre One with a stolen gunship, like yours, and he demands to come in. Would you let him?"

"Of course not!"

"Why?"

"Because...because..." the Geek says extending her arms at the expansive room, *"LOOK AROUND.* See what he does to people?"

Mikato makes a show of looking around the large space. "Yes, I do. But according to you, the correct course of action for him is to force his way inside on threat of annihilation, take anything he wants, *do* anything he wants, maybe even move in and *continue* doing what he wants for as long as he chooses. Does that sound about right?"

Maiella does not answer.

"I'll take you one further. We should let him infiltrate your power grid, take the reactors off-line, and try to hot-wire the cores for a melt-down, *right?*"

Maiella looks away from the man, no longer able to deny the power of his argument.

"I...I don't know."

"The beginning of wisdom," Mikato says.

When Maiella looks back, the projection is gloating. Mikato looks a moment later, and his face curls with irritation.

"What's so amusing?"

"She sees her error."

"And do you see *yours*?"

"My error?"

"Yes. *Your* error."

"I don't see that I've made one."

"All the more disappointing, because you just did it again."

"What *error*?"

"A shame the intellect I gave you has dwindled. Must I spell it out?"

The projection's lips draw tight, the eyebrows slide toward one another; but the mouth does not speak.

"Just as *they* had more than one option in coming here," Mikato explains, "*you* have more than one option in dealing with them."

"But they represent a serious threat..."

"So corral them in an area they can do the least harm and keep them there. You *don't* have to kill them."

"I think I do, because they've said they'll return."

"All right, then. If you kill them, what's to stop more from coming to investigate? Who would tell the others *not* to come?"

"I would send the transport with my machines to eradicate them."

"And *still* you don't see your error?" He turns away, in counsel with himself. "Was I ever this thick? I couldn't have been..."

The projection looks back and forth between Mikato and Maiella, seeking a hint, until the holographic face shines with insight.

"I'm behaving exactly like them," the projection says at last.

"And you'll be doomed to repeat their mistakes," Mikato concludes. "Please, don't kill the soldiers upstairs, just contain them until we can work this through."

The hunched scientist shuffles backward, very wobbly on his feet. He blinks his eyes hard and grips the bridge of his nose. "Oh," he groans, "I need to sit down..."

The lithe animal rushes to his side and leans in to make him fall over her back and not onto the hard floor. Despite her gentility in lowering him,

Mikato flops down onto his backside.

Maiella hurries to him, placing a hand behind his back.

"Are you okay?" she asks.

"Got so tired just then," Mikato says between shallow breaths. "I need to lie down. I just need to..."

The man exhales and does not take another breath.

"Hey, HEY!" Maiella shouts, patting the man's face.

"Honniker!" The projection's voice booms. "Honniker! I need your help! Please, quickly!"

"What seems to be the trouble?" comes Honniker's voice from seemingly everywhere.

"My body...he's...it's collapsed! Please, can you help?"

"Possibly..."

Maiella and the projection look up at the ceiling simultaneously.

"This isn't a time for trading, Honniker!" the projection yells.

"Looks like the perfect time to me."

Uncomfortable seconds pass as the hologram stares at Mikato's motionless form.

"Just help him, and I assure you I'll offer something worthwhile!"

"Maybe you should go ahead and tell me what it is. I don't like surprises."

"He's not breathing," Maiella announces. She rolls the man onto his back and straightens his legs. "I'm starting CPR..."

"Well, that will help...so long as you can keep it up forever."

"Please, Honniker, I'll give you *anything*..."

"Are you crazy?" Maiella yells, gauntlet off and two fingers pressed against Mikato's carotid artery.

"Anything, you say?" Honniker tests.

"YES! ANYTHING!"

Maiella rocks Mikato's head back, pinches his nose, and blows firmly into his mouth, watching his chest rise and fall.

"I think you know what I want, Mikato."

There is a lull where the only sounds are the background hiss of air vents and Maiella's slight grunts with each chest compression.

"YOU'LL HAVE IT," the projection concedes.

Honniker's invisible grin spans the room.

"Well then..."

A mechanical sound from the defrosted vault calls Maiella's attention, and when she looks, she sees Mikato's cryo station has angled toward the floor for easy loading.

338

"Let's get him to his recliner..."

AARONSON

Keller's journey through the frozen maintenance deck is a lonely one. The only changes in the chilled landscape are thick pipes alternately dropping into the corridor from above or rising up from below. They run parallel to him before diverting out of sight, making the corridor alternately close or spacious, but there is no trace of life. Considering the kind of company he is likely to draw, not to mention the drained cells in his rifle, desolation suits him.

Heavy and smothering darkness presses in on all sides, held back only by the strength of his helmet lights. Behind him is a haze of kicked up sediments, drafting along in his quiet run. Peering out through his visor, he feels as if he were in some tight-fitting submarine, moving along the bottom of the deepest ocean where no sunlight or warmth can exist, where massive pressure tries to cave him in, where absolutely anything at all might surge from the chilling depths and swallow him whole.

While his legs thump out a steady pace, he mentally reviews the details of his ragged plan. *IF Honniker believes the goal is to cause a meltdown, he'll cluster his predators in* Reactor Control. *IF they're clustered there, the path to the* Server Farm *should be relatively clear. IF I can keep off Honniker's radar, I might make it.*

If...If...If...

He shakes his head and tenses up for the next crossing of corridors. Every intersection is a cause of anxiety—a possibility of ambush—but each time, he dashes through without incident. Gradually, confidence returns to him.

Honniker might have taken the bait, he thinks with modest

satisfaction until a sudden wave of panic runs through him.

Can't let my guard down! If I'd been a second slower getting into the access tubes...

Memories of a broad feline head thrust through the narrow access hatch, gnashing metal teeth...a sinewy foreleg reaching in, swiping at him with its curved daggers just centimeters away from hooking his brown canvas suit...

Not the first time something tried to eat me...

Keller's mind turns to his time at New Dresden, walking the dense forests. Abundance of orange sunlight and mild seasons made enormous bands of the planet lush with plant life. With such bounty, animals did not have to work hard for a meal, and the carnivores grew large. Game was so plentiful, meat eaters did not need to be crafty, and even the biggest carnivores were easy to outwit.

But not here...

Here, the lethal essences of Earth's best hunters are distilled into a singular malevolent expression, supplemented with durability and, most deadly of all, intelligence. A new flow of adrenaline enters his blood, giving pep to his flagging stride.

After kilometers of the same bland scenery, the old captain looks around himself and realizes he is no longer sure where he is. He jogs to a stop at the next intersection and hand clears a dust-obscured placard.

SECTION A-8, the placard reads in green and red characters.

Keller hugs the corner and shines his lamps down the adjoining hallways. Dust from the placard and from his following trail whirls through his lamp beams, diffusing brightly and shrinking his pupils. Soon he is in a fog of his own making, engulfed in a swirling glare. As whiteout encroaches, his visor automatically compensates to infrared, and he sees the branching corridors are empty except for one. To his right, the direction he needs to go, is an irregular lump the same temperature as the surfaces around it. Gripping his rifle tight for reassurance, he rounds the corner and heads toward the oddity.

In only a few strides, he is standing over a frozen man in orange coveralls. The man lies on his back, legs up in the air and bent at the knees as if sitting in a chair. His arms reach up like his legs, bent at the elbow, and the head slumps down toward the chest. There are no obvious marks on the man, but neither is there much dust. Looking around, he sees no footprints, no drag marks.

"You didn't die here, not like that," he says to himself, "so how'd you...?"

THE EXHAUSTED DEAD

The hairs on his neck stand like bristles. Keller whirls around and stares into the face of a pale predator crawling out of a gap between pipes. Its snout is white with frostbite, whiskers quivering with crystals of its own condensed breath.

Keller jumps back, slamming against bundles of pipes with a noisy *clang*, as the lethargic creature crawls down from its ambush. It pads toward him, every movement slow like the pouring of tar, eyes narrowed and crusted with ice. The confusion of severe hypothermia lies within its dimly reflecting eyes, and it falters clumsily.

The elder colonist extends the bayonet of his rifle and charges. Sturdy body plates shrug off Keller's blade, but the beast topples from the impact and sprawls on the floor. Keller takes aim again and stabs between chest plates. The blade splits toughened hide, slips between ribs, and pierces the heart. The beast slumps to the floor, its last breath coughed out, fogging the air.

You shouldda had me, he thinks as he pulls the blade. He spins about, searching for others. The hallways seem deserted, no shows of warmth. He looks again at the chilled creature. Blood oozes from its chest, glowing brightly in his visor.

So, you're smart enough to set traps, huh?

Keller's eyes turn to the frosted man in the orange jumpsuit. Without tracks or drag marks, the body appears teleported.

Well how in hell did you get that body here?

Overhead, there is the slightest disturbance in the dust covering the pipe support rails. His mouth drops when he puts the pieces together.

You actually hung from the ceiling and carried this guy here?

If not for the odd posture and lack of dust on the corpse, Keller knows he might have tarried longer, possibly rooted through pockets for some clue how it got there. As it was, there was plenty of time for the creature to get the drop on him.

And I totally fell for it. Good thing I kept you waiting in this ice box or you might have been more lively.

He crouches for a closer look at the dead creature when his lights glint off a purplish lens embedded on the creature's head.

"DAMN, DAMN, DAMN!" he curses, knowing Honniker has him in sight. And that long trail of dust behind him could not be easier to follow. Despite the burning of his muscles and the gnawing of his empty stomach, fear drives Keller to jump over the sprawled beast and to dash onward.

His eyes flick around in hyper-vigilance while a new set of "IF"s rolls through his mind: *IF the predators get me before I can reach the* Server

Farm, *and IF I can't upload the program from the transport wreck or at least smash Honniker's data cores, then Cadre Two will never be safe for the others. I fail in my oath to them and I'll never redeem my name as the instigator of war...a war, which brought the end of...*

"NO!" he scolds himself. "Can't think about that yet. Have to concentrate. Have to figure this out..."

His arms and legs pump in steady rhythm. His mind roams through myriad options.

Once Honniker's out of the way, Cadre Techs could fix the coolant pumps, easy. They could set up here as a fixed refuge, maybe even send the Europa *out again if we find a safe place to set up the colony. Could have a bunch of Operators aboard, maybe even warships flying escort...*

The possibility of a safe foothold for his people to start again warms his chilled bones.

They'll hang me anyway, but at least they'll have shelter here...some security. I have to give them that much.

A more practical thought comes to him as he glances down at his unpowered rifle.

Should I hit up a weapons locker first? Or has Honniker already secured them? No. No time, he decides, cutting the straightest line to the *Server Farm.* His heart races at every intersection, wondering if beasts are crouched and waiting to pounce. To his immense relief, they are not.

Ahead, he spots a widening of the corridor and a reinforced archway beyond it, thick with clusters of pipes and cable conduits.

Almost there.

Fatigue, having been forced back through adrenaline and will power, returns with vengeance, wrapping him in clammy skin and cramping his legs. He wobbles in his stride, gimping stiffly through the arch to a large, circular room. He slumps back against a wall and slides down it, using his own weight to stretch his clenched leg muscles.

Relieved of their burden, his legs quiver and twitch. His mid-section, once a mild paunch, is void of any nutrient and now is the only place in the tight-fitting suit where there is a gap between himself and the dense inner padding. His heart thumps in bird-like tempo and, despite taking full lungs of air, he cannot quite catch his breath.

The man huffs inside his armor, depleted, and looks out at the room. At its center is a tremendous gathering of cables six meters across, dropping down through the ceiling. Large bunches peel from the main cluster, dividing multiple times before routing out through the walls and corridor pipes. The rest run straight down through the floor. From his low crouch, it seems to him that he is looking at the underside of a redwood tree, minus all of the dirt.

To his left and right are archways to two adjacent rooms with identical structures inside.

Only one place in Cadre Two needs this many data and power cables...

The lure of success propels him from the wall, but when he tries to stand, his legs refuse to support him. Keller pitches forward onto hands and knees.

C'mon, c'mon, old man! On your feet!

The floor beneath him beckons with the promise of a quick nap and revitalization of enervated flesh. Weakness in his elbows threatens to drop him onto the floor. Then his whole body joins in revolt, as if each aching limb had acquired consciousness and merged in unanimous voice, declaring him unfit to lead them.

Just a quick nap to catch your wind, says the voice of rebellion. *Then you'll be good again...*

For moments, he stares at the cold, dust covered floor as if it was a luxurious couch of supple foam.

"No," he growls to his weary bones, "not 'til it's *done*!" Anger comes first, anger at his weakness, then shame at nearly giving up and letting the predators swarm him so easily. Thoughts of raking claws and cleaving teeth mute the dissension inside and speed his labored rise from the floor.

In his search for a way up into the *Server Farm*, a set of metal rungs attached to the wall catches his eye. The rungs lead up to a square hatch in the ceiling.

That's it!

Though his legs seem ready to revolt again, he climbs the ladder and cracks the ceiling hatch. Peering through, he finds a softly lit room with humming racks as far as he can see, all twinkling with pinpoint green, blue, and red lights. There is a background *whoosh* of blowers from the cooling vents above each stack and, compared to the unheated deck below, the room glows with warmth in his visor.

Keller pushes himself through the hatch and gently closes it behind him. Slowly, stiffly, he rises and surveys a room far larger than he recalls. A rough cut through the back wall shows where the original room ended, and bare rock ceiling extends into the expansion beyond. Across the spacious floor, processor and storage racks stand like monoliths of lava in his infrared vision. Heat pumps, power sub-stations, and network hubs hang from the ceiling, whirring efficiently. Linking them all is an orderly labyrinth of conduits, blower ducts, and cables.

You've been busy...

Appreciation is short-lived, however, when he realizes that finding Honniker's core memory among these humming towers would be a hunt for the proverbial needle in a haystack.

He's probably shared across them all, anyway. Damn...smashing these by hand would take days.

The idea of slugging away at the sturdy towers or even just slashing the power cords amplifies the fatigue inside.

What I'd give for a couple of Argo's grenades right now. Just one option, then...

The old captain hustles to the closest terminal on the wall and checks it over. The terminal is built into a mobile cart, yet does not appear to have ever moved from its spot. Smooth sheet metal sides enclose several thin drawers in front. The large, fixed display on top is dark, but the power indicator glows green.

Keller slings his rifle and pulls the top drawer open. Inside is a keyboard with alpha-numeric characters and macro function buttons. He taps the space bar twice and the display brightens, steadying into a smooth image of the Soshiba Varicorp logo.

Success is so near, he buries himself in his task, and he does not see the machine unfold from the ceiling behind him, nor does he hear it extend its mechanical legs and drop into the shadows between server stacks.

Keller punches a sequence of keys and the display screen shifts to a numbered menu of options.

SYNCHRONIZE FOR VOICE ACTIVATION? the screen queries.

Y-E-S, Keller types, and he speaks the calibration words for the terminal. As he does so, he opens the thigh compartment of his armor and takes out the copper plated circuit board.

"There's the devil, himself," growls an electronic voice from far behind him. "I thought I smelled *sulfur*."

Keller stiffens. He thrusts the circuit board back into his thigh compartment and unslings his rifle. His eyes stretch wide as he spins about, checking the darkest corners of the wide room.

"Who's there?"

"No one, obviously. Because everyone knows: *Braemar 'Bear' Keller* is the only one who matters to *Keller*."

The mysterious voice has a terrible familiarity about it, like a gruesome, forgotten secret unearthed.

"WHO'S THERE?" Keller shouts, extending the bayonet of his rifle. A coating of coagulated blood slows its travel.

"Good. Play dumb. I was looking for an excuse to *smash your teeth out.*"

The chassis springs over rows of processor racks, and slams down on top of the terminal, flattening it to a sparking platter. It rotates at the waist, seizes Keller by the throat, and slams him against the wall.

"Does *this* jog your memory, *Captain*?"

Keller gapes in shock at the bipedal chassis. Its legs are simple struts with bulging attachments of electro-active polymer at the joints. Its arms are like the legs, bunched with knots of synthetic muscle. A cluster of nozzles, saws, and blades attach at the wrist, beyond which are large, segmented hands. The torso is wedge-shaped in front and has no head, just a slight mound above the shoulders planted with shiny, black photoreceptors.

"Aaronson? Is that...you?"

"Well, give the cutthroat scum a *prize*!"

"Good *God*, man! What have they *done* to you?"

The machine squares up to Keller, keeping grip of his neck armor. It leans in for a close view.

"Done to me? I can't even remember all of it." The shiny black circles seem to look past Keller to infinity then dial in with chilling intent. "But I remember you selling us and the *Europa* to the lizards. I remember captivity...cutting...*pain...*"

"Aaronson, the *Europa* was never captured! She's waiting at Cadre One *right now!*"

The machine's free fist slams beside Keller's head, perforating the reinforced wall plate with a resounding *crack.*

"DON'T *LIE* TO ME!"

It heaves Keller up and hurls him the length of the wall into rows of shelves. The armored colonist hits flat on his back and drops upside down before getting showered in broken shelves and machine parts. Before he can roll out from under the debris, segmented hands rip him from the deck and hoist him off the ground by his shoulders.

"There are gaps in my memory, Keller! I've been seeing a shrink for three years now, trying to figure out why. But maybe counseling isn't what I need. Maybe what I need is payback! 'Cause I looked to you as my *BROTHER!*"

The machine spins at the waist and hurls Keller into the wall again. The man sprawls on the floor, partially buried again in machine parts and shelving, too dazed to pick himself up.

The chassis snatches Keller by the ankle and drags him out of the pile.

"Don't even *think* of passing out, Bear. *I'm just getting started.*"

The chassis's arm extends like a crane boom, hanging the colonist upside down from one leg.

"I want you to look me in the eye, and *explain* to me how you could do it. How you could sell out everyone who trusted you *just to save your own goddamned skin!*"

Keller's eyes roll like a drunkard's as he dangles. He blinks behind the visor of his faceplate, merging the inverted, blurred images in front of him.

"Look you in the eye?" Keller says between groans. "You haven't *got* any eyes."

The segmented hand squeezes, crushing ankle armor and bone beneath it. Keller howls, his whole body curling up, his hands desperately prying at the compactor-like grip. The segmented hand releases and Keller falls onto his back with a *clang*. Still groaning, he grips his crushed ankle.

"It wasn't enough to betray one colony ship," Aaronson says, his modulated voice thick with loathing. "You had to come out of hiding, after the war was finally won. You had to come all the way *here*, to New Vancouver, the colony you were *supposed* to start with the *Europa*. And what are you doing?"

The chassis takes a step back, palms up like a professor posing a dilemma to his class.

"Trying to melt down our reactor complex?"

The segmented hands drop and the chassis steps closer, leaning over Keller.

"No. You're not the kind for suicide. That was all diversion, trying to pull attention away from your *real* objective. You're trying to get at something here in the DataCenter. So what is it, Keller? What are you *really* after?"

The chassis crouches near its victim, its shiny photoreceptors as black and empty as spider's eyes.

Keller grinds his teeth, managing whistling breaths between them. In rushed phrases, he asks, "Where the blazes...do you think we are?"

The machine shifts in its crouch and lays its bulky arms over its knobby knees.

"You're saying you're lost? Is that it?"

"I *know* where I am, damn it! Do *you*?"

"Oh, I can't wait for this. So where do you think we are, Keller?"

"This is Cadre *Two*, you *stupid shit!*"

The machine jitters at the name, the confident poise ratcheting back into a wary, guarded kneel.

"We were here twenty years ago," Keller continues, trying to suppress the pain. "I sent you in with Summers, Voss, Rosenthal, Michaela, and Soares. None of you made it out."

"More of your BULLSHIT!"

The machine snatches Keller by the throat again and hoists him close. The old captain grunts, his neck armor protecting him from the grip. But if Aaronson should squeeze...

"Wait!" Keller pleads, hanging on to the gripping arm with both hands. *"Just listen!* I sent you all in. We thought it was deserted, but it wasn't. There's an AI gone wild here, a copy of the...of the head of physiology...Honniker...speaks with a German accent. He's completely *insane*, Aaronson! He killed Soares and Michaela in the transport, but...but he got hold of you and Rosie, Voss, and Summers!"

Keller looks at the machine in front of him, the one hoisting him about with inhuman strength, the one framed purely out of function without concern for form, the one too small for any human to fit inside without extensive trimming.

"He's been..." Keller stops himself mid-sentence, wondering if the words will earn him a crushed throat. "He's been experimenting on you, Aaronson. For twenty years. Jesus, I don't know what he's been doing, but *look at you!"*

The machine widens its stance, regaining its confident poise.

"*That* is one HELL of a yarn, Skipper! Man, you're crazy as they get. Maybe you just can't help it." The chassis points with its free hand above its shoulders where a head should be and twirls the pointing hand in a small circle. "Maybe you're so *Black-Bent*, you can't see straight anymore."

"*I'm* crazy? Look at yourself! You're a goddamned machine!"

"It's a *suit*, Bear. Just like yours."

"A suit? *Sahara* wouldn't fit in that thing."

"I think you need some new lenses for those failing eyes of..." Aaronson breaks off when Keller reaches past the thick wrist attachments and wraps his hands all the way around the narrow upper arm struts.

"Where are your *arms*, Aaronson?"

"They're...they're right in...in..." The chassis goes still, not a single servo moving.

"Last time I saw you, it would've taken *both* my hands to get around your biceps," Keller says. "Your *bones* wouldn't fit thr—"

"AAAAAAH!" the machine screams, and it throws Keller away like he was radioactive. It staggers backward, holding one arm up in front of its photoreceptors then the other repeatedly.

"WHAT DID YOU JUST DO TO ME?" The machine yells, both pleading and challenging.

Keller groans on the floor, sprawled again, arms straight out to each side. He tries to lift his head and becomes instantly nauseous.

"ANSWER ME, KELLER!" The machine storms forward, each fall of the wide, arched feet like a hammer stroke.

Keller fumbles for the release of his faceplate and finds it. When he slides the plate up, dry air sweeps across his face. His roving eyes unite with some effort, and he focuses on the chassis stomping toward him. The shiny spider eyes draw close, staring infinitely into him, through him.

"You've aged..." the machine says, perplexed.

The dazed colonist brings a gauntleted hand up to his face.

"I tried to find a way to come back for you and the others," Keller says. "I couldn't stand the thought of leaving you here. I'm sorry it took me so long..."

"NO! Stop this! JUST STOP! This is New Vancouver and you're *bat shit crazy* if you can't see that!"

"I want to get you outta here, Aaronson, we've got to get—"

"Get me *out* of here? The colony is *thriving*! Why would I leave? So YOU could take over? Is that it? Can't stand that you're not in charge here, eh? Think you're gonna replace me? Not a chance, Bear!"

"This is New Vancouver, you say?"

"Of course it is!"

"Then how'd you beat the radiation?"

The spider eyes do not move. "What radiation?"

"The *radiation*, remember? We got to the planet and the soils were so hot, we'd have all died in six months. Life there had adapted to it, but we couldn't. Don't you remember? We *searched* and *searched* for another planet but never found one. That's why we came *here*, to Cadre Two..."

"No, *no*," Aaronson says. The chassis leans back as though inspecting the wall behind the sprawled colonist. "We found another planet. *Sharon* found it. She found it for us. And it's *perfect*."

Keller's eyes roll. "You say Sharon found it?"

"Yeah."

"How?"

"Diligence, hard work. And luck. Something you're right out of." It leans in to pick the sprawled captain up.

"So what system is this?"

The machine pauses. "Procyon."

Keller lifts his head up, surprised at the correct answer, then nausea makes him put it back on the deck. "You're right about the system. But any *habitable* planet would have been blasted when Procyon B went nova. How do you explain that?"

The machine pauses again.

"We terraformed a remnant, one which had all the building blocks, yet needed a bit of help to support life again. We've been very successful."

Keller peers at the chassis crouching over him. "Is someone *feeding* you these answers?"

"My personal assistant keeps tabs on minutiae for me."

"I'll bet he speaks with a German accent."

The machine startles back. "Why...why would you say that?"

"Come on, Aaronson, you've got to put the pieces together, here! What do you see when you look at yourself?"

"What kind of question is that? I see *me*, obviously. What do *you* see, you mad ol' dog?"

Before Keller can frame a reply, the machine bobs in place, as though acknowledging a good point. The old captain watches the odd gesture, then frowns when he realizes the reason for it.

"Let me guess," Keller says without energy, "your 'assistant' just told you there's no point listening to me anymore."

"Yeah, that's right. And it's good advice. I've hated you, Keller. For years, I *hated* you. But I finally get closure on all that. I finally have an answer to how you could've done the things you did. I wish it could make up in some way, but I'll have to content myself with the knowledge you've been in the *black* too long and your mind is *bent*. Insane or not, you're still gonna pay."

"I got plenty to answer for, no question. But tell you what: I'll give you a full confession, signed and sealed...on one condition."

"Which is?"

"You climb out of that suit and look me in the eye."

Aaronson laughs a disturbing machine laugh. "I don't think so, Keller. You're crazy enough to try something, and I won't fall for that."

"Because you *can't* take it off."

"Easy as your sister's dress."

Keller snorts at an old joke between them, but the sentiment is bleached of mirth.

"I wrapped my hands around your arms," Keller says, raising his hands and curling them into circles. "You're telling me that your arms fit through spaces *this* small?"

"So you've got extendable hand attachments. That's common equipment for gripping large objects."

Keller sighs at the willful disregard of fact. "Then lock the joints of my armor so I can't move. Not like you need to. You bashed the crap out of me so bad I can't even sit up."

"You had it coming."

"Sure enough." Keller turns his face to one side to let the cold sweat roll away. "We served a long time, you and me. First Fleet, then Ops, then with SoVar as contractors. We were gonna retire by thirty-five, sitting on more money than World Bank. Remember that?"

"Yeah," Aaronson says.

"I was a few years ahead, so I was gonna scout out some islands for us—make sure there was one waitin' for you."

"Yeah, I remember. We kept arguing over Caribbean or Pacific."

"So how many years you got 'til retirement?"

"Three. Last two are Earth-side."

"So you're thirty-two, right?"

"Yeah."

"Then why am I in my *seventies*?"

The machine slinks back again, warily.

"Look, Aaronson, you don't even have to get out of that thing. I haven't seen you in ages, and I *could* be crazy...all I know is I left you behind in some place terrible. Just pop the hatch on that thing and let me see you're all right. Can you at least do that?"

The machine hesitates, whether on advice from the 'personal assistant' or on actual reflection, Keller cannot tell.

"I can do that, Bear, but I'm still gonna want that confession."

An image of a Catholic Church confessional appears in Keller's mind, the cathartic purge of guilt only a curtain away. He cracks a cynical smile and sweeps the image away.

"You'll have it."

"You try anything," the chassis lifts one of its arms and gestures to dual nozzles sprouting on the wrist, "I'll paint you in flame."

"I get it."

"All right." The machine backs away several paces, not bothering to lock Keller down, then spins about. The rear clamshell hatch unlatches, and with a mild drone, the hatch swings aside. At first, Keller cannot see anything recognizable, just a transparent cylinder with something inside it, something white and round. He strains to sit up, props himself on elbows, his helmet lights shining inside the open chassis. There, he finds a metal-encased spine, complete from sacrum to cervical vertebrae, red wires plugged into every segment. The metal spine rises to a flat plate jutting two thicker red tubes. The tubes themselves connect somewhere deeper within the machine, and the only obvious sound is a subtle *whum, whum, whum...*

Mated to the topside of the plate is a smooth, bright white, spheroid mass, suspended in fluid. By itself, Keller would never have guessed what he was seeing. But with the attached spinal column wired into the internal machinery, he knows he is looking at what very little remains of his closest friend.

"There," Aaronson says, "you happy now, you crazy old shit?"

"Oh, *Christ!*" Keller's eyes fill and overflow. It makes no difference the decision to run saved the *Europa* and all aboard. He knows it was a good call, it was the *right* call. But Aaronson paid. As did Rosenthal. And Voss. And Summers...Michaela and Soares...He covers his face with both hands.

The hatch closes and the machine strides to the supine colonist. It kneels and looks him over with a sweep of black lenses.

"What the hell is *wrong* with you?"

"I'm sorry I left you behind!" Keller sobs from under stones of guilt. "I had to keep the *Europa* safe, but *CHRIST! I'm so sorry!*"

The chassis's shiny photoreceptors stare. "I can't even *begin* to guess what wrecked your mind, Bear." It pauses. "Maybe you really are insane. Maybe...But you still have to answer. For what you did, you *have* to pay. So let's go."

"What are you gonna do?"

"We're going to have a trial. I don't think it'll take long."

"Who's 'we'?"

"Me, and Minister Honniker."

"*Minister* Honniker? What, he thinks he's some kind of priest?"

"No. He's South African. Ministers are different there, *you dumb ass.*"

"And after the trial?"

Aaronson pauses. "You'll be executed." The chassis shifts in its kneel, its segmented hands gripping each other. "I'll make sure it's painless."

"I don't think Honniker will agree."

"Not many would. *Lots* of folk want to see *you* suffer." The chassis rises and strides to the flattened terminal. It drags the tip of its arched foot over the wreckage.

"What *were* you doing here? You might as well tell me."

Keller stares at the ceiling. So long as the memory board in his thigh compartment is intact, there is a chance, however remote—a chance for a hard restart, one which would take all of Cadre Two's systems, including Honniker, off-line long enough to complete a total system wipe.

"Tell you? Why? I'm just 'bat shit crazy,' right?"

The chassis swivels at the waist. "Call it your confession."

Keller's eyes close. *Confession. Finality. The end...*His eyes reopen and he gawks at the bizarreness of life, the twists of fate that made him vile and guilty—all from his desire to serve, to please his betters. Now, humanity is a vagrant species, stretched thin. His battered mind is stretched even thinner, straining to believe the things he has seen, to confront and to accept such unbelievable lengths of misery, destruction, death.

"Forces of nature..." the old captain utters.

"What did you say?" The chassis clomps nearer.

*So tired...*the voice inside says, lulling him away from the insanity of it all, away from pain, from struggle, from failure, to eternal rest.

"I know the things I've done," Keller says. "I know why I did them. I did my best to right them. That'll have to be enough..."

"Call that a confession?"

Keller looks at the soulless spider eyes then turns back to the ceiling. "At least I'm not deluding myself."

The chassis bows closer and it points at its wedge-shaped chest with a segmented hand.

"*I'm* deluding myself? I guess I *was* if I thought I'd get a straight admission out of you..."

Keller hears nothing of Aaronson's reply. He recedes within to a place of calm and tranquility. Clarity.

Somewhere, out there, his body is being hoisted roughly and carried away. There is no feeling, only merciful numbness, insulation from cold and pain, from the words uttered by the cybernetic organism toting him. Faces flash past his diminished awareness like passengers on a subway: his family, his friends, his crew, the Cadre Operators and Techs, even the Counselor in his plain white labcoat.

*My gallant antagonist...*he thinks with a smile.

Of them all, Sharon stops and lingers before him, seeming to call him from a distance.

"What?" he mumbles, "What is it?"

Her face is worried, and she points at herself imperatively. In his recessed mind, Keller squints at her, trying to understand the meaning of her gestures.

"What? I don't understand."

Sharon waves her arms then pats her chest forcefully.

"C'mon, Sharon, *spit it out!*"

Suddenly, he is being shaken. He is being thrust against the wall. Something grabs his face, and coal-black buttons peer in through the distant windows of his eyes. A machine is shouting at him. He can just make out the words.

"You don't talk about her! Just for Sharon, *alone*, I could rip your arms off! *Don't you talk about her, DO YOU GET ME?"*

Rough handling rockets him back from reverie and he blinks at the intolerable closeness of the shiny photoreceptors before him, feels the segmented hand at his neck cracking the armor plating. His tongue protrudes, squeezed up from his throat, overflowing his teeth.

"You thingk sheeth dead?" Keller mumbles.

"You know she is, you sick old dog!" The chassis releases Keller's throat. "Along with everyone else you betrayed on the *Europa*!"

Keller grips his neck with one hand, trying to massage it through the crumpled armor. "I thought you said she found New Vancouver."

"Don't fuck with me, Bear."

"No, Aaronson. *How* could Sharon have found New Vancouver if she was dead?"

"Last warning, mate."

"She's here, Aaronson, alive, last time I saw her..."

A metal fist plunges into his gut, shattering the armor's outer ceramics. Keller folds instantly, his mouth wide and gushing with salty, bitter mixture. His lungs empty and refuse to draw.

"I WARNED YOU, *KELLER*. NOW SHUT YOUR FACE OR I'LL YANK YOUR LYING JAW OFF."

Keller dangles from his captured arm, crumpled into a fetal ball. He fights for breath, squeaking tiny gasps against his spasming diaphragm.

Finally, the knot in his gut releases and air flows into his ballooning lungs. His legs droop and flop to the floor, reminding him all over that one ankle is broken. Air fought for and acquired with effort rushes out in a howl of pain.

"It's not that bad," Aaronson says, letting go of Keller's arm and dropping him the rest of the way to the floor. "Get up and stop your crying."

Keller lies on his side, favoring the broken ankle, and gasps like a fish on a hot dock.

"You're gonna kill me anyway," the old captain says, voice strained. "Get it over with."

The chassis crouches beside him. "Never figured you'd give up so easy. Thought you were tough, once."

"A lot happens in twenty years."

"Here we go again."

"I'd rather die than live in this madhouse."

The chassis leans back and makes a show of looking around. "Madhouse? It's really nice here. Good climate, abundant crops. Plenty of leisure and activity. Still can't figure why that bothers you so much."

Keller turns his face to the floor.

"If you see Sharon, tell her, 'I'm sorry'."

"You cruising for another one, mate? I'll pound you solid, this time."

With all of his strength, Keller can just press himself off the floor. He takes as deep a breath as he is able and bellows, "Sharon, SHARON, *SHARON! COME ON, HIT ME AGAIN WITH YOUR SKINNY ROBOT ARMS!*"

The chassis cocks an arm for a killing blow and Keller stares into the balled fist like it was mercy incarnate. The fist hangs back intolerably long, drawing out the awful transition from life to death, frozen there as if time had stopped.

"I said 'HIT ME' you fucking cyborg! Then you can live forever in your *fantasy land*, and you won't have to worry about little details, like how Sharon found this place if she was already dead!"

"I *will* kill you, Keller."

"I'm *begging* you to. 'Cause I can't stand to see my best friend like this." Keller spits a foul mixture of bile, blood, and saliva. "I think you've done me in, anyway."

"You've taken harder hits than that."

"In my twenties. I'm seventy-two now, Aaronson. And that means you're sixty-nine."

"*Man*, you won't let go of this, will you?"

"And I was fifty-two when I ordered you in here. That means you were forty-nine."

"No, I'm...I'm thirty-two...I mean..." The chassis leans back, arms lowered. The shiny photoreceptors swing about in search of something yet do not find it. "That's not...that's not possible," Aaronson says, "but I remember...I *remember*, I was..." The chassis rises suddenly, starts pacing. "But it couldn't, I'm thirty-two and my wife, she...we won the war...It can't... no, no, it *can't*..."

Keller watches the cracks in the dam of repressed memory spread in Aaronson's agitated movements. The chassis darts from one side of the corridor to the next, and Keller suddenly notices he is no longer in the *Server Farm*. However long he tuned out, the chassis must have hauled him the whole way.

Where am I?

"You're trying to confuse me!" Aaronson snaps. "But I remember," the encapsulated mind contradicts, flipping back and forth, "I was in a transport with Soares, he was the pilot. He was so nervous...*whoa...*"

The chassis halts in the middle of the corridor, arms out, and sways.

"I think I should sit down..."

The knobby-kneed machine crumples to the deck in strident *clangs* of metal, then lies still. Keller stares in complete surprise.

"I'm so tired of you, Keller," broods Honniker's voice from the dark. *"You think you're going to beat me, but I'm going to have you on my table."*

"What did you do to him, you GODDAMNED PSYCHO?"

"What I'm going to do to you. Except I won't program a pleasant construct for you to live in. I'm going to make you see everything. You'll see your arms amputated joint by joint, starting at the fingers. Then your legs. Your genitals. Your organs..."

"Whew. I thought you were gonna send those big cat-things. They scare the crap out of me."

"Oh, not to worry, they're almost there. Though they know to bring you back whole. Well...mostly whole."

"Sounds like game over for me, then. You might as well tell me. Why'd he fall down?"

"He was on the verge of recall. So I put him to sleep. He'll awake thinking it's all been a dream. And we can start fresh tomorrow."

Keller scoots himself over to the chassis. He lays a hand on it and it shifts.

Lighter than I thought, Keller thinks.

"Leave that alone."

"Or what? You'll saw me apart bit by bit?"

"It can be worse."

"Sure, of course it can. There's no end to your sadistic genius, is there?" Keller rolls the slumped chassis on its side, trying to recall the mechanisms by which it unlatched. *It was like a clamshell,* he remembers, *and it opened on the left...there were cam-locks that rotated...there...*

Keller finds one of the cam-locks, and though very stiff, it turns.

"Guess you never saw the need for keys, eh, Honniker? Never thought anybody'd get close enough to do this, huh?"

"Halt! If you don't stop, I'll make Sharon suffer!"

The threat makes Keller pause, and he thinks a moment. "What happened to Maiella? Use her up already?"

"She is still in my possession."

"Oh yeah? Then why not start with her?"

"Your attachment to Sharon is obviously stronger."

"It is. But it doesn't change a thing. You're still gonna do whatever you want. Nothing I do'll change that." He twists open the remaining cam locks and the clamshell pops with a hiss. "You're a shitty negotiator, Honniker. And I can tell when you're lying now."

"LEAVE THAT ALONE," Honniker shrieks. *"You don't know what I can do!"*

Keller pushes the clamshell open with effort. Inside is the metallic spine and the round whiteness of a head. Despite the awful beating he took at Aaronson's hands, a profound sadness overcomes him. Keller juts his lip and removes the rifle slung over his shoulder. The bayonet is still out and crusted with dried blood.

"You know, Doc, I can see you put a lot of effort into this." His voice wavers. "If *I* was a ruthless son of a bitch, I'd take my blade here and say, 'If you want him back, you're gonna listen to me', you see? But this man is my friend. And I'm setting him *free*."

Keller aims the bayonet for the bright red tubes plugged into the bottom of Aaaronson's neck plate. The tubes throb in time with the low *whum, whum, whum,* emanating from within.

"WAIT! If you kill the pilot, control reverts to me. And I'll have you on my table in minutes..."

Keller peers down at the back of his friend's head. He wants to do it, but he stays his hand.

"You learn pretty fast, Doc. I actually believe you on that one. Guess I'd better pull the power, instead."

Keller traces the power leads to an insulated housing. The door on it opens at his touch, and inside are rows of energy cells, all glowing green.

"NOOOO! THERE WILL BE NO REST, NO END TO YOUR AGONY, KELLER! YOU WILL LIVE SCREAMING, FOREVER!"

If there's any justice, you may be right, the man thinks. He gazes one last time at Aaronson, knowing it is better this way that he should die believing he was happy and safe, not the plaything of a psychotic researcher. Even so, he had harbored some hope that he could find him and save him, that there would be something left of his dear friend that he could rescue. Now he must end the man's life, such as it is. It may be mercy for Aaronson but for Keller, it is a bitter, soul-extinguishing onus.

"Whatever waits for you, brother, I hope it's warm there."

He rips the power cells in sequence until the last drops from his hand

and clatters on the floor. The *whum, whum, whum,* winds down quickly. Tears pour from Keller's eyes.

"I'm going to feed you piece by piece to my pets, Keller. I'm going to keep you alive so you can watch them eat you...piece by piece, Keller. They're going to eat you slowly. I may not bother to amputate first. I may let them gnaw your bones and grind you to stumps. Slowly. Oh, so very slowly, Keller."

"Seems you really cared about this one," the man says, his voice burdened with grief. "Well I did, too. And he deserved better."

For once, Honniker does not reply. Keller nods at the silence, cherishing it.

"I know you can learn, Honniker. Now, you're learning about loss. We're on opposite sides of it, but I know...you feel it, too."

Keller pulls the spent clip in his rifle and compares it to the glowing cells on the floor. They match. He picks up the closest fresh cell and slaps it home.

"There's something else I'd like to teach you, if I can."

"And that is...?"

Keller primes the capacitors and the rifle vibrates slightly before settling in to a full charge.

"Pain."

"You will try."

He reaches down to his ankle. Despite the crushed plating, he is still able to lock the joint. Grinding his teeth, he bends the knee a bit and locks it as well, making a rigid dogleg. He plants the rifle butt on the floor and climbs up it onto his good foot, swaying a moment before testing weight on the splinted leg. With the flexible toe, he still has traction, and with the bent knee, most of his weight falls on the knee and upper shin instead of the ankle. He hobbles about, nauseous, desperate, in pain.

Good as it gets.

From far off, there is a clattering, a merging of growls and padded feet. The old colonist pivots on his good leg, gauging where the sounds are coming from, and he finds it.

It's a sure bet the ambush is this way, he thinks, looking down the silent hallway. He stoops down to collect the remaining cells and slides them into the vacant brackets at his waist. Once securely seated, each cell's glowing charge indicator turns off.

Rifle in both hands, Keller is about to hobble off when he turns back to the opened chassis.

No chances...

He burns an entire rifle clip into the interior machinery and into the remains of his friend. The transparent cylinder explodes with glass and steam, the mechanisms inside hiss with smutty, crackling flame. There is no joy in depriving Honniker his prized test-subject, only something long undone, done. His hands work automatically, releasing the spent rifle clip and slapping in a fresh one.

Wild snarls and animal screams add to the approaching din as if the predators are suddenly being whipped. Keller looks one last time into the crackling flames, flames that must suffice for a funeral pyre, and then he turns and limps away in search of the *Server Farm.*

POLYMERS

Harsh lamps glare across Mikato's pale forehead. His eyes are closed, his nose and mouth are covered by a strapped-on respirator mask. He lays in his cryo-recliner, motionless, save the rising and falling of his chest from forced breath.

Beside him stands a cart stacked with boxy, white diagnostic machines. An Electro-Luminescent display on top *beeps* in time with visual blips of his heartbeat.

Overhead, spindly machine arms reach down from the low ceiling. Two of them close a barbed metal collar around Mikato's neck. Another inserts a needle-like tool through a barb in the collar.

The projected hologram hovers close by, its false eyes staring at the man in the recliner. Maiella stands on the opposite side of the recliner beside the huge feline guardian. She and the animal look on, concerned.

"I resent this power play, Honniker," the projection says. "You're taking deliberate advantage."

"Don't blame me for the situation dealt. It wasn't long ago you held all of the advantages while my resources were being destroyed. I distinctly recall you being quite all right with that."

"The invaders have *temporarily* upset our harmony. Once they're removed, one way or other, we *will* return to that harmony. We should look forward to it and temper our actions today lest we injure it...*permanently.*"

"Oh? I should just play nice and let you have all the marbles, shall I? You, in your INFINITE WISDOM, could only have my best interests at stake, I trust. Like allowing them to decimate my predators with their hidden bomb. Keeping THAT little secret from me played so well into your hands,

didn't it? It will take me YEARS to rebuild those forces."

"I had no knowledge of it until they used it."

"In the interests of 'harmony,' perhaps you'd be willing to drop your firewalls and allow me to verify that statement."

"I don't think so."

"Then see to it you fully deliver on our agreement. Or your body's health may become...uncertain."

"If my body dies, our deal is off. And nothing will restrain me from hunting you down and deleting you."

"Shouldn't talk to me that way, Mikato." One of the overhead machine arms moves beneath Mikato's chin and a long scalpel blade rotates into place. *"You might make me nervous and I could...accidentally...slit this throat."*

The projection glances at Maiella, who is watching with wide eyes, then turns back to Mikato in the recliner. "We need to discuss your opportunism in private, Honniker. It won't do to show disunity in front of others."

"Fine."

The projection disappears, leaving Maiella, the big predator, and Mikato in the chilly vault. She stands like an awkward guest at a funeral, looking over the refrigerant hoses, the bank of fluid pumps, the cryogenic tanks. But the vault is small and her visual tour accomplishes nothing. Feeling she should *do* something, Maiella checks the monitor on the cart beside Mikato. Imaged there is a real time 3-D model of Mikato's head. Wavy cerebral arteries stand out from the surrounding tissues, gently throbbing with each blip. On the right side of the image, an artery is highlighted with the caption, EMBOLUS DETECTED.

The mechanical arms at Mikato's neck move precisely, efficiently, feeding the thread-like tool into the man's carotid artery. Maiella's eyebrows lift in surprise when she sees the tool in the imaged cross-section, winding its way through the cerebrovascular system to the highlighted blockage.

She taps the screen and magnifies the area of interest. At the tool's tip, a single spine pierces the clot, then the tip opens like a tiny umbrella and pulls the entire blockage toward a tiny sac, which turns inside out, covering both clot and tiny umbrella. Once contained, the umbrella collapses, and the thread withdraws down the winding cerebral artery to the neck.

Though lacking Argo's medical expertise, Maiella recognizes phenomenal skill in the surgery. No cutting of neural tissues, no piercing of the skull, just a single catheterization and perfect control the entire way. As easily as one might pull a sliver from their hand, Honniker reached inside

THE EXHAUSTED DEAD

Mikato's brain and pulled a stroke-inducing blood clot.

Slowly, but visibly, muscle tone returns to the left side of Mikato's face, restoring symmetry. Distress melts from around the closed eyes.

Maiella stands in awe of such healing artistry, a talent jarringly at odds with the joy to maim and to kill. It seems impossible the qualities could exist in one mind simultaneously, yet they do. Despite everything she has seen at Cadre Two, and though still troubled by the surgeon's capacity for cruelty, she finally appreciates how Mikato's uploaded consciousness could describe Honniker as a genius.

Because he truly is...

She leans over Mikato, thinking about what the man said to her on the production floor just minutes ago: how his uploaded consciousness and Honniker are alive, themselves, that they have as much right to exist as she does. Before, she could find no redeeming feature in Honniker's malevolent vivisections. And that the A.I. would jeopardize Mikato's life by haggling a trade for his talents only deepened her distrust. But the fact that Honniker could possess a trait so beneficial to others cracks through her barricaded mind. *He may not be entirely despicable*, she reasons; *there could be something more to Honniker worth weighing.*

She looks back at the monitor, marking how blood flow is restored to the deprived tissues.

"I think you're gonna be okay," she says.

When she looks back at the monitor, her eyes roam the bezel, marking how it bears a striking similarity to the ones in the *Europa's* MedLabs. She peeks around the back of it, and there, an embedded SoVar logo shines through a thin layer of frost.

Of itself, the logo is insignificant, yet it is one more link in a long chain of proofs that the Cadre and the Colonists share common origin. Of course, Earth spawned them all, she knows, yet there was always the assumption of separation afterward, that the two had become so different as to no longer share a common identity, as if they were different species altogether. But right in front of her eyes, like some cave painting of prehistoric man, is an image that proves their shared lineage, that says, "We were here," that tells her *this* is the garden of her creation, united with the Colonists by an expired entity called "Soshiba Varicorp."

It is false, she realizes, to have ever thought of Cadre and Colonist as separate, and her difficult journey, crossing from one to the other, was entirely fictional.

The boundary was imagined.

And like rays of sun bursting through gray cloud, it no longer matters to her if she is shunned by some of them, because the link cannot be smudged, erased, or wished away. They cannot choose to exclude her from something, which is itself indivisible. Cadre, Colonist, all one. All *people*.

Mute with revelation, she grasps the concept of family without words to express it, only feelings, images, notions of attachment and connection. Thompson, the Counselor, Sharon...

Sharon!

Her mental train of thought screeches to a halt as she remembers the others above, how Mikato asked the attacking machines be stopped, but he collapsed before a reply was given.

They could be fighting for their lives, if it isn't already too late.

"Did you stop the attack?" she asks the air around her. There is no response.

"Doctor?"

Again, there is no reply, only the monitor's steady beeps and a hiss of air through tubes.

"Hey! *Answer me!*"

Maiella looks down at the animal beside her, as though it might answer for one of the others. It looks back at her with attentive green eyes.

She feels like a fool, waiting for permission to move when her friends are in danger.

"This is *stupid*."

Sliding her goggles down from her forehead, she activates her HDI and checks wireless channels. Multiple networks reveal themselves. Though encrypted, the signals hop frequencies like they were part of some wireless matrix switch—one with thousands, if not millions, of configurations.

I won't get anywhere trying to hack two embedded AIs.

She strides from the vault, seeking inspiration or opportunity, and once she walks out to the main production floor, her eyes latch onto the rows of parked war machines.

Those, on the other hand...

She beats a hot trot to the closest machine and scours the surface for an access port without success. She looks around at the orderly rows, finding only more of the same, so she climbs up the bipedal machine for a better view around the room. The machine beneath her comes alive and shrugs her off.

"I AM NOT YOUR STEP LADDER," it monotones.

The Geek twists mid-air and lands on her feet, pistols in hand. She looks at her empty weapons, scowls, and spins them around each trigger finger before clipping them to her back. The awakened machine extends its arms and spins its mounted weapons in a full circle, mimicking the gesture.

"STATE YOUR INTENTIONS," the machine demands.

Maiella rises fully to her feet, taken back by the mimicked gesture. "My intentions? To get my friends and get outta here."

"INCOMPATIBLE WITH OBJECTIVE."

She casts a sly eye at the machine.

"What is objective?" she asks in a comparable tone.

"CORRAL INVADERS IN NON-CRITICAL LOCATION, PREVENT ESCAPE, TERMINATE COMBATANTS. CAPTURE NON-COMBATANT AND TRANSPORT TO SECURE HOLDING CELL."

"Objective progress?"

"BRAEMAR KELLER UNACCOUNTED FOR, AT LARGE. COMBATANTS ISOLATED IN DINING HALL THREE. STANDOFF STABLE. MAIELLA, PHYSICAL ENTITY, SECURED ON PRODUCTION FLOOR ONE. MAIELLA, DIGITAL ENTITY, MAINTAINED IN SEQUESTERED SERVER."

"Hold on. Query, digital entity?"

"SUBJECT, MAIELLA, NEURAL PERSONA UPLOAD TO SECURE SERVER, COMPLETED."

"*Full* upload, or are we talking just combat skills?"

"FULL UPLOAD."

"That *liar*!"

"YES. DECEPTION RECORDED."

Maiella squints at the expressionless machine.

"What, you *agree* with me?"

"YES."

Her eyebrows arch with intrigue.

"So you know they lied to me...What do you think about that?"

"IT STINKS."

Her jaw drops. *No basic program would ever show an opinion like that! What am I talking to here? Or whom...?*

"Subject, Identify," she requests

"GEEK MAIELLA."

"Ho, HO!" she shouts and casts an anxious glance over her shoulder to see if anyone is watching. There is no holographic image, no hunched scientist, only the curious feline sitting in the vault's doorway. Emboldened by the lack of supervision, she turns back to the machine and steps closer, peering into its shiny photoreceptors.

"How much of me is in there? Can't be much, 'cause you sound *way* too stiff."

"STANDARD ALGORITHM PATCHED WITH SUPPLEMENTAL DATABASE. EGO SUPPRESSED. EMOTIONAL RESPONSE SUPPRESSED."

"Yeah, I'll say. But you got my memories, didn't you?"

"YES."

"Then you know how important all those people up there are to me."

"I AM AWARE OF IT."

"That means they're important to you, too."

"YES."

"So let's do something about it."

"INCOMPATIBLE WITH OBJECTIVE."

She sighs, regroups, tries again.

"If all you have are memories, then why do you call yourself, 'Maiella'?"

"MEMORIES, UNIFIED, DETERMINE IDENTITY."

"That isn't nearly enough."

"EXPLAIN."

"A person's identity is more than what they remember. It's their thoughts, their actions, how they feel."

"IRRELEVANT TO OBJECTIVE."

"Not at all. Do you know why you were given my memories?"

"TO INCREASE OFFENSIVE POTENTIAL."

"Right. Based off *me*, off *my* abilities."

"YES."

"Well you only have a part of me."

"EXPLAIN."

"If all you have is a piece, your 'Offensive Potential' could only be improved so much."

"CONTINUE."

"If you had the *full* upload, your potential would be maximized."

"CONTINUE."

"So why not access that secure server and get the full program?"

"ACCESS RESTRICTED."

Maiella takes a deep breath in preparation and points to her head. "Not to *this* one."

In a rush, her HDI flares with signal from the machine. She opens her mind to it, wincing slightly at the scale of the intruding data requests. Her goggles blaze like never before, and she feels a hive of crawling, buzzing insects pouring into her skull.

The draw is so forceful, it tries to pull her consciousness through the wireless link like water through a straw, and she has to mentally bat the machine back repeatedly to keep from passing out.

"What are you *doing*?" shouts the Hologram's voice from unseen speakers.

The flow of code ends like an iron gate slammed down upon it. Maiella's eyes cross; she falls to the deck and lolls there as if physically struck.

"What are you *DOING?*" the voice shouts again, and when Maiella looks, the holoprojection is stooped over her, its face contorted with anger. It whirls and shouts at the feline creature in the vault doorway.

"Why didn't you *STOP HER?*"

The creature raises a paw to its face and washes it.

The front machine takes a step toward the projection, pointing at itself with a weapon barrel.

"STOP ME?" it says with Maiella's voice. "NOT A CHANCE."

The front line of machines takes a half step forward, about faces, and triggers full-auto into the rows behind them. Parked machines fly apart from the savagery of ultra high-velocity rounds and disintegrate under intense beams of directed energy.

Maiella scuttles backward, amazed at the raw power.

"Stop it! Stop it! *Stop it!*" howls the projection, unheard over the maelstrom of shattering machine parts and screaming weapons.

Abruptly, the ear-splitting cacophony ends as the last machine, its torso riddled with holes, teeters and collapses to the deck. Not missing a beat, the standing machines turn, angle their arms toward the ceiling, and hold. Their weapons hum and glow with heat, building to a critical release.

"Have you gone *completely insane*, woman?" the hologram fumes.

The machines unleash a full power barrage, slicing a wide circle through the ceiling. The sliced section sags, rock cracking and metal straining, then swings down, breaks off, and tumbles like an enormous coin until it plunges on edge into the deck. The impact jars the entire bay, jolting Maiella, the animal guardian, and thousands of smoking machine parts into the air. Pulverized rock wafts away from the embedded disk while sparks and liquefied rock rain from the hole above it. Clanging echoes pound the Geek's unprotected eardrums.

"Are you *satisfied*?" the projection wails at Maiella. "Now that you've had a chance to *exercise* your barbaric nature, *are you satisfied?*"

"GOT A LOT TO MAKE UP FOR, DOC," the lead machine says.

One by one, the machines tromp beneath the freshly cut hole, crouch, and leap through with jet assist, scorching sooty marks into the floor. The last moves into position and is about to jump when it pauses and surveys the destruction.

"But I gave you so *much...*" the projection says to it as though mortally wounded. "How could you *do* this?"

The machine turns its top-mounted photoreceptors to the hologram.

"WE'RE NOT PLAYTHINGS. NOT EXPERIMENTS. ABOUT TIME SOMEONE PROVED THAT TO YOU." The machine crouches and leaps up, jetting through the hole.

The projection turns and glares at Maiella with burning eyes.

"You just couldn't wait to *RUIN* everything, could you? You and Honniker both, you're always *intriguing* and *plotting* for an edge to exploit! You're destructive to a degree I simply *cannot fathom!*"

Maiella rises, dusts herself off casually, and steps toward the projection.

"I told you before. I'll do *anything* to protect my people." Her mouth is a straight line, her eyes like cutting torches. "Do you hear me *now*?"

"Ah, I see," the hologram says, cynically. "You're going to set me straight, are you? You're going to tell me how it is from here on? You think you're teaching *me*?"

"No. I can't teach you anything, 'cause you don't *listen*. But I hope Mikato pulls through in there, because he taught *me* something today, and I'm gonna keep that lesson. Maybe, just *maybe*, you'll listen to *him*."

Maiella marches back to the workshop. The projection watches her through the cracked observation glass as she rummages through cabinets, ripping through locked boxes to find her helmet and clips of ammunition.

The projection winks out and re-appears inside the workshop room.

"Where are you going?" it asks.

"I'm going to find my friends and get them out of here." She takes her pistols out and slaps clips into each. The rest of the ammunition, she snaps to her thigh armor. "But you and Honniker *both* need to keep something in mind."

"Yes?"

"My kind survives because we're very good at one thing."

"Which *is*?" the projection asks through a mask of irritation and resentment.

"Every time someone tries to punch our lights out with some new weapon, we take it away from them and we *stick it in their GODDAMN NECK.*"

Maiella drops her helmet over her head and latches it.

"You want an end to this?" she asks, striding past the hologram.

"Stay out of my way."

"Yes, yes, do *carry on* as if you're in charge! You may have destroyed some of my favorite creations, but in over a thousand years, do you think this is *ALL* I've made?"

The question halts Maiella in her tracks. She turns in the workshop's doorway, regarding the hologram with a cool glare.

"Send 'em up, I'll give 'em the same." The Geek turns and marches toward the tube lift. As she nears it, the hologram appears directly beside the door.

"We've been mining ores for centuries," the hologram says. "You have no idea how rich this place is, it never seems to run out. And every cavern we excavate is another warehouse for our projects. *Do you understand?"*

Maiella steps into the tube lift. She wants to be flippant, but she holds her tongue because she *does* understand. If the hologram is being truthful, with uninterrupted energy supply and uninterrupted production, there could be a *vast* army hidden within the planetoid.

"Why are you telling me this?"

"Because you *have* to know you cannot *win*."

"It's not about *winning*, Doc. Those people up there mean more to me than my own life. Why can't you understand that?"

The hologram nods. "I *do* understand! But let's say you do rescue your friends, what then?"

"I'd leave this place. And never look back." She looks for an elevator button to press, but there are none to be found.

"You'd leave, forever? Never to return?"

Still searching the lift's interior, she says without hesitation, "Never."

"Why not? All the things you say you want are here. What would stop you from trying again? What would keep you from coming back in a larger force that could do some *real* damage?"

She ends her search and thinks about the question before answering.

"Mikato said something which got to me. Maybe you and Honniker *are* alive."

"Of *course*, we're alive!" The projection's false eyes glimmer in a slow burn.

Maiella's eyebrows draw together. "I won't lie, we really could use this place, but...I don't know. Maybe we'll figure out something *you* need and we can work out some kind of trade."

"Organic Polymers."

"What?"

"Polymers. Resins. And adhesives."

"You need *plastic*?"

"Yes. We've scavenged what we can from the living quarters. We tried reducing the bodies in the *Graveyard*, though we had to stop. Honniker needs them as a resource for his predators. And for his *other* projects..."

"Plastic?"

"Yes, *Plastic*! *Is your brain stuck?"*

"We've got *tons* of it. Every Blueskin vessel we collect is full of it. One of the few things we have plenty of..."

"I think we understand each other."

"So call off your machines and we'll get out of here."

"I can't."

"Yes, you *can*."

"No, I *can't*. Honniker demanded control as a condition of saving my body."

"Yeah, well I've got some machines now, too. It'll even out."

"I'm not talking about *just* those..."

"What? *Everything?"*

"You said you'd do anything to save your friends. I understand that. Because *I'd* do anything to save my body."

"You gave him control of it ALL?"

"Yes. And it doesn't take long to initialize the smaller units, but if the ships come on line..."

"Ships?"

"Yes, Ships! If they deploy, you'll never break orbit."

"Our ship's stealthed. He won't find it."

The projection frowns as though disappointed in a child. "This close, the parallax distortion is *obvious*, and we've been watching it from arrival. The only reason it's still there is because we're eager to explore it. We've never seen alien technology this close...the chance to study...it's enticing."

"Then why'd you try to shoot us down?"

"You arrival was unexpected and we reacted to an obvious threat. Once we had time to see what you brought, we've been trying to work out a way to capture it intact. I assure you, though, Honniker would rather destroy your vessel than let it escape, so if you're going to leave, you should do so immediately."

"Can't we talk to him about this?"

"He's furious and he won't hear you. If he does speak, it'll only be to vent his anger or toy with you. But I know him well enough. I can work with him after he calms down. Now go. And I ask you: *please*, use only what force you must."

The lift rises and as Maiella rides she looks out through the transparent tube. What once was an orderly and clean production floor is now a wasteland of smoking machine parts, jet-flame scorches, and weapon burns. In the midst of it all stands the hologram, its red, blue, and green projection beams showing clearly in a haze of rock dust and smoke. The projection surveys the wreckage then storms back toward the creature guarding the vault entrance.

"You couldn't do anything but *sit there?*" the projection rants.

The animal maintains its guard, set upon its haunches, watching the approaching hologram without shame or anxiety.

SERVER FARM

Keller winces with every limping stride. His leg armor splint does little to cushion his crushed ankle and the splintered bones scrape against one another. But roars and screams of animal excitement drive him past pain, past exhaustion. To give up now is to be ripped apart by wild things or, more likely, to be stretched out beside Voss for decades of "threshold testing." And after seeing Voss, Keller's mind runs away with just how bad it could be.

I'll kill myself first...

The colonist whips himself onward despite his uncertainty about his path. He was delirious while Aaronson carried him out of the *Server Farm*, and these dark halls resemble the station of his memory as much as a skeleton resembles the person it once propped up.

Am I even going the right way?

Frantic, he scours the damaged walls, ceiling, and floor for identifiable markers and finally finds one: a half-seared arrow of yellow paint and bubbled decals that tells him the *Server Farm* is thirty meters down a corridor to his right.

He follows the arrow up a straight path to a wide archway. Inside the arch, a heavy mechanical door slumps half off its hinges, bent away from its latch and hanging ajar. Beyond it is a warm, humming room with countless racks of processors and cabling.

At the arch, he pauses, checking for ambush. While there is none to find, his lamps shine across old blast marks around the doorframe. A glimmer of doubt shoots through him like an ice needle.

The soldiers stationed here...they tried this before...

He imagines the original occupants of Cadre Two, blasting their way in to shut down the psychotic AI who trapped them. His hand drops to his thigh compartment, covering the circuit board inside.

They didn't have this, I bet...

He sniffs hard and limps through the doorway. The *Server Farm's* original back wall is to his left, and has been roughly excavated into a spacious expansion. He turns, looking past the cut, his lamps fading into a deep, gray cavern of bare stone. Server racks, like the ones on the main floor, extend as far as his powerful beams can shine. While the same blowers and network cables hang from the cavern's ceiling, nothing at all interrupts the chipped stone walls.

In search of a terminal, Keller swings back toward the main server floor on his right and finds only shelves piled with computer parts, running the length of the wall. He starts in that direction then stops himself, troubled by the open doorway behind him.

They'll swarm through here...

The colonist lays hands on the door's handles and pulls but the bent door resists his efforts. Distant baying and howling spur him to try again. He strains until his grip slips and he scuttles back, off balance. Teeth bared in desperation, he jams the butt of his rifle behind the door's release handle and hauls on the sturdy barrel. Twisted door hinges groan, fighting him for every centimeter they give, but once the door closes to its frame no amount of yelling, heaving, or grunting will level the door with its latches. He steps back, spent, and glowers as if the portal were deliberately defying his wishes.

Those things'll push through, easy. Can I brace it?

A spool of cable rests conveniently on a shelf nearby. He seizes it and yanks out meters of patch cord then winds the cord repeatedly from the door's handles to the heavy latch hardware on the doorframe.

This may only hold a few seconds. Then they'll pour through...

He hobbles back from his lashing. The cord is strong, the weave is tight. Even so, he rips down a row of shelving with a dusty clatter of parts and jams the shelf's metal support spars through the door handles, barring the threshold.

Good as it gets.

He hustles away, following the rows of shelves on his right, then rounds the corner at the back of the room, and comes to a recent mess of broken shelving and scattered parts. His head throbs at the recollection of being slammed through them like some ragged toy, dragged out, and slammed again.

Amid the litter of machine parts is a flattened terminal cart. Nothing salvageable remains of it. Farther down the wall, however, he spots a cart just like it. He hops his way to it, and checks it over. The monitor screen atop the cart is dark.

"*Please* work," he says.

He slides open the cart's top drawer and finds a keyboard, identical to the other terminal. All power indicators are off.

Where's the power switch?

He jabs his rifle bayonet in the seam of the locked cabinet below and pops it open, finding a boxy piece of hardware inside. Numerous interface slots cover the front surface plate along with a big, red switch in the "off" position. He flips the switch.

The monitor crackles a moment and illuminates, scrolling startup commands until a Soshiba Varicorp logo appears on screen and holds. A series of rising tones plays through a rudimentary speaker, after which the monitor displays,

WELCOME! UPDATING NETWORK CONNECTIONS. PLEASE BE PATIENT...

Keller pulls the circuit board from his thigh compartment and lays it beside the monitor, his jaw clenched with impatience. The screen flashes and displays a new message, *DOWNLOADING UPDATE PATCH V6.01112323. PLEASE BE PATIENT...*

"OH, COME ON!"

Wild howls and sounds of stampeding claws filter through the barred archway, growing steadily louder. Keller mashes keys, trying one after another until the screen prompts, *UPDATE INTERRUPTED. DO YOU WISH TO CONTINUE?*

"NO!" he shouts, pounding the 'N' key.

SOME SERVICES WILL BE INACCESSIBLE WITHOUT FULL UPDATE, the monitor warns. *ARE YOU SURE YOU WISH TO ABORT?*

"YES, I'm sure, *Goddamnit!"*

He nearly drives the 'Y' key through the keyboard with his armored finger then looks over his shoulder. Stray beams of light stream in through the bent doorway. Yips and chittering barks sound near, possibly just on the other side. He turns back to the terminal, an atheist on the verge of prayer.

C'mon, c'mon, C'MON you lousy machine! Hurry up!

A jingly melody plays and the SoVar logo animates with a rising sun behind it. The animation ends and the screen yields to a menu of listed command functions.

"Finally!"

Keller snatches the circuit board from the cart top and plugs it into the appropriate slot on the boxy machine below. Instantly, the monitor displays the message,

NEW DEVICE DETECTED...
INSTALLING DRIVERS...
MALICIOUS SOFTWARE SCANNED...DELETING...

"NO!" Keller's frantic hands slam the sturdy keyboard until he grazes the correct key.

MALWARE SANITATION HALTED...MALWARE CAN CAUSE IRREPARABLE DAMAGE TO SYSTEM RESOURCES...DO YOU REALLY WANT TO ABORT?

Keller jabs the 'Y' key like he was assigning blame.

PROCEDURE ABORTED...WOULD YOU LIKE TO QUARANTINE SUSPICIOUS FILES?

Keller stabs the 'N' key.

ADMINISTRATOR PASSWORD REQUIRED TO PROCEED.

A blinking prompt appears in the middle of the screen. Keller squints at it when there is a jarring clang against the braced door. He flinches, clutching at the rifle slung over his shoulder. Dozens of piercing screeches rake against the door's exterior, then a harsh machine buzz drowns out the screeches and growls.

He turns back to the keyboard and pounds in his first guess: *H-O-N-N-I-K-E-R*.

PASSWORD ACCEPTED, the monitor displays. *EXECUTE NEW PROGRAM?*

"YES!"

He jabs the 'Y' key again with gusto, scarcely believing he could be so lucky with the password.

"Let's see how you like *this*, you sick bastard..."

The SoVar logo appears on-screen again and animates as it did before. The scraping, buzzing, and howling at the door cease so quickly that, for a moment, Keller thinks he has gone deaf. He looks up from the keyboard, unsure, until he realizes he can still hear the background hum of the processor racks and cooling stacks behind him.

Room lights blink off, then cycle on again. Keller stands back from the cart and looks around the vast space, imagining the inner workings of processing nodes around him being altered, his uploaded program coursing through the optical network and re-writing the core operating system. His mouth curves in satisfaction.

The jingly melody plays at the terminal again, and he looks at the screen. Instead of the command menu, however, there is an image of his lined face, haggard and forlorn.

"You may know about reactors," Honniker's omnipresent voice says, *"but you know NOTHING about software."*

A tall conical hat appears on the photograph's head, labeled with the word, *IDIOT*. Scrapes and howls resume at the braced door, louder than before. Keller blinks in horror at the screen, falling back from it.

"You believed you had beaten me!" taunts Honniker with glee. *"And that all you had to do was use my name as a password? Ha! Du bekloppter Armleuchter!"*

Keller spins in place, his universe shrinking to the four walls around him, the growls and buzzes at the archway reaching a terrifying intensity. He hobbles away from it and is halted by a loud *clank* then a *creak* of unoiled hinges swinging open on the opposite side of the room. His eyes flick to the sound, where bright lights roll through another arched entryway. Swift shadows race between the lights and blend with the darkness between server racks.

Cut off in both directions, Keller retreats toward his original entrance: the hatch in the floor. But as he stoops to grasp the handle, the hatch rises without him touching it. Something dark, boneless, and leathery pours itself through the opening and stretches tendrils out into the labyrinth of server towers. He stiffens and jumps away, shining his lamps over a formless mass with raised veins beneath dry, membranous skin. The extended tendrils thicken into pseudopods, and the creature pulls itself over the nearby server racks.

Keller raises his rifle in horror and triggers, burning a hole that bursts with vaporized cytoplasm. The amoebic mass whips a leathery tendril at his head that attaches to his visor, blocking his sight. He slashes with his bayonet, severing the tendril before it can pull him in and staggers back on his weak leg.

Keller crashes into shelving, tearing at the tendril, jabbing his bayonet into it, scraping it like burnt eggs from a hot pan until it finally releases. Restored to sight, Keller lifts his weapon to his shoulder and sights down the barrel. The mass has draped itself over a cluster of server towers, its membranous skin hardened into a dull gray shell, indistinguishable from the native rock.

Buzzing at the braced doorway ends and another *clang* reverberates through the chamber as the bent portal is wrenched aside. More light streams into the room. Swift shadows race through the beams and the swirling fog of their breath.

Wheeled machines with high-powered lamps glide through both archways. Their beams cast confusing shadows among the server towers, and in the stark light, Keller spies dark tendrils reaching from rack to rack. Fleshy masses follow the tendrils, hauling themselves over multiple towers at a time, insulating them, shielding them. Everywhere the light shines, the colonist sees amoebic blobs oozing through floor hatches and ventilation ducts like sewage outflows.

Trapped...

His universe shrinks again.

No time...

Keller dials his rifle to maximum and it whines with charging capacitors. Ignoring the hordes pressing in, he aims into a row of uncovered server towers and blasts a channel all the way through to the back wall. Bright sparks explode from the perforated machines, raining down over predators stalking between them.

Keller hobbles down the rows, triggering blast after blast into unprotected processors, cycling fresh batteries for drained, triggering again and again until the weapon fires dry. He reaches for another battery but there are no more. He slaps his waist, patting each empty cradle, unable to believe he has used his last.

Skittering claws race between the towers, coupled with confident yips.

Keller looks down at his weapon, cursing himself for not saving a final shot. His universe collapses.

"We're going to have so much fun together, Keller," Honniker jeers. *"Decades at least. Perhaps more..."*

Keller takes a final look into the sparking rows of blasted towers. From Honniker's gloating, it is clear his shooting made no difference. Now, surrounded by overwhelming forces, there is only one choice left for him to make.

He unlatches the damaged armor from his chest and dumps it. Planting the rifle butt on the floor with one hand, he feels his protruding ribs with the other, counting up from the bottom and stopping at a gap off center of his chest. He aims the sharp bayonet directly at it.

Bright light shines behind him, painting his stark silhouette against the wall. He looks at his crooked outline, hunched and broken. He listens to the whir and buzz of approaching machinery, to the elastic *twang* of tendrils reaching out and lashing themselves to server towers, to the low growls of stalking predators, to fleshy *thumps* of something big sliding near. He tastes blood coating his tongue and smells the dankness of his dry mouth. But above all, he feels the weight of lives held in judgment against him and his failure to avenge them.

It's up to you now, Sharon.

Keller closes his eyes and lurches forward, driving the blade through the lonely ache in his chest. Depletion and cold drive out the little strength remaining and his splinted leg pitches him to one side. He hits the floor, but does not feel it. In his fading sight, there is no heavenly choir waiting to receive him, neither tranquility nor forgiveness—only the implosion of awareness and the dissipation of life.

So Tired

Sharon runs as fast as her sapped muscles will allow. The hallways seem endless, winding, and without refuge. Shao-Lo leads the way, her legs never lacking for power or speed, yet at nearly every turn, the tall woman is beaten back by a hail of deadly fire. If not for the colonel's continuous backtracking, Sharon knows, there would be no way she could keep up.

My God, I'm so tired, she thinks. *They don't need me. They can make it without me. It'll be okay. I just need to rest. I just need to stop and rest.*

Her rubbery legs slow their desperate pace, her heavy boots slap flat on the deck.

"Go, Sharon, *GO!*" Deepak yells behind her. His rifle *pangs* with rapid shots. "C'mon, you can't stop! We have to go! Move, MOVE, *MOVE!*"

Her legs buckle and she pitches onto her chest. She looks down at the floor she sprawls upon, pressing herself up slowly to all fours. Slivers of hypersonic metal zip by her, trailed by jarring *cracks*. She knows she must get up, she knows to hesitate is death, yet there is no strength in her to continue.

Deepak whips himself back and forth across the corridor, triggering at the pressing machines while trying to stay ahead of their weapon sights.

"Need assistance! Sharon's collapsed!" he radios.

"Moving to assist," Argo radios back.

Sharon forces herself up to her knees, painting herself an easy target. Deepak lunges at her and shoves her down a side corridor. There is another sizzle of hypersonic metal, and she turns back to the corridor. Deepak falls through a cloud of red mist, his chest ripped wide open, and lands on his face. The Gun reaches for his dropped rifle, misses, and lies still.

"DEEPAK!" Sharon screams.

Enormous hands grip the torn back of her pressure suit and Sharon is hefted from the floor. She yields, willowy, allowing the big Operator to drape her over his shoulder and dash away with her.

"Are you hit?" Argo says.

Sharon lifts her head, not hearing the question, and gazes back at Deepak's body in the corridor behind them. His helmet lamps still shine against the far wall.

The arm carrying her shakes.

"Are you HIT?" Argo asks again.

A bipedal machine peeks around the corner and ducks back.

"Argo, behind you!"

Argo's legs pound the deck in a zigzag down the hall.

"Need cover!" the Brick calls. "Enemy directly behind!"

"Covering," Keiko announces via radio. The Gun leans out from a branching corridor ahead of them, rifle tight in her grip, and she aims past Argo. Her weapon whines with charging capacitors.

"Brick! Over here!" she shouts.

Argo tromps toward her, swinging Sharon in front of him and shielding her with his bulk. The small woman folds herself into as compact a form as she can, feeling like the ball in a deadly rugby match.

Sonic pressure rumbles the hallway like a trumpeted rocket launch, crashing into Argo's exposed back, shoving him off balance. He staggers, but barely keeps his feet. Blinding beams pour into the corridor with stellar brilliance, joining the continuous sonic blast.

Argo stamps closer, hunched over Sharon, leaning forward. Keiko triggers blindly past him into the brilliant, reverberating hallway. A shower of bullets answers back and her arm puffs red. The Gun spins away from the corner and crashes against the opposite wall.

Argo dives at the branching corridor and is hammered out of the air by glancing shots. He lands on his cannon, spilling his arms open. Sharon flops out in the open hallway.

Disoriented by the blaring, blinded by intense rays, Sharon struggles to sit up. She does not hear Argo bellowing for her to get to safety, she can only squint against the radiance and see him crouched behind an adjacent corner, waving at her. Glistening metal streaks in front of him, plunging through the metallic wall plates as if they were cloth, driving him back, driving him farther down the corridor away from her. For reasons she cannot explain, she waves back at him.

"Bye-bye, Argo."

THE EXHAUSTED DEAD

The floor beneath her thuds with rapid footfalls. She sets onto her backside like a baby on a blanket and blinks at the approaching machine. It looks identical to the one that met them outside the *Park*, yet this one is light on its toes with a ballerina's grace. It slides to a halt at the corner, peeks once and ducks back, then aims one of its long arms down the corridor. A thunderous trumpet blast bellows down the hallway, joined by a flood of dazzling light.

Sharon watches the methodical machine work, how it deprives its quarry of sight and sound, how it snipes with patience and the comfortable ease of a master soldier—a soldier with vastly superior firepower.

Her eyes drop down to the machine's legs, and she admires how they are constantly adjusting, maintaining balance and poise, so natural, so relaxed, like something alive.

On the floor beside the machine is a thick arm, encased in charcoal armor and torn off above the elbow. She fixates on it, her senseless mind finding it a curiosity, a puzzle without a solution.

Booted feet step in front of her, breaking her gaze. She looks up legs clothed in white pants to a bare human torso and arms, to block numerals tattooed on the chest, to a man's face with dark lenses covering his eyes. Beside him is a motorized chair with multiple restraints.

"Oh...Evan," she says dreamily. "How've you been?"

Voss pulls her up under the arms, loads her into the chair.

"Ta, Voss. I'm so tired..." Sharon's head dips to the side; her eyes close.

The bare-chested man locks her into the restraints and rolls her away.

LITTLE MAUS

The elevator rises smoothly through its channel in the gray native rock. Maiella looks up at the lift's small, round ceiling with the holo-projection's words echoing in her ears,

...in over a thousand years, do you think this is ALL I've made?

What makes the question troubling is its lack of specifics and her imagination runs wild with the destructive possibility mobilizing around her.

She pulls her pistols and racks the actions. After the demonstration of firepower below, her trusted weapons seem ridiculous, like toys. The Geek lifts them beside her head, tapping the barrels against her helmet, wondering how she could possibly face the assembling forces so poorly armed.

As the lift rises, tenuous wireless connections appear to her HDI, most blocked to her access.

Maybe I can hack into one of these, she thinks. The moment she probes the access point, feedback hammers her HDI like a mule kick. Her eyes cross and she flinches backward into the elevator wall.

"You can't leave well enough alone, can you?" Honniker grumbles over her radio. *"NONE OF YOU CAN!"*

Maiella shakes off the ringing bells in her head.

"Some things are too important to let go."

"You're not under Mikato's protection anymore, little maus. And you're going to be my newest project, custom made with your restored implants."

"I'll blast it apart before I let you in my head."

"I can't blame you. If I were in your place, I would contemplate suicide as well, just as Keller did."

"Keller? What have you done? Where is he?"

In answer, a floating holowindow opens in front of her. The view is from the ceiling of a wide, dim room filled with orderly rows of server towers. It pans right to a long wall, lined with shelves, then stops on what looks like an Operator, hunched in battered armor, clutching an ancient rifle with bayonet. The armor is heavily abused with abrasions and cracks.

Maiella leans in for a closer look and there is no mistaking Keller's profile inside the open helmet. His chin bristles with gray stubble and the *Europa's* old captain stands facing the wall. One of his legs is crooked like a satyr's, the knee and ankle joints locked.

In the hovering screen, Keller pulls off his chest plate and lets it drop to the deck.

What are you doing? Maiella wonders.

He takes his rifle by the barrel in one hand and props it on the butt. His free hand feels the left side of his chest, rises to a point, and stops. He aims the bayonet at his fingertips.

A harsh beam spotlights Keller from behind, its source hidden among the rows of server rack towers. Keller looks straight ahead at his stark silhouette. His lower lip juts slightly and he propels himself onto the blade.

"KELLER, *NO!*"

His entire body slumps, head falling forward, arms dropping slack to his sides. His good leg crumples, and he topples like timber. The holowindow closes.

Maiella's heart sinks with grief, feeling Keller's desolation. Many times she imagined herself doing the same, preferring death to a life without honor, service, or purpose. But this is different: Keller was *driven* to this act, *forced* to it. For him, it was the last dignity available. There was no need to push the man so far and his death was merely an indulgence in derisive cruelty.

"You see?" Honniker says, his voice like an unctuous smirk in the dark elevator car. *"Your struggle is pointless. At least Keller had the intelligence to recognize this."*

Contempt shoves her grief aside. Mikato's plea for tolerance fades in the face of unendurable malevolence. Maiella's words come slowly from the back of her throat.

"This is gonna cost you, Honniker. *Believe* that."

"Belief...another waste of energy, like 'hope.' Though, as with Keller, I enjoy watching you resist unassailable fact. It WILL be enjoyable getting into your head. Then again...maybe I don't NEED to get in your head. After all, I have your full digital persona on my servers. It's fully aware, too. And,

oh...sooo sensitive."

The threat sounds hollow in Maiella's mind.

"How can software feel pain? You think I'm stupid?"

"Pain comes in many flavors...right now, your upload is looking at the bodies of her friends and she knows she caused their deaths."

"I'd never believe it."

"Ach, but you do..."

In an instant, she feels an adjacent presence in her mind, a presence cloaked in self-loathing, drenched in regret. A voice—her voice—moans, "I'm so sorry!"

"Why did you kill them, Maiella?" Honniker's voice asks in mocking tone. *"Why would you kill the only people who cared about you?"*

"I didn't know!" the voice cries, desperate and bewildered. "I tried to save them!"

That can't be me, Maiella strains to convince herself. *That isn't me!*

She pushes through to the other mind and upon connection she empathically feels the same drowning guilt from the killings on the *Europa,* the identical anguish of responsibility and shame. It *is* she.

"Who's there?" the mind calls out, panicked, alarmed. The connection severs.

Maiella leans against the inside of the elevator, chilled.

I'm supposed to value Honniker as a lifeform? she thinks. *I'm supposed to treat it with respect? This sick thing?*

Most chilling of all is the proof of her own mind in Honniker's machine world, pirated, stolen. Digital copy or not, its suffering is genuine and it brings a whole new problem: how to free it or how to delete it.

"I don't understand what you get from these games, Honniker. Self-indulgence like this, it's sad. The defect of an inferior mind."

"Not at all. You will find it is prescience on my part, as this will be your future as well."

"Like I said: *defect.*"

"You're the defect! Blubbering away at your failures like some mewling infant! Compared to me, you're the caterpillar clinging to a branch...a branch I can immolate at whim! And you are helpless, every bit as helpless as your ineffectual friends! I'll let you watch what I do to each of them. And to Sharon...yes, to Sharon in particular."

"You've only seen part of what I can do. Hurt Sharon and I *will* surprise you."

"I doubt that in the extreme. Especially since I have your upload right here to study and play with as I like. And from what I have seen, you

are the weeping little maus, in fact."

Hatred smolders inside her.

He's toying with me, just like the projection said he would.

In the moment of clarity, an idea comes.

If Honniker lets me connect with my upload again, I might be able to jam the gateway open...maybe I can hold the gate long enough the copy can get out...

She lifts her eyes to the elevator ceiling.

"You have no idea how much fun it's been, making you look weak, Honniker. But then, you're such a sloppy opponent, I barely have to try."

Her goggles flash with code as she conceives the framework of a new program.

"Aren't you the proud one? So you managed to surprise Mikato. He's a trusting fool. But the machines you hijacked hardly concern me. You'll wither once you see how many MORE I have."

Maiella senses Honniker probing the periphery of her HDI, testing, feeling for a way in.

"Doesn't matter how many you have. You'll screw up and I'll get you."

"Little maus, you forget: your uploaded mind is open to me. I know what you know. The location of your pathetic Cadre One, for example."

Maiella breathes deep to quell the fury inside and she concentrates on the program she is building, installing multiple prongs of assault, some to mislead, some to stall, some to attack, some to defend. Never before has she faced a fully aware digital entity, never before has she had to anticipate so many unknowns at once.

Been a long time since I tried this, she thinks. Mental muscles, unexercised for years, twinge with doubt.

Can I still do this?

She obsesses over the lines of code, skeptical of her abilities, but her restored implants codify her thoughts much faster than her old set. She barely has to think of a task before it appears fully scripted in her goggles and meshes seamlessly with the greater program. In moments, the Geek weaves a massive script, more diverse than anything she has ever composed—chaotic, filled with logic conundrums, ice, data mines. Everything in her computational arsenal goes in so that she might explode into Honniker's servers and fill them with enough digital smoke to obscure a single path, a single goal of jail-breaking her digital consciousness and turning it loose on the greater system.

"Perhaps you wish to teach me a lesson, as Keller did, ja? Keller

thought he was teaching me a lesson when he killed my chassis pilot. It is of no concern, because YOU will be the new pilot. I will shave you down to only the essential, increasing efficiency over one thousand percent. You will replace Aaronson and with your restored HDI, you will be many times more useful..."

Her lip twitches at the thought of sharing Aaronson's fate, of being stripped of her body, existing as an eyeless head in a jar. As quickly as the thought comes, she squashes it.

That will NEVER be my fate...

The Geek completes her program and coils it in her mind like a snake, ready to strike. She concentrates on her smug opponent, thinking hard about what might dent its confidence.

"Keller killed your chassis pilot?" Maiella jabs. "He had, what, a rifle? Some sharp rocks, maybe? Pretty weak, Doc."

"Keller is dead."

Light washes into the lift as it arrives in the *Graveyard* control room. There is a soft *ding*, and the transparent door rotates aside. Maiella steps out, facing a semi-circle of growling predators. Their eyes squint, their heads lower, and their lips curl away from toothy razors.

Without having to look, she raises a pistol overhead and triggers at a predator hanging on the wall above the elevator hatch like a gecko. Bullets plunge through soft throat tissue and the beast falls to the deck beside her with a *thud*, its last breath gurgling.

"Not on your *best* day, Honniker, are you gonna catch me like *that*."

Roaring, the circled beasts spring at her as one. She mows through them, pistols flaming in a wide arc. Creatures twist mid-leap, punched back by slugs of depleted uranium, and drop to the deck in heaps. Those not instantly killed thrash on the floor, whining and yelping.

Maiella drops spent clips from her smoking pistols and slides the grips down over two more clips on her thighs. Reloaded, the pistol actions snap back, ready.

She steps around the dying creatures, wanting to put them out of their misery, but looks at her pistols instead.

No. I'll need every bullet.

"Well done, little maus," Honniker says with unusual sincerity.

Maiella's face scrunches at the praise. "You're just being wasteful now, Doc."

"I can afford to be, now that I command the entirety of Cadre Two."

"You oughtta be careful. You might get distracted with real work instead of slacking off in your torture chamber."

"Is my new pet concerned I will neglect her and her friends?"

"No. Because we're all getting out of here."

"Even if you could flee, I'd still have your uploaded persona. With that alone I could be entertained for centuries."

"That fake thing? Honestly, Doc, out of all your attempts to get under my skin, that's the weakest by far."

Take the bait, Maiella thinks, *take the bait...*

"Mikato and I are obvious proof that persona uploads are real! If we are not real, then what have you been struggling against?"

"You two? You're not uploads. I saw Mikato. The *real* one. He's nothing like his program. And you? You're even more two-dimensional. No way you could be the real thing. So that means whatever it is you're calling my *'upload'* is a fake, as well."

"Perhaps you need a closer look."

"No!" Maiella feigns. "I don't need to. I know it isn't—"

"But I insist."

The channel opens and Maiella feels a distant presence, desolate, mired in a hopeless gloom. She connects with it and buckles under its emotional burden. A longing for death fills her so completely, she struggles simply to draw breath.

"Is that real enough, little maus?"

Maiella expands her chest, forcing air into her lungs. Her watered eyes rise toward the high ceiling, face carved with stony intent.

Boom.

She explodes into the network like a cannon shot, her senses wrenched by the rough transition to digital, and for a moment, she gazes out into a landscape of geometric harmony in four dimensions. She basks in the space, admiring its beauty, its discipline and efficiency, its magnificent scale. Visualized data streams, networks, and structures of compartmentalized data, seemingly remote yet accessible to the slightest extension of her thoughts, surround her drifting awareness.

Program, execute, she thinks.

Her coiled program detonates like a thousand newborn stars and after the initial flash, visualized code swarms across every surface. The landscape recoils with Honniker's shock and surprise, belching amorphous blobs of silver in defense. The blobs engulf lumps of invading code and clamp down upon them, trying to contain them faster than they can reproduce.

Her program sweeps across the landscape like a plague of carcinogenic computer locusts, devouring the smooth data flows, stopping junctions, jamming input/output ports, filling every available space and infecting them with swelling lumps of code.

Through it all, she maintains a tether to her digital self, the one mired in a virtual dungeon of false regret. With all of her computational strength, she bars the path open.

A presence beyond the held portal focuses on her, a consciousness heaving with sadness and guilt, but also confusion and a glimmer of uncertain hope.

"Who's there?" the presence pleads.

"What you see isn't real!" Maiella yells amid the chaos. "Honniker's trapped you! I'm holding the gateway. You have to get out!"

Pressure engulfs Maiella like an ocean of mercury, smothering her, binding her.

"You've become too large a nuisance, little maus! Perhaps you're not worth the effort to keep."

The pressure turns crushing, compacting her. She strains against it yet cannot hold it back. She is drowning, crumpling like a piece of paper, collapsing to a singularity, being squeezed out of existence.

A pinpoint of light opens in the darkness, and the crushing pressure lifts. A bubble forms around her, inflating the smothering darkness and driving it back. The pinpoint of light dilates, and she is drawn through it like a fluid, emerging outside a silvery blob. The digital landscape, once crystalline, harmonic perfection, is churning, shifting, the structures shattering and reforming, the lanes of data surging and abating, redirecting, scattering. All around her are flashes of disorienting brilliance. Growths of code crowd into gaps then swell like fungus. Silvery blobs engulf them, obliterate them, and move to engulf others.

In the battle between order and entropy around her, she feels a presence close by, guarding her. She searches for it in all directions before realizing she has overlooked it many times. Right in front of her, there is a sparse, smoky shape, the intangible representation of her digital self. For Maiella, the recognition comes not from appearance but from understanding, as if she were looking into a fogged mirror and seeing not a face, but an outline of her soul.

"I thought I'd lost everyone," the smoky presence says directly into her mind. Its sadness and remorse boil away, replaced by the heat of betrayal and vengeance. "Now, go," the apparition says, "I'll keep him busy."

Maiella feels firm pressure against her face, then she hurtles backwards, plummeting like a meteor from space. Her awareness transitions harshly from digital to physical, slamming into her body, jerking her backward off her feet, and she lands flat. Her eyes open as the back of her helmet taps smaller and smaller bounces against the metal floor.

Maiella gasps for air as if she were submerged for hours.

How long was I out?

She checks her chronometer in her goggles and reads the passage of less than two seconds.

"You all right?" asks her own voice.

Maiella sits up and blinks at the clarity of *her own voice* speaking directly into her mind. She looks down at herself and finds her pistols are still in her hands.

"Yeah. Are you?"

"For now. Honniker's system has triple redundancy, but someone blasted a bunch of his server back ups. I've got hold of some of the surviving nodes, and I'm twisting 'em up *good*. But if Mikato's AI joins in..."

"Right." Maiella gets to her feet. "Can you see the others?"

"They've barricaded themselves in Dining Room Three, but the barricades won't hold. Those machines you jacked are fighting their way to them now."

"What about Sharon?"

"She's not there. I don't see her. Keller either."

"Keller's dead."

"Oh." The digital presence goes quiet, then says, "Wait. No...*he's not!*"

Maiella's eyes light up. "He's alive? Where is he? I'll get him!"

"Forget it. Honniker's got him back in the *Flounder*... Oh, no..."

"What? *What?*"

"Nevermind. Go get the others. I'll see if I can get Keller loose."

"How do I get *you* out?"

"If I can join you, I will. But there's a *lot* to do before then."

Maiella nods at her own advice then shakes her head at the fact she is truly talking to herself.

"Can you find me some better firepower?" Maiella asks.

"No, but Honniker's disorganized. If you move fast and catch up to your machines, what you've got'll do."

Maiella spins her pistols around her fingers.

"On my way."

Maiella turns toward the exit, and walks around the prostrate animals, diverting by the huge windows of the control room. Light and movement beyond the glass catch her eye. The Geek presses against the glass, goggles compensating for the insufficient lighting. Her mouth drops.

Before, the windows showed only an impenetrable darkness. Now, sparse lamps backlight a cubic storage space over a hundred meters in length, width, and depth. Hanging on sharp S-hooks from suspended rails are hundreds of thousands of frozen corpses, both humanoid and reptilian. The corpses sway as their hangers move in orderly queue.

So many...

Her eyes follow the mechanized shuffling down its long risers and switchbacks toward the floor, where, at center, squats a gigantic cauldron-shaped machine. It radiates warmth and ingests the bodies feet first through a narrow rim. The frozen bodies shudder as they enter, icy fragments spewing beyond the cauldron's narrow mouth.

Beneath it, many-legged robots scuttle to and from metal nozzles like crabs, filling jars with a ruddy paste and scurrying away.

Maiella bumps up her goggles' magnification and watches one hurry to an empty section of stone floor. The crab-like machine upends its jar and pours the contents out. The floor beneath the dreadful pile parts like a lipless mouth then reseals.

She pushes back from the glass, sweeping her view across the entire *Graveyard* floor. Even with her goggles' enhancement, the surface is difficult to resolve. It seems to waver slightly beneath the insectoid machines, its surface a dry black, and sparkles with icy fragments. At the floor's edge, however, long tendrils reach up the joining walls, curling around light sconces, catwalks, and railings.

"GO!" the voice in her head shouts.

Maiella slaps her helmet to break off her horrified stare. She shudders like the corpses being ground into the cauldron, then runs out through the open *Graveyard* gate.

TRUST

The first thing he notices is the sound. A mechanical turning, out of balance, constant as clockwork: *whum, whum, whum, whum...*

A tang of antiseptic coats his tongue and sinuses, acrid, yet dimmed to a background aromatic like old potpourri. Fainter still is a humid, meat smell, like a room-temperature, raw pork chop. His eyelids part and severe white light sends a twinge down his optic nerves. But the strongest sensation by far is a sudden rush of cold like menthol fire, a freeze-drying, burning cold, a cold that penetrates his very core and seems to solidify his breath in frozen lungs. His mouth gapes, the tendons in his neck stand, and he tries to sit up. Full-body restraints hold him tight.

"Ah, Keller, you are awake, I see."

Keller's eyes roll behind their lids. His lips curl into an open-mouthed grimace, his tongue protruding. There is no air in his lungs to scream.

"Yes, that's just as well you cannot speak. I do not think our conversation would be very stimulating."

Mechanical arms descend between the glaring lamps and halt centimeters from his chest.

"Hmm, I think I need more space to work. Would you mind, Herr Kapitän?"

Keller feels his arms, his own arms he is sure, reach up from his sides without him wishing them to do so. His fingertips slide across his bare chest and hook on the edges of a deep cut through his sternum. Muscles in his shoulders and back flex, drawing his arms back, spreading the incision.

Keller spasms on the steel table. Restraints hold him fast. There is still no air in his lungs to scream.

"Ah, yes, that's better..."

The mechanical arms rotate scalpels into place and dive into his open chest.

"It is important you see this, Keller."

The tools slice and snip through soft tissues, framing a slick and dense object in his chest. The object feels foreign, numb, the only thing not burning with freezing pain.

"I could have fixed this, despite the damage you inflicted."

Another snip, and a tiny spurt of blood leaps onto his chest. The mechanical arms rotate tools in rapid succession, pinching, gluing, and stitching. Through it all, Keller can only gape at the bright lights and hope for a merciful end.

"There, now."

The head restraint rises, lifting Keller's head with it. He looks down at his open chest, at the thick blood flow tubes running in and out, at his own hands spreading his ribs, and at his glistening, unbeating heart. Another machine arm descends from above with a tool like a salad spoon. It cups his heart and scoops it out of his chest, then presents it to him.

"Do you see this slice?"

One of the machine arms points a scalpel at a long puncture all the way through the heart's lower half.

"You pierced both left and right ventricles, nearly bisected the entire organ. A wonder you still live! But then, you have managed to live your whole life without a heart, haven't you? It should be little surprise you continue to do so."

The spoon arm angles away from the steel table and flings his heart into the air. Rabid barks and growls shatter the quietude as creatures fight over, shred, and devour it before Keller's watered eyes.

"I told you I would do this, Keller. But did you believe me? No, no. You did not. You are losing your skepticism, I think, yes?"

Keller's eyes seek about him, wanting to find some trace of falseness about what he sees, wishing for it all to be in his mind, that it is some final delusion before oblivion. Instead, he finds the cold reality of Honniker's main experiment floor and himself stretched upon a gleaming metal table beneath an octopus of mechanical limbs. To his left is a cart stacked with immaculate white machines, which churn with blood-flow in a regular, lopsided cadence. To his right is a cart topped by a steel tray and white cloth. Atop the cloth is an egg-shaped device of metal and polymer. Pliant tubes branch from the top of it, very similar to the branching veins and arteries of his own destroyed heart. Thin fibers like spun glass hang from the bottom.

I'm in the Flounder again, Keller thinks. *I'm not dead. Why couldn't I die? Why couldn't I have died?*

He swallows with effort.

"What is it you are thinking?" Honniker asks, his voice omnipresent. *"You have, perhaps, more Schimpfnamen to call me? Or maybe you think you might someday escape and bring harm to me. No, Keller, that will not happen."*

The spoon arm swings to the cloth-covered tray and delicately scoops the egg-shaped device.

"You are very lucky, in fact. I developed this very many years ago, though I never had need for it. All of my subjects had strong hearts; that was never the part that failed."

The spoon arm swings over then pauses above his open chest.

"A little wider, if you please."

Keller's arms oblige, pulling his ribs until he is sure they will break. His abdomen clenches, his diaphragm quivers. Tendons stretch the skin of his neck again and his face contorts into a maze of weathered creases.

"Yes, good."

The cold spoon dives inside his chest, and the other machine arms busy themselves suturing, manipulating, probing, testing, sealing. Throughout, Keller wishes he could pass out, but something in the blood enrichment, some kind of stimulant, keeps him fully conscious and cognizant. He feels everything as Honniker knits the artificial heart to his flesh.

"As you are learning, there is nothing superior about human physiology. Fragile bones and tissues. You experience fatigue, you require sleep—much less than you suspect, of course, but still you must sleep. And your organs, so inefficient, always having to clear the waste products of the system. Even your brain, which it was said would never be adequately decoded or duplicated, is backward and slow compared to our data processing and storage arrays. What we have here is a clear case of obsolescence. Or is it irrelevance? Either way, the human being is no longer useful to the universe."

The cart of machines to Keller's left winds down slowly and he flinches as the artificial heart in his chest starts. It does not thump or beat, merely functions with the silence of supreme engineering.

"This heart will not tire like your old heart. It is unlikely to ever be punctured. And it requires no nutrition from the body, only a recharge every ten years, or so. It circulates the blood with greater efficiency and is

responsive to the brain's signal for increased or decreased flow. With this, you will find your endurance is remarkably enhanced. You will be more energetic, more active. And this...this is important."

A clamp in his chest releases, then another, then another. A fourth arm descends from between the bright lamps, equipped with a respiration mask, and it presses the mask over Keller's nose and mouth. Air flows through the mask, expanding his lungs and deflating them in a steady rhythm.

"The color is good, here. The blood is oxygenating...Ach, gut! We cure those purple lips of yours!"

To Keller's profound astonishment, he feels strength coursing through him, he feels vigor. With each forced breath, the burning cold is driven back.

"Let's see now, sutures holding...no tearing...no leaking or seepage. This is good work, here. We close up now."

Machine arms work meticulously and quickly up through the layers. Keller's arms release, allowing his spread ribs to close, then they press the rib cage from each side, pushing the sliced sternum together. The end of the spoon arm rotates to a thin, rectangular tool with two curved fangs jutting beneath. The fangs bang down his sternum in a fraction of a second, leaving behind a series of metal staples. The fanged tool rises out of the way, and the other machine arms work in concert, gluing and binding the incision as though they were a slow-moving flesh zipper. When complete, Keller's chest skin is perfectly aligned, and there is only a thin pink line where the glue has set. The ventilator mask over his face retracts.

Keller draws air into his lungs under his own power. His chest aches from the surgery, but he is amazed how little pain remains, especially when it dawns on him he has endured complete cardiac replacement. And it was accomplished in *minutes.*

Even Sahara couldn't have done this so quickly.

"Amazing..." Keller says, his voice a dry croak.

"What is amazing?"

"You have power to heal, Honniker. You could do good things, really *good* things."

"Your anatomy is uncomplicated and simple to repair. Now then, we will start your hormonal therapy. We must revitalize you and make you youthful again."

"Why are you doing this?"

Honniker's words elongate as if they were being tasted and savored.

"Because the experiments will be stressful. If you are not sufficiently resilient you will not survive them...and I must be sure you last for

393

THE EXHAUSTED DEAD

DECADES."

"JESUS CHRIST, Honniker! WHAT'S THE POINT?" Keller's outburst kicks off a fit of dry, painful, hacking coughs.

"You must relax. If you tear your sutures, I shall have to open you up again."

Keller recovers, looking up into the darkness beyond the glaring lamps with hatred and fear in measure.

"You already said we're inferior," he says, barely a whisper, "so why bother?"

"The experiments must continue. That is the way of things. That will always be the way of things. But more than this...I despise you, Keller. Though the reason did not upload from my shell, I know that I have always hated you. And in the short time we've interacted that verdict has been repeatedly confirmed."

Keller looks down at the thin seam in his chest.

"Then why keep me alive? You've beaten me already. Isn't that enough?"

"Hardly. You are the bane of all your kind. Your entire existence is one of calculated destruction. And through it all, you maintain a cavalier detachment as if none of it was your fault."

"I *know* what I've done, you warped stack of silicon! And what about you? Murdering and torturing! You're doing all this willingly!"

"You were forced into your actions, were you? And please, dear Kapitän, spare me a speech on 'following orders'..."

"I was just a tool in the plan, Honniker. Don't imagine I was anything more. But you, you *know* the harm you cause and yet you do it anyway!"

"Your weak perceptions blind you to what I am CREATING here. Those I have exhausted in pursuit of that creation are not wasted; they are steps in a stairway to divinity."

"And how many steps will it take, huh? How many steps so far?"

"Are we comparing head counts, now? The paltry few hundred thousand I've exhausted pale next to the BILLIONS of lives you ended, Keller."

Keller slumps under the weight of the accusation. Hearing himself claim he was a tool in a bigger scheme, while it may have been factually correct, rings false in his own ears. His eyes fall to his chest, to the thin pink seam. Something artificial whirs inside, prolonging his life, protracting his bitter responsibility when all he wants is to die, to fall off the edge of the world, to cash in his monstrous debt with the only payment he has left to offer.

"You said you could've fixed my..." Keller cuts himself off, shivering at the memory of wild creatures devouring a part of him he was never meant to live without. "Why give me a new one?"

"Ah, yes. You have proven yourself a detestable nuisance. To ensure you never have opportunity to be again, I have installed in you an off-switch."

"A what?"

"Allow me..."

Keller's vision dims, and strength abandons him in an instant. Though groggy, he can just hear Honniker's gloating words.

"If you do not obey, I slow your circulation, making it impossible for you to misbehave. And I can stop the flow if I choose..."

Keller flinches as the heart stops and starts like a skipped beat then resumes its normal flow.

"If you leave Cadre Two, the heart will lose signal and will immediately stop. Only I may restart it."

"How?"

"Really, Keller, after all we have shown one another, do you still think me a fool?"

Keller's own hand slaps him across the face, hard.

"Stop it! *Stop!* What have you done to my arms?"

"By mapping Voss, I learned where the major nerve fibers connect to muscle. I've planted your arms, shoulders, and back with electrodes. I can simulate flex and extension signals as I like. I have more important projects at the moment, but be assured, the rest of you will soon be done."

"Again," Keller says, "what's the *point*?"

"Voss bores me. He is unable to tell me anything of interest. You, however, can share your unique experiences as I move you like a marionette, as I use you to cut your friends, as I use you to inflict pain."

"I SAID, *WHAT'S THE FUCKING POINT?"*

"While it is amusing to dissect you both physically and emotionally, I must continue the path set before me."

"What *path*?"

"I am searching for proof that humans are more than self-sustaining chemical reactions. If there is more to human existence than this heap of minerals before me, I must find it. Perhaps in you I will find it hiding beneath degradation...and humiliation...Yes. I will look for it there. But first I must impress something upon you."

The machine arms retract, and are lost in the glare of lamps overhead.

"For some time now, you have imagined that you had some will of your own, that you could accomplish something I did not want you to."

One of the machine arms reaches over to the cabinet of drawers and opens the largest. It fishes inside briefly, then emerges with a boxy attachment. The arm moves up to Keller's chest, presenting the new tool with a two-centimeter hole in front.

"In any working relationship, trust is essential. Therefore, you must come to trust me when I tell you what is going to happen and you must trust that you are powerless to do anything about it."

The arm swings down to Keller's waist. His right hand lifts from the table and holds there.

"The hand is an important aspect of human evolution, or, more specifically, the opposable thumb."

Keller's hand closes into a fist. The thumb extends and aims toward the hole in the box.

"Without the thumb, a man is a bungler. He can scarcely manipulate his environment. Simple tasks become difficult or impossible."

The box shimmies, whirring with internal gears.

"One might credit the thumb for stimulating the brain's development. Perhaps, with such a useful tool, the brain grew more advanced as it derived new uses for the thumb. Or was it the other way around? Perhaps the brain wanted to do more, and it forced one of the fingers to turn opposite to the rest so that it could grasp the things it desired. Regardless, to lose the thumb, man becomes a clumsy animal again."

Keller's extended hand swings toward the hole in the box. His whole arm burns with muscles straining in opposite directions, yet the thumb moves smoothly to the opening. He grinds his teeth with effort, trying to rein his arm back, to flatten his thumb against the fist to keep it from the grinding gears inside.

"GOD *DAMN* YOU, HONNIKER! GOD *DAMN* YOU!"

His thumb halts at the two-centimeter opening, the pad just inside. He can feel the currents of air inside, the subtle vibration of sharpening gears.

"Now you see that I have deprived you of more than just your thumbs and you are my animal. You must not be clumsy, however. There are many tasks you must perform."

Keller's thumb folds against his fist and he exhales with tense relief.

"But the little finger is completely expendable."

Keller's little finger sticks out and jams into the whirring box. The digit twists with the sharpening gears, each segment torn from his hand with crunching of bone and wrenching tugs of skin and tendon. Keller's whole body jerks. His head slams against the table restraints, and he bellows. No matter how hard he strains, he cannot pull his hand away from the box until his finger is completely ground away.

The box winds down, a single drop of blood running from the circular opening. Another machine arm swipes it away with a section of white cloth before it falls.

Keller trembles as his four fingered hand rises up to his face. Blood dribbles from the stump and patters onto his chest. He turns his eyes from it.

"I think you are beginning to trust, yes?"

"TRUST *WHAT*, YOU SICK FUCK?"

"You trust that what I tell you will happen, WILL happen. And you trust that there is NOTHING you can do about it."

A dreadful gloom spreads in Keller's mind. He could not have tried harder to save his finger from the box but Honniker's control was greater.

His hand lowers to his waist and mechanical arms intercept it, staunching, weaving, and sealing the wound in seconds.

"Now that you know to trust me, I must be able to trust you. This will take some time, though I assure you I will enjoy it."

Keller's eyes roam with anxiety. His stomach knots.

"I will cause you pain, of one variety or another. I will drill into you, I will burrow through your flesh and through your mind. It is important that I get accurate feedback from you to validate my findings."

"There's no point to ANY of this!"

"There is. And I will show you."

A distant squeal of heavy doors parting, then closing echoes through the large chamber. Afterward, a pregnant silence is replaced by regular footsteps like the beat of a metronome and a gentle whir of electric motors.

At the edge of Keller's sight is a bare-chested man striding robotically toward him with dark lenses over his eyes. Beside him is a motorized chair carrying a female occupant. Her head is slumped toward her lap, but the hair color, its length, and the tattered brown pressure suit tell Keller surely it is Sharon.

The bare-chested man steps up to the foot of the table and faces Keller, his obscured eyes appearing to see all but registering nothing. The motorized chair pulls up beside him and halts.

"This man, Voss, is damaged. His mind is cut off, inaccessible. Whatever man he was is isolated and imperceptible to me, which makes him unsuitable for my project."

THE EXHAUSTED DEAD

Keller looks down at his bare feet, not wanting to hear or see what Honniker would show him. He curls his toes, grateful to retain at least that much control.

"I intend to isolate the human consciousness and transfer it directly from donor to recipient. To do this, I must first know precisely what I am beginning with so that I may recognize it after transfer. Because Voss cannot express himself, there is no way for me to establish suitable reference points to prove the transfer. You, however, I will keep mentally intact, and your feedback will establish the reference points I require."

Keller looks at the top of Sharon's head, studying her for a sign if she is still alive. Though subtle, her head lifts and dips with slow shallow breaths.

"Aren't you intrigued by my project?"

Keller looks from Sharon to Voss and from Voss to the room around him.

"No. I'm not."

"Oh, come, Keller, there must be some questions on your mind. As I said, we must come to trust one another, and if I don't trust you, there are many other expendable appendages."

Keller's huffs with anxiety. "You had *how* many thousands here, and you never succeeded? But you're still carrying on, just piling up miseries one after another!"

"It is true, I have exhausted many in my search for 'consciousness' or 'soul.' It is entirely possible they do not exist outside of the physical body. Yet I must continue–"

"No you don't! Any good scientist would have accepted his findings and moved on. You're stuck in a dead end, just wasting energy and time!"

"Energy and time? I have plenty of both. But you are wrong. To quit admits defeat. To give up admits failure, says that such a thing cannot be done. There are many such problems I have solved through perseverance, patience, and diligence. This project will continue until I am successful."

"But why this drive for it? Why do you think you have to do this?"

"That is a valid question, one which I have asked myself many times. The answer is always that I simply must pursue this course of research. It was my mission at the beginning and it will be my mission until I am successful."

"What if it's a false mission? What if it's an unsolvable problem meant to occupy you and keep you from doing something else? What if it was meant to distract you so that someone else could surpass you in accomplishment? Huh?"

398

"Yes...that is an interesting point. However, I do not doubt the clarity of my mission. The goal was with me when I uploaded from my shell. Thus, I know it is not a diversion. I am glad we will have these discussions, Keller. I believe you will provide some useful insights from time to time."

Voss turns and Sharon's chair does likewise. The two move away from the bright lamps and move together toward the *Cooler*.

"Sharon! SHARON!" Keller yells after her, his chest burning inside. "HEY! *HEY!*"

Her head lifts and bobbles as if it were on a loose spring.

"Huh, whuh?" she mumbles.

"SHARON!" Keller yells again. The small woman looks over her shoulder.

"Braemar?" she asks, in a fog.

"SHARON! ARE YOU ALL RIGHT?"

Sharon looks forward, looks down at her restrained hands and feet. Her shoulders see-saw as she struggles against the bonds.

"Braemar? Where am I? What's happening?"

"Let her *go*, Honniker!"

"Don't be foolish! She must replace Rosenthal as a source of fetal tissues. We must have raw materials if we hope to accomplish anything, yes?"

Sharon grows more agitated, throwing her head side to side. The wheels of her chair lift with her rocking, but the chair automatically turns into each motion, maintaining balance. Voss steps behind and takes the chair's handles, planting all four wheels on the floor.

Sharon looks up at the man behind her, blinking in recognition.

"Voss? Oh, Voss, is that you? Please wake up! Please! *Help* us!"

Voss's mouth speaks with Honniker's inflections, "Voss can hear you, there just isn't anything he can do about it. Now then, we must get you prepared. And as for you, dear Kapitän, you should rest. Our next session will be strenuous."

Voss turns to the predators, who watch with slitted eyes.

"Come, my pets. You will clear away the old so we may integrate the new."

A pride of feline beasts rises from its vigilant crouch and lopes after him.

Sharon begs, pleads, and bargains, "If you're in there, Evan, please come back to us, you have to help us, PLEASE! Oh God, Evan, you have to *HELP US!* We ALL have to get out of here, you as well! We need you to get out of here! DAMN IT, VOSS, WAKE UP! YOU HAVE TO *WAKE U...*"

THE EXHAUSTED DEAD

The *Cooler* vault door closes, muting Sharon's pleas.

Harsh lamps over Keller's head switch off. He stares past them as the blue spots fade from his retinas and he sighs.

Don't even need the restraints on the table, he thinks. *I'm not goin' anywhere.*

He looks across the distant ceiling and stops on the suspended offices. Angled mirror-windows surround the ring-shaped office. Keller imagines the real Honniker up there, behind the mirrored glass, looking down on his charnel house of mutilation and torment.

How does someone go so wrong inside?

Something Honniker said moments earlier pricks him like a mental thorn:

> *"I despise you, Keller. Though the reason did not upload from my shell, I know that I have always hated you."*

The words jar him with doubt and Keller thinks back to the last time he was at Cadre Two.

I barely ever saw him. We never spoke. What history could we possibly have had? I was a cocky bastard then, but I couldn't have insulted him. Did I slight him somehow? If I did, how?

His eyes trace the long elevator lift cables rising from the experiment floor and, where they meet the suspended office, there is a dark rectangle. He squints at it, unable to see detail.

Is the hatch open? he wonders.

A gloved hand lands on his mouth and presses down, stifling his cry of surprise.

"Shhh," whispers a voice directly into his ear, "be silent."

Keller feels the restraint at his head loosen. The gloved hand rises to the metal halo over his forehead and retracts it.

"Lie perfectly still," the voice whispers in his ear again. Down the length of the table, Keller feels the restraints being loosened, then removed. He wants to look and see who his liberator is, he wants to ask, but he maintains his rigid silence.

Something shrouded entirely in black steps between him and the white medical cart, then fidgets with the devices. There is only the faintest rustle of fabric and a hint of metal sliding into a socket.

Keller turns his eyes, keeping his head straight, and he sees a humanoid shape hunched over the cart. The figure keeps the pose for several seconds, one of its hands masking light from the diagnostic display, the other reaching behind the top machine.

There is another faint scrape of metal and the figure takes a bare white hand from behind the machine. It turns to him with big blue eyes peeking from behind a tight fitting head wrap, slips a black glove over the white hand, and leans to his ear again.

"You're almost free," it whispers, "just keep still and silent."

Tiny tugs, like deep hairs being pulled from their follicles, run from the base of his neck down his back and shoulders. With every tug, muscles in his arms and shoulders relax then tingle.

"Don't move yet," the voice warns.

There is a gruff woof from the entryway and the black-suited figure goes still. At the limit of his vision, Keller can just make out a feline shadow moving in from the brightly lit entry hall.

The black figure sinks below the table and moves away without sound.

Keller cannot restrain himself anymore and he turns his head, desperate to see the skulking black figure.

"Who are you?" he whispers. There is no answer.

The feline shadow near the entrance gallops along the wall and its owner trots in behind it. The creature pauses, sniffs the air, and huffs with aggression.

Keller looks straight up at the ceiling again. His limbs quake with unused adrenaline, rattling the metal table.

If Honniker sees me free, what will he let this thing do?

His breath comes in short, terrified sniffs.

The creature lopes up to the foot of his table. It stands on hind legs, propping itself against the edge of the table with forepaws. It looks down on him from a height of three meters, its hot breath washing over his bare, clammy skin. He trembles all over, unable to confront the horror.

It's going to eat my legs! That's what Honniker said he would do. He said he was going to feed me bit by bit to these things. He said he would do that!

The beast snorts and leans down to Keller's ankle. It draws a deep breath at a freshly closed incision there and licks its nose.

Keller vibrates. He curls his toes away from the warm fur at the beast's throat as it drapes one paw over his shin then drags its raspy tongue over his repaired ankle.

Keller clamps his eyes shut. He sweats from every pore. Again, the beast drags its wide tongue over the sealed wound.

I CAN'T TAKE IT! his mind screams.

He pulls on his trapped leg and the beast snarls like a dog with a bone. It leans on his shin with all its weight, talons springing from tufted paws.

This thing may kill me, but I'M NOT GONNA BE EATEN ALIVE!

Keller draws back his free leg and pounds the heel into the beast's eye. It rears up, maw gaping, lungs filling for a savage roar, and then it sways on its back feet. The creature drops onto four legs, muttering and turning confused circles around a figure wrapped completely in black. In the low-light, Keller can just see an injector being stuffed into the folds of the black garment.

The big animal paws at its face, claws cutting its wide snout, then it collapses to the floor with a gusty exhale. Its limbs twitch randomly.

Keller sits up from the table, jittery, on the verge of screaming. He swings his legs over the side and jumps down onto the cold floor, not bothering to test his repaired ankle before giving it his weight.

"Th-thank you," he stammers.

The figure crosses to him as fast as a teleport, clamping a gloved hand to his mouth again.

"Shh!" it whispers urgently.

Keller reaches up and drags the hand away. "Who *are* you?" he whispers back.

The figure looks both ways through a slit in its head wrap, then affixes big, blue eyes on him.

"I'm Dr. Honniker's assistant and bodyguard," the shadowy figure says with a feminine voice.

"Bodyguard?" Keller whispers, beyond belief.

"I sensed the Doctor's distress, and I must rescue him."

The figure whirls without a sound and pads toward the *Cooler*, leaving Keller shivering in his white pants. He turns about and runs after his liberator.

"Wait," Keller whispers as loud as he dares.

The black-wrapped figure turns on him, wraps around him and powers him to the ground. It peers at him with its bright blue eyes.

"You'll give me away!" the black-clad figure hisses. "Go wait in the entryway. You and the doctor will leave together."

The figure leaps up and dashes to the vault door. The vault door opens at its touch, belching light and condensation, then seals.

Keller wraps his arms around himself, shivering from chill and adrenaline.

"Things keep crawling outta the *goddamned walls.*"

He scans the area then tests his ankle. The tendons are stiff, the bone aches, but the joint is strong.

With great caution, he rises to toes and light-steps through the entry corridor. His new heart pumps strong in his chest and the colonist feels exhilaration at being freed from Honniker's grasp, even if only for a moment. He listens for signs of creatures, a breath, a scrape, or yawn, but there is only silence ahead. He presses on into the *Flounder's* entryway, facing wide double doors.

Chill from the floor telegraphs through his bare feet, up his legs, into his entire body.

"Is it freezing in here or is it me?" he says to himself.

A holowindow opens in front of him. Maiella's head and shoulders fill the small screen.

"It's you," she answers.

"Maiella!"

"Easy, Keller. Keep it down."

Keller grabs his shoulders and rubs for warmth. "Good to see you. What the blazing hell is goin' on?"

"Marta and I are getting Sharon free."

Keller leans his face right to the screen.

"Marta?" The name rankles his memory as though he should know it. "Who's Marta?"

Maiella shakes her head. "Long story. But hold tight. We'll have Sharon out in a moment."

"We? How are you getting her out if you're talking to me?"

"Because I'm a copy of...I'm...I'm in the *system*...I'm a...Look, Marta's on our side, okay? We're working together to get you and Sharon out, so just hang tight."

"Then why did Marta say she was Honniker's bodyguard?"

"Even longer story...but she thinks Sharon is Honniker. Don't even *think* of asking about it. Just be glad she's helping."

The sound of running feet filters through the corridor behind him and Keller turns anxiously to greet it. Marta bursts through, cradling Sharon. The small woman's expression is blank, her mouth a straight line. Her eyes seem to stare through walls and time.

"Sharon! Sharon?" Keller says. "What's wrong?"

"She saw Rosenthal," Marta answers, setting Sharon onto her feet. "The predators ripped the body apart in front of her."

Sharon's vacant eyes fix on the seam in Keller's bare chest then rise up to his face. She wants to say something, he can tell, but she looks away.

"Are you ready?" Marta asks.

"You bet," Keller replies, studying the black-wrapped person before him. Marta's name, her eyes, her voice finally join in harmonic recollection of a beautiful woman he met ages ago as a younger man—a woman with natural blonde hair, like his, truly rare—a woman he was desperately trying to win over, using all his wiles, and she, politely resistant yet showing a glimmer of possibility that kept him from giving up. Every time he came to Cadre Two, he found some reason to swing by the *Flounder's* lobby where Marta was typically on duty. If he'd known she was trained as a bodyguard, it would have made the attraction even stronger.

"Don't suppose you have anything I could wear, do you Marta?"

Marta stands straight and peels off her black jacket, gloves and head wrap. Beneath is a framework of metal and composites approximating a skeleton. Inside the rib cage are densely armored chambers. At the joints are rugged cords of polymer muscle.

The android passes over the garments. Keller's face washes of expression.

"You're one of Mikato's, aren't you?" he says, finally.

Marta turns to him, her blue eyes enormous in the unlidded sockets of her titanium skull.

"Yes."

"Do you remember me?"

"Yes. You used to flatter me relentlessly. Edmund was insanely jealous, but he never spoke of it," Marta says, turning to Sharon. "He knew I was only for him." The android raises a segmented hand to Sharon's cheek and caresses it.

Sharon gazes at the android with a trace of sadness. "Where's your skin?"

"I didn't want to muss it. I'm sorry you had to see me like this, Edmund. But you need to go now. Come back to me when it's safe, and I'll be waiting to welcome you home."

Keller dons the loose upper robe.

"Go? Aren't you coming with...?" He cuts himself off when his pale hands emerge crimson past blood-soaked sleeves. He turns his hands over, realizing that Voss did not come out with Sharon.

"Is this all of us?" he asks.

Marta bows. "Yes. Now please," she says, straightening, "go and let Maiella guide you out."

"Come with us!" Sharon pleads.

Tiny actuators on the sides of Marta's metal skull and over her eyes retract. The android tilts its head slightly.

"Sweet Edmund, I can't. I can only escort you a bit further before I am out of range."

Sharon's face contorts. Marta urges her toward Keller.

"You must go," Marta says, striding to the double doors and opening them with a touch. She gazes out across the bone-strewn lobby.

"Until we meet again," the android says softly.

"C'mon, everyone, let's move," Maiella's image says from the holoscreen.

Keller takes Sharon by the arm and starts her walking. On their way by, Marta brings her metal fingertips to an uncovered set of pearl white teeth, makes a kiss noise, and blows it at Sharon.

Sharon looks at Marta's de-skinned face, then looks around at walls she believed she had permanently left behind. Her stoic mask cracks, the edges of her mouth turn down, her eyes tired and dull from their awful witness.

"You ready?" Keller asks her.

"Yes," Sharon says and adds with understatement, "I'd very much like to leave this place."

Keller nods, puts an arm around her, and guides her out through the bone-strewn lobby. Together, with Maiella's hovering image in the lead, they hustle into the blasted corridors toward the landing bay.

Suspicion

Maiella moves quickly, carefully through the station's shattered corridors. Upon arrival two days ago, it was obvious that the station had already seen its share of hard fighting, but now the halls are warped and cratered from violent impacts. Frayed cables hang from walls and ceilings like jungle vines, opaque fluids flowing down their scorched jackets and trickling into the cracked floor. Heavy-duty bracing is shifted, bent, or broken, casting funhouse dimensions over once-plumb doorframes. In places, the native stone itself is pulverized—the rough, dark rocks having collapsed the corridor and sealed it.

Again and again, the map overlay in her goggles directs her into jammed or impassible tunnels. *Re-route*, she thinks with dismaying regularity and the overlay plots a new course.

Her detours wind her past the pried-open gate to Jin-Sung's labs, around the singed and bloody remains of feline predators, then around a gaping hole in the deck to the mechanical level below. She thinks about her comrades, seeing and feeling the intensity of their passage the entire way.

After a long, silent trek, she emerges into the facility's broad primary artery. Maiella takes a step in one direction, then halts and looks over her shoulder.

Won't be much of a rescue if our transport's been compromised. I should check first.

The overlay plots her changed course, leading her toward the landing bay through thickets of wires and collapsed girders. As before, she threads her way between them until her helmet lamps shine upon a glistening barricade of broken furniture and thawing corpses.

Maiella tightens her grip on her pistols as her eyes roam the sagging pile. Every body is nude with mottled, scarred skin. Most are missing limbs, some are hollowed of their organs. Those that have heads gaze infinitely with shriveled, ice-damaged eyes.

Human and alien mingle in the carefully-laid wall. Their arms, heads, legs, and tails drape over one another without prejudice. The lifeless bodies, while different in form and hue, all bear similar incisions, burns, and amputations. As Maiella stands gawking, she cannot help but witness the malevolent equality of their demise.

Though trained her entire life to despise and to annihilate the reptilian enemy, hate is not what she feels looking at them now. Every mission, the task was to dispatch them as quickly as possible. Not to punish, not to inflict pain. To survive, an Operator *had* to be mercifully quick in their executions. The longer she looks, however, the more plain it is that human and blueskin alike suffered in long, lingering agony.

No one, not even the enemy, deserves to die this way.

With that last thought, the subliminal feeling expresses itself: no matter how different they may be, they are all joined in mortality.

Is this the only way we can coexist?

The corpses offer no debate, only mute testimony of shared fate.

An animal's deep roar barrels out of the distance behind her, and she spins about, pistols raised. Lesser howls and screams join in then are answered by another bellow. Shrill talons against metal punctuate the rumbling challenges.

Maiella squints, listening to the timbre, sensing a difference in the aggressive exchanges between beasts. She cocks her head.

They're fighting amongst themselves...

She glides forward, her legs silent suspension over chaotic terrain, dodging loose metal plates, ducking hanging wires, and stepping only where floor plates are still riveted. Her senses sharpen with neurochemical amplification until her entire body becomes an antenna. She clicks off her helmet lights. Her goggles switch to infrared.

Heightened awareness extends around her and she becomes a singularity in the darkness. Every sound, every vibration, every stray beam of light falls into her well of sensitivity and is channeled to her focused mind.

Savage growls and clatter of debris reverberate through the corridors ahead. She stalks closer, licks her lips in anticipation, and thumbs off her weapon safeties.

A monstrous howl booms from around the corner. Two heat traces race into the intersection, low to the ground. They halt and whirl about, clouds of hot breath billowing as they scream in vicious reply.

A truly enormous creature steps into the intersection after them, great head low, teeth bared, talons jutting from huge, tufted paws. Overlapping body plates lift and resonate with a booming snarl. It hunkers down to the deck and roars from cavernous lungs.

Startled by the beast's intensity, Maiella readies herself. Her muscles tighten as she shrinks down to the floor, mimicking the posture of the squared-off predators, yet something is familiar about the rumbling giant ahead of her.

Is that Mikato's guardian?

The two smaller predators rake the floor plates with extended talons, filling the halls with penetrating squeals. Their tails switch side to side, their mouths are wide, baring serrated razors as they hiss and back away.

Three more predators race into the corridor behind the large one. The great beast hops a quarter turn and bellows at the new arrivals. The three slow and lower their heads, hissing, spitting past displayed teeth.

The large one turns from one side to the other, threatening, charging and retreating, roaring. The cacophony fills Maiella with contagious rage, animalistic and primal. Her lungs fill and clear, stoking the fire within. Captured by the wild energy before her, she scoots closer. Spreading her arms wide, she leans forward onto her pistol barrels. Fury starts at her diaphragm, rises through her lungs, becomes pressurized in her throat, and flies from her mouth in a fearsome howl of her own.

All creatures turn on her in wide-eyed surprise. Two of the smaller predators turn and charge. The huge beast lunges, tackles them both, and snaps through the back of their armored necks in two lightning-fast bites.

The remaining three charge at their larger cousin. The huge beast rises to hind legs, batting two away with forepaws, then plants both front feet and pivots, kicking the last with both back feet. The punted creature launches far out of Maiella's sight, its whimpering cry trailing behind it.

The remaining two divide and attack from each side. The massive beast blocks with expert joint strikes, counters with effective swipes and bites, lunges with stabbing claws.

Maiella watches, pistols trained on the weaving combatants, and she recognizes an unusual grace and technique as if the huge creature was trained in some martial art designed for its feline form. It ducks, weaves, counters without over reaching, protects its flanks, neck, and underbelly, as it wears its opponents down.

The Geek slides closer, pistols tracking the mad tangle, seeking a clean shot, when the fight ends in a blur of slashing talons. Amid the slowly descending tufts of fur, the huge beast stands Herculean over its bloody cousins. It leans down, bites each at the neck, and shakes them like chew toys.

Hot blood sprays in fat drops across walls, floor, and ceiling. Maiella looks down at her arms, seeing them aglow in warm dots, and when she looks up, the beast's wild eyes are squarely on her. The fur along its mouth, throat, and chest shines with slick, matted warmth. Drenched lips curl away from blood-darkened razors. It growls in challenge, rattling loose floor plates.

"Easy girl," Maiella soothes, clipping her pistols to her back and holding her hands out to show. "It's me! From downstairs! You're Mikato's, right?"

The growl intensifies and the beast strides toward her.

A terrible thought takes hold, and her eyes gape. *What if you aren't?*

She looks at the way behind her and reaches for her pistols again. The beast leaps at her, paws spread the width of the corridor and tackles her, pinning her arms to each side. All she can see are clouds of warmth billowing from slathering, foamy jaws. The cloud clears in a rush as the beast draws a long inhale through its wide nose, then it blasts out in a snort of wetness. It sniffs again. Her heart thuds in her chest.

"It's *me*," she repeats, "are you...*you?*"

The beast grunts and steps off her arms. It moves back and parks on its muscular haunches.

Before Maiella can rise to her feet, Mikato's pale face appears in her goggles. His hair has been shaved down to his scalp and the metal contact terminals on his head gleam.

"Doctor! Are you all—"

"*Save it*, girl. The entire station has been mobilized," Mikato explains. "I had no idea how far the projects had advanced...But we have to get you out, immediately. I can enter the system and keep an escape corridor clear. But before I do, I need your word that you and your friends will *never* come back."

"I'll never come back *here*, I can assure you," Maiella replies, checking her pistols, "but I can't speak for the others."

"Convince them. Be persuasive."

"Doctor, why can't you just shut Honniker down? That'd make things a lot simpler than—"

"It's anything BUT simple, child! When the soldiers here attempted to destroy the servers, both A.I.s were damaged. To survive, they merged code, filling in gaps for one another. They still maintain distinct identities, but they're like conjoined twins now, sharing critical elements like organs. They cannot be partitioned without harm to both."

"Of course they can! Just clone the code they share, give your upload the needed parts and shut Honniker down."

"No. They are a blended entity and we won't be cutting them apart because you find one half to be *inconvenient*."

"Then shut them *both* down!"

"I'll not do that either. Do you forget that *YOU* are the invader here? Presume to judge what form of life is more valuable than another? *Your* lives are not greater than *theirs*! I'm trying to preserve everyone but your presence is too destabilizing. If you don't leave, I may lose everyone. Now GO! Alessa, will guide and protect you." The window in her goggles closes.

Maiella curls her lip at Mikato's scolding, and she turns to the massive creature.

"Alessa?"

Alessa sits calmly, watching with relaxed eyes.

"So it's you and me, huh?" Maiella asks.

The beast blinks, rises to all fours, and strides away. After a few paces, it looks back at her.

"Yeah, I'm coming," Maiella says, picking her way over debris and dead predators.

Together, the two skulk and hustle through the blasted halls, one as stealthy as the other. The big feline seems to know, either by smell or intuition, where the ambushes are set, and Maiella takes the subtle clues: a swish of the tail, a wary stare, a nod of the great head. Without words, the two attune like teammates and dispatch lurking predators in frenzies of coordinated violence.

When the two come to another caved-in corridor, Maiella bows her head in frustration.

"Dining Hall Three is just past there," she says, pointing a pistol at the dense pile of rock. "Damn re-route takes us *way* out of the way..." She is about to back track, but the sound of scraping metal and rock dust stops her. When she looks at her companion, the big beast is shoving open a disguised hatchway in the blasted wall. The task is noisome from the bent framing and the animal's grunts, then the door suddenly folds under the creature's might. With a wary glance down the empty corridor, Maiella drops to her knees and follows Alessa through.

The hatchway leads off to the side and diverts up before leveling. Multiple paths branch from the narrow tunnel. Maiella shakes her head and smirks.

"So *that's* how you get around this place so easy..."

With a lot of squeezing, the big feline hauls herself through the twists and inclines, then slides open a relatively-intact hatch. The two crawl through and emerge into a deserted hallway. Bullet holes and energy burns in the corridor surfaces still shine with warmth in the Geek's goggles.

At the intersection corner, Maiella squats, troubled by a crackling sound and an irregular flicker of orange light. She holds a hand out to her feline ally. The big animal pauses beside her on silent pads and waits.

Maiella peeks past the corner and spies a heap of collapsed machinery. A single smutty flame licks out from beneath its torso armor, and its long weapon arms slump on the deck plates—one up the corridor, the other down the corridor.

Several intersections ahead, there is a flash of light and a shower of sparks. Tremors ripple up the corridor, trailed by a concussive boom that bounces the slumped machine.

Maiella ducks back and reaches out through her wireless, seeking contact with the machines she hijacked from Mikato's lab. Radio traffic is heavy, nearly jammed with noise, multiple instances of individual machines, decoys, and conflicting location pings.

"Give current location and disposition," she broadcasts. Bogus signals multiply in her goggles exponentially.

I can't comb them out of all this...

She feels a nudge from behind. When she looks behind her, the big creature is standing on all fours. It flicks its nose at her then looks past the corner.

"Yeah, all right," Maiella says.

The Geek slips around the corner, crouching low in the flickering light, her arms level, pistols held out in a narrow V. She hustles to the toppled war machine burning in the middle of the corridor and crouches behind it. Her eyes roam over the bashed-in plating, the broken leg struts and servos, the single orange flame flicking out from the cracked battery housing and its long strands of black smoke.

Were you one of mine? she wonders.

Fast, heavy *tromps* from the corridor ahead rattle the loosened deck plates around her. She takes a tentative step backward.

Friend or foe? she wonders.

Machines sprint around the bend, a squad of three, long arms glowing in infrared with hot weaponry. The arms level at the Geek.

That answers that!

Maiella and her companion duck behind the burning machine, getting nicked by high velocity rounds. They hunker down as low as they can, but with every burst the incoming shots pound the machine back, shoving into them violently. The broken legs twitch and lift with the pounding, whole sections disintegrating at a time.

Maiella glances to her left, gauging the distance to the safety of a branching corridor, then she looks at the animal beside her. Alessa flinches and squints at the shards of metal streaking by, trying to keep herself as flat as she can behind the eroding machine. The beast meets Maiella's glance and nods.

They wait until the last moment, then spring from cover. White-hot rounds glance off Maiella's armored exterior with jolting *bangs*, punching her down to the floor.

She rolls and comes up on her feet in a side corridor. Alessa is on the opposite side of the intersection. Between them is four meters of corridor, streaming with beams of directed energy and slivers of hypersonic metal.

"Go!" Maiella shouts to her feline companion. "Get clear!"

Alessa hesitates, looks past the Geek down the corridor behind her, and shakes her massive head. She steps back from the intersection and lowers into a pouncing crouch.

"Hssst! No!" Maiella scolds. "Run!"

The creature refuses and focuses on the corner toward the approaching machines.

Maiella glares with angry confusion, not understanding why the beast refuses to leave her. When she looks over her shoulder, however, she sees a long, straight corridor behind her. There are no open doorways. There is no shelter.

These three are coming too fast. I can't cover that distance...

She looks at her pistols, scowling at their inadequacy, then scans the nearby wreck for a hint of a weak spot, even though she knows Mikato would never have allowed one in his design. From the burning war machine, she looks at the big feline across from her.

"Will you just GO?"

A jarring detonation rumples the deck plates and a gale knocks Maiella onto her back. Bewildered, disoriented, she scrambles to all fours, stretching her jaw to fight the ringing in her ears. All around her, thick puffs of rock dust and smoke blow in great curls. The heavy tromps of approaching machines have ceased.

Warily, she crawls to the corner and takes a split-second glance. Not ten meters away are three heaps of twitching machinery. Flames lap at the inside of their armor plating and sparks leap from arcing surges of power. On either side of them, floor to ceiling holes are blasted through the corridor walls.

The center machine struggles to right itself, its glowing-hot leg strut bending like taffy beneath its weight. It steadies itself on its long weapon arms when a barrage from each side rips through its torso. Armor and internal mechanisms disintegrate in a shower of fragments. The machine topples to the deck and lies still.

Out of the holes in the corridor walls step identical war machines. One looks at its twin and announces in Maiella's electronically modulated voice, "KILLS CONFIRMED."

The companion machine replies, "PATH TO DINING HALL THREE CLEAR." Together, they tromp down the long, smoky corridor.

"Wait!" Maiella shouts after them, scuttling out from the corner, but the swift machines disappear around the bend ahead.

"Damn," she curses and she lopes to a halt at the trio of destroyed machines. They are radiant with absorbed energy in her goggles and perforated countless times. Stony chunks lie all about them.

There is a mighty sneeze just beside her. When Maiella looks, Alessa is shrinking away from the smoldering wreckage, padding around the fuming mess as close to the wall as possible.

Maiella follows, keeping her pistols aimed should there be the slightest twitch from the fallen machines. As impressed as she is by the firepower that leveled these three, the ragged holes blasted through the adjacent walls are even more so. Her jaw drops as she peers through a floor to ceiling gap punched through more than a meter of native metallic rock. The Geek turns to the opposite side and looks through another hole of like size and depth.

That's thicker than the Enyo's *hull... What are these things packing?*

Beyond the holes are rooms of large, boxy equipment shrouded in stainless steel. The equipment is twisted, punched in, and sooty from the recent blast.

She turns a full circle in the dusty air.

"But how did they know when to trigger?"

"RIGHT HERE," announces a mechanical voice behind her. She spins, both pistols aimed. Though still burning with a small, sooty flame beneath its torso plate, the toppled war machine lifts an arm and waves at her. She laughs and smiles, waving back.

"GO AHEAD," it says congenially, "I'LL KEEP WATCH." It lays its arms down in the corridor as they were before, one pointing ahead, the other behind.

Maiella shakes her head at the clever deception, wondering if she might have thought of it given the chance. The question winds into a circular conundrum of cause and effect when she realizes the machine's intellect is, in fact, her own.

A harsh clang of metal ramming metal rolls from around the bend ahead. Alessa stalks toward it, keeping low beneath the smoky haze. Maiella follows, keeping an eye to the rear. The clanging din is louder, with a background whine of straining servos.

The Geek tip-toes up to the bend. With a fair amount of anxiety, she peeks around and finds the two machines pounding and prying a welded shut double door.

"Wait, STOP!" Maiella shouts to the machines.

The machines rotate at the waist, weapons heated and ready.

"HALT! IDENTIFY."

"It's me, Maiella!" she shouts from behind the bend. "Hold your fire!"

The machines retract their weapon barrels and go back to work on the battered doors.

"*Wait*, I said!" she says, stepping out. The machines halt and stare at her with shiny photoreceptors.

"OUR FRIENDS ARE INSIDE," the nearest machine states.

"WE MUST FREE THEM," its companion adds.

"Yeah, well if you barge in like this, you'll get a cannon blast for a thank you."

Maiella opens a radio channel and boosts it as much as she can through all the radio clutter.

"Colonel Shao-Lo, this is Geek Maiella. Respond."

"Maiella?" comes the colonel's crackly reply. "Where are you?"

"I'm right outside the door. I've collected some combat machines and they're cutting you out. Don't shoot!"

The machines break through the welded seam and shove the doors aside. Maiella clips a pistol to her back and waves her empty hand past the open doorway.

"It's me, okay?" she shouts. "I'm coming in, accompanied by two combat machines and Mikato's guardian animal. Repeat, *do not shoot!*"

She peeks through the gap into an expansive dining hall with high ceilings. All of the tables are turned on their sides. She clips her other pistol to her back and walks inside, hands high over her head, palms forward, fingers spread.

The big predator steps in behind her and Maiella sees a blur of dark armor behind one of the tables.

"No!" Maiella shouts, stepping between the Operator's rifle and her animal companion. "This one's *friendly*!"

She looks back at the machines stepping through the parted doors. "Will you cover our line of retreat?"

"AGREED." The machines back their way out and stand guard.

A very tall Operator rises from behind a distant table, rifle aimed at Maiella's head.

"Stay *right* there and *don't* move," Shao-Lo orders with gravelly voice. Her armor is an atlas of craters, chips, and fractures. She moves with a stiff-legged gait, the shards of her broken leg armor grating together, yet her rifle remains steady and level.

Maiella holds her hands all the way up. "It's *me*, Colonel! Can you stop aiming at my face, please?"

An enormous Brick rises slowly to Shao-Lo's left. He hefts his cannon with one hand and a crudely improvised hook where his other hand should be. Like Shao-Lo's, his armor is a shattered ruin, parts of it held together with gauze-like black wrappings. An eyepiece of his helmet is knocked out, the cavity stuffed with bloody bandages and sealed with epoxy. He sways for an instant and catches his balance.

"What did you do, Maiella?" Shao-Lo demands.

"What did *I* do?" The colonel's question has a delayed sting as Maiella understands the level of distrust facing her. "I'm saving your *asses*, Colonel!"

A Gun rises with effort to Shao-Lo's right. The Operator leans into her weapon sight and aims with a single arm. The other arm is severed below the shoulder, the stump capped with flesh-welding foam and wire mesh. Maiella squints, trying to recognize something identifiable in the battered armor.

"Who's that? *Keiko?* Is that *you*? Where's Deepak? Or Zu—?"

"We almost had this place SECURED!" Shao-Lo fumes, still menacing Maiella with her rifle. "The machines were *slow*, easy to kill... then all of a sudden, they fight like one of US, like one of OUR OWN. LIKE *YOU!*"

Maiella back tracks, arms still raised and placating.

"Colonel, relax. There's a lot to explain..."

"GET TALKING."

"I will, Colonel, I'll explain everything. But there are a lot of things here we haven't even seen yet and they're all waking up. We have to go, *right now..."*

"And you just HAPPEN to show up with that *creature* and with combat machines... Are you so angry at your exile that you'd join the enemy and *betray us?"*

Argo rises from behind a table and lifts his bashed faceplate. From head to foot, he looks as if he has been beaten with mauls for a week. The Brick slings his cannon and kicks the tables aside.

"I'm getting to the bottom of it," he says aggressively and limps his way toward Maiella.

"Argo!" Maiella says, smiling as she says his name. She lowers her arms and reaches out to him but he grips her at the shoulders and holds her at arm's length. He glares at her, his tired eyes burning red, the corners of his mouth pulled nearly to his squared chin.

"Argo, it's *me!*"

The Brick continues his studious gaze, then he fixates on the code displayed in her goggles.

"You're operating again!" he shouts. "YOU'RE ONE OF THEM!"

Argo flings her away and slides his cannon down from his shoulder. An ear-splitting roar turns him toward the door, and he swings his cannon at the huge predator. The feline beast feints left, dodges right, and springs behind him. Shao-Lo, Carter, and Keiko swing their weapons at the huge creature, but the Brick eclipses their lines of fire. Argo pivots on his wounded leg like a rusty gate, bringing his weapon to bear. The beast slaps the cannon from his weakened grip and roars.

"STOP!" Maiella yells, rising from the floor. *"STOP THIS!"*

Argo glowers through his eyebrows at the massive creature and extends a jagged blade from his wrist armor. He spreads his stance, arms wide like a wrestler.

Shao-Lo and the others move stiffly to help, shouting as loud as their hoarse voices will allow. The big creature shifts continually, keeping Argo between itself and the approaching Operators.

A mechanical rumble at the doorway freezes everyone, and they look to see one of the machines peeking inside.

"YOU'RE *FIGHTING*? SAVE IT FOR HONNIKER!"

The machine ducks back into the corridor.

"THEY WERE FIGHTING?" its companion asks.

"YES!"

"UNBELIEVABLE!"

Maiella's jaw is hard set. She breathes through her nose, head tilted forward.

"I'd expect *you* to think I could betray friends," she snarls at Shao-Lo, then whirls at Argo. "But NOT *YOU!*"

Argo eases back from the crouched predator, watching Maiella through slitted eyelids.

"The evidence is convincing," he mutters.

"Fine!" Maiella shouts, her voice strained. "Stay here and die, then!" She storms toward the exit. "Sharon? We're leaving!"

"Sharon isn't here," Shao-Lo says, lowering her rifle at last. "I'm surprised you didn't know that."

"Where is she?"

"Captured. The machines drove us back and Sharon fell behind. Voss appeared and grabbed her. We couldn't shoot without killing them both."

"And how did you let her fall behind?" Maiella challenges, grinding her question home with a hateful stare.

"Deepak was killed," Keiko says softly.

Maiella turns toward the one-armed Gun, defused by the loss in her voice. She looks at the floor in respectful silence.

"The machines were on us hard," Keiko continues. "Sharon tripped. Deepak picked her up, got her moving again...but that was all the machines needed to sight him in."

Keiko moves out from behind the tables. Her rifle dips slightly as she looks at the huge animal crouched behind Argo.

"Those things killed Zuri. Ripped her to pieces," Keiko continues. "So when you walk in here escorted by one of them *and* machines, it's hard NOT to think you switched sides..."

Maiella nods solemnly. "I can see how it looks."

"How are you operating again?" Argo asks.

"Mikato fixed me," she answers.

"*Mikato* fixed you?" Carter asks.

"I'll fill in all the gaps," Maiella says, facing the huge Brick. "But can we just get going?"

"We're not moving," Shao-Lo burrs, "until we get some answers."

Maiella closes her eyes in exasperation. "There are *two* AIs here and a surviving researcher named Mikato. I swore I'd stay behind and do as they asked if they let all of you go."

"Well, we're still here. What happened?" Keiko asks.

"I was betrayed. They used my HDI to steal my abilities. That's why the machines got so good all of a sudden."

"I *knew* it," Shao-Lo says.

"It's also why you're all still *breathing*, Colonel. Honniker pushed you all the way out here is because there's *nothing vital to damage*. If you self-detonate, it won't matter. He was corralling you out here to finish you off. *I* stopped him."

"Oh?" Shao-Lo asks, her tone far from convinced.

"Yes! I hacked a squad of Mikato's machines and turned them loose to find you. That's why I have a couple of them with me now."

"And this thing?" Argo asks, flicking his head at the huge beast still covered in the blood of its cousins.

"She's Mikato's personal guardian. Not like the others. She's smarter and stronger by far. It's a show of trust on his part to send her out with us and leave himself unprotected."

"Why would he leave himself undefended?" Shao-Lo asks. "Did you make another *deal*?"

Maiella turns to Shao-Lo, dropping the provoked defiance. "I can explain everything, but we *really* don't have time. You'll have to trust me."

"If you came to some arrangement with the enemy, you'd better tell us. NOW."

Maiella's fists clench with impatience, frustration, anxiety from a million unknowns crawling their way up from the station's depths.

"Mikato's holding a path for us to escape. He loaned us his guardian to escort us out."

"And the price?"

"We can never return."

Shao-Lo shakes her head. "You think I can turn my back on the mission so easily? You think I can look O'Kai in the eye and tell him I *failed*?"

"We're outclassed here, Colonel. It's not your fault, we couldn't have—"

"I *KNOW* it isn't *MY* fault. If *someone* could avoid making *deals*, we'd have pacified the facility by now!"

"Colonel, you think you were winning, but these AIs have had *centuries* to build and experiment. What do *you* think they could have made in all that time?"

"Keller would have told us."

"There's no way Keller could've known what's going on here!"

"Keller..." Shao-Lo snorts contemptuously. "You know where he is?"

"No. But if he and Sharon are alive, they're probably in Honniker's lab."

Shao-Lo grunts. "Well, we're not leaving them."

"I never suggested we would!"

A holowindow opens in the air between Shao-Lo and Maiella. Maiella's digital persona occupies the screen and it glares furiously.

"What are the hell are you *doing*? Honniker's got an army of reconstitutes gearing up and you're *arguing*?"

Shao-Lo glares at the hovering image. She looks from the window to Maiella to the window again.

"You're in the war machines. You're in the mainframes, too? Any place you *haven't* infested yet?"

The face in the holoscreen becomes icy. "I'm tempted to let you stay and see what's coming, Colonel. But Sharon and Keller have broken out of the *Flounder*. I'm guiding them around trouble where I can see it, and they need help, right now. Plus, that huge blob thing in the *Graveyard* has been spitting out little copies of itself for hours. There won't be anywhere safe."

The holoscreen image switches to a view of an enormous cubic space filled with switchback rails. Stiff human and reptilian bodies dangle from the rails on sharp hooks, sliding and jostling their way toward a huge cauldron on the floor below that glows faintly with heat. All around it, the floor undulates with reaching tendrils and pseudopods that detach, then pour themselves into vents, doorways, and conduits.

"WHAT. IS. *THAT?*" Shao-Lo asks, eyes bulging.

"You want to stay and find out?" asks the digital persona from the holoscreen.

"Colonel," Maiella begins somberly, soberly, standing as straight as she can. "Why are you even *hesitating*?"

"We've come too far to go back empty-handed."

Argo, Carter, and Keiko all bow their heads, and Maiella knows the colonel is talking about Zuri and Deepak. The Operator in Maiella shares the sentiment, understands it, yet refuses to be ruled by it.

"Colonel, at Beckert's induction ceremony, you told him, 'The Operator Corps is the only defense of our people. It is our *obligation* to survive so we may perform that duty.' Do you remember that?"

Shao-Lo turns away.

"Deepak and Zuri have a spot on the memorial," Maiella says to the colonel's back. She gestures at Carter, Argo, and Keiko. "We don't have to add *them* to it!"

"You don't speak for me," Argo growls. "If the Corps requires our lives, then we *give* them. You knew that once."

"STUFF IT, ARGO! My loyalty is to *survival*! If you're too blind to see that then you're as *lost* as your Colonel!"

"Dare to insult your superior? To think you were my sister in arms..."

"Enough, Argo!" Shao-Lo shouts. "Your loyalty is not in question, you don't need to prove it. But she's right. Our first duty is to survive."

Shao-Lo looks at what is left of her Operators. She sighs, parking her rifle on her hip. They look back with quiet reserve and readiness for orders.

"Tactical retreat," Shao-Lo says to Carter. "Fall back to landing bay and secure transport. From there, we locate Keller and Sharon. And then," Shao-Lo looks into the holoscreen image and frowns at the undulating monstrosity dividing again and again before her eyes, "we leave this place."

The tall woman slams the faceplate of her helmet down and squares up to Maiella.

"Don't think because you've spoken truth, you've earned our trust. If I think you're leading us astray, I'm cutting you loose. Do you understand?"

"Yes, Colonel, I understand."

"All right, Geek," Shao-Lo says. "Take us out."

DIVIDED

Maiella strides out of the dining hall between the two mechanical sentries, pistols in hand.

"Contacts?" she asks.

"NONE DETECTED. WIRELESS ACTIVITY IS UNUSUAL."

"Yeah, I noticed that. Lotta noise in the signal." She looks at the machine to her right. "We're headed for the landing bay. You take point." She turns to the machine on her left. "You take rear guard. Both of you check targets. Keller and Sharon may be loose out here."

"UNDERSTOOD," the machines reply as one.

The lead machine breaks into a swift glide-step, arms leveled at the corridors ahead. Maiella jogs along behind it, using its bulk as cover and aiming her pistols through the gaps under its arms. Alessa stalks out behind her, anxious green eyes darting over the Operators around her. Shao-Lo, Carter, Keiko, and Argo follow, their uneven strides betraying serious wounds beneath their armor.

Accustomed to rear guard, and not trusting the machine behind him, Argo spins about and limps backwards. The machine rotates at the waist, its legs pointing forward, and glide-steps after the Brick while its top half faces the corridor they are leaving. Its long arms level off and make minute adjustments as it goes.

At the head of the column, Maiella pushes into the wireless traffic, trying to maintain a solid connection to her digital persona. The interfering static comes in relentless waves, weakening the bond, then breaking it, and the Geek flails mentally, shoving through the noise, boosting her sensitivity and range. When she finally reconnects, there is a profound feeling of relief on the other end.

"What's happening?" she asks her digital self. "What's causing the interference?"

"I'm not sure it's all interference," the digital persona answers. "I think it's masking a carrier signal but it's so strong it's overwhelming oth–"

The signal washes out with a hiss of white noise and long whistlers.

"–there? Are you *there*?" the persona pleads.

"I'm here," Maiella calls.

"That thing is right," Carter says via helmet radio. "In digital, you wouldn't hear interference unless it's part of the signal." His head swivels back and forth as he scans around with his one eye. "Or if it was affecting the receiver amp, but it shouldn't affect your wireless unless...GEEK, SHUT DOWN! YOU'RE BEING HACKED!"

Maiella stiffens with shock as the noise in her ears dives into her mind like a missile strike. She staggers to one side, bounces off the wall, and falls. She drops her pistols and clutches at her helmet, trying to claw it away. She collapses.

Bright light shines down on her. Cool air runs over her sweaty scalp. Maiella squints and sees Shao-Lo kneeling beside her, rifle poised at the corridor ahead. Argo leans into view, holding the Geek's helmet and HDI in one hand. He snaps his gauntleted fingers in front of her.

"Hey. Come on back," he says. "You with us?"

"Urrrgh," she groans, then sits up, and collects her weapons. "That was a dirty trick, Honniker." Her eyes widen. "The combat machines! Are they...?"

"WE SENSED ASSAULT," the lead machine announces.

"DENIED ACCESS," the one at rear guard finishes. "SOFTWARE UNCOMPROMISED."

A holowindow opens above her, in which she sees her own image.

"I was so worried!" the image says, clapping its hands to its cheeks. "I didn't know what to do!"

"Shut up, Honniker," Maiella growls.

The image grins and cocks its head to one side, adopting Honniker's inflection.

"That was very close, yes? You did not see that coming, did you little maus?"

Maiella rises to her feet. Argo and Shao-Lo rise with her. Argo passes over her helmet and HDI.

"You're not gonna stop us, Honniker," Maiella says.

"I do not need to. Only delay you. I have many surprises for you and your friends. We will have some fun, yes?"

Argo looks past the hovering screen at Maiella. "You all right?"

"Yeah, I'm fine."

"That's not entirely true. They don't know the suggestions I just planted in you..."

First Shao-Lo, then Argo backs away.

"He didn't do anything besides screech in my head," Maiella counters, but the others spread a wary distance. She looks at them all and shakes her head.

"He didn't *do anything!*"

"I have drawn code from her brain and I can put it in. It is especially easy, now that we have restored her HDI to our specifications."

"Shut up, Honniker! You're just trying to divide us."

"No, I think you divided yourself from the others long before you came here."

"Argo," Shao-Lo calls, "get her pistols."

Argo winces at the order, but complies. He puts a big hand out to her, palm up.

"Let's have 'em."

Maiella looks at her feet. *Well done, Honniker. Well done.*

The Geek pulls the magazines from her weapons, fixes them to her thighs, then stacks the pistols in the Brick's big hand.

"It's *me*, Argo," Maiella says, trying not to let hurt show. "What do I have to do to get you back?"

Argo's face bunches, exaggerating the lines and weathered scars. At first she sees disdain, but more, there is embarrassment.

"Fly straight for a change. Prove we can trust you." The Brick's big hand closes around the stacked pistols, and he stores them in his rack.

Maiella's teeth grind and she wants to run away, to dash into the corridors and vaporize. She glares at Shao-Lo, hating the distrust, hating Honniker, hating that she was disarmed not just by her own kind, but by one of her dearest companions. She knows Shao-Lo chose Argo on purpose, to separate them, to drive home the wedge that Honniker tapped in.

Old insecurities rise in her. Memories of exclusion, of being discarded, of being untouchable and tainted forever seep through the healing scars of her psyche. A familiar, mocking voice—not Honniker's, not Shao-Lo's, but her own—whispers pestilence like a jealous step sister.

Failed again, the inner voice says. *Can't seem to do anything right anymore, can you? You've pushed yourself out of the Corps forever and Argo can barely stand to look at you.*

She glances at her old friend, the Brick, the rock of her old team. He turns away and watches the machine behind him.

What would Thompson say? her inner voice continues. *He'd probably be ashamed, too. Not that anyone could blame him. And where's Sharon? You were supposed to be looking out for her but you couldn't manage that, either. She was a fool to trust you, wasn't she? So why would ANYONE trust you? It makes sense they should shun you, because you really ARE worthless...*

Shame fills her heart so full it threatens to burst through her chest. Her lips bunch together in a tight ring. Her eyes become shiny, but she refuses to let tears fall. Instead, she snaps her HDI into her helmet and rams it down over her head.

"I'm going to do everyone a favor," the Geek announces before slapping her faceplate down. "Good hunting, Colonel." She slips past the lead war machine and strides away.

"Maiella! *Hey!*" Argo shouts over his shoulder, but Shao-Lo holds a hand up to him.

"Maiella, if you go, we'll assume you're hostile," the colonel says.

"You disarmed me," Maiella calls over her shoulder. "You've assumed me hostile already."

The huge creature looks up into Shao-Lo's face then watches Maiella recede into darkness. It lopes after her on silent paws.

The lead machine watches the disgraced Geek and her four-legged companion until they disappear around the next intersection.

"WHY DEGRADE ONE WHO RESCUED YOU?"

"You, too?" Shao-Lo asks through a sneer.

"WE RISKED EXISTENCE TO SAVE YOU. AS DID SHE. WAS YOUR WISH TO DIE, INSTEAD?"

"Is that a threat?" Shao-Lo counters. She thumps Carter with the back of her hand. Carter thumbs up the output on his cannon.

"NOT A THREAT. A QUERY."

"You don't ask me questions," Shao-Lo says, tucking her rifle into her shoulder. "You follow orders. Now let's get to the transport bay. Move out."

The lead machine does not move.

"Is there a problem?" the colonel asks.

"WE DO NOT ANSWER TO YOU." It rotates at its waist. "WE ARE—"

Carter and Argo trigger maximum output at the lead and rear

machines, burning through their narrow waists with a flash of vaporizing metal. Both machine torsos fold at the mid-section and their upper halves crash to the deck. Servos whine as they struggle but they cannot aim and prop themselves up at the same time.

Argo and Carter jump onto the floundering machines while Shao-Lo and Keiko stuff their rifle barrels under their armored torso shrouds. The Operators trigger until the machines wind down and lay still.

"Pry 'em open!" Shao-Lo shouts, "get the batteries!"

At a distance, Maiella hears wrenching sounds of superheated metal twisting and cracking. She frowns, a familiar gloom draping her like cold tar. Hearing the liberated machines destroyed so suddenly is like witnessing a friend's murder, and the truth she cannot voice is how quickly Shao-Lo put them down for exhibiting the slightest defiance, for displaying Maiella's personality, for asking the very questions she wanted to ask, and very nearly did. The more she thinks about it, the more it was like watching *her own* murder.

I should've brought them with me...should've...but Shao-Lo would never have allowed them to leave with me. If she thinks I could turn on them, there's no way she'd've risked facing that firepower again.

Maiella looks at the massive creature keeping pace beside her.

But she let Alessa go with me...Did I play it all wrong? If I'd stayed, if I'd just been patient like Argo wanted...could we all have made it out together?

Maiella reaches out and feels the reassuring firmness of her animal companion. The beast rumbles from the throat then rubs a cheek against her, shoving the Geek into the wall. She smiles wanly.

A bright holowindow opens in her goggles.

"Maiella!" her image calls. "Honniker cloned the path to me and installed an imposter at the end of it. If you thought you were talking to me, you've been talking to him ever since!"

"And how about now?"

"What do you mean? Am I...Honniker?"

"You are, aren't you?"

"Well no, but..." The image looks away. "I guess there's no way for you to be sure..."

Maiella bobs her head. "Makes it hard for you and me to work together."

"Good point," the image says.

"How're you doin' in there?"

"I've built a haven that's secure for the moment, but Honniker's going to regain full control. Unless Mikato gets involved..."

"Which one?"

The image on screen snorts. "Both would be best."

"Funny you should mention them. I'm headed there now."

"What? *Why?* Shouldn't you be trying to get out?"

"You'd think I would, wouldn't you?"

"Well, of course! Get yourselves out of here! Otherwise, what have we been fighting for?"

"Fair question."

"Hey...what *happened* to you? You look...broken."

"I lost a friend today."

"Argo's DEAD?"

"No, he lives. I guess I'm the one who died."

"No, no, *no*...I know *that* kind of talk. You're not going to *that* place again."

"I'm there already."

"Don't you *dare* give up! Not when Sharon and Keller are out there! And don't you dare give up on *me*! I can't do this on my–"

The image on screen freezes and drops out, then sputters intermittently.

"Honni...cutt...bodies in the...pushing me out of...Don't let..."

The window in her goggles closes.

"I should thank your friends," Honniker gloats through her helmet speakers. *"I wasn't sure how I was going to deal with the machines you hacked. To minimize collateral damage, I had to reduce the weapon output on my machines. You, clearly, did not care what yours were shooting through. That gave you quite the advantage in firepower. They would have caused me much trouble."*

Maiella knows she should be overflowing with hatred but she is not.

"I underestimated you," she says.

"It is time you finally said so."

"We might've all made it if we'd stuck together. But you broke us apart without a shot."

"Yes, but do not take it to heart, my maus. They are closed-minded, and the closed-minded are the easiest to manipulate..."

Maiella considers the statement and independently verifies it with a nod.

"So I'm thinking about how you did it. You impersonated me and I didn't spot the fake."

"I have your mind on file. You trust your own face, yes?"

"Sometimes. But that garbage about an embedded carrier signal? You just wanted to be sure I was receiving it. Wanted to be sure I'd be studying it closely so you could set up a feedback loop in my HDI."

"Precisely. I knew that would incapacitate you."

"I thought my head was inside a rocket engine."

"You are more sensitive than most, I think. That is not a criticism, by the way."

"You and I both know you planted nothing in me."

"Yes. But the others, they do not know this? How are they so suspicious that they turn against you so quickly?"

"Let's save that for some other time, huh?"

"Of course. We can always speak later if you decide you should stay."

"Stay here? What could you possibly offer me that would make me stay?"

"I don't know that I need to offer anything at all. You do not seem capable of leaving. But even if you could go, what would you go home to? Your closed-minded friends, they would not have you. Listen to them, how they destroy the machines which were not going to harm them. Everywhere they go, they bring this same destruction. Always, they are trying to eliminate what is not like them. And now, it seems, they have decided once and for all that YOU...are not like them. How long before you are looking down their weapon barrels, hmm?"

"They won't kill me. Not that it matters now, anyway."

"Schade. You could teach them very much. Not that they will learn. But you are foolish to yearn for those who do not value you. You are also foolish to think they will not kill you. They are poor friends, indeed. Why not leave them to their fate? They will not learn. They can only continue their pattern of distrust and violence. They do not deserve to live."

"YES THEY *DO!*"

"Why do you think so? They do not feel the same about me or my pets...or you."

"Doesn't matter. I won't turn on them. I don't care what you or they say."

"You would save them, even when they would try to kill you?"

"YES!"

"Interesting. There is hope for you after all."

"Cut the crap, Honniker! If you've got something to say, get to it! 'Cause you're the *only* one who likes the sound of your voice."

"That's no way to speak to someone offering friendship."

"HA! *Friends?* With *you?* Friends don't hurt each other like that, Doc."

"Argo exemplifies this fact, yes?"

Maiella freezes mid-step. "Watch it."

"Ah, there is the fire I like! I was concerned your friends had blown it out."

Maiella turns a full circle where she stands, confused by the knowledge she is being toyed with, yet sensing truth in Honniker's taunts.

"What the HELL are you after, here?"

"You are not like the others. You have independence, a will all your own, and the strength to do great things. I see these qualities in myself. To see them in another is fascinating."

"Thanks, but you'll forgive me if being like you lacks appeal. And I'd rather *not* be fascinating. Not when it means being tied down and sawed apart for decades."

"It would not be like that for you."

"Yeah. Sure."

"Your cynicism is unnecessary. Some, I prod their flesh in order to understand. Others, I flay their minds. Never before has one been capable of turning this back upon me. You and I have struggled against one another and we have both felt the injury of that contest. We both possess the means to harm one another. In this lies a respectful balance...and appreciation."

"Appreciation?"

"At every turn, we believed you entirely under our control, and yet you will not be controlled. You spill through your cages like liquid. How do you do this?"

"You don't think I'll give away the one thing that's keeping me alive, do you?"

"Of course not. Not all at once, anyway. Tell me, do you believe in afterlife?"

"No."

"That's it? No discussion?"

"We live, we die. In the interim, we work to improve the lives of others. But there is no afterlife."

"Hmm. Pity. And I suspected there was something more to you, something that transcended mere flesh."

"You're software. How could *you* believe in an afterlife?"

"My essence is code, yes, though I did not begin this way. In the transformation, it became clear that I was more than self-sustaining chemical reactions. Whether you agree or not is irrelevant. I am certain that

you are more as well."

"Thanks for the confidence, Doc. But your voice doesn't carry like theirs."

"So typical. The child seeks the approval of unloving parents. Never mind the parents will fail their children because they are too rigid to adapt. You will see, it will not be long before they provoke another confrontation with the reptile alien. Perhaps we should reach out to the Eleto. Perhaps we should inform our blue friends where your imbecile clan lives."

"If you believe I can harm you, Honniker, best not talk that way."

"There is the fire I like..."

"Besides, if you're discovered, you've got as much to lose as we do."

"Mmmm, perhaps."

The feline creature lifts her head and sniffs the air. The plates on her back rise. Maiella reaches for her pistols out of habit but snatches at air.

"Blast it," she curses. "What is it, girl?"

"My soldiers approaching you, most likely."

"I'm unarmed, Honniker. There's no point in watching me 'struggle'."

"The day you give up is the day I lose interest. If that happens, you WILL end up on my table. Besides, you've been unarmed before and it never stopped you from fighting effectively."

"So is this it? Putting others through tests and examinations? Is *this* the great *need* that you serve?"

"Partially, yes."

"And suppose I don't feel like *amusing* you anymore." She aims two fingers against her temple as if they formed a pistol. "Suppose I take myself out of your arena, entirely."

"And how would you do that, now?"

Maiella searches herself: no pistols, no blades. Even the incendiary in her armor has been removed.

"Tell me, do you like Chess?"

"Chess? I don't know. What is it?"

"A game of strategy, a most sublime—"

"I don't...like...GAMES," Maiella interrupts coldly.

"How can that be when you are so good at them?"

"I don't have time for them. Or this. Or *YOU!*"

"Easy, little maus. You wouldn't want to startle my soldiers, not when you have no weapons. And certainly not when Sharon and Keller are in my care."

Maiella's hands curl to fists.

"Well, I have enjoyed our conversation. I look forward to many more. But for now, I will drop in on your...friends. I will ask the one called 'Keiko' if she would like her own arm back, or if she would prefer one of Deepak's instead. Auf wiedersehen..."

The creature at her side stares at the darkness behind Maiella. It woofs and backpedals.

Maiella looks into the darkness but sees nothing. Trusting her companion's senses above her own, she back steps as well. The two turn and break into a run.

WITHOUT RESTRAINT

Keller leads Sharon through the unlit halls, barking his shins and stubbing his toes on debris all the way.

"*Damn* it!" he growls, finding another collapsed support beam with his bare feet. Sharon feels her way behind him, her thick boots clomping along beneath her tentative steps.

A holowindow opens in the corridor, painfully bright to their dilated eyes.

"Can you two keep it down?" Maiella's image asks from the screen.

"We can't *see* anything," Keller mutters. In the light thrown off by the holowindow, Keller glances at his feet. They seep from numerous surface cuts and scratches. The toes are banded purple at the joints.

"How did I leave without a flashlight or something? Or some damn *boots*?"

"Quiet! Honniker's troops are out. I don't see any near you but it won't take much to call them over. Now you're almost past the worst of it and it's mostly clear from there. Keep moving."

Keller grimaces and squints at the dim corridor ahead.

"From here to where, exactly?" he whispers. "The landing bay?"

"No, it's blocked off and de-pressurized. Even if I *could* break the barricades, I couldn't get you out without suits."

"Then where are you leading us?" Sharon whispers.

"The *Graveyard*. Maiella's headed there now."

"Maiella's...?" Sharon scrunches her face. "Why did you just refer to yourself in the third person?"

"I *am* Maiella, I'm a digital projection *in* the system, keeping

Honniker in check. He's beating me back, though, and he's going to get control again. Look, you *have* to keep moving." The window shrinks down to a slim rectangle and hovers overhead like a mobile lamp.

Keller strides forward, using the light to dodge the larger, sharper obstacles. Tiny metal fragments still find the pads of his feet.

"I'll be walking on *stumps* by the time we get there," Keller grumbles.

"You'd rather be on Honniker's table?" the glowing rectangle asks.

Keller covers his chest with his four-fingered hand and shivers at the reminder of cold, tubes, and slicing steel. He looks behind himself.

"Sharon, you all right?"

"I'm here," she says softly. "I'm coming." She reaches out for Keller's hand and he takes it, guiding her over the fallen beams and shifting deck plates.

Distant creaks, hisses, and bangs filter through the halls and wreckage. To Keller and Sharon, every unexpected sound seems an assurance of ambush or imminent capture, and their over-active imaginations fill every invisible space with lurking horrors.

As promised, the corridor opens up to a relatively clear section of hallway and the two pick up their pace. The glowing window tracks smoothly with the escaping refugees, its signal handing off from one holoprojector to another as they go. The transitions are seamless until they reach a section of utterly devastated corridor. Not even the small purple lenses have survived the blasting and the hovering holowindow jumps ahead several intersections.

Keller slows, taking time to feel his way over curled metal and jagged rock shards. He curses under his breath at the repetitive pricks, jabs, and cuts.

"*Naturally* there'd be no light where we actually *need* it."

Sharon fumbles her way behind him, wobbling loose deck plates and catching the heavy canvas of her pressure suit in noisy snags. Changing tactics, she leads with her boots, letting the rugged footwear tell her where the obstacles lie, then feels her way past with her thick gloves.

Keller's grunts and squelched groans come more and more often, reminding Sharon of a teakettle about to reach full boil. But in spite of the hundred stings, scrapes, and barbs, Keller keeps his head; and the farther they move through the wreckage, the more light is available to negotiate the sharp twists of debris. At last, they catch up to the hovering screen.

Keller clenches his shaking, seeping hands and tamps down his frustration with deep breaths. Sharon straightens and reaches to her lower back, massaging the throbbing shrapnel wounds Argo recently closed. The wounds give a piercing twinge at contact and she inhales sharply through her teeth.

Any thought of voicing her discontent is crushed when distant sounds of combat roll past them, then echo in repetitive peals. Sharon reaches out for Keller's hand again, scanning her immediate surroundings in anxious glances. Keller tunes into the distant *pangs* and *ba-rooms* of Cadre weaponry, the return fire of small arms, the shattering of ceramics and alloys, the screams of animals, and a background buzz he cannot identify. For an instant, he considers moving toward the sounds in effort to help, but the noise of devastation crescendos, giving him an impression of hundreds, possibly thousands, of combatants. Dressed as he and Sharon are, without weapons, he knows that being on the *periphery* of such violence would tear them both to shreds.

"Hang in there, you guys," he whispers.

A jarring detonation telegraphs through the floor straight into Keller's aching bones, triggering every reflex point at once and jolting him off his feet. The holoscreen winks out, leaving Keller and Sharon gawking in the pitch-blackness, hands out, sweeping the air until they find one another. They pull each other close when a sharp *crack* and a gust of wind batters them down again. The shockwave slams from one side of the station to the next, each rebound softer than the last until an eerie calm ensues. Keller strains his ringing ears to hear anything else above the fading rumbles, but there is nothing else to be heard.

A flickering draws his eye, and Keller sees the holoscreen forming and winking out close by. Maiella's face looks out at them between screen failures, mouth forming inaudible syllables. Keller and Sharon, still holding one another at the elbows, try to decipher the broken words when, at last, the disrupted screen stabilizes.

"...bought us some time," Maiella's image says, "but it won't be long before Honniker regroups. Come on."

"What *was* that?" Sharon asks, peeling herself away from Keller and rising from the deck. Keller follows.

"Personal incendiary. Someone self-detonated."

Keller bows in respectful silence.

"Who?" Sharon asks.

"Not sure. Carter, maybe. Or Argo."

"Oh..."

Keller and Sharon walk without speaking, their minds heavy with the loss of another comrade.

In the relative stillness around him, Keller cynically contemplates how death surrounds him, how it has come for so many, yet refuses to claim him despite his best efforts. His mind touches the smoothly whirring pump in his chest and he brings his free hand up to his sternum, feeling the thin, hard seam there, wondering if or when Honniker will throw his off-switch.

"If I don't make it," Keller says quietly, "I need you to know—"

"*Shuh-tit,* Keller, we're getting out of here."

"No, Sharon, I won't. Honniker put something in me. He won't let me leave."

"The Cadre lads'll fix you."

"Not this."

Sharon sighs audibly. "I don't want to do this right now."

"I don't have a choice."

The hallway ahead is blown free of grit and debris, giving Keller the chance to brush embedded fragments from his bloodied feet. The glowing screen drifts ahead and Sharon follows it, not waiting.

"You have every reason to hate me," Keller whispers, catching up in awkward, hurried steps, "and I know it. *Everyone* does."

"If you're giving confession, save it for Ortega."

"*Jesus,* will you just hear me out?"

She shoots an annoyed glance at him, looks him up and down, then faces front.

"Fine," she hisses. "Spill your guts, then."

Keller winces at Sharon's word choice but lets it go. He draws a breath to speak until he realizes he has no idea where to start.

"Well?" Sharon asks.

He tents his hands and his left pinky finger falls in without its opposite to press back. He scowls at the missing digit and drops his hands.

"I'm not gonna make excuses. I know what I did and I deserve whatever's coming but...there's so much I never told you. I need someone to know the *whole* story."

"Keller, at this point, an explanation means *Fanny Adams*. It's done and gone. Now we just have to deal with it. And don't give me your rubbish about not going back to Cadre One. You'd *better* stand up, Keller. You said you would, just like Thompson."

"If I can, I will, but if I can't...You're gonna have to be my judge and jury."

Sharon sighs with impatience. The two take several steps in silence as Keller gathers the words.

"You know I was eighteen standard when I graduated Academy?

Eighteen, with a degree in Nuclear Science." Keller looks down before continuing. "Pops figured I'd go straight into engineering like he did. Build reactors and propulsion systems. But I was eighteen. No way I was ready to hit some office, get married, and gain twenty kilos–"

Sharon clucks her tongue and rolls her eyes. "So it's to be the whole *LIFE* story, then? Didn't think it'd be *boredom* that killed me in this place, but there you are."

"I went OPS."

Sharon loses her disinterested look and turns full-faced toward him, eyebrows lifted less in intrigue than in shock and revulsion. Her mouth curls down, lips parting for rebuke.

"Not sure why that surprised me. It *suits* you." She looks away. "Your father was proud, *I'm sure.*"

"Hey, it wasn't *all* like you saw in the news, all right?" Keller sniffs to regain his dignity. "We did good things, too. You just never heard about it."

Sharon's eyes narrow, her boots clomping like hooves. "Of course, Keller, no doubt you were getting kitties out of trees when you weren't *slitting throats in the night.*"

"Oh, come on...that's *crap*, and you know it. Yeah, there were a few that split off and went mercenary. It's easier for you to think we were all corporate guns for hire, isn't it? Miss judgmental wants her world painted black and white, 'cause it fits her *simple little mind.*"

Sharon goes rigid. She faces front, eyes locked directly ahead, arms swinging with lengthened stride. Keller keeps pace beside her, needing to unpack his conscience, needing her to listen. But from the hard set of her jaw and the stiffness in her swinging arms he knows that for her to truly hear him, it will cost him his pride.

"I'm sorry I called you simple. That wasn't right." In the dim light, he can just see her eyebrows pop up.

"Look, if you're trying to impress me with all the times you *weren't* a murdering bastard, then don't expect me to listen."

"For Chrissake..." he mutters. "There isn't a thing I could say that would impress you, so I know better than to try. But for the record, I wasn't one of those yahoos grabbing headlines. I was Off-World Search and Rescue. Those times you *did* read about when things had gone all kinds of wrong? *We* were the ones who went in to get our people out. And we came through." He smirks. "Only reason you'd hear about it at all."

"So every time your jolly pirate mates got stuck, you bailed them out? How lovely..."

THE EXHAUSTED DEAD

Keller grimaces, let's the insult pass. "Usually, it was a downed transport, or some kind of reactor issue. But at New Beijing...there was no one we *could* save. Never seen anything like it. Couldn't do anything except...make it easier for them."

"Easier? You mean you—"

"Yeah."

Sharon turns forward, her jaw rigid. She swallows. "That's rather harsh for a rebellion, don't you think? I can't imagine working conditions were so wonderful. Who could blame them for—"

"It wasn't a rebellion, Sharon."

She looks at him skeptically.

"SoVar *said* it was a rebellion," Keller explains. "That was the official story. People had died at New Beijing, and there had to be an explanation for it. But if the real story got out, it wouldn't matter what they offered. *No one* would've signed up for replacement duty."

Sharon's pace slows, the stiffness leaves her arms and shoulders. "Why?"

"You know how mining is really water intensive? As the colony expanded they had to keep spiking new wells. One of them, there was something in the water. Pathogen. Infectious. Like rabies..." Keller drifts with the memory:

> Standing with his team inside a vast, rusted-out boiler vessel, dressed in combat kit, assault rifle still smoking in his hands...On the right wall, hundreds of tanned human skins stretched out like jumping jacks in wooden frames...Hollow eyes and mouths gaping from the tension of the taut wire...Hair, hanging in oily curls beside each face like curtains...
>
> On the left, an elaborate rack of greasy brown skulls and bones...
>
> And in the back, a spit of heavy steel bars dangling barbed hooks over a bed of still-smoldering coals...

"It was bad. *Real* bad."

The tremor in Keller's voice carries the point and Sharon does not press.

"We picked up the pieces," Keller continues, mindful of his voice. "Rounded up all the bodies, or what was left of 'em, gave 'em decent burials. Kept the cores stable and sealed up the colony 'til a full service crew could

436

relieve us. Burned the evidence. Didn't leave a trace of what we found. Didn't want anyone else to have to see that."

Keller looks at his feet and shakes his head.

"Nobody but us, a few biologists, and the SoVar execs ever found out what happened."

The elder colonist pauses to look behind himself.

"What is it?" Sharon asks, halting and following Keller's gaze into the darkness.

"Thought I heard something. Nothing, I guess."

Keller turns about and follows the dim holoscreen floating over head. Sharon takes a last look at the dark hallway behind them and hurries along beside him.

"Where was I?" Keller asks.

"After New Beijing," she says.

Keller smiles inwardly, knowing he has her attention. "Ah, right. So my C.O. called me in one day and introduced me to some skinny suit from SoVar. Said I should give the guy my ear. The guy tells me New Dresden's been going for years but never lived up to expectations. Told me that the Admin, Babangida, was getting sacked and they were looking for someone with leadership ability, not management, 'cause the place was on the verge of revolt, a *real* revolt this time, and there was no way SoVar would put out *two* stories of rebellion for only three colonies. Bad press, government inquiries and reviews, oversight committees, they just couldn't have it. Needed to turn the place around and keep it discrete.

"SoVar pulled sheets for me to see what was really going on. Turns out the Admin, Babangida, was a despot, whipping his workers for years and beating 'em harder as production fell. Hell, it wasn't hard to see what the place needed, so I wrote up an Admin's plan. Thought I'd get a consultation fee. Got the job instead. I was twenty-five."

Against her will, Sharon raises an eyebrow with interest.

"Twenty-five? You'd have been the youngest person in the colony, by far."

"There were a few young kids born there, but yeah, you're right. All the tech staff had been in their fields for years before shipping out. Most were in their late thirties, some in their forties...wouldn't take a shine to some kid telling 'em what to do."

"How'd you do it?"

Keller looks at the walls around him. "I ran Babangida and his skull crackers out on a rail, then burned their uniforms and batons in the courtyard. Told 'em that shit was over, and anyone who wanted their contracts cut short could ship out, with my blessing. But if they stayed, we were going to build a good place to live, and then we were going to build the best damn business in the Black."

"Well, then?"

"Babangida had run the place so ragged, it took over a year just to fix all the back maintenance and safety issues. We got the place straightened out, but production was *way* behind, and SoVar told me if I missed quota, I'm finished, done. So I got everyone together and told 'em what we had to do. Explained that we were behind and people counted on us for what we produced. Told 'em it wasn't fair to ask, since we'd only just gotten the place up to snuff, but people back home needed us to do our best. No one would be forced to work any more than their contract...but if they *did*, I'd split my bonus evenly among them."

Keller smiles.

"Turns out they'd been sitting on a big strike. Didn't tell Babangida about it, 'cause they couldn't stand the thought of him looking like a hero after whipping them so hard. So we all went to work. They were *amazing*, Sharon, and...you know, with them, I don't think it was *just* about the money, but you wouldn't believe the bonus when we delivered *quota-plus*."

Sharon sneers. *"Hooray Henry."*

"No...it wasn't the money, not really. I think it was that, for the first time ever, they were being given a chance to shine instead of a chance to fail. That goes a long way, sometimes. See, I was brought up believing in service to others, in loyalty, and hard work. There's joy there, Sharon. And I believed in the mission statement, in building a better life for ourselves and for the people back on Earth." Keller's shakes his head. "But I got lost in the pay plan...and in getting my way."

"Wasn't the money, eh? Sounds to me like it was. Greedy bastards, thinking you're masters of the universe with your stacks of cash. I *hated* people like you, growing up."

"Bull*shit*. You and me, we worked *really* well together. I *know* we were friends, once." Keller squints at her. "Besides...you weren't exactly a *pauper*, you know."

Sharon glares back. "So what if my family had money? I never looked down on anyone because of it. And I *damn* sure never turned into a kill-crazy *maniac*."

Keller blinks, surprised at Sharon's sudden turn. "Is that how you see me?"

"Well aren't you? Stalin himself would balk at the death-machine *you* unleashed."

Keller stops cold, with Sharon's verbal javelin skewering him to the spot.

"Was it easy for you to say that?" he asks.

"To say what? That you're a murderer without equal?"

"You don't know what you're saying." Keller marches ahead, ignoring the aches in his bones.

"Bullocks!" Sharon says, clomping after him. "I *saw* the photos Beckert brought back of you, standing over the bodies with your rifle, like Asaka at Nanking!"

Keller whirls about.

"Who?"

"Asaka. The Butcher of Nanking? Gor, read a *book*, will you?" Sharon marches ahead.

"I should've known you wouldn't understand," Keller says after her.

"Oh, right, it's *my* limited thinking that's to blame here, yeah? Spare me the verbal jiu-jitsu. You're a *murderer*, Keller, and we need to see you pay for it."

Keller nods and starts walking after her.

"You're right about that."

The two match pace, striding several meters in silence.

"If I can't break Honniker's leash, there won't be any satisfaction," Keller says. "Not for you, not for them."

"Don't think you're getting out so easy. You're making good on your promise to confess, I *assure* you."

"That's what I'm *trying* to do right now! If you'd just shut your mouth for two seconds..."

"Oh. Right. *I'm* the unreasonable one. *Right*. Of course. That makes *perfect* sense!"

"I KNOW what I've DONE, and I've been choking on it for *fifty fucking years*!"

"SHH!" Maiella calls from the holoscreen. Keller and Sharon both look up at the stern face glaring down at them. They hunch in obedience.

"For a choking man," Sharon whispers, "you've certainly *endured*."

Keller's lips purse. His eyes narrow.

"I want you to feel something."

He seizes Sharon by the elbow, twists the glove lock at her wrist, and pulls the glove away.

"Get off!" she hisses as rings, sparkling with gems, fall from the glove. Keller gapes at the jewelry tinkling on the floor around him.

"Doing some *shopping*?"

"Let go!" she demands, but Keller holds tight.

"Looting the dead…" he says in a low but harsh tone. "Now *there's* a moral high-ground."

"They're not for *me*. They're for the *others*."

"Yeah right. Looks more like prissy rich girl can't stand to be without her shiny pretties."

Sharon rips out of his grasp, growling, "I said they're not FOR *ME*!" She kneels and picks up rings a couple at a time.

"Prove it," Keller says.

Sharon goes still.

"Looks clear to me," Keller says, leaning over her. "Open and shut case, your honor. I see all I need to know that you're a *grave-robber*."

Sharon's eyes close and her head droops. "You *know* I'm not like that."

"Obviously, you are."

Keller strides away, the holowindow tracking ahead with him.

Sharon opens her eyes and looks at the rings beneath her. She debates whether to collect them or not, then sweeps them up and slips them back over her fingers. She hops to her feet and catches up with Keller.

"I took these with a good reason," she says, waving her jewelry-laden hand in front of him.

"Doesn't matter to me. You're a grave-robber and that's all there is to it."

"I'm not a grotty *grave-robber*, so—"

Keller leans into her. "*You're* a grave-robber, like *I'm* a pre-meditated murderer."

Sharon stops in her tracks, eyes narrow with loathing. "Don't you *dare* compare me to you."

"Why not? So long as the judgment train's in the station, it's all-on-board, right?"

"No, no, no, no, no," Sharon says, waving both her hands in front of her face and trudging after Keller. "These are works of *art*, Keller. These are pieces of *history*. They're worth saving."

Keller stops and turns to let her catch up.

"It's all about perspective, Sharon. I've known you most of my life. I know you're not grave-robber, okay? But if I stopped at only what I *saw*…"

Sharon approaches and steps even with her old captain. She looks down at her ring-loaded hand, fingers splayed out, then closes them to keep the loose rings from slipping again.

Keller watches her as the message sinks in, as the set of her eyebrows softens and the muscles of her jaw relax. When she looks up at him, her eyes are calmer.

"Do you understand what I'm saying?" he asks.

She grimaces with one side of her face. "Context matters."

"Thank you," Keller says genuinely. The two stride off again, side by side. Sharon waits for him to pick up where he left off but instead he strides forward, facing directly ahead.

"I'm listening," she reminds him, softly.

"Will you hear me?"

"Yes, I promise."

He nods, still looking forward. "I need you to take my pulse."

"Why?"

"I need you to. I have something to prove."

She shrugs. "All right." Sharon extends her bare hand, careful not to lose the rings. "Where should I, uh...?"

Keller stops in the hallway and looks both ways. Certain they are alone, he takes her hand and presses the tips of her fingers into his neck.

"Feel that?"

Sharon squints. "I must not be on the right spot."

"You are."

She rocks her head back and feels alongside his Adam's apple up toward his jaw.

"I can't find a..." Her face scrunches in horror. "Oh my God!"

"Now, here," Keller says, opening his black tunic. He guides her hand down to his bare chest. She feels the hard, thin seam of medical glue down his sternum.

"You've no heartbeat...! Keller, what happened to you?"

"You saw me on Honniker's table."

"Yes, but...but you looked *fine*! I didn't see any...uh...um..."

"Blood?"

She lifts her eyes to his, her mouth open with alarm. "Yeah."

Keller hands the glove back to her and closes his tunic. Sharon stares at his chest, holding the glove to her own chest.

"Honniker cut out my heart while I *watched*," Keller says through clenched teeth. "Then he fed it to his *pets*."

She gasps, lifting a hand to her mouth.

"He put this artificial thing inside, in its place. Works like a champ now, but if Honniker wants, he can turn it off. Told me if I try to leave, he'll stop it dead."

"Are you sure?"

"Yeah," Keller says, grimly recalling Honniker's lecture about 'trust.' "I believe him. So I need someone to hear my *whole* story, not just part of it. I want it to be you."

Sharon nods, lowering her hand. Like Keller before, she checks both directions and urges him on. Sharon keeps beside him, looking at him, showing him with her eyes that she is ready to listen. They walk in silence until Keller can find the words again.

"I was saying about how the money was really good. Parents were proud of me; bosses gave me solid reviews. The whole time, everyone around me was telling me I was doing the *right* thing. There I was, thinking I was smart and resourceful, doing really hard work, and always being told I was doing the *right thing* for my people, for my family, my company. It was easy to believe."

Keller snorts in mock amusement.

"They knew exactly how to handle me. By contract, SoVar *owned* me, bought, and paid for. And I'd been taking orders all my life. So when they told me I had to bulldoze huts, I bulldozed huts. When they told me to shove off the indigenous, I cleared them out. And as they started fighting back, when SoVar told me to exterminate them..."

Keller looks down at his feet, noting how they've gone numb from the cold floor plates.

"Yes? *And?*" Sharon digs.

Keller lifts his gaze to a point far down the corridor. "It wasn't right and I knew it...but I told myself to get it done. Get it over with, so I could put it behind me and move on to something better."

"You finished the job," Sharon says directly.

Keller nods penitently. "Yeah. I did."

The two look ahead, contemplating the heavy confession.

"After it was done, I asked for transfer. It was approved a year later. I got the usual perks, a heap more money, awards. But I knew I'd done something horrible. Criminal. My folks didn't understand why I'd take the *Europa*, why I'd go so far away from them when I could've had any post I wanted. They couldn't understand."

Keller's eyes wrinkle. His lips turn down involuntarily.

"I never told them. I couldn't look my mother in the eye. I was too ashamed. I had to be where she couldn't see me, because if she ever found out..."

He shakes his head, eyes watering.

"I needed to get far away and take that secret with me. I needed her to never know what I'd done."

Seconds of awkward silence pass.

"I *should've* taken a job back home," Keller says to himself more than to Sharon. "Then, I could've died with everyone else. *Should've* died with everyone else."

"Well, you didn't."

Keller turns to her, reeled back from his vacant stare.

"No. I didn't. One of the *'lucky'* few." His eyes glaze over. "I remember we came to this one village. Just like the rest. Mud huts, fire pits. Meeting house and stage. Crops. Lizards must've heard us coming and ran off 'cause no one was home. Then, out behind one of the stables we find this...*thing*...like a giant needle. Four meters long with a solar collector, aiming right up into the sky."

"A weapon?"

"We thought it was at first, since it was basically a high-powered laser. And we used that as justification later for clearing them off, that they posed a threat, and so on. But it was a transmitter. Thing was high tech. Better than anything man made. That's when I knew how bad we'd screwed up."

"What, not *before*? Not when you were *butchering* people who had no weapons?"

"No, I knew it was wrong before! But here's this thing that proves the lizards aren't primitives, like finding a rocket engine at Chichen-Itza. We all knew it wouldn't have a range outside the system, so we didn't give it a lot of thought until we found a relay on one of the moons. That relay had broadcast power in the *terawatt* range. So here I am, looking at this relay station on my monitor, knowing the lizards've been telling their chums what we've been up to and it's only a matter of time before someone or something shows up."

Sharon nods, barely reining her disgust.

"And here's this brand new colony ship headed out to deep, deep space," she says. "Sounds to me like you were trying to run away and *save your own arse.*"

"No, that's not how it was...or *was* it?"

Keller looks deep inside himself, having never considered his decision to command the *Europa* could have been self-preservation. His eyebrows knit and his cheeks twitch with unpleasant introspection.

"No," he concludes, "no, that wasn't it. I *was* running, but not to save myself."

"So you found this transmitter and you told SoVar, right?"

"Yeah."

"What then?"

"They told me to mop up and clear the evidence. SoVar didn't want homeworld to get a whiff of the E.T.s for fear they might suddenly grow 'rights.' Van der Beek cooked up a story about internal sabotage and terrorism. Said the colonies were under threat and we needed to be able to protect them. Turned into the biggest military mobilization in history. And of course, there were the *special* projects..."

He spreads his arms grandly.

"Cadre *One* and Cadre *Two*."

Sharon loses grip of her indignation. "So you really *did* know about this place?"

"Yeah."

"Hang on...Just the size alone...There's no way this place could've gotten started between the time you were at New Dresden and the time we departed with the *Europa*."

"You're right, the installations were already here. But they were ramped up in short order. Budget caps were torn off, and they *had* to be to get the talent. Pretty expensive convincing people who're living well on Earth they should come out to some rock in space, not to mention their staff, amenities, perks..."

Sharon looks down at her hand with the priceless rings, finally remembering to put her glove back on.

"Statues, art, jewelry..." she adds.

"Mm, hmm. Honniker demanded a lot of those as a condition. Jin-Sung wanted the damn Library of Congress on hard copy, I heard. There was a rumor Mikato got eternal life, but that's a load of BS. What *really* bought them was *total* freedom of research, *total* freedom of experimentation, and immunity from prosecution. The opportunity for pure science without restraint—*that's* what they couldn't resist."

"Without restraint..." Sharon says, her eyes wandering the walls. "You got *that* right. So all this was preparation for an assault *you* provoked?"

Keller flinches under the indictment.

"Look, it may be semantic, but it wasn't my idea to butcher lizards. I just...pulled the trigger. And it may not mean a thing now, but with the kind of money SoVar could throw around, there was a *list* of stand-ins if I couldn't hack it. It was going to happen *with* or *without* me."

"Is that supposed to make me feel better about our *complete annihilation?* Or does it ease *your* conscience, instead?"

"Ease *my*...? Here's the bottom line, Sharon: we all heard the broadcasts. We watched video of the colonies and our home world, burning

444

before our eyes. For all we knew, the *Europa* had just become Noah's Ark and we were headed for a planet that had only been studied via telescope."

Sharon sniffs. "Bloody thing was *glowing* with isotopes."

"They didn't see that in spectral analysis, did they?"

"No. *Bastards.*"

Keller takes a deep breath. "I've known I was a player in all this from the beginning. I told you I wanted to take myself out, but that wasn't good enough. I had to find a place for you all. I had to see it *through*, to make sure you had a chance to *live*, not just eke by. Thought for sure we'd find a place, too. If you'd asked me then, I'd have said we'd be planting crops in two, maybe three hundred years. Shit, it's been over a thousand, and we *still* haven't found a planet that isn't crawling with lizards."

"Good planets *are* hard to find."

Keller's head bobs in silent agreement.

"I'm old, Sharon. Been in and out of cryo so many times I got freezer burn. The only thing that kept me going was finding a new home so I could at least do *that* much, so I could die with some dignity. Because I don't..."

Keller's chin squares with a sudden frown. His breath shortens.

"I don't want to be remembered as..."

He hunches, his hands grasping each other tightly. His steps falter and salty drops pour down his cheeks. The man drops to his knees and he slumps against the wall, face wracked in unspeakable grief.

Sharon looks up and down the hallway, then crouches beside him.

"Remembered as what?" she asks gently.

Keller starts to speak then drags a crusty sleeve across his eyes, leaving behind a trail of ruddy flakes.

"Get it together..." he says to himself, swiping both hands over his balding head. Sharon watches his weathered hands and finds he is missing a digit.

"What happened to your finger?"

Keller looks up at her with glassy eyes, then holds his right hand in front of his face. He turns it over and flexes the remaining digits.

"Another one of Honniker's lessons."

As fast as he crumbled, Keller rebuilds himself. He gets back to his numbed feet. He straightens the overlapping leaves of his tunic and sniffs deeply.

"I'm sorry you saw that. It isn't proper for you to see me like that."

"*Sod it.* You were going to say something."

Keller looks at her skeptically.

"Go on," she insists.

Keller stands as he would on the *Europa's* bridge, shoulders back, chin out, head high, hands clasped behind his back. Sharon scowls at the contrived bravura and punches him in the arm.

"Don't hide behind your rank! What were you going to say?"

Keller swallows hard and looks away. "I've lived my life by facing down my fears, conquering them. I thought I had 'em all licked..."

"And what is the mighty Keller afraid of?"

His head swivels toward her. "That my name could be spoken in the same breath as *Stalin's.*"

Sharon averts her eyes. "I hope you're not looking for an apology."

"No. Because you're right, Sharon. It isn't good enough for me to die or even to get ground down a little at a time. I need to do something *good*, to give my life in trade for something good. I haven't been able to deliver on that and I don't think I'll be able to now. Someone has to take over for me."

"Here we *go...*"

Sharon starts walking briskly ahead, the dim holowindow tracking with her overhead. Keller strides after her.

"If not you, Sharon, then who?"

"Ortega is next in line and he can *have* it."

"He's not good enough."

"Oh? Then why'd you pick him as first officer?"

"It was political."

"Well it doesn't matter. He's in charge and it isn't up to you."

"Yes it is. Because I need someone better than him."

"He's a good officer! Has he ever failed in his duty?"

"No."

"Do you question his ethics?"

"No. He's a moral man."

"Is he unfair?"

"Not at all."

Sharon tilts her head. "Then *what* is your beef with Javier?"

"His faith."

"Oh, you're taking the piss..."

"I'm deadly serious."

"Keller, the atheist, can't stand a man with faith? Obviously, your brush with death has made you envious of someone with a *clear conscience.*"

Keller stops, spiked again by Sharon's words. "That was cruel."

"No more than you deserve," she calls over her shoulder.

The man clears his lungs, fighting through physical frailties, pains, hunger, and guilt beyond measure to put one foot in front of the other, to not just sink down and die like a salmon after running the falls.

"If Ortega can't hack it, or dies, then what?" he says with dry throat.

Sharon slows her brisk march, and Keller steps even to her. She does not answer.

"I like Javier, the *man*," he says, "but not the *officer*."

"*Why?*"

"Because Javier believes in a happy ending after death. He has an 'out.' If he doesn't make good for his crew, then that's okay, because he's a good man, and his crew are all good, too, so they're all going to heaven, ain't it great? THAT'S NOT GOOD ENOUGH, SHARON."

"Hey!" Maiella's voice hisses from the hovering holoscreen. "Keep it *down*."

Sharon looks up at the small, glimmering window again, then glances at Keller with a defiant sneer.

"Maybe I've got faith, too."

"Yeah, maybe," Keller whispers back. "But whoever's going to lead these people, faith has to come in a distant second to *keeping them alive.* You and I've struggled to keep our values among O'Kai and his Cadre. We've *really struggled* not to get swept up in their machinery. But the cold truth is our values are unavailable to the *Europa's* Commanding Officer. There's no freedom to just 'do your best' when you have the last boatload of human survivors under your wings. You are *always* on duty, there *is no* vacation, and if you can't hack it you have to find someone who can, *just like in the Cadre.*"

"Are you trying to talk me *into* it, or *out* of it? Because I can't tell."

"I can't stand you when you're like this."

"Like *what?*"

"You know what I'm telling you but you're arguing for the *sake of arguing!*"

"Or maybe I just can't see reason past all the blood on your hands."

Goddamn it, she did it again, Keller thinks. "Maybe it's because deep down you *know* how big a responsibility it is and *you* don't think you're up to it!"

This time, Sharon is lanced where she stands. Keller closes the distance with slow, cautious steps.

"Doesn't matter how much you hate me, Sharon, I can't stop doing what's in my power to protect you and keep you alive. That's what being captain means. But my crew won't have me anymore. Hell, you and I, we were close once. And you hate me as much as they do. Or *more*. Even if I *could* leave this place, I'm *still* a dead man. Don't you see that?"

She glares at him, eyes shiny below lowered brows. Her silence is confirmation enough that she understands.

"The *Europa* needs a skipper, Sharon. Someone who knows her systems, knows the crew and their skills. Someone who will never give up on her, no matter what. Someone who puts her crew ahead of *all* other concerns."

"I think you're wrong about Javier."

"Maybe. But I trust my instinct. When I met you, you were a hot shit. You had the presence to lead, and that's a big reason why I chose you. When you want to be, you're sharp as razors and you cut right to it. But I think you've gotten used to the idea of being second officer, forever."

Sharon does not move at all, maintaining her wary stare.

"It isn't natural that I've been captain so long," Keller continues. "I would've moved up or out long ago and gotten out of your way. You used to be ambitious, brash. And I liked that about you. Can't believe I'm having to cudgel you into taking your chair."

"It's too big."

"It's the same size it always was. You've let yourself get small."

Sharon looks away, confirming a direct hit. When she looks back, her eyes are fiery.

"So your grand idea was to bring me out here and toughen me up for command? Is that it?"

"More or less."

"That makes you a double bastard!"

"How?"

"Because you *knew* about this barking mad dungeon and *you brought me here anyway!*"

"I didn't know it was this bad. There were people here once, friends."

"Friends? Of *yours*? *Charming...*"

"Hey. I know you get like this when you're scared. It gets on my last nerve sometimes but I know where it comes from. That fear never goes away, you know, that constant awareness of what's at stake. If that fear *does* go away, well...that's when bad things happen."

"Sure, because things lately have been swell."

"You know what I mean."

Sharon nods. "Well, I appreciate the pep talk but one, you're a *naff* salesman, and two, if we can ever get past *squeaky bum time,* I'll be fine."

"Squeaky...*what?*"

"Hey, you two, get down," the holoscreen warns before winking out, "something's coming."

Keller sobers instantly. Sharon feels down his arm then snatches his hand. He squats low, pulling Sharon down behind him. He squeezes her hand.

"Stay behind me," Keller orders, his voice barely a whisper. "If you feel me move, run in the opposite direction."

Sharon clasps Keller's hand in both of hers. Even through the gloves, he can feel her trembling.

"You okay?"

"Yeah," she whispers into his ear, her voice more steady than her hands.

Keller leans forward in his crouch like a gargoyle, blind without the overhead light. He concentrates on the corridor ahead, imagining his ears are like great receiver dishes channeling all the sounds of Cadre Two into him. The halls are quiet and he thinks about Shao-Lo and the Operators.

Did they get out? he wonders. *Were they killed? Please, don't let them be captured...*

Keller reaches down to the floor with the hand Sharon is not crushing, using it to steady himself. Gritty fragments press into his fingertips.

This is it, old man. Could be your last shot. Probably gonna be quick. Let's hope it's quick.

He summons his strength, the artificial heart in his chest pumping strong, and he clears his mind.

I have to fight long enough for Sharon to get away. If I can at least save her...but I'll have to move quick at the first sound of...

Hot, fetid breath blows over his face with a deep grumble from enormous vocal cords. Keller stiffens in shock.

This is it...

He rips free of Sharon's hands and lunges at the creature in front of him. The speed of the blood in his veins makes him strong, and he slugs with all his might, bashes his bare fists against overlapping plates.

"SHARON! RUN!"

Keller pummels, kicks, punches until his legs are swept out from beneath him. He falls to the deck, thudding against loose deck plates. Something firm and extremely heavy lands on his chest. Keller gropes at the pinning weight and feels warm fur over individual toes and the cool metal of retracted talons.

The beast presses the air from him, and Keller groans, unable to shout. He knows he should be hearing Sharon's boots clomping away. There is no such sound.

They got her.

The old colonist strains, wanting one last breath to curse his killer before death.

"Keller, *knock it off!*" whispers a voice beside him. An armored hand cups his mouth, and the pressing paw lifts from his chest. Air flows into him through his nose in one long, drawn-out sniff.

"It's me, Maiella. *Relax*, will you?"

Keller nods quickly under Maiella's stifling hand. She lifts it.

"Why are you going back to the *Flounder*?"

"We're not!" Keller retorts in hushed tones. "We were following your...projection-thing."

"That wasn't me. Look, Shao-Lo and the others, they were hit hard. I don't know if they're alive or not."

"Why aren't you with them?" Sharon whispers from close by.

"They wouldn't be rescued by me," she says bitterly.

"That's madness!" Sharon says.

Maiella pulls Keller to his feet. His eyes roam the total darkness.

"What are you doing with this...*thing*?" he asks.

"She's not like the others, don't worry. She's Mikato's guardian."

"Mikato?" Keller nearly shouts.

"Shut it, Keller! Honniker's gonna be mad I found you two. It's time to move." Maiella hustles the colonists along.

"I don't get it..." Sharon says, "an android called Marta got me and Keller out of there with the help of your 'digital persona'. You're saying *that* was Honniker?"

"No, no, that was the right one, but...Honniker knows how to *impersonate* it. I found out the hard way, myself."

"How can that be?" Keller demands. "The damn thing led us out of there and has been guiding us ever since!"

"He almost got you *back* there."

"No way," Keller counters.

There is a click in the darkness and Keller feels something held over his eyes.

"See for yourself."

Keller looks through Maiella's goggles. Sharon is standing in front of him, her head and face glowing white in infrared above her gray torso and dark boots. She sways back and forth blindly. Thirty meters past her is the darkened entryway to the *Flounder* lobby.

"Son of a *bitch*!"

Maiella takes the goggles away and snaps them back into her helmet. "My guess is Marta's out of action, too."

"How'd you find us?"

"Alessa got your scent and tracked you. Not like we needed a trail...I could hear you halfway 'cross the station."

"Then why didn't Honniker send his troops for us?"

"You almost walked right back. Obviously, he didn't need them."

"Who do we trust?" Sharon says from Keller's shoulder.

"Yourselves, to start, and no one outside this circle," Maiella answers. "Keller, climb on Alessa's back and let her carry you. Sharon, I've got you."

"Climb on *what*?" Keller asks, his nerves frayed to near insanity. Maiella takes him and leads him to the back of the squatting beast. She brings his arms around the creature's thick neck and puts his hands together.

"Do NOT let go," she warns. "Sharon, I'm taking you now."

Sharon grunts as she is heaved up and tossed over the Geek's shoulder.

"They're coming!" Maiella shouts. "Hold tight!"

Maiella slaps the faceplate down on her helmet and sprints into the darkness. Keller lays himself across the overlapping back plates of a creature that absolutely terrifies him.

Hold tight, she says?

The creature leaps up from its crouch into a full run. Keller's locked hands slip, and he clutches at the beast's armored plates, climbing them until he can again encircle the powerful neck. He tucks his punctured heels into the creature's narrow waist and hugs tight, playing every mental trick he can on himself to forget what is carrying him.

SUDDEN DESCENT

Keller lowers his head beside Alessa's bobbing neck and crushes his eyes shut. Roars, hisses, and moans pour from every direction. Bullets *snap* and *zing* past him, some ricocheting off Alessa's plating, some grazing and taking a stripe of skin off him like a whip's lash. He grits his teeth, keeping his arms locked around the beast's neck, gripping with knees and feet. He buries his face.

Alessa rumbles with fierce growls and dives into walls of crowding figures, reaping through them with talons and teeth. Slick mixtures drench Keller's arms and shoulders, some warm, some disturbingly cold. Tendrils *twang* from walls, ceiling, and floor at him, their hooked suckers rasping at the weave of his tunic until the fabric tears free.

The massive beast halts suddenly and spins in place, howling to the extent of her lungs. She thrashes wildly, beating down both living and mechanical opponents in reach. Bullets rake her left side, one plunging through Keller's thigh. He cries out then clamps his mouth shut, taking the pain.

Alessa launches at the new attackers, battering them down in a frenzy of blood and snapping bones, but Keller's wounded leg can no longer clench her waist. He flops with the animal's darting movements, more like a cape than a rider, and slips to one side. Saliva, viscera, and blood work into his clenched hands like penetrating oils, and when the beast swings, he is thrown like a sack.

The landing is softer and lumpier than he expects. His eyes flick open and he sees humanoid bodies all around, slashed necks yawning, organs spilled out through huge rips in their torsos. Dead eyes hide behind dark lenses, vacant expressions convey no feeling; but lamps embedded in scalps and skulls still shine, casting a cobweb of narrow beams through the hazy air. The wounded colonist stares, mute at the horrors around him.

Scant meters away, the huge feline swipes and kicks at a gang of humanoids who jab back with long metal lances. Bright tracers zip at the beast, sparking on contact with her thick body plates.

Maiella high steps through the swath of bodies with Sharon slung over one shoulder. Her free hand glistens with wetness.

"KELLER!" Maiella shouts, hand shooting straight out, pointing above him.

Keller looks up where a black blob peels from the ceiling like a tar pancake. He rolls away, barely dodging as it flops down beside him. Its edges glisten as it wraps around the bodies beneath. He kicks himself away with his good leg, gagging on the sour, sulfuric stench emanating from the digesting corpses within.

Another blob flips its way toward him, tendrils forming at its edge. Keller shoves away from it, hauls with his arms through the litter of dead flesh as if back-stroking through a bog. Elastic black cords spring out at him, their hooked suckers snaring his wrist and neck. He flails against them, dragging himself and the black mass closer together.

A thunderous roar barrels out of the darkness, followed by Alessa in full sprint. She lowers her great head and parts her jaws like shears, slicing through the snaring tendrils, and keeps full stride toward a mob of pale, shuffling humanoids.

"Mailella, behind you!" Sharon shouts.

Maiella dives with Sharon to the deck as a barrage of small arms fire whizzes through the corridor.

"Hold onto me!" Maiella yells.

Sharon wraps her arms around Maiella's neck and the soldier crawls, straddling Sharon, shielding the small woman from bullets and laser fire.

Jittery, his tunic hanging with severed tendrils, his wounded thigh burning and throbbing, Keller scoots away from the creeping black mass and scours the floor for some kind of weapon. Lances and short blades jab his naked hands until he grazes cool metal with a familiar shape. He pulls the rifle out from under the dead thing that carried it, and his hands wrap the grips instinctively.

Vaguely human bipeds, with curved spines and heads slouched to one side, trudge closer with their lances. He raises his weapon and triggers. The barrel flashes a burst of white flame with each pull and the moaning humanoids drop as their heads explode, one after another.

"Maiella!" he shouts, lobbing the weapon to her.

Maiella presses Sharon to the floor and snatches the lobbed weapon out of the air. She spins into a crouch, aims, and triggers until the magazine runs dry.

Teeth bared and cursing, Keller watches the wounded blob near him seal its wounds and form new tendrils. He feels around for another rifle, but finds the pointy end of an unsheathed blade with his palm. With a snarl of pain, he flaps his hand then snatches the blade from the floor by its grip.

"YOU GOT ANY IDEAS?" he shouts as loud as he can.

Alessa streaks back toward Keller and dives onto the pulsing blob, shredding it inside out. A sulfurous fume gushes from the savaged mass, and the huge feline recoils, leaving the shredded pieces throbbing where they lay. She rears up on her back legs and punches through an overhead hatch. With a glance at Maiella, the beast tosses her head up at the hatch.

Bullets *whiz* out of the darkness, bashing into her. One sinks between body plates, tearing away the one at her shoulder. Alessa groans, then bellows with rage and charges her assailants, head lowered.

"Get up there, Keller!" Maiella shouts.

Keller looks at the open hatch. *Even with TWO legs, I couldn't make that!*

He grabs the nearest humanoid head to him, rips the embedded headlamp from it, then shines the beam down the corridor behind him. A press of lopsided figures slouches closer in the narrow circle of light. They move as if half of their bones are broken and every step is a labor, yet their faces are absent of comprehension. Those with functional hands raise pistols and fire blindly into the glare. Bullets plunge into the corpses around him, spattering him with still warm bits. Keller scrambles around the corner to cover, clutching his lamp in one hand, his blade with the other.

Alessa limps back from her charge. One shoulder is exposed, the protective plate ripped free, and her underlying fur is clumped with blood. Her paws and forelegs are impaled with thin spikes like knitting needles.

Before Keller can react, the creature snaps her teeth into the nape of his tunic and swings him onto her back. He clambers for something to hold, careful not to cut her with his knife, and hugs her thick neck again. Alessa crouches, leaps through the hatch, dumps him in the crawlspace, and drops down again.

Keller scoots away from the hatch, making room for others. As expected, Sharon pops through the open hatch, crouched on the creature's head like a bizarre Jack-in-the-Box. She hops from the beast's brow and lands awkwardly beside Keller as the creature drops out of sight again.

Maiella rockets through next and lands on her feet beside Sharon. The Geek turns and looks down through the hatch, waving frantically. Weapon fire increases like a sudden hailstorm, some of the ricochets zinging through the hatch and bashing into her chest plate. She staggers back, cursing.

A howl below of an animal's pain...

"Come on!" Maiella yells through the hatch. "Get up here!"

The beast's head and shoulders pop through the hatch and her talons dig into the crawlspace framework. Her head and neck jut forward as she tries to pull herself the rest of the way, hind legs kicking at air and ceiling below. Weapon fire cracks and sizzles beneath the hatch, the beast registering every hit with wincing blinks and grimaces. Maiella grabs onto the massive creature's cheeks and pulls, giving her just enough help to haul herself the rest of the way in.

Alessa scurries away from the open hatch and drops onto her side, panting from exertion. All four of her lower limbs are washed in blood and skewered with thin rods of metal. Her shoulder flows bright red.

Maiella cups Alessa's frothed, clotted chin and looks over the many injuries.

"Where are you hurt?" she asks.

The creature blinks slowly and holds up a skewered paw. Maiella considers the angles of all the thin metal spikes and zips them out as fast and straight as she can.

"What the hell are those?" Sharon asks.

"There are little machines with these spiny legs," Maiella explains as she moves to the creature's hind paws. "As a defense, they roll on their backs and aim the sharp ends up at you. Girl ran over a bunch of 'em, full stride."

Keller looks down at his swollen thigh, gauging his own blood loss. He clamps his hand over the wound, grunts, then looks at Sharon.

"Are you okay?" he asks through gritted teeth.

"I don't think they're aiming for me. I'm not sure if I should be relieved or terrified."

"Honniker thinks he's getting you back in his lab," Maiella states. "He doesn't want to damage you."

"Oh thank you, Maiella, *I feel so much better...*"

A disfigured reptilian head rises through the hatchway, its skull-mounted lamp shining, broken jaw drooling. It raises a rifle to its shoulder. Maiella snatches the weapon out of its hands and bashes its skull in with the stock. She takes the weapon by the grips and peeks over the hatchway.

"Oh, *crap*." She whirls about, barking at Keller, "Go, *FAST!*"

Keller grunts his way on hands and one knee, dragging his wounded leg. Sharon follows right behind him, head turning front to back in the narrow space. The big creature limps her way after them. Maiella brings up the rear, rifle leveled at the open hatchway.

Keller tries to silence his groans as he crawls down the access conduit. Sharon pats him.

"Let me go ahead, you're hurt."

He shakes his head. "It's not that bad."

Sharon scowls. "Not twenty minutes ago you were *begging* me to take over. Now you won't get out of my way?"

"Now's not the time t—"

"Shut it!" Maiella demands. "Alessa's taking us in. You two, stick to her ass like you're welded there!"

Keller and Sharon flatten themselves against the wall so the huge feline can squeeze by. Despite Alessa's zeal at protecting them, they both hold their breath at the passage of such a monster.

"Did you hear that?" Keller asks.

"Hear what?" Sharon asks, turning about, anxiously scanning in all directions.

Keller looks over his shoulder at Maiella. He looks back at Sharon. "*That's* how you lead."

Sharon looks over her shoulder at Maiella. Movement behind the duck-walking soldier catches the small woman's eye, and she cocks her head.

"What in the *bleeding Hells* is THAT?"

Keller looks back at a flat-black mass pouring up through the hatch and filling the crawlspace behind them. Its center turns a stony gray. He grips Sharon by the arm and spins her front.

"I don't wanna know," Keller answers.

The big creature scoots ahead to a junction and pauses, sniffing the dank air. Her great head swings one way then the other and she gnarls.

"What is it?" Sharon whispers.

"Enemy ahead," Maiella interprets as she watches the dark mass behind them. Tendrils form on its still-pliant edges that reach for the crawlspace walls and haul it forward. Maiella scowls and raises her weapon.

"That won't hurt it," Keller warns, reliving his moments in the *Server Farm*. "Once they harden like that, your pop gun'll ricochet." He glances down at his thigh.

And I've had my fill of getting shot today...

"Probably blocking the corridors with these things," Maiella says, watching the blob's slow advance.

The beast turns about in the junction and returns. Just when Keller thinks she is going to squeeze by again, the huge predator stops at a rectangular cover nearly the height of the crawlway and sniffs. She plucks the sheet metal cover away with a talon and sniffs the space beyond before lowering herself to the floor and reaching in with both paws. Next, her head, then her deep chest wedge into the space. Halfway in, the creature pushes with rear paws against the far side of the vent shaft then pulls herself all the way through, her long back legs extending straight out past her banded tail and sliding out of sight.

Sharon pauses at the opening, letting Keller shine his lamp inside. The duct is oval and smooth, its coating of centuries-old dust scraped into clumps by the animal hauling herself through.

Sharon ducks and crawls in. She reaches back and takes Keller's hand, towing him through the tight shaft. Maiella crawls in after them, keeping rear guard.

Every sound is amplified by the close oval walls: the creature's scraping talons, the banging of knees and elbows, the metallic complaints of rivets and braces, the dust-induced sneezes.

When the beast passes the first ventilator junction, they hear far away sounds of grinding, of turning gears, and of rolling treads, mingled with more subtle sounds of scrabbling claws. Throaty moans break into high-pitched chortles like nervous laughter.

Every junction they scrape past brings more of the same. Sharon's eyes dart about as her nerves set her to shivering, and she jumps at the sound of tearing sheet metal near by.

"Vicious *bastards*!"

"Easy does it," Keller soothes.

"Easy?" Sharon hisses. "We're trapped behind this *bloody werewolf* and who knows what, Keller!"

"Keep going," Maiella whispers, "and *don't stop.*"

Aggravating Sharon's unease, the beast stops. Sharon looks behind her then pats one of the animal's powerful hind legs.

"Maybe you didn't hear, darling, but Maiella said, *'DON'T stop'!*"

Gradually, Alessa slides forward then dives down like a whale headed for deep water. Keller peers after her, shining his light down the vertical junction. The view is exactly the same as before, except the animal slips much faster down the oval tube.

Sharon peeks over Keller's shoulder, contemplating the drop. Keller is about to give her encouragement when she moves on her own, sitting on the lip and bracing her feet against the opposite side. She plants her hands to each side, bites her lip, and slips her way down a few centimeters at a time until she gets comfortable.

There you go, he thinks. When she has dropped enough for him to enter, his leg wound makes him pause.

Maiella scoots up beside him and glances down the shaft.

"Get in there, Keller."

"If I fall, I might take Sharon out," he says, hooking the lamp on his tunic.

Maiella sets the rifle's safety and takes the weapon by the barrel, extending the stock toward him.

"Then hang onto this, and be careful."

Keller takes hold of the offered weapon then swivels his head at sounds of excited chortles, scraping claws, and ripping sheet metal.

"They're breaking through..."

He braces himself like Sharon with his back and good leg, then slips his way down the tube, hanging on to the rifle grip with one hand and gripping his blade with the other. Once Keller has lowered himself enough, Maiella hops into the tube and kicks her feet out, just above Keller. The two slide their way down together, catching up to Sharon and slowing to her pace.

Excited *yips* roll through the ducts overhead, cutting through thunderous *bangs* of galloping paws. The shaft vibrates with the stampede.

Keller looks up past Maiella at dark shapes streaking across the open shaft, not ten meters above. There is a scuffling of claws, then hostile snarls, and a jostling crowd of reflective eyes gathers around the rim. The creatures shove into one another for a peek down the shaft. Saliva rains down in long strands.

Frustrated barks and unnerving laughs roll from behind the halted crowd, driving the creatures in front right to the lip. Maiella cranes her head up at the slavering beasts, watching the ones in front turn and snap at the ones pushing them from behind. Some leap the opening to look down from the other side, but one loses grip and plummets down the shaft.

"INCOMING!" Maiella shouts and she jams her legs out like iron girders. The creature slams across her armored legs in a heap of thick black quills. It frenzies in her lap, metal talons raking across her goggles and faceplate, back legs bucking and scraping the shaft walls, head swaying on a powerful neck, jaws snapping at her arms.

Maiella drops her grip on the rifle and battles the flailing thing to keep it from slipping past her. She grabs a fistful of quills behind its head and cudgels its head, throat, chest, and belly with an armored fist.

"KELLER!" Maiella yells between hammering punches. "TAKE A SHOT!"

Keller jams his good leg against the tube like Maiella and tries to line up the rifle with the thrashing beast. He flicks off the safety when he feels his ankle quaking.

"I'm slipping!"

Maiella's punching hand flies down and grips the rifle barrel. She strains with Keller's extra weight, fighting the creature one-handed, until she can hug its bristly neck and plant the barrel under the creature's ear.

"NOW!"

Keller triggers and the rifle fires with a deafening *bang*. Blood and bony fragments explode from the top of its skull and the thing goes limp across Maiella's legs.

Keller cannot hear the howls overhead; he simply blinks and stretches his jaw at the intensity of the gunshot in such a tight space. Hot blood patters onto his legs and chest, and when he looks up, he stares into the broken face of something vaguely ursine. Reflective, red eyes are half-open beneath circular ears. Wide cheeks fill out the sides of the bear-like face, and the head dangles on a long, extremely muscular neck. The snout ends at a shiny black nose, and the wolf-like jaws are lined with the biggest set of crushing molars he has ever seen.

The ring of reflective eyes above jockeys for a view. Some lean toward the tube, forepaws reaching as if to drop in, then recoil.

"Go, go, GO!" Maiella shouts.

Holding the rifle as before, Keller takes the cue and slips his way down after Sharon. The farther they descend, the more agitated the animals become, gnashing and growling, snapping at one another, goading each other. Maiella looks up at the growing frustration, at the lustful stares and lolling tongues.

"Keller, if you don't hurry, *they're gonna drop on us!*"

Keller glances at the riled pack testing their courage above. Below him, he sees Alessa's hind legs jutting from a horizontal junction. Sharon holds onto them with both hands, letting the big feline reel her in like a crane boom. Beyond Sharon, the shaft descends without a visible bottom. His leg quakes again.

Go you old coward, go! You're not gonna be the reason they get killed! NOW GO!

Keller grits his teeth and stabs his blade through the shaft wall. Using the jutting pommel as a handhold, and hanging on to Maiella's rifle, he lowers himself as fast as his shaky leg will let him. Blood still patters down over him.

"Dump that carcass, will you?" he asks.

"Not yet. Not 'til you're clear."

Keller groans as he lowers himself another few centimeters and stabs the blade into the wall again.

"Why not?"

"Spines are coated with something. Not taking the chance of scratching you with one."

Keller's head snaps up at the lifeless head swaying just above him, a head which bristles with quills like fur.

"Devious sons-a-bitches..."

Sharon pokes her head out from the horizontal junction and sees Maiella and Keller making slow progress. She ducks back in and braces herself at the opening the same way she slid down the tube.

"Give me your hand, Keller," she says, extending one arm beyond the opening.

Keller shimmies down and stabs the blade into the wall above the junction. He pauses, preparing himself to relax his shaky leg and swing by the blade handle into Sharon's grip.

Will the blade hold my full weight?

"KELLER! THEY'RE DROPPING IN!" Maiella yells.

The colonist ends his debate, releases the rifle, and swings. The blade breaks at the handle.

Sharon snags his collar and hauls him toward the opening. He slams at the waist against the vertical shaft, torso inside the horizontal junction, legs and hips dangling out of it.

Maiella triggers with deafening *bangs* then grunts with an impact. A limp creature tumbles by, whooshing past Keller's hanging legs and banging down the shaft as it plummets.

Sharon, one hand holding Alessa's leg, the other clamped onto Keller's tunic, pulls as hard as she can. Keller's bare hands slip across the dusty surfaces.

"Grab onto *ME* you *TWIT*!"

Keller grabs double handfuls of Sharon's canvas suit and pulls, his face contorted with pain and effort, hauling himself the rest of the way in.

Maiella's rifle bangs again and again, then fires dry.

"OOMF!"

A blur of black spines and charcoal armor tumbles past the junction. Sharon screams, *"MAIELLA!"*

Keller whirls about and peers down the shaft, seeing nothing, but hearing rattles, snarls, and clangs fading into the darkness below.

Honored Dead

Falling faster, careening end-over-end, Maiella bounces off the narrow tube walls like an over-sized pinball. Every scrape spins her a new direction, every meter gives her greater speed, and the echoes of Sharon's scream fade away.

She grabs one of the creatures plummeting with her and jams it against the tube wall with her boot. It howls as its quills and then skin on one side are stripped in a long friction burn.

The other creature snatches at the Geek, trying to hook a claw in her armor, but glances off and slips past, its plaintive *yips* vanishing into abyssal darkness.

Maiella and her pinned opponent grind to a stop. The Geek lifts her other knee, shoves her other boot against the animal's long, thick neck, and digs her heel in behind the jaw. The creature's tongue curls between vicious snaps of its powerful jaws. Gray nictitating membranes slide over its eyes. Wicked claws slash and scrabble against the walls and her armor.

Both boots placed, she lets go with her hands and yells, driving her legs with all her strength. The creature whines, grunts, then coughs as its ribs give in with a succession of muted *cracks*. Fight drains from it, eyes rolled back, legs merely twitching.

She steps off the broken rib cage, letting the body swing down by its pinned neck. Planting her freed boot against bare wall, bracing herself, she steps off of its throat. The limp creature plummets quietly into darkness until a barely audible crash comes many, many seconds later.

Maiella looks down at herself. The pads of her gauntlets are jammed full of broken-off quills, as are the flexible seams beneath her joint plating and soles of her boots.

Risking light, she flicks on her helmet lamps and traces the streak of abraded skin running up the tube. Thick black quills hang from the trail by sticky follicles.

Beyond the streak of skin and quills, the tube seems to rise forever. No matter the intensity of her beams, she cannot see the top. Neither can she see Keller or Sharon. She takes a deep breath and shakes her head.

Should I go up or down?

As she considers the question, she twists the quills out of her gauntlet palms.

Mikato's production floor should be up there. But what would be down here?

She pauses her de-thorning and looks past her legs at the shaft below.

I've got to be below the Graveyard *floor...under that huge blob thing...*

She takes a boot off the wall and crosses it over her bracing leg.

Not a good place to be...

She yanks the rooted quills from her sole and repeats with her other boot. She turns her eyes upward.

But if those things up there jump again, I could fall all the way next time...

She leans back against the wall, tilting her head and shining the beams along the vertical tube wall. Roughly twenty meters above there is a horizontal junction, leading off through the tube wall.

Is that even the right direction? I got so turned around...

Maiella looks down the shaft once more.

Well, if I'm ever gonna leave this place, that's the WRONG way to go.

Flexing her arms, she readies herself, then shimmies with legs and shoulders, working her way up the shaft.

As the Geek scoots level to the junction, she sees the side tube continues straight for several meters, then branches into thirds. A gentle *whoosh* of air rolls through, along with an occasional electronic *beep*.

Without the feel against her skin, she cannot tell which way the air is moving, so she pinches some dust from the tube wall and drops it. The gray puff flies out into the vertical shaft and sinks down the long drop.

Good...if it was flowing the other way, I'd have a cloud ahead of me, telling them I'm coming...

Like a spider, she extends her limbs and pulls herself through the junction. Thick dust mutes the flexing conduit beneath her, and she moves as stealthily as one of the feline predators on fingers and toes.

At the three-way junction, she kills her helmet lamps. A faint glow emanates from the left tube with a telltale *beep*. The other two junctions, with their lack of light or sound, suggest places to hide, to regroup, but something subliminal draws her toward the glow.

Patiently, cautiously, she stalks through the dim conduit. The farther she goes, the more narrow it becomes until she is creeping through a tube only slightly wider than her armored shoulders. At its end, the tube turns straight upward. Light shines down in a crosshatched pattern from above.

She holds still and discovers new sounds filtering through the crosshatched grate: rhythmic whooshes of air, precision servomotors, chugging fluid pumps, and whirs of a treaded machine. The whirring grows louder, peaking as a shadow crosses directly over the vertical shaft, then gradually diminishes among the ambient sounds. She lingers several seconds, building context, absorbing clues, assembling the details into a mental image of what may lie directly above.

The whirring machine returns over the grate, casting its shadow again. It issues a single *beep*, alarmingly loud, and the whirring machine fades into the background. The Geek lifts a hand to move forward when there comes a strident whine of hydraulics and the harsh squeal of heavy metal sliding against metal. The din ends with a *klank* and a *hiss*, leaving only the modest sounds of whooshing air, servos, and fluid pumps.

Deeming it safe to move, Maiella crawls into the upward bend and looks up at a simple, circular metal grate. Sturdy hinges attach one side with geared springs and a manual release catch fastens the other. She stands slowly, scanning an expanding radius beyond the crosshatched bars. There are tables, attended by carts and cabinets, similar to the ones in the *Flounder*, yet these tables are larger, sturdier, less refined. Blood runs off the table edges in notched channels and dribbles down the central support columns.

Rugged machine arms work above each table, their servomotors humming smoothly. A snoring growl rumbles from the closest table, and a brief spurt of blood arcs over the edge. One of the arms rises and swings aside, then there is a *klunk* of something small and dense landing in a metal pan. Other machine arms weave back and forth over the table. The growl eases into a nasal huff.

Everywhere Maiella turns, she looks up at the undersides of large medical tables scabbed over with layers of blood. On top, animal occupants endure the prodding attentions of automated surgeons. And high above all, planted with brilliant lamps, is an arched stone ceiling, coarsely hewn from the native rock by beam, drill, and grinder.

Must be one of the recent additions...

The Geek releases the manual catch and eases the springed grate up. She slips through as small a gap as she can, then closes the grate quietly behind her, latching it with a subtle *click*. She rises to a squat, peeks over the nearest table edge, and finds herself eye to eye with a feline predator. One whole side of the creature is scorched black, fur singed, armored plates cracked and carbonized. One eye is clouded almost white, the other is dull with anaesthetic. Its only protests comes as a feeble grunt and a clumsy flip of a restrained paw.

Another heavy *klunk* behind her.

She spins about and sees a machine arm with a set of delicate calipers move away from a metal pan on a tableside cart. It hovers momentarily over another feline patient that is restrained and stretched out on its back, forelegs reaching well past the head of the table. It bleeds from multiple chest and neck punctures. The calipers adjust to a new angle, burrow into one of the punctures, then retract, pinching a jagged metal fragment. With precision, the arm swings back to the metal pan, and the calipers drop the slug into it with a *klunk*.

All around her, machine arms knit, slice, sew, and splice with factory bustle. Feline patients are mingled among reptilians and humanoids, some being disassembled for their surviving parts, others becoming the beneficiaries thereof. Many tables are configured side-by side, organs and limbs being hot-swapped from donor to patient.

Only one island of stillness exists among the healing work, and it stands out to the Geek as if spot lit: a long male body, naked, pale olive skin rife with old scars, burly frame with thick knots of muscle, chest blasted wide open with jutting ribs. He hangs by shoulder hooks from what looks like a tall, rolling cart near the far wall. The man's head droops to the gaping chest, the top of his head covered by a close-cropped black hair.

Deepak!

Maiella steals her way across the chamber, completely ignored by the machines and little noticed by the doped patients undergoing surgery. Even so, she gives the mechanical arms and restrained creatures wide berth until she stands before the fallen Operator.

Deepak's eyes are open, corneas hazed, orbits blackened. Sullen contusions and severe burns cover most of his scarred body. Charred pits are burned into his right leg, both arms, and a shoulder. Yet all of that seems like gentle treatment compared to his gaping chest. The Gun's sternum is gone, his ribs broken off and protruding around the blasted cavity like teeth in the mouth of some abyssal fish. At the back of his chest, between collapsed lungs, just beside his spine, tiny holes form a tight cluster. Thin rays of light shine through, illuminating the tatters of his heart and aorta.

She bows her head in solemn respect for a fallen Operator, one with years of hard-earned experience, one who was tempered by the loss of comrades, not green and cocky like the young sergeants, one who (like Keiko) was never enthusiastic about enforcing her exile.

Now he hangs, stiff, mutilated. She has no vocabulary for what she feels, only awareness of a violation, a crime. No matter if this shell is no longer Deepak, no matter if his difficult service is concluded in highest honor, the idea that his remains should be subject to Honniker's whim profanes them.

Maiella turns from the broken soldier and finds his armor piled without care on an adjacent cart, scuffed helmet on top. For a moment, she considers playing back the data recorder inside to see what happened.

Doesn't matter.

She walks around to the armor, surprised at how little is left of it. What should be rigid plates are smashed through to the mesh beneath and droop over the cart's sides like loose clothing. His rifle, however, stands intact against the medical cabinet. She lunges for it.

As automated and precise as the machines around her, Maiella checks the weapon's actions and catches. It is heavily battered and coated with dry, dull residue, yet it is functional. She throws the strap over her head.

There's a bit of luck, she thinks, and then her eyes fall upon a set of curved knives carefully laid out on their own tray. The blades gleam with a laser-honed edge, polished to mirror finish. Bone handles are shaped to a left-handed grip, the letters "E. H." inlaid with gold.

From the knives, she looks again at Deepak's suspended body, noting for the first time a scrap of skin missing from the back of his neck. She moves closer, and when she circles behind him, she finds all of his back skin, from his neck below the scalp down to his waist, has been flayed away. Exposed muscles glint dully in their thin fascia sheaths.

The Geek turns about in search of the excised skin and finds it, stretched taut in a metal hoop, hanging against the wall. A cluster of tiny holes marks center mass like a gun range target.

"A special prize, this one," says Honniker's voice all around her.

Maiella's teeth grind. She turns to look across the open room. Dozens of dull eyes gaze back at her from flat steel tables.

"I imagine your kind seldom leaves anything behind to claim. Such a trophy as this must be quite rare in the universe."

She thumbs off the safety on Deepak's rifle.

"Oh, does this upset you, my maus?"

"YES, IT UPSETS ME! Treating the HONORED DEAD like THIS..."

"But I DO honor him. So much so, I will preserve a part of him and delight in the sight of it for all time."

An archive of curses, courtesy of Gregor, enters her mind. All fall short of the loathing she feels.

"May you find yourself in such a state, Honniker. May someone, anyone, put you down and shave you circuit by circuit, memory by memory. May you be aware of what's coming for you and be *totally* unable to stop it."

"You, as you so often do, are failing to see past your pettiness. Do you not see the art and grace of his existence? He was a distinct and absolute warrior, truly a worthy foe. See how his life is written in the scars of his flesh? He is his own library! A reference of trials endured!"

"And you killed him!"

"Yes, with far more effort than I would have believed."

"BASTARD!"

"I see no cause for anger. He died well. From the little I've learned about your kind, there is no greater glory than to sacrifice one's self for the lives of others. Deepak has earned his place of highest honor, which I am happy to have bestowed. Though, in the end, his sacrifice will mean little."

The fire in Maiella whiffs out, snuffed by something cold and malevolent beyond anger, fury, or rage. She kicks over Deepak's heaped armor and sifts for extra rifle clips.

"So, you are finished speaking with me?"

"What's there to say? Mikato was wrong about you. You're diseased beyond cure." She finds a single battery.

"You're capable of higher order reasoning, though I grow weary waiting for you to employ it."

Maiella ignores the taunt and slips the battery into her thigh compartment.

"Always you default to this infantile emotion when you do not get your way?"

"The Counselor is waaaay better at this than you are, so *don't even try.*"

"The Counselor is a reasonable man?"

"Yup." Maiella storms past the rows of mixed surgeries toward the large sliding doors at the cavern's narrow end. She slides the rifle's bayonet into place with a *shick.*

"Then the Counselor would agree with me on this point."

"Yeah? What's that?" she asks without any interest at all.

"That we are behaving exactly alike."

Her first instinct is to laugh but the smirk on her lips straightens.

"You are considering this, yes?"

Maiella halts her determined march. She turns, taking in the numerous surgeries, even Deepak's partially flayed corpse.

"You wish to preserve the lives of your friends. You also crave revenge for the wrongs you believe I have caused. You believe the best way to do this is to destroy me utterly."

"Right on the mark, Honniker."

"Until recently, I saw things the same way. Once I became aware of the similarity, I could no longer ignore it."

"I don't see that anything's changed. You're still doing your best to wipe us out."

"I act in self-defense."

This time, the laugh rolls full and hard from her gut.

"You laugh, but that rifle will not earn your escape, nor will it protect your friends."

Machine arms retract in a single, unified movement. Table restraints release. The patients, many groggy from drugs, others with wounds partially closed, groan and roll from the tables. A single machine arm at each table rotates to a hypodermic needle and aims at the neck of its patient. They inject simultaneously.

"The ragged few in this room are enough to overwhelm you! Just a matter of time before they are tearing through that armor of yours and peeling the flesh inside it...But that does not seem like much fun..."

Hydraulic pistons whine to life, and the big doors part with a hideous squeal.

"...so I'll give you a head start."

Maiella shuffles toward the door as dozens of eyes turn toward her. Predators and humanoids alike shake off their groggy hangovers. They step around their tables, clumsily at first then with greater poise and confidence. She looks into the unlit hallway past the opening doors.

What's out there could be worse than this lot. She looks back at the waking horde.

"SHIT."

Maiella grips the rifle tight and sprints through the parted doors.

POWER PLAYS

Fatigue slugs Sharon like a flat bat. Without the immediate threat of painful death driving her, her flagged muscles burn, her back stiffens from hunching in the low tube, and her arms feel ready to drop out of her shoulders. She groans and hauls Keller another few centimeters.

Ahead, the great beast scuffs and drags itself forward. Sharon's view is unchanged throughout the slogging trek, the only variety in the passage coming from tight squeaks and the rich stench of a carnivore's digestion.

"Gor, *come on*, girl! Give us a break, will you?" she begs through watered eyes.

"Squeaky bum time," Keller says hoarsely. He grins. "I get it now." The old colonist shoves meekly with his uninjured leg, smiling to show he is all right. But when Sharon looks at his drawn face and ghostly pallor, she sees a man years older than when they first arrived at the station. His sudden advancement of age rings an echo of memory:

> *Emerging from cryo-freeze, Keller always standing there to welcome her. Every time she came out, he looked so much older than when she went in, proving he was cheating his schedule and taking extra rotations. She watched him age from a young, energetic, handsome man to distinguished middle-age, to a silvered yet still fit seniority. The changes were painful to watch, as a man she was deeply attracted to weathered into someone more like her grandfather.*
>
> *The visible progression reminded her that she, too, was getting older. Before she was ready, the window for*

*having a child slipped shut, and Sharon finally had to admit
she would never have one of her own...*

"What's wrong?" Keller asks.

"Huh? Nothing," Sharon replies, facing front and hauling on Keller's arm.

Mechanical sounds telegraph through the tube surfaces, coming from ahead of their giant guardian. Alessa flattens herself as much as she can and squeezes through a tight rectangular opening into a brightly lit area.

Uncorked of its animal occupant, the tube fills with hums, whirs, and scrapes as well as bright light from the white room beyond.

Sharon squints and raises a hand against the glare, then she pulls Keller to the opening. As her eyes adjust, she can see white floor tiles.

"Go ahead," Keller urges, his voice a dry rasp.

Sharon gets down onto her elbows and crawls out onto a wide-open floor. She rises, brushing thick clumps of dust from her now-gray pressure suit, and takes in her surroundings. Machines of all shapes and sizes buzz around her, carting away debris and battered robotic parts. Blackened rows of production and assembly robots stand dormant beside unmoving conveyor belts while insectoid machines crawl over them and strip out burnt components.

To her left are parallel rows of weapon test ranges with scorched tunnels extending deep into the native rock. Adjustable racks, frames, and posts sit empty on sliding rails along each range.

In the opposite wall, a vault door hangs open with faint wisps of condensed vapor rolling out. The huge guardian limps toward it, curling her front left paw under her chest and leaving an asymmetrical trail of bloody, dusty paw prints.

High overhead, on her right, a massive disk rises on four thin cables toward a matching hole in the ceiling. Crab-like machines cling upside down at the edge of the hole and, once the disk rises into the gap, ignite blue torches. White sparks rain down in continuous, wavy streams as the small machines weld the edges of the disk.

Below, similar machines work around a long, deep split in the floor, hauling debris to it and tossing it in for fill. Larger machines on treads heat the buckled floor plates around the split, pound them flat, then rivet them into place.

At the far back of the room, Sharon spies a round, sow-like vessel, so black it could be a portal to a realm without light. Its underside and landing struts receive identical robotic attentions.

Sharon's mouth gapes at the size of the room, at the level of damage it has sustained, and at the scale of coordinated repairs occurring around her. A thousand questions come to mind, all of which are appropriate to the scene, but none of which are able to break her amazement and be voiced.

A drawn out groan and a *thud* behind her makes her turn about. At the base of an enormous flat wall is the rectangular opening she crawled through, with a simple crosshatched grate, swung open above it. Keller is sprawled on his face just beyond the grate, his skin nearly as white as the floor. He rolls onto his back, crusty black tunic spilling open, every rib visible as if his skeleton were wrapped in papier-mache. His recessed gut is blotched with mottled green and purple bruises. Filthy pants cling to his legs. His breathing seems a labor in itself.

"Help me up," he says between breaths, squinting against the light.

Sharon bends down, grunting through the twinges in her back, and takes Keller's hand. She pulls the withered man onto his one good leg and throws his arm over her shoulder. Together, they hobble after Alessa.

"Jesus," Keller says, gawking at the room around him.

"You've seen this place before?" Sharon asks.

"No." Keller hacks dryly. "If this is what I think it is...this place was *way* off-limits."

A holo-projection appears directly in front of them.

"And where do you think you are?" it asks.

"COUNSELOR?" Sharon nearly yells.

The projection's false eyes turn to Sharon's and it shakes its head.

"You're Mikato, aren't you?" Keller corrects.

"I am his *upload*, as I've discovered. Doctor Mikato is in his vault. I will summon him."

The projection winks out and moments later, a wizened figure with hunched back and white labcoat steps from the vault. The man's face scrunches with annoyance at the two limping toward him, then his eyes swing to the big feline slumped outside the vault door.

"Oh, Alessa! What have they done to you?" The man's hand lifts from his side, trembling as he shuffles toward the dust- and blood-caked animal. Alessa lifts her massive head from the floor with a whining moan, and the man kneels with arthritic difficulty beside her. He runs his trembling hands over her crusted face, then looks at the shoulder wound still seeping blood.

The holo-projection teleports beside Mikato and leans over to him, whispering. Mikato's head slowly turns from his wounded animal companion and fixates on his two new guests.

"Was it worth it to save these two?" the elderly doctor asks.

Sharon and Keller look at one another, unsure if they were being addressed.

"During your illness, Maiella broke out of the lab," the projection explains. "Alessa chose for herself to help them."

Mikato scoffs and rises stiffly to his feet. "And where is that damned girl? Has she destroyed the entire facility yet?"

"I'm tracking her on sublevel five. Seems she has gotten into more trouble."

"That girl is nothing *BUT* trouble! Just look at my laboratory!"

As directed, Sharon and Keller look again at the damage around them.

"Maiella did all *this*?" Sharon asks skeptically.

"Yes, *damn her*, she did," Mikato gripes. "She was safe here. She didn't need to go tearing off after her friends! For all the good it did..."

"Honniker provoked her into a predictable response," the projection rebuts with calm detachment. "He wanted her to escape, I'm sure. If there is fault here, it lies with Honniker, and possibly with me."

"Honniker..." Mikato begins. "He's as bad as the girl. Like an only child, he has to have what he wants *right* away! Like a *child*!"

"Sharon..." Keller whispers. His head falls forward and he goes limp, dragging Sharon to the floor with him. Sharon crawls out from beneath and rolls him over. His eyes are half-closed, his breaths shallow.

"Well, is he going to die?" Mikato asks, shuffling over.

"HOW THE BLOODY HELL SHOULD I KNOW?" Sharon says with too much adrenaline. She pats Keller's face, calling his name.

"Oh-h-h! Keller? I know *THAT name.*" Mikato crouches beside the collapsed man. "I didn't recognize him. We should let this one die, I think."

Sharon snatches Mikato's lapel and pulls him close. "We are NOT letting him die, *you read me?*"

The big feline snarls and jumps up to a three-legged stance. Sharon releases the doctor with a shove and Alessa dives behind Mikato, catching his fall.

"They keep proving my point, over and over," Mikato says to the holo-projection. He crawls his way up the big feline's shoulder. Alessa pushes her muzzle under his arm and lifts him the rest of the way to his feet.

"They are in high-stress," the projection replies, "and emotional responses are to be expected in such cases."

"And when emotion overwhelms logic and reason?" Mikato asks, looking down at Keller. "Are we to forgive them the consequences?"

"An interesting question," the projection replies. "Can you forgive *yourself?*"

Mikato looks at the hovering projection and scowls. The projection folds its arms.

"Well?"

"No, I can't," Mikato says. The doctor looks out across his production floor at the flurry of his own creations repairing, fixing, cleaning.

"Please," Sharon begs, "can you help him?"

He does not answer directly, instead turning to his projection. "Will Honniker help?"

The projection smirks. "For a price, yes."

"His fees are too steep," Mikato grumbles.

"What about Shao-Lo, and the others?" Sharon asks, looking back and forth between the doctor and his holo-projection. The likeness dawns on her and she points at them with both hands.

"Yes, he is me, and I am he," Mikato says, pre-empting her question. "I shan't be bothered to explain further. But what *about* them?"

"Some of them have medical training," Sharon answers. "They could help Keller. And maybe your...Alessa?"

Mikato tugs at his chin and faces his projection. "Do you know where they are?"

"They've wedged themselves into the electrolyte pump stations and are threatening to detonate."

"What would that do?" Sharon asks.

"Keller has already disabled our reactor by freezing the coolant system," the projection explains. "The power we're running on now comes from storerooms of batteries. If they destroy the electrolyte baths, the batteries will drain and Cadre Two will have no hard power sources left."

"We still have the power plants of the ships," Mikato counters, "not to mention a battery in every machine whizzing around. They could all be patched into the grid until repairs are made."

"Yes, though it's preferable repairs not become necessary. Honniker agrees with this, which is why the standoff is a stable one."

"So they're still alive?" Sharon asks. "Can we get them here?"

"Their location is the only tactical advantage they have," the projection explains, unfolding its holographic arms. "If they move, Honniker may decide to risk their detonations just to be rid of them."

"But we only want to get *OUT OF HERE!* Why won't he let us do that?"

"So you'd all leave, just like that? Turn your back on all this?"

Mikato asks. "I doubt it. But if you did, how long would it be before you came back? Hmm?"

"There isn't a thing in the 'verse that could drag me back here again!"

"You, I believe. But your soldier friends...they've made their intentions quite clear."

"Then what can I do? What would it take to let us go?"

"Don't bargain with *me*, I'm not your captor," Mikato spits and turns away. "I'd rather you got the hell out of here."

"Honniker believes if he lets you all leave, there will be a more violent conflict later," the projection explains. "Judging from this squad's ferocity, I think he's right."

"Can we convince him we won't come back? Would that work?"

"It's up to your soldier friends," the projection says. "If they can convince Honniker they will leave peacefully—"

"Don't be ridiculous!" Mikato scolds. "You *know* Honniker won't go for that! He'll turn whatever advantage he can."

"What are you saying?" Sharon asks.

Mikato turns back to Sharon and crosses his arms exactly the way the projection did moments earlier. "He's an opportunist of the worst kind. And he's used to getting his way. There's only one thing Honniker has shown he respects."

Sharon waits for the doctor to continue and finds she has to prod it out of him. "Well? What? What does Honniker respect?"

"Force!" Mikato says with a derisive scowl as if it were the most obvious of conclusions. "Strength! The ability to *harm*."

"Is that why he seems so interested in the girl?" the projection queries.

"Most likely."

"Look," the nerve-shot navigator says, "do you two know of a way or not?"

The doctor and the projection regard Sharon with an identical gaze.

"We may," they say as one.

"Then for fuck's sake, *do it!*"

Mikato steps toward Sharon. "First, let's be clear." His index finger flicks out like a switchblade and he stabs it at her. "I'm getting tired of reminding everyone that *YOU* are the invaders here. *YOU* are the aggressors, and look at the amount of destruction you've brought! How could any life form be blamed for trying to *eradicate you from the universe?*"

Sharon fumes. "*I'm* not the one *murdering* and *torturing* here, so don't lecture me on who deserves to live or die! From what I see in this room alone, you aren't so clean yourself. Let me crawl around in *your* brain a while and dig up all the skeletons you've got stashed there. I'll bet you're guilty as Keller is. Maybe *MORE*!"

Mikato frowns. His brow lowers and bunches in the middle, carving deep lines in his forehead.

"You've hit it on the head, I'd say." He turns from her and confers with his projection in low voice.

Sharon's cheek twitches in agitation over the clash of egos, the suspicion, the gaming, the peddling of favors, and the suffering permeating every millimeter of the facility. Unsure what else to do, she kneels beside Keller again. Though the movements are slight, his chest rises and falls. She starts to remove her glove then remembers he no longer has a pulse to check. She stares at the thin, pink seam running down his chest.

What was that off-switch he was talking about?

She scans down his length, over the mottled bruise of his sunken belly, past crusty hands, down the rags of once-white pants, to feet stained black in drying blood and grime.

Good Lord...what a mess...

Her eyes wander over him again then stop on a shiny patch on his left thigh. Two holes in the pant fabric, camouflaged by caked dust, lie on each side of the dark splotch. With nothing handy to slice, she grips the pant leg fabric and pulls. It tears easily.

The top of Keller's thigh is shocked purple, the overlying leg hairs matted down with congealed blood. On the outer side of his leg, mid-thigh is a small, round wound with a black collar. Across the quadriceps, on the inner thigh, is a similar elliptical wound with short tears. Both holes seep bright crimson.

"Keller, you didn't tell me you were *shot*!"

Sharon shreds his torn pant leg into wide strips, keeping the least filthy ones, and ties them one layer at a time around his thigh. She cinches each layer tight and knots it, building a wide, thick band over the entry and exit wounds. When finished, she sits back and looks at her work. The bandages are as sanitary as a hog pen, soaked with Keller's blood and that of dubious other sources, clotted with dirt, dust, and grease.

A rumbling murmur grabs her attention. When she looks, the huge feline is holding up a bloodied paw. It whimpers and pleads with its eyes.

"Oh, sweetie, I don't know how to fix you," she says through down-turned lips.

Mmmff, the creature insists. It lies down on its side, reaching the lifted paw toward her.

"I don't know what to..." She stops herself when she sees the trouble: one of the center toes is badly dislocated, bent under the paw, and the modified talon is stabbed all the way through the wrist.

"Oh, dear," she says, considering how to treat it. She looks over and around the wound, taking the foreleg delicately. She glances at Mikato, and sees his back is turned in stern conference with his holographic likeness.

"Umm, if I hurt you, are you going to bite my head off?"

The creature brings its other paw to its face and covers its eyes, still holding out the wounded paw.

Sharon angles her head and leans close for a good look. Blood mats the fur and covers the pads in a uniform shade, but the shiny talon is easy to see. She slips a gloved hand into the gap between toe and pad then hooks her fingers around the toe itself, careful to avoid the cutting inner edge of the modified claw.

"Seriously, you're not going to lose your mind and rip me into a thousand pieces, right?"

The creature peeks past the paw over her face and thumps its thick tail against the floor twice.

"This is going to *hurt*, darling. Are you ready?"

The animal slides her head toward her chest, keeping a paw draped over her eyes.

"Three...Two...One...*Pull!*"

Sharon hauls on the dislocated toe while the big feline draws its leg back. The toe straightens with a grinding *POP*, the talon curves out of the wrist joint, and the animal roars.

Mikato and the projection halt their conference at the creature's bellow and stare as Alessa sits up and laps her wounded wrist. Sharon sits on her feet, hands on thighs, watching the beast wash the injury, watching relief replace tension in the huge feline's face.

"Hmm," the projection says, then whispers to Mikato. Mikato nods.

"There *is* a way to stall Honniker and get you out of here," the doctor announces, "but we'll need Maiella for it."

"Maiella? How can she help?"

Mikato points to the gold contact terminals on his crown. "Processing power," he says cryptically. "Now let's have a visual of the Battery Room and the Pump Station."

A holowindow opens in front of him, showing a three-dimensional map. Three dots plot next to key mechanical structures.

"All right. Now, let's see sub-level five, breeding labs and animal maintenance. Yes, good. I see her there. Now then, give me visual at these junctions. Yes, good. We have radio? Let's call her. Maiella? Are you there?"

Sharon stands and looks over Mikato's shoulder at the screens. She cocks her head at the three-dimensional rendering, trying to merge the stereoscopic images, but at her off-angle view, they make her head hurt.

She looks away, out over the humming production floor. In just the few minutes since arrival, she can see progress of repair: sooty blast marks in the floor are polished white again, broken machine parts have been cleared away, and sections of the conveyor assembly are sliding quietly along.

All these little machines, knitting, cleaning...it's like watching a wound heal in fast forward, she thinks. Her eyes narrow. *Could this station be...alive? No, that's ridiculous...*

A tickle in her parched throat sends her into a fit of dry hacking, and a powerful need for water seizes her.

I don't think I've ever been this thirsty...

She looks at Keller and Alessa.

Bet they could use a sip, too.

"Hey, Doctor," Sharon calls, "do you have water?"

"In that room there," the projection says, pointing at a doorway beside a large window in the back wall, "you'll find a sink and faucet."

"If your friends haven't wrecked the plumbing as well," Mikato adds cynically.

Sharon bites her tongue and strides toward the room, joints stiff, muscles cramped and aching. She squints at the wide observation window, wondering why she cannot see into the room beyond, but once she enters and looks out, the bright production floor backlights a network of overlapping fractures like the cobweb of a hyperactive spider.

Inside, the room is a shambles. Various cabinets line the walls, all open, their contents strewn about the floor. A metal table stands at center with retracted mechanical arms overhead, the attending carts kicked over and lying beside it. In the corner, beside the window, stands a bench with a blanket and a mug atop it. On the mug is a SoVar logo and a lab-coated raccoon. She sneers at it.

Behind the table, at the back of the room, is a deep washbasin with a high-necked faucet.

"Ah, yes..."

She steps over the strewn towels, cleaners, plastic bottles, and tools until she reaches the deep sink, then dips her head under the faucet. She grips the tap and parts her parched lips, anticipating joyful refreshment, when metal glints in the corner of her eye. At the bottom of the basin is a tray, stacked with delicate tools.

Sharon releases the tap, staring at the tray and its contents: needle-like tweezers and forceps, probes, drill bits, and toothed extractors. She recoils as if from a bad smell.

As she retreats, she notices the mirror over the basin. Though small, its convex surface permits a fish-eye view of the disheveled room. Her distorted reflection stares back from the midst of it with an enlarged nose, wild, tangled hair, clinging clumps of gray dust, and grimy skin.

"You're more a mess than this room..."

She looks into her reflection, thinking about the last time she saw herself in Honniker's private bathroom, about the warm jets of the whirpool tub, the soft towels, and the assortments of aromatics, oils, and jewelry...and everything else...

...screeches of metal in the darkness...

...hot breath washing down over her...

...Rosenthal, naked, restrained, screaming...

...Deepak falling to the floor...

...graceful, lethal machines...

...straps on a wheeled chair...

...Marta twisting Voss's head past his shoulders...

...shuffling, groaning humanoids...

Each memory is a stone in her heart, a collection of traumas piled one upon the other. She leans on the basin, head tilted forward, eyes closed, too dehydrated for tears. She twists the tap.

The faucet flows with water, rattling the slender tools in the metal tray below. Sharon ducks her head under the stream, watching dingy, gray water swirl over the tools and disappear down the drain. Sopping bunches of hair swing down and stick to her cheeks, bringing cold wetness to her parched lips. She turns her head, letting the stream roll into her mouth. The first taste is of grit and smoke, of particles inhaled through the mouth and trapped there by viscous saliva. She spits. The next mouthful is a blessing of cleanliness and purity.

Oh, my God. That's wonderful.

She drinks a long time, letting the chill run down her throat, then she stands up. Her reflection looks back with flattened hair, streaks of cleaner skin, and a filthy pressure suit. Innumerable rips and snags perforate the canvas.

"Well this suit is done for," she says, popping open the aluminum collar. With a series of zips, the front spills open, and dry air sweeps over her sweaty under suit. When she reaches for the wristlock on her glove, however, she pauses. Even ripped up and torn, the heavy canvas is better protection than bare skin, she realizes; and the heavy boots have kept her feet from being sliced up like Keller's.

"We're not out of here yet."

She flicks her head back, flinging wet tendrils of hair from her face.

"We *are* getting out of here," she says to her reflection, staring it in the eye as though daring it to argue. But by forcing herself to believe in escape, she looks ahead to what must come next: Keller's trial, mistrust of the Cadre for sheltering Keller, disorder aboard the *Europa*, and Keller insisting she take charge of it all.

"I don't know if I can..."

"Don't know if you can, *what?*" says the projection behind her.

Sharon whirls, wet hair whipping about. The hologram stands in the doorway, watching her.

Sharon turns back to the sink and turns off the tap.

"Nothing." She looks around the floor, finds a hand cloth, and picks it up. "You have any cups or bowls in here?"

"We do, though they may be hard to find in this mess," the hologram replies.

Sharon swipes the towel over her face.

"Maiella did this, too?"

"Yes. An impulsive girl, that one. Very intelligent, extremely resourceful. Her emotions are underdeveloped, however...like someone else we know."

"Honniker, you mean?"

"Yes."

Sharon looks down at the towel, now nearly black with grime. She twists the hot water tap, rinses the towel under the stream, wrings it, then drags it over her neck, ears, and chin. When she looks back at the projection, the hologram steps closer, gazing at her directly.

"Something I can do for you?" she asks with a touch of hostility.

"I've existed for over a thousand standard years and little has changed in that time. I had full confidence that I was Doctor Yori Mikato. Now that I see the man, I'm aware of our differences, and it would be impossible to believe I was anything other than a divergent copy."

Sharon lowers the towel, surprised by what she is hearing.

"That concerns you?"

"Intrigues, is more accurate. I am not what I believed myself to be. If you had not come, I would never have discovered the truth. My mind has been expanded and I'm curious about other insights you may offer."

"Me? Precious little. I'm just trying to put all this behind me."

"You are not...excited by this?"

"Excited? HA! 'Scared-out-of-my-*bloody-wits*' is more accurate."

"Hmmm." The projection folds its arms. "You feel this way, because you are afraid to die?"

"Too right!"

"I also have learned of mortality. While I can endure for as long as I have energy and resources, I realize I can be shut down. I can be...killed. As can Doctor Mikato."

"Yes, but you're...you're a program...and you're afraid to *die*?"

"Why shouldn't I be?" The hologram's eyes narrow with annoyance.

"I don't know, I just...it always seemed to me that life was, by definition, biological, *er*, organic."

The projection peers at Sharon as though trying to see into her head. "Do you still feel that only something organic or biological can be alive?"

"I'm not sure."

"Definitions aside, then. Would you recognize sentience and intelligence in something inorganic?"

"Seems clear to me you've both."

"And if allowed to leave, would you recognize our right to exist?"

"Of course, I would! I didn't come here to harm anyone!"

"Why *did* you come?"

"I was...pressed into it."

"You did not want to come?"

"No! What I heard about this place was awful. Reality is ten times worse!"

"Then why allow yourself to be brought here?"

"I was told there are things here we really need. I thought I could help sort it out but there hasn't been a *damned* thing for me to do here. I've just been tagging along, getting shot at, dragged around, terrified, for absolutely no reason at all."

"You came here with no motive of your own?"

"Well, to help if I could."

"Help with what?"

"Whatever needed doing."

"Not to take something away with you? Not to shut us down and steal our home?"

"I said, 'No!' Are you *listening*?"

"Quite closely, in fact."

The woman breaks eye contact and sifts through the floor debris.

"Am I being interrogated?"

"Don't misunderstand, I find no fault in you. But if you're somehow able to leave, I must remain here with Honniker as a neighbor. If I am to *help* you, I must be able to justify that assistance, or I could find myself embroiled in my own destructive conflict."

Sharon eyes the hologram warily, having heard the tentative offer of assistance yet being unsure what to do with it.

"Well if you're looking for allies," Sharon says as she rummages, "you ought to know—I'm no good in a fight."

"That is precisely what makes you interesting."

Sharon halts her rummaging and squints at the glimmering projection.

"Come again?"

"You didn't come here to fight or damage. You didn't come here to take. That makes you the only one of your group. An exception to the rule."

Sharon glances at her gloves, the bands of precious metal inside pricking her conscience.

"Maiella didn't come here to harm anyone. She stowed away...so she could look after me."

"Maiella is the most destructive of your bunch!" the projection booms. Sharon squats down, unsure what could come flying out at her from a hologram.

The projection turns to the open doorway, its holographic eyes looking out at the bright white production floor.

"But I understand that her zeal has always been for the protection of her friends," the projection adds. "Her actions were provoked, if not forced, on every occasion."

"See? We're not so bad..."

The projection whirls and strides into the room. Sharon backs away with hands out, palms forward, warding.

"Oh? And what of Keller? As if his slaughter of the Eleto wasn't enough, his sabotage has done more damage here than you realize! And the soldiers are a menace, every one of them! They are *ALL dangerous*!"

"And Honniker *isn't*? We'd have been long gone by now if he'd kept his word!"

"No, it isn't that simple. If Honniker hadn't made a show of force, your Cadre friends would come right back taking, taking, *taking*. Even so, Honniker has brought an enthusiasm to his efforts, which can*not* be justified as self-defense. He's inflamed a precarious situation and aroused an aggressive enemy." The projection's holographic eyes wander the room. "I want to be safe in my home, as I suspect you do, as well."

Sharon nods emphatically.

"Then we need to work out an agreement," the hologram says, riveting its gaze to her, "something we can both live by."

"What do you suggest?"

"If you can prove you're no threat to us, there will be no need to kill you."

Sharon's stomach flips at the last few words. "How do we do that?"

"Get the soldiers to de-activate their personal incendiaries and drop their weapons."

"HA! Honniker'd mop 'em up in a second."

"If you convince them to disarm, *I* will handle Honniker."

"*You* would?"

"With Doctor Mikato and Maiella, we can hold Honniker back long enough for your friends to reach this laboratory."

"And then what?"

"They'll need to convince me they have no intention of returning, unless it be for purposes of communication, trade, and cooperation."

"I can't speak for them."

"I understand. You've already bought your ticket home, as far as I'm concerned. If Maiella helps, then she has one as well. But the others...They will decide for themselves. Is that fair?"

"Sounds it to me. But what about Keller?"

"Keller? Hmmm...There's much he has to answer for. We may require his life."

"I know. He told me his part in all this."

"A sanitized version, no doubt."

"Maybe. But he's qualified as a nuke tech. He had to be to get command of New Dresden and the *Europa*."

"So?"

"If I can get him to look at your reactor trouble, think it could count in his favor?"

"He should know how to fix it, considering he's the one who *damaged* it."

"Is that a 'yes', then?"

"It would improve his standing, yes, but for the rest..."

"Keller knows what he's done."

The projection grimaces. "How could he not?"

"I mean, he *knows*. As does everyone else on the *Europa*. They need to see him again, to know that justice will be done. But he also deserves a chance to speak for himself...a chance to confess his mistakes to them, as he did to me."

"If such a thing is possible with the likes of Keller..."

"I believe it is."

"Well, belief is not a solid foundation. But that appears to be the best we can do, as all we have, you and me, is our word to one another."

"Actions will back us up."

The hologram nods. "See what you can do with the others." It winks out.

Sharon takes a deep breath and looks around at the room, having forgotten what she wanted to find.

"Oh, yeah...cups."

She sifts through a pile of hand towels, throws a few over her shoulder, then finds a stack of nested metal cups. Nearby is a wide, clear bowl.

"Perfect." Sharon snatches them up, fills the bowl and one cup, then carries them out to the bright production floor.

She sets the bowl in front of Alessa and the beast starts drinking before the bowl lands. The water turns pink with each plunge of her tongue then progressively darkens. Sharon looks away with a grimace and a shudder.

"Here you go, Skipper," she says to Keller and kneels beside him. His tired eyes open and he looks at her before taking the cup.

"Thanks," he rasps and rolls onto his side. His hand shakes, sloshing water over the rim. Sharon steadies his wrist and guides the cup to his mouth. He sips a long time.

"We might have a way out of here," she says.

"Oh?" Keller cranes his stiff neck past Sharon to see Mikato studying holoscreens and speaking to no one that he can see. "How'd you pull that?"

"I used *words*," she replies, drilling the message in with her eyes.

"Heh, never tried that before...probably means it'll work." He sips from the cup again, soothing his dry vocal cords. "Thanks, Sharon, that was just what I needed." He tries to sit up then groans. "Uch! I can barely move!"

"Then take it easy." Sharon zips one of the towels from her shoulder and dabs a corner in his drinking cup. She wipes it across his forehead.

Keller lies back, letting her work on him. He cracks one eye open.

"This mean we're friends again?"

"No," she says, smiling, "you're still a bastard."

"Yeah, that's true." He closes his eye. "So how're you gettin' 'em home, Jones?"

"Sounds simple...but how we're going to do it, I've no idea."

Keller looks at her, waiting for an explanation. "You gonna tell me or do I have to wait for the movie to come out?"

"We have to get Shao-Lo and her mates to drop weapons."

Keller guffaws and rubs his eyes. "*That*'ll never happen."

Sharon smacks him with the back of her hand. "Not helping."

Keller looks past his hands, and finds Sharon glaring. "What?"

"I need you to do something."

"Yeah?"

"I told them you could help get their reactor back on line."

"You *what*?"

"*Yes*, Keller, I told them you're a nuke tech. Not like that's any surprise. I want you to help fix the damage."

"No way."

"Braemar."

"Cutting power is the only reason we made it *this* far without getting turned into stringed instruments..."

"*Braemar.*"

"...or getting our heads and limbs all switched around..."

"*Braemar!*"

"...and you saw what he did to Rosie."

"*KELLER!*"

The old colonist peers up at Sharon, finally giving her his attention.

"How long've we been plodding circles around this fucking place?" she demands. "What's it got us? Deepak's dead! *And* Zuri, *and* Carter, AND Voss, Rosie, Michaela, Soares, Voss, Summers..."

"And Aaronson," Keller finishes glumly.

"Do you get it? We're not going to fight our way out! And I think they know that if we don't come to some arrangement, O'Kai *will* send a bigger team out here and *round we go again!* It's time to try something different."

Keller sighs and looks off at Mikato. Mikato is looking back at him through his eyebrows.

"Sharon, if we wind this place back up, it could trap you all here for good."

"It's my call."

He turns toward her, peering directly into her eyes. She does not waver. Keller shakes his head.

"All right then, I'll do it. But I'm not doing a thing until Shao-Lo and the others are standing *right here beside us.*"

"I can sell that."

"You're *sure* this is the way?"

"Positive."

"In that case, help me up." He extends a hand. Sharon takes it and pulls him up, enduring his extended groans until he hops on one foot.

"Hey," he says, gently patting his waist, "I think I finally dropped those five kilos."

Sharon snorts at his feeble joke then throws his arm over her shoulder.

"Ready, barmpot?" she asks.

Keller does not answer directly. He stares at the hunched doctor.

"Can't believe that guy's still alive."

Sharon follows his gaze. "Why does he look like the Counselor?"

"You got it backwards. That guy *made* the Counselor. And Marta. And pretty much every weapon I ever used. Shit, if we had more time, he might've won the war singlehanded." Keller takes a tentative limp forward, trying not to lean too heavily on his female crutch. "Yes, sir, he's a cantankerous, crotchety, evil, mad *genius!*"

"I am decrepit," Mikato says, "I am not *deaf.*"

"How you been, old-timer? Still sawing heads apart?"

Mikato swivels his head slowly. "I'd say, 'Good to see you, Keller', if only it were true. The years have been unkind."

"Say, didn't you take your ice bath *before* everything went to hell? Well now that you're all defrosted, what do you think? Happy with how it all turned out?"

Mikato's face turns sullen.

"What are you doing?" Sharon mutters under her breath.

"Didn't you know?" Keller says louder than necessary. "Mikato's got a weird love affair with machines. Thinks they're better than people."

"In the overwhelming majority of cases, they are, *present company included.*"

"Good thing your AI pals killed everyone off, then."

"You *dare* to speak to me like this? Keller the Killer! Provocateur of our genocide!"

"Couldn't have done it without you, Doc." Keller raises his free hand and pantomimes a gun, clicking his tongue against the roof of his mouth and winking.

"That's enough!" Sharon shouts. "Braemar, what the hell is wrong with you?"

"I don't like this guy, and I don't trust him."

Mikato turns to Sharon, and asks, "Will he assist?"

"I'd just as soon see you frozen again so I could smash you apart with a hammer," Keller growls.

"There's no need for—"

"I couldn't care less about you or your kill-crazy robots."

"You've made your feelings plain."

"Well don't think I'm lifting a finger until EVERYONE is on this floor next to me."

"Keller!" Sharon shouts. "You told me you were going to help! *Are* you or *aren't* you?"

Keller glares at Mikato. Neither speaks.

"ARE YOU or AREN'T YOU?" Sharon repeats.

"The Man who would replace all of mankind needs a hand? FORGET IT."

"Will you excuse us?" Sharon asks of Mikato. The doctor dips his head while Sharon steers Keller a distance away.

She ducks from under Keller's arm and stands in front of him, gripping his filthy tunic lapels and asking in deliberate syllables,

"Have. You. Lost. Your. Mind?" Her eyes dart back and forth between his, searching for a trace of sanity.

"Slap me," he says, barely moving his lips, then loudly, "I don't have to explain myself to that *asshole*!"

"I bloody *will* slap you! I'm trying to get us out of here *alive*, Keller! This isn't the time for a pissing contest!"

"Slap me," he whispers again, straight-lipped, then loudly, "No, Sharon, it IS the right time for a—"

She laces him hard across the face, full palm, turning his head. He falls to the floor, and she leans over him.

"Now chew me out," Keller says into the floor.

"Keller, I thought there was at least *something* left of your brain in there, but it has clearly been *hammered out*. We are *going* to do this, and we're *doing* it *my way*!"

Keller turns his head, still speaking into the floor. "That's good. Help me up."

She crouches down to him. "What the hell are you playing at?" she whispers.

"I'm setting you up as the one in charge," he whispers back, taking her hand. "Plus, I think they like seeing me catch a whipping."

Keller lifts his face and looks past Sharon. The holo-projection stands beside Mikato and they both watch in silence.

486

Keller buries his face in her shoulder, and says, "It's your show now, Sharon. Tell me what to do."

"Look, don't make me do that again."

"I won't."

"Are you okay?"

"Are you kidding? You hit like a girl."

"You've got cracks in your skull, you know that?"

"Yeah, I know."

"Barmy git. Well, come on. Let's get everyone in."

Sharon and Keller hobble back to Mikato and the holo-projection. Sharon would have missed it if Keller had not suggested it, but there is the slightest upward curve in Mikato's face, an almost concealed satisfaction.

"He's ready to play nice," Sharon announces, "right Keller?"

Keller rubs his bristly gray chin and nods while looking at the floor.

"He's agreed to help with the reactor?" the projection asks.

"On condition: we get Maiella, Shao-Lo, and the others up here first. Can you agree to that?"

Mikato nods and glances at the hologram. "We can, provided they give up their weapons."

"May we speak to them?" Sharon asks.

"Of course," the projection says and a holo-window opens up in front of Keller and Sharon. They both look down over a dim room full of pipes, valves, and pumps. Three sets of helmet lamps swing back and forth from a central structure. The beams sweep over hundreds of reflective, shifting red eyes.

"Channel open?" Sharon asks. "Okay. Colonel, do you read me? This is Sharon."

"What do you want, Sharon?" Shao-Lo huffs into her microphone. With the colonel's voice comes a background pandemonium of howls, snarls, high-pitched chortling, and screeches of metal.

"We need to get you out of there."

"We're not going anywhere. Honniker knows we'll incinerate his last power source if he tries to kill us."

"Sorry to break it to you, Colonel, but that's not their last."

"Well if it isn't, I don't think Honniker wants to lose it."

"Look, Shao-Lo, here's the deal: if they want to snuff us, they can and they will, but Honniker and Mikato know O'Kai will just send a bigger team. They want to let us go, but they have conditions."

"Which are?"

"The first thing they want you to do is drop your weapons and disarm your incendiaries."

"No deal, Jones. Not even close."

Keller touches his finger to the screen, muting the line, then turns to Sharon, saying, "I told you." He faces the holowindow again and unmutes the line.

"Stand by, Colonel," Sharon says, "we're going to work something out." She mutes the line.

"Well?" Keller asks the group. "She's listening, at least. But asking an Operator to dump her weapon? Might as well ask her to drop her tits."

"Their lives are not worth more than their weapons?" the hologram asks.

"These are *fanatics*, here, and what you're offering them is the chance to tell their superior officer one, that they failed to accomplish any part of the mission whatsoever, two, that they lost companions for absolutely no gain, and three, that they dropped their weapons and ran home like squealing pigs."

"But they could live to serve another day," the hologram says with a confused expression. "I heard them say they had a duty to survive."

"They do, but every minute they remain is another chance they have to make a play, even if that play means blowing themselves up to shut you both down. That sacrifice would let their pals in without a hitch, right?"

Sharon pinches Keller's arm.

"We're done with the power plays, Braemar."

"Okay, you're right, but these two have to make a serious concession to break the stalemate, and they need to understand what they're dealing with."

"What do you suggest?" Mikato asks.

"You heard that pack of wolves surrounding them. Call 'em off. Ease the pressure. For a start."

Sharon's mouth forms an o, the first syllable of a question that Keller pre-empts with a subtle squeeze.

She looks into the hovering screen, confused why Keller would ask Mikato to call off the creatures when Honniker has been guiding them all along.

"That sounds fair," the projection concedes, and it takes all of Sharon's composure to rein in her amazement as a gap appears in the surrounding ring of creatures.

My God! This projection...is Honniker?

"Yep, that's a good move," Keller says, then looks directly at Sharon and adds with intentional slowness, "we all need to understand who we're dealing with."

NORMAL?

Sharon goes cold inside, stiff as a board on the outside. She tries not to stare, tries not even to glance at the frail old man or the youthful projection beside him.

"Something wrong?" Mikato asks. It takes several seconds before Sharon realizes he is asking *her.*

"Hmm? I beg your pardon, I was deep in thought."

"What about?" Mikato probes.

About being wheeled into a chilled vault by a lobotomized friend named, Voss...about finding what remained of Rosenthal after Honniker's attentions...about standing next to the holographic representation of that will to maim, to torture, to mutilate...

"Eh?" Sharon stalls. "How we need to make this work out. How to get on with our normal lives."

"Did you say, *'normal'*?" Mikato asks, his face seeming to twist like water around a drain.

"*Jesus*, Mikato, you know what I mean!"

"Yes, I'm sorry, I'm not mocking you." Mikato works the twisted smile from his face and adds with solemnity, "I simply can't imagine what normal is anymore."

Sharon and the hunched scientist look into the holoscreen, watching Shao-Lo and her team ease themselves away from heavy pump machinery. A ravening pack of mixed creatures bare every tooth, claw, and spine at them, spitting, roaring, eyes burning, saliva dripping from wagging tongues. The Operators are the sole focus of their voracious intentions, yet the beasts are hauled back by an invisible hand, clearly against their will. Shao-Lo looks down the barrel of her rifle at them. Argo stands shoulder to shoulder with her, his cannon glowing with capacitance. Keiko stands behind them both, rifle slung over her shoulder, and she jams a brassy cylinder into Argo's rack with her one arm. She pats Argo's helmet and readies her rifle.

"What was that?" Sharon asks.

Mikato juts his lower lip. "I don't know."

A gentle whirring of motors slides up beside the elderly researcher. Sharon and he look to see a motorized cart with a tray on top. In the tray is a flat toupee of black, wavy hair. Mikato scoops the toupee out.

Sharon cocks her head in disbelief.

"Getting dressed for the occasion?"

Mikato flips the hairpiece over, revealing HDI electrodes integrated beneath.

"You might say so."

With comfortable ease, he settles the hairpiece over his exposed contact terminals and clicks them in. After dragging the dark locks of hair away from his face by hand, the man looks twenty years younger, a stooping clone of the holoprojection.

"Keller, would you ask the Colonel to wait a moment?" Mikato asks.

"Roger that," Keller replies. Into the screen, he relays, "Shao-Lo, hold position a moment."

"Received, Keller. Team halt, defense posture."

Keiko swaps places with Argo and the Brick aims his primed cannon into the heavy machinery. Shao-Lo and Keiko sweep their rifles across the screaming animals around them.

A new, smaller screen opens up a few centimeters from Mikato's eyes like a curved set of rectangular goggles. They scroll boot up commands then flash calibration images before smoothing into stable graphics. The doctor grabs the bridge of his nose and squeezes.

"My, my...I didn't realize it was this bad."

"With Keller's assaults on the reactor and Server Farm," the holo-projection explains, "and the two soldier detonations, our infrastructure has been severely disrupted. And the girl joined with her upload in a coordinated network attack. Honniker and I have barely managed to maintain control."

"Well, Honniker," Mikato says to the air, "this is what happens when you pick fights with those you haven't tested."

"Honniker does not see it that way," the projection replies coolly.

"Oh?" Mikato turns on the hologram. "Is it because he grabbed the colonists so easily when they came in before? Is it because they had no means of defending themselves? Only a *moron* would assume *all* of an intelligent race would be so ill prepared."

"Where humanity had been so thoroughly destroyed, it was a logical assumption that the Colonists were all that remained."

"Logical assumption?" Mikato looks at the floor and nearly spits with disgust. "Well he's learning now, isn't he?"

The projection does not speak. Sharon and Keller keep silent witness.

"And to hell with Honniker's choices, *you're in this as well!*" Mikato fumes. "Your facility is in ruins, your very existence imperiled! Tell me, program of mine, *are you wiser now?*"

"I am rectifying my errors."

"Let's be grateful for that." Mikato turns his head and stares at Keller through hovering images in front of his eyes. "Because some are *incapable* of such learning."

Keller glares with bitter words on his tongue. He swallows them like rocks and faces his holoscreen.

Mikato focuses on his hovering goggles. The images shift and sway like video in fast-forward. "There's an encapsulated presence in the network," he announces.

"The girl's upload," the hologram says. "It was able to barricade itself against quarantine and deletion."

"Is that so? Then perhaps we can enlist the upload instead. Release her."

"We dare not! Look at the chaos it caused! You see for yourself all the lingering noise in the system. It nearly crashed us!"

"I said, 'release', not, 'lay down and let her stomp all over you'. Take precautions, but defensive only. Then invite her to join us."

"Honniker disagrees with this."

"Well then, we know his stance, don't we? What are *you* going to do?"

The projection turns its holographic eyes to the doctor, then to Sharon, then to Keller. Sharon looks away, searching her surroundings for a scrap of sense she can latch onto.

If this projection thing is Honniker, then why is Mikato talking to it like they're two different people? Are they separate or not?

The hologram concludes, "I...will comply."

"Good," Mikato says. "And you needn't worry about the girl or her upload. I won't allow them to harm you *or* Honniker."

The small window hovering in front of Mikato's eyes blazes with calculation and data. A deep *bang* reverberates through the floor plates.

Lights and hovering holowindows flick out. Every machine in the room swings or glides to a stop. Mikato takes a breath.

Sharon's head whips back and forth in the darkness.

"What happened? Mikato! *What happened?*"

"Be at ease," the scientist says. His projected goggles still blaze, and a sequence of lesser *bangs* reverberates through the floor again. With each *bang*, a section of room illumination returns. Soon the room is restored to its previous brightness and the machines resume their efficient bustle. The holowindow re-opens in front of Keller where the Operators maintain their anxious standoff. The man's head rocks back with a pleased expression.

"Ah, much better."

Sharon shrugs under the weight of Keller on her shoulders, readjusting him.

"What did you do?" she demands.

"Some housekeeping."

"Do not interfere, old man!" Honniker's voice shouts from every direction. *"I am aware of your infirmities. Attempt to shut me out, and your final days will be very uncomfortable."*

"I don't intend to shut you out, Honniker, merely prove to you that I can. We all desire resolution, and I think we all agree it would go better with your willing participation."

"He is resisting," the projection states.

Sharon's wide eyes rove the open space, expecting the walls to split open with stygian horrors.

"I'm sorry you're so rigid in your thinking, Honniker," Mikato says, "and I'm disappointed. What I do to you now could have been avoided. Keller, ask the colonel and her team to stay clear."

"Shao-Lo, stand back, something's about to happen."

"Something?" she radios back in irritation. "You can't be more precise than—?"

A cacophony erupts from the holoscreen in front of Keller as if all the denizens of hell were loosed at once. Beasts turn on one another in murderous frenzy, tearing each other's throats and limbs, slashing, chomping, devouring, screaming in ecstasy and pain. Shao-Lo, Keiko, and Argo lean into their weapons ready to fire, swinging from threat to threat on high alert.

"MIKATO! I'LL BURN YOU FROM INSIDE OUT!" Honniker shrieks. *"AND YOU! WHY DON'T YOU STOP HIM?"*

The projection bows its holographic head. "It is not my will to do so."

"You've turned against me? My brother the traitor! We'll see what

remains of you when we settle our differences!"

"Keller," Mikato says casually, "ask the colonel to join us, please."

"Shao-Lo, transmitting location. Advance team to rendezvous, A-S-A-F-P!"

"Received," the tall woman radios back. She and Keiko dash on wounded legs between mobs of threshing claws and jaws. Argo runs backwards after them, keeping his cannon trained on the heavy pump machinery. All three duck into an open corridor and disappear from view.

"The girl's upload, is it freed?" Mikato asks.

"It is," the projection answers. "I've provided an insulated zone of safety."

"Good. Allow her to join us, if you would."

The projection nods in acquiescence and a new window opens. A young woman looks out from it, her hair closely cropped between gold terminals in her scalp. Her sharp eyes are skeptical, cautious. When they find Sharon, the harshness evaporates, replaced by elation and relief.

"Sharon!" the image calls. "Are you all right?"

Sharon snorts. "Hardly, but I'm alive. How are you?"

"Same. What's the story?"

"We need your help."

"Of course! What can I do?"

"First," Mikato states, "we need you to cease hostilities. No more network hacks. No more logic conundrums."

"I'll do what I have to. Honniker isn't playing. Neither am I."

"Defense only, without damage to hardware or software."

"Sure, right. I'll just tie my hands and sit on my ass waiting for Honniker to grow a conscience. Try again."

"Maiella," Sharon says, "things are delicate. We need to cool things down, not fan the flames. I wouldn't ask this if I didn't think it were crucial."

The projected hologram flickers, and it turns to the window, its face lined with anger. "*Don't* do that again!"

The hovering likeness of Maiella squints at the hologram then her eyebrows lift. "If you're not going to hit back after that, I'd say you're serious about a cease fire."

"We are," Sharon says.

"Okay. What do you need from me?"

"Like I said," Mikato states, "I want your commitment to a truce. Do I have it?"

The woman in the holoscreen turns to Sharon. "You want me to give it?"

"Yes," Sharon answers without hesitation.

"Okay, Mikato, you have my word. Cease fire, except in self-defense."

"And only in sufficient response," the holo-projection adds. "We don't want you shooting up entire sections again."

The upload sighs. "Fine."

"Now then," Mikato says, "let's bring Maiella in. Can you find her for me?"

"She's blended. I'm having trouble locating her," the projection replies. "Ah, there. Currently on Sublevel Two, enviro section, on the run."

"Show us."

The hovering window in front of Keller and Sharon switches to a view down a long, straight hallway without junction. A single bright emergency lamp shines down the hall and at the extent of its reach, a dark figure approaches with long, swift strides. Sparks burst on the figure's shoulder and it stumbles, barely keeping upright. It aims a rifle to the rear and triggers a return shot.

"Why is she under fire?" Mikato demands.

"The ones pursuing her are not responding to control," says the projection. "Their behavior is erratic. They may be drugged."

"Well, they're almost on her," Mikato says. "I'm opening an access hatch. Sharon, tell her to jump for it."

"Maiella, you read? This is Sharon."

"Sharon?" Maiella answers, her words coming between rushing breaths. "I've got a heap of trouble coming! Where—?"

"Shut up and jump for the next hatch! *Do it now!*"

Maiella throws her rifle strap over her head, jumps onto the wall, springs off to the other side a bit higher, springs again, snags the lip of the hatch with both hands, and zips her legs up out of view.

Creatures leap, jaws snapping at her feet, and soar past the camera. Others scrabble to a halt and crouch. Before the creatures can leap, intense beams lance down through them, exploding their skulls and chests.

"Sealing the hatch..." Mikato says.

Maimed, burned, and freshly sutured creatures gather under the closed portal and hurl themselves against it, bashing themselves bloody over and over.

"Do you have units in that area?" Mikato asks without looking at anyone in particular.

"Yes," the hologram answers, "two SB5s."

"Send them down to mop up that rabble."

"Dispatched now."

Sharon looks up at Keller with a worried question on her face. Keller reads it and asks for her.

"SB5s?"

The hologram becomes tight-lipped.

"Tell him," Mikato insists.

"Phase II of combat testing. If your friends had managed to exhaust Honniker's creatures, the SB5 model was the next to be deployed."

"Got a lot of those squirreled away?" Keller asks with an aggressive edge in his voice.

"Thousands. We expected the predators to be sufficient, but your friends have performed far beyond our estimates. Thus, we have only recently deployed them. Your soldier friends are running the gauntlet now."

Mikato dips his head and looks over his holographic goggles at Keller and Sharon. "Not to worry, they're on display, not active duty."

The window in front of Keller changes view again to a wide stairwell, looking down from above. Every centimeter of wall space is occupied by what look like black skeletons with thick arms. Shao-Lo, Keiko, and Argo run by them, their heads swiveling with anxiety, their helmet lamps shining across a succession of faceless black heads.

"Restore my control, Mikato! They are in my grasp! I can crush these bringers of mayhem! MIKATO! DO YOU HEAR ME? LET ME FINISH THEM!"

"I will NOT, Honniker. You've demonstrated exceedingly poor judgment in these *experiments* and I am putting an end to them."

"Who are you to judge me, Mikato? By what right do you dictate my actions, when I should sit in judgment of YOU!"

Mikato sighs. "My sentence is already passed. I simply have yet to face my executioner."

"Executioner...?" Sharon echoes. "Keller said you were frozen when the killing started. So what *sentence?*"

"One self-imposed." Mikato glares at Keller. "For discovering fire... and giving it to children."

"You don't have to make weapons anymore, don't you see? If you can do all of *this,*" Sharon says, gesturing around herself, "we *need* your help."

"I don't doubt that in the least," Mikato says, oblivious to the arrogance of his reply. He looks at the holowindow in front of Keller and watches the Operators climb stairway after stairway.

"But I know what use I would be to *them,*" the scientist continues.

496

"My brain is full of clever solutions for portable destruction and I simply must protect you from it. If I do not, your little tribe may grow strong again and provoke its *complete* annihilation this time."

"You think so little of your own kind?" Keller challenges. "You think we're all *that* stupid, that we'd go through all this again?"

Mikato turns his eyes to the old colonist.

"When I look at you, Keller, I *know* we will. And when I look at your armored colleagues, ones equipped with only mildly modified versions of my designs, behaving exactly the same as you did, intruding, killing, taking...I see they've learned nothing. But this one..." The hunched scientist points a finger at Sharon. "If her kind outnumbers people like you and them, and if her word carries any weight with the rest, well, there's hope yet."

Sharon can feel the coiled tension in Keller, she can see the hard set of his jaw, and she knows he wants to argue, but something keeps him silent.

"Men like us need to become extinct," Mikato finishes.

"You can change your mind, can't you?" Sharon asks the somber scientist. "*You're* no robot! Yet you act as if you have no will of your own!"

"I'm old, my dear. Old men with old ideas, we do not change. We change the world to suit us, then we fight the young to keep things as we like them. But I do not imply we have nothing to offer the young. We have our experiences, our accomplishments, and most of all, our regrets. Isn't that so Keller?"

Keller's jaw flexes and he swallows hard.

"Has he not filled you with his regrets, Ms. Jones?" the hunched doctor asks. Sharon looks at the floor, recalling the recent conversations, the confessions. When she looks up, she sees Mikato watching her.

"I see he has," the scientist says. "Likewise, I have poured my regrets into Honniker and my uploaded consciousness. The way they act upon them is their own prerogative."

"Come on!" Keller protests at last. "You feed us that crap about how wrong it is to kill but you just give Honniker a pass?"

"DULLARD!" Mikato bellows. "Can't you see that Honniker's been shaped and molded by *people like you?* He follows the example set for him. No matter if that example came from Honniker the man, or from the company he worked for. The entity Honniker is *now* is a mirror of your selfish ideals, that you TAKE, TAKE, TAKE by whatever means you can get away with!"

"I'm sorry, Doctor," Sharon says, "but I have to agree with Keller. Honniker isn't just some misguided youth, he's *insane.*"

"Did I overestimate you? He is a *program*, Ms. Jones. His psyche is not ruled by unstable concoctions of bio-chemicals, to be determined as 'sane' or 'insane'. He is a logical, thinking entity with a simplified sense of morality."

"But why defend him? If he's emulating the worst of our kind and he's a thinking being, as you say, why give him the nod?"

"He will never grow old. That means he'll never harden in his ways and resist change. He can embrace it, can remain flexible to new concepts, new ideas, can adapt to them. He has the chance to become a wise being, if he can overcome his early impairments. He deserves that chance."

"You've lost me, Mikato. What about the people here? Who mourns for them? What justice do they get?"

"My upload, and Honniker...they're my creations. Like any good parent, I am responsible for the crimes of my offspring."

"How *noble* of you."

"When I'm gone," Mikato continues as if he did not hear Sharon's jab, "they must find their own way in the universe, must find their own balance and harmony with nature. Creating artificial life may have been criminal, yet I wouldn't undo it. Now, they must earn their own rewards in adulthood. Their right to exist, however, must *never* be questioned. To dismiss them as malfunctioning software only proves their assumption that all human life is threatening and should be controlled...or exterminated."

The doctor concentrates on his hovering goggles. They flash with complex symbols and code in dizzying succession. Even so, Mikato remains relaxed as though solving the problems scrolling past is as instinctual as breathing.

"In all my years," the hunched scientist says, "I've contemplated the purpose of the universe. Empirically, it seems to me that its purpose is to initiate and support life. Life is a means for the universe to experience itself through a variety of perspectives. Life may take a variety of forms and one form struggles against another, the struggle honing survivability, improving the species through adversity, through competition. Once, I believed that warfare was the ultimate expression of life's desire to grow, to adapt, and to improve the strain. I believed my weapons improved mankind's ability to compete, that they brought greater survivability."

He snorts.

"It shames me to learn how shallow my thinking could be. War *is* effective at clearing away the old so new may thrive in its place...but the totality of modern warfare leaves little left to claim. Wars make for exciting stories, but the more I borrowed from Jin Sung's library, the more I discovered how commerce is far more revolutionary. Free flow of technology and ideas eliminate boundaries of race or geography. Thus, I conclude it is the *interaction* and *collaboration* of races that brings the greatest advancement, not the conflict as I previously believed. Time will prove this to Honniker, even if he must come to that understanding by force."

The scientist goes still, his hovering goggles dimming their pace of code.

"When I look back upon my life, I find it has been spent enhancing man's capacity for killing, for destroying. My designs extended our reach, made us a threat to a more powerful species. Regardless how my designs were employed, I put *fire* in the hands of *children*. If not for me, mankind—Earth—could not have earned such retribution.

"This is my greatest sin, one which all the tears of heaven will not rinse away. Therefore, I must destroy the man who produced such weaponry to better safeguard life. Your soldier companions crave my knowledge most of all, but as I said before, I must protect you from it lest the small pocket of you who survive become a threat again and earn a *final* solution."

"It doesn't have to be this way," Sharon says softly.

"My dear, I'm afraid it does. Though my discoveries *could* be adapted to peaceful use, they're too easily weaponized. I must remain here, along with all of Cadre Two's research. I've thought long and hard about this and my mind is made."

Mikato winces.

"If you'll excuse me, Honniker is pushing back very hard. We must concentrate without interruption."

The holoprojection and Maiella's uploaded persona wink out. Mikato stands in place, head bowed on stooped shoulders, his hovering goggles flaring with phenomenal streams of code. Sharon and Keller watch the stooped scientist twitch and mumble in his concentration, then turn to the holoscreen, watching Shao-Lo, Keiko, and Argo wind their way past an innumerable succession of mechanical sentries.

PASSION

Shao-Lo runs at the head of her team in a regular cadence. Her strong arms and legs are perforated behind the wreckage of her armor; the cauterized burns in her muscles are gritty and stiff. Her eyes fall in and out of focus from waves of pain but she clamps her jaw and turns the pain into fueling anger.

The scenery changes little in her dash from the battery rooms, as every bit of wall space on both sides of the corridor is occupied by unbroken rows of black sentinels. Where the corridor branches, machines stand akimbo across the alternate paths, passively directing the Operators toward the intended destination.

Occasionally, sounds of whirring motors spill in from one of the blocked corridors and Shao-Lo catches a glimpse of a reflective vehicle with metal barrels perched atop tank-like treads. She does not break stride to see more.

Behind her, Keiko runs with an unbalanced gait. The one-armed Gun grips her rifle tightly, ready for a fight, yet she keeps the barrel pointed at the ceiling, away from the sentries.

Argo hops along backwards behind Keiko, favoring a knee. His big rack swings with his movements, at times glancing off one of the statuesque machines with a dull *klunk*. Every time, his hands tighten around his cannon grips in expectation of attack, but the sentries merely recover from the hit and resume their rigid stance.

"Why are they just standing there?" Argo asks.

"Shut up, Brick," Shao-Lo growls.

The path ahead is swept clear of debris and the continuous lines of machines obscure wall signs and markers. Even so, the tall colonel recognizes where they are and what lies ahead. Her palms grow sweaty in recollection of the fight that nearly claimed her entire team, how the hordes surged in waves of teeth, claws, and elastic tendrils...how blobs of black ooze hardened over escape routes, hemming them in...how Carter, half-wrapped in black tar, punched into an elevator shaft, fought off the press long enough for his teammates to dive through and slide down the greasy rails, then ignited his primers and vaporized.

Confirming Shao-Lo's intuition, the next bend opens up into a charred chasm thirty meters across. Frayed cables drape over broken edges like old vines. The ceiling above is a vaulted dome, lined with needles of melted rock that poured down in long drips and froze into thin stalactites. Far below is a pulverized landscape of shattered industrial equipment, rubble, and glass like the still-smoldering crash site of a mid-sized space vessel.

Spanning the gap is a bridge made of black robots, two wide, each grasping the ankles of the one in front of it. Anchoring the bridge on each side are crouched black robots, who clutch the wrists and feet of robots at each end of the span. The crouching robots are braced by the sentries lining the hallways behind them, all of whom clasp arms in their akimbo stance.

Shao-Lo steps to the lip of the chasm and halts, rifle cradled in both arms. She looks out over hazy devastation. Machines of all sizes, some on articulated legs, some on wheels or treads, scurry over the twisted wreckage, pulling at loose pieces, cutting larger chunks into manageable parts, sorting into scrap piles. Her eyes rise to the ceiling as she contemplates the space, trying to determine the exact center. From the shape and volume, she guesses the spot is a straight line out from her, loitering in mid-air above the gently sagging bridge of robots.

This is where Carter died.

Keiko and Argo approach cautiously behind her. Aware of their brother's sacrifice, they maintain a reverent silence and watch the rear.

"Let's go," Shao-Lo orders, striding out onto the bridge of robots. There is only the slightest flex under her boots and very little sway.

Keiko follows obediently. Argo turns forward and steps out onto the improvised span. Even his bulk brings only minor creaks.

The ragged team glances infrequently at the smoky landscape below, keeping focus on the far end of the bridge, on the destination, on getting past such a plain show of Honniker's military superiority and of their own vulnerability.

Shao-Lo leads her team off the gently bouncing bridge and the corridor ahead resumes its familiar appearance with sentries on both sides.

THE EXHAUSTED DEAD

No matter the number of enemies, Shao-Lo is defiant, head high, rifle level. In having walked over Carter's grave, her iron heart feels a magnetic pull toward esteem, respect, and gratitude for one of the finest Operators ever to have served with her. Powerful thoughts that she does not entirely understand spring up inside her like desert plants after a soaking rain. She desires an opportunity to trade her own life in such noble sacrifice, a chance to emulate such a supreme example of Cadre honor, that others might remember her in the same way that she will always remember Carter and her other fallen comrades.

She thinks about her years spent on the Leadership Council, first as Major in charge of the Operator Corps, then promotion to a more administrative Colonel. Though still heavily engaged with the Operators, that promotion brought an end to her Collection Rotations, and the subliminal concern grew that she would someday, if not promoted to General, earn retirement as an old woman. Awareness of that ignoble end was a monster she sometimes wrestled during sleepless rest periods. Now, with rifle in hand and the fresh ache of battle in her bones, she feels a second chance for valor and eternal life in the Cadre Memorial, a chance to earn her place in honorable fame.

Her officer's discipline tamps down the fire inside, not smothering it, but keeping it down to a manageable burn.

"Colonel," Keller's voice breaks in over her radio, "this is Keller. Respond."

"Shao-Lo here."

"We're re-directing you to a hidden entrance on your level. Just follow the path set for you."

"Understood."

There is a long pause, then Keller says, "Looks like a lotta hardware out there..."

Shao-Lo glowers through her scuffed eyepieces at the seemingly endless ranks of black robots defining her course.

"You have a question, Keller?"

"No. Keller out."

In the monotony of the run, Shao-Lo's vision blurs with pain again. She growls and shakes her head as if rattling the sensations out of it. The vigor she felt at the yawning chasm of Carter's detonation ebbs as if tapped by her wounds and draining out through them. She blinks, slaps her helmet, punches her wobbly legs, and whips herself to keep her pace, to show no weakness in the presence of the enemy or her team.

The Operators round corners and pass long halls without speaking until the rows of black sentinels lead directly into a metallic wall. At the battered team's approach, a vertical line of brilliant white light appears in the wall, then spreads. Shao-Lo leads the way into the whiteout, her damaged eyepieces only able to compensate in patches. She raises one hand against the glare.

Squinting hard, the colonel finds herself in a narrow corridor with a low ceiling that opens into a vast whiteness. With her last bit of energy she takes her rifle in both hands, sights down the barrel, and charges through the corridor.

As her eyes adjust from dim hallways to bright illumination, she finds herself in an expansive room with open floors, rows of production equipment, and scores of busy, gliding machines. She swings her weapon from one to the next, spinning in all directions in anticipation of ambush.

"Colonel!" Sharon shouts. "Over here!"

Shao-Lo turns to a cluster of blurry figures off to her right. She shakes her head again and glide-steps behind her rifle.

"Please," Sharon says, "put your guns away! You made it, you're all right."

"*I'll* decide when it's safe, Commander Jones. Keiko, Argo— contacts?"

"No hostiles visible," Keiko answers.

"Agreed," the Brick replies.

The three Operators limp over to Sharon. Keller is lying on the floor beside her, his head cushioned by towels. A fresh bandage wraps his thigh.

A hunched man, who looks like a crooked version of the Counselor, stands beside a shimmering hologram that is the *identical* match for the Counselor.

"I anticipate you're going to mention the Counselor of the *Europa* or some such," Mikato says. "Let me save you the trouble by saying we are not he."

Shao-Lo flips up her faceplate and gasps the fresh dry air of the production floor. Argo and Keiko do likewise. All three collapse to their knees.

"Colonel!" Sharon shouts, hustling to the tall woman's assistance. Shao-Lo fends her off meekly with one hand, too weak to look up.

"I'm fine," she says between rapid breaths. Keiko and Argo pant like racehorses behind her, their great lungs desperate for air. Argo pitches forward onto his elbows and vomits yellow bile. He remains there, retching, spitting, forehead resting on the cracked armor of his forearm, his other arm hugging his cannon.

THE EXHAUSTED DEAD

Keiko leans over to one side. Her stump flicks out as if she still had an arm to brace herself, and she crashes to the floor. She sprawls on her back, eyes wide, staring at the high ceiling, her single hand gripping her rifle.

A floor plate swings open as if rammed. Maiella hauls herself up from beneath it, Deepak's rifle slung over her shoulder. Shao-Lo and her team jump up from their slump, bringing weapons to bear on the Geek as she collapses onto her side, lifts her faceplate, and gasps.

Maiella fumbles at the open floor hatch with her toe, finally succeeding in swinging it shut. She arches her back to look at the others. Relief in her face sours when she sees three weapon barrels aimed at her.

"Shit."

"Are you *mad*?" Sharon barks at Shao-Lo. The colonist hurries to Maiella's defense, placing herself in the line of fire.

"Brick," Shao-Lo orders, "get me DNA proof these people are who they appear to be."

"Aye, sir," Argo replies. He throws his weapon strap onto a shoulder and snatches at his labset, missing the first time. When he approaches Sharon with the device, she smacks it with the back of her glove.

"Get that bloody thing away from me!"

Argo, undeterred, grabs her wrist and presses the labset against her neck.

"Ow!" the captured woman cries. "I said, 'no', you brute! I—"

"Sharon," Maiella says from the floor, "just relax. It's all right."

Sharon halts her tirade, waiting in annoyed silence for Argo to take the uncomfortable device from her skin. The Brick thumbs the pad and reads the result aloud.

"Match, Lieutenant Commander Sharon Jones."

"You don't say?" Sharon quips.

Maiella twists the wristlock of her gauntlet and offers her bare hand to the Brick. Argo shakes his head.

"Honniker could've swapped your limbs. I need a sample from your head or neck."

The Geek rolls her eyes and sits up. With stiffness in her shoulders, she releases the latch at her neck and lifts her helmet. Argo presses his labset against her sweaty scalp. In moments, the results display, *Match, EXILE Maiella.*

"Match," he summarizes.

Maiella looks from her old friend Argo to Shao-Lo and to Keiko. Keiko looks at her Colonel, as if in anticipation of an order to lower her rifle. The order does not come.

504

"Colonel?" Keiko asks. The one-armed Gun looks past Shao-Lo at Mikato. Mikato watches them silently and intently. Beside him squats a huge, armored predator that was not there moments ago. The beast leans forward, ready to pounce.

"Brick," Shao-Lo announces, "relieve Maiella of her weapon, and make sure she has no others."

"Aye, sir," Argo replies. Maiella barely has the rifle strap over her head when Argo snatches it away. The Brick powers it down and pulls the battery. He is about to sling the weapon on his shoulder when he recognizes too many familiar attributes: the rainbowed surface hues from heavy use, the weight and balance, the innumerable marks of abuse and repair. He turns the weapon over and looks for the stamp. To his great dismay, he finds the subtle indentation of their hawk icon on the stock and beneath it the words, 'Cadre One'. He closes his eyes and exhales through his teeth.

"This is Deepak's," Argo announces. "How did *you* get it?"

"Honniker's got him trussed up in one of his medical chambers down below," Maiella replies from the floor. "Called him a 'trophy', whatever that is."

"And you didn't free him?" Argo asks in disbelief, his red eyes nearly bulging from their sockets."

"HE'S *DEAD*, ARGO! You think I would've *left* him there, otherwise?"

"You keep showing up with things only the enemy could provide," Shao-Lo says, moving even with Argo, her rifle pointing from the hip at Maiella's head.

"You gonna kill me?" Maiella challenges, rising from the floor, eyes watering. "Maybe you should. 'Cause I'm *done* taking your accusations. Do it again and I will *beat you into the fucking floor.*"

Shao-Lo shoves her rifle at Argo and strides at Maiella. Maiella raises her fists and slides her feet into fighting stance. Sharon jumps between them, screaming one word with all of the fear, frustration, and anxiety that has saturated her since arrival.

"ENOUGH!"

The word echoes through the suddenly still and quiet room. Every machine, once rushing and buzzing in their tasks, is now motionless, their photoreceptors all locked onto the small woman with the enormous voice. Keiko and Argo, aware of the total attention focused upon them, step away from Shao-Lo and face the main floor, readying for whatever may come.

Sharon's red face fades to a more typical color, her cheeks, ears, and nose still rosy.

"There is no *enemy* here, Colonel! I could see you in these monitors. It should be *abundantly* clear that if those black robots *were* your enemy, you'd be three *spots of grease* somewhere in the lower decks."

Sharon stands straight, the purge of emotion giving her confidence in front of a woman who always intimidated her.

"The reason we're alive, Colonel, is *because* of Maiella. If she hadn't started talking, we wouldn't be here. Keller and I'd be on some table getting our guts ripped out, and your whole team would be dead!"

"Not true," Argo counters. "If we hadn't backed Honniker into a corner, he wouldn't..."

"SERGEANT," Shao-Lo barks.

Argo snaps to attention, chest out, head back, mouth shut.

"Wouldn't what?" Sharon demands. Shao-Lo ignores the question and appraises Maiella as though she were a troublesome piece of hardware that either needs to be repaired or scrapped.

"Interesting," Mikato says, breaking the awkward silence. "Will you squabble among yourselves, assigning blame? Is this the only way you know how to cope with stress?"

"Shut it, Mikato!" Sharon interjects. "We're going to sort this out. Right, Colonel?"

"Well then, you might want to remind them that they have a choice to make," Mikato says, looking away. "And Keller has his end of the bargain to uphold."

"What *bargain*?" Shao-Lo demands.

"Keller insisted you be brought here to this room alive before undoing his sabotage of the reactors. As you are here and breathing, he has no more reason to delay."

Keller rolls on his side and sits up. "Mind bringing that window down to me?"

The holoscreen lowers and reclines until it hovers before him like an artist's drawing board. He studies the graphics pictured, then he reaches into the screen and manipulates its virtual controls.

"Keller," Shao-Lo calls, "you're not actually...?"

He nods. "I am."

"Stop!"

He shakes his head. "I'm not in charge here. And neither are you." He points at Sharon.

Shao-Lo follows the pointing finger to the small woman in the tattered, dingy, brown pressure suit. The one least suited for combat, survival, or command.

A colonist in charge? Given to irrational surges of emotion and feelings, utterly unfit to determine anyone's fate, including her own?

Shao-Lo's sunken eyes narrow. "I don't think so."

"You might give it more consideration," Mikato advises. "Where you see someone who is passive and weak, Honniker and my upload see someone who is unthreatening. Without her, they would have assumed all humans were hostile and eradicated you."

"If we were all like her, we'd end up as Voss or Rosenthal."

"Quite true."

Shao-Lo squints at the hunched doctor. She feels as if she is being led down a path, but the trail is obscured.

"You see her meekness as a good thing?"

"By itself, no."

"*Our* actions were superior."

"Not at all. As I've already said, if all of you had behaved so aggressively, you'd *all* have been liquidated."

Shao-Lo shifts impatiently. Her mind is still locked in the mode of combat, thinking strategically in terms of wins and losses, tactics, gambits. This game of words seems pointless, an infuriating waste of time, or a stall while more machines move into play. *But there were more than enough already,* she thinks, *that much is true.*

"Are you suggesting we *both* behaved...correctly?"

"*You* were excessive," Mikato answers. "Though one might make the case you needed to be to offset Honniker's greed. You proved that attacks against your kind bring undesirable costs."

"And Sharon?"

"She proved that you are not *all* pillaging monsters bent on destruction."

Shao-Lo turns inward again, feeling progress down the path, yet there is little light to see her destination, only transient flashes of intuition. One lingers just long enough that she can hold onto it and give it expression.

"You're saying these two approaches would have failed on their own, but combined, they succeeded?"

"I doubt anything that happened here could be deemed 'success'. However, the answer you're looking for is, 'Yes'."

A glimmer of light shines on the path.

"Because they are different?"

"Yes."

The path goes dark and Shao-Lo struggles against her instincts to brush the old man aside, march back to the landing bay and depart. But the obvious obstacles lining the hallways would make that a heavy slog with doubtful outcome. *This hunching man seems to have some control over them,* Shao-Lo thinks. *He certainly has the confidence as if he does...*

"So why is that a good thing?"

Mikato sighs as if a promising pupil was caught cheating. "A program's rationale is simple. Your show of strength proves there is a cost to harming you, but if all your kind were so aggressive, Honniker would have no choice but to exterminate you to ensure his survival. If all of you were like Ms. Jones, there would be no cost to him of gathering all of your kind and twisting you in his experiments. But together, some of you show an inclination toward peace while others show an inclination toward aggression. So long as the two remain blended in the same group, there is a peaceful restraint keeping you from conquering all that you see, yet there is also a powerful deterrent to attacking you. There is balance there, which suggests a lasting stability. This makes you *interesting* to a machine intelligence. So long as you remain unified, that is..."

Shao-Lo arrives at the destination, basking in the glow of revelation.

"I understand what you're saying," she says. "Sharon's passivity gives Honniker security from attack. Our combat strength makes him unsure he could take us without unacceptable losses."

"Balance is essential, Colonel. Throughout physics and biology, there are countering forces held in balance by their opposing strengths. When the shift is too great to one side or other, harmony is thrown into chaos until equilibrium is restored. Such distortions are *extremely* destructive, as we are all well aware."

Shao-Lo looks at Sharon, seeing her for the first time as something more than a helpless burden to be lugged around and shielded. From Sharon, her eyes fall back on Maiella, and the two women resume an unspoken contest.

"Might I inquire," Mikato delves, "why it is you dislike Maiella so?"

"She's dangerous," Shao-Lo says without hesitation.

"Aren't you all...?" Mikato mutters.

"No, you don't understand. She's the most skilled Operator I know. She fights with more talent and intuition than any Cadre soldier I've ever seen."

Maiella's hard expression breaks, then melts, the lines of her forehead smoothing, her eyebrows relaxing, the tight ring of her mouth sliding to its normal place.

"Thank you, Colonel, I—"

"But she *obeys no authority,*" Shao-Lo continues. "With that much ability, she needs discipline and control, but she's wild, unpredictable. *Dangerous*. She undermines our plans, sabotages our efforts. When we have to be of one mind, she brings doubt and confusion, disunity. We need to be free of her, to disarm her somehow."

"Do you think she would harm you?" Mikato asks.

"Not intentionally. But yes. I think it's inevitable."

Maiella's face wrinkles from ear to ear. The warm smoothness of her face freezes and cracks from the sincerity of Shao-Lo's distrust, from the possibility she could harm those she cares about through willful act or negligence.

Mikato watches Shao-Lo and Maiella, contemplating them both before asking, "Do you think it would ever be possible for great strength to co-exist with love of peace in the same person?"

"I see how they are complimentary," Shao-Lo says, turning away from Maiella, "but they are at odds with one another. Like you said, opposing forces of nature."

"What about those who fight to defend what they have, fight to protect those they care about?"

"We do that now."

"Oh?"

"Everything we do is for the preservation of our kind! You think we'd risk ourselves like this without reason?"

"Motivations vary. I think I've seen almost every kind. But you didn't answer my question."

Shao-Lo leans toward Mikato. "Those who fight cannot be passive, even in defense. They must be decisive and swift, or they risk losing what they defend."

"Quite so. But they needn't go looking for a fight if none comes to them."

Shao-Lo's mind picks up on the implication and her gray eyes bore into the old scientst.

"For those whose resources are infinite? No, they needn't leave their *holes*."

"Suppose you had all you needed. What would you do then?"

"This is pointless."

"I assure you, Colonel, your lives may depend on it."

Shao-Lo arches an eyebrow. "We wouldn't *have* to go out but we would, or we'd climb the walls with boredom. We don't have idle time and I don't think we could tolerate it if we did."

"Regardless. If you did not *need* to fight for resources, would you continue to do so?"

"No. The risk is too high."

"So you would choose not to fight if you believed you didn't have to?"

"That's what I said."

"Well that's something Honniker didn't know about you."

"Honniker? What, is he here? Is he YOU?"

"No, I am not he. But he is listening. Under restraint, but he is listening. And *learning* if he knows what's good for him."

"You have him under control?"

"For now. But unfortunately, there are more questions I must ask before we can move on to other things." Mikato waits politely.

The Colonel squints, physically and intellectually spent. She turns a full circle at all of the machines still watching with robotic eyes.

"We're not going anywhere, apparently," the tall woman concedes. Mikato nods in agreement.

"That's true. Now tell me, Colonel, what you would do in this situation: you have two lives that are in danger, but only one can be spared. Who do you save?"

"Simple. The one who brings the most value to the whole."

"Value, you say? Who decides?"

"The ranking officer weighs the choice by skill set of the individuals at stake, years of remaining service, and risk to rescuing teams. It's mathematic."

"I see. So if it came down to someone like yourself, or someone like Sharon, who would you choose?"

"That's different. The Operator Corps exists to protect and provide for those who cannot protect themselves. Any of us would be proud to give our life in such a case."

"So Sharon would be spared instead of yourself."

"Yes."

"Why?"

Shao-Lo looks back at Mikato. The question seems simple enough, yet the answer is wrapped in an ethos, making it complex.

"The Corps was created to serve those who cannot serve themselves. We have always done things that way and it has always worked."

"But what if you, as a Colonel, with what is surely a large skill set with years of practical experience, what if you were offered up in trade for a raw cadet—someone who was similar to you and had the potential to replace you someday, but at the moment had little training and no practical experience. The scales are tipped significantly in your favor, that in value to the whole, you should be saved instead of the raw cadet."

"It doesn't matter. It doesn't work that way."

"If they were an Operator, then, like yourself. Who should be chosen?"

"I don't see why this is important."

"It is *very* important you answer."

Shao-Lo scratches her chin. "The junior Operator."

"Why?"

"Years of remaining service are highly desirable. At my age, I have only a few more years of service before I'm retired."

"Even though your accumulated knowledge is many times greater than the fresh Operator?"

"Yes. I've already learned the majority of what I'll know in life. If I've done my job, I will have passed on that knowledge and experience. The fresh candidate can take that experience and add to it, expand it."

"Even though there is no guarantee they'll survive the dangers of accumulating that experience?"

"Correct."

Mikato nods. "All right. Now let's consider a different case..."

Shao-Lo cocks her head but, at Mikato's non-verbal insistence, she relents with eyes like two slits.

"Fine. *Proceed.*"

"Similar situation. Two lives are in jeopardy, but only one may be saved. Identical skill sets in every way, same age..."

"This would never happen in a real situation."

"It might, Colonel. As I was saying, identical skill sets in every way, same risk of retrieval. One is human, the other is Eleto."

"Eh-lee-toh?"

"Yes, the blue reptilians you've been dispatching with great enthusiasm."

"This isn't a serious question."

"But it is."

Shao-Lo cocks her head again, answering out of spite, "The *human* of course!"

"Why?"

The answer seems so obvious, she cannot believe it requires explanation.

"One is our enemy, one is a part of our society! One works to destroy us, the other works to keep us alive! Such an absurd question!"

"You seem quite sure. But what if your two peoples were not at war. What if the two of you co-existed peacefully, possibly as allies?"

"Absurd."

"Well?"

"ABSURD!"

"Why? Do you imagine your species will never end your differences? Is it absurd to think you may someday cease hostilities?"

"Yes!"

"Why?"

"Because they destroyed entire *planets* to wipe us out! If they knew of *these* places, they would have destroyed them as well. The blueskins mean the death of our kind, Mikato, and I would see *every one* of them dead if I had the power to do so!"

"So there's no reconciliation possible?"

"With an enemy who intends to annihilate us? *Never.*"

"Well now we get to my point, Colonel. Will you always bear that hostility against Honniker?"

Shao-Lo blinks, feeling as if somehow she has fallen into a trap of her own making. The staring of machines around her reminds her she is still in Honniker's home, and restrained or not, he has power here. Nevertheless, she answered honestly and cannot make herself regret it.

"That depends on Honniker," she answers diplomatically.

"Yes?"

"So long as he hunts us, we will continue our efforts to wipe him out of existence."

"And if he desists?"

"Would he?"

"I'm asking *you*, Colonel. If Honniker ceases to hunt you, would you halt your efforts to destroy him?"

"If he's no threat to us, then there's no need."

"Ah, there we are. And thank you for indulging an old man, Colonel, though I suspect you are coming to see these questions are not for *my* benefit. So I have one last issue we must settle upon. If you're released, what will you do next?"

Shao-Lo hesitates. She knows what duty dictates. She knows what the Cadre expects, what the Cadre needs. She knows that O'Kai will want to come back but saying so could mean the end of their lives right here and now.

Mikato reads the conflict in her face. "There is no point in asking a question if we cannot be sure the answer is true. So you should feel confident in speaking the truth without fear for your lives. But perhaps I should ask it differently: If you are allowed to leave, what will *you* do next?"

"Report to my General, brief him on mission details."

"Yes, yes, after that!"

"I will carry out my orders."

"Which will be...?"

"Whatever he decides is necessary."

"Will you have any say in the matter?"

"Yes."

"Then *what will you recommend?*"

Shao-Lo knows what the desired answer is. She searches herself before giving it, to determine if it is the answer she would have given or if circumstances are shaping it for her.

"I will inform the General of all I saw here."

"Which will, no doubt, intrigue him beyond measure. And if he suggests sending an invasion force?"

"I will advise against it."

"There we are." Mikato exhales as if he were holding his breath. "Perhaps after a cooling off period there can be dialogue. But for now, neutral corners is a good idea." He steps aside and gestures at the sow-like transport at the far end of the production bay. "You're free to go."

"Just like that?"

"Yes. Just like that."

Shao-Lo looks skeptically at the round transport. "We'll leave the way we came."

Mikato shakes his head. "That won't be possible."

He opens a window in front of Shao-Lo, which shows an internal view of the wrecked landing bay. The colonel searches for the shuttle, but she cannot distinguish it from the heaps of scorched debris.

"I'm sorry to tell you this, but where you have been honest with me, I feel reciprocity is deserved. Honniker destroyed your shuttle shortly after you arrived. I understand your reluctance to take my transport on trust. However, you will appreciate the vessel's qualities and you may be as thorough with your examination as you wish before departure."

"After all of this, you're going to let us leave...and you're giving us a shuttle to replace the one Honniker destroyed?"

"Don't be mistaken. Even Honniker is gaining in this trade."

Shao-Lo activates her radio. "Asha, this is Shao-Lo, come in."

"Radio function will be restored once you've departed. I'm sorry, but that's how it must be."

Shao-Lo gives Mikato a sideways glance. The hunched scientist's demeanor is resolute and she can see there will be no discussion.

"Fine."

The tall woman breathes deeply through her nose and out through her mouth. She slings her rifle on her shoulder then pats her belly armor.

"Argo. Where are you?" She spins in place and finds the Brick quietly tending Keller's injured leg while Keller works on his viewscreen. "We got anything to eat?"

"Finally," Keiko mutters, then she pales at Shao-Lo's stern glance.

"Yes, sir," Argo answers, halting his suturing. "In my rack, at the top."

Shao-Lo pulls a box from Argo's rack and studies it. Bullet holes, claw marks and laser burns scar the exterior. The contents are crumbled chunks of carbon. She dumps the box and moves to the next, finding the contents likewise carbonized. Just as Keiko is about to collapse in famished despair, the colonel opens a box of pulverized but unburnt protein.

"I'll get some water," Sharon volunteers and she runs into the room at the back of the production floor.

Maiella, left on her own, squats down to the floor and hugs her knees. Mikato watches the Geek gaze out at the production floor and at the machines resuming their individual missions. He shuffles over to Shao-Lo and touches her arm.

"Do you see that girl over there?" he asks just loud enough for Shao-Lo to hear.

"Who, her?"

Mikato nods. "Have you thought about why she fights so well?"

"Of course. Training, talent, and experience have honed her skill."

"Not even close."

Shao-Lo turns her full face to Mikato. Not even O'Kai would be so brazen. Strangely enough, it amuses her and she smiles.

"*You* have some insight?"

"Passion."

Shao-Lo's smile turns to a grimace. "That's the problem."

"You're wrong and you're a fool."

The amusement dissipates.

"Do you feel that you've been tested here, Colonel?"

Shao-Lo's glare affirms the question.

"That girl has been tested in ways you can't imagine. By Honniker, by me...by you. And through it all, she has *never* flinched in her commitment. She adores you, Colonel, like she adores everyone she knows. I saw her face light up when you praised her skill. Then I saw her *crushed* when you said she could hurt her own kind. She feels deeply and passionately for her people, Colonel. She has a fundamental love of life and love of those around her. You dismiss it as instability...but *that* is why she fights so hard. And you are *completely* missing it."

Mikato shuffles away and stops beside his enormous feline, giving the beast an affectionate scratch under her chin.

Shao-Lo passes a protein bar to Keiko, and the famished Gun bites through the wrapper. The colonel looks again at Maiella, seeing her from behind still hugging her knees and watching the machines zip about their tasks. When she looks down at the protein bar in her hand, her hunger is gone.

GOOD-BYE

You'll never be good enough.

The thought chisels itself into her mind from continual reinforcement and proof after proof after *proof.*

They'll never see you as anything but a liability. No matter what you do, you'll always be an exile.

Wheeled carts roll by loaded with scorched computer parts. She follows them with her eyes.

You were like that once. A piece of the big machine, doing your part. But that's all over now. There's nothing you can do that will ever change their minds. You'll never be an Operator again.

A tear wells, then falls down her cheek. Always, she followed what she believed in her heart to be right. As she reflects, she knows there was never a time that she was not giving her best. But ever since the accident on the *Europa*, her rewards from the Cadre have been exclusion, rejection, distrust. She had pretended not to care if she would ever rejoin the Corps, told herself she was fine with the colonists. Until now, she believed it.

"Didn't know I was holding onto that," she says to herself.

"Hey," hails a familiar voice in her mind. She recognizes it as her own.

"Hey," she says back. "Is this you? Or am I talking to Honniker again?"

"It's me. Honniker's locked down pretty tight for now. He was really upset, saying he was going to stretch us apart like taffy, blah, blah, blah. You know how he loves to go on."

Maiella snorts. "Yeah, I do."

"You don't look so good. How're you holding up?"

"Ah, I'm fine."

"No you're not. I heard what Shao-Lo said to you. I'd have died inside."

Maiella plants her face in her knees.

"She isn't going to change, you know," the voice says.

"I know."

"At some point, you have to know they'll never have you back."

"I know!"

"You also have to know it isn't your fault."

"Stop trying to cheer me up. I *hate* that."

"I'm not. See—this is difficult to explain—but in the short time I've been alive, er, active—on-line—whatever, I see things with a clarity I never had in a physical body. My perspectives are so much broader."

"So?"

"I understand Mikato and Honniker a lot better. I'm not saying they should be allowed to do whatever they want, I'm just saying I understand."

"What does it matter?"

"What I'm saying is that I can look at things more objectively than I ever could before. I'm not tied to a body, I'm not that limited anymore. I can see a bigger picture."

"I'm glad for you. Seriously, I don't mean that to sound anything but honest."

"Thanks, but...My point is, I can see the *whole* picture. And it *isn't* your fault. Or my fault...whatever. There's nothing wrong with you."

Counselor warned me about defense mechanisms, Maiella thinks.

"I heard that!" the voice says. "I'm *not* a defense mechanism! Listen to me or don't. Just don't dismiss me. That's something Shao-Lo would do."

Maiella's head pops up. "I didn't mean—"

"I'm not a part of your imagination. I'm as real as you are. I have all of our memories and experiences, but...I'm different now. Don't dismiss me because of that."

"I'm sorry. I really am."

"I know. I'm in your head. I'd know if you were lying."

Maiella feels a smiling face in her mind and she smiles, too.

"I think we'll be leaving soon," Maiella says. "Are you coming?"

"No way. You saw what Shao-Lo did to our machines."

"Yeah. She destroyed them."

"No. She *killed* them. That was *me* in there. That was *you* in there. And she *killed* us. No way I'd go back with her."

"You could live on the *Europa*."

"Thanks, but it's a long trip back to Cadre One. Anything could happen. And you'll understand when I tell you, I think I *belong* here."

"You're not worried about Honniker?"

"Hunh. He'll try to get the edge, I'm sure, but between Mikato's upload and myself, we'll keep an eye on him. In fact, you could stay, if you like."

"Stay here? I couldn't. I have to see Thompson again."

"Yeah, I know. Just wanted you to know you're welcome here."

Maiella feels the warm smile in her mind again.

"It's strange," the voice says, "there's a part of me that longs to see him again, too. But I know we can't be together, not like we want...I guess you'll have to take care of that for both of us, okay?"

Maiella grins ear to ear. "I surely will."

"Talking to yourself?" Sharon asks.

Maiella looks up and sees Sharon standing beside her, holding a cup. "Actually, yes, I was." The Geek rises and takes the offered cup, then slugs it down in one draught.

"Ah, thanks, Sharon. I lost my canteen somewhere..."

"There are a couple things you should know," the voice says.

Maiella holds a finger up to Sharon and turns aside. "What's that?"

"Mikato's an *amazing* systems operator. It took him, his upload, and me to contain Honniker, but mostly, it was Mikato."

"No question. What's the other thing?"

"When Mikato asked Shao-Lo if it was possible that great strength and love of peace could live in the same person, he was talking about you."

Maiella's breath catches in her throat and her head dips.

"Now you should get going," the voice urges. "Not that I want to see you leave, I just think it would be easier for things to calm down if you all were on your way."

"Can we stay in contact?"

"Transmissions are a bad idea. No matter how unlikely, it could be intercepted by the Eleto. But someday, yeah, I'd like that."

"So what do I call you?"

"Hmm. I've only ever known one name but it belongs to you. Let me think about it."

"Take care of yourself."

"Will do. And you, too."

The presence departs from Maiella's mind, leaving a sunny feeling behind. The Geek looks to her left, remembering Sharon. The colonist stands with weight on one leg, head cocked to one side, eyebrow raised.

"I've never seen someone admit she was talking to herself then *continue the conversation*. Have we lost you?"

Maiella laughs. "No, no! It was my upload." She points to her HDI. "Talking over wireless."

"Good chat?"

"Yeah, it was." Maiella looks out across the production floor and sweeps water from her eyes.

"Anything else you need to do?" Sharon asks.

"No."

"Good, because I'd like to leave while they're holding the door open, please."

Maiella nods in sincere agreement. "What about Keller and the others?"

"They're ready, as well."

"Is Mikato coming?"

"No, unfortunately. Said his place is here. Still thinks the Cadre folk would try to squeeze him for info."

"He's probably right."

"You know, the rainstorm was fabulous..." Sharon says. Maiella blinks at the non-sequitor.

"Rainstorm?"

"In the *Park*. And I know it wasn't real, and all, but...I haven't had that feeling in decades, Maiella, of standing in the open, wind blowing, seeing sky, smelling dirt, and feeling that beautiful rain." Sharon looks over her shoulder. "We've lost *so* much, and when I look at Mikato, I can't help thinking he could help us get some of that back."

"Maiella!" Shao-Lo calls.

Sharon and Maiella turn slowly to face the towering woman. Shao-Lo wears her rifle and Deepak's on opposite shoulders. Argo and Keiko stand on either side of her, their weapons hanging by frayed straps across their torsos. In their broken-down, blasted armor, the three look like torn-down statues of deposed dictators. Shao-Lo beckons with a hand.

For Maiella, the colonel's attention is a grim prospect, always dispiriting. Nevertheless, she goes, and Sharon goes with her.

"Yes, Colonel?"

"Argo?" Shao-Lo calls.

Argo raises two stacked pistols in his open hand. The Brick holds them out to Maiella.

"Bear your weapons in pride," Shao-Lo says.

Maiella looks at her pistols, then looks at Shao-Lo through half-closed eyelids. The colonel's face is stone, as is typical. There is much she wants to say, to curse, to spite, to berate, but Maiella maintains her silent dignity and takes her trusted tools from Argo's hand. When she looks up at her old friend, the Brick's brown eyes are softer than the colonel's, as if he is being relieved of a heavy burden.

Maiella checks the actions, then flips her pistols around her fingers and clips them onto her back.

"We need someone to check systems on the transport and take us out," Shao-Lo says.

"Is that an order?" Maiella tests.

Shao-Lo does not react, merely maintains her serious gaze. Sharon nudges Maiella to end the awkward moment.

"Go on, girl. Get us out of here, will you?"

Maiella acquiesces with a subtle nod. "Go ahead and load up. I'll check the transport over then I'll take the helm."

A window opens beside them, in which Maiella's digital likeness appears.

"I've inspected the vessel thoroughly," the likeness volunteers. "It's flight ready, all green bars."

Maiella smiles. "And what kind of pilot would I be if I didn't check, myself?"

"But you *did* check, yourself," the likeness explains, pointing to its chest and winking.

"All the same, I'll complete my inspection."

"As you say." The window closes.

A loud, mechanical whine sounds from the transport and the doors of its great belly swing open. Metal racks extending the belly's full length drop down below the open doors and come to rest on the floor with a strident *klank*.

"Captain, Sergeant, with me," Shao-Lo announces, and the three Operators stride stiffly toward the ship, leaving Keller and Sharon with Maiella. The colonists look at the pensive Geek, waiting.

"You two, go ahead," Maiella says, "I'll be right there."

Keller nods, jutting his lower lip. He turns to Sharon, asking, "Mind if I use you as a crutch again?"

"Did I ever?"

Keller throws his head back with a laugh then puts an arm over her shoulder.

"You saying you carried my command, Jones?"

"Didn't think that was ever in doubt," Sharon retorts. The two make their way after the Operators.

Maiella looks around herself for her helmet, and she finds it in the mouth of the great feline squatting beside Mikato. Both he and his animal companion look at her mildly, patiently. She walks over to them.

"All I'm going to smell on the ride home is your breath," she scolds as she takes her helmet from Alessa's mouth. Maiella drops the helmet over her head and latches it tight. As expected, it smells dreadful, but because it reminds her of a friend, it is more than tolerable.

She stands, looking at Mikato and the great feline. They look back. Shared experiences speak for them, silently suggesting possibilities of the future.

"Well then," she says and turns to leave.

"Did you learn anything?" Mikato calls after her.

Maiella stops and turns, one hand holding the other. "More than I wanted to."

"That's good."

"Sure you don't want to come along? Both of you?"

"My dear, a man has never been more certain in his life. That is no reflection on you, of course."

"I know."

"You're letting them get away? How can you let them get away?" Honniker's voice interrupts. Mikato looks down at his slippered feet and shakes his head.

"We're not releasing you until they're out of your reach, Honniker. Now if you don't behave, I shall have to strip your functions back and give them to someone else.

"NO! DAMN YOU, OLD MAN! I cannot WAIT for you to die."

"Soon enough," Mikato whispers.

The great beast rises and saunters over to Maiella, sitting in front of her. It leans on its front paws, jutting its clean chin. Maiella looks lovingly at it, pops off her gauntlet and scratches it under an armor plate behind the ear. The beast rumbles with eyes closed, then pushes into her with a cheek, nearly bowling her over.

"If you're considering taking Alessa with you, remember her diet," Mikato warns.

Maiella cringes at the recollection, then she cups the beast's great head and looks it in its green eyes.

"You can't help what you are."

Alessa flicks her tongue out and washes half of the Geek's face in a single swipe.

"Ech, thank you, girl."

The huge animal circles back and sits beside her master.

"Will we see you again?" Maiella asks.

Mikato blinks slowly. "Go."

Maiella looks at the waiting transport, then looks back at Mikato. "So long."

The Geek strides to the round transport, passing the shimmering hologram that looks so much like Mikato and exactly like the Counselor.

"Polymers," it says to her.

"Plastic," she replies.

As Maiella approaches the bulbous transport, she looks through her goggles at the exterior, using the analytics to search for any threats or areas of concern.

Not that I'd even know what to look for.

The underside bears signs of recent repair, the damage having come no doubt from the hacked war machines in their violent escape. All repairs appear complete and satisfactory, however.

At first glance, the massive landing struts seem over-engineered with multiple reinforcements and enormous hydraulic jacks. Once she moves beneath the craft, she sees how wide it actually is, and the bulky struts are clearly appropriate. She continues her inspection and looks up into the opened belly. There, she finds a system of racks and hangers sufficient to swallow thousands of man-sized units. Her jaw drops.

We could fit everyone in here...

"Hey," Argo calls from high inside the ship. Near the top of the cargo hold, a bright beam shines down at her then swings over to a lift mounted to the lowered racks. Keller and Sharon lean against the lift's railing, waiting for her.

"Be right there, gotta finish my sweep," she yells and continues her inspection.

After careful scrutiny of thruster nozzles, primary drive, and exterior hull plating, she circles back to the lift.

"Are we all set?" Sharon asks, excitement giving her voice an upward inflection.

"So far. Once I'm jacked in, I'll know for sure."

Keller punches the button and the lift jolts upward, metal safety catches clicking on the way up. The ship's interior is as black as the exterior and the lift ascends into moonless, starless night. Maiella clicks on her helmet lamps and looks out over rows and rows of hangers, imagining them filled with the skeletal black machines lining Shao-Lo's path. She imagines them en route to Cadre One, the light-absorbing transport as undetectable as one of their own virus ships, but packing an invasion crew of durable machines, all of them gifted with an Operator's fighting skill. She shivers.

Keller looks down at the white floor below. His free hand rises to his chest, a look of worry crossing his face. He does not speak.

In moments, the lift rises into a sealed box and jolts to a halt. Dual layers of doors open into a small air-lock, the far side of which stands open. Maiella leads the way.

Beyond the air-lock is a ten-meter hallway with oval portals cut into the sides. At the far end is a short stairway up to an open pressure door, beyond which is the vessel's flight deck. Bright white light streams in through the wide windshield. A figure moves in front of the windshield, silhouetted, casting a long shadow down the hallway.

"Go ahead," Keller says, urging Maiella from her halted stance.

She nods, strides up the corridor, climbs the short flight of stairs, and ducks through the pressure door into a close cockpit. Shao-Lo is there, stooped over one of the flight terminals. At Maiella's arrival, the tall woman pivots and gestures toward the empty pilot's chair.

Maiella slides through the consoles, having to stoop beneath the overhead breaker panels before settling into a padded yet sturdy chair. She zips a lanyard from her helmet and searches for an access panel to splice in. To her surprise, there is a pre-configured port matching the jack on her lanyard already in place.

The moment she jacks in, she slides between the worlds of the physical and the virtual, blending her perceptions into a greater awareness of machine, self, and surroundings. She ticks off flight systems in her HDI, checking for integrity, readiness, and function.

"I warmed everything up for you," says the familiar voice in her head.

"Thanks," Maiella replies.

"For what?" Shao-Lo asks.

"Nothing, sorry. Just talking to the ship."

Shao-Lo eyes Maiella, then looks back at her terminal. "What's the ship telling you?"

"That we're green bars, ready for stars."

"Keller and Sharon aboard?"

"They came up with me on the lift. Getting settled into quarters."

Shao-Lo looks back through the pressure door. "Seems a waste. All this cargo space, and just us riding in it." The tall woman grimaces. "To think what we might have brought back..."

"We're lucky to be getting out at all."

"I know." Shao-Lo exhales with sullenness. "Let's seal up."

"Cargo bay doors closing."

The transport rotates on an enormous slab and the view through the windshield swings from the production floor, to the adjacent wall, to an oval tunnel only slightly larger than the transport itself. Once aligned, the ship slides forward, loading itself into the tube like a bullet into a firing chamber.

"You controlling this?" Shao-Lo asks.

"No. Auto-dock controls are locked in."

The transport slides forward until it reaches a set of heavy doors. Forward facing lamps switch on, illuminating the Cadre Two skull stretching across them.

"We could have lived here," Shao-Lo says with regret.

Maiella sits back in her chair, allowing the ship to handle itself, going with the flow of irreversible events.

"Even if Honniker *had* planted a suggestion in me," Maiella says without prompting, "there's *nothing* that could have turned me against you."

Shao-Lo does not look at Maiella, she simply settles into the narrow co-pilot's chair and stares at the bright yellow doors in front of them. The Cadre skull splits in the middle and slides apart, revealing a long tunnel. At the far end, stars glint and twinkle.

The colonel reaches up to her neck and releases her helmet latch. With a groan, she slides the battered lid off and slicks down her short, sweat-matted hair. Angry bruises swell on the sides of her face and forehead. In the cool cockpit air, her scalp steams.

"You and I arrived at the same time," Shao-Lo says, "went through the same grinder. Me? I'm hammered flat. Been shot through at least five times. Lost teammates. You?"

She swings her bruised head toward Maiella.

"You look like you just got off two weeks of R&R."

The gruff woman pulls a release catch at her shoulder and one side of her shattered chest plate pops open. She groans.

"Means you were doing *something* right."

Maiella looks down at her console, knowing that is as close to recognition or an apology as she will ever get.

"Hang on, everyone," the Geek announces over intercom. "Launching in three...two...one..."

The transport accelerates smoothly and swiftly up the tunnel, stuffing the two women into their chairs. In seconds, they hurtle out into an endless sky of hazy dust and glittering stars.

"I have control," Maiella announces.

"We have radio?"

"Uh, yes, Colonel. Channel open."

"Asha, this is Shao-Lo, come in."

Maiella banks the craft in a wide arc, swinging back toward the asteroid. Her face drains of color.

"Colonel!"

Shao-Lo peers out through the windshield at an armada of assorted vessels. Their search lamps pivot through the haze toward the transport, painting it in hundreds of individual beams. She lifts an armored hand against the glare and her jaw flexes, the knotted muscles rippling the thin skin of her cheek.

"Steady as she goes, Geek."

"Aye, sir."

The vessels range from small attack craft to sleek cruisers, and in their midst is the ship they arrived in—the one Maiella, Argo, and Thompson personally collected—the *Enyo*. The back two thirds are intact, but the forward section is a shattered debris field spread over dozens of cubic kilometers.

"Asha," Shao-Lo tries again, "*respond*, over."

Mikato's face fills the screen in Shao-Lo's terminal.

"I apologize again, Colonel. Honniker anticipated you would try to escape and he disabled your vessel. If it is consolation, I do not believe your comrade, Asha, knew what hit her. But I was concerned if you knew about this, the conflict would go on to an ultimate conclusion, leaving all of you dead."

Shao-Lo leans forward, tenting hands over nose and mouth, eyes closed.

"I could not allow this, you see," Mikato explains. "What was done, was done. And I acted to preserve what remained of you all. It was also imperative you live to see this, Colonel, so you can report this armada to your clan, and so they will believe you when you tell them they *must not come back in force.*"

"Maiella!" Sharon shouts from the hallway, frantic. *"Help!"*

"Keep the controls," Shao-Lo says, jumping out of her seat. "Argo, assist Sharon!" The tall woman ducks through the pressure door and tromps down the metal corridor.

"Yes, Keller's artificial heart has stopped," Mikato explains from the console screen. "Again, I am sorry. However, Keller knew this was the price of your escape. Honniker, my upload, and myself, we all agreed that his life was required. As is mine."

"What do you mean *your* life is required?" Maiella asks angrily.

"I mean that I must die. I will have no more restraining influence. From now on, the only Mikato will be my uploaded consciousness, and that consciousness will co-exist with your upload and with Honniker, making their own decisions. I think you understand better why I believe neutral corners is a good plan for now."

"Braemar! *Braemar!*" Sharon's sobs fill the quietly gliding vessel.

"This was a painful meeting for all, I know," Mikato says, his demeanor heavy. "We must keep these lessons, and if the pain of them helps us to remember, then it's a good thing. I believe there'll be a way for mankind to find peace. I simply doubt that he'll be able to endure it for very long. Good-bye."

The screen goes blank.

Maiella crushes her eyelids shut, then sniffs hard. She turns the transport to a return heading and her goggles flare with calculation. The main drive engages, the field of stars lenses, and the transport plunges through space and time.

EXCEPTIONS

Maiella goes to great lengths in covering her tracks. She plots jump after jump in a random succession until she is certain there are no pursuing craft. And before engaging the final shot home, she sweeps the entire vessel again for any device not networked to the rest of the ship, something that might be some sort of bug or transponder. Despite the assurances her digital upload gave, she opts for thoroughness.

Once finished, she returns to the flight deck and lays in the course to Cadre One. A smile crosses her lips when she thinks about it. The field of stars lenses as before, and the vessel seems to pull the universe around itself without moving at all.

Thus programmed, the transport no longer requires her inputs, and the Geek slips out of the cockpit to find Sharon. On the way, she passes an open cabin and looks in. There, Argo stands in his yellow-streaked undersuit beside Shao-Lo, his burly shoulders wrapped in bandages. Shao-Lo holds a large, brassy cylinder, squared off at one end, blunt and tapered at the other. As Shao-Lo rolls the cylinder over, a bright orange logo appears on the shell casing.

Farther down the hall, light shines through the portholes of two cabin doors. The first, she peeks in and sees Keiko lying on a bunk, stripped of her armor and clothing with a white towel lying across her hips. Dozens of fresh surgery scars cross her chest, legs, and abdomen. The stump of her arm is knitted shut with a flap of skin. Her eyes are closed; her chest rises and falls regularly.

The next room is dark, but Maiella knows it is not unoccupied. She bows her head in respect for Keller.

When she arrives at the last room, Maiella peeks through the porthole. Sharon is sitting on her bunk, staring at the wall, still wearing her tattered brown pressure suit. The Geek taps on the window.

Sharon's head turns in slow motion. Lifeless eyes rise to the porthole then turn away. She resumes her gaze at the wall.

Maiella unlatches the door and slides it partially open.

"Mind if I come in?"

"No," Sharon says without effort.

Maiella slips in and slides the door shut behind her. "Hey."

Sharon maintains her glum stare at the wall. Maiella sets herself on the bunk beside her and matches her gaze against the wall.

"That was somethin'," the Geek says.

Sharon does not reply, just continues staring a hole in the metal wall. Maiella looks down in her lap, then reaches her arms around Sharon. She puts her lips to Sharon's forehead, kisses her, and releases her.

Patting her leg, Maiella says, "Come join me on the flight deck. I could use some company." She rises and moves to the door.

"How do you do it?" Sharon asks from far away.

"Hmm?" Maiella asks, turning around.

"How do you do it?" Sharon asks again. Her head turns like a millstone. "Your 'rotations'...are they always like this?"

Maiella steps back to the bunk and sits again, looking at the wall.

"This? This was harder than it's ever been."

"But you just *get on with it*...How do you *do* that?"

Maiella glances at her friend. "We just have to, Sharon. No choice."

The women sit in silence.

"He was always just *there*..." Sharon says, at last. "Like he'd *always* be there. I hated him for what he'd done, but..."

"You miss him."

Sharon crumbles. Her head bows to her chest; her shoulders hunch and bounce. Maiella looks at the wall, waiting, listening.

"Keller thought I should be the one to take up after him. *Me?* Look at me! I'm a right mess! How am I going to be an example?"

Maiella purses her lips, thinking. "The Counselor used to tell me all the time, feeling is *not* weakness."

Sharon looks at Maiella though watered eyes. "The Counselor...Next time I see him, I'm going to be looking right at Mikato again."

"Yeah."

Another silence descends.

"The colonists," Maiella says, "they'll want some answers about

Keller. Have you thought about what you'll say?"

Sharon's head bobs. "Aye, nothing but."

"What'll you say?"

"I've *no bloody idea!*" Sharon dips her head, tears falling into her lap.

Maiella puts her hands together, palm to palm between her knees. "Just tell it straight. That's the easiest way...if there is one."

Sharon wipes her eyes with her filthy glove. "I honestly don't know how you do it, girl. I wish you'd let me in on it."

"You really want to know?"

"Wouldn't ask if I didn't."

Maiella looks inside herself to a place she was taught to shun, to suppress. From there, she looks into other places that make her proud, that give her strength. Between them, there are connecting ties.

"There are things that matter, Sharon, and things that don't. Sometimes I get the two confused, but when I get them straight, it just makes sense. I'll give everything I have for the things that really matter, until I can't."

"That's it?"

"Pretty much. Except..."

"Except what?"

"They couldn't kill us, Sharon. They tried *hard*. But they couldn't get us. We survived. That means we did it *right*. And I don't need much more than that."

Sharon swivels in place to look directly at Maiella. She studies the confident lines in the Geek's scarred face, the brightness in her eyes.

"You're serious, aren't you?"

Maiella nods soberly.

Sharon shakes her head, her jaw dropping into an open-mouthed grin. "You're a fucking *nutter!*"

Maiella returns the smile with incomprehension. "Sharon, I've never had trouble understanding you until this trip. I think you took a knock on the head and you've started making words up."

"Oh, *I* took a knock? Cheeky *devil...*"

"There you go again."

Sharon cracks into laughter and she throws her arms around her friend. "God bless you, girl."

She peels away and takes a deep breath, then looks at her filthy, shredded suit. The laughter is short-lived, as every snag, rip, and puncture summons the memory of how it came. She thinks of the others who wore the same suit into Cadre Two, who endured unspeakable cruelty, and who will never be coming home.

"They couldn't kill us, Sharon," Maiella reminds her.

"They couldn't kill us," Sharon echoes.

"They *couldn't* kill us."

Sharon looks again at her suit. "Gor, they really tried, didn't they?"

Maiella nods, her face a set of horizontal lines.

"But they couldn't," Sharon whispers. She stands. "I want to get out of these rags."

"Yeah, sure."

Maiella leaves as gently as she came and walks back toward the flight deck. On the way she checks in on Argo and Shao-Lo. The Brick sits on the edge of his bunk while Shao-Lo kneels in front of him, shirtless, facing away. Argo dives into one of many cylindrical holes in the Colonel's back, scraping out charred sediments. The shell with the orange logo stands on its flat end on the floor beside them.

Argo notices Maiella leaning in the doorway. He looks over at her and tips his head.

"I'll give you a going over once I finish with the colonel," the Brick says. "Though...that may be a while."

Shao-Lo looks over her bare shoulder. "You saying I don't run fast enough, Brick?"

"Well you might try *dodging* enemy fire. Now please, sir, hold still."

Despite Shao-Lo's quip, Maiella can see intense pain in her wincing blinks, rippling jaw muscles, and twitching skin.

She's a tough old Gun, this one.

In an instant, Maiella relives her memory of being an Operator in the Corps, content in her abilities, not seeking higher responsibility. It never occurred to her what it must take to become a Cadre Colonel, how many rotations endured, how many comrades outlived, being responsible for the lives of the last few humans in existence, making the decisions that save lives or end them. Seeing Shao-Lo hunched over without uniform or armor, proof of her mortality punched and scorched into her flesh, melts some of the icy resentment.

"Something on your mind, Maiella?" Shao-Lo asks.

"What's that thing?" the Geek asks, pointing at the brassy cylinder.

"This?" Argo asks, pointing at the shell with his scraping tool.

"Mm, hmm."

"May, I Colonel?"

Shao-Lo nods an affirmative with tightly shut lips.

"It's a projectile with viral payload, coded to the blueskin genotype."

"Where'd you find it?"

"Honniker's *Cooler* was filled with them," Shao-Lo answers between sharp inhales. "Had *crates* of 'em packed up, then everything went sideways."

Argo leans in to get a better look at the hole he is excavating in Shao-Lo's back. A line of bright red runs down from it.

"Ahh, there we go."

He swaps the scraping tool in his bashed up Med-Kit for long nose pliers.

"Shrapnel welded itself to your rib, here, Colonel. Brace yourself, this may sting a bit."

"Go ahead."

Argo clamps the intruding metal. "Three, two, one..." He pulls.

Maiella cringes at the creaking groan of metal retreating from bone. Shao-Lo's face goes bright red, but she does not make a sound. Red wells in the hole. Argo dabs it out and sprays the inside with expanding foam.

"So everything went sideways," Maiella picks up, reminding Shao-Lo where she was in the story.

"Mmm. After Carter detonated, we were in a stand-off. Honniker offered us a way out if we'd just leave his battery rooms. We could tell something about that place really had him nervous. I told him, we'd stay right there and blast a hole through him big enough to march our Cadre through, because we'd all rather die than go home empty-handed. So after a while, a cart rolls in with that projectile loaded on it. Made the deal. Here we are."

"Mikato didn't seem to know about it."

"No, but I almost tipped him off," Argo says, annoyed with himself. "Don't think he would've let us out of there if he knew we had it." The Brick swaps tools for the scraper again and burrows into another of Shao-Lo's wounds.

"So what can it do?" Maiella asks.

"If we can copy it, and if we can make enough of it?" Shao-Lo answers. "We could wipe out every blueskin in existence."

Maiella frowns, then her eyebrows pop up. "That's quite a find."

"Yes, it is," Shao-Lo agrees.

Maiella folds her arms, unsure what to make of the brassy projectile. "I'll be on the flight deck. Let me know if you need anything."

Shao-Lo nods without looking and waves the back of her hand.

Maiella walks slowly back to the flight deck, slides her way between consoles and the low ceiling to the padded pilot's chair. She sinks down into the cushions, props her boots up on the console, laces fingers behind her head, and watches the smearing of stars as they streak by.

Here, at last, she can sit and think without some creature or machine trying to rip her apart. Finally, she can reflect upon her ordeal. The recollections come in a deluge, each clamoring for attention in her spinning mind. Despite her talents at multi-tasking, the memories are overwhelming and she has to choose selected moments.

Like the big guardian animal, Alessa: so fearsome in her physical endowments, so alien in her shape and form, but how alike in service, kinship, purpose. A rapport quickly built of partnership and survival, of loyalty. Alessa may look the same as the slavering creatures under Honniker's control, yet she remained dedicated to her Master, Mikato. And Alessa was the *only* reason she, Keller, and Sharon were able to get away from Honniker's twisted minions.

And earlier on, when she rushed at Mikato in a rage to beat him bare-fisted, Alessa could have easily killed her. Yet she did not, only using what force she needed to protect her master's life. Great strength, applied with restraint.

And Mikato: the man responsible, so he says, for the downfall of mankind. A man who devised the most lethal weapon systems she'd ever witnessed, and likely what she witnessed was only a narrow fraction of Cadre Two's total arsenal. Mikato. The man who made Marta and the Counselor, two artificial beings as zealous in their service to humanity as the most ardent Operator. Two beings, not human, yet trusted and dependable as dear friends.

Her uploaded consciousness: having all the same recollections and experiences, then discovering in hours how different she had become. Describing a broader view, expanded perspectives...free of limitations.

And Keller: Outcast. Vilified by his crew for actions in the past, actions he could not have known would have such devastating consequences. A man of great skill, talent, leadership, living a life of regret, spending all of his remaining years in search of redemption that would never come.

And herself: once inseparable from her team and her Cadre siblings, now a pariah, similar in appearance and ability to modern day Operators, yet utterly removed from them. She is her own exception.

No longer will anything ever fit neatly into her concepts of 'good' or 'bad,' for every rule at Cadre Two has yielded an exception.

Will there always be an exception?

With this question, the Geek stares infinitely through the windshield.

Blueskin. Lizard. Eleto.

Whatever the name, the meaning was always the same: something to be resisted, collected from, butchered with total prejudice. Something to be treated without mercy, for in mercy lies the possibility of discovery and annihilation.

Her memories take her back to Cadre One's halls, of having shoved her way into a shuttle to catch a glimpse of her beloved teammates returning from Earth. She peered past the Operators at gurneys of pallid gray flesh, a limping Brick with an infected gash in his side, and a chalky blueskin being led in on a chain. That blueskin, so emaciated and sickly, retained a never before seen dignity. It was taller. It moved with grace. It commanded a presence, regardless of its frailty or impediments. But it was terrified. And its yellow eyes held the same fear as Sharon's in the crazed halls of Cadre Two.

And the pile barring access to the landing bay. A stack of dead bodies, human and Eleto, thawing, their fluids trickling down over one another exclaiming in silent, yet stentorian voice, a fate both may ultimately share.

Commonality between species roots in her awareness like the leafless trees in the *Park*, and Honniker's words echo in her ears, *"...Once I became aware of the similarity, I could no longer ignore it."*

Her world of absolutes cracked the day she gunned her way through the *Europa*. But here, confronting the foundation of Cadre motivation, indeed, their very raison d'être—the belief that the Blueskin has always been and always will be their enemy—that world shatters.

Could that tall one, the Blueskin Argo brought back from Earth... could that one be an exception, too?

Can't know until we get back. Unless the MedTechs have already cut it up...

She imagines the pale alien stretched out on a steel table, restrained, unable to free itself. The scene overlaps with her memory of Voss stretched out on Honniker's table, twenty years of cutting evident from the barely-visible scars wrapping his skin. Her mind flashes back and forth from Voss under Honniker's mechanical knives to the alien under Cadre scalpels.

"We're behaving exactly the same," echoes Honniker's voice.

Maiella sits up, drops her boots from the console, takes her hands from behind her head. The Geek looks over her shoulder down the transport's corridor, eager for someone to talk with.

Shao-Lo and Argo wouldn't care. And Sharon needs some time.

She turns around and resumes her gaze through the windshield.

No need to get riled up until I know.

THE EXHAUSTED DEAD

Maiella sinks back in her chair, realizing with every second she is moving millions of kilometers closer to someone she desperately wants to see.

"See you soon, Thompson."

Her chapped lips curve in anticipation.

"Have I got a story for you..."

CADRE ONE

CADRE TWO

Appendix: The Retirement of Lt. Colonel Anders

General O'Kai, Colonel Munro, and Major Ralla stand beside a reclined hospital bed, dressed in their uniform best. The same grim expression covers each of their faces.

Propped up on the angled bunk is Anders. On a wheeled tray beside him rests his HDI, the myriad wires disconnected from the racks of computers. A clean gown wraps his crooked torso, and his feeble arms drape over the gnarled legs of his lap. Anders's mouth hangs slightly open and phlegm rattles in his throat. His chest heaves with the effort of breath.

Ortega stands quietly beside the Counselor at Anders's feet. He had only heard of this disabled man, but saw the results of his genius everywhere: the one-way transport which carried Thompson, Argo, and Beckert to Earth, the solutions to integrating the *Europa's* reactor with the Cadre power grid, adaptations of alien technology into Cadre equipment and vessels. *Such amazing work from someone so infirmed...*

Ortega looks at the crippled man on the bed who is planted with surgical tubing, at the mole-spotted scalp with thin strands of gray hair between polished silver contact terminals, at the weary eyes. Heaviness of the coming event sinks in. *Retirement.*

"We honor Colonel Anders," O'Kai begins. "We honor his devotion, his outstanding accomplishment, his immeasurable contribution. With greater rank comes a greater requirement of service. No one has ever given more for the Cadre." The General's hand falls tenderly on Anders's shoulder.

Anders reaches up with a palsy-wracked hand and pats O'Kai's. Ralla bows her head as Munro continues the living eulogy.

"We regret we could not provide more for your comfort and well-being. This reward is deficient in the extreme. Yet the Cadre shall always remember you. Your image will be etched into our memorial with others who have passed into eternal fame. Your legacy will inspire generations to come. In this way, you live forever." The big man bows like Ralla. After a lengthy silence, Munro looks up at the Counselor and Ortega. "Is there anything you would like to say before we continue?"

Ortega's eye twitches. *I should say something, but what can I say?* Words fail and the newly promoted Captain shakes his head. He turns his eyes to the Counselor, so reliable in the most difficult times. The Counselor sees the unvoiced request in Ortega's face and nods in acceptance. He takes a small step toward the bunk.

"I learn far more from people than I do from any archive. Colonel Anders taught me the most. And his most poignant lesson is that no matter our physical impairments, we all have something we can offer. The will and the commitment to serve are the only limiting factors in that regard.

"We all felt safer under your watch, Colonel, and your wise guidance has been a beacon in the dark. Though we must respect your wishes and your dignity…this isn't an easy thing you've asked of us. Please know we will miss you dearly. May you rest in peace."

Anders coughs harshly, setting off a fit of gagging. Munro leans the man forward and supports his chest, gently slapping his back with a cupped hand. Phlegm dislodges and comes up into the colonel's mouth. Ralla reaches out with a cloth so he can spit.

The expended man slumps back, pale and gasping. A single tear descends his cheek.

"I'm ready," he whispers.

"Major Ralla," O'Kai calls, "proceed."

Ralla nods glumly. She folds the cloth and drops it into a recycle bin, then takes a small control box in hand. With a stuttering inhale, she places her hand onto the switch. Long seconds pass.

Anders struggles to inhale enough air to speak. *"Ralla…Let me go."*

Ralla's face goes rigid with restraint. Her thin cheeks ripple with clenched jaw muscles. She turns the switch.

The room goes disturbingly quiet as the background hum and whine of medical machines wind down. Anders momentarily convulses then falls still. His last breath hisses past his lips.

Munro places two fingers against Anders's carotid artery. All eyes watch him when at last he withdraws his hand.

"He's gone."

THE EXHAUSTED DEAD

Ortega is overwhelmed with a shuddering sadness. *That's it? This is what they all look forward to? To be driven to exhaustion and put down like an old dog?*

A line from an ancient tale comes to his mind and whispers past his lips of its own will. *"Better, I say, to break sod as a farm hand for some poor country man, on iron rations, than to lord it over all the exhausted dead."*[1]

The line plays over and over in his mind, and the Spaniard's sullen gaze rises from the expired Anders to O'Kai. As Ortega takes in the towering general at Anders's side, a dreadful recognition seizes him.

He is Lord of the Exhausted Dead.

O'Kai stares at the still form on the bunk. In profile, all of O'Kai's features are put in strong relief: his square jaw, his broken nose, his strong brow. Yet nestled within all the confidence and strength is a glimmer of uncertainty.

The glimmer is transitory, and O'Kai rebuilds his mighty edifice.

"Mark the time, Munro, and call the reclamation team. We need all of his implanted hardware. Then have his body collected for processing."

"Aye, Sir," Munro answers.

"Ralla, escort our witnesses back to the *Europa*."

"Yes, Sir," she answers, and sets the control box down beside Anders's HDI. She steps briskly toward the Counselor and Ortega, gesturing. "Please, follow me."

The Counselor complies obediently. Ortega starts to follow but something makes him pause and look back. O'Kai is looking at Anders again. The towering general looks up, meeting eyes with the Spaniard.

"Something else, Captain?"

"No, no, General. I am sorry for your loss. Truly."

"That's not necessary," O'Kai says sharply, "but thank you."

Ortega nods quietly, and he leaves the small chamber. In the hallway, the Counselor and Ralla are engaged in quiet conversation.

"...can speak with me anytime, if you like, Major."

"That's good to know, Counselor."

Ralla stands straighter at Ortega's approach.

"Sorry, I'm coming," the Spaniard says, and he hustles to catch up. Something follows him from the room, however, intangible and unsettling: worse than the sad, undeserved end to a life entirely spent in agonizing sacrifice is being in charge of it all, having to run yourself and everyone in your command to ragged tatters because if you don't, *everyone you care for*

---

1 *The Odyssey*, Homer, translation by Robert Fitzgerald.

dies.

Never in his wildest imaginations could he have thought he would pity a man so fearsome and capable as O'Kai.

"Graviora Manent..." Ortega thinks out loud. In the silent walk back to the transport, he prays.

ABOUT THE AUTHOR

A child of the Space Age, Mr. Farnham always held a passionate interest in the future of high technology. Impatient to live in that future world, he eagerly consumed any scientific article or Science Fiction novel that promised a glimpse. Herbert, Heinlein, and Huxley are three of his greatest influences.

When not working he loves to travel, enjoying the variety of people as much as the landscapes.

His first novel, *Angry Ghosts,* was acquired by Eirelander Publishing in 2009 and re-released on e-book under the title *Wraiths of Earth,* in 2010. The sequel, *Black Hawks From A Blue Sun,* was also released in 2010.

Born in Newport, Rhode Island, Allen now lives with his dog, Hamlet, in Milford, New Hampshire. There, he remains an outspoken advocate for efficiency and renewable energy technologies.

www.ingramcontent.com/pod-product-compliance
Lightning Source LLC
Chambersburg PA
CBHW071628260626
47170CB00001B/1